Esquire's

BIG BOOK
OF FICTION

Esquire's

BIG BOOK
OF FICTION

edited by

Adrienne Miller

Context Books New York 2002

www.contextbooks.com

Designer: Johanna Roebas
Jacket design: Carol Devine Carson

Context Books
368 Broadway
Suite 314
New York, NY 10013

Library of Congress Cataloging-in-Publication Data

Esquire's big book of fiction / edited by Adrienne Miller.
p. cm.
ISBN 1-893956-26-1 (pbk. : alk. paper)
1. Short stories, American. 2. American fiction—20th century.
3. United States—Social life and customs—20th century—Fiction.
I. Miller, Adrienne. II. Esquire.
PS648.S5 E87 2002
813'.010805—dc21

2002003457

ISBN 1-893956-26-1

9 8 7 6 5 4 3 2 1

Manufactured in Canada

For Arnold Gingrich

Contents

Introduction
by Adrienne Miller   xiii

Towel Season
Ron Carlson   1

The Song of Grendel
John Gardner   15

The Snows of Kilimanjaro
Ernest Hemingway   44

Adult World (I)
David Foster Wallace   69

Adult World (II)
David Foster Wallace   89

Incarnations of Burned Children
David Foster Wallace   95

CONTENTS

A Jewish Patient Begins His Analysis
Philip Roth   99

Parker's Back
Flannery O'Connor   109

The Jeweler
Pete Dexter   131

All the Pretty Horses
Cormac McCarthy   140

Downstream
Antonya Nelson   183

The B.A.R. Man
Richard Yates   203

The Things They Carried
Tim O'Brien   218

Marry the One Who Gets There First:
Outtakes from the Sheidegger-Krupnik Wedding Album
Heidi Julavits   238

The Celebrity
John Dos Passos   257

The Remobilization of Jacob Horner
John Barth   266

Soldier's Joy
Tobias Wolff   287

CONTENTS

The Bullet's Flight
Denis Johnson   308

Memento Mori
Jonathan Nolan   313

The Lonesome Vigilante
John Steinbeck   328

Monhegan Light
Richard Russo   336

Fleur
Louise Erdrich   358

The Widow Ching—Pirate
Jorge Luis Borges   373

Neighbors
Raymond Carver   380

Lightning Man
David Means   387

The Visit to the Museum
Vladimir Nabokov   397

Hardy in the Evening
Tony Earley   408

Morning in America
Tony Earley   411

CONTENTS

Rock Springs
Richard Ford   414

Behold the Husband in His Perfect Agony
Barry Hannah   437

After the Storm
John Updike   460

Heart of a Champion
T. Coraghessan Boyle   479

Verona: A Young Woman Speaks
Harold Brodkey   487

His Son, in His Arms, in Light, Aloft
Harold Brodkey   494

The Misfits
Arthur Miller   514

The Last Generation
Joy Williams   534

The Beggar Said So
Isaac Bashevis Singer   550

Cutting Losses
Thomas McGuane   561

A Man in the Way
F. Scott Fitzgerald   587

CONTENTS

Plains of Abraham
Russell Banks   593

Bess
Jayne Anne Phillips   614

Among the Paths to Eden
Truman Capote   627

I Look Out for Ed Wolfe
Stanley Elkin   641

The Deep Sleep
Aleksandar Hemon   670

The Language of Men
Norman Mailer   688

Under the Pitons
Robert Stone   700

The Eighty-Yard Run
Irwin Shaw   730

In the Men's Room of the Sixteenth Century
Don DeLillo   746

The Death of Justina
John Cheever   758

The Wish
Joanna Scott   770

About the Authors   785

Introduction

More than two thousand short stories have appeared in *Esquire* since Arnold Gingrich created the magazine in 1933. Reading through the stories in this collection, one is struck by how simple and powerful the magazine's goals have been for the fiction it publishes. Through eight decades and an even greater number of editorial staffs, *Esquire*'s taste in fiction has remained consistently (and mercifully) immune to faddishness. The vision has been simple: Publish stories that take hold of you and don't let go.

From the first, *Esquire* has endeavored to introduce new voices to its readers. The magazine published early short stories by Don DeLillo, Raymond Carver, Saul Bellow, Richard Ford, Philip Roth, Annie Proulx, Tim O'Brien, T. Coraghessan Boyle, Denis Johnson, and J.D. Salinger. About Salinger it's worth noting that in 1941, when the author was just twenty-two, *Esquire* published one of his first pieces, "The Heart of a Broken Story." In 1945, six years before the publication of *The Catcher in the Rye*, the magazine ran another story of his called "This Sandwich Has No Mayonnaise," which is a kind of postscript to *Catcher*. Vincent Caulfield, Holden's brother, is the narrator, and in this story, Holden is missing in action in the Pacific, presumed dead.

Raymond Carver was an unknown writer when *Esquire* ran "Neighbors" in 1971. A genius and a revolutionary, Carver created new characters and a new language with which to write about them. He continues, for better or worse, to be a monumental influence on writers, many of whom are probably neither geniuses nor revolutionaries but whose dads are paying for their grad school. In 1999 and 2000, *Esquire* ran three previously unpublished Carver short stories, discovered by his widow Tess Gallagher and one of our editors.

The magazine has also published pieces by Graham Greene, Sinclair Lewis, Robert Penn Warren, Bernard Malamud, Gore Vidal, William Faulkner, James Baldwin, Italo Calvino, Thomas Mann, Rebecca West, John Irving, Evelyn Waugh, Tennessee Williams, Paddy Chayeksy, William H. Gass, Chester Himes, and Robert Graves. Excerpts from *The Crying of Lot 49*, by Thomas Pynchon; Richard Yates's masterpiece *Revolutionary Road*; and Stanley Elkin's *Boswell*. Truman Capote's *Breakfast at Tiffany's*, Jim Harrison's *Legends of the Fall*, and Dylan Thomas's play *A Child's Christmas in Wales* were all published in the magazine in their entirety.

As with its nonfiction, *Esquire* has regularly taken big risks with its short stories. Most of them have been successful. (Let us not speak, however, of a certain rather risky late-eighties *Esquire* cover featuring a novelist wearing a ninja's outfit.) Consider, for instance, John Gardner's grand philosophical allegory *Grendel*. It is no small feat that a Chaucer-obsessed medievalist with an axe to grind about "values" would find a home in a commercial magazine.

In a different vein entirely, there is Barry Hannah, whose stories from *Airships* are today rightly viewed as essential and canonical— though they were nothing less than radical when they were first published in *Esquire*. And then there is the inimitable Mr. Brodkey. Harold Brodkey: that marvelously arrogant abuser of the colon! "Verona: A Young Woman Speaks" is an astonishing performance, both emotionally and punctuationally, in addition to being a convincing example (there aren't many of them) of the "female perspective" written by a male author. Flannery O'Connor was being largely ignored by the old-boy network when *Esquire* published "Why Do the Heathens Rage?" and "Parker's Back."

Recently, *Esquire* has published a stylistically broad range of stories, from the more traditional, like pieces by Ron Carlson—the bringer of great relief with his large-hearted stories about characters who actually *don't* give in to their own worst impulses—to the technically innovative, stories like the brilliantly sustained folktale "Lightning Man" by David Means and "The Wish" by Joanna Scott.

No introduction to a collection of *Esquire* fiction would be complete without a Hemingway-Fitzgerald story. It is fairly well known that Ernest Hemingway was, for a time, a contract writer for the magazine. In 1936, as the story goes, he had missed a deadline for a nonfiction column and sent in a short story instead. The story in question was that triumph of sado-masochism, "The Snows of Kilimanjaro." The original *Esquire* version of the story was famously cruel to F. Scott Fitzgerald; "The rich were dull and they drank too much . . ." it read. "He remembered poor Scott Fitzgerald and his romantic awe of them and how he had started a story once that began, 'The very rich are different from you and me.' And how someone had said to Scott, Yes they have more money." (In future printed versions of the story, including the one in this anthology, Fitzgerald's name has been changed to "Julian.") The slight put further stress upon the two writers' already, shall we say, "demanding" friendship, but Fitzgerald continued on as a frequent contributor to the magazine.

There is a short story called "Porcupines at the University," by Donald Barthelme, and in it there are three questions: "Are these porcupines wonderful? Are they significant? Are they what I need?" That's how I chose these stories: They're the ones that got a yes, a *yes*, and a YES.

—*Adrienne Miller*

Esquire's

BIG BOOK
OF FICTION

Towel Season

Ron Carlson

Suddenly it was June, and there were strange towels in the house. There were stacks on the table in the entry; two or three towels, Edison knew, were not their towels. In the hall, he'd step over large, striped piles of strange, wet towels waiting to be washed. The kids, Rebecca and Toby, pedaled home in bathing suits, alien towels hung from their necks. Twice, Edison tripped as he sidled through the laundry room carrying his files, his feet tangled in a great heap of these damp things. The commotion brought Leslie from the kitchen, and she looked down at him, the absent-minded professor, his papers around his head. "You're kind of too young for this kind of thing," she said. He didn't look uncomfortable. She knew if she left him there and went back to her potato salad, there was a good chance he'd simply go to sleep. He was up past one almost every night working on his largest mathematical project. This was his final experimental journey for the firm; if it worked, he was going to be able to go on and on toward the edge. If not, he would join all the other middle-level engineers.

"Whose towels are these?"

The answer was, depending on the day, the Hanovers', the Plums', the Reeds'; close-radius towels, the Hanovers and their pool just down the street, the Plums and their pool around the corner, and the Reeds and their pool not three blocks from the elementary where all the children (nine total) of these people attended.

"These, dear, are the Plums', and we'll be returning them this evening when we go over there for a cookout, so get your work done." She picked up his files and laid them on his chest. "Okay? Swimming? Drinks on their patio? Remember? Don't worry—when the time comes, I'll drive us all over."

Edison crawled to his feet. "All right." Leslie watched him go into his study, and then she stuffed the towels in the washer. He was working on the most advanced and important calculations of his life. The firm kept only one or two theoretical mathematicians, and this project would determine if Edison would make the cut.

The summer developed into these dinners and all the shifting towels. That night, they loaded the car and drove five hundred yards to the Plums' and drifted with the Hanovers and the Reeds toward the gate, carrying their coolers and casseroles and Tupperware containers and the bundle of towels. They seemed like zombies in a fog to Edison, because he was in a fog most of the time himself, working so many hours at his computer screen, and inside the greetings continued, even though they'd all seen one another at the Reeds' three nights ago. Edison and Allen Reed opened bottles of Corona and sat out on the picnic table in the steady heat of the season. These outings always disoriented Edison, who saw them as some kind of puzzle. Part of him was still at his green screen, mulling equations, while he watched the children spill into the green pool and the women set out the food.

"How's the project going, Ed?" Allen asked him. Reed, large and tan, was an applications engineer for the firm. Ed looked at the man's skin, so dark from the sun it seemed part of the strangeness. What kind of engineer has such a tan? Allen Reed was about five years older than Edison and had an affectionate condescension for theoretical math.

"I'm working every day," Edison said. He was looking at the bench where all the towels had gathered in stacks: fourteen towels. There was no way they were going home with the right families. Folded there in multicolored order, they seemed part of some problem Edison had solved this week or dreamed of or was working on now.

"Yes, well, you let me know when they find a market for chaos and its theory, and I'll come over with my slide rule and give you a hand." Allen was going to pat Edison on the shoulder, which he did with people he was kidding, but he saw that Edison was about two seconds from getting the joke. They were all used to these odd moments with Edison.

The thing that was said about Edison at least once every party, after he'd been asked a question and then waited five or ten seconds to answer, or after one of his rare remarks, was "I'm glad I'm not a genius," which was meant as a kind of compliment and many times simply as a space filler after some awkwardness.

And even early in the summer, on the way home from a cookout, Toby, who was six years old, started crying, and, when questioned about his grief, stuttered in a whisper, "Daddy's a genius!" He cried as Leslie carried him to the house in one of the large, pale-blue towels that Edison knew was not theirs, and he cried himself to sleep.

Undressing for bed, Leslie said, "Ed, can you lighten up a little, fit in? These are my friends."

"Sure," he said as she got into bed beside him. "I think I can do that." A long moment later, he turned to Leslie and said, "But I'm not a genius. I'm just in a tough section of this deal now. Can you tell Toby? I'm just busy. I need to finish this project."

"I know you do," she whispered. "What should I tell him it's like?" When they were dating, he'd begun to try to explain his work to her in

3

metaphors, and she'd continued the game through his career, asking him for comparisons that she'd then inhabit, embellish. Right after they were married and Edison was in graduate school, he'd work late into the night in their apartment and crawl into bed with the calculations still percolating in his head. "What's it like?" Leslie would ask. "Where are you now?" She could tell he was remote, lit. They talked in territories.

"I've crossed all the open ground, and the wind has stopped now. My hope is to find a way through this next place."

"Mountains?"

"Right. Okay, mountains—blank, very few markings." He spoke carefully and with a quiet zeal. "They're steep, hard to see."

"Is it cold?"

"No, but it is strange. It's quiet." Then he'd turn to her in bed, his eyes bright, alive. "I'm way past the path. I don't think anyone has climbed this route before. There are no trails, handholds."

Leslie would smile and kiss him in that close proximity. "Keep going," she'd say. "Halfway up that mountain, there's a woman with a cappuccino cart and a chicken-salad sandwich—me."

Then a smile would break across his face, too, and he would see her, kiss her back, and say it: "Right. You."

Now in bed, Edison said, "Tell him it's like . . ." he paused and ran the options, "playing hide-and-seek."

"At night. In the forest?"

"Yes," he was whispering. "It's a forest, and parts of this thing are all over the place. It's going to take a while."

The Hanovers' party was like all the parties, a ritual that Edison knew well. The kids swam while the adults drank, then the kids ate and went off into the various corners of the house primarily for television, then the adults ate their grilled steaks or salmon or shish kebab and drank a new wine while it got dark and they flirted. It was easy and harmless, and whoever was up was sent to the kitchen or the cooler for more potato salad or beer and returned and gave whatever man or woman whatever he or she had asked for and said as a husband or wife might, "There you are, honey. Can I get you anything else, dear?" And maybe there'd be some nudging, a woman punctuating the sentence with her hip at a man's shoulder or a man taking a woman's shoulders in both hands possessively.

At some point, there'd be Janny Hanover and Scott Plum coming out of the house holding hands and Janny announcing, "Scott and I have decided to elope," with him saying, "I've got to have a woman who uses mayonnaise on everything." In their swimsuits in the dark, arms around each other's waists, now parting and rejoining the group, they did look as if it were a possibility. The eight adults were interchangeable like that, as swimsuit silhouettes, Edison thought, except me—I'm too skinny and too tall; I'd look like a woman's father walking out of the patio doors like that. I'd scare everybody. Around the pool, the towels glowed in random splashes where they'd been thrown. Edison listened to the men and women talk, and when they laughed, he tried to laugh, too.

Days, while Leslie took Toby and Becky to the shoe store, the orthodontist, and tennis lessons, Edison worked on his project. He was deep in the fields, each problem more like a long, long hike. He had to go way into each to see the next corner and then there to see forward. He had to keep his mind against it the entire time; one slip and he'd have to backtrack. Edison described his work to Leslie now the same way he began to think of it: following little people through the forest, with some weaving through the trees, some hiding behind trees and changing clothes, emerging at different speeds. He had to keep track of them all, shepherd them through the trees and over a hill that was not in sight quite yet and line them up for a silver bus. The silver bus was Leslie's contribution. He'd work on butcher paper with pencils, and then after two or three o'clock, he would enter his equations into the computer and walk out into his house, his face vague, dizzy, not quite there yet.

Summer began in earnest, and women began stopping by with towels. Edison would hear Janny Hanover or Paula Plum call from the front hall, the strange female voices coming to him at first from the field of numbers progressing across the wide paper. "Don't get up! It's just me! See you tonight at the Reeds'!" and then the door would shut again, and Edison would fight with his rising mind to stay close to the shifting numerals as they squirmed and wandered. He felt, at such moments, as if he were trying to gather a parachute in a tricky and persistent wind.

Some days, there'd be a tan face suddenly at his study door, Paula Plum or Melissa Reed, saying, "So this is where the genius does it" and placing two or three folded towels on the chair. The incursion was always more than Edison could process. He looked up at the woman wearing a hot-pink tank top, sunglasses in her hair, and felt as if he'd been struck. The calculation bled, toppled. Edison felt involved in some accident, his hands collapsed, his heartbeat in his face. Then she was gone, whoever she had been, singing something about tonight or tomorrow night at the Plums' or the Reeds', and Edison found himself dislocated, wrecked. His children knew not to barge in that way, because it meant his day's work would vanish, and he'd spend hours looking out the front window or walking the neighborhood in the summer heat. The chasm between his pencil figurings and the figures of the real world was that, a chasm, and there was no bridge.

At the Reeds' and the Plums', while the kids splashed in the pool and Scott flirted with Melissa and Allen with Paula, silhouettes passing in and out of the house as summer darkness finally fell, while everyone was fed grilled meat of all kinds and Paula Plum's tart potato salad, word got out that Edison was brusque, at least not hospitable, and Janny Hanover lifted her wine to him, saying, "Why, darling, you looked absolutely like I was going to steal your trigonometry!" Edison smiled at her, feeling Leslie's gaze; he'd promised he would try to do better. Holding this smile was pure effort.

"And you looked at me like you didn't even know who I was," Paula added.

Edison didn't know what to say, held the smile, tried to chuckle, might have, and then it became painfully clear that he should say something. He couldn't say what he thought: *I don't know who you are.* The faces glowed in a circle around him, the healthy skin, all those white teeth. "Well, my heavens," and there was a pause that they all knew they would fall into, and people knew they would have to do something—cough, get up for more beer, make a joke. He'd done this to this group a dozen times already this summer, what an oddball. Then he spoke: "Do you ladies go through the neighborhood surprising every geek who's double-checking his lottery numbers?"

And the pause sparked and Dan Hanover laughed, roared, and the laughter carried all of them across, and it was filled with gratitude and something else that Edison saw in Leslie's eyes, something about him: He'd scored a point. There was a new conviviality through the night, more laughter, the men brought Edison another beer, Leslie was suddenly at ease. Children drifted in and out of the pool, docking between their parents' legs for a moment before floating away, dropping towels here and there. Edison, the new center of the group, felt strange—both warm and doomed.

The following days were different from any he'd known. People treated him . . . how? Cordially, warmly—more than that. This new fellowship confused him. He'd obviously broken the code and was inside now. His research crashed and vanished. At the butcher paper with his pencils, he was like a man in the silent woods at night, reaching awkwardly for things he could not see. "I'm going in circles."

"Is any of it familiar? Is there a moon?" Leslie asked. "Shall I honk the horn of the silver bus? Start a bonfire?"

"There's no light, no wind. I'm stalled."

"Go uphill. You'll see the horizon."

But he didn't. In the work he'd done, all the linkages had been delicate, and after two days the numbers paled and dried and the adhesive dissipated, and while he stared at the sheet, the ragged edge of the last figures, it all ran away. He was going to have to turn around, follow the abstruse calculations back until he could gather it all again. Edison left the room. He walked the long blocks of his neighborhood in the heat, lost and stewing.

Days, he began to ferry the kids around and was surprised to start learning the names of their friends, the young Plums, the Hanover girl, the Reed twins. He was surprised by everything—the pieces of a day, the way they fit and then fled. He'd wait in the van at the right hour, and the children would wander out of the movie theater and climb in. It was a wonder. He started cooking, which he'd always enjoyed, but now he started cooking all the time. Permutations on grilled-cheese sandwiches, variations on spaghetti.

He delivered towels, returning stacks of cartoon characters to the Hanovers, Denver Broncos-logo towels to the Plums, who had transferred from Colorado, and huge, striped things to the Reeds, always trading for his family's mongrel assemblage. He became familiar with the women, dropping in on them at all daytime hours, calling through the front doors: "Man in the house," and hearing, after a beat, Janny or Melissa or Paula call, "Thank heaven for that. Come on in." If the kids were in the car, he'd drop the towels and greetings and hurry out; if not, sometimes there was coffee. Melissa Reed put a dollop of Jägermeister in hers; Janny Hanover drank directly out of a liter Evian bottle, offering him any of her husband's ales (Dan was a member of Ale of the Month); Paula made him help her make lemonade from scratch. All of the women were grateful for the company. These visits and the weekend parties made Edison in his new life feel as if he were part of a new, larger family, with women and children everywhere; he was with people more than he'd ever been.

In bed, he didn't want to talk; his hands ran over Leslie in his approach. She held him firmly, adjusted, asked, "What is it like now, the project?" Edison put his head against her neck, stopped still for a beat, and then began again working along her throat. "Ed, should I worry about you? Where are you with the research?" He lifted away from her in the dark, and then his hand descended and she caught it. She turned toward him now, and he pulled to free his hand, but she held it. It was an odd moment for them. "Edison," she said. "What is going on?" They were lying still, not moving. "Are you okay? Have you stumbled on a log and hit your head on a sharp outcropping? Has a mighty bear chased you up a nasty tree? Did he bite you? Should I call that helicopter they use in the mountains?" He could hear the smile in her voice. "What do you need me to do? Where are the little people?" It was clear he was not going to answer. "They're waiting for you. Go get them. And I'm waiting, too, remember? By the silver bus. You'll make it, Ed." But when she let go of his hand and kissed him, he held still one second and then simply turned away.

The project needed to be done this season; it couldn't smolder for another year. They'd take him off it and have him counting beans in the group cubicles. They put you out on the frontier like this once, and when you came back beaten you joined one of the teams, your career in close orbit, the adventure gone.

Meanwhile, he fled the house. He'd stand close to Paula at the counter while they squeezed the lemons, their arms touching; he began having a drop of Jäger with Melissa; and when Janny Hanover would see him to the door, they'd hug for five seconds, which is one second over the line. He could feel her water bottle against his back.

Some afternoons, Leslie would stand in the doorway of his little study and see the spill of pencils where they'd been for days. She kept the hallway clear of laundry, but he never went to that corner of the house anymore. They circled each other through the days. In bed, he was silent. She tried to open him: "Okay, mister, should I try to drive the bus closer, honk the horn? You want me to bring in some of those all-terrain vehicles? Some kind of signal? We're running low on crackers."

After a moment, he said, "I'm not sure."

"Can you see any landmarks, stars?"

"Not really," he answered. "I can't." His voice was flat, exhausted, trying to imagine it all. "It's steep. It's too dark. I'm having some trouble with my footing."

"I know you are. Everybody does," Leslie said, opening her eyes and looking at his serious face. "Keep your own path. Dig your feet in. Try."

* * *

9

Paula wanted to know if he really worked for the CIA; Janny wanted to know if his IQ was really 200; Melissa asked him if she should get implants. She was drinking her laced coffee at the kitchen table, and she simply lifted her shirt. The fresh, folded towels stood on the corner of the table. The afternoons he was home between errands were the worst. Now his calculations seemed a cruel puzzle, someone else's work, dead, forgotten, useless.

Edison was a shining light at the parties, sharing recipes and inside information on the children. There was always someone talking at his right hand, a man or a woman; he was open now yet still exotic. His difference was clear: He was the only man still not settled, the only man still *becoming*, unknown, and it gave him an allure that Leslie felt, and she watched him the way you watch the beast in a fairy tale—to see if it is really something very good in other clothing. Certainly, the parties were less of a strain for her now, not having to worry about Edison's strangeness, his potential for gaffes, but his new state strained everything else.

By August, the women's familiarity with Edison was apparent. At the cookouts, they spoke in a kind of shorthand, and others had to ask them to back up, explain, if they were to understand at all. Janny Hanover let her hand drift to Edison's shoulder as they talked. Paula Plum began using certain words she'd learned from him: *vector, valence, viable*. Melissa Reed returned from a weeklong trip (supposedly to see her parents in Boulder) with four new swimsuits and a remarkable bust line.

Then, suddenly, it was Labor Day, an afternoon different from the hundred before it only in mind; that is, as Edison swept the pool patio and washed the deck chairs and cleaned the grill, he knew summer was, in some way, over. But he wanted the exercise there in his yard, the broom, the hose, the bucket of suds, the sun a steady pressure, and as he wiped the tables and squared the furniture, he thought: No wonder Scott and Dan and Allen like this. The pool was clean, a diamond-blue, and there wasn't a crumb on the deck. Edison wandered around another half hour, and then he put his tools away with great care.

That evening, the women did a slow dance around him. He felt it in confused pushes and pulls; he watched the children in the pool, their groupings and regroupings, and then he'd have a new cold beer in his hand, talking again to Scott Plum about chlorine. He sat in the circle of his friends on folding chairs in the reflected swimming-pool light, with Paula or Janny right behind him, hip against his shoulder, and he held everyone's attention now, describing with his hands out in the air a game he'd designed to let the children choose who got to ride in the front seat. "It's called First Thumb," he said, lifting his thumbs from each fist, one then the other. Edison named the different children and how they played the game, and who had gotten to sit in the front seat today and how. His hands worked like two puppets. Because the women laughed, the men smiled, and Janny pulled Edison's empty beer bottle out of his hands and replaced it with a full one.

"You're too much," Dan Hanover said. "This is a hell of a summer for you. I'll be glad when you get this spec project done and get over to give us a hand in applications." He leaned forward and made his hands into a ring, fingertip to fingertip. "We've got engine housings—"

"Not just the housings, the whole acceptor," Allen Reed interrupted. "And the radial displacement and timing has a huge window, anything we want. We've got carte blanche, Ed."

"*Fund*-ing! You'd be good on this team," Dan Hanover said.

"Solve," Allen Reed said, tapping Edison's beer bottle with his own, "for x."

Wrapped in a towel like a little chieftain, Toby waddled up and leaned between his father's legs for a moment, his wet hair sweet on Edison's face. Then he called his sister's name suddenly and ran back to play.

"Right." Edison did not know what to say. He picked up Toby's wet towel in both hands and looked at the men.

Later, as the party was breaking up and the friends clustered at the gate, Dan Hanover said, "It's a relief to have you joining the real world," and Allen Reed clamped his arm around Edison and said, "It's been a good run. You're a hell of a guy."

Melissa Reed took his upper arm against her new bosom and said, "Don't listen to him, Edison. He says that because you remind him of what he was like ten years ago." She squeezed his arm and kissed him on the lips, but his face had fallen.

That night, after everyone had left, Edison was agitated and distracted while they cleaned up. He shadowed Leslie around the deck and through the house, and, at some point, he dumped a load of towels in the laundry room and continued on into his room. After Leslie had cleared the patio, blown out all the candle lanterns, and squared the kitchen away, she found Edison at his desk. She stood in the doorway for a minute, but he was rapt on his calculations.

He was there through the night, working, as he was in the morning and all the long afternoon. He accepted a tuna sandwich about midday. She found him asleep at 5:00 P.M., his face on the large sheet of paper, surrounded by his animated figurings and the nubs of six pencils.

She helped him into bed, where he woke at midnight with a tiny start that opened Leslie's eyes. "Greetings," she said.

His voice was rocky and uneven. "I went back in. I walked all the way over the low hills, and I climbed up and back over and into the woods—I found the same woods—and I gathered most of the little people. They're like children; I mean, sometimes they follow, and so now I think I'm headed the right way." He sighed heavily and she could hear the fatigue in his chest.

"Get some sleep."

He was whispering. "I don't have them all, and I see now that's part of it; I'm not sure you ever get them all. There are mountains beyond these I didn't even know about."

Leslie lay still. He knew she was awake.

"But that's for another time. Now I can keep these guys together and come down. Do you see? I can wrap this up." She was silent, so he added, "There weren't any bears."

"Stop," she said quietly. "You don't want that game."

12

"It took all night, but I was able to find them because I knew you were waiting." Leslie could hear the ghost of the old exhilaration in his voice.

"Edison," she said, taking his hand. "I'm not there. You need to understand that I'm not at the silver bus anymore. I waited. I saw you give up. Why would I wait?"

"Where'd you go?" There were seconds between all the sentences. "Where are you?"

She spoke slowly. "I don't know. I'm . . . it's way north. I'm living in a small town, in an apartment above the hardware store."

He rose to an elbow, and she could feel him above her as he spoke. "What's it like there? How far is it?"

"I just got here. No one knows me. It's getting colder. I wear a coat when I walk to the library in the afternoons. I've got to get the kids from school."

Edison lay back down, and she heard the breath go out of him. "In town," he said, "are the leaves turning?"

"Listen." Now she rolled and covered him, a knee over, her arm across his chest. "My landlord asked about you."

"Who? He asked about me?"

"Where my husband was." Leslie put her hand on his shoulder and pulled herself up to kiss him. Held it. "How long I'd be in town."

"And you told him I was lost? He likes you."

"He's a nice man." Leslie shifted up again and now spoke, looking down into his eyes. "He said no one could survive in those hills. Winter comes early. He admired you, your effort." She kissed him. "But you weren't the first person lost to the snow."

"He's been to your place?" Edison's arms were up around her now, and she moved in concert with him.

"He's the landlord." She kissed him deeply, and her hands were moving. "He likes my coffee."

"I always liked your coffee." Edison shifted and pulled her nightshirt over her head, her sudden skin quickening the dark.

"Edison," Leslie whispered. "You're not a hell of a guy; you're not like any of them. You don't need to join the team. Any team." She had been still while she spoke, and now she ran her hand up, finally stopping with her first finger on his nose. "Don't solve for x. Just get all your little people to the bus and drive to town." She pressed her forehead against his. "I left the keys."

"I know where they are," he said. His hand was at her face now, too, and then along her hip, the signal, and he turned her, rolled over so that he looked down into her familiar eyes.

"Were you scared?" she asked. "What was it like when it started to snow and you were still lost?"

"Everything went white. I wanted to see you again." His every word sounded against her skin, her hair. "It didn't seem particularly cold, but the snowflakes, when they started, there were trillions."

The Song of Grendel

John Gardner

The old ram stands looking down over rockslides, stupidly triumphant. I blink. I stare in horror. "Scat!" I hiss. "Go back to your cave, go back to your cow shed—whatever." He cocks his head like an elderly, slow-witted king, considers the angles, decides to ignore me. I stamp. I hammer the ground with my fists. I hurl a skull-size stone at him. He will not budge. I shake my two hairy fists at the sky and I let out a howl so unspeakable that the water at my feet turns sudden ice and even I myself am left uneasy. But the ram stays; the season is upon us. And so begins the twelfth year of my idiotic war.

The pain of it! The stupidity!

"Ah, well." I sigh, and shrug, trudge back to the trees. Do not think my brains are squeezed shut, like the ram's, by the roots of horns. Flanks atremble, eyes like stones, he stares at as much of the world as he can see and feels it surging in him, filling his chest as the melting snow fills dried-out creek beds, tickling his gross, lopsided balls and charging his brains with the same unrest that made him suffer last year at this time, and the year before, and the year before that. (He's forgotten them all.) His hind parts shiver with the usual joyful, mindless ache to mount whatever happens near—the storm piling up black towers to the west, some rotting, docile stump, some spraddle-legged ewe. I cannot bear to look. "Why can't these creatures discover a little dignity?" I ask the sky.

The sky ignores me, forever unimpressed. Him too I hate, the same as I hate these brainless budding trees, these brattling birds.

Not, of course, that I fool myself with thoughts that I'm more noble. Pointless, ridiculous monster crouched in the shadows, stinking of dead men, murdered children, martyred cows. "Ah, sad one, poor old freak!" I cry, and hug myself, and laugh, letting out salt tears, he he!, till I fall down gasping and sobbing. (It's mostly fake.) The sun spins mindlessly over-head, the shadows lengthen and shorten as if by plan. Small birds, with a high-pitched yelp, lay eggs. The tender grasses peek up, innocent yellow. It was just here, this shocking green, that once when the moon was tombed in clouds, I tore off sly old Athelgard's head.

Such are the tiresome memories of a shadow-shooter, earth-rim-roamer, walker of the world's weird wall. "Waaah!" I cry, with another quick, nasty face at the sky, mournfully observing the way it is, bitterly remembering the way it was, and idiotically casting tomorrow's nets. "Aargh! Yaww!" I reel, smash trees. Disfigured son of lunatics. The big-boled oaks gaze down at me yellow with morning, beneath complexity. "No offense," I say, with a terrible grin, and tip an imaginary hat.

It was not always like this, of course. On occasion it's been worse.

No matter. No matter.

The doe in the clearing goes stiff at sight of my horridness, then remembers her legs and is gone. It makes me cross. "Blind prejudice!" I bawl at the splintered sunlight where half a second ago she stood. I wring my fingers, put on a long face. "Ah, the unfairness of everything," I say, and shake my head. It is a matter of fact that I have never killed a deer in all my life, and never will. Cows have more meat and, locked up in pens, are easier to catch. It is true, perhaps, that I feel some trifling dislike of deer but no more dislike than I feel for other natural things—discounting men. But deer, like rabbits and bears and even men, can make, concerning my race, no delicate distinctions. That is their happiness: they see all life without observing it. They're buried in it like crabs in mud. Except men, of course. I am not in a mood, just yet, to talk of men.

So it goes with me day by day and age by age, I tell myself. Locked in the deadly progression of moon and stars. I shake my head, muttering darkly on shaded paths, holding conversation with the only friend and comfort this world affords: my shadow. Wild pigs clatter away through brush. A baby bird falls feet-up in my path, squeaking. With a crabby laugh, I let him lie, kind heaven merciful bounty to some sick fox. So it goes with me, age by age by age. (Talking, talking. Spinning a web of words, pale walls of dreams, between myself and all I see.)

The first grim stirrings of springtime come (as I knew they must, having seen the ram), and even under the ground where I live, where no light breaks but the red of my fires and nothing stirs but the flickering shadows on my wet rock walls, or scampering rats on my piles of bones, or my mother's fat, foul bulk rolling over, restless again—molested by nightmares, old memories—I am aware in my chest of tuber-stirrings in the black-sweet duff of the forest overhead. I feel my anger coming back, building up like invisible fire, and at last, when my soul can no longer resist, I go up—as mechanical as anything else—fists clenched against my lack of will, my belly growling, mindless as wind, for blood. I swim up through the fire-snakes, hot dark whalecocks prowling the luminous green of the mere, and I surface with a gulp among churning waves and smoke. I crawl up onto the bank and catch my breath.

It's good at first to be out in the night, naked to the cold mechanics of the stars. Space hurls outward, falcon-swift, mounting like an irreversible injustice, a final disease. The cold night air is reality at last: indifferent to

17

me as stone. I lie there resting in the steaming grass, the old lake hissing and gurgling behind me, whispering patterns of words my sanity resists. At last, heavy as an ice-capped mountain, I rise and work my way to the inner wall, beginning of wolfslopes, the edge of my realm. I stand in the high wind balanced, blackening the night with my stench, gazing down to cliffs that fall away to cliffs, and once again I am aware of my potential: I could die. I cackle with rage and suck in breath.

"Dark chasms!" I scream from the cliff edge, "seize me!" "Seize me to your foul black bowels and crush my bones!" I am terrified at the sound of my own huge voice in the darkness. I stand there shaking, whimpering.

I sigh, depressed, and grind my teeth. I toy with shouting some tidbit more—some terrifying, unthinkable threat, but my heart's not in it. "Missed me!" I say with a coy little jerk and a leer, to keep my spirits up. Then, with a sigh, a kind of moan, I start very carefully down the cliffs that lead to the fens and moors and Hrothgar's hall. Owls cross my path as silently as raiding ships, and at the sound of my foot, lean wolves rise, glance at me awkwardly, and, neat of step as lizards, sneak away. I used to take some pride in that—the caution of owls when my shape looms in, the alarm I stir in these giant northern wolves. I was younger then. Still playing cat and mouse with the universe.

I move down through the darkness, burning with murderous lust, my brains raging at the sickness I can observe in myself as objectively as might a mind ten centuries away. Stars, spattered out through lifeless night from end to end, like jewels scattered in a dead king's grave, tease, torment my wits toward meaningful patterns that do not exist. I can see for miles from these rock walls: thick forest suddenly still at my coming—cowering stags, wolves, hedgehogs, boars, submerged in their stifling, unmemorable fear.

I sigh once more, sink down into silence, and cross it like dark wind. Behind my back, at the world's end, my pale slightly glowing fat mother sleeps on, old, sick at heart, in our dingy underground room. Life-bloated, baffled, long-suffering hag. Guilty, she imagines, of some unremembered, perhaps ancestral crime. (She must have some human in her.) Not that she thinks. Not that she dissects and ponders the dusty mechanical bits of her miserable life's curse. She clutches at me in my sleep as if to crush me. I break away. "Why are we here?" I used to ask her. "Why do we stand this putrid, stinking hole?" She trembles at my words. Her fat lips shake, "Don't ask!" her wriggling claws implore. (She never speaks.) "Don't ask!" It must be some terrible secret, I used to think. I'd give her a crafty squint. She'll tell me in time, I thought. But she told me nothing.

And so I come through trees and towns to the lights of Hrothgar's meadhall. I am no stranger here. A respected guest. Eleven years now and going on twelve I have come up this clean-mown central hill, dark shadow out of the woods below, and have knocked politely on the high oak door, bursting its hinges and sending the shock of my greeting inward like a cold blast out of a cave. "Grendel!" they squeak, and I smile like exploding spring. The old Shaper, a man I cannot help but admire, goes out the back window with his harp at a single bound, though blind as a bat. The drunkest of Hrothgar's thanes come reeling and clanking down from their wall-hung beds, all shouting their meady, outrageous boasts, their heavy swords aswirl like eagles' wings. "Woe, woe, woe!" cries Hrothgar, hoary with winters, peeking in, wide-eyed, from his bedroom in back. His wife, looking in behind him, makes a scene. The thanes in the meadhall blow out the lights and cover the wide stone fireplace with shields. I laugh, crumple over; I can't help myself. In the darkness, I alone see clear as day. While they squeal and screech and bump into each other, I silently stack up my dead and withdraw to the woods. I eat and laugh and eat until I can barely walk, my chest hair matted with dribbled blood, and then the roosters on the hill crow, and dawn comes over the roofs of the houses, and all at once I am filled with gloom again.

"This is some punishment sent us," I hear them bawling from the hill.

My head aches. Morning nails my eyes.

"Some god is angry," I hear a woman keen. "The people of Scyld and Heorogar and Hrothgar are mired in sin!"

My belly rumbles, sick on their sour meat. I crawl through blood-stained leaves to the eaves of the forest, and there peek out. The dogs fall silent at the edge of my spell, and where the king's hall surmounts the town,

19

the blind old Shaper, harp clutched tight to his fragile chest, stares futilely down, straight at me.

A few men, lean, wearing animal skins, look up at the gables of the king's hall, or at the vultures circling casually beyond. Hrothgar says nothing, hoar-frost-bearded, his features cracked and crazed. Inside I hear the people praying—whimpering, whining, mumbling, pleading—to their numerous sticks and stones. He doesn't go in. The king has lofty theories of his own.

"Theories," I whisper to the bloodstained ground. "They'd map out roads through Hell with their crackpot theories!"

They wail, the whole crowd, women and men, a kind of song, like a single quavering voice. The song rings up like greasy smoke and their faces shine with sweat and something that looks like joy. The song swells, pushes through woods and sky, and they're singing now as if by some lunatic theory they had won. I shake with rage. The red sun blinds me, churns up my belly to nausea. I cringe, clawing my flesh, and flee for home.

I used to play games when I was young—it might as well be a thousand years ago. Explored our far-flung underground world in an endless war game of leaps into nothing, ingenious twists into freedom or new perplexity, quick whispered plotting with invisible friends, wild cackles when vengeance was mine. I nosed out, in my childish games, every last shark-toothed chamber and hall, every black tentacle of my mother's cave, and so came at last, adventure by adventure, to the pool of firesnakes. I stared, mouth gaping. They were grey as old ashes; faceless, eyeless. They spread the surface of the water with pure green flame. I knew—seemed to have known all along—that the snakes were there to guard something. Inevitably, after I'd stood there a while rolling my eyes back along the dark hallway, my ears cocked for my mother's step, I screwed my nerve up and dove. The firesnakes scattered as if my flesh were charmed, and so I discovered the sunken door, and so I came up, for the first time, to moonlight.

I went no farther, that first night. But I came out again, inevitably. I played my way farther out into the world, vast cavern aboveground, cautiously darting from tree to tree challenging the terrible forces of night on tiptoe. At dawn I fled back.

I lived those years, as do all young things, in a spell. At times the spell would be broken suddenly: on shelves or in hallways of my mother's cave, large old shapes with smoldering eyes sat watching me. A continuous grumble came out of their mouths; their backs were humped. Then little by little it dawned on me that the eyes that seemed to bore into my body were in fact gazing though it, wearily indifferent to my slight obstruction of the darkness. Of all the creatures I knew in those days, only my mother really looked at me.

She loved me.

I was her creation. We were one thing, like the wall and the rock growing out from it. Or so I ardently, desperately affirmed. When her strange eyes burned into me, I was intensely aware of where I sat, the volume of darkness I displaced, the shiny-smooth span of packed dirt between us, and the shocking separateness from me in my mama's eyes. I would feel, all at once, alone and ugly, almost—as if I'd dirtied myself—obscene. The cavern river tumbled far below us. Being young, unable to face these things, I would bawl and hurl myself at my mother and she would reach out her claws and seize me, though I could see I alarmed her (I had teeth like a saw) and she would smash me to her fat, limp breast as if to make me part of her flesh again. After that, comforted, I would gradually ease back out into my games. Crafty-eyed, wicked as an elderly wolf, I would scheme with or stalk my imaginary friends, projecting the self I meant to become into every dark corner of the cave and the woods above.

One morning I caught my foot in the crack where two old tree trunks joined. "Owp!" I yelled. "Mamma! Waa!" I looked at the foot in anger and disbelief. It was wedged deep, as if the two oak trees were eating it. Pain flew up through me like fire up the flue of a mountain. I lost my head. I bellowed for help. "Mama! Waa! Waaa!" I bellowed to the sky, the forest, the cliffs, until I was so weak from loss of blood I could barely wave my arms. "I'm going to die," I wailed. "Poor Grendel! Poor old Mama!" I wept and sobbed. "Poor Grendel will hang here and starve to death," I told myself, "and no one will ever miss him!" The thought enraged me. I hooted. I thought of my mother's foreign eyes, staring at me from across the room; I thought of the cool, indifferent eyes of the others. I shrieked in fear; still no one came.

"Please, Mama!" I sobbed as if heartbroken.

I slept, I think. When I woke and looked up through the leaves overhead there were vultures. I sighed, indifferent. I tried to see myself from the vultures' viewpoint. I saw, instead, my mother's eyes.

That night, for the first time, I saw men.

It was dark when I awakened—or when I came to, if it was that. I was aware at once that there was something wrong. There was a smell, a fire very different from ours, pungent, painful as thistles to the nose. I opened my eyes and everything was blurry, as though underwater. There were lights all around me, like some weird creature's eyes. They jerked back as I looked. Then voices, speaking words. The sounds were foreign at first, but when I calmed myself, concentrating, I found I understood them: it was my own language, but spoken in a strange way, as if the sounds were made by brittle sticks, dried spindles, flaking bits of shale. My vision cleared and I saw them, mounted on horses, holding torches up. Some of them had shiny domes (as it seemed to me then) with horns coming out, like a bull's. They were small, these creatures, ridiculous but, at the same time, mysteriously irritating, like rats. Their movements were stiff and regular, as if figured by logic. They had skinny, naked hands that moved by clicks.

I tried to move. They all stopped speaking at the same instant, like sparrows. We stared at each other.

One of them said—a tall one with a long black beard—"It moves independent of the tree."

They nodded.

The tall one said, "It's a growth of some kind, that's my opinion. Some beastlike fungus."

They all looked up into the branches.

A short fat one pointed up into the tree with an ax. "Those branches on the northern side are all dead there. No doubt the whole tree'll be dead

22

before midsummer. It's always the north side goes first when there ain't enough sap."

They nodded, and another one said, "See there where it grows up out of the trunk? Sap running all over."

They leaned over the sides of their horses to look, pushing the torches toward me. The horses' eyes glittered.

"Have to close that up if we're going to save this tree," the tall one said. The others grunted, and the tall one looked up at my eyes, uneasy. I couldn't move. He stepped down off the horse and came over to me, so close I could have swung my hand and smashed his head if I could make my muscles move. "It's like blood," he said, and made a face.

Two of the others got down and came over to pull at their noses and look.

"I say that tree's a goner," one of them said.

They all nodded, except the tall one. "We can't just leave it rot," he said. "Start letting the place go to ruin and you know what the upshot'll be."

They nodded. The others got down off their horses and came over. The fat one said, "Maybe we could chop the fungus out."

They thought about it. After a while the tall one shook his head. "I don't know. Could be it's some kind of a oak tree spirit. Better not to mess with it."

They looked uneasy. There was a hairless, skinny one. He stood with his arms out, like a challenged bird, and he kept moving around in jerky little circles, bent forward, peering at everything, at the tree, at the woods around, up into my eyes. Now suddenly he nodded. "That's it! King's right! It's a spirit!"

"You think so?" they said. Their heads poked forward.

"Sure of it," he said.

"Is it friendly, you think?" the king said.

The hairless one peered up at me with the fingertips of one hand in his mouth. The skinny elbow hung straight down, leaning on an invisible table while he thought the whole thing through. His black little eyes stared straight into mine, as if waiting for me to tell him something. I tried to speak. My mouth moved, but nothing would come out. The little man jerked back. "He's hungry!" he said.

"Hungry!" they all said. "What does he eat?"

He looked at me again. His tiny eyes drilled into me and he was crouched as if he were thinking of trying to jump up into my brains. My heart thudded. I was so hungry I could eat a rock. He smiled suddenly; a holy vision had exploded in his head. "He eats *pig*!" he said. He looked doubtful. "Or maybe pigsmoke. He's in a period of transition."

They all looked at me, thinking it over, then nodded.

The king picked out six men. "Go get the thing some pigs," he said. The six men said, "Yes sir!" and got on their horses and rode off. It filled me with joy, though it was all crazy, and before I knew I could do it, I laughed. They jerked away and stood shaking, looking up.

"The spirit's angry," one of them whispered.

"It always has been," another one said. "That's why it's killing the tree."

"No, no, you're wrong," the hairless one said. "It's yelling for pig."

"Pig!" I tried to yell. It scared them.

They all began shouting at each other. One of the horses neighed and reared up, and for some crazy reason they took it for a sign. The king snatched an ax from the man beside him and, without any warning, he hurled it at me. I twisted, letting out a howl, and it shot past my shoulder.

"You're all crazy," I tried to yell, but it came out a moan. I bellowed for my mother.

"Surround him!" the king yelled. "Save the horses!"—and suddenly I knew I was dealing with no dull mechanical beasts, but with thinking creatures, patternmakers, the most dangerous things I'd ever met. I shrieked at them, trying to scare them off, but they merely ducked behind bushes and took long sticks from the saddles of their horses, bows and javelins. "You're all crazy," I bellowed, "you're all insane!" I'd never howled more loudly in my life. Darts like hot coals went through my legs and arms and I howled more loudly still. And then, just when I was sure I was finished, a shriek ten times as loud as mine came blaring off the cliff. It was mother! She came roaring down like thunder, screaming like a thousand hurricanes, eyes as bright as dragon fire, and before she was within a mile of us, the creatures had leaped to their horses and galloped away. Big trees shattered and fell from her path; the earth trembled. Then her smell poured in like blood into a silver cup, filling the moonlit clearing to the brim, and I felt the two trees that held me falling, and I was fumbling, free, into the grass.

I woke up in the cave, warm firelight flickering on walls. My mother lay picking through the bone pile. When she heard me stir, she turned, wrinkling her forehead, and looked at me. I tried to tell her all that had happened, all that I'd come to understand. She only stared, troubled at my noise. "The world resists me and I resist the world," I said. "That's all there is."

The fire in mother's eyes brightens and she reaches out as if some current is tearing us apart. "The world is all pointless accident," I say. Shouting now, my fists clenched. Her face works. She gets up on all fours, brushing dry bits of bone from her path, and, with a look of terror, rising as if by unnatural power, she hurls herself across the void and buries me in her bristly fur and fat. I sicken with fear. "My mother's fur is bristly," I say to myself. "Her flesh is loose." Buried under my mother I cannot see. She smells of wild pig and fish. "My mother smells of wild pig and fish," I say. What I see I inspire with usefulness, I think, trying to suck in breath, and all that I do not see is useless, void. I observe myself observing what I observe. It startles me.

(Talking, talking, spinning a skin, a skin. . . .)

I can't breathe, and I claw to get free. She struggles. I smell my mama's blood and, alarmed, I hear from the walls and floor, the booming booming of her heart.

It wasn't because he threw that battle-ax that I turned on Hrothgar. That was mere midnight foolishness. I dismissed it, thought of it afterwards only as you remember a tree that fell on you or an adder you stepped on by accident, except of course that Hrothgar was more to be feared than a tree or snake. It wasn't until later, when I was full-grown and Hrothgar was an old, old man, that I settled my soul on destroying him—slowly and cruelly. Except for his thanes' occasional stories of seeing my footprints, he'd probably forgotten by then that I existed.

Oh, I heard them at their meadhall tables, their pinched, cunning rats' faces picking like needles at a boaster's words, the warfalcons gazing down, black, from the rafters, and when one of them finished his raving threats, another would stand up and lift his ram's horn, or draw his sword, or sometimes both if he was very drunk, and he'd tell them what *he* planned to do. Now and then some trivial argument would break out, and one of them would kill another one, and all the others would detach themselves from the killer as neatly as blood clotting, and they'd consider the case and they'd either excuse him, for some reason, or else send him out to the forest to live by stealing from their outlying pens like a wounded fox. At times I would try to befriend the exile, at other times I would try to ignore him, but they were treacherous. In the end, I had to eat them. As a rule, though, that wasn't how all their drinking turned out. Normally the men would howl out their daring, and the evening would get merrier, louder and louder, the king praising this one, criticizing that one, no one getting hurt except maybe some female who was asking for it, and eventually they'd all fall asleep on each other like lizards, and I'd steal a cow.

Darting unseen from camp to camp, I observed a change come over their drunken boasts. It was late spring. Food was plentiful. Every sheep and goat had its wobbly twins, the forest was teeming, and the first crops of the hillsides were coming into fruit. A man would roar, "I'll steal their gold and burn their meadhall!," shaking his sword as if the tip were afire, and a man with eyes like two pins would say, "Do it now, Cowface! I think you're not even the man your father was!" The people would laugh. I would back away into the darkness, furious at my stupid need to spy on them, and I would glide to the next camp of men, and I'd hear the same.

Then once, around midnight, I came to a hall in ruins. The cows in their pens lay burbling blood through their nostrils, with javelin holes in their necks. None had been eaten. The watchdogs lay like dark wet stones, with their heads cut off, teeth bared. The fallen hall was a square of flames and acrid smoke, and the people inside (none of them had been eaten either) were burned black, small, like dwarfs turned dark and crisp. The sky opened like a hole where the gables had loomed before, and the wooden benches, the trestle tables, the beds that had hung on the meadhall walls were scattered to the edge of the forest, shining charcoal. There was no sign of the gold they'd kept—not so much as a melted hilt.

Then the wars began, and the war songs, and the weapon-making. If the songs were true, as I suppose at least one or two of them were, there had always been wars, and what I'd seen was merely a period of mutual exhaustion.

I'd be watching a meadhall from high in a tree, night birds singing in the limbs below me, the moon's face hidden in a tower of clouds, and nothing would be stirring except leaves moving in the light spring breeze and, down by the pigpens, two men walking with their battle-axes and their dogs. Inside the hall I would hear the Shaper telling of the glorious deeds of dead kings—how they'd split certain heads, sneaked away with certain precious swords and necklaces—his harp mimicking the rush of swords, clanging boldly with the noble speeches, sighing behind the heroes' dying words. Whenever he stopped, thinking up formulas for what to say next, the people would all shout and thump each other and drink to the Shaper's long life. In the shadow of the hall and by the outbuildings, men sat whistling or humming to themselves, repairing weapons: winding bronze bands around gray ash spears, treating their sword blades with snakes' venom.

Then suddenly the birds below me in the tree would fall silent, and beyond the meadhall clearing I'd hear the creak of harness leather. The watchmen and their dogs would stand stock-still, as if lightning-struck; then the dogs would bark, and the next instant the door would bang open and men would come tumbling, looking crazy, from the meadhall. The enemies' horses would thunder up into the clearing, leaping the pig fences, sending the cows and the pigs away mooing and squealing, and the two bands of men would charge. Twenty feet apart they would slide to a stop and stand screaming at each other with raised swords. The leaders on both sides held their javelins high in both hands and shook them, howling their lungs out. Terrible threats, from the few words I could catch. Things about their fathers and their fathers' fathers, things about justice and honor and lawful revenge.

Then they would fight. Spears flying, swords whonking, arrows raining from the windows and door of the meadhall and the edge of the woods. Horses reared and fell over screaming, ravens flew, crazy as bats in a fire; men staggered, gesturing wildly, making speeches, dying or sometimes pretending to be dying, sneaking off. Sometimes the attackers would be driven back, sometimes they'd win and burn the meadhall down, sometimes they'd capture the king of the meadhall and make his people give weapons and gold rings and cows.

It was confusing and frightening, not in a way I could untangle. I was safe in my tree, and the men who fought were nothing to me, except of course that they talked in something akin to my language, which meant that we were, incredibly, related. I was sickened, if only at the waste of it: all they killed—cows, horses, men—they left to rot or burn. I sacked all I could and tried to store it, but my mother would growl and make faces because of the stink.

The fighting went on all that summer and began again the next and again the next. Sometimes when a meadhall burned the survivors would go to another meadhall and, stretching out their hands, would crawl unarmed up the strangers' hill and would beg to be taken in. They would give the strangers whatever weapons or pigs or cattle they'd saved from destruction, and the strangers would give them an outbuilding, the worst of their food, and some straw. The two groups would fight as allies after that, except that now and then they betrayed each other, one shooting the other from behind for some reason, or stealing the other group's gold some midnight, or sneaking into bed with the other group's wives and daughters.

I watched it, season after season. Sometimes I watched from the high cliff wall, where I could look out and see all the meadhall lights on the various hills across the countryside, glowing like candies, reflected stars. With luck, I might see on a soft summer night as many as three halls burning down at once. That was rare, of course. It grew rarer as the pattern of their warring changed. Hrothgar, who'd begun hardly stronger than the others, began to outstrip the rest. He'd worked out a theory about what fighting was for, and now he no longer fought with his six closest neighbors. He'd shown them the strength of his organization, and now, instead of making war on them, he sent men to them every three months or so, with heavy wagons and back slings, to gather their tribute to his greatness. They piled his wagons high with gold and leather and weapons, and they kneeled to his messengers and made long speeches and promised to defend him against any foolhardy outlaw that dared to attack him. Hrothgar's messengers answered with friendly words and praise of the man they'd just plundered, as if the whole thing had been his idea, then whipped up the oxen, pulled up their loaded back slings, and started home.

And now when enemies from farther out struck at kings who called themselves Hrothgar's friends, a messenger would slip out and ride through the night to the tribute-taker, and in half an hour, while the enemy bands were still shouting at each other, still waving their ash spears and saying what horrible things they would do, the forest would rumble with the sound of Hrothgar's horsemen. He would overcome them: his band had grown large, and for the treasures Hrothgar could afford now to give them in sign of his thanks, his warriors became hornets. New roads snaked out. New meadhalls gave tribute. His treasure hoard grew till his meadhall was piled to the rafters with brightly painted shields and ornamented swords and boars-head helmets and coils of gold, and they had to abandon the meadhall and sleep in the outbuildings. Meanwhile, those who paid tribute to him were forced to strike at more distant halls to gather the gold they paid to Hrothgar and a little on the side for themselves. His power overran the world, from the foot of my cliff to the northern sea to the impenetrable forests south and east.

One night, inevitably, a blind man turned up at Hrothgar's temporary meadhall. He was carrying a harp. I watched from the shadow of a cow shed, since on that hill there were no trees. The guards at the door crossed their axes in front of him. He waited, smiling foolishly, while a messenger went inside. A few minutes later the messenger returned, gave the old man a nod, and—cautiously, feeling ahead of himself with his crooked bare toes like a man engaged in some strange, pious dance, the foolish smile still fixed on his face—the blind old man went in. A boy darted up from the weeds at the foot of the hill, the harper's companion. He too was shown in.

The hall became quiet, and after a moment Hrothgar spoke, tones low and measured—of necessity, from too much shouting on midnight raids. The harper gave him back some answer, and Hrothgar spoke again. I glanced at the watchdogs. They still sat silent as tree stumps, locked in my spell. I crept closer to the hall to hear. The people were noisy for a time, yelling to the harper, offering him mead, making jokes, and then again King Hrothgar spoke, white-bearded. The hall became still.

The silence expanded. People coughed. As if all by itself, then, the harp made a curious run of sounds, almost words, and then a moment later, arresting as a voice from a hollow tree, the harper began to chant.

> *Lo, we have heard the honor of the Speardanes,*
> *nation-kings, in days now gone,*
> *how those battle-lords brought themselves glory.*
> *Oft Scyld Shefing shattered the forces*
> *of kinsmen-marauders, and dragged away their*
> *meadhall-benches, terrified earls—after first men found him*
> *castaway. (He got recompense for that!)*
> *He grew up under the clouds, won glory of men*
> *till all his enemies sitting around him*
> *heard across the whaleroads his demands and gave*
> *him tribute. That was a good king!*

So he sang—or intoned, with the harp behind him—twisting together like sailors' ropes the bits and pieces of the best old songs. The people were hushed. Even the surrounding hills were hushed, as if brought low by language. He knew his art. He was king of the Shapers, harp-string scratchers.

That was what had brought him over wilderness, down his blind man's alleys of time and space, to Hrothgar's famous hall. He would sing the glory of Hrothgar's line and gild his wisdom and stir up his men to more daring deeds. For a price.

He sang of battles and marriages, of funerals and hangings, the whimperings of beaten enemies, of splendid hunts and harvests. He sang of Hrothgar, hoarfrost white, magnificent of mind.

When he finished, the hall was as quiet as a mound. I too was silent, my ear pressed tight against the timbers. Even to me, incredibly, he had made it all sound true and very fine. Now a little, now more, a great roar began, an exhalation of breath that swelled to a rumble of voices and then to the howling and clapping and stomping of men gone mad on art. They would seize the oceans, the farthest stars, the deepest secret rivers in Hrothgar's name! Men wept like children: children sat stunned. It went on and on, a fire more dread than any visible fire.

I crossed the moors in a queer panic, like a creature half insane. I knew the truth: *A man said, "I'll steal their gold and burn their meadhall!" and another man said, "Do it now!"*

Thus I fled, ridiculous hairy creature torn apart by poetry—crawling, whimpering, streaming tears, across the world like a two-headed beast, like a mixed-up lamb and kid at the tail of a baffled, indifferent ewe—and I gnashed my teeth and clutched the sides of my head as if to heal the split, but I couldn't.

At the top of the cliff wall I turned and looked down, and I saw all the lights of Hrothgar's realm and the realms beyond that, that would soon be his, and to clear my mind, I sucked in wind and screamed. The sound went out, violent, to the rims of the world.

I clamped my palms to my ears and stretched up my lips and shrieked again. Then I ran on all fours, chest pounding, to the smoky mere.

The Shaper remains, though now there are nobler courts where he might sing. The pride of creation. He built this hall by the power of his songs.

The boy observes him, tall and solemn, twelve years older than the night he first crept in with his stone-eyed master. He knows no art but tragedy—a moving singer. The credit is wholly mine.

Inspired by winds (or whatever you please) the old man sang of a glorious meadhall whose light would shine to the ends of the ragged world. The thought took seed in Hrothgar's mind. It grew. He called all his people together and told them his daring scheme. He would build a magnificent meadhall high on a hill, with a view of the western sea, a victory seat to stand forever as a sign of the glory and justice of Hrothgar's Danes. There he would sit and give treasures out, all wealth but the lives of men and the people's land. And so his sons would do after him, and his sons' sons, unto the final generation.

I listened, huddled in the darkness, tormented, mistrustful. I knew them, had watched them; yet the things he said seemed true. He sent to far kingdoms for woodsmen, carpenters, metalsmiths, goldsmiths—also carters, victuallers, clothiers to attend to the workmen—and for weeks their uproar filled the days and nights. I watched from the vines and boulders two miles off. Then word went out to the races of men that Hrothgar's hall was finished. He gave it its name. From neighboring realms and from across the sea came men to the great celebration. The harper sang.

I listened, felt myself swept up. I knew very well that all he said was ridiculous, not light for their darkness but flattery, illusion, a vortex pulling them from sunlight to heat, a kind of midsummer burgeoning, waltz to the sickle. Yet I was swept up. "Ridiculous!" I hissed in the black of the forest. I snatched up a snake from beside my foot and whispered to it, "I knew him *when*!" But I couldn't bring out a wicked cackle, as I'd meant to do. My heart was light with Hrothgar's goodness, and leaden with grief at my own bloodthirsty ways. I backed away, crablike, farther into darkness, backed away till the honey-sweet lure of the harp no longer mocked me. Yet even now my mind was tormented by images. Thanes filled the hall and a great silent crowd of them spilled out over the surrounding hill, smiling, peaceable, hearing the harper as if not a man in all that lot had ever twisted a knife in his neighbor's chest.

"Well then he's changed them," I said, and stumbled and fell on the root of a tree. "Why not?"

I listened, tensed. No answer.

"He reshapes the world," I whispered, belligerent. "So his name implies. He stares strange-eyed at the mindless world and turns dry sticks to gold."

A little poetic, I would readily admit. His manner of speaking was infecting me, making me pompous. "Nevertheless," I whispered crossly— but I couldn't go on, too conscious all at once of my whispering, eternal posturing.

In the hall they were laughing.

Men and women stood talking in the light of the meadhall door and on the narrow streets below; on the lower hillside boys and girls played near the sheep pens, shyly holding hands. A few lay touching each other in the forest eaves. I thought how they'd shriek if I suddenly showed my face, and it made me smile, but I held myself back. They talked nothing, stupidities, their soft voices groping like hands. I felt myself tightening, cross, growing restless for no clear reason, and I made myself move more slowly. Then, cir- cling the clearing, I stepped on something fleshy, and jerked away. It was a man. They'd cut his throat. His clothes had been stolen. I stared up at the hall, baffled, beginning to shake. They went on talking softly, touching hands, their hair full of light. I lifted up the body and slung it across my shoulder.

Then the harp began to play. The crowd grew still.

The harp sighed, the Shaper sang, as sweet-voiced as a child.

He told how the earth was first built, long ago: said that the greatest of gods made the world, every wonder-bright plain and the turning seas, and set out as signs of his victory the sun and moon, great lamps for light to land- dwellers, kingdom torches, and adorned the fields with all colors and shapes, made limbs and leaves and gave life to every creature that moves on land.

The harp turned solemn. He told of an ancient feud between two brothers which split all the world between darkness and light. And I, Gren- del, was the dark side, he said. The terrible race god cursed.

I believed him. Such was the power of the Shaper's harp! Stood wriggling my face, letting tears down my nose, grinding my fists into my streaming eyes, even though to do it I had to squeeze with my elbow the corpse of the proof that both of us were cursed, or neither, that brothers had never lived, nor the god who judged them. "Waaa!" I bawled.

Oh what a conversion!

I staggered out into the open and up toward the hall with my burden, groaning out, "Mercy! Peace!" The harper broke off, the people screamed. (They have their own versions, but this is the truth.) Drunken men rushed me with battle-axes. I sank to my knees, crying, "Friend! Friend!" They hacked at me, yipping like dogs. I held up the body for protection. Their spears came through it and one of them nicked me, a tiny scratch high on my left breast, but I knew by the sting it had venom on it and I understood, as shocked as I'd been the first time, that they could kill me—eventually *would* if I gave them a chance. I struck at them, holding the body as a shield, and two fell bleeding from my nails at the first little swipe. The others backed off. I crushed the body in my hug, then hurled it in their faces, turned, and fled. They didn't follow.

I ran to the center of the forest and fell down panting. My mind was wild. "Pity," I moaned, "O pity! Pity!" I wept—strong monster with teeth like a shark's—and I slammed the earth with such force that a seam split open twelve feet long. "Bastards!" I roared, "Sons of bitches! Monsters!" Words I'd picked up from men in their lunatic rages.

Two nights later I went back. I was addicted. The Shaper was singing the glorious deeds of the dead men, praising war. He sang how they'd fought me. It was all lies. The sly harp rasped like snakes in cattails, glorifying death. I snatched a guard and smashed him on a tree, but my stomach turned at the thought of eating him.

"Woe to the man," the Shaper sang, "who shall through wicked hostilities shove his soul down into the fire's hug! Let him hope for no change: he can never turn away! But lucky the man who, after his deathday, shall seek the Prince, find peace in his father's embrace!"

"Ridiculous!" I whispered through clenched teeth. How was it that he could enrage me so? I knew what I knew, the mindless, mechanical bruteness of things, and when the Shaper's lure drew my mind away to hopeful dreams, the dark of what was, and always was, reached out and snatched my feet.

I got up and felt my way back through the forest and over to the cliff wall and back to the mere and to my cave. I lay there listening to the indistinct memory of the Shaper's songs. My mother picked through the bone pile, sullen. I'd brought no food.

"Ridiculous," I whispered.

She looked at me, and whimpered, scratched at the nipples I had not sucked in years. She was pitiful, foul, her smile a jagged white tear in the firelight.

I clamped my eyes shut, listened to the river, and after a time I slept.

It was the height of summer, harvest season in the first year of what I have come to call my war with Hrothgar. The night air was filled with the smell of apples and shucked grain, and I could hear the noise in the meadhall from a mile away. I moved toward it, drawn, as always, as if by some kind of curse. I meant not to be seen that night.

I had no intention of terrifying Hrothgar's thanes for nothing. I hunkered down at the edge of the forest, looking up the long hill at the meadhall lights. I could hear the Shaper's song.

I no longer remember exactly what he sang. I know only that it had a strange effect on me: it no longer filled me with doubt and distress, loneliness, shame. It enraged me. It was their confidence, maybe—their blissful, swinish ignorance, their bumptious self-satisfaction and, worst of all, their *hope.* I went closer, darting from cowshed to cowshed and finally up to the wall. I found a crack and peeked in. I do remember what he said, now that I think about it. Or some of it. He spoke of how god had been kind to the Scyldings, sending so rich a harvest. The people sat beaming, bleary-eyed and fat, nodding their approval of god. He spoke of god's great generosity in sending them so wise a king. They all raised their cups to god and Hrothgar, and Hrothgar smiled, bits of food in his beard. The Shaper talked of how god had vanquished their enemies and filled up their houses with precious treasure, how they were the richest, most powerful people on earth, how here and here alone in all the world men were free and heroes were brave and virgins were virgins. He ended the song, and people clapped and shouted their praise and filled their golden cups.

Then a stick snapped behind me, and the same instant, a dog barked. A helmeted, chain-mailed guard leaped out at me, sword in two hands above his head, prepared to split me.

I was as surprised as the guard. We both stared.

Then, almost the same instant, the guard screamed and I roared like a bull gone mad to drive him off. He let go of the sword and tried to retreat, walking backward, but he tripped on the dog and fell. I laughed, a little wild, and reached out fast as a striking snake for his leg. In a second I was up on my feet again. He screamed, dangling, and then there were others all around me. They threw javelins and axes, and one of the men caught the guard's thrashing arms and tried to yank him free. I held on, and laughed again at Hrothgar's whispering and trembling by the meadhall door, at everything—the oblivious trees and the witless moon. I'd meant them no harm, but they'd attacked me again, as always. They were crazy.

I wanted to say, "Lo, god has vanquished mine enemies!"—but that made me laugh harder, though even now my heart raced and, in spite of it all, I was afraid of them. I backed away, still holding the screaming guard. They merely stared, with their weapons drawn, their shoulders hunched against my laughter. When I'd reached a safe distance I held up the guard to taunt them, then held him still higher and leered into his face. He went silent, looking at me upside down in horror, suddenly knowing what I planned. As if casually, in plain sight of them all, I bit his head off, crunched through the helmet and skull with my teeth and, holding the jerking, blood-slippery body in two hands, sucked the blood that sprayed like a hot, thick geyser from his neck. It got all over me. Women fainted, men backed toward the hall. I fled with the body to the woods, heart churning—boiling like a flooded ditch—with glee.

Some three or four nights later I launched a raid. I burst in when they were all asleep, snatched seven from their beds, and slit them open and devoured them on the spot. I felt a strange, unearthly joy. It was as if I'd made some incredible discovery, like my discovery long ago of the moonlit world beyond the mere. I was transformed. I was a new focus for the clutter of space I stood in: if the world had once imploded on the tree where I waited, trapped and full of pain, it now blasted outward, away from me, screeching terror. I had become, myself, the mama I'd searched the cliffs for once in vain. I had *become* something. I had hung between possibilities before, between the cold truths I knew and the heart-sucking conjuring tricks of the Shaper; now that was passed: I was Grendel, Ruiner of Mead-halls, Wrecker of Kings!

But also, as never before, I was alone. I do not complain of it (talking, talking, complaining, complaining, filling the world I walk with words). But I admit it was a jolt.

It was a few raids later. The meadhall door burst open at my touch exactly as before, and, for once, that night, I hesitated. Men sat up in their beds, snatched their helmets, swords, and shields from the covers beside them, and, shouting brave words that came out like squeals, they threw their legs over the sides to stumble toward me. Someone yelled, "Remember this hour, ye thanes of Hrothgar, the boasts you made as the meadbowl passed! Remember our good king's gift of rings and pay him with all your might for his many kindnesses!"

Damned pompous fools. I hurled a bench at the closest. They all cowered back. I stood waiting, bent forward with my feet apart, flat-footed, till they ended their interminable orations. I was hunched like a wrestler, moving my head from side to side, making sure no sneak slipped up on me. I was afraid of them from habit, and as the four or five drunkest of the thanes came toward me, shaking their weapons and shouting at me, my idiotic fear of them mounted. But I held my ground. Then, with a howl, one plunged at me, sword above his head in both fists. I let it come.

I closed my hand on the blade and snatched it from the drunken thane's hand and hurled it the length of the hall. It clattered on the fireplace stones and fell to the stone floor, ringing. I seized him and crushed him. Another one came at me, gloating in his bleary-eyed heroism, maniacally joyful because he had bragged that he would die for his king and he was doing it. He did it. Another one came, reeling and whooping, trying to make his eyes focus.

I laughed. It was outrageous: they came, they fell, howling insanity about brothers, fathers, glorious Hrothgar and god. But though I laughed, I felt trapped, as hollow as a rotten tree. The meadhall seemed to stretch for miles, out to the edges of time and space, and I saw myself killing them, on and on and on, mechanically, without contest. I saw myself swelling like bellows on their blood.

All at once I began to smash things—benches, tables, hanging beds—a rage as meaningless and terrible as everything else.

Then—as a crowning absurdity—my salvation that moment—came the man the thanes called Unferth.

He stood across the hall from me, youthful, intense, cold sober. He was taller than the others; he stood out among his fellow thanes like a horse in a herd of cows. His nose was as porous and dark as volcanic rock. His light beard grew in patches.

"Stand back," he said.

The drunken little men around me backed away. The hall floor between us, Unferth and myself, lay open.

"Monster, prepare to die!" he said. Very righteous. The wings of his nostrils flared and quivered like an outraged priest's.

I laughed. "Aargh!" I said. I spit bits of bone.

He glanced behind, making sure he knew exactly where the window was. "Are you right with your god?" he said.

I laughed somewhat more fiercely. He was one of those.

He took a tentative step toward me, then paused, holding his sword out and shaking it. "Tell them in Hell that Unferth, son of Ecglaf, sent you, known far and wide in these Scannian lands as a hero among the Scyldings." He took a few side steps, like one wrestler circling another, except that he was thirty feet away. The maneuver was ridiculous.

"Come, come," I said. "Let me tell them I was sent by Sideways-Walker."

He frowned, trying to puzzle out my speech. I said it again, louder and slower, and a startled look came over him. Even now he didn't know what I was saying, but it was clear to him, I think, that I was speaking words. He got a cunning look, as if getting ready to offer a deal—the look men have when they fight with men instead of poor stupid animals.

He was shaken, and to get back his nerve he spoke some more. "For many months, unsightly monster, you've murdered men as you pleased in Hrothgar's hall. Unless you can murder me as you've murdered lesser men, I give you my word those days are done forever! The king has given me splendid gifts. He will see tonight that his gifts have not gone for nothing! Prepare to fall, foul thing! This one red hour makes your reputation or mine!"

I shook my head at him, wickedly smiling. "Reputation!" I said, pretending to be much impressed.

His eyebrows shot up. He'd understood me; no doubt of it now. "You can talk!" he said. He backed away a step. My talking changed the picture.

I nodded, moving in on him. Near the center of the room there was a trestle table piled high with glossy apples. An evil idea came over me—so evil it made me shiver as I smiled—and I sidled across to the table. "So you're a hero," I said. He didn't get it, and I said it twice more before I gave up in disgust. I talked on anyway, let him get what he could, come try for reputation when he pleased. "I'm impressed," I said. "I've never seen a live hero before. I thought they were only in poetry. Ah, ah, it must be a terrible burden, though, being a hero—glory reaper, harvest of monsters! Everybody always watching you, weighing you, seeing if you're still heroic. You know how it is—he he! Sooner or later the harvest virgin will make her mistake in the haystack." I laughed.

I picked up an apple and polished it lightly and quickly on the hair of my arm. I had my head bowed, smiling, looking up at him through my eyebrows.

"Dread creature—" he said.

I went on polishing the apple, smiling. "And the awful inconvenience,"

I said. "Always having to stand erect, always having to find noble language! It must wear on a man."

He lifted his sword to make a run at me, and I laughed—howled—and threw an apple at him. He dodged, and then his mouth dropped open. I laughed harder, threw another. He dodged again.

"Hey!" he yelled. A forgivable lapse.

And now I was raining apples at him and laughing myself weak. He covered his head, roaring at me. He tried to charge through the barrage, but he couldn't make three feet. I slammed one straight into his pockmarked nose, and blood spurted out like joining rivers. It made the floor slippery, and he went down. *Clang!* I bent double with laughter. Poor Jangler—Unferth—tried to take advantage of it, charging at me on all fours, snatching at my ankles, but I jumped back and tipped over the table on him, half burying him in apples. He screamed and thrashed, trying to see if the others were watching. He was crying, only a boy, famous hero or not, a poor miserable virgin.

"Such is life," I said, and mocked a sigh. "Such is dignity!" Then I left. I got more pleasure from that apple fight than from any other battle in my life.

I was sure, going back to my cave, the he wouldn't follow. They never did. But I was wrong; he was a new kind of Scylding. He must have started tracking me that same morning. A driven man, a maniac. He arrived at the cave three nights later.

I was asleep. I woke up with a start, not sure what it was that had awakened me. I saw my mother moving slowly and silently past me, blue murder in her eyes. I understood instantly, and I darted around in front to block her way. I pushed her back.

There he lay, gasping on his belly like a half-drowned rat. His face and throat and arms were a crosshatch of festering cuts, the leavings of fire-snakes. His hair and beard hung straight down like seaweed. He panted for a long time, then rolled his eyes up, vaguely in my direction. In the darkness he couldn't see me, though I could see him. He closed his hand on the sword hilt and jiggled the sword a little, too weak to raise it off the floor.

"Unferth has come!" he said.

I smiled.

He crawled toward me, the sword noisily scraping on the cave's rock floor. Then he gave out again. "It will be sung," he whispered, then paused again to get wind. "It will be sung year on year and age on age that Unferth went down through the burning lake—" He paused to pant. "—and gave his life in battle with the world-rim monster." He let his cheek fall to the floor and lay panting for a long time, saying nothing. It dawned on me that he was waiting for me to kill him. I did nothing. I sat down and put my elbows on my knees and my chin on my fists and merely watched. He lay with his eyes closed and began to get his breath back. He whispered: "It's all very well to make a fool of me before my fellow thanes. All very well to talk about dignity and noble language and all the rest, as if heroism were a golden trinket, mere outward show, and hollow. But such is not the case, monster. That is to say—" He paused, seemed to grope; he'd lost his train of thought.

I said nothing, merely waited, blocking my mother by stretching out an arm when she came near.

"Even now you mock me," Unferth whispered. I had an uneasy feeling he was close to tears. If he wept I was not sure I could control myself. His pretensions to uncommon glory were one thing. If for even an instant he pretended to misery like mine. . . .

"You think me a witless fool," he whispered. "Oh, I heard what you said. I caught your nasty insinuations. 'I thought heroes were only in poetry,' you said. Implying that what I've made of myself is mere fairy-tale stuff." He raised his head, trying to glare at me, but his blind stare was in the wrong direction, following my mother's pacing. "Well, it's not, let me tell you." His lips trembled and I was certain he would cry: I would have to destroy him from pure disgust, but he held it. He let his head fall again and sucked for air. A little of his voice came back: "Poetry's trash, mere clouds of words, comfort to the hopeless. But this is no cloud, no syllabled phantom that stands here shaking its sword at you."

I let the slight exaggeration pass.

But Unferth didn't. "Or lies here," he said. "A hero is not afraid to face cruel truth." That reminded him, apparently, of what he'd meant to say before. "You talk of heroism as noble language, dignity. It's more than that, as my coming here has proved. No man above us will ever know whether Unferth died here or fled to the hills like a coward. Only you and I and god will know the truth. That's inner heroism."

"Hmmm," I said. It was not unusual, of course, to hear them contradict themselves.

He looked hurt and slightly indignant. He'd understood.

"Wretched shape—" he said.

"But no doubt there are compensations," I said. "The pleasant feeling of vast superiority, the easy success with women—"

"Monster!" he howled.

"And the joy of self-knowledge, that's a great compensation! The easy and absolute certainty that whatever the danger, however terrible the odds, you'll stand firm, behave with the dignity of a hero, yea, even to the grave!"

"No more talk!" he yelled. His voice broke. He jerked his head up. "Does *nothing* have value in your horrible ruin of a brain?"

I waited. The whole foolish scene was his idea, not mine.

I saw the light dawning in his eyes. "I understand," he said. I thought he would laugh at the bottomless stupidity of my cynicism, but while the laugh was still starting at the corner of his eyes, another look came, close to fright. "You think me deluded. Tricked by my own walking fairy tale. You think I came without a hope of winning—came to escape indignity by suicide!" He did laugh now, not amused: sorrowful and angry. The laugh died quickly. "I didn't know how deep the pool was," he said. "I had a chance. I knew I had no more than that. It's all a hero asks for."

I sighed. The word *hero* was beginning to grate. He was an idiot. I could crush him like a fly, but I held back.

"Go ahead, scoff," he said, petulant. "Except in the life of a hero, the whole world's meaningless. The hero sees values beyond what's possible. That's the *nature* of a hero. It kills him, of course, ultimately. But it makes the whole struggle of humanity worthwhile."

42

I nodded in the darkness. "And breaks up the boredom," I said.

He raised up on his elbows, and the effort of it made his shoulders shake. "One of us is going to die tonight. Does *that* break up your boredom?"

"It's not true," I said. "A few minutes from now I'm going to carry you back to Hrothgar, safe and sound. So much for poetry."

"I'll kill myself," he whispered. He shook violently now.

"Up to you," I answered reasonably, "but you'll admit it may seem at least a trifle cowardly to some."

His fists closed and his teeth clenched; then he relaxed and lay flat.

I waited for him to find an answer. Minutes passed. It came to me that he had quit. He had glimpsed a glorious ideal, had struggled toward it and seized it and come to understand it, and was disappointed. One could sympathize.

He was asleep.

I picked him up gently and carried him home. I laid him at the door of Hrothgar's meadhall, still asleep, killed the two guards so I wouldn't be misunderstood, and left.

He lives on, bitter, feebly challenging my midnight raids from time to time (three times this summer, innumerable times in the dreary twelve years that have passed since that idiot apple fight)—lives on, poor Unferth, crazy with shame that he alone is always spared, and furiously jealous of the dead. I laugh when I see him. He throws himself at me, or he cunningly sneaks up behind, sometimes in disguise—a goat, a dog, a sickly old woman—and I roll on the floor with laughter. So much for heroism. So much for the harvest virgin. So much for Shapers' dreams.

They talk of a man who will get me sure, some super super-hero men call Beowulf. Terrific.

Come, fierce stranger.

Soon.

The Snows of Kilimanjaro

Ernest Hemingway

Kilimanjaro is a snow-covered mountain 19,710 feet high, and is said to be the highest mountain in Africa. Its western summit is called by the Masai "Ngàje Ngài," the House of God. Close to the western summit there is the dried and frozen carcass of a leopard. No one has explained what the leopard was seeking at that altitude.

"The marvelous thing is that it's painless," he said. "That's how you know when it starts."

"Is it really?"

"Absolutely. I'm awfully sorry about the odor though. That must bother you."

"Don't! Please don't."

"Look at them," he said. "Now is it sight or is it scent that brings them like that?"

The cot the man lay on was in the wide shade of a mimosa tree and as he looked out past the shade onto the glare of the plain there were three of the big birds squatted obscenely, while in the sky a dozen more sailed, making quick-moving shadows as they passed.

"They've been there since the day the truck broke down," he said. "Today's the first time any have lit on the ground. I watched the way they sailed very carefully at first in case I ever wanted to use them in a story. That's funny now."

"I wish you wouldn't," she said.

"I'm only talking," he said. "It's much easier if I talk. But I don't want to bother you."

"You know it doesn't bother me," she said. "It's that I've gotten so very nervous not being able to do anything. I think we might make it as easy as we can until the plane comes."

"Or until the plane doesn't come."

"Please tell me what I can do. There must be something I can do."

"You can take the leg off and that might stop it, though I doubt it. Or you can shoot me. You're a good shot now. I taught you to shoot didn't I?"

"Please don't talk that way. Couldn't I read to you?"

"Read what?"

"Anything in the book bag that we haven't read."

"I can't listen to it," he said. "Talking is the easiest. We quarrel and that makes the time pass."

"I don't quarrel. I never want to quarrel. Let's not quarrel anymore. No matter how nervous we get. Maybe they will be back with another truck today. Maybe the plane will come."

"I don't want to move," the man said. "There is no sense in moving now except to make it easier for you."

"That's cowardly."

45

"Can't you let a man die as comfortably as he can without calling him names? What's the use of slanging me?"

"You're not going to die."

"Don't be silly. I'm dying now. Ask those bastards." He looked over to where the huge, filthy birds sat, their naked heads sunk in the hunched feathers. A fourth planed down, to run quick-legged and then waddle slowly toward the others.

"They are around every camp. You never notice them. You can't die if you don't give up."

"Where did you read that? You're such a bloody fool."

"You might think about someone else."

"For Christ's sake," he said, "That's been my trade." He lay then and was quiet for a while and looked across the heat shimmer of the plain to the edge of the bush. There were a few Tommies that showed minute and white against the yellow and, far off, he saw a herd of zebra, white against the green of the bush. This was a pleasant camp under big trees against a hill, with good water, and, close by, a nearly dry water hole where sand grouse flighted in the mornings.

"Wouldn't you like me to read?" she asked. She was sitting on a canvas chair beside his cot. "There's a breeze coming up."

"No thanks."

"Maybe the truck will come."

"I don't give a damn about the truck."

"I do."

"You give a damn about so many things that I don't."

"Not so many, Harry."

"What about a drink?"

"It's supposed to be bad for you. It said in Black's to avoid all alcohol. You shouldn't drink."

"Molo!" he shouted.

"Yes Bwana."

"Bring whiskey-soda."

"Yes Bwana."

46

"You shouldn't," she said. "That's what I mean by giving up. It says it's bad for you. I know it's bad for you."

"No," he said. "It's good for me."

So now it was all over, he thought. So now he would never have a chance to finish it. So this was the way it ended in a bickering over a drink. Since the gangrene started in his right leg he had no pain and with the pain the horror had gone and all he felt now was a great tiredness and anger that this was the end of it. For this, that now was coming, he had very little curiosity. For years it had obsessed him; but now it meant nothing in itself. It was strange how easy being tired enough made it.

Now he would never write the things that he had saved to write until he knew enough to write them well. Well, he would not have to fail at trying to write them either. Maybe you could never write them, and that was why you put them off and delayed the starting. Well he would never know, now.

"I wish we'd never come," the woman said. She was looking at him holding the glass and biting her lip. "You never would have gotten anything like this in Paris. You always said you loved Paris. We could have stayed in Paris or gone anywhere. I'd have gone anywhere. I said I'd go anywhere you wanted. If you wanted to shoot we could have gone shooting in Hungary and been comfortable."

"Your bloody money," he said.

"That's not fair," she said. "It was always yours as much as mine. I left everything and I went wherever you wanted to go and I've done what you wanted to do. But I wish we'd never come here."

"You said you loved it."

"I did when you were all right. But now I hate it. I don't see why that had to happen to your leg. What have we done to have that happen to us?"

"I suppose what I did was to forget to put iodine on it when I first scratched it. Then I didn't pay any attention to it because I never infect. Then, later, when it got bad, it was probably using that weak carbolic solution when the other antiseptics ran out that paralyzed the minute blood vessels and started the gangrene." He looked at her. "What else?"

"I don't mean that."

47

"If we would have hired a good mechanic instead of a half-baked Kikuyu driver, he would have checked the oil and never burned out that bearing in the truck."

"I don't mean that."

"If you hadn't left your own people, your goddamned Old Westbury, Saratoga, Palm Beach people to take me on—"

"Why I loved you. That's not fair. I love you now. I'll always love you. Don't you love me?"

"No," said the man. "I don't think so. I never have."

"Harry, what are you saying? You're out of your head."

"No. I haven't any head to go out of."

"Don't drink that," she said. "Darling, please don't drink that. We have to do everything we can."

"You do it," he said. "I'm tired."

Now in his mind he saw a railway station at Karagatch and he was standing with his pack and that was the headlight of the Simplon-Orient cutting the dark now and he was leaving Thrace then after the retreat. That was one of the things he had saved to write, with, in the morning at breakfast, looking out the window and seeing snow on the mountains in Bulgaria and Nansen's secretary asking the old man if it were snow and the old man looking at it and saying, No, that's not snow. It's too early for snow. And the secretary repeating it to the other girls, No, you see. It's not snow and them all saying, It's not snow we were mistaken. But it was the snow all right and he sent them on into it when he evolved exchange of populations. And it was snow they tramped along in until they died that winter.

It was snow too that fell all Christmas week that year up in the Gauertal, that year they lived in the woodcutter's house with the big square porcelain stove that filled half the room, and they slept on mattresses filled with beech leaves, the time the deserter came with his feet bloody in the snow. He said the police were right behind him and they gave him woolen socks and held the gendarmes talking until the tracks had drifted over. In Schruns, on Christmas day, the snow was so bright it hurt your eyes when you looked out from the weinstube and saw everyone coming home from church. That was where they walked up the sleigh-smothered urine-yellowed road along the river with the steep pine hills, skis heavy on the shoulder, and where they ran that great run down the glacier above the Madlener-haus, the snow as smooth to see as cake frosting and as light as powder and he remembered the noiseless rush the speed made as you dropped down like a bird. They were snowbound a week in the Madlener-haus that time in the blizzard playing cards in the smoke by the lantern light and the stakes were high all the time as Herr Lent lost more. Finally he lost it all. Everything, the skichule money and all the season's profit and then his capital. He could see him with his long nose, picking up the cards and then opening, "Sans Voir." There was always gambling then. When there was no snow you gambled and when there was too much you gambled. He thought of all the time in his life he had spent gambling. But he had never written a line of that, nor of that cold bright Christmas day with the mountains showing across the plain that Barker had flown across the lines to bomb the Austrian officers' leave train, machine-gunning them as they scattered and ran. He remembered Barker afterwards coming into the mess and starting to tell about it. And how quiet it got and then somebody saying, "You bloody, murderous bastard." Those were the same Austrians they killed then that he skied with later. No not the same. Hans, that he skied with all that year, had been in the Kaiser-Jägers and when they went hunting hares together up the little valley above the sawmill they had talked of the fighting on Pasubio and of the attack on Pertica and Asalone and he had never written a word of that. Nor of Monte Corno, nor the Siete Communi, nor of Arsiero. How many winters had he lived in the Voralberg and the Alberg? It was four and then he remembered the man who had the fox to sell when they had walked into Bludenz, that time to buy presents, and the cherry pit taste of good kirsch, the fast-slipping rush of running powder-snow on crust, singing "Hi Ho said Rolly!" as you ran down the last stretch to the steep drop, taking it straight, then running the orchard in three turns and out across the ditch and onto the icy road behind the inn. Knocking your bindings loose, kicking the skis free and leaning them up against the wooden wall of the inn, the lamplight coming from the window where inside, in the smoky, new-wine smelling warmth, they were playing accordion.

"Where did we stay in Paris?" he asked the woman who was sitting by him in a canvas chair, now, in Africa.

"At the Crillon. You know that."

"Why do I know that?"

"That's where we always stayed."

"No. Not always."

"There and at the Pavilion Henri-Quatre in St. Germain. You said you loved it there."

"Love is a dunghill," said Harry. "And I'm the cock that gets on it to crow."

"If you have to go away," she said, "is it absolutely necessary to kill off everything you leave behind? I mean do you have to take away everything? Do you have to kill your horse, your wife and burn your saddle and your armour?"

"Yes," he said. "Your damned money was my armour. My Swift and my Armour."

"Don't."

"All right. I'll stop that. I don't want to hurt you."

"It's a bit late now."

"All right. I'll go on hurting you. It's more amusing. The only thing I ever really liked to do with you I can't do now."

"No, that's not true. You liked to do many things and everything you wanted to do I did."

"Oh for Christ sake stop bragging will you?"

He looked at her and saw her crying.

"Listen," he said. "Do you think that it is fun to do this? I don't know why I'm doing it. It's trying to kill to keep yourself alive I imagine. I was all right when we started talking. I didn't mean to start this, and now I'm crazy as a coot and being as cruel to you as I can be. Don't pay any attention, darling, to what I say. I love you, really. You know I love you. I've never loved

50

anyone else the way I love you." He slipped into the familiar lie he made his bread and butter by.

"You're sweet to me."

"You bitch," he said. "You rich bitch. That's poetry. I'm full of poetry now. Rot and poetry. Rotten poetry."

"Stop it. Harry, why do you have to turn into a devil now?"

"I don't like to leave anything," the man said. "I don't like to leave things behind."

It was evening now and he had been asleep. The sun was gone behind the hill and there was a shadow all across the plain and the small animals were feeding close to camp; quick dropping heads and switching tails, he watched them keeping well out away from the bush now. The birds no longer waited on the ground. They were all perched heavily in a tree. There were many more of them. His personal boy was sitting by the bed.

"Memsahib's gone to shoot," the boy said. "Does Bwana want?"

"Nothing."

She had gone to kill a piece of meat and, knowing how he liked to watch the game, she had gone well away so she would not disturb this little pocket of the plain that he could see. She was always thoughtful, he thought. On anything she knew about, or had read, or that she had ever heard.

It was not her fault that when he went to her he was already over. How could a woman know that you meant nothing that you said; that you spoke only from habit and to be comfortable. After he no longer meant what he said, his lies were more successful with women than when he had told them the truth.

It was not that he lied as that there was no truth to tell. He had his life and it was over and then he went on living it again with different people and more money, with the best of the same places, and some new ones. You kept from thinking and it was all marvelous. You were equipped with good insides so that you did not go to pieces that way, the way most of them had, and you made an attitude that you cared nothing for the work you used to do, now that you no longer do it. But, in yourself, you said that you would write about these people; about the very rich; that you were really not one of them but a spy in their country; that you would leave it and write of it and for once it would be written by someone who knew what he was writing of. But he would never do it, because each day of not writing, of comfort, of being that which he despised, dulled his ability and softened his will to work so that, finally, he did no work at all. The people he knew now were all much more comfortable when he did not work. Africa was where he had been happiest in the good time of his life so he had come out here to start again. They had made this safari with the minimum of comfort. There was no hardship; but there was no luxury and he had thought that he could get back into training that way. That in some way he could work the fat off his soul the way a fighter went into the mountains to work and train in order to burn it out of his body.

She had liked it. She said she loved it. She loved anything that was exciting, that involved a change of scene, where there were new people and where things were pleasant. And he had felt the illusion of returning strength of will to work. Now if this was how it ended, and he knew it was, he must not turn like some snake biting itself because its back was broken. It wasn't this woman's fault. If it had not been she it would have been another. If he lived by a lie he should try to die by it. He heard a shot beyond the hill.

She shot very well this good, this rich bitch, this kindly caretaker and destroyer of his talent. Nonsense. He had destroyed his talent himself. Why should he blame this woman because she kept him well? He had destroyed his talent by not using it, by betrayals of himself and what he believed in, by drinking so much that he blunted the edge of his perceptions, by laziness, by sloth, and by snobbery, by pride and by prejudice, by hook and by crook. What was this? A catalog of old books? What was his talent anyway? It was a talent all right but instead of using it, he had traded on it. It was never what he had done, but always what he could do. And he had chosen to make his living with something else instead of a pen or a pencil. It was strange too, wasn't it, that when he fell in love with another woman, that woman should always have more money than the last one? But when he no longer was in love, when he was only lying, as to this woman, now, who had the most money of all, who had all the money there was, who had had a husband and children, who had taken lovers and been dissatisfied with them, and who loved him dearly as a writer, as a man, as a companion and as a proud possession; it was strange that when he did not love her at all and was lying, that he should be able to give her more for her money than when he had really loved. We must all be cut out for what we do, he thought. However you make your living is where your talent lies. He had sold vitality, in one form or another, all his life and when your affections are not too involved you give much better value for the money. He had found that out but he would never write that, now, either. No, he would not write that, although it was well worth writing.

Now she came in sight, walking across the open toward the camp. She was wearing jodhpurs and carrying her rifle. The two boys had a Tommie slung and they were coming along behind her. She was still a good-looking woman, he thought, and she had a pleasant body. She had a great talent and appreciation for the bed, she was not pretty, but he liked her face, she read enormously, liked to ride and shoot and, certainly, she drank too much. Her husband had died when she was still a comparatively young woman and for a while she had devoted herself to her two just-grown children, who did not need her and were embarrassed at having her about, to her stable of horses, to books, and to bottles. She like to read in the evening before dinner and she drank scotch and soda while she read. By dinner she was fairly drunk and after a bottle of wine at dinner she was usually drunk enough to sleep.

That was before the lovers. After she had the lovers she did not drink so much because she did not have to be drunk to sleep. But the lovers bored her. She had been married to a man who had never bored her and these people bored her very much.

Then one of her two children was killed in a plane crash and after that was over she did not want the lovers, and drink being no anaesthetic she had to make another life. Suddenly she had been acutely frightened of being alone. But she wanted someone that she respected with her.

It had begun very simply. She liked what he wrote and she had always envied the life he led. She thought he did exactly what he wanted to. The steps by which she had acquired him and the way in which she had finally fallen in love with him were all part of a regular progression in which she had built herself a new life and he had traded away what remained of his old life. He had traded it for security, for comfort too, there was no denying that, and for what else? He did not know. She would have bought him anything he wanted. He knew that. She was a damned nice woman too. He would as soon be in bed with her as anyone; rather with her, because she was richer, because she was very pleasant and appreciative and because she never made scenes. And now this life that she had built again was coming to a term because he had not used iodine two weeks ago when a thorn had scratched his knee as they moved forward trying to photograph a herd of waterbuck standing, their heads up, peering while their nostrils searched the air, their ears spread wide to hear the first noise that would send them rushing into the bush. They had bolted, too, before he got the picture.

Here she came now.

He turned his head on the cot to look toward her. "Hello," he said.

"I shot a Tommie ram," she told him. "He'll make you good broth and I'll have them mash some potatoes with the Klim. How do you feel?"

"Much better."

"Isn't that lovely? You know I thought perhaps you would. You were sleeping when I left."

"I had a good sleep. Did you walk far?"

"No. Just around behind the hill. I made quite a good shot on the Tommie."

"You shoot marvelously you know."

"I love it. I've loved Africa. Really. If *you're* all right it's the most fun that I've ever had. You don't know the fun it's been to shoot with you. I've loved the country."

"I love it too."

"Darling you don't know how marvelous it is to see you feeling better. I couldn't stand it when you felt that way. You won't talk to me like that again, will you? Promise me?"

"No," he said. "I don't remember what I said."

"You don't have to destroy me. Do you? I'm only a middle-aged woman who loves you and wants to do what you want to do. I've been destroyed two or three times already. You wouldn't want to destroy me again, would you?"

"I'd like to destroy you a few times in bed," he said.

"Yes. That's the good destruction. That's the way we're made to be destroyed. The plane will be here tomorrow."

"How do you know?"

"I'm sure. It's bound to come. The boys have the wood all ready and the grass to make the smudge. I went down and looked at it again today. There's plenty of room to land and we have the smudges ready at both ends."

"What makes you think it will come tomorrow?"

"I'm sure it will. It's overdue now. Then, in town, they will fix up your leg and then we will have some good destruction. Not that dreadful talking kind."

"Should we have a drink? The sun is down."

"Do you think you should?"

"I'm having one."

"We'll have one together. *Molo, letti dui whiskey-soda!*" she called.

"You'd better put on your mosquito boots," he told her.

"I'll wait till I bathe. . . ."

While it grew dark they drank and just before it was dark and there was no longer enough light to shoot, a hyena crossed the open on his way around the hill.

"That bastard crosses there every night," the man said. "Every night for two weeks."

"He's the one makes the noise at night. I don't mind it. They're a filthy animal though."

55

Drinking together, with no pain now except the discomfort of lying in one position, the boys lighting a fire, its shadow jumping on the tents, he could feel the return of acquiescence in this life of pleasant surrender. She *was* very good to him. He had been cruel and unjust in the afternoon. She was a fine woman, marvelous really. And just then it occurred to him that he was going to die.

It came with a rush; not as a rush of water nor of wind; but a sudden evil-smelling emptiness and the odd thing was that the hyena slipped lightly along the edge of it.

"What is it, Harry?" she asked him.

"Nothing," he said. "You had better move over to the other side. To windward."

"Did Molo change the dressing?"

"Yes. I'm just using the boric now."

"How do you feel?"

"A little wobbly."

"I'm going in to bathe," she said. "I'll be right out. I'll eat with you and then we'll put the cot in."

So, he said to himself, we did well to stop the quarreling. He had never quarreled much with this woman while with the women that he loved he had quarreled so much they had finally, always, with the corrosion of the quarreling, killed what they had together. He had loved too much, demanded too much, and he wore it all out.

He thought about alone in Constantinople that time, having quarreled in Paris before he had gone out. He had whored the whole time and then, when that was over, and he had failed to kill his loneliness, but only made it worse, he had written her, the first one, the one who left him, a letter telling her how he had never been able to kill it . . . How when he thought he saw her outside the Regence *one time it made him go all faint and sick inside, and that he would follow a woman who looked like her in some way, along the Boulevard, afraid to see it was not she, afraid to lose the feeling it gave him. How everyone he had slept with had only made him miss her more. How what she had done could never matter since he knew he could not cure himself of loving her. He wrote this letter at the Club, cold sober, and mailed it to New York asking her to write him at the office in Paris. That seemed safe. And that night missing her so much it made him feel hollow and sick inside, he wandered up past Taxim's, picked a girl up and took her out to supper. He had gone to a place to dance with her afterward, she danced badly, and left her for a hot Armenian slut, that swung her belly against him so it almost scalded. He took her away from a British gunner subaltern after a row. The gunner asked him outside and they fought in the street on the cobbles in the dark. He'd hit him twice, hard, on the side of the jaw and when he didn't go down he knew he was in for a fight. The gunner hit him in the body, then beside his eye. He swung with his left again and landed and the gunner fell on him and grabbed his coat and tore the sleeve off and he clubbed him twice behind the ear and then smashed him with his right as he pushed him away. When the gunner went down his head hit first and he ran with the girl because they heard the M.P.'s coming. They got into a taxi and drove out to Rimmily Hissa along the Bosphorus, and around, and back in the cool night and went to bed and she felt as overripe as she looked but smooth, rose-petal, syrupy, smooth-bellied, big-breasted and needed no pillow under her, and he left her before she was awake looking blousy enough in first daylight and turned up at the Pera Palace with a black eye, carrying his coat because one sleeve was missing. That same night he left for Anatolia and he remembered, later on that trip, riding all day through fields of the poppies that they raised for opium and how strange it made you feel finally and all the distances seemed wrong, to where they had made the attack with the newly arrived Constantine officers, that did not know a god-damned thing, and the artillery had fired into troops and the British observer had cried like a child. That was the day he'd first seen dead men wearing white ballet skirts and upturned shoes with pompons on them. The Turks had come steadily and lumpily and he had seen the skirted men running and the officers shooting into them and running then themselves and he and the British observer had run too until his lungs ached and his mouth was full of the taste of pennies and they stopped behind some rocks and there were the*

Turks coming as lumpily as ever. Later he had seen the things that he could never think of and later still he had seen much worse. So when he got back to Paris that time he could not talk about it or stand to have it mentioned. And there in the café as he passed was that American poet with a pile of saucers in front of him and a stupid look on his potato face talking about the Dada movement with a Romanian who said his name was Tristan Tzara, who always wore a monocle and had a headache, and, back at the apartment with his wife that now he loved again, the quarrel was over, the madness all over, glad to be home, the office sent his mail up to the flat. So then the letter in answer to the one he'd written came in on a platter one morning and when he saw the handwriting he went cold all over and tried to slip the letter underneath another. But his wife said, "Who is that letter from, dear?" and that was the end of the beginning of that. He remembered the good times with them all, and the quarrels. They always picked the finest places to have quarrels. And why had they always quarreled when he was feeling best? He had never written any of that because, at first, he never wanted to hurt anyone and then it seemed as though there was enough to write without it. But he had always thought that he would write it finally. There was so much to write. He had seen the world change; not just events; although he had seen many of them and had watched the people, but he had seen the subtler change and he could remember how the people were at different times. He had been in it and he had watched it and it was his duty to write of it; but now he never would.

"How do you feel?" she said. She had come out from the tent now after her bath.

"All right."

"Could you eat now?" He saw Molo behind her with the folding table and the other boy with the dishes.

"I want to write," he said.

"You ought to take some broth to keep your strength up."

"I'm going to die tonight," he said. "I don't need my strength up."

"Don't be melodramatic, Harry, please," she said.

"Why don't you use your nose? I'm rotted halfway up my thigh now. What the hell should I fool with broth for? Molo bring whisky-soda."

"Please take the broth," she said gently.

"All right."

The broth was too hot. He had to hold it in the cup until it cooled enough to take it and then he just got it down without gagging.

"You're a fine woman," he said. "Don't pay any attention to me."

She looked at him with her well-known, well-loved face from *Spur* and *Town and Country*, only a little worse for the drink, only a little worse for the bed, but *Town and Country* never showed those good breasts and those useful thighs and those lightly small-of-back-caressing hands, and as he looked and saw her well-known pleasant smile, he felt death come again. This time there was no rush. It was a puff, as of a wind that makes a candle flicker and the flame go tall.

"They can bring my net out later and hang it from the tree and build the fire up. I'm not going in the tent tonight. It's not worth moving. It's a clear night. There won't be any rain."

So this was how you died, in whispers that you did not hear. Well, there would be no more quarreling. He could promise that. The one experience that he had never had he was not going to spoil now. He probably would. You spoiled everything. But perhaps he wouldn't.

"You can't take dictation, can you?"

"I never learned," she told him.

"That's all right."

There wasn't time, of course, although it seemed as though it telescoped so that you might put it all into one paragraph if you could get it right.

There was a log house, chinked white with mortar, on a hill above the lake. There was a bell on a pole by the door to call the people in to meals. Behind the house were fields and behind the fields was the timber. A line of lombardy poplars ran from the house to the dock. Other poplars ran along the point. A road went up to the hills along the edge of the timber and along that road he picked blackberries. Then that log house was burned down and all the guns that had been on deer foot racks above the open fireplace were burned and afterwards their barrels, with the lead melted in the magazines, and the stocks burned away, lay out on the heap of ashes that were used to make lye for the big iron soap kettles, and you asked Grandfather if you could have them to play with, and he said, no. You see they were his guns still and he never bought any others. Nor did he hunt anymore. The house was rebuilt in the same place out of lumber now and painted white and from its porch you saw the poplars and the lake beyond; but there were never any more guns. The barrels of the guns that had hung on the deer feet on the wall of the log house lay out there on the heap of ashes and no one ever touched them.

In the Black Forest, after the war, we rented a trout stream and there were two ways to walk to it. One was down the valley from Triberg and around the valley road in the shade of the trees that bordered the white road, and then up a side road that went up through the hills past many small farms, with the big Schwartzwald houses, until that road crossed the stream. That was where our fishing began. The other way was to climb steeply up to the edge of the woods and then go across the top of the hills through the pine woods, and then out to the edge of a meadow and down across this meadow to the bridge. There were birches along the stream and it was not big, but narrow, clear and fast, with pools where it had cut under the roots of the birches. At the Hotel in Triberg the proprietor had a fine season. It was very pleasant and we were all great friends. The next year came the inflation and the money he had made the year before was not enough to buy supplies to open the hotel and he hanged himself.

You could dictate that, but you could not dictate the Place Contrescarpe where the flower sellers dyed their flowers in the street and the dye ran over the paving where the autobus started and the old men and the women, always drunk on wine and bad marc; and the children with their noses running in the cold; the smell of dirty sweat and poverty and drunkenness at the Café des Amateurs and the whores at the Bal Musette they lived above. The Concierge who entertained the trooper of the Garde Republicaine in her loge, his horsehair-plumed helmet on a chair. The locataire across the hall whose husband was a bicycle racer and her joy that morning at the Cremerie when she had opened L'Auto and seen where he placed third in Paris-Tours, his first big race. She had blushed and laughed and then gone upstairs crying with the yellow sporting paper in her hand. The husband of the woman who ran the Bal Musette drove a taxi and when he, Harry, had to take an early plane the husband knocked upon the door to wake him and they each drank a glass of white wine at the zinc of the bar before they started. He knew his neighbors in that quarter then because they all were poor. Around that Place *there were two kinds; the drunkards and the sportifs. The drunkards killed their poverty that way; the sportifs took it out in exercise. They were the descendants of the Communards and it was no struggle for them to know their politics. They knew who had shot their fathers, their relatives, their brothers, and their friends when the Versailles troops came in and took the town after the Commune and executed anyone they could catch with calloused hands, or who wore a cap, or carried any other sign he was a working man. And in that poverty, and in that quarter across the street from a Boucherie Chevaline and a wine cooperative he had written the start of all he was to do. There never was another part of Paris that he loved like that, the sprawling trees, the old white plastered houses painted brown below, the long green of the autobus in that round square, the purple flower dye upon the paving, the sudden drop down the hill of the rue Cardinal Lemoine to the River, and the other way the narrow crowded world of the rue Mouffetard. The street that ran up toward the Pantheon and the other that he always took with the bicycle, the only asphalted street in all that quarter, smooth under the tires, with the high narrow houses and the cheap tall hotel where Paul Verlaine had died. There were only two rooms in the apartment where they lived and he had a room on the top floor of that hotel that cost him sixty francs a month where he did his writing, and from it he could see the roofs and chimney pots and all the hills of Paris.*

From the apartment you could only see the wood and coal man's place. He sold wine too, bad wine. The golden horse's head outside the Boucherie Chevaline where the carcasses hung yellow, gold and red in the open window, and the green-painted cooperative where they bought their wine; good wine and cheap. The rest was plaster walls and the windows of the neighbors. The neighbors who, at night, when someone lay drunk in the street, moaning and groaning in that typical French ivresse *that you were propaganded to believe did not exist, would open their windows and then the murmur of talk.*

"Where is the policeman? When you don't want him the bugger is always there. He's sleeping with some concierge. Get the Agent." Till someone threw a bucket of water from a window and the moaning stopped. "What's that? Water. Ah, that's intelligent." And the windows shutting. Marie, his femme de menage, protesting against the eight-hour day saying, "If a husband works until six he gets only a little drunk on the way home and does not waste too much. If he works only until five he is drunk every night and one has no money. It is the wife of the working man who suffers from this short-ening of hours."

"Wouldn't you like some more broth?" the woman asked him now.

"No, thank you very much. It is awfully good."

"Try just a little."

"I would like a whiskey-soda."

"It's not good for you."

"No. It's bad for me. Cole Porter wrote the words and the music. This knowledge that you're going mad for me."

"You know I like you to drink."

"Oh yes. Only it's bad for me."

When she goes, he thought. I'll have all I want. Not all I want but all there is. Ayee he was tired. Too tired. He was going to sleep a little while. He lay still and death was not there. It must have gone around another street. It went in pairs, on bicycles, and moved absolutely silently on the pavements.

No, he had never written about Paris. Not the Paris that he cared about. But what about the rest that he had never written?

What about the ranch and the silvered gray of the sagebrush, the quick, clear water in the irrigation ditches, and the heavy green of the alfalfa. The trail went up into the hills and the cattle in the summer were shy as deer. The bawling and the steady noise and slow moving mass raising a dust as you brought them down in the fall. And behind the mountains, the clear sharpness of the peak in the evening light and, riding down along the trail in the moonlight, bright across the valley. Now he remembered coming down through the timber in the dark holding the horse's tail when you could not see and all the stories that he meant to write.

About the half-wit chore boy who was left at the ranch that time and told not to let anyone get any hay, and that old bastard from the Forks who had beaten the boy when he had worked for him stopping to get some feed. The boy refusing and the old man saying he would beat him again. The boy got the rifle from the kitchen and shot him when he tried to come into the barn and when they came back to the ranch he'd been dead a week, frozen in the corral, and the dogs had eaten a big part of him. But what was left you packed on a sled wrapped in a blanket and roped on and you got the boy to help you haul it, and the two of you took it out over the road on skis, and sixty miles down to town to turn the boy over. He having no idea that he would be arrested. Thinking he had done his duty and that you were his friend and he would be rewarded. He'd helped to haul the old man in so everybody could know how bad the old man had been and how he'd tried to steal some feed that didn't belong to him, and when the sheriff put the handcuffs on the boy he couldn't believe it. Then he'd started to cry. That was one story he had saved to write. He knew at least twenty good stories from out there and he had never written one. Why?

"You tell them why," he said.

"Why what, dear?"

"Why nothing."

She didn't drink so much, now, since she had him. But if he lived he would never write about her, he knew that now. Nor about any of them. The rich were dull and they drank too much, or they played too much backgammon. They were dull and they were repetitious. He remembered poor Julian and his romantic awe of them and how he had started a story once that began, "The very rich are different from you and me." And how someone had said to Julian, Yes they have more money. But that was not humorous to Julian. He thought they were a special glamorous race and when he found they weren't it wrecked him just as much as any other thing that wrecked him.

He had been contemptuous of those who wrecked. You did not have to like it because you understood it, he could beat anything, he thought, because no thing could hurt him if he did not care.

All right. Now he would not care for death. One thing he had always dreaded was the pain, he could stand pain as well as any man, until it went on too long, and wore him out, but here he had something that had hurt frightfully and just when he had felt it breaking him, the pain had stopped.

He remembered long ago when Williamson, the bombing officer, had been hit by a stick bomb someone in a German patrol had thrown as he was coming in through the wire that night and, screaming, had begged everyone to kill him. He was a fat man, very brave, and a good officer, although addicted to fantastic shows. But that night he was caught in the wire, with a flare lighting him up and his bowels spilled out into the wire, so when they brought him in, alive, they had to cut him loose. Shoot me, Harry. For Christ sake shoot me. They had had an argument one time about our Lord never sending you anything you could not bear and someone's theory had been that meant that at a certain time the pain passed you out automatically. But he had always remembered Williamson that night. Nothing passed out Williamson until he gave him all his morphine tablets that he had always saved to use himself and then they did not work right away.

Still this now, that he had, was very easy; and if it was no worse as it went on there was nothing to worry about. Except that he would rather be in better company.

He thought a little about the company that he would like to have.

No, he thought, when everything you do, you do too long, and do too late, you can't expect to find the people still there. The people all are gone. The party's over and you are with your hostess now.

I'm getting as bored with dying as with everything else, he thought.

"It's a bore," he said out loud.

"What is, my dear?"

"Anything you do too bloody long."

He looked at her face between him and the fire. She was leaning back in the chair and the firelight shone on her pleasantly lined face and he could see that she was sleepy. He heard the hyena make a noise just outside the range of the fire.

"I've been writing," he said. "But I got tired."

"Do you think you will be able to sleep?"

"Pretty sure. Why don't you turn in?"

"I like to sit here with you."

"Do you feel anything strange?" he asked her.

"No. Just a little sleepy."

"I do," he said.

He had just felt death come by again.

"You know the only thing I've never lost is curiosity," he said to her.

"You've never lost anything. You're the most complete man I've ever known."

"Christ," he said. "How little a woman knows. What is that? Your intuition?"

Because, just then, death had come and rested its head on the foot of the cot and he could smell its breath.

"Never believe any of that about a scythe and a skull," he told her. "It can be two bicycle policemen as easily, or be a bird. Or it can have a wide snout like a hyena."

It had moved up on him now, but it had no shape anymore. It simply occupied space.

"Tell it to go away."

It did not go away but moved a little closer.

"You've got a hell of a breath," he told it. "You stinking bastard."

It moved up closer to him still and now he could not speak to it, and when it saw he could not speak it came a little closer, and now he tried to send it away without speaking, but it moved in on him so its weight was all upon his chest, and while it crouched there and he could not move, or speak, he heard the woman say, "Bwana is asleep now. Take the cot up very gently and carry it into the tent."

He could not speak to tell her to make it go away and it crouched now, heavier, so he could not breathe. And then, while they lifted the cot, suddenly it was all right and the weight went from his chest.

It was morning and had been morning for some time and he heard the plane. It showed very tiny and then made a wide circle and the boys ran out and lit the fires, using kerosene, and piled on grass so there were two big smudges at each end of the level place and the morning breeze blew them toward the camp and the plane circled twice more, low this time, and then glided down and leveled off and landed smoothly and, coming walking toward him, was old Compton in slacks, a tweed jacket and a brown felt hat.

"What's the matter, old cock?" Compton said.

"Bad leg," he told him. "Will you have some breakfast?"

"Thanks. I'll just have some tea. It's the Puss Moth you know. I won't be able to take the Memsahib. There's only room for one. Your lorry is on the way."

Helen had taken Compton aside and was speaking to him. Compton came back more cheery than ever.

"We'll get you right in," he said. "I'll be back for the Mem. Now I'm afraid I'll have to stop at Arusha to refuel. We'd better get going."

"What about the tea?"

"I don't really care about it you know."

The boys had picked up the cot and carried it around the green tents and down along the rock and out onto the plain and along past the smudges that were burning brightly now, the grass all consumed, and the wind fanning the fire, to the little plane. It was difficult getting him in, but once in he lay back in the leather seat, and the leg was stuck straight out to one side of the seat where Compton sat. Compton started the motor and got in. He waved to Helen and to the boys and, as the clatter moved into the old familiar roar, they swung around with Compie watching for warthog holes and roared, bumping, along the stretch between the fires and with the last bump rose and he saw them all standing below, waving, and the camp beside the hill, flattening now, and the plain spreading, clumps of trees, and the bush flattening, while the game trails ran now smoothly to the dry water holes, and there was a new water that he had never known of. The zebra, small rounded backs now, and the wildebeest, big-headed dots seeming to climb as they moved in long fingers across the plain, now scattering as the shadow came toward them, they were tiny now, and the movement had no gallop, and the plain as far as one could see, gray-yellow now and ahead old Compie's tweed back and the brown felt hat. Then they were over the first hills and the wildebeest were trailing up them, and then they were over mountains with sudden depths of green-rising forest and the solid bamboo slopes, and then the heavy forest again, sculptured into peaks and hollows until they crossed, and hills sloped down and then another plain, hot now, and purple brown, bumpy, with heat and Compie looking back to see how he was riding. Then there were other mountains dark ahead. And then instead of going on to Arusha they turned left, he evidently figured that they had the gas, and looking down he saw a pink sifting cloud, moving over the ground, and in the air, like the first snow in a blizzard, that comes from nowhere, and he knew the locusts were coming up from the South. Then they began to climb and they were going to the East it seemed, and then it darkened and they were in a storm, the rain so thick it seemed like flying through a waterfall, and then they were out and Compie turned his head and grinned and pointed and there, ahead, all he could see, as wide as all the world, great, high, and unbelievably white in the sun was the square top of Kilimanjaro. And then he knew that there was where he was going.

Just then the hyena stopped whimpering in the night and started to make a strange, human, almost crying sound. The woman heard it and stirred uneasily. She did not wake. In her dream she was at the house on Long Island and it was the night before her daughter's debut. Somehow her father was there and he had been very rude. Then the noise the hyena made was so loud she woke and for a moment she did not know where she was and she was very afraid. Then she took the flashlight and shone it on the other cot that they had carried in after Harry had gone to sleep. She could see his bulk under the mosquito bar but somehow he had gotten his leg out and it hung down alongside the cot. The dressings had all come down and she could not look at it.

"Molo," she called, "Molo! Molo!"

Then she said, "Harry, Harry!" Then her voice rising, "Harry! Please, Oh Harry!"

There was no answer and she could not hear him breathing.

Outside the tent the hyena made the same strange noise that had awakened her. But she did not hear him for the beating of her heart.

Adult World (I)

David Foster Wallace

Part One. The Ever-Changing Status of the Yen

For the first three years, the young wife worried that their lovemaking together was somehow hard on his thingie. The rawness and tenderness and spanked pink of the head of his thingie. The slight wince when he'd first enter her down there. The vague hot-penny taste of rawness when she took his thingie in her mouth—she seldom took him in her mouth, however; there was something about it that she felt he did not quite like.

For the first three to three-and-a-half years of their marriage together, this wife, being young (and full of herself (she realized only later)), believed it was something about her. The problem. She worried that there was something wrong with her. With her technique in making love. Or maybe that some unusual roughness or thickness or hitch down there was hard on his thingie, and hurt it. She was aware that she liked to press her pubic bone and the base of her button against him and grind when they made love together, sometimes. She ground against him as gently as she could force herself to remember to, but she was aware that she often did it as she was moving towards having her sexual climax and sometimes forgot herself, and afterwards she was often worried that she had selfishly forgotten about his thingie and might have been too hard on it.

They were a young couple and had no children, though sometimes they talked about having children, and about all the irrevocable changes and responsibilities that this would commit them to.

The wife's method of contraception was a diaphragm until she began to worry that something about the design of its rim or the way she inserted or wore it might be wrong and hurt him, might add to whatever it was about their lovemaking together that seemed hard on him. She searched his face when he entered her; she remembered to keep her eyes open and watched for the slight wince that may or may not (she realized only later, when she had some mature perspective) have actually been pleasure, may have been the same kind of revelational pleasure of coming together as close as two married bodies could come and feeling the warmth and closeness that made it so hard to keep her eyes open and senses alert to whatever she might be doing wrong.

In those early years, the wife felt that she was totally happy with the reality of their sexlife together. The husband was a great lover, and his attentiveness and sweetness and skill drove her almost mad with pleasure, the wife felt. The only negative part was her irrational worry that something was wrong with her or that she was doing something wrong that kept him from enjoying their sexlife together as much as she did. She worried that the husband was too considerate and unselfish to risk hurting her feelings by talking about whatever was wrong. He had never complained about being sore or raw, or of slightly wincing when he first entered her, or said anything other than that he loved her and totally loved her down there more than he could even say. He said that she was indescribably soft and warm and sweet down there and that entering her was indescribably great. He said she drove him half insane with passion and love when she ground against him as she was getting ready to have her sexual climax. He said nothing but generous and reassuring things about their sexlife together. He always whispered compliments to her after they had made love, and held her, and considerately regathered the bedcovers around her legs as the wife's sexual heartrate slowed and she began to feel chilly. She loved to feel her legs still tremble slightly under the cocoon of bedcovers he gently regathered around her. They also developed the intimacy of him always getting her Virginia Slims and lighting one for her after they had made love together.

The young wife felt that the husband was a simply wonderful lovemaking partner, considerate and attentive and unselfish and virile and sweet, far better than she probably deserved; and as he slept, or if he arose in the middle of the night to check on foreign markets and turned on the light in the master bathroom adjoining their bedroom and inadvertently woke her (she slept lightly in those early years, she realized later), the wife's worries as she lay awake in their bed were all about herself. Sometimes she touched herself down there while she lay awake, but it wasn't in a pleasurable way. The husband slept on his right side, facing away. He had a hard time sleeping due to career stress, and could only fall asleep in one position. Sometimes she watched him sleep. Their master bedroom had a nightlight down near the baseboard. When he arose in the night she believed it was to check the status of the yen. Insomnia could cause him to drive all the way downtown to the firm in the middle of the night. There were the rupiah and the won and the baht to be monitored and checked, also. He was also in charge of the weekly chore of grocery shopping, which he habitually also performed late at night. Amazingly (she realized only later, after she had had an epiphany and rapidly matured), it had never occurred to her to check on anything.

She loved it when he gave oral sex but worried that he didn't like it as much when she reciprocated and took him in her mouth. He almost always stopped her after a short time, saying that it made him want to be inside her down there instead of in her mouth. She felt that there must be something wrong with her oral sex technique that made him not like it as much as she did, or hurt him. He had gone all the way to his sexual climax in her mouth only twice in their marriage together, and both the times had taken practically forever. Both the times took so long that her neck was stiff the next day, and she worried that he hadn't liked it even though he had said he couldn't even describe in words how much he liked it. She once gathered her nerve together and drove out to Adult World and bought a Dildo, but only to practice her oral sex technique on. She was inexperienced in this, she knew. The slight tension or distraction she thought she felt in him when she moved down the bed and took the husband's thingie in her mouth could have been nothing but her own selfish imagination; the whole problem could be just in her head, she worried. She had been tense and uncomfortable at Adult World. Except for the cashier, she had been the only female in the store, and the cashier had given her a look that she didn't think was very appropriate or professionally courteous at all, and the young wife had taken the dark plastic bag with the Dildo to her car and driven out of the crowded parking lot so fast that later she was afraid her tires might have squealed.

The husband never slept in the nude—he wore clean briefs and a T-shirt.

She sometimes had bad dreams in which they were driving someplace together and every single other vehicle on the road was an ambulance.

The husband never said anything about oral sex together except that he loved her and that she drove him mad with passion when she took him in her mouth. But when she took him in her mouth and flattened her tongue to suppress the well-known Gag Reflex and moved her head up and down as far as her ability allowed, making a ring of her thumb and first finger to stimulate the part of his shaft she could not fit in her mouth, giving him oral sex, the wife always sensed a tension in him; she always thought she could detect a slight rigidity in the muscles of his abdomen and legs and worried that he was tense or distracted. His thingie often tasted raw and/or sore, and she was concerned that her teeth or saliva might be stinging him and subtracting from his pleasure. She worried about her technique at it, and practiced in secret. Sometimes, during oral sex in their lovemaking together, she thought it felt as if he was trying to have his sexual climax quickly so as to have the oral sex be over A.S.A.P. and that that was why he couldn't for so long, usually. She tried making pleased, excited sounds with her mouth full of his thingie; then, lying awake later, she sometimes worried that the sounds she had made had perhaps sounded strangled or distressing and had only added to his tension.

This immature, inexperienced, emotionally labile young wife lay alone in their bed very late on the night of their third wedding anniversary. The husband, whose career was high-stress and caused insomnia and frequent awakenings, had arisen and gone into the master bathroom and then downstairs to his study, then later she had heard the sound of his car. The Dildo, which she kept hidden at the bottom of her sachet drawer, was so inhuman and impersonal and tasted so horrid that she had to all but force herself to practice with it. Sometimes he drove to his office in the middle of the night to check the overseas markets in more depth—trade never ceased somewhere in the world's many currencies. More and more often she lay awake in bed and worried. She had become woozy at their special anniversary dinner and had nearly spoiled their evening together. Sometimes, when she had him in her mouth, she became almost overwhelmed with fear that the husband wasn't enjoying it, and would have an overwhelming desire to bring him to his sexual climax A.S.A.P. in order to have some kind of selfish 'proof' that he enjoyed being in her mouth, and would sometimes forget herself and the techniques she had practiced and begin bobbing her head almost frantically and moving her fist frantically up and down his thingie, sometimes actually sucking at his thingie's little hole, exerting actual suction, and she worried that she chafed or bent or hurt him when she did this. She worried that the husband could unconsciously sense her anxiety about whether he enjoyed having his thingie in her mouth and that it actually was this that prevented him from enjoying oral sex together as much as she enjoyed it. Sometimes she berated herself for her insecurities—the husband was under enough stress already, due to his career. She felt that her fear was selfish, and worried that the husband could sense her fear and selfishness and that this drove a wedge into their intimacy together. There was also the riyal to be checked at night, the dirham, the Burmese kyat. Australia used the dollar but it was a different dollar and had to be monitored. Taiwan, Singapore, Zimbabwe, Liberia, New Zealand: all deployed dollars of fluctuant value. The determinants of the ever-changing status of the yen were very complex. The husband's promotion had resulted in the new career title Stochastic Currency Analyst; his business cards and stationery all included the title. There were complex equations. The husband's mastery of the computer's financial programs and currency software were already legendary at the firm, a colleague had told her during a party while the husband was using the bathroom again.

She worried that whatever the problem with her was, it felt impossible to sort out rationally in her mind to any true degree. There was no way to talk about it with him—there was no way the wife could think of to even start such a conversation. She would sometimes clear her throat in the special way that meant she had something on her mind, but then her mind froze. If she asked him whether there was anything wrong with her, he would believe she was asking for reassurance and instantly would reassure her—she knew him. His professional specialty was the yen, but other currencies impacted the yen and had to be continually analyzed. Hong Kong's dollar was also different and impacted the status of the yen. Sometimes at night she worried she might be crazy. She had ruined a previous intimate relationship with irrational feelings and fears, she knew. Almost in spite of herself, she later returned to the same Adult World store and bought an X-rated videotape, storing it in its retail box in the same hiding place as the Dildo, determined to study and compare the sex techniques of the women in the video. Sometimes, when he was asleep on his side at night, the wife would arise and walk around to the other side of the bed and kneel on the floor and watch the husband in the dim glow of their nightlight, study his sleeping face, as if hoping to discover there some unspoken thing that would help her stop worrying and feel more sure that their sexlife together pleased him as much as it pleased her. The X-rated videotape had explicit color photos of women giving their partners oral sex right there on the box. *Stochastic* meant random or conjectural or containing numerous variables that all had to be monitored closely; the husband joked sometimes that it really meant getting paid to drive yourself crazy.

Adult World, which had one side of marital aids and three sides of X-rated features, as well as a small dark hall leading to something else in the rear and a monitor playing an explicit X-rated scene right there above the cash register, smelled horrid in a way that reminded the wife of absolutely nothing else in her life experience. She later wrapped the Dildo in several plastic bags and put it out in the trash on the night before Trash Day. The only significant thing she felt she learned from studying the videotape was that the men often seemed to like to look down at the women when the women had them in their mouth and see their thingie going in and out of the woman's mouth. She believed that this might very well explain the husband's abdominal muscles tensing when she took him in her mouth—it could be him straining to raise up slightly to see it—and she began to debate with herself whether her hair might be too long to allow him to see his thingie go in and out of her mouth during oral sex, and began to debate whether or not to get her hair cut short. She was relieved that she had no worries about being less attractive or sexual than the actresses in the X-rated videotape: these women had gross measurements and obvious implants (as well as their own share of slight asymmetries, she noted), as well as dyed, bleached, and badly damaged hair that didn't look touchable or strokable at all. Most notably, the women's eyes were empty and hard—you could just tell they weren't experiencing any intimacy or pleasure and didn't care if their partners were pleased.

Sometimes the husband would arise at night and use the master bathroom and then go out to his workshop off the garage and try to unwind for an hour or two with his hobby of furniture refinishing.

Adult World was all the way out on the other side of town, in a tacky district of fast food and auto dealerships off the expressway; neither time she had hurried out of the parking lot did the young wife see any cars she ever recognized. The husband had explained before their wedding that he had slept in clean briefs and a T-shirt ever since he was a child—he was simply not comfortable sleeping in the nude. She had recurring bad dreams, and he would hold her and speak reassuringly until she was able to get back to sleep. The stakes of the Foreign Currency Game were high, and his study downstairs remained locked when not in use. She began to consider psychotherapy.

Insomnia actually referred not to difficulty falling asleep but to early and irrevocable awakening, he had explained.

Not once in the first three-and-a-half years of their marriage together did she ask the husband why his thingie was hurt or sore, or what she might do differently, or what the cause was. It simply felt impossible to do this. (The memory of this paralyzed feeling would astound her later in life, when she was a very different person.) Asleep, her husband sometimes looked to her like a child on its side sleeping, curled all tightly into itself, a fist to its face, the face flushed and its expression so concentrated it looked almost angry. She would kneel next to the bed at a slight angle to the husband so that the weak light of the baseboard's nightlight fell onto his face and watch his face and worry about why, irrationally, it felt impossible to simply ask him. She had no idea why he put up with her or what he saw in her. She loved him very much.

On the evening of their third wedding anniversary, the young wife had fainted in the special restaurant he had taken her to to celebrate. One minute she was trying to swallow her sorbet and looking at the husband over the candle and the next she was looking up at him as he knelt above her asking what was wrong, his face smooshy and distorted like the reflection of a face in a spoon. She was frightened and embarrassed. The bad dreams at night were brief and upsetting and seemed always to concern either the husband or his car in ways she could not pin down. Never once had she checked a Discover statement. It had never even occurred to her to inquire why the husband insisted on doing all the grocery shopping alone at night; she had only felt shame at the way his generosity highlighted her own irrational selfishness. When, later (long after the galvanic dream, the call, the discreet meeting, the question, the tears, and her epiphany at the window), she reflected on the towering self-absorption of her naiveté in those years, the wife always felt a mixture of contempt and compassion for the utter child she had been. She had never been what one would call a stupid person. Both times at Adult World, she had paid with cash. The credit cards were in the husband's name.

The way she finally concluded that something was wrong with her was: either something was really wrong with her, or something was wrong with her for irrationally worrying about whether something was wrong with her. The logic of this seemed airtight. She lay at night and held the conclusion in her mind and turned it this way and that and watched it make reflections of itself inside itself like a fine diamond.

The young wife had had only one other lover before meeting her husband. She was inexperienced and knew it. She suspected that her brief strange bad dreams might be her inexperienced Ego trying to shift the anxiety onto the husband, to protect itself from the knowledge that something was wrong with her and made her sexually hurtful or unpleasing. Things had ended badly with her first lover, she was well aware. The padlock on the door of his workshop off the garage was not unreasonable: power tools and refinished antiques were valuable assets. In one of the bad dreams, she and the husband lay together after lovemaking, snuggling contentedly, and the husband lit a Virginia Slims and then refused to give it to her, holding it away from her while it burned itself all the way down. In another, they again lay contentedly after making love together, and he asked her if it had been as good for him as it had for her. The door to his study was the only other door that stayed locked—the study contained a lot of sophisticated computer and telecommunications equipment, giving the husband up-to-the-minute information on foreign currency market activity.

In another of the bad dreams, the husband sneezed and then kept sneezing, over and over and over again, and nothing she did could help or make it stop. In another, she herself was the husband and was entering the wife sexually, ranging above the wife in the Missionary Position, thrusting, and he (that is, the wife, dreaming) felt the wife grind her pubis uncontrollably against him and start to have her sexual climax, and so then he began thrusting faster in a calculated way and making pleased male sounds in a calculating way and then feigned having his own sexual climax, calculatingly making the sounds and facial expressions of having his climax but withholding it, the climax, then afterwards going into the master bathroom and making horrid faces at himself while he climaxed into the toilet. The status of some currencies could fluctuate violently over the course of a single night, the husband had explained. Whenever she woke from a bad dream, he always woke up too, and held her and asked what was the matter, and lit a cigarette for her or stroked her side very attentively and reassured her that everything was all right. Then he would arise from bed, since he was now awake, and go downstairs to check the status of the yen. The wife liked to sleep in the nude after lovemaking together, but the husband almost always put his clean briefs back on before using the bathroom or turning away onto his side to sleep. The wife would lie awake and try not to spoil something so wonderful by driving herself crazy with worry. She worried that her tongue was rough and pulpy from smoking and might abrade his thingie, or that unbeknownst to her her teeth were scraping his thingie when she took the husband in her mouth for oral sex. She worried that her new haircut was too short and made her face look chubby. She worried about her breasts. She worried about the way her husband's face sometimes seemed to look when they made love together.

Another bad dream, which recurred more than once, involved the downtown street the husband's firm was on, a view of the empty street late at night, in a light rain, and the husband's car with its special license plate she'd surprised him with at Christmas driving very slowly up the street towards the firm and then passing the firm without stopping and proceeding off down the wet street to some other destination. The wife worried about the fact that this dream upset her so much—there was nothing in the scene of the dream to explain the crawly feeling it gave her—and about the way she could not seem to bring herself to talk openly to him about any of the dreams. She feared that she would feel somehow as if she were accusing him. She could not explain this feeling, and it gnawed at her. Nor could she think of any way to ask the husband about exploring the idea of psychotherapy—she knew he would agree at once, but he would be concerned, and the wife dreaded the feeling of being unable to explain in any rational way to ease his concern. She felt alone and trapped in her worry; she was lonely in it.

During their lovemaking together, the husband's face sometimes wore what sometimes seemed to her less an expression of pleasure than of intense concentration, as if he were about to sneeze and trying not to.

Early in the fourth year of their marriage, the wife felt herself becoming obsessed with the irrational suspicion that her husband was sexually climaxing into the master bathroom's toilet. She examined the toilet's rim and the bathroom trash basket closely almost every day, pretending to clean, feeling increasingly out of control. The old trouble with swallowing sometimes returned. She felt herself becoming obsessed with the suspicion that her husband maybe took no genuine pleasure in their lovemaking together but was concentrated only on making her feel pleasure, forcing her to feel pleasure and passion; lying awake at night, she feared that he took some kind of twisted pleasure in imposing pleasure on her. And yet, just experienced enough to be full of doubts (and of herself) at this innocent time, the young wife also believed that these irrational suspicions and obsessions could be merely her own youthful, self-centered Ego displacing its inadequacies and fears of true intimacy onto the innocent husband; and she was desperate not to spoil their relationship with insane displaced suspicions, like the way she had failed and wrecked the relationship with her previous lover because of irrational worries.

And so the wife fought with all her strength against her callow, inexperienced mind (she then believed), convinced that any real problem lay in her own selfish imagination and/or her inadequate sexual persona. She fought against the worry she felt about the way, nearly always, when she had moved down his body in the bed and taken him in her mouth, the husband would nearly always (it seemed then), after waiting with tense and rigid abdominal muscles for what felt somehow like the exact minimum considerate amount of time with his thingie in her mouth, would always reach gently down and pull her gently but firmly back up his body to kiss her passionately and enter her from below, gazing into her eyes with a very concentrated expression as she sat astride him, she sitting always slightly hunched out of embarrassment at the slight asymmetry of her breasts. The way he would exhale sharply in either passion or displeasure and reach down and pull the wife up and slide his thingie inside her in one smooth motion, the gasp sharp as if involuntary, as if trying to convince her that merely having his thingie in her mouth drove him mad with desire to be all the way up inside her down there, he said, and to have her, he said, 'right up close' against him instead of 'so far away' down his body. This nearly always made her feel somehow uneasy as she sat astride him, hunched and bobbing and with his hands on her hips and sometimes forgetting herself and grinding down with her pubic bone against his pubis, fearful that the grinding plus her weight on him could cause injury but often forgetting herself and involuntarily bearing down at a slight angle and grinding against him with less and less caution, sometimes even arching her back and thrusting out her breasts to be touched, until the moment he nearly always—nine times out of ten, on average—gave another gasp of either passion or impatience and rotated slightly onto his side with his hands on her hips, rolling her gently but firmly over with him until she was all the way beneath him and he ranged over her and either still had his thingie deep in her or else reentered her smoothly from above; he was very smooth and graceful in the movements and never hurt her when changing positions and rarely had to reenter, but it always caused the wife some worry, afterwards, that he almost never came to his sexual climax (if indeed he ever really did come to his climax) from beneath her, that as he felt his climax building inside himself he seemed to feel an obsessive need to rotate and be inside her from above, from the familiar Missionary Position of male dominance, which although it made his thingie feel even more deeply inside her down there, which the wife enjoyed very much, she worried that the husband's need to have her beneath him at the sexual climax indicated that something she did when sitting astride him and moving either hurt him or denied him the sort of intense pleasure that would lead to his sexual climax; and so the wife to her distress sometimes found herself preoccupied with worry even as they finished and she began to have another small aftershock of climax while grinding gently against him from below and searching his face for evidence of a truly genuine climax there and sometimes crying out in pleasure beneath him in a voice that sounded, she sometimes thought, less and less like her own.

The sexual relationship the wife had had prior to meeting her husband had occurred when she was a very young woman—hardly more than a child, she realized later. It had been a committed, monogamous relationship with a young man whom she had felt very close to and who was a wonderful lover, passionate and giving and very skilled (she had felt) in sexual technique, who was very vocal and affectionate during lovemaking, and attentive, and had loved to be in her mouth for oral sex, and had never seemed hurt or sore or distracted when she forgot herself and ground against him, and always closed both his eyes in passionate pleasure when he began to move uncontrollably into his sexual climax, and whom she had (at that young age) felt that she loved and loved being with and could easily imagine marrying and being in a committed relationship with forever—all until she had begun, late in the first year of their relationship together, to suffer from irrational suspicions that the lover was imagining making love with other women during their lovemaking together. The fact that the lover closed both his eyes when he experienced intense pleasure with her, which at first had made her feel sexually secure and pleased, began to worry her a great deal, and the suspicion that he was imagining being inside of other women when he was inside of her became more and more of a dreadful conviction, even though she also felt that it was groundless and irrational and only in her mind and would have hurt the lover's feelings just terribly if she had said anything to him about it, until finally it became an obsession, even though there was no tangible evidence for it and she had never said anything about it; and even though she believed the whole thing was

almost surely just in her mind, the obsession became so terrible and overwhelming that she began to avoid making love with him, and began having
sudden irrational bursts of emotion over trivial issues in their relationship,
bursts of hysterical anger or tears that were in fact bursts of irrational worry
that he was having fantasies about sexual encounters with other women.
She had felt, towards the end of the relationship, as if she were totally inadequate and self-destructive and crazed, and she came away from the relationship with a terrible fear of her own mind's ability to torment her with
irrational suspicions and to poison a committed relationship, and this
added to the torment she felt about the obsessive worrying that she was
now experiencing in her sexual relationship with her husband, a relationship that had also, at first, seemed to be more close and intimate and fulfill-
ing than she could rationally believe she deserved, knowing about herself
all (she believed) she did.

Part Two. Yen4U

She once, as an adolescent, in an Interstate rest-stop women's room, on a
wall, above and to the right of vending machines for tampons and feminine
hygiene products, had seen, surrounded by the coarse declamations and
crudely drawn genitalia and the simple and somehow plangent obscenities
inscribed there in varied anonymous hands, standing out in both color and
force, a single small red felt-tip block-capital rhyme,

> IN DAYS OF OLD
> WHEN MEN WERE BOLD
> AND WOMEN WEREN'T INVENTED
> THEY ALL DRILLED HOLES
> IN ROADSIDE POLES
> AND STOOD THERE QUITE
> CONTENTED[,]

tiny and precise and seeming somehow—via something about the tiny
hand's precision against all that surrounding scrawl—less coarse or bitter

than how simply sad, and had remembered it ever since, and sometimes thought of it, for no apparent reason, in the darkness of her marriage's immature years, although, to the best of her later recollection, the only real significance she had attached to the memory was that it was funny what stuck with you.

Part Three. Adult World

Meanwhile, back in the present, the immature wife fell deeper and deeper inside herself and inside her worry and became more and more unhappy.

What changed everything and saved everything was that she had an epiphany. She had the epiphany three years and seven months into the marriage.

In secular psychodevelopmental terms, an epiphany is a sudden, life-changing realization, often one that catalyzes a person's emotional maturation. The person, in one blinding flash, 'grows up,' 'comes of age.' 'Put[s] away childish things.' Releases illusions gone moist and rank from a grip of years' duration. Becomes, for good or ill, a citizen of reality.

In reality, genuine epiphanies are extremely rare. In contemporary adult life, maturation and acquiescence to reality are gradual processes, incremental and often imperceptible, not unlike the formation of renal calculus. Modern usage usually deploys *epiphany* as a metaphor. It is usually only in dramatic representations, religious iconography, and the 'magical thinking' of children that achievement of insight is compressed to a sudden blinding flash.

What precipitated the young wife's sudden blinding epiphany was her abandonment of mentation in favor of concrete and frantic action.* She abruptly (within just hours of deciding) and frantically telephoned the ex-lover whom she'd formerly been in a committed relationship with, now by all accounts a successful associate manager at a local auto dealership, and implored him to agree to meet and talk with her. Placing this call was one of

*(In this, her epiphany accorded fully with the Western tradition, in which insight is the product of lived experience rather than mere thought.)

the most difficult, embarrassing things the wife (whose name was Jeni) had ever done. It appeared irrational and risked seeming totally inappropriate and disloyal: she was married, this was her former lover, they had not exchanged a word in almost five years, their relationship had ended badly. But she was in crisis—she feared, as she put it to the ex-lover over the telephone, for the very soundness of her mind, and needed his help, and would, if necessary, beg for it. The former lover agreed to meet the wife for lunch at a fast food restaurant near the auto dealership the following day.

The crisis that had galvanized the wife, Jeni Roberts, into action was itself precipitated by nothing more than another of her bad dreams, albeit one that comprised a kind of compendium of many of the other bad dreams she'd suffered during the early years of her marriage. The dream was not itself the epiphany, but its effect was galvanic. The husband's car slowly passes his downtown firm and proceeds off down the street in a light rain, its YEN4U license plate receding, followed by Jeni Roberts's car. Then Jeni Roberts is driving on the heavy-flow expressway that circumscribes the city, trying desperately to catch up with the husband's car. Her wipers' beat matches that of her heart. She cannot see the car with its special personalized license plate anywhere up ahead but feels the particular special sort of anxious dream-certainty that it is there. In the dream, every other vehicle on the expressway is symbolically associated with emergency and crisis—all six lanes are filled with ambulances, police cars, paddywagons, fire engines, Highway Patrol cruisers, and emergency vehicles of every conceivable description, sirens all singing their heart-stopping arias and all their emergency lights activated and flashing in the rain so that Jeni Roberts feels as though her car is swimming in color. An ambulance directly in front of her will not let her by; it changes lanes whenever she does. The nameless anxiety of the dream is indescribably horrid—the wife, Jeni, feels she simply must (wiper) must (wiper) *must* catch the husband's car in order to avert some kind of crisis so horrible it has no name. A river of what looks to be sodden Kleenex flows windblown along the expressway's breakdown lane; Jeni's mouth feels full of raw hot sores; it is night and wet and the whole road swims with emergency colors—spanked pinks

and slapped reds and the blue of critical asphyxia. It is when they are wet
that you realize why they call Kleenex *tissue*, flowing by. The wipers match
her urgent heart and the ambulance still, in the dream, will not let her pass;
she slaps frantically at the steering wheel in desperation. And now in the
window at the rear of the ambulance, as if in answer, appears a lone splayed
hand at the glass, pressing and slapping at the glass, a hand reaching up
from some sort of emergency stretcher or gurney and opening spiderishly
out to stroke and slap and press whitely against the rear window's glass in
full view of Jeni Roberts's Accord's retractable halogen headlights so that
she sees the highly distinctive ring on the ring finger of the male hand
splayed frantically against the emergency glass and screams (in the dream)
in recognition and cuts hard left without signaling, cutting off various other
emergency vehicles, to pull abreast of the ambulance and tell it to please
stop because the stochastic husband she loves and must somehow catch up
to is inside on a stretcher ccaselessly sneezing and slapping frantically at
the window for someone he loves to catch up and help; but then (such is
the dream's motive force that the wife actually *wets the bed*, she discovers on
waking) and but then as she pulls abreast on the left of the ambulance and
lowers her passenger window with the Accord's automatic feature in the
rain and gesticulates for the ambulance driver to lower his own window so
she can implore him to stop it's (in the dream) the *husband* driving the
ambulance, it's his left profile at the wheel—which the wife has always
somehow been able to tell he prefers to his right profile and customarily
sleeps on his right side partly with this fact in mind, though they'd never
spoken openly about the husband's possible insecurities about his right
profile—and but then as the husband turns his face toward Jeni Roberts
through the driver's window and lit-up rain as she gesticulates it seems to
be both *him* and *not him*, her husband's familiar and much-loved face distorted and pulsed with red light and wearing a facial expression indescribable as anything other than: Obscene.

It was this look on the face that (slowly) turned left to look at her from
the ambulance—a face that in the very most enuretic and disturbing way
both *was* and *was not* the face of the husband she loved—that galvanized

Jeni Roberts awake and prompted her to gather every bit of her nerve together and make the frantic humiliating call to the man she had once thought seriously of marrying, an associate sales manager and probationary Rotarian whose own facial asymmetry—he had suffered a serious childhood accident that subsequently caused the left half of his face to develop differently from the right side of his face; his left nostril was unusually large, and gaped, and his left eye, which appeared to be almost all iris, was surrounded by concentric rings and bags of slack flesh that constantly twitched and throbbed as irreversibly damaged nerves randomly fired— was what, Jeni had decided after their relationship foundered, had helped fuel her uncontrollable suspicion that he had a secret, impenetrable part to his character that fantasized about lovemaking with other women even while his healthy, perfectly symmetrical, and seemingly uninjurable thingie was inside her. The ex-lover's left eye also faced and scanned a markedly different direction than did his dextral, more normally developed eye, a feature that was somehow advantageous in his auto sales career, he tried to explain.

Galvanic crisis notwithstanding, Jeni Roberts felt awkward and very nearly mortified with embarrassment as she and the ex-lover met and selected their meal options and sat down together in a windowside booth of molded plastic and made radically incongruous small talk while she prepared to try to ask the question that would accidentally precipitate her epiphany and a whole new less innocent and self-deluded stage of her married life. She had decaf in a disposable cup and put in six prepackaged creamers as her former sexual partner sat with his entree's styrofoam box unopened and gazed both through the window and at her. He had a ring on his pinkiefinger and his sportcoat was unbuttoned, and the white shirt beneath the coat bore the distinctive furrows of an oxfordcloth dress shirt that had only recently been removed from its retail packaging. The sunlight through the big window was noon-colored and made the crowded franchise feel like a greenhouse; it was hard to breathe. The associate sales manager watched as she started the tops of the creamers with her teeth to safeguard her nails and removed them and placed them in the foil ashtray and dumped the thimblefuls of creamer into the disposable cup and stirred them in with a complimentary square-tipped stirrer one after another, the look in his developmentally appropriate eye the puddly look of nostalgia. She was still profligate with the creamer. She had both a wedding band and a diamond engagement ring, and the rock wasn't cheap by a long shot. The former lover's stomach hurt and eye-flesh ticced especially bad now because of how now they were in the dreaded last three bank days of the month and Mad Mike's Hyundai put unbelievable pressure on reps to move units in the last three days so they could go on that month's books and inflate the books for the clowns in the regional office. The young wife cleared her throat several times in her special way that the man solely responsible for the performance of all Mad Mike's reps remembered all too well, doing the dry nervous thing with her throat to communicate the fact that she recognized how inappropriate a question like this was going to appear now at this juncture, with them with their unhappy history and now no longer in any way even like marginally connected, and her happily married, and that she felt embarrassed but was also in some kind of she was saying genuine inner-crisis-type situation about something, and desperate—the way usually only serious credit problems made people look desperate and trapped like this—with her eyes with that drowning look in them of she was begging him not to take advantage of her desperate position in any way including judgment or ridicule at her expense. Plus and how she always drank her coffee with two hands around the cup even in a hot environs like this one here. Hyundai-U.S.'s volume, margins, and financing terms were among the countless economic conditions affected by fluctuations in the value of the yen and related Pacific currencies. The young wife had spent an hour at the mirror in order to choose the shapeless blouse and slacks she wore, actually taking her soft contacts back out in order to wear her glasses as well, and nothing on her face in the window-light but a quick dab-and-blot of gloss. The expressway's heavy flow glittered through the window that lit up her right side with sun; and through the glass the Mad Mike's lot, with its plastic pennants and a man in a wheel-chair with his wife or like nurse getting worked by fat Kidder in the hospi-tal gown and arrow-through-head-prosthesis the reps all had to wear on the days Messerly was there to keep tabs, lay also within the divided purview of the booth's former lover—who still loved her, Jeni Ann Orzolek of Market-ing 204, and not his current fiancée, he realized with the sickening wince of a mortal wound reopened—and just beyond it, shimmering in the heat, the Adult World lot, with its all makes and classes of vehicle day and night, moving them through like Mad Mike Messerly could only fantasize.

Adult World (II)

Part: 4
Format: Schema
Title: One Flesh

'As blindingly sudden and dramatic as any question about any man's sexual imagination is going to appear, it was not the question itself which caused Jeni Roberts's epiphany and rapid maturation, but what she found herself gazing at as she asked it.'

> —PT. 4 epigraph, in same stilted mode as 'Adult World (I)' [→ highlights format change from dramatic/stochastic to schematic/ordered]

1a. Question Jeni Roberts asks is whether Former Lover had indeed in their past relationship ever fantasized about other women during love-making w/ her.

    1a(1) Inserted at beginning of question is participial phrase 'After apologizing for how irrational and inappropriate it might sound after all this time . . .'

1b. At some point during J.'s question, J. follows F.L.'s gaze out fast-food window & sees husband's special vanity license plate among vehicles in Adult World lot: → epiphany. Epiph unfolds more or less independently as facially asymmetric F.L. responds to J.'s question.

1c. Flat narr description of J.'s sudden pallor & inability to hold decaf steady as J. undergoes sddn blndng realization that hsbnd is a Secret Compulsive Masturbator & that insomnia/yen is cover for secret trips to Adult World to purchase/view/masturbate self raw to XXX films & images & that suspicions of hsbnd's ambivalence about 'sexlife together' have in fact been prescient intuitions & that hsbnd has clearly been suffering from inner deficits/psychic pain of which J.'s own self-conscious anxieties have kept her from having any real idea [point of view (1c) all objective, exterior desc only].

2a. Meanwhile F.L. is answering J.'s orig question in vehement neg, tears appearing in eye: holy shit no, god, no, no, never, had loved her always, was never as fully *'there'* as when he & J. were making love [if in J.'s p.o.v., insert 'together' after 'love'].

    2a(1) At emotional height of dialogue, tears streaming down ½ face, F.L. confesses/declares that he still loves J., has all this time, 5 yrs, in fact sometimes still thinks of J. while making love to his current fiancée, which causes him to feel guilty (i.e. 'like I'm not really *there*') drng sex w/ fiancée. [Direct transcription of F.L.'s whole answer/confession → emotional focus of scene is off J. while J. undergoes trauma of sddnly realizing hsbnd is Secret Compulsive Masturbator → avoids nasty problem of trying to convey epiphany in narr expo.]

2b. Coincidence [N.B.: too heavy?]: F.L. confesses that he also still sometimes secretly masturbates to memories of former lovemaking w/ J.,
sometimes to point of making himself raw/sore. [→ F.L.'s 'confession'
here both reinforcing J.'s epiph w/r/t male fantasy & providing her w/
much-needed injection of sexual esteem (i.e. it 'wasn't her fault').
[N.B. re Theme: implicit sadness of F.L. making soul-rending confession of love while J. is ½-distracted by trauma of (1b)/(1c)'s epiph; i.e.
= further networks of misconnection, emotional asymmetry.]]

    2b(1) Tone of F.L.'s confession trmndsly moving & high-affect, & J.
        (even tho traumatized w/r/t (1b)/(1c)'s shattering epiphany)
        never for one nanosec doubts the truth of what F.L. says; feels
        she 'really did know this man' & c.

        2b(1a) Narr [*not* J.] notes sudden appearance of red &
            demonic-looking gleam in hypertrophic iris of
            F.L.'s left ['bad'?] eye, which could be either trick of
            light or genuine demonic gleam [= p.o.v. shift/narr
            intrusion].

2c. Mnwhile F.L., interpreting J.'s pallor & digital palsy as requital/posi-
tive response to his declarations of enduring love, begs her to leave
hsbnd for him, or alternatively (*'at least'*) to proceed now to Holiday
Inn just down the expressway & spend rest of afternoon making passionate love [→ w/ dmnc sinistral gleam & c.].

2d. J. (still gone 100% pale à la Dostoevsky's Nastasya F.) abruptly acqui-
esces w/r/t adulterous Holiday Inn interlude [tone flat = " 'Mm, OK,"
she said.']. F.L. buses tray w/ uneaten entrée & empty cup & creamers
& c., follows J. out into fast-food pkng lot. J. waits in Accord while
F.L. attempts to sneak own Ford Probe [N.B.: too heavy?] out of
M.M. Hyundai lot w/o Messerly or sales reps seeing him leave early on
high-pressure end-of-month sales day.

    2d(1) J.'s precise mtvation for acquiescing to Holiday Inn interlude
        left opaque [→ entails that (2d) is in p.o.v. of F.L. only].
        Comic dscrptn of F.L. crawling along row of vehicles on
        hands & knees in attempt to slip into Probe unseen from

M.M. showroom has undercurrent of creepiness [→ congruence w/ subthemes of secrecy, creepy incongruity, opaque shame].

3a. J.'s Accord fllws F.L.'s Probe down xprsway toward Hday Inn. Sudden sun-shower forces J. to activate wipers.

3b. F.L. turns into Hday Inn lot, expects to see J.'s Accord turn in behind him. Accord does *not* turn in, continues down xprsway. [Abrupt p.o.v. change →] J., driving across town toward home, imagines F.L. leaping out of Probe & running dsprtly across Hday Inn lot in downpour to stand at roaring edge of xprsway & watch Accord recede, gradually disappearing in traffic. J. imagines F.L.'s wet/forlorn/asymm image dwndlng in rear-view mirror.

3c. Nearly home, J. finds herself weeping for F.L. & F.L.'s dwndlng image instead of for self. Weeps for hsbnd, '. . . how *lonely* his secrets must make him' [p.o.v.?]. Notes this & speculates on significance of 'weeping for' [= 'on behalf of'?] men. Bgning (3c), J.'s thoughts & spclations evince new sophistication/comprehension/maturity. Pulls into home's driveway feeling '[. . .] queerly exultant.'

3d. Narr intrusion, expo on Jeni Roberts [same flat & pedantic tone as ¶s 3, 4 of 'A.W.(I)' PT. 3]: While following F.L.'s teal/aqua Probe down xprsway, J. hadn't 'changed mind' about having secret adulterous sex w/ F.L., rather merely '. . . realized it was unnecessary.' Understands that she has had life-changing epiphany, has '. . . bec[o]me a woman as well as a wife' & c. & c.

    3d(1) J. hereafter referred to by narr as 'Ms. Jeni Orzolek Roberts'; hsbnd referred to as 'the Secret Compulsive Masturbator.'

4a(I) Epiloguous expo on J.O.R. → extension of narrative arc: 'Ms. Jeni Orzolek Roberts, from that day forward, kept the memory of her lover's desperate, ½-wet face faithfully shaped within her' & c. Realizes hsbnd has 'interior deficits' that '. . . ha[ve] nothing to do with her as a wife[/woman]' & c. Survives this aftershock of epiphany, + various other standard aftershocks. [Possible mentn of psychotherapy, but now in upbeat terms: psychth now 'freely chosen' rather than 'straw dsprtly clutched at.'] J.O.R. establishes separate investment portfolio w/ substantial positions in gold futures & large-cap mining stock. Quits smoking w/ help of transdermal patches. Realizes/gradually accepts that hsbnd loves his secret loneliness & 'interior deficits' more than he loves[/is able to love] her; accepts her 'unalterable powerless-ness' over hsbnd's secret cmplsions [possible mention of esoteric Support Group for spouses of S.C.M.'s—any such thing? 'Mast-Anon'? 'Co-Jack'? (N.B.: *avoid easy gags*)]. Realizes that true well-springs of love, security, gratification must originate within self*; and w/ this realization, J.O.R. joins rest of adult hmn race, no longer 'full of herself'/'immature'/'irrational'/'young.'

4a(II) Marriage now enters new, more adult phase ['honeymoon over' an easy gag?]. Never once in sbsqnt yrs of marriage do J.O.R. & hsbnd discuss his S.C.M. or interior pain/loneliness/'deficits' [N.B.: hammer home fiduciary pun]. J.O.R. doesn't know whether hsbnd even suspects she knows about his S.C.M. or Discover charges at Adult World; she finds she does not care. J.O.R. reflects w/ amused irony on new 'significance' of persistent adlscnt mem-ory of rest-stop graffito. Hsbnd[/'the S.C.M.'] continues to arise & leave master bdrm in wee hrs; sometimes J.O.R. hears his car start as she '. . . stirs only slightly and returns at once to sleep' & c. Ceases worrying w/r/t whether hsbnd enjoys 'sexlife' w/her; con-tinues to love ['?] hsbnd even tho she no longer believes he's 'wonderful' [/'attentive'?] lvmking partner. Sex between them finds its own level; by 5th yr it's appr every 2 weeks. Their sex now characterized as 'nice'—less intense but also less scary [/'lonely']. J.O.R. ceases to search hsbnd's face drng sex [→ metaphor: Theme → eyes closed = 'eyes open'].

---

*[N.B.: narr tone here mxmly flat/affectless/distant/dry → no discernible endorse-ment of cliché.]

4a(II(1)) Taking 'authentic responsibility for self,' J.O.R. '. . . gradually begins exploring masturbation as a wellspring of personal pleasure' & c. Revisits Adult Wld svrl times; becomes almost a rglr.
Purchases 2nd dildo [N.B.: 'dildo' now not captlzd], then 'Penetra-
tor!!$^{®}$' dildo w/ vibrator, later 'Pink Pistollero$^{®}$ Pistol-Grip Mas-
sager,' finally 'Scarlet Garden MX-1000$^{®}$ Vibrator with Clitoral
Suction and Fully Electrified 12 Inch Cervical Stimulator'
['$179.99 retail']. Narr inserts that J.O.R.'s new dresser/vanity
ensemble contains no sachet drawer. [Ironies: J.O.R.'s new hi-tech
mastrbtory appliances are (a) manufactured in Asia & (b) displayed
on Adult Wld wall labeled MARITAL AIDS (2 hvy/obvious?).] By
marriage's 6th yr, hsbnd frqntly away on 'emergency trips to the
Pacific Rim'; J.O.R. mastrbting almost daily.

>   4a(II(1a)) Narr intr, expo: J.O.R.'s most frequent/pleasurable
>   mastrbtion fantasy in 6th yr of marriage = a faceless,
>   hypertrophic male figure who loves but cannot have
>   J.O.R. spurns all other living women & chooses
>   instead to mastrbte daily to fantasies of lvmking w/
>   J.O.R.

4a(III) Concl ¶: 7th, 8th yr: Hsbnd mastrbtes secretly, J.O.R. openly. Their
now-bimonthly sex is '. . . both a submission to and celebration of
certain freely embraced realities.' Neither appears to mind. Narr:
binding them now is that deep & unspoken complicity that in adult
marriage is covenant/love → 'They were now truly married,
cleaved,** one flesh, [a union that] afforded Jeni O. Roberts a cool,
steady joy. . . .'

4b. Concl [embed]: '. . . were ready thus to begin, in a calm and mutually
respectful way, to discuss having children [together].'

**[/'cloven'? (*avoid ez gag*)]

Incarnations of Burned Children

David Foster Wallace

The Daddy was around the side of the house hanging a door for the tenant when he heard the child's screams and the Mommy's voice gone high between them. He could move fast, and the back porch gave onto the kitchen, and before the screen door had banged shut behind him the Daddy had taken the scene in whole, the overturned pot on the floortile before the stove and the burner's blue jet and the floor's pool of water still steaming as its many arms extended, the toddler in his baggy diaper standing rigid with steam coming off his hair and his chest and shoulders scarlet and his eyes rolled up and mouth open very wide and seeming somehow separate from the sounds that issued, the Mommy down on one knee with the dishrag dabbing pointlessly at him and matching the screams with cries of her own, hysterical so she was almost frozen. Her one knee and the bare little soft feet were still in the steaming pool, and the Daddy's first act was to take the child under the arms and lift him away from it and take him to the sink, where he threw out plates and struck the tap to let cold wellwater run over the boy's feet while with his cupped hand he gathered and poured or flung more cold water over his head and shoulders and chest, wanting first to see the steam stop coming off him, the Mommy over his shoulder invoking God until he sent her for towels and gauze if they had it, the Daddy moving quickly and well and his man's mind empty of everything but purpose, not yet aware of how smoothly he moved or that he'd ceased to hear the high screams because to hear them would freeze him and make impossible what had to be done to help his child, whose screams were regular as breath and went on so long they'd become already a thing in the kitchen, something else to move quickly around. The tenant side's door outside hung half off its top hinge and moved slightly in the wind, and a bird in the oak across the driveway appeared to observe the door with a cocked head as the cries still came from inside. The worst scalds seemed to be the right arm and shoulder, the chest and stomach's red was fading to pink under the cold water and his feet's soft soles weren't blistered that the Daddy could see, but the toddler still made little fists and screamed except now merely on reflex from fear the Daddy would know he thought possible later, small face distended and thready veins standing out at the temples and the Daddy kept saying he was here he was here, adrenaline ebbing and an anger at the Mommy for allowing this thing to happen just starting to gather in wisps at his mind's extreme rear still hours from expression. When the Mommy returned he wasn't sure whether to wrap the child in a towel or not but he wet the towel down and did, swaddled him tight and lifted his baby out of the sink and set him on the kitchen table's edge to soothe him while the Mommy tried to check the feet's soles with one hand waving around in the area of her mouth and uttering objectless words while the Daddy bent in and was face to face with the child on the table's checkered edge repeating the fact that he was here and trying to calm the toddler's cries but still the child breathlessly screamed, a high pure shining sound that could stop his heart and his bitty lips and gums now tinged with the light blue of a low flame the Daddy thought, screaming as if almost still under the tilted pot in pain. A minute, two like this that seemed much longer, with the Mommy at the Daddy's side talking sing-song at the child's face and the lark on the limb with its head to the side and the hinge going white in a line from the weight of the canted door until the first wisp of steam came lazy from under the wrapped towel's hem and the parents' eyes met and widened—the diaper, which when they opened the towel and leaned their little boy back on the checkered cloth and unfastened the softened tabs and tried to remove it resisted slightly with new high cries and was hot, their baby's diaper burned their hand and they saw where the real water'd fallen and pooled and been burning their baby all this time while he screamed for them to help him and they hadn't, hadn't thought and when they got it off and saw the state of what was there the Mommy said their God's first name and grabbed the table to keep her feet while the father turned away and threw a haymaker at the air of the kitchen and cursed both himself and the world for not the last time while his child might now have been sleeping if not for the rate of his breathing and the tiny stricken motions of his hands in the air above where he lay, hands the size of a grown man's thumb that had clutched the Daddy's thumb in the crib while he'd watched the Daddy's mouth move in song, his head cocked and seeming to see way past him into something his eyes made the Daddy lonesome for in a strange vague way. If you've never wept and want to, have a child. Break your heart inside and something will a child is the twangy song the Daddy hears again as if the lady was almost there with him looking down at what they've done, though hours later what the Daddy won't most forgive is how badly he wanted a cigarette right then as they diapered the child as best they could in gauze and two crossed handtowels and the Daddy lifted him like a newborn with his skull in one palm and ran him out to the hot truck and burned custom rubber all the way to town and the clinic's ER with the tenant's door hanging open like that all day until the hinge gave but by then it was too late, when it wouldn't stop and they couldn't make it the child had learned to leave himself and watch the whole rest unfold from a point overhead, and whatever was lost never thenceforth mattered, and the child's body expanded and walked about and drew pay and lived its life untenanted, a thing among things, its self's soul so much vapor aloft, falling as rain and then rising, the sun up and down like a yoyo.

A Jewish Patient Begins His Analysis

Philip Roth

So deeply imbedded was she in my consciousness that for the first few years of school I believed that each of my teachers was actually my mother in disguise. I would rush for the door when the last class was over, wondering if I could possibly make it home to our apartment before she had successfully managed her transformation. That she turned out to be back in the kitchen by the time I arrived, and baking the cookies for my afternoon milk, did not cause me to doubt my fantasy; it only deepened my respect for her powers. It was always a relief not to have caught her between identities, though I never seemed able to stop making the effort. I knew that my father and sister were innocent of my mother's real nature, and the burden of betrayal that I thought would fall to me if I ever came upon her unawares was more than I wanted to bear. I actually feared I might somehow be done away with if I were to catch sight of her flying in from school through the bedroom window, or causing herself to emerge limb from limb out of her invisible state and into her apron.

Of course when she asked me to tell her all about my day in school, I did so with the utmost scrupulosity. I did not pretend to understand all the implications of her ubiquitousness, but that it had to do with finding out the kind of little boy I was when I thought Mommy wasn't really around was indisputable. One consequence of this bizarre deification, which lasted from kindergarten into the second grade, is that I became an unnecessarily honest little boy, meticulous in all things, as you will see.

And I became brilliant too. Of my sluggish, sallow, overweight, older sister, my mother would say (in Hannah's presence, of course—honesty was her policy), "The child is no genius, but then we don't ask the impossible. God bless her, she works hard, she applies herself to her limit, and so whatever she gets is all right." Of me, with her long Egyptian nose, her springy orange hair, her eyes the delicious color of the crust of honey cake, her clever babbling mouth, of me—so unmistakably the descendant of the pale redheaded Polish Jews of whom she was the first to be born in America—of me, my mother said, with characteristic restraint, "This *bandit*? He doesn't even have to open the book—'A' in everything. Albert Einstein the Second!"

And how did my father take to all this? He suffered from constipation. He drank mineral oil and milk of magnesia. He chewed Ex-Lax. He turned to suppositories. He tried All-Bran morning and night, and ate mixed dried fruits by the pound bag. He learned to brew senna leaves in a saucepan and, with sour face and prayerful heart, sat at the kitchen table, his body engorged by now with his own waste, and drank off the evil-smelling stuff. I remember that when they announced over the radio the explosion of the first atomic bomb he said aloud, "Maybe that would help me." But all catharses were in vain for that man; his insides were gripped by the hand of outrage and frustration. I was the favorite.

To make life harder for him, he loved me himself. He too saw in me the family's opportunity to be "as good as anybody." Saw in me our chance to be honored and respected—though the only way he knew to talk of these ambitions was in terms of money. "Don't be dumb like your father," he would say, as though it were a joke, "don't marry beautiful, don't marry love—marry rich!" How he loathed being so looked down upon! Like a dog he worked for a future he simply was not slated to have. It was his bad luck to have been left at the gate without even knowing how to punctuate an English sentence, or a sentence in any language, for that matter. And then he was a Jew in the employ of a billion-dollar Protestant outfit, or institution, as they liked to think of themselves: "The Most Benevolent Financial Institution in America" is a phrase I remember hearing my father repeat from time to time to his awestruck little boy. Oh, before his children he spoke with reverence of Boston and Northeastern Mutual: they had paid him a wage during the Depression; they gave him stationery with his own name printed beneath the company's insignia—a Pilgrim Father with arm outstretched toward Plymouth Rock; every spring they sent him and my mother for a free weekend in Atlantic City, to a fancy *goyische* hotel no less; there, along with all the other insurance agents who had met their A.E.S. (annual expectation of sales) to be intimidated by the desk clerk, the waiter, the bellboy, not to mention the puzzled paying guests.

He believed in what he was selling, another drain on his energies. He took his lunch on the run and often ate dinner hours after we did, so dedicated was he to searching out the insured in his district—the most impoverished around—who were in danger of letting their stinking thousand-dollar policies lapse. He talked himself hoarse trying to get illiterate black men to comprehend the necessity of "having an umbrella for a rainy day." To the stupidest Poles and most violent Irishmen in all of Jersey City my father brought news of that marvelous day when the tiny infant, still in its cradle, would be starting off on "the wonderful adventure of college."

They laughed at him. They didn't listen. They heard him knock and told him, "Go away, nobody home." They set their dogs to sink their teeth into his persistent Jewish ass. And still, over the years, he managed to accumulate from The Company enough plaques and scrolls and medals honoring his salesmanship to cover an entire wall of the windowless dark hallway where the Passover dishes were stored in cartons and the "Oriental" rugs laid away in thick wrappings of heady tar paper over the summer. If he squeezed blood from a stone, wouldn't The Company reward him with a miracle of its own? Might not The President up in The Home Office hear of his accomplishment and turn him overnight from an agent at five thousand a year to a district manager at fifteen? But where they had him they kept him. Who else would work such a territory so hard, and with such results? Moreover, there had not been a Jewish manager in the entire history of Boston and Northeastern, and my father, with his seventh-grade education, wasn't exactly suited to be the Jackie Robinson of the insurance business.

N. Everett Lindabury, President of Boston and Northeastern Mutual, had his picture hanging in our hallway. The framed photograph had been awarded to my father after he had sold his first million dollars' worth of insurance. Mr. Lindabury, The Home Office . . . my father made it sound like Roosevelt in the White House in Washington . . . and all the while how he hated their guts, Lindabury's particularly, with his corn-silk hair and his crisp, confident New England speech, and the four sons simultaneously in Harvard College, oh the whole bunch of them up there in Massachusetts, *shkutzim* fox hunting and playing polo and sailing around in boats—so I heard him at night, bellowing with indignation from behind his bedroom door—and keeping him from being a man in the eyes of his wife and children. What wrath! What fury! And there was really no one to unleash it on—except himself. "Why can't I move my bowels—I'm up to my ass in prunes! Why do I have these headaches! Where are my glasses! Who took my hat!"

In that ferocious, that self-annihilating way in which so many Jewish men of his generation served their families, my father served my mother, my sister Hannah, and particularly me. Where he had been imprisoned, I would fly: that was his dream. My own was its corollary: in my liberation would be his—from ignorance, from exploitation, from anonymity. To this very day our destinies are still scrambled together in my imagination: there are still occasions when upon reading in some book a passage that impresses me with its wisdom or beauty my first reaction is, "I'll send him a copy. Of course. If only he reads this, then he'll understand—" Of course. He will understand. He will know. He will be lifted, strengthened. He will tell Everett Lindabury just what he can do with that Fabian Bachrach photograph of himself. . . . In my freshman year of college, when I was even more his son, I once tore the subscription blank out of one of the literary magazines I had just begun to discover in the library, filled in his name and our Jersey City address, and sent him an anonymous gift subscription. But when I came sullenly home at Christmastime to visit and condemn, *The Kenyon Review* was nowhere to be found. *Hygeia, Collier's, Look,* but where was his *Kenyon Review?* Gone! I thought angrily. Thrown out unopened, discarded unread by this *schmuck* father of mine, this Philistine, this lackey, this ignoramus!

I remember the Sunday morning when, on the big dirt field in back of my school, I pitched a baseball at my father and waited to see it go flying off high above my head. It is spring. I am eight, in possession of my first "mitt" and hardball, and a regulation bat I cannot actually swing all the way around. But the hitting, you see, I am going to leave to him. He wears square gold-rimmed spectacles; his hair is a wild bush the color and texture of steel wool; his teeth sit in a glass in the bathroom smiling at the toilet all night—but at the dinner table he can make the muscles in his arms as hard as stone if I ask him to. Though it is Sunday he has been out since early morning in his hat, coat, bow tie and black shoes, carrying under his arm the massive black insurance book that tells who owes the most Benevolent Financial Institution in America how much. Looking (I realize now) not unlike Harpo Marx, down with his book goes my harried and undiscourageable father into the colored neighborhood by the docks. Sunday morning is the best time to catch red-handed those unwilling (and unable) to fork over the ten or fifteen cents necessary to meet their weekly premium payments. He lurks about where he knows the husbands sit out in the sunshine with their bottles of Morgan Davis wine. He emerges from alleyways like a shot to catch between home and church the pious cleaning women, who are off in other peoples' houses during the daylight hours of the week, and in hiding from him on the weekday nights. "Uh-oh, Mr. Insurance Man here!" Even the children begin to run—the *children*, he cries in despair, so tell me what hope is there for these people? How will they ever get anywhere in this world if they ain't even able to grasp the meaning of life insurance? Don't they see enough death every day to know "they's all" going to die too? Don't they give a crap for the loved ones they leave behind? Please, what kind of man is it—I tell you I don't believe he even exists—who can think to die and leave penniless behind him a helpless child, a grief-struck wife. . . .

The glove, the ball, and bat are a birthday gift of—who else?—a rich uncle on my mother's side, who has twice taken me with him and his two oily self-satisfied little boys to see a ball game, once to watch the Jersey City Giants play the Syracuse Chiefs, a doubleheader, and the second time all the way to Yankee Stadium.

My father steps up to the plate in his coat and his brown fedora. "Okay, big-shot ballplayer," he says to me in a slightly weary voice, and grasps the bat somewhere near the middle—and with his left hand where his right hand should be. My heart is sinking fast already, but I hurl the ball nevertheless, and so discover that on top of all the other things I have surmised about him, he isn't "King Kong" Charlie Keller either.

It was my mother who could accomplish anything, who herself had to admit that it might even be that she was actually too good. She could make Jell-O with sliced peaches in it. She could bake a cake that tasted like a banana. Weeping, she grated her own horseradish rather than buy the *pishacks* they sold in a bottle at the store. She watched closely the absent-minded butcher to be certain that he did not forget to put her chopped meat through the kosher grinder. She telephoned all the other women in the building drying clothes on the back lines—called even the divorced *goy* on the top floor one magnanimous day—to tell them rush, take in the laundry, a drop of rain had fallen on our windowpane. For mistakes she checked my sums; for holes, my socks; for dirt, my nails—nothing, nothing escaped her. She even dredged the deepest recesses of my ears by pouring cold peroxide into my head. It tingled and popped like ginger ale, and brought to the surface, in bits and pieces, the hidden stores of wax. A semimedical procedure like this takes time, of course; it takes effort, to be sure; but where health and cleanliness is concerned, she will not spare herself and sacrifice others. She lights candles for our dead. She seems to be the only one who goes to that cemetery who has the common sense, the common decency, to clear off the weeds from the graves of our dead. The first hint of heat and she has mothproofed everything wool in the house, rolled and bound the rugs and dragged them off to my father's trophy room. She is never ashamed of her house; a stranger could walk in and open any closet, any drawer, and she would have nothing to be ashamed of. You could eat off her bathroom floor, if that should ever become necessary. When she loses at mah-jongg she takes it like a sport, not-like-the-others-whose-names-she-won't-mention-it's-too-petty-to-even-talk-about-let's-just-forget-she-even-brought-it-up. She sews, she knits, she darns—she irons better than the *shvartze*, to whom, of all her friends who each possess a piece of this grinning, childish old lady's black hide, she alone is good. "I'm the only one who's good to her. I'm the only one who gives her a whole can of tuna for lunch. I can't be a stingy person, I'm sorry. I can't live like that, excuse me. Esther Wasserman leaves forty cents in nickels around the house when Mary comes and counts up afterward to see it's all there. Maybe I'm too good," she whispers to me, meanwhile running scalding water over the dish from which Mary has just eaten her lunch, alone like a leper, "but I couldn't do a thing like that." Once Mary chanced to come back into the kitchen while my mother was still at the faucet sending steamy, germ-slaughtering torrents over the knife and fork that had passed between the *shvartze's* thick pink lips. "Oh, you know how hard it is to get mayonnaise off silverware these days, Mary," says my mother, thinking fast, and in that way, she tells me later, has managed to spare the colored woman's feelings.

When I am bad I am locked out of the apartment. I stand at the door hammering and hammering until I swear I will turn over a new leaf. But what is it I have done? I shine my shoes every evening, carefully I do it on a sheet of last night's *Jersey Journal* that I lay over the linoleum; afterward I never fail to close the lid on the tin of polish. I roll the toothpaste tube from the bottom—Hannah doesn't—after cleaning my teeth morning and night, brushing them always in circles and not, as Hannah improperly does, up and down. Hannah bites at her cuticles and practically drives my mother crazy with it; I don't. I say "Thank you," I say "You're welcome," I say "I beg your pardon," I say "May I?" When Hannah balks I voluntarily and out of my turn set the table, remembering always forks on the left, knives and spoons on the right, and napkin folded into a triangle. I never eat *milchigs* off a *flaishedige* dish, never, never, never. Nonetheless, there is not a month that goes by when I don't do something so inexcusable that I am told to pack a bag and leave. But what could it possibly be? Mother, it's me, the little boy who spends the whole week before school begins beautifully lettering in English script the names of his subjects on his colored course dividers, who patiently fastens reinforcements to a term's worth of three-ringed paper, lined and unlined both. I carry a comb and a hankie at all times; my pockets are empty of junk; if I used a ruler I could not get the bows of my laces to correspond more perfectly; never do my knicker stockings drag at my shoes, I see to that; my homework is completed two weeks in advance. Let's face it, Ma—I am the smartest little boy in the history of that school. Teachers go home happy to their husbands because of me. So what is it I have done? Can anybody tell me? I am so awful she will not have me in her house a minute longer. When I once called my sister a rat, my mouth was immediately washed with a cake of brown laundry soap; this I understand. But banishment? What could I possibly have done!

Because she is good she will pack a lunch for me to take along but then out I go and what happens is not her business.

Okay, I say, if that's how you feel! (For I have the taste for melodrama too; I am not in this family for nothing.) I don't need a bag of lunch! I don't need anything!

I don't love you anymore, not a boy like you. I'll live alone here with Daddy and Hannah, says my mother, a genius really at phrasing things just the right way to kill you. Hannah can set up the mah-jongg tiles for the ladies on Monday night. We won't be needing you anymore.

Who cares! And out the door I go, into the long dim hallway. Who cares? I will sell newspapers on the streets in my bare feet. I will ride where I want on freight cars and sleep in open fields, I think—and then it is enough for me to see the empty milk bottles standing by our welcome mat for the immensity of all I have lost to come breaking over my head. "I hate you!" I holler. "You stink!" To this filth, to this heresy booming through the corridors of the apartment building where she is vying with twenty other Jewish women to be the patron saint of self-sacrifice, my mother has no choice but to throw the double lock on our door. This is when I start to hammer to be let in. I drop to the doormat to beg forgiveness for my sin (which is what again?) and promise her nothing but perfection for the rest of our lives, which at that time I believe will be endless.

Then there are the nights I will not eat. My sister, who is three years older than I am, assures me that what I remember is fact: there were times when I would refuse to eat.

But can a mother submit to such idiocy?

Without food how will I fight off bronchitis and pneumonia in the cold winter months and polio all the rest of the year?

Don't I realize she is only asking me to do something for my own good?

Wouldn't she give me the food out of her mouth? Don't I know that?

I don't want the food from her mouth. I don't even want the food from my plate.

A child with my sweet temperament, with my accomplishments, my future—am I to be encouraged in such willfulness? From Hannah she is used to it. From Hannah she is not even so concerned. But me, with all the gifts that God has lavished on me, am I to be allowed to think that I can just starve myself to death for no good reason in the world?

Do I want people to look down on a skinny little funny-looking boy all my life, or look up to a man?

Do I want to be pushed around and made fun of, or do I want to command respect?

Which do I want to be, weak or strong, a success or a failure?

I just don't want to eat. I don't want any.

So my mother sits down in a chair beside me with a long bread knife in her hand. It is made of stainless steel, and has little sawlike teeth. Which do I want to be, weak or strong, a success or a failure?

Oh, Doctor, why, why oh why would a mother pull a knife on her own son? I am seven, eight, nine years old, I have no complicated sense of strategy. How do I know she really wouldn't use it? What am I supposed to do, try bluffing her out, at eight? Someone waves a knife in my direction, I believe they intend to cut me up. *But why?* What in hell is the matter with her? What can she possibly be thinking? How crazy can she possibly be? Only yesterday she set down her iron on the board and *applauded* while I stormed around the kitchen rehearsing my role as Christopher Columbus in the third-grade production of *Land, Ho!* I am the star actor of the school—they cannot put on a play without me. Once they tried, when I had my appendix out, and my teacher later told my mother it was a fiasco. Oh how, how can she spend such glorious afternoons in that kitchen, polishing silver, chopping liver, threading new elastic into the waistband of my little jockey shorts—and feeding me all the while my cues from the mimeographed script, playing Queen Isabella to my Columbus, Betsy Ross to my Washington, Mrs. Pasteur to my Louis—how can she rise with me on the crest of my art during those dusky beautiful hours after school, and then at night, because I will not eat some string beans and a baked potato, point a bread knife at my heart?

And why doesn't my father stop her?

Parker's Back

Flannery O'Connor

Parker's wife was sitting on the front porch floor, snapping beans. Parker was sitting on the step, some distance away, watching her sullenly. She was plain, plain. The skin on her face was thin and drawn as tight as the skin on an onion and her eyes were gray and sharp like the points of two ice picks. Parker understood why he had married her—he couldn't have got her any other way—but he couldn't understand why he stayed with her now. She was pregnant and pregnant women were not his favorite kind. Nevertheless he stayed as if she had him conjured. He was puzzled and ashamed of himself.

The house they rented sat alone save for a single tall pecan tree on a high embankment overlooking a highway. At intervals a car would shoot past below and his wife's eyes would swerve suspiciously after the sound of it and then come back to rest on the newspaper full of beans in her lap. One of the things she did not approve of was automobiles. In addition to her other bad qualities, she was forever sniffing up sin. She did not smoke, dip, drink whiskey, use bad language or paint her face, and God knew some paint would have improved it, Parker thought. Her being against color, it was the more remarkable she had married him. Sometimes he supposed that she had married him because she meant to save him. At other times he had a suspicion that she actually liked everything she said she didn't. He could account for her one way or another; it was himself he could not understand.

She turned her head in his direction and said, "It's no reason you can't work for a man. It don't have to be a woman."

"Aw, shut your mouth for a change," Parker muttered.

If he had been certain she was jealous of the woman he worked for he would have been pleased, but more likely she was concerned with the sin that would result if he and the woman took a liking to each other. He had told her that the woman was a hefty young blonde; in fact she was nearly seventy years old and too dried up to have an interest in anything except getting as much work out of him as she could. Not that an old woman didn't sometimes get an interest in a young man, particularly if he was as attractive as Parker felt he was, but this old woman looked at him the same way she looked at her old tractor—as if she had to put up with it because it was all she had. The tractor had broken down the second day Parker was on it and she had set him at once to cutting bushes, saying out of the side of her mouth to the nigger, "Everything he touches, he breaks." She also asked him to wear his shirt when he worked; Parker had removed it even though the day was not sultry; he put it back on reluctantly.

This ugly woman Parker married was his first wife. He had had other women but he had planned never to get himself tied up legally. He had first seen her one morning when his truck broke down on the highway. He had managed to pull it off the road into a neatly swept yard on which sat a peeling two-room house. He got out and opened the hood of the truck and began to study the motor. Parker had an extra sense that told him when there was a woman nearby watching him. After he had leaned over the motor a few minutes, his neck began to prickle. He cast his eye over the empty yard and porch of the house. A woman he could not see was either nearby beyond a clump of honeysuckle or in the house, watching him out the window.

Suddenly Parker began to jump up and down and fling his hand about as if he had mashed it in the machinery. He doubled over and held his hand close to his chest. "Goddamnit!" he hollered. "Jesus Christ in hell! Jesus God Almightydamn! Goddamnit to hell!" he went on, flinging out the same few oaths over and over as loud as he could.

Without warning a terrible bristly claw slammed the side of his face and he fell backward on the hood of the truck. "You don't talk no filth here!" a voice close to him shrilled.

Parker's vision was so blurred that for an instant he thought he had been attacked by some creature from above, a giant hawk-eyed angel wielding a hoary weapon. As his sight cleared, he saw before him a tall rawboned girl with a broom.

"I hurt my hand," he said. "I *hurt* my hand." He was so incensed that he forgot that he hadn't hurt his hand. "My hand may be broke," he growled, although his voice was still unsteady.

"Lemme see it," the girl demanded.

Parker stuck out his hand and she came closer and looked at it. There was no mark on the palm and she took the hand and turned it over. Her own hand was dry and hot and rough and Parker felt himself jolted back to life by her touch. He looked more closely at her. I don't want nothing to do with this one, he thought.

The girl's sharp eyes peered at the back of the stubby reddish hand she held. There emblazoned in red and blue was a tattooed eagle perched on a cannon. Parker's sleeve was rolled to the elbow. Above the eagle a serpent was coiled about a shield and in the spaces between the eagle and the serpent there were hearts, some with arrows through them. Above the serpent there was a spread hand of cards. Every space on the skin of Parker's arm, from wrist to elbow, was covered in some loud design. The girl gazed at this with an almost stupefied smile of shock, as if she had accidentally grasped a poisonous snake; she dropped the hand.

"I got most of my other ones in foreign parts," Parker said. "These here I mostly got in the United States. I got my first one when I was only fifteen years old."

"Don't tell me," the girl said. "I don't like it. I ain't got any use for it."

"You ought to see the ones you can't see," Parker said and winked.

Two circles of red appeared like little apples on the girl's cheeks and softened her appearance. Parker was intrigued. He did not for a minute think that she didn't like the tattoos. He had never yet met a woman who was not attracted to them.

Parker was fourteen when he saw a man in a fair, tattooed from head to foot. Except for his loins, which were girded with a panther hide, the man's skin was patterned in what seemed from Parker's distance—he was near the back of the tent, standing on a bench—a single intricate design of brilliant color. The man, who was small and sturdy, moved about on the platform, flexing his muscles so that the arabesque of men and beasts and flowers on his skin appeared to have a subtle motion of its own. Parker was filled with emotion, lifted up as some people are when the flag passes. He was a boy whose mouth habitually hung open. He was heavy and earnest, as ordinary as a loaf of bread. When the show was over, he had remained standing on the bench, staring where the tattooed man had been, until the tent was almost empty.

Parker had never before felt the least motion of wonder in himself. Until he saw the man at the fair, it did not enter his head that there was anything out of the ordinary about the fact that he existed. Even then it did not enter his head, but a peculiar unease settled in him. It was as if a blind boy had been turned so gently in a different direction that he did not know his destination had been changed.

He had his first tattoo sometime after—the eagle perched on the cannon. It was done by a local artist. It hurt very little, just enough to make it appear to Parker to be worth doing. This was peculiar too, for before he had thought that only what did not hurt was worth doing. The next year he quit school because he was sixteen and could. He went to the trade school for a while, and then he quit the trade school and worked for six months in a garage. The only reason he worked at all was to pay for more tattoos. His mother worked in a laundry and could support him, but she would not pay for any tattoo except her name on a heart, which he had put on, grumbling. However, her name was Betty Jean and nobody had to know it was his mother. He found out that the tattoos were attractive to the kind of girls he liked but who had never liked him before. He began to drink beer and get in fights. His mother wept over what was becoming of him. One night she dragged him off to a revival with her, not telling him where they were going. When he saw the big lighted church, he jerked out of her grasp and ran. The next day he lied about his age and joined the Navy.

Parker was large for the tight sailor's pants but the silly white cap, sitting low on his forehead, made his face by contrast look thoughtful and almost intense. After a month or two in the Navy, his mouth ceased to hang open. His features hardened into the features of a man. He stayed in the Navy five years and seemed a natural part of the gray mechanical ship, except for his eyes, which were the same pale slate color as the ocean and reflected the immense spaces around him as if they were a microcosm of the mysterious sea. In port Parker wandered about comparing the run-down places he was in to Birmingham, Alabama. Everywhere he went he picked up more tattoos.

He had stopped having lifeless ones like anchors and crossed rifles. He had a tiger and a panther on each shoulder, a cobra coiled about a torch on his chest, hawks over his thighs, Elizabeth II and Philip over where his stomach and liver were, respectively. He did not care much what the subject was so long as it was colorful; on his abdomen he had a few obscenities but only because that seemed the proper place for them. Parker would be satisfied with each tattoo about a month, then something about it that had attracted him would wear off. Whenever a decent-sized mirror was available, he would get in front of it and study his overall look. The effect was not of one intricate arabesque of colors but of something haphazard and botched. A huge dissatisfaction would come over him and he would go off and find another tattooist and have another space filled up. The front of Parker was almost completely covered but there were no tattoos on his back. He had no desire for one anywhere he could not readily see it himself. As the space on the front of him for tattoos decreased, his dissatisfaction grew and became general.

After one of his furloughs, he didn't go back to the Navy but remained away without official leave, drunk, in a rooming house in a city he did not know. His dissatisfaction, from being chronic and latent, had suddenly become acute and raged in him. It was as if the panther and the lion and the serpents and the eagles and the hawks had penetrated his skin and lived inside him in a raging warfare. The Navy caught up with him, put him in the brig for nine months and then gave him a dishonorable discharge.

After that Parker decided that country air was the only kind fit to breathe. He rented the shack on the embankment and bought the old truck and took various jobs which he kept as long as it suited him. At the time he met his future wife, he was buying apples by the bushel and selling them for the same price by the pound to isolated homesteaders on back-country roads.

"All that there," the girl said, pointing to his arm, "is no better than what a fool Indian would do. It's a heap of vanity." She seemed to have found the word she wanted. "Vanity of vanities," she said.

Well what the hell do I care what she thinks of it? Parker asked himself, but he was plainly bewildered. "I reckon you like one of these better than another anyway," he said, dallying until he thought of something that would impress her. He thrust the arm back at her. "Which you like best?"

"None of them," she said, "but the chicken is not as bad as the rest."

"What chicken?" Parker almost yelled at her.

She pointed to the eagle.

"That's an eagle," Parker said. "What fool would waste their time having a chicken put on themself?"

"What fool would have any of it?" the girl said and turned away. She went slowly back to the house and left him there to get going. Parker remained for almost five minutes, looking agape at the dark door she had entered.

The next day he returned with a bushel of apples. He was not one to be outdone by anything that looked like her. He liked women with meat on them, so you didn't feel their muscles, much less their old bones. When he arrived, she was sitting on the top step and the yard was full of children, all as thin and poor as herself; Parker remembered it was Saturday. He hated to be making up to a woman when there were children around, but it was fortunate he had brought the bushel of apples off the truck. As the children approached him to see what he carried, he gave each child an apple and told it to get lost; in that way he cleared out the whole crowd.

The girl did nothing to acknowledge his presence. He might have been a stray pig or goat that had wandered into the yard and she too tired to take up the broom and send it off. He set the bushel of apples down next to her on the step. He sat down on a lower step.

"Hep yourself," he said, nodding at the basket; then he lapsed into silence.

She took an apple quickly as if the basket might disappear if she didn't make haste. Hungry people made Parker nervous. He had always had plenty to eat himself. He grew very uncomfortable. He reasoned he had nothing to say so why should he say it? He could not think now why he had come or why he didn't go before he wasted another bushel of apples on the crowd of children. He supposed they were her brothers and sisters.

She chewed the apple slowly but with a kind of relish of concentration, bent slightly but looking out ahead. The view from the porch stretched off across a long incline studded with ironweed and across the highway to a vast vista of hills and one small mountain. Long views depressed Parker. You look out into space like that and you begin to feel as if someone were after you, the Navy or the Government or Religion.

"Who them children belong to, you?" he said at length.

"I ain't married yet," she said. "They belong to momma." She said it as if it were only a matter of time before she would be married.

Who in God's name would marry her? Parker thought.

A large barefooted woman with a wide gap-toothed face appeared in the door behind Parker. She had apparently been there for several minutes.

"Good evening," Parker said.

The woman crossed the porch and picked up what was left of the bushel of apples. "We thank you," she said and returned with it into the house.

"That your old woman?" Parker muttered.

The girl nodded. Parker knew a lot of sharp things he could have said, like "You got my sympathy," but he was gloomily silent. He just sat there, looking at the view. He thought he must be coming down with something.

"If I pick up some peaches tomorrow I'll bring you some," he said.

"I'll be much obliged to you," the girl said.

Parker had no intention of taking any basket of peaches back there, but the next day he found himself doing it. He and the girl had almost nothing to say to each other. One thing he did say was, "I ain't got any tattoo on my back."

"What you got on it?" the girl said.

"My shirt," Parker said. "Haw."

"Haw haw," the girl said politely.

Parker thought he was losing his mind. He could not believe for a minute that he was attracted to a woman like this. She showed not the least interest in anything but what he brought until he appeared the third time with two cantaloupes. "What's your name?" she asked.

"O.E. Parker," he said.

"What does the O.E. stand for?"

"You can just call me O.E.," Parker said. "Or Parker. Don't nobody call me by my name."

"What's it stand for?" she persisted.

"Never mind," Parker said. "What's yours?"

"I'll tell you when you tell me what them letters are the short of," she said. There was just a hint of flirtatiousness in her tone and it went rapidly to Parker's head. He had never revealed the name to any man or woman, only to the files of the Navy and the Government, and it was on his baptismal record which he got at the age of a month; his mother was a Methodist. When the name leaked out of the Navy files, Parker narrowly missed killing the man who used it.

"You'll go blab it around," he said.

"I'll swear I'll never tell nobody," she said. "On God's holy word I swear it."

Parker sat for a few minutes in silence. Then he reached for the girl's neck, drew her ear close to his mouth and revealed the name in a low voice.

"Obadiah," she whispered. Her face slowly brightened as if the name came as a sign to her. "Obadiah," she said.

The name still stank in Parker's estimation.

"Obadiah Elihue," she said in a reverent voice.

"If you call me that aloud, I'll bust your head open," Parker said. "What's yours?"

"Sarah Ruth Cates," she said.

"Glad to meet you, Sarah Ruth," Parker said.

Sarah Ruth's father was a Straight Gospel preacher but he was away, spreading it in Florida. Her mother did not seem to mind Parker's attention to the girl so long as he brought a basket of something with him when he came. As for Sarah Ruth herself, it was plain to Parker after he had visited three times that she was crazy about him. She liked him even though she insisted that pictures on the skin were vanity of vanities and even after hearing him curse, and even after she had asked him if he was saved and he replied that he didn't see it was anything in particular to save him from. After that, inspired, Parker had said, "I'd be saved enough if you was to kiss me."

She scowled. "That ain't being saved," she said.

Not long after that she agreed to take a ride in his truck. Parker parked it on a deserted road and suggested to her that they lie down together in the back of it.

"Not until after we're married," she said—just like that.

"Oh, that ain't necessary," Parker said and as he reached for her, she thrust him away with such force that the door of the truck came off and he found himself flat on the ground. He made up his mind then and there to have nothing further to do with her.

They were married in the County Ordinary's office because Sarah Ruth thought churches were idolatrous. Parker had no opinion about that one way or the other. The Ordinary's office was lined with cardboard file boxes and record books with dusty yellow slips of paper hanging on out of them. The Ordinary was an old woman with red hair who had held office for forty years and looked as dusty as her books. She married them from behind the iron grille of a stand-up desk and when she finished, she said with a flourish, "Three dollars and fifty cents and till death do you part," and yanked some forms out of a machine.

Marriage did not change Sarah Ruth a jot and it made Parker gloomier than ever. Every morning he decided he had had enough and would not return that night; every night he returned. Whenever Parker couldn't stand the way he felt, he would have another tattoo, but the only surface left on him now was his back. To see a tattoo on his own back he would have to get two mirrors and stand between them in just the correct position and this seemed to Parker a good way to make an idiot of himself. Sarah Ruth, who, if she had had sense, could have enjoyed a tattoo on his back, would not even look at the ones he had elsewhere. When he attempted to point out especial details of them, she would shut her eyes tight and turn her back as well. Except in total darkness, she preferred Parker dressed and with his sleeves rolled down.

"At the judgment seat of God, Jesus is going to say to you, 'What you been doing all your life besides have pictures drawn all over you?' " she said.

"You don't fool me none," Parker said. "You're just afraid that hefty girl I work for'll like me so much she'll say, 'Come on, Mr. Parker, let's you and me. . . .' "

"You're tempting sin," she said, "and at the judgment seat of God you'll have to answer for that too. You ought to go back to selling the fruits of the earth."

Parker did nothing much when he was at home but listen to what the judgment seat of God would be like for him if he didn't change his ways.

When he could, he broke in with tales of the hefty girl he worked for. " 'Mr. Parker,' " he said she said, " 'I hired you for your brains.' " (She had added, "So why don't you use them?")

"And you should have seen her face the first time she saw me without my shirt," he said. " 'Mr. Parker,' she said, 'you're a walking panner-rammer!' " This had, in fact, been her remark but it had been delivered out of one side of her mouth.

Dissatisfaction began to grow so great in Parker that there was no containing it outside of a tattoo. It had to be his back. There was no help for it. A dim half-formed inspiration began to work in his mind. He visualized having a tattoo put there that Sarah Ruth would not be able to resist—a religious subject. He thought of an open book with HOLY BIBLE tattooed under it and an actual verse printed on the page. This seemed just the thing for a while; then he began to hear her say, "Ain't I already got a real Bible! What you think I want to read the same verse over and over for when I can read it all?" He needed something better even than the Bible! He thought about it so much that he began to lose sleep. He was already losing flesh—Sarah Ruth just threw the food in the pot and let it boil. Not knowing for certain why he continued to stay with a woman who was both ugly and pregnant and no cook made him generally nervous and irritable, and he developed a little tic in the side of his face.

Once or twice he found himself turning around abruptly as if someone were trailing him. He had had a granddaddy who had ended in the state mental hospital, although not until he was seventy-five, but as urgent as it might be for him to get a tattoo, it was just as urgent that he get exactly the right one to bring Sarah Ruth to heel. As he continued to worry over it, his eyes took on a hollow, preoccupied expression. The old woman he worked for told him that if he couldn't keep his mind on what he was doing, she knew where she could find a fourteen-year-old colored boy who could. Parker was too preoccupied even to be offended. At any time previous, he would have left her then and there, saying dryly, "Well, you go ahead on and get him then."

Two or three mornings later he was baling hay with the old woman's sorry baler and her broken-down tractor in a large field, cleared save for one enormous old tree standing in the middle of it. The old woman was the kind who would not cut down a large old tree just because it was a large old tree. She had pointed it out to Parker as if he didn't have eyes and told him to be careful not to hit it as the machine picked up hay near it. Parker began at the outside of the field and made circles inward toward it. He had to get off the tractor every now and then and untangle the baling cord or kick a rock out of the way. The old woman had told him to carry the rocks to the edge of the field, which he did when she was there watching. When he thought he could make it, he ran over them. As he circled the field his mind was on a suitable design for his back. The sun, the size of a golf ball, began to switch regularly from in front to behind him, but he appeared to see it both places as if he had eyes in the back of his head. All at once he saw the tree reaching out to grasp him. A ferocious thud propelled him into the air, and he heard himself yelling in an unbelievably loud voice, *"God above!"*

He landed on his back while the tractor crashed upside down into the tree and burst into flames. The first thing Parker saw were his shoes, quickly being eaten by the fire; one was caught under the tractor, the other was some distance away, burning by itself. He was not in them. He could feel the hot breath of the burning tree on his face. He scrambled backward, still sitting, his eyes cavernous, and if he had known how to cross himself he would have done it.

His truck was on a dirt road at the edge of the field. He moved toward it, still sitting, still backward, but faster and faster; halfway to it he got up and began a kind of forward-bent run from which he collapsed on his knees twice. His legs felt like two old rusted rain gutters. He reached the truck finally and took off in it, zigzagging up the road. He drove past his house on the embankment and straight for the city, fifty miles distant.

Parker did not allow himself to think on the way to the city. He only knew that there had been a great change in his life, a leap forward into a worse unknown, and that there was nothing he could do about it. It was for all intents accomplished.

The artist had two large cluttered rooms over a chiropodist's office on a back street. Parker, still barefooted, burst silently in on him at a little after three in the afternoon. The artist, who was about Parker's own age— twenty-eight—but thin and bald, was behind a small drawing table, tracing a design in green ink. He looked up with an annoyed glance and did not seem to recognize Parker in the hollow-eyed creature before him.

"Let me see the book you got with all the pictures of God in it," Parker said breathlessly. "The religious one."

The artist continued to look at him with his intellectual, superior stare. "I don't put tattoos on drunks," he said.

"You know me!" Parker cried indignantly. "I'm O.E. Parker! You done work for me before and I always paid!"

The artist looked at him another moment as if he were not altogether sure. "You've fallen off some," he said. "You must have been in jail."

"Married," Parker said.

"Oh," said the artist. With the aid of mirrors the artist had tattooed on the top of his head a miniature owl, perfect in every detail. It was about the size of a half-dollar and served him as a showpiece. There were cheaper artists in town but Parker had never wanted anything but the best. The artist went over to a cabinet in the back of the room and began to look over some art books. "Who are you interested in?" he said. "Saints, angels, Christs or what?"

"God," Parker said.

"Father, Son or Spirit?"

"Just God," Parker said impatiently. "Christ, I don't care. Just so it's God."

The artist returned with a book. He moved some papers off another table and put the book down on it and told Parker to sit down and see what he liked. "The up-to-date ones are in the back," he said.

Parker sat down with the book and wet his thumb. He began to go through it, beginning at the back where the up-to-date pictures were. Some of them he recognized—the Good Shepherd, Forbid Them Not, The Smiling Jesus, Jesus the Physician's Friend, but he kept turning rapidly backward and the pictures became less and less reassuring. One showed a gaunt green dead face streaked with blood. One was yellow with sagging purple eyes. Parker's heart began to beat faster and faster until it appeared to be roaring inside him like a great generator. He flipped the pages quickly, feeling that when he reached the one ordained, a sign would come. He continued to flip through until he had almost reached the front of the book. On one of the pages a pair of eyes glanced at him swiftly. Parker sped on, then stopped. His heart too appeared to cut off; there was absolute silence. It said as plainly as if silence were a language itself, *Go back*.

Parker returned to the picture—the haloed head of a flat stern Byzantine Christ with all-demanding eyes. He sat there trembling; his heart began slowly to beat again as if it were being brought to life by a subtle power.

"You found what you want?" the artist asked.

Parker's throat was too dry to speak. He got up and thrust the book at the artist, opened at the picture.

"That'll cost you plenty," the artist said. "You don't want all those little blocks though, just the outline and some better features."

"Just like it is," Parker said, "just like it is or nothing."

"It's your funeral," the artist said, "but I don't do that kind of work for nothing."

"How much?" Parker asked.

"It'll take maybe two days' work."

"How much?" Parker said.

"On time or cash?" the artist asked. Parker's other jobs had been on time, but he had paid.

"Ten down and ten for every day it takes," the artist said.

Parker drew ten one-dollar bills out of his wallet; he had three left in.

"You come back in the morning," the artist said, putting the money in his own pocket. "First I'll have to trace that out of the book."

"No, no!" Parker said. "Trace it now or gimme my money back," and his eyes blared as if he were ready for a fight.

The artist agreed. Anyone stupid enough to want a Christ on his back, he reasoned, would be just as likely as not to change his mind the next minute, but once the work was begun he could hardly do so.

While he worked on the tracing, he told Parker to go wash his back at the sink with the special soap he used there. Parker did it and returned to pace back and forth across the room, nervously flexing his shoulders. He wanted to go look at the picture again but at the same time he did not want to. The artist got up finally and had Parker lie down on the table. He swabbed his back with ethyl chloride and then began to outline the head on it with his iodine pencil. Another hour passed before he took up his electric instrument. Parker felt no particular pain. In Japan he had had a tattoo of the Buddha done on his upper arm with ivory needles; in Burma, a little brown root of a man had made a peacock on each of his knees using thin pointed sticks, two feet long; amateurs had worked on him with pins and soot. Parker was usually so relaxed and easy under the hand of the artist that he often went to sleep, but this time he remained awake, every muscle taut.

At midnight the artist said he was ready to quit. He propped one mirror, four feet square, on a table by the wall and took a smaller mirror off the lavatory wall and put it in Parker's hands. Parker stood with his back to the one on the table and moved the other until he saw a flashing burst of color reflected from his back. It was almost completely covered with little red and blue and ivory and saffron squares; from them he made out the lineaments of the face—a mouth, the beginnings of heavy brows, a straight nose, but the face was empty; the eyes had not yet been put in. The impression for the moment was almost as if the artist had tricked him and done the Physician's Friend.

"It don't have eyes," Parker cried out.

"That'll come," the artist said, "in due time. We have another day to go on it yet."

Parker spent the night on a cot at the Haven of Light Christian Mission. He found these the best places to stay in the city because they were free and included a meal of sorts. He got the last available cot and because he was still barefooted, he accepted a pair of secondhand shoes which, in his confusion, he put on to go to bed; he was still shocked from all that had happened to him. All night he lay awake in the long dormitory of cots with lumpy figures on them. The only light was from a phosphorescent cross glowing at the end of the room. The tree reached out to grasp him again, then burst into flame; the shoe burned quietly by itself; the eyes in the book said to him distinctly *Go back* and at the same time did not utter a sound. He wished that he were not in this city, not in this Haven of Light Mission, not in a bed by himself. He longed miserably for Sarah Ruth. Her sharp tongue and ice-pick eyes were the only comfort he could bring to mind. He decided he was losing it. Her eyes appeared soft and dilatory compared with the eyes in the book, for even though he could not summon up the exact look of those eyes, he could still feel their penetration. He felt as though, under their gaze, he was as transparent as the wing of a fly.

The tattooist had told him not to come until ten in the morning, but when he arrived at that hour, Parker was sitting in the dark hallway on the floor, waiting for him. He had decided upon getting up that, once the tattoo was on him, he would not look at it, that all his sensations of the day and night before were those of a crazy man and that he would return to doing things according to his own sound judgment.

The artist began where he left off. "One thing I want to know," he said presently as he worked over Parker's back, "why do you want this on you? Have you gone and got religion? Are you saved?" he asked in a mocking voice.

Parker's voice felt salty and dry. "Naw," he said, "I ain't got no use for none of that. A man can't save his self from whatever it is he don't deserve none of my sympathy." These words seemed to leave his mouth like wraiths and to evaporate at once as if he had never uttered them.

"Then why. . . ."

"I married this woman that's saved," Parker said. "I never should have done it. I ought to leave her. She's done and gone and got pregnant."

"That's too bad," the artist said. "Then it's her making you have this tattoo."

"Naw," Parker said, "she don't know nothing about it. It's a surprise for her."

"You think she'll like it and lay off you a while?"

"She can't hep herself," Parker said. "She can't say she don't like the looks of God." He decided he had told the artist enough of his business. Artists were all right in their place but he didn't like them poking their noses into the affairs of regular people. "I didn't get no sleep last night," he said. "I think I'll get some now."

That closed the mouth of the artist but it did not bring him any sleep. He lay there, imagining how Sarah Ruth would be struck speechless by the face on his back and every now and then this would be interrupted by a vision of the tree of fire and his empty shoe burning beneath it.

The artist worked steadily until nearly four o'clock, not stopping to have lunch, hardly pausing with the electric instrument except to wipe the dripping dye off Parker's back as he went along. Finally he finished. "You can get up and look at it now," he said.

Parker sat up, but he remained on the edge of the table.

The artist was pleased with his work and wanted Parker to look at it at once. Instead Parker continued to sit on the edge of the table, bent forward slightly but with a vacant look. "What ails you?" the artist said. "Go look at it."

"Ain't nothing ail me," Parker said in a sudden belligerent voice. "That tattoo ain't going nowhere. It'll be there when I get there." He reached for his shirt and began gingerly to put it on.

The artist took him roughly by the arm and propelled him between the two mirrors. "Now *look*," he said, angry at having his work ignored.

Parker looked, turned white and moved away. The eyes in the reflected face continued to look at him—still, straight, all-demanding, enclosed in silence.

"It was your idea, remember," the artist said. "I would have advised something else."

Parker said nothing. He put on his shirt and went out the door while the artist shouted, "I'll expect all of my money!"

Parker headed toward a package shop on the corner. He bought a pint of whiskey and took it into a nearby alley and drank it all in five minutes.

Then he moved on to a pool hall nearby which he frequented when he came to the city. It was a well-lighted barnlike place with a bar up one side and gambling machines on the other and pool tables in the back. As soon as Parker entered, a large man in a red-and-black checkered shirt hailed him by slapping him on the back and yelling, "Yeyyyyyy boy! O.E. Parker!"

Parker was not yet ready to be struck on the back. "Lay off," he said, "I got a fresh tattoo there."

"What you got this time?" the man asked and then yelled to a few at the machine, "O.E.'s got him another tattoo."

"Nothing special this time," Parker said and slunk over to a machine that was not being used.

"Come on," the big man said, "let's have a look at O.E.'s tattoo," and while Parker squirmed in their hands, they pulled up his shirt. Parker felt all the hands drop away instantly and his shirt fell again like a veil over the face. There was a silence in the poolroom which seemed to Parker to grow from the circle around him until it extended to the foundations under the building and upward through the beams in the roof.

Finally someone said, "Christ!" Then they all broke into noise at once. Parker turned around, an uncertain grin on his face.

"Leave it to O.E.!" the man in the checkered shirt said. "That boy's a real card!"

"Maybe he's gone and got religion," someone yelled.

"Not on your life," Parker said.

"O.E.'s got religion and is witnessing for Jesus, ain't you, O.E.?" a little man with a piece of cigar in his mouth said wryly. "An o-riginal way to do it if I ever saw one."

"Leave it to Parker to think of a new one!" the fat man said. "Yyeeeeeeyyyyyyy boy!" someone yelled and they all began to whistle and curse in compliment until Parker said, "Aaa shut up."

"What'd you do it for?" somebody asked.

"For laughs," Parker said. "What's it to you?"

"Why ain't you laughing then?" somebody yelled.

Parker lunged into the midst of them and like a whirlwind on a summer day there began a fight that raged amid overturned tables and swinging fists until two of them grabbed him and ran to the door with him and threw him out. Then a calm descended on the pool hall as nerve-shattering as if the long barnlike room were the ship from which Jonah had been cast into the sea.

Parker sat for a long time on the ground in the alley behind the pool hall, examining his soul. He saw it as a spiderweb of facts and lies that was not at all important to him but which appeared to be necessary in spite of his opinion. The eyes that were now forever on his back were eyes to be obeyed. He was as certain of it as he had ever been of anything. Throughout his life, grumbling and sometimes cursing, often afraid, once in rapture, Parker had obeyed whatever instinct of this kind had come to him—in rapture when his spirit had lifted at the sight of the tattooed man at the fair, afraid when he had joined the Navy, grumbling when he had married Sarah Ruth.

The thought of her brought him slowly to his feet. She would know what he had to do. She would clear up the rest of it, and she would at least be pleased. His truck was still parked in front of the building where the artist had his place, but it was not far away. He got in it and drove out of the city and into the country night. His head was almost clear of liquor and he observed that his dissatisfaction was gone, but he felt not quite like himself. It was as if he were himself but a stranger to himself, driving into a new country though everything he saw was familiar to him, even at night.

He arrived finally at the house on the embankment, pulled the truck under the pecan tree and got out. He made as much noise as possible to assert that he was still in charge here, that his leaving her for a night without word meant nothing except it was the way he did things. He slammed the car door, stamped up the two steps and across the porch and rattled the doorknob. It did not respond to his touch. "Sarah Ruth!" he yelled. "Let me in."

There was no lock on the door and she had evidently placed the back of a chair against the knob. He began to beat on the door and rattle the knob.

He heard the bedsprings creak and bent down and put his head to the keyhole, but it was stopped up with paper. "Let me in!" he hollered, bamming on the door again. "What you got me locked out for?"

A sharp voice close to the door said, "Who's there?"

"Me," Parker said. "O.E."

He waited a moment.

"Me," he said impatiently. "O.E."

Still no sound from inside.

He tried once more. "O.E.," he said, bamming the door two or three more times. "O.E. Parker. You know me."

There was a silence. Then the voice said slowly, "I don't know no O.E."

"Quit fooling," Parker pleaded. "You ain't got any business doing me this way. It's me, old O.E., I'm back. You ain't afraid of me."

"Who's there?" the same unfeeling voice said.

Parker turned his head as if he expected someone behind him to give him the answer. The sky had lightened slightly and there were two or three streaks of yellow floating above the horizon. Then as he stood there, a tree of light burst over the skyline.

Parker fell back against the door as if he had been pinned there by a lance.

"Who's there?" the voice from inside said and there was a quality about it now that seemed final. The knob rattled and the voice said peremptorily. "Who's there, I ast you?"

Parker bent down and put his mouth near the stuffed keyhole. "Obadiah," he whispered and all at once he felt the light pouring through him, turning his spiderweb soul into a perfect arabesque of colors, a garden of trees and birds and beasts.

"Obadiah Elihue!" he whispered.

The door opened and he stumbled in. Sarah Ruth loomed there, hands on her hips. She began at once, "That was no hefty blond woman you was working for and you'll have to pay her every penny on her tractor you busted up. She don't keep insurance on it. She came here and her and me had us a long talk and I . . ."

Trembling, Parker set about lighting the kerosene lamp.

"What's the matter with you, wasting that kerosene this near daylight?" she demanded. "I ain't got to look at you."

A yellow glow enveloped them. Parker put the match down and began to unbutton his shirt.

"And you ain't going to have none of me this near morning," she said.

"Shut your mouth," he said quietly. "Look at this and then I don't want to hear no more out of you." He removed the shirt and turned his back to her.

"Another picture," Sarah Ruth growled. "I might have known you was off after putting some more trash on yourself."

Parker's knees went hollow under him. He wheeled around and cried, "Look at it! Don't just say that! *Look* at it!"

"I done looked," she said.

"Don't you know who it is?" he cried in anguish.

"No, who is it?" Sarah Ruth said. "It ain't anybody I know."

"It's Him," Parker said.

"Him who?"

"God!" Parker cried.

"God? God don't look like that!"

"What do you know how he looks?" Parker moaned. "You ain't seen him."

"He don't *look*," Sarah Ruth said. "He's a spirit. No man shall see his face."

"Aw listen," Parker groaned, "this is just a picture of Him."

"Idolatry!" Sarah Ruth screamed. "Idolatry. Inflaming yourself with idols under every green tree! I can put up with lies and vanity but I don't want no idolator in this house!" and she grabbed up the broom and thrashed him across the shoulders with it.

Parker was too stunned to resist. He sat there and let her beat him until she had nearly knocked him senseless and large welts had formed on the face of the tattooed Christ. Then he staggered up and made for the door.

She stamped the broom two or three times on the floor and went to the window and shook it out to get the taint of him off it. Still gripping it, she looked toward the pecan tree and her eyes hardened still more. There he was—who called himself Obadiah Elihue—leaning against the tree, crying like a baby.

The Jeweler

Pete Dexter

The old man ordered the soup of the day again, homemade noodles and chicken served with bread and a glass of house wine, and wiped at his nose with his napkin the whole time he ate. It was February, and everybody on the East Coast had the flu. The old man looked like he should have been home in bed, but his habits were set deep. At ten to six every morning, for instance, he stepped out of his front door in his bathrobe and slippers to retrieve the *Inquirer*. Two hours later he came out again, dressed in an overcoat, and walked to the end of his block and caught the SEPTA bus to work. Twice this week he'd given his seat to young women. Exactly at 1:00 he left the store, walked the four blocks to the restaurant, and had his soup of the day and wine, always sitting at the same table near the kitchen. The tab always came to six dollars, and he always left a dollar for the waitress. She had a snake tattooed around the fleshy part of her arm, and beneath it the name *Jerry* was written in script.

The man who had been keeping track of the old man's habits was named Whittemore, and he noticed the hair in his plate as soon as the waitress set it on the table. The hair lay across his fish and was anchored at one end in a little white paper cup of tartar sauce, moving slightly in the air from the overhead fan, like something dying in bed but not quite dead. He moved closer and saw that most of the hair was black, but out toward the end, away from the tartar sauce, there was a bulb of root where it was brown.

The waitress was a blonde, so the hair had come from the kitchen, which was worse in a way than if it had just belonged to the waitress herself. She had the tattoo, of course, and a stud in her nose—a small pearl—and a stained blouse, but this was the human being, after all, that they'd sent out to greet the public. Christ knew what they looked like back in the kitchen.

"Is everything all right, hon?" She came back to his table empty-handed from the other side on the way to the kitchen. Whittemore looked up and saw the back of the stud glistening inside her nose. A week ago, when he first walked in and saw the pearl, he thought it was some kind of growth.

"It's fine," he said.

She put a hand on her hip and he noticed her fingers. Cloudy, yellow nails, the skin itself stained dark. He wondered if she was also a photographer, had her hands in chemicals in her off-hours. Or maybe just a Camel smoker. The point was, who could eat the food after they saw her hands? He shuddered suddenly, remembering that he'd been having ideas about this same girl earlier in the week. He remembered the exact words that came into his head: *She looks up for anything.*

"You don't eat much," she said.

"Too much stress."

She nodded, as if that made perfect sense, and then gave him a little wink. "I'm the same way," she said. "I just come in to calm my nerves."

*   *   *

The old man knew he was caught and was no trouble in the parking lot or in the car on the way out of town.

His name was Eisner, and whatever he was stealing, he hadn't been spending any of it on his clothes. He sat in the passenger seat in a suit that must have been fifty years old, wearing a bow tie and a starched white shirt, chewing Smith Brothers cough drops. They passed city hall and he cleared his throat.

"It used to be there was no skyscrapers in the whole city," he said. "It was a local ordinance, nothing taller than the Billy Penn. That was the law." A moment passed, and he shifted in his seat. "The place wasn't as dark then," he said.

A little snot teardrop glistened beneath one of the old man's nostrils, moving up and down as he breathed, and Whittemore felt himself edging away. He tried to remember if he'd touched him in the parking lot. He wasn't worried about the door. He'd followed him out, but he knew he'd covered his hand with his sleeve. He did that without thinking now, and he hadn't shaken hands with anybody since his mother's funeral. Not that it came up much anymore, but when it did, he would cough into his fist and tell whoever it was that he might be coming down with the flu. Nobody got past that, and nothing human had touched him in a long time.

They were on the parkway now, headed toward the river. Whittemore looked up and saw the art museum half a mile ahead, ancient and dead even in the sunlight; it could have been waiting for them both. The old man moved again, the air stirring with germs.

"A tan like that, you must travel a lot," Eisner said. They passed the museum and headed west, along the Schuylkill and past the boathouses. Then he said, "Myself, I'm a creature of habit. I stay put." And then he sneezed into his hands.

Whittemore gave him his handkerchief, which Eisner used to dry his fingers and then his eyes. And when he could see again, he looked out his window, away from the river into Fairmount Park. "During the war," he said, "there were supposed to be Japs that lived back in there in cardboard boxes and ate people's dogs. . . ." It was quiet for a little while, and then he said, "I guess they decided they'd rather take their chances in the park."

Against his will, Whittemore began thinking about his visit to the doctor before he left Seattle. The doctor was Japanese—which is what brought it to mind—and said he didn't think the memory lapses were anything to worry about, that they were related to stress. The doctors in Seattle saw a lot of stress, of course, all those fucking owls to worry about, domestic partners who couldn't get on the major medical at Boeing. Whittemore had noticed that it was about twelve years ago when the doctors quit saying *You're fine.* Now it was always *I don't think it's anything to worry about.* Which smelled of insurance. Every day, he saw the world dividing itself into a billion insurance policies, everybody trying to set things up in some way that made them safe.

"Myself, what I don't like is hotels," Eisner said. "Strange mattresses, peepholes in the doors, somebody's always got their hand out. People drool on the pillowcase, it soaks through, even a hundred-dollar hotel." He dabbed at his nose with the handkerchief and said, "Rich people drool as much as anybody else, maybe more, when you think about it. And the strangers walking up and down the halls? No reflection on you, but the more human beings I see from out of state, the less hope I have for the future."

Whittemore had frozen, though, at the mention of hotel pillows. How could he have missed that? It seemed dangerous in some way that the old man had thought of it and he hadn't. Ahead of them, a Rolling Rock delivery truck dropped into a pothole that must have broken half the bottles inside.

"You care to know how this happened?" the old man said a little later.

Whittemore began to say no, that it wasn't any of his business. The old man was popping his toast every two minutes as it was. Instead, he shrugged. He'd been having queer feelings again, even before he left Seattle, like it was all out of his hands.

"There wasn't any reason," the old man said. "That's the big joke. I'm seventy-six years old; they don't have anything I want. Nothing. No reason but the twins themselves. The future-is-ours, dot-com-generation, bastard twins." He looked at him quickly and said, "Kids, I'm talking about. Nothing personal. You want a cough drop?"

Whittemore shook his head no and wondered for the next mile why the old man would think he needed a cough drop.

"Paul and Bonnie, I would cut off my right hand before I took a cent. But then they crashed their car on the Black Horse Pike—going to the shore for a weekend in the middle of winter, for Christ's sake, just like that, they're gone—and the twins take over before they're even in the ground. Forty-two years these people were my friends, they were like my family, but the truth is they didn't spend enough time at home. The business was too important. That's all I'll say about it, end of story. They didn't spend enough time at home."

Whittemore nodded, as if he agreed with that, although he hadn't met the boys himself. That wasn't the way it was done. He worked for himself. There were people in the middle, and everything went through them—the money and the jobs. It was cleaner all the way around.

"Cheating people who've been coming into the store forty years, that's how this happened. Cheating young people come in to buy a wedding ring. Ruining their parents' good reputation. What's that worth? What's the price these days on a good reputation?"

They'd been in the car half an hour now, and the houses in the distance were bigger and had rolling lawns and iron fences. Then a golf course. "You play golf?" the old man said, and a moment later Whittemore grabbed at his knee and ran the outside wheels off onto the shoulder of the road.

The sensation wasn't painful as much as eerie. Like something in there was being unscrewed. It happened on airplanes and in the movies, anywhere Whittemore had to sit still. He took vitamins, rode his bicycle three times a week, did sixty push-ups every morning, and never got through the rest of the day without a twinge somewhere, without thinking this might be it.

"You know I taught these little bastards how to play? Did they tell you that?" The old man was warming to the subject now. "They got to have the best clubs, right from the first day. New leather bags, new shoes. God forbid they should play in tennis shoes. Fourteen years old, and they're riding around in carts like old men. . . ."

Eisner wiped at his eyes again and then stared out the window, watching someone swing, just wanting to see a golf swing, moving a little in his seat as the swell of the fairway began to eclipse the golfer. "Cheat?" he said. "They embarrass you to death."

The course disappeared, and Eisner sneezed again. Some of it blew out beneath the handkerchief and spotted his pants. "Did you say you played? I get nervous, I can't remember what people tell me."

"A little. I used to play a little."

"Then you know what I'm talking about."

They passed into Lancaster County, and a few minutes later turned off the highway onto a road so faded that there was hardly a road left. Weeds were growing in the lane markers. They saw an Amish pulled to the side who had broken an axle on his buggy. He was up front, calming the horse; a woman was nursing a baby in the shadows of the backseat.

"I hear Titleist is coming out with a new ball, twenty extra yards off the tee," Eisner said.

Whittemore saw the dirt road that he'd picked earlier and began slowing for the turn. The old man's voice was shaking so badly, he could hardly get this out: "Myself," he said, "I wouldn't mind trying it. You get up in years like me, you can use the extra distance."

And that was as close as he came to asking for anything.

Whittemore pulled the car to the side of the road and sat still a minute, thinking it over. "What if you had to go away?"

"Me?" Eisner said. "Where am I going to go?"

"Someplace else," Whittemore said. "The other side of the world."

The old man took a minute putting it together. "You mean like the Poconos?" he said.

Whittemore went to Seventh Street that same afternoon to return the five thousand in person. That was the only chance he saw, to talk to them in person. Something like this—but not exactly this—had happened once before and been negotiated. That was the word the people in the middle used, *negotiated*. It meant they waited three or four months, gave you enough time to think maybe they'd forgotten, and then a couple of guys who laughed at everything came around with their softball bats and their twenty-pound biceps and pimples on their shoulders and brought you back into the world of hospitals and medical science. He couldn't remember now exactly what it had been like. This time, though, unless he could head it off, things would have to be explained, which was a more serious word to the people in the middle.

The jewelers took him upstairs to their office—they seemed to be in a hurry to get him off the showroom floor—and while one of them closed the door, the other one took off his coat, dropped into the chair behind his desk, hung his health-club arms over the sides—the kid wanted him to notice his arms—and stared at him as if he were trying to make up his mind. He was the one who did the talking.

"So?" the kid said.

Right away, he saw for himself what the old man meant.

"We put the five thousand up front, right? I told your people, you're late, you forfeit the back end. That simple."

Whittemore looked from one of them to the other. Identical, but he could already tell who was who.

"No comprende?" the kid said.

He began to tell them that the back end didn't matter, that he hadn't done it anyway, but he stopped himself, waiting to see where this would go. "The deal was ten," he said. "Five in front, five after it's done. That was the agreement."

The kid shook his head, and then he and his brother glanced at each other again. "It's like I told your people. Time constraints have been violated. The agreement's changed."

Whittemore sat dead still, looking from one of the twins to the other.

"I know what you're thinking," the kid said. "I know everything you're thinking, and it's like I told your people, my brother and I have left instructions with our lawyers, sealed instructions to be opened in the event any-thing unfortunate happened. That occurs, the lawyers open an envelope, which spells out all the details of the whole situation. Names, dates, times, everything. If we so much as slip in the shower."

They waited for him a moment, then smiled as the message settled. One of them, then the other.

"You two shower together?"

"Just a hypothesis, something to consider," the kid said.

Whittemore considered their jewelry: Rolex watches half an inch thick, diamond rings, gold bracelets and neck chains. The one at the book-case was wearing cuff links. He wondered if it was part of the jewelry busi-ness that you had to look like a Gypsy coming out a hotel window, or if these two just liked to twinkle when they moved, separate themselves from the world at large.

The kid in the chair looked at his brother, who had walked over to the window. The little glances reminded him of the way lovers reach out to touch hands without even knowing they're doing it. "I mean, look at your-self," the one in the chair said, "coming in here like this . . ."

Whittemore nodded at him, but the kid misunderstood. But then, he misunderstood everything. "It's a Mexican standoff, man," he said. "Now get your ass out of here before I call the police."

He shot the one at the window first and then turned slowly to the one who did the talking, giving him a moment to reflect on his Mexican standoff.

Afterward, he stayed in the room a little longer than he should have, the cordite stinging his nose, studying the posture of the bodies, down to the exact position of the fingers when everything had stopped moving. He sat down behind the desk in the kid's chair, taking the weight off his knees.

The one at the window had been a nail biter.

He thought of the old man and wondered how long it would be before he got homesick and showed up at the restaurant. His hands had shaken, but that was all. No crying, no regrets. There in the front seat, Whittemore had suddenly remembered how he'd let the guys who laughed at every-thing position his legs across the kitchen chairs just so and that one of his knees—he wasn't sure even then which one—hadn't dislocated the first time they came down on it, or the second, or the third.

He'd taken Eisner to a bus stop anyway.

Eisner got out and was around the car at Whittemore's window in what seemed like the same instant, tapping at the window, brimming tears, and Whittemore rolled it down to see what he wanted, and he came in like death itself, glistening tears and snot, right through the window, his hands, his head, his shoulders, and shit the sheets if Whittemore didn't just sit there and let the old man hug him.

All the Pretty Horses

Cormac McCarthy

The Hacienda de Nuestra Señora de la Purísima Concepción was a ranch of fourteen thousand hectares situated along the edge of the Bolsón de Cuatro Ciénagas in the state of Coahuila. The western sections ran into the Sierra de Anteojo to elevations of nine thousand feet but south and east the ranch occupied part of the broad barrial or basin floor of the bolsón and was well watered with natural springs and clear streams and dotted with marshes and shallow lakes or lagunas. In the lakes and in the streams were species of fish not known elsewhere on earth and birds and lizards and other forms of life as well all long relict here for the desert stretched away on every side.

La Purísima was one of very few ranches in that part of Mexico retaining the full complement of six square leagues of land allotted by the colonizing legislation of eighteen twenty-four and the owner Don Héctor Rocha y Villareal was one of the few hacendados who actually lived on the land he claimed, land that had been in his family for one hundred and seventy years. He was forty-seven years old and he was the first male heir in all that new world lineage to attain such an age.

He ran upwards of a thousand head of cattle on this land. He kept a house in Mexico City where his wife lived. He flew his own airplane. He loved horses. When he rode up to the gerente's house that morning he was accompanied by four friends and by a retinue of mozos and two packanimals saddled with hardwood kiacks, one empty, the other carrying their noon provisions. They were attended by a pack of greyhound dogs and the dogs were lean and silver in color and they flowed among the legs of the horses silent and fluid as running mercury and the horses paid them no mind at all. The hacendado halloed the house and the gerente emerged in his shirt-sleeves and they spoke briefly and the gerente nodded and the hacendado spoke to his friends and then all rode on. When they passed the bunkhouse and rode through the gate and turned into the road upcountry some of the vaqueros were catching their horses in the trap and leading them out to saddle them for the day's work. John Grady and Rawlins stood in the doorway drinking their coffee.

Yonder he is, said Rawlins.

John Grady nodded and slung the dregs of coffee out into the yard.

Where the hell do you reckon they're goin? said Rawlins.

I'd say they're goin to run coyotes.

They aint got no guns.

They got ropes.

Rawlins looked at him. Are you shittin me?

I dont think so.

Well I'd damn sure like to see it.

I would too. You ready?

They worked two days in the holding pens branding and earmarking and castrating and dehorning and inoculating. On the third day the vaqueros brought a small herd of wild three year old colts down from the mesa and penned them and in the evening Rawlins and John Grady walked out to look them over. They were bunched against the fence at the far side of the enclosure and they were a mixed lot, roans and duns and bays and a few paints and they were of varied size and conformation. John Grady opened the gate and he and Rawlins walked in and he closed it behind them. The horrified animals began to climb over one another and to break up and move along the fence in both directions.

That's as spooky a bunch of horses as I ever saw, said Rawlins.

They dont know what we are.

Dont know what we are?

I dont think so. I dont think they've ever seen a man afoot.

Rawlins leaned and spat.

You see anything there you'd have?

There's horses there.

Where at?

Look at that dark bay. Right yonder.

I'm lookin.

Look again.

That horse wont weigh eight hundred pounds.

Yeah he will. Look at the hindquarters on him. He'd make a cow horse. Look at that roan yonder.

That coonfooted son of a bitch?

Well, yeah he is a little. All right. That other roan. That third one to the right.

The one with the white on him?

Yeah.

That's kindly a funny lookin horse to me.

No he aint. He's just colored peculiar.

You dont think that means nothin? He's got white feet.

That's a good horse. Look at his head. Look at the jaw on him. You got to remember their tails are all growed out.

Yeah. Maybe. Rawlins shook his head doubtfully. You used to be awful particular about horses. Maybe you just aint seen any in a long time.

John Grady nodded. Yeah, he said. Well. I aint forgot what they're supposed to look like.

The horses had grouped again at the far end of the pen and stood rolling their eyes and running their heads along each other's necks.

They got one thing goin for em, said Rawlins.

What's that.

They aint had no Mexican to try and break em.

John Grady nodded.

They studied the horses.

How many are there? said John Grady.

Rawlins looked them over. Fifteen. Sixteen.

I make it sixteen.

Sixteen then.

You think you and me could break all of em in four days?

Depends on what you call broke.

Just halfway decent greenbroke horses. Say six saddles. Double and stop and stand still to be saddled.

Rawlins took his tobacco from his pocket and pushed back his hat.

What you got in mind? he said.

Breakin these horses.

Why four days?

You think we could do it?

They intend puttin em in the rough-string? My feelin is that any horse broke in four days is liable to come unbroke in four more.

They're out of horses is how come em to be down here in the first place.

Rawlins dabbed tobacco into the cupped paper. You're tellin me that what we're lookin at here is our own string?

That's my guess.

We're lookin at ridin some coldjawed son of a bitch broke with one of them damned mexican ringbits.

Yeah.

Rawlins nodded. What would you do, sideline em?

143

Yep.

You think there's that much rope on the place?

I dont know.

You'd be a woreout sumbuck. I'll tell you that.

Think how good you'd sleep.

Rawlins put the cigarette in his mouth and fished about for a match. What else do you know that you aint told me?

Armando says the old man's got horses all over that mountain.

How many horses.

Somethin like four hundred head.

Rawlins looked at him. He popped the match with his thumbnail and lit the cigarette and flipped the match away.

What else? said Rawlins.

That's it.

Let's go talk to the man.

They went to work on the green colts daybreak Sunday morning, dressing in the half dark in clothes still wet from their washing them the night before and walking out to the potrero before the stars were down, eating a cold tortilla wrapped around a scoop of cold beans and no coffee and carrying their fortyfoot maguey catchropes coiled over their shoulders. They carried saddle blankets and a bosalea or riding hackamore with a metal noseband and John Grady carried a pair of clean gunnysacks he'd slept on and his Hamley saddle with the stirrups already shortened.

They stood looking at the horses. The horses shifted and stood, gray shapes in the gray morning. Stacked on the ground outside the gate were coils of every kind of rope, cotton and manila and plaited rawhide and maguey and ixtle down to lengths of old woven hair mecates and hand plaited piecings of bindertwine. Stacked against the fence were the sixteen rope hackamores they'd spent the evening tying in the bunkhouse.

Rawlins stuffed the last of the tortilla in his jaw and wiped his hands on his trousers and undid the wire and opened the gate.

John Grady followed him in and stood the saddle on the ground and went back out and brought in a handful of ropes and hackamores and squatted to sort them. Rawlins stood building his loop.

I take it you dont give a particular damn what order they come in, he said.

You take it correctly, cousin.

You dead set on sackin these varmints out?

Yep.

My old daddy always said that the purpose of breakin a horse was to ride it and if you got one to break you just as well to saddle up and climb aboard and get on with it.

John Grady grinned. Was your old daddy a certified peeler?

I never heard him claim to be. But I damn sure seen him hang and rattle a time or two.

Well you're fixin to see some more of it.

We goin to bust em twice?

What for?

I never saw one that completely believed it the first time or ever doubted it the second.

John Grady smiled. I'll make em believe, he said. You'll see.

I'm goin to tell you right now, cousin. This is a heathenish bunch.

The horses were already moving. He took the first one that broke and rolled his loop and forefooted the colt and it hit the ground with a tremendous thump. The other horses flared and bunched and looked back wildly. Before the colt could struggle up John Grady had squatted on its neck and pulled its head up and to one side and was holding the horse by the muzzle with the long bony head pressed against his chest and the hot sweet breath of it flooding up from the dark wells of its nostrils over his face and neck like news from another world. They did not smell like horses. They smelled like what they were, wild animals. He held the horse's face against his chest and he could feel along his inner thighs the blood pumping through the arteries and he could smell the fear and he cupped his hand over the horse's eyes and stroked them and he did not stop talking to the horse at all, speaking in a low steady voice and telling it all that he intended to do and cupping the animal's eyes and stroking the terror out.

Rawlins took one of the lengths of siderope from around his neck where he'd hung them and made a slipnoose and hitched it around the pastern of the hind leg and drew the leg up and half hitched it to the horse's forelegs. He freed the catchrope and pitched it away and took the hackamore and they fitted it over the horse's muzzle and ears and John Grady ran his thumb in the animal's mouth and Rawlins fitted the mouthrope and then slipnoosed a second siderope to the other rear leg. Then he tied both sideropes to the hackamore.

You all set? he said.

All set.

He let go the horse's head and rose and stepped away. The horse struggled up and turned and shot out one hind foot and snatched itself around in a half circle and fell over. It got up and kicked again and fell again. When it got up the third time it stood kicking and snatching its head about in a little dance. It stood. It walked away and stood again. Then it shot out a hind leg and fell again.

It lay there for a while thinking things over and when it got up it stood for a minute and then it hopped up and down three times and then it just stood glaring at them. Rawlins had his catchrope and was building his loop again. The other horses watched with great interest from the far side of the potrero.

These sumbucks are as crazy as a shithouse rat, he said.

You pick out the one you think is craziest, said John Grady, and I'll give you a finished horse this time Sunday week.

Finished for who?

To your satisfaction.

Bullshit, said Rawlins.

By the time they had three of the horses sidelined in the trap blowing and glaring about there were several vaqueros at the gate drinking coffee in a leisurely fashion and watching the proceedings. By midmorning eight of the horses stood tied and the other eight were wilder than deer, scattering along the fence and bunching and running in a rising sea of dust as the day warmed, coming to reckon slowly with the remorselessness of this rendering of their fluid and collective selves into that condition of separate and helpless paralysis which seemed to be among them like a creeping plague. The entire complement of vaqueros had come from the bunkhouse to watch and by noon all sixteen of the mesteños were standing about in the potrero sidehobbled to their own hackamores and faced about in every direction and all communion among them broken. They looked like animals trussed up by children for fun and they stood waiting for they knew not what with the voice of the breaker still running in their brains like the voice of some god come to inhabit them.

When they went down to the bunkhouse for dinner the vaqueros seemed to treat them with a certain deference but whether it was the deference accorded the accomplished or that accorded mental defectives they were unsure. No one asked them their opinion of the horses or queried them as to their method. When they went back up to the trap in the afternoon there were some twenty people standing about looking at the horses—women, children, young girls, and men—and all waiting for them to return.

Where the hell did they come from? said Rawlins.

I dont know.

Word gets around when the circus come to town, dont it?

They passed nodding through the crowd and entered the trap and fastened the gate.

You picked one out? said John Grady.

Yeah. For pure crazy I nominate that bucketheaded son of a bitch standin right yonder.

The grullo?

Grullo-lookin.

The man's a judge of horseflesh.

He's a judge of craziness.

He watched while John Grady walked up to the animal and tied a twelvefoot length of rope to the hackamore. Then he led it through the gate out of the potrero and into the corral where the horses would be ridden. Rawlins thought the horse would shy or try to rear but it didnt. He got the sack and hobbleropes and came up and while John Grady talked to the horse he hobbled the front legs together and then took the mecate rope and handed John Grady the sack and he held the horse while for the next quarter hour John Grady floated the sack over the animal and under it and rubbed its head with the sack and passed it across the horse's face and ran it up and down and between the animal's legs talking to the horse the while and rubbing against it and leaning against it. Then he got the saddle.

What good do you think it does to waller all over a horse thataway? said Rawlins.

I dont know, said John Grady. I aint a horse.

He lifted the blanket and placed it on the animal's back and smoothed it and stood stroking the animal and talking to it and then he bent and picked up the saddle and lifted it with the cinches strapped up and the off stirrup hung over the horn and sat it on the horse's back and rocked it into place. The horse never moved. He bent and reached under and pulled up the strap and cinched it. The horse's ears went back and he talked to it and then pulled up the cinch again and he leaned against the horse and talked to it just as if it were neither crazy nor lethal. Rawlins looked toward the corral gate. There were fifty or more people watching. Folk were picnicking on the ground. Fathers held up babies. John Grady lifted off the stirrup from the saddle horn and let it drop. Then he hauled up the cinchstrap again and buckled it. All right, he said.

Hold him, said Rawlins.

He held the mecate while Rawlins undid the sideropes from the hackamore and knelt and tied them to the front hobbles. Then they slipped the hackamore off the horse's head and John Grady raised the bosalea and gently fitted it over the horse's nose and fitted the mouthrope and headstall. He gathered the reins and looped them over the horse's head and nodded and Rawlins knelt and undid the hobbles and pulled the slipnooses until the siderope loops fell to the ground at the horse's rear hooves. Then he stepped away.

John Grady put one foot in the stirrup and pressed himself flat against the horse's shoulder talking to it and then swung up into the saddle.

The horse stood stock still. It shot out one hindfoot to test the air and stood again and then it threw itself sideways and twisted and kicked and stood snorting. John Grady touched it up in the ribs with his bootheels and it stepped forward. He reined it and it turned. Rawlins spat in disgust. John Grady turned the horse again and came back by.

What the hell kind of a bronc is that? said Rawlins. You think that's what these people paid good money to see?

By dark he'd ridden eleven of the sixteen horses. Not all of them so tractable. Someone had built a fire on the ground outside the potrero and there were something like a hundred people gathered, some come from the pueblo of La Vega six miles to the south, some from farther. He rode the last five horses by the light of that fire, the horses dancing, turning in the light, their red eyes flashing. When they were done the horses stood in the potrero or stepped about trailing their hackamore ropes over the ground with such circumspection not to tread upon them and snatch down their sore noses that they moved with an air of great elegance and seemliness. The wild and frantic band of mustangs that had circled the potrero that morning like marbles swirled in a jar could hardly be said to exist and the animals whinnied to one another in the dark and answered back as if some one among their number were missing, or some thing.

When they walked down to the bunkhouse in the dark the bonfire was still burning and someone had brought a guitar and someone else a mouth-harp. Three separate strangers offered them a drink from bottles of mescal before they were clear of the crowd,

The kitchen was empty and they got their dinner from the stove and sat at the table. Rawlins watched John Grady. He was chewing woodenly and half tottering on the bench.

You aint tired are you, bud? he said.

No, said John Grady. I was tired five hours ago.

Rawlins grinned. Dont drink no more of that coffee. It'll keep you awake.

When they walked out in the morning at daybreak the fire was still smoldering and there were four or five men lying asleep on the ground, some with blankets and some without. Every horse in the potrero watched them come through the gate.

You remember how they come? said Rawlins.

Yeah. I remember em. I know you remember your buddy yonder.

Yeah, I know the son of a bitch.

When he walked up to the horse with the sack it turned and went trotting. He walked it down against the fence and picked up the rope and pulled it around and it stood quivering and he walked up to it and began to talk to it and then to stroke it with the sack. Rawlins went to fetch the blankets and the saddle and the bosalea.

By ten that night he'd ridden the entire remuda of sixteen horses and Rawlins had ridden them a second time each. They rode them again Tuesday and on Wednesday morning at daybreak with the first horse saddled and the sun not up John Grady rode toward the gate.

Open her up, he said.

Let me saddle a catch-horse.

We aint got time.

If that son of a bitch sets your ass out in the stickers you'll have time.

I guess I'd better stay in the saddle then.

Let me saddle up one of these good horses.

All right.

He rode out of the trap leading Rawlins's horse and waited while Rawlins shut the gate and mounted up beside him. The green horses stepped and sidled nervously.

This is kindly the blind leadin the blind, aint it?

Rawlins nodded. It's sort of like old T-bone Watts when he worked for daddy they all fussed about him havin bad breath. He told em it was better than no breath at all.

John Grady grinned and hooted the horse forward into a trot and they set out up the road.

Midafternoon he'd ridden all the horses again and while Rawlins worked with them in the trap he rode the little grullo of Rawlins's choice up into the country. Two miles above the ranch where the road ran by sedge and willow and wild plum along the edge of the laguna a young girl rode past him on a black Arabian saddle horse.

He heard the horse behind him and would have turned to look but that he heard it change gaits. He didnt look at her until the Arabian was alongside his horse, stepping with its neck arched and one eye on the mesteño not with wariness but some faint equine disgust. She wore english riding boots and jodhpurs and a blue twill hacking jacket and she carried a riding crop. She passed five feet away and turned her fine-boned face and looked full at him. She had blue eyes and she nodded or perhaps she only lowered her head slightly to better see what sort of horse he rode, just the slightest tilt of the broad black hat set level on her head, the slightest lifting of the long black hair. She passed and the horse changed gaits again and she sat the horse more than well, riding erect with her broad shoulders and trotting the horse up the road. The mesteño had stopped and sulled in the road with its forefeet spread and he sat looking after her. He'd half meant to speak but those eyes had altered the world forever in the space of a heartbeat. She disappeared beyond the lakeside willows. A flock of small birds rose up and passed back over him with thin calls.

That evening when Antonio and the gerente came up to the trap to inspect the horses he was teaching the grullo to back with Rawlins in the saddle. They watched, the gerente picking his teeth. Antonio rode the two horses that were standing saddled, sawing them back and forth in the corral and pulling them up short. He dismounted and nodded and he and the gerente looked over the horses in the other wing of the corral and then they left. Rawlins and John Grady looked at each other. They unsaddled the horses and turned them in with the remuda and walked back down to the house carrying their saddles and gear and washed up for supper. The vaqueros were at the table and they got their plates and helped themselves at the stove and got their coffee and came to the table and swung a leg over and sat down. There was a clay dish of tortillas in the center of the table with a towel over it and when John Grady pointed and asked that it be passed hands from both sides of the table took up the dish and it was handed down in this manner like a ceremonial bowl.

Three days later they were in the mountains. The caporal had sent a mozo with them to cook and see to the horses and he'd sent three young vaqueros not much older than they. The mozo was an old man with a bad leg named Luis who had fought at Torreón and San Pedro and later at Zacatecas and the boys were boys from the country, two of them born on the hacienda. Only one of the three had ever been as far as Monterrey. They rode up into the mountains trailing three horses apiece in their string with packhorses to haul the grub and cooktent and they hunted the wild horses in the upland forests in the pine and madroño and in the arroyos where they'd gone to hide and they drove them pounding over the high mesas and penned them in the stone ravine fitted ten years earlier with fence and gates and there the horses milled and squealed and clambered at the rock slopes and turned upon one another biting and kicking while John Grady walked among them in the sweat and dust and bedlam with his rope as if they were no more than some evil dream of horse. They camped at night on the high headlands where their windtattered fire sawed about in the darkness and Luis told them tales of the country and the people who lived in it and the people who died and how they died. He'd loved horses all his life and he and his father and two brothers had fought in the cavalry and his father and his brothers had died in the cavalry but they'd all despised Victoriano Huerta above all other men and the deeds of Huerta above all other visited evils. He said that compared to Huerta Judas was himself but another Christ and one of the young vaqueros looked away and another blessed himself. He said that war had destroyed the country and that men believe the cure for war is war as the curandero prescribes the serpent's flesh for its bite. He spoke of his campaigns in the deserts of Mexico and he told them of horses killed under him and he said that the souls of horses mirror the souls of men more closely than men suppose and that horses also love war. Men say they only learn this but he said that no creature can learn that which his heart has no shape to hold. His own father said that no man who has not gone to war horseback can ever truly understand the horse and he said that he supposed he wished that this were not so but that it was so.

Lastly he said that he had seen the souls of horses and that it was a terrible thing to see. He said that it could be seen under certain circumstances attending the death of a horse because the horse shares a common soul and its separate life only forms it out of all horses and makes it mortal. He said that if a person understood the soul of the horse then he would understand all horses that ever were.

They sat smoking, watching the deepest embers of the fire where the red coals cracked and broke.

Y de los hombres? said John Grady.

The old man shaped his mouth how to answer. Finally he said that among men there was no such communion as among horses and the notion that men can be understood at all was probably an illusion. Rawlins asked him in his bad spanish if there was a heaven for horses but he shook his head and said that a horse had no need of heaven. Finally John Grady asked him if it were not true that should all horses vanish from the face of the earth the soul of the horse would not also perish for there would be nothing out of which to replenish it but the old man only said that it was pointless to speak of there being no horses in the world for God would not permit such a thing.

They drove the mares down through the draws and arroyos out of the mountains and across the watered grasslands of the bolsón and penned them. They were at this work for three weeks until by the end of April they had over eighty mares in the trap, most of them halterbroke, some already sorted out for saddlehorses. By then the roundup was underway and droves of cattle were moving daily down out of the open country onto the ranch pastures and although some of the vaqueros had no more than two or three horses to their string the new horses stayed in the trap. On the second morning of May the red Cessna plane came in from the south and circled the ranch and banked and dropped and glided from sight beyond the trees.

An hour later John Grady was standing in the ranch house kitchen with his hat in his hands. A woman was washing dishes at the sink and a man was sitting at the table reading a newspaper. The woman wiped her hands on her apron and went off into another part of the house and in a few minutes she returned. Un ratito, she said.

John Grady nodded. Gracias, he said.

The man rose and folded the newspaper and crossed the kitchen and came back with a wooden rack of butcher and boning knives together with an oilstone and set them out on the paper. At the same moment Don Héctor appeared in the doorway and stood looking at John Grady.

He was a spare man with broad shoulders and graying hair and he was tall in the manner of norteños and light of skin. He entered the kitchen and introduced himself and John Grady shifted his hat to his left hand and they shook hands.

María, said the hacendado. Café por favor.

He held out his hand palm upward toward the doorway and John Grady crossed the kitchen and entered the hall. The house was cool and quiet and smelled of wax and flowers. A tallcase clock stood in the hallway to the left with brass weights that moved slowly behind their casement doors. He turned to look back and the hacendado smiled and extended his hand toward the dining room doorway. Pásale, he said.

They sat at a long table of english walnut. The walls of the room were covered with blue damask and hung with portraits of men and horses. At the end of the room was a walnut sideboard with some chafingdishes and decanters set out upon it and along the windowsill outside taking the sun were four cats. Don Héctor reached behind him and took a china ashtray from the sideboard and placed it before them and took from his shirt pocket a small tin box of english cigarettes and opened them and offered them to John Grady and John Grady took one.

Gracias, he said.

The hacendado placed the tin on the table between them and took a silver lighter from his pocket and lit the boy's cigarette and then his own.

Gracias.

The man blew a thin stream of smoke slowly downtable and smiled.

Bueno, he said. We can speak english.

Como le convenga, said John Grady.

Armando tells me that you understand horses.

I've been around em some.

The hacendado smoked thoughtfully. He seemed to be waiting for more to be said. The man who'd been sitting in the kitchen reading the paper entered the room with a silver tray carrying a coffee service with cups and creampitcher and a sugar-bowl together with a plate of bizcochos. He set the tray on the table and stood a moment and the hacendado thanked him and he went out again.

Don Héctor set out the cups himself and poured the coffee and nodded at the tray. Please help yourself, he said.

Thank you. I just take it black.

You are from Texas.

Yessir.

The hacendado nodded again. He sipped his coffee. He was seated sideways to the table with his legs crossed. He flexed his foot in the chocolatecolored veal boot and turned and looked at John Grady and smiled.

Why are you here? he said.

John Grady looked at him. He looked down the table where the shadows of the sunning cats sat in a row like cutout cats all leaning slightly aslant. He looked at the hacendado again.

I just wanted to see the country, I reckon. Or we did.

May I ask how old are you?

Sixteen.

The hacendado raised his eyebrows. Sixteen, he said.

Yessir.

The hacendado smiled again. When I was sixteen I told people I was eighteen.

John Grady sipped his coffee.

Your friend is sixteen also?

Seventeen.

But you are the leader.

We dont have no leaders. We're just buddies.

Of course.

He nudged the plate forward. Please, he said. Help yourself.

Thank you. I just got up from the breakfast table.

The hacendado tipped the ash from his cigarette into the china ashtray and sat back again.

What is your opinion of the mares, he said.

There's some good mares in that bunch.

Yes. Do you know a horse called Three Bars?

That's a thoroughbred horse.

You know the horse?

I know he run in the Brazilian Grand Prix. I think he come out of Kentucky but he's owned by a man named Vail out of Douglas Arizona.

Yes. The horse was foaled at Monterey Farm in Paris Kentucky. The stallion I have bought is a half brother out of the same mare.

Yessir. Where's he at?

He is enroute.

He's where?

Enroute. From Mexico. The hacendado smiled. He has been standing at stud.

You intend to raise racehorses?

No. I intend to raise quarterhorses.

To use here on the ranch?

Yes.

You aim to breed this stallion to your mares.

Yes. What is your opinion?

I dont have a opinion. I've known a few breeders and some with a world of experience but I've noticed they were all pretty short on opinions. I do know there's been some good cowhorses sired out of thoroughbreds.

Yes. How much importance do you give to the mare?

Same as the sire. In my opinion.

Most breeders place more confidence in the horse.

Yessir. They do.

The hacendado smiled. I happen to agree with you.

John Grady leaned and tipped the ash from his cigarette. You dont have to agree with me.

No. Nor you with me.

Yessir.

Tell me about the horses up on the mesa.

There may be a few of them good mares still up there but not many. The rest I'd pretty much call scrubs. Even some of them might make a half-decent cowhorse. Just all around usin kind of a horse. Spanish ponies, what we used to call em. Chihuahua horses. Old Barb stock. They're small and they're a little on the light side and they dont have the hindquarters you'd want in a cutting horse but you can rope off of em. . . .

He stopped. He looked at the hat in his lap and ran his fingers along the crease and looked up. I aint tellin you nothing you dont know.

The hacendado took up the coffeepitcher and poured their cups.

Do you know what a criollo is?

Yessir. That's a argentine horse.

The hacendado studied him.

Do you know a book called *The Horse of America*, by Wallace?

Yessir. I've read it front to back.

The hacendado nodded and stubbed out his cigarette and pushed back his chair. Come, he said. I will show you some horses.

They sat opposite on their bunks with their elbows on their knees leaning forward and looking down at their folded hands. After a while Rawlins spoke. He didnt look up.

It's a opportunity for you. Aint no reason for you to turn it down that I can see.

If you dont want me to I wont. I'll stick right here.

It aint like you was goin off someplace.

We'll still be workin together. Bringin in horses and all.

Rawlins nodded. John Grady watched him.

You just say the word and I'll tell him no.

Aint no reason to do that, said Rawlins. Its a opportunity for you.

In the morning they ate breakfast and Rawlins went out to work the pens. When he came in at noon John Grady's tick was rolled up at the head of his bunk and his gear was gone. Rawlins went on to the back to wash up for dinner.

The barn was built on the english style and it was sheathed with milled one by fours and painted white and it had a cupola and a weather vane on top of the cupola. His room was at the far end next to the saddleroom. Across the bay was another cubicle where there lived an old groom who'd worked for Rocha's father. When John Grady led his horse through the barn the old man came out and stood and looked at the horse. Then he looked at its feet. Then he looked at John Grady. Then he turned and went back into his room and shut the door.

In the afternoon while he was working one of the new mares in the corral outside the barn the old man came out and watched him. John Grady said him a good afternoon and the old man nodded and said one back.

When he took the mare back to the barn the old man was pulling the cinchstrap on the black Arabian. The girl stood with her back to him. When the shadow of the mare darkened the bay door she turned and looked.

Buenas tardes, he said.

Buenas tardes, she said. She reached and slid her fingers under the strap to check it. He stood at the bay door. She raised up and passed the reins over the horse's head and put her foot in the stirrup and stood up into the saddle and turned the horse and rode down the bay and out the door.

That night as he lay in his cot he could hear music from the house and as he was drifting to sleep his thoughts were of horses and of the open country and of horses. Horses still wild on the mesa who'd never seen a man afoot and who knew nothing of him or his life yet in whose souls he would come to reside forever.

They went up into the mountains a week later with the mozo and two of the vaqueros and after the vaqueros had turned in in their blankets he and Rawlins sat by the fire on the rim of the mesa drinking coffee. Rawlins took out his tobacco and John Grady took out cigarettes and shook the pack at him. Rawlins put his tobacco back.

Where'd you get the readyrolls?

In La Vega.

He nodded. He took a brand from the fire and lit the cigarette and John Grady leaned and lit his own.

You say she goes to school in Mexico City?

Yeah.

How old is she?

Seventeen.

Rawlins nodded. What kind of a school is it she goes to?

I dont know. It's some kind of a prep school or somethin.

Fancy sort of school.

Yeah. Fancy sort of school.

Rawlins smoked. Well, he said. She's a fancy sort of girl.

No she aint.

Rawlins was leaning against his propped saddle, sitting with his legs crossed sideways onto the fire. He looked at the cigarette.

Well, he said. I've told you before but I dont reckon you'll listen now any more than you done then.

Yeah. I know.

I just figure you must enjoy cryin yourself to sleep at night.

John Grady didnt answer.

This one of course she probably dates guys got their own airplanes let alone cars.

You're probably right.

I'm glad to hear you say it.

It dont help nothin though, does it?

Rawlins sucked on the cigarette. They sat for a long time. Finally he pitched the stub of the cigarette into the fire. I'm goin to bed, he said.

Yeah, said John Grady. I guess that's a good idea.

They spread their soogans and he pulled off his boots and stood them beside him and stretched out in his blankets. The fire had burned to coals and he lay looking up at the stars in their places and the hot belt of matter that ran the chord of the dark vault overhead and he put his hands on the ground at either side of him and pressed them against the earth and in that coldly burning canopy of black he slowly turned dead center to the world, all of it taut and trembling and moving enormous and alive under his hands.

What's her name? said Rawlins in the darkness.

Alejandra. Her name is Alejandra.

Sunday afternoon they rode into the town of La Vega on horses they'd been working out of the new string. They'd had their hair cut with sheep-shears by an esquilador at the ranch and the backs of their necks above their collars were white as scars and they wore their hats cocked forward on their heads and they looked from side to side as they jogged along as if to challenge the countryside or anything it might hold. They raced the animals on the road at a fifty-cent bet and John Grady won and they swapped horses and he won on Rawlins's horse. They rode the horses at a gallop and they rode them at a trot and the horses were hot and lathered and squatted and stamped in the road and the campesinos afoot in the road with baskets of garden stuff or pails covered with cheesecloth would press to the edge of the road or climb through the roadside brush and cactus to watch wide eyed the young horsemen on their horses passing and the horses mouthing froth and champing and the riders calling to one another in their alien tongue and passing in a muted fury that seemed scarcely to be contained in the space allotted them and yet leaving all unchanged where they had been: dust, sunlight, a singing bird.

Although the night was cool the double doors of the grange stood open and the man selling the tickets was seated in a chair on a raised wooden platform just within the doors so that he must lean down to each in a gesture akin to benevolence and take their coins and hand them down their tickets or pass upon the ticketstubs of those who were only returning from outside. The old adobe hall was buttressed along its outer walls with piers not all of which had been a part of its design and there were no windows and the walls were swagged and cracked. A string of electric bulbs ran the length of the hall at either side and the bulbs were covered with paper bags that had been painted and the brushstrokes showed through in the light and the reds and greens and blues were all muted and much of a piece. The floor was swept but there were pockets of seeds underfoot and drifts of straw and at the far end of the hall a small orchestra labored on a stage of grainpallets under a bandshell rigged from sheeting. Along the foot of the stage were lights set in fruitcans and colored crepe that smoldered throughout the night. The mouths of the cans were lensed with tinted cellophane and they cast upon the sheeting a shadowplay in the lights and smoke of antic demon players and a pair of goathawks arced chittering through the partial darkness overhead.

John Grady and Rawlins and a boy named Roberto from the ranch stood just beyond the reach of light at the door among the cars and wagons and passed among themselves a pint medicine-bottle of mescal. Roberto held the bottle to the light.

A las chicas, he said.

He drank and handed off the bottle. They drank. They poured salt from a paper onto their wrists and licked it off and Roberto pushed the cob stopper into the neck of the bottle and hid the bottle behind the tire of a parked truck and they passed around a pack of chewing gum.

Listos? he said.

Listos.

She was dancing with a tall boy from the San Pablo ranch and she wore a blue dress and her mouth was red. He and Rawlins and Roberto stood with other youths along the wall and watched the dancers and watched beyond the dancers the young girls at the far side of the hall. He moved along past the groups. The air smelled of straw and sweat and a rich spice of colognes. Under the bandshell the accordion player struggled with his instrument and slammed his boot on the boards in countertime and stepped back and the trumpet player came forward. Her eyes above the shoulder of her partner swept across him where he stood. Her black hair done up in a blue ribbon and the nape of her neck pale as porcelain. When she turned again she smiled.

He'd never touched her and her hand was small and her waist so slight and she looked at him with great forthrightness and smiled and put her face against his shoulder. They turned under the lights. A long trumpet note guided the dancers on their separate and collective paths. Moths circled the paper lights aloft and the goathawks passed down the wires and flared and arced upward into the darkness again.

She spoke in an english learned largely from school books and he tested each phrase for the meanings he wished to hear, repeating them silently to himself and then questioning them anew. She said that she was glad that he'd come.

I told you I would.

Yes.

They turned, the trumpet rapped.

Did you not think I would?

She tossed her head back and looked at him, smiling, her eyes aglint. Al contrario, she said. I knew you would come.

At the band's intermission they made their way to the refreshment stand and he bought two lemonades in paper cones and they went out and walked in the night air. They walked along the road and there were other couples in the road and they passed and wished them a good evening. The air was cool and it smelled of earth and perfume and horses. She took his arm and she laughed and called him a mojado-reverso, so rare a creature and one to be treasured. He told her about his life. How his grandfather was dead and the ranch sold. They sat on a low concrete watertrough and with her shoes in her lap and naked feet crossed in the dust she drew patterns in the dark water with her finger. She'd been away at school for three years. Her mother lived in Mexico and she went to the house on Sundays for dinner and sometimes she and her mother would dine alone in the city and go to the theater or the ballet. Her mother thought that life on the hacienda was lonely and yet living in the city she seemed to have few friends.

She becomes angry with me because I always want to come here. She says that I prefer my father to her.

Do you?

She nodded. Yes. But that is not why I come. Anyway, she says I will change my mind.

About coming here?

About everything.

She looked at him and smiled. Shall we go in?

He looked toward the lights. The music had started.

She stood and bent with one hand on his shoulder and slipped on her shoes.

He rode back alone with the smell of her perfume on his shirt. The horses were still tied and standing at the edge of the barn but he could not find Rawlins or Roberto. When he untied his horse the other two tossed their heads and whinnied softly to go.

The hacendado had bought the horse through an agent sight unseen at the spring sales in Lexington and he'd sent Armando's brother Antonio to get the animal and bring it back. He was a deep chestnut in color and stood sixteen hands high and weighed about fourteen hundred pounds and he was well muscled and heavily boned for his breed. When they brought him in the trailer in the third week of May and John Grady and Señor Rocha walked out to the barn to look at him John Grady simply pushed open the door to the stall and entered and walked up to the horse and leaned against it and began to rub it and talk to it softly in spanish.

Le gusta? said the hacendado.

John Grady nodded. That's a hell of a horse, he said.

In the days to follow the hacendado would come up to the corral where they'd shaped the manada and he and John Grady would walk among the mares and John Grady would argue their points and the hacendado would muse and nod and walk away a fixed distance and stand looking back and nod and muse again and walk off with his eyes to the ground to a fresh vantage point and then look up to see the mare anew. But there were two things they agreed upon wholly and that were never spoken and that was that God had put horses on earth to work cattle and that other than cattle there was no wealth proper to a man.

They stabled the stallion away from the mares in a barn up at the gerente's and as the mares came into season he and Antonio bred them. They bred mares almost daily for three weeks and sometimes twice daily and Antonio regarded the stallion with great reverence and great love and he called him caballo padre and like John Grady he would talk to the horse and he conspired with John Grady in telling the hacendado that the horse needed to be ridden to keep it manageable. Because John Grady loved to ride the horse. In truth he loved to be seen riding it. In truth he loved for her to see him riding it.

He'd go to the kitchen in the dark for his coffee and saddle the horse at daybreak with only the little desert doves waking in the orchard and the air still fresh and cool and he and the stallion would come sideways out of the stable with the animal prancing and pounding the ground and arching its neck. They'd ride out along the ciénaga road and along the verge of the marshes while the sun rose riding up flights of ducks out of the shallows or geese or mergansers that would beat away over the water scattering the haze and rising up would turn to birds of gold in a sun not yet visible from the bolsón floor.

He'd ride sometimes clear to the upper end of the laguna before the horse would even stop trembling and he spoke constantly to it in spanish in phrases almost biblical repeating again and again the strictures of a yet untabled law. Soy comandante de las yeguas, he would say, yo y yo sólo. Sin la caridad de estas manos no tengas nada. Ni comida ni agua ni hijos. Soy yo que traigo las yeguas de las montañas, las yeguas jóvenes, las yeguas salvajes y ardientes. While inside the vaulting of the ribs between his knees the darkly meated heart pumped of whose will and the blood pulsed and the bowels shifted in their massive blue convolutions of whose will and the stout thighbones and knee and cannon and the tendons like flaxen hawsers that drew and flexed and drew and flexed at their articulations and of whose will all sheathed and muffled in the flesh and the hooves that stove wells in the morning groundmist and the head turning side to side and the great slavering keyboard of his teeth and the hot globes of his eyes where the world burned.

There were times in those early mornings in the kitchen when he returned to the house for his breakfast with María stirring about and stoking with wood the great nickelmounted cookstove or rolling out dough on the marble countertop that he would hear her singing somewhere in the house or smell the faintest breath of hyacinth as if she'd passed in the outer hall. And sometimes she would ride in the mornings also and he knew she was in the dining room across the hall by herself and Carlos would take her breakfast tray to her with coffee and fruit and once riding in the low hills to the north he'd seen her coming along the ciénaga road two miles away and he had seen her riding in the parkland above the marshes and once he came upon her leading the horse through the shallows of the lakeshore among the tules with her skirts caught up above her knees while redwing blackbirds circled and cried, pausing and bending and gathering white waterlilies with the black horse standing in the lake behind her patient as a dog.

He'd not spoken to her since the night of the dance at La Vega. She went with her father to Mexico and he returned alone. There was no one he could ask about her. By now he'd taken to riding the stallion bareback, kicking off his boots and swinging up while Antonio still stood holding the trembling mare by the twitch, the mare standing with her legs spread and her head down and the breath rifling in and out of her. Coming out of the barn with his bare heels under the horse's barrel and the horse lathered and dripping and half crazed and pounding up the ciénaga road riding with just a rope hackamore and the sweat of the horse and the smell of the mare on him and the veins pulsing under the wet hide and him leaning low along the horse's neck talking to him softly and obscenely. It was in this condition that all unexpectedly one evening he came upon her returning on the black Arabian down the ciénaga road.

He reined in the horse and it stopped and stood trembling and stepped about in the road slinging its head in a froth from side to side. She sat her horse. He took off his hat and passed his shirt sleeve across his forehead and waved her forward and put his hat back on and reined the horse off the road and through the sedge and turned so that he could watch her pass. She put the horse forward and came on and as she came abreast of him he touched the brim of hat with his forefinger and nodded and he thought she would go past but she did not. She stopped and turned her wide face to him. Skeins of light off the water played upon the black hide of the horse. He sat the sweating stallion like a highwayman under her gaze. She was waiting for him to speak and afterward he would try to remember what it was he'd said. He only knew it made her smile and that had not been his intent. She turned and looked off across the lake where the late sun glinted and she looked back at him and at the horse.

I want to ride him, she said.

What?

I want to ride him.

She regarded him levelly from under the black hatbrim.

He looked out across the sedge tilting in the wind off the lake as if there might be some help for him in that quarter. He looked at her.

When? he said.

When?

When did you want to ride him?

Now. I want to ride him now.

He looked down at the horse as if surprised to see it there.

He dont have a saddle on.

Yes, she said. I know.

He pressed the horse between his heels and at the same time pulled on the reins of the hackamore to make the horse appear uncertain and difficult but the horse only stood.

I dont know if the patrón would want you to ride him. Your father.

She smiled at him a pitying smile and there was no pity in it. She stepped to the ground and lifted the reins over the black horse's head and turned and stood looking at him with the reins behind her back.

Get down, she said.

Are you sure about this?

Yes. Hurry.

He slid to the ground. The insides of his trouserlegs were hot and wet.

What do you aim to do with your horse?

I want you to take him to the barn for me.

Somebody will see me at the house.

Take him to Armando's.

You're fixin to get me in trouble.

You are in trouble.

She turned and looped the reins over the saddlehorn and came forward and took the hackamore reins from him and put them up and turned and put one hand on his shoulder. He could feel his heart pumping. He bent and made a stirrup of his laced fingers and she put her boot into his hands and he lifted her and she swung up onto the stallion's back and looked down at him and then booted the horse forward and went loping out up the track along the edge of the lake and was lost to view.

He rode back slowly on the Arabian. The sun was a long time descending. He thought she might overtake him that they could change the horses back again but she did not and in the red twilight he led the black horse past Armando's house afoot and took it to the stable behind the house and removed the bridle and loosed the cinch and left it standing in the bay saddled and tied with a rope halter to the hitchingrail. There was no light on at the house and he thought perhaps there was no one home but as he walked back out down the drive past the house the light came on in the kitchen. He walked more quickly. He heard the door open behind him but he didnt turn to look back to see who it was and whoever it was they did not speak or call to him.

The last time that he saw her before she returned to Mexico she was coming down out of the mountains riding very stately and erect out of a rainsquall building to the north and the dark clouds towering above her. She rode with her hat pulled down in the front and fastened under her chin with a drawtie and as she rode her black hair twisted and blew about her shoulders and the lightning fell silently down through the black clouds behind her and she rode all seeming unaware down through the low hills while the first spits of rain blew on the wind and onto the upper pasturelands and past the pale and reedy lakes erect and stately until the rain caught her up and shrouded her figure away in that wild summer landscape: real horse, real rider, real land and sky, and yet a dream withal.

The dueña Alfonsa was both grandaunt and godmother to the girl and her life at the hacienda invested it with oldworld ties and with antiquity and tradition. Save for the old leatherbound volumes the books in the library were her books and the piano was her piano. The ancient stereopticon in the parlor and the matched pair of Greener guns in the italian wardrobe in Don Héctor's room had been her brother's and it was her brother with whom she stood in the photos taken in front of cathedrals in the capitals of Europe, she and her sister-in-law in white summer clothes, her brother in vested suit and tie and panama hat. His dark moustache. Dark spanish eyes. The stance of a grandee. The most antique of the several oilportraits in the parlor with its dark patina crazed like an old porcelain glazing was of her greatgrandfather and dated from Toledo in seventeen ninety-seven. The most recent was she herself full length in formal gown on the occasion of her quinceaños at Rosario in eighteen ninety-two.

John Grady had never seen her. Perhaps a figure glimpsed passing along the hallway. He did not know that she was aware of his existence until a week after the girl returned to Mexico he was invited to come to the house in the evening to play chess. When he showed up at the kitchen dressed in new shirt and canvas pants María was still washing the supper dishes. She turned and studied him where he stood with his hat in his hands. Bueno, she said. Te espera.

He thanked her and crossed the kitchen and went up the hall and stood in the diningroom door. She rose from the table where she was sitting. She inclined her head very slightly. Good evening, she said. Please come in. I am señorita Alfonsa.

She was dressed in a dark gray skirt and a white pleated blouse and her gray hair was gathered up behind and she looked like the schoolteacher she in fact had been. She spoke with an english accent. She held out one hand and he almost stepped forward to take it before he realized that she was gesturing toward the chair at her right.

Evenin, mam, he said. I'm John Grady Cole.

Please, she said. Be seated. I am happy that you have come.

Thank you mam.

He pulled back the chair and sat and put his hat in the chair beside him and looked at the board. She set her thumbs against the edge and pushed it slightly toward him. The board was pieced from blocks of circassian walnut and birdseye maple with a border of inlaid pearl and the chessmen were of carved ivory and black horn.

They were well into the second game and he had taken both knights and a bishop when she made two moves in succession that gave him pause. He studied the board. It occurred to him that she might be curious to know if he would throw the game and he realized that he had in fact already considered it and he knew she'd thought of it before he had. He sat back and looked at the board. She watched him. He leaned forward and moved his bishop and mated her in four moves.

She smiled again. Where did you learn to play chess?

My father taught me.

He must be a very good player.

She watched him, not unkindly. She smiled.

Alejandra will be in Mexico with her mother for two weeks. Then she will be here for the summer.

He swallowed.

Whatever my appearance may suggest, I am not a particularly old-fashioned woman. Here we live in a small world. A close world. Alejandra and I disagree strongly. Quite strongly in fact. She is much like me at that age and I seem at times to be struggling with my own past self.

She broke off. She set the cup and saucer to one side. The polished wood of the table held a round shape of breath where they'd stood that diminished from the edges in and vanished. She looked up.

You see that I cannot help but be sympathetic to Alejandra. Even at her worst. But I wont have her unhappy. I wont have her spoken ill of. Or gossiped about. I know what that is. She thinks that she can toss her head and dismiss everything. In an ideal world the gossip of the idle would be of no consequence. But I have seen the consequences in the real world and they can be very grave indeed. They can be consequences of a gravity not excluding bloodshed. Not excluding death. I saw this in my own family. What Alejandra dismisses as a matter of mere appearance or outmoded custom . . .

She made a whisking motion with the imperfect hand that was both a dismissal and a summation. She composed her hands again and looked at him.

Even though you are younger than she it is not proper for you to be seen riding in the campo together without supervision. Since this was carried to my ears I considered whether to speak to Alejandra about it and I have decided not to.

She leaned back. He could hear the clock ticking in the hall. There was no sound from the kitchen. She sat watching him.

What do you want me to do? he said.

I want you to be considerate of a young girl's reputation.

I never meant not to be.

She smiled. I believe you, she said. But you must understand. This is another country. Here a woman's reputation is all she has.

Yes mam.

There is no forgiveness, you see.

Mam?

There is no forgiveness. For women. A man may lose his honor and regain it again. But a woman cannot. She cannot.

They sat. She watched him. He tapped the crown of his seated hat with the tips of his four fingers and looked up.

I guess I'd have to say that that dont seem right.

Right? she said. Oh. Yes. Well.

She turned one hand in the air as if reminded of something she'd misplaced. No, she said. No. It's not a matter of right. You must understand. It is a matter of who must say. In this matter I get to say. I am the one who gets to say.

The clock ticked in the hall. She sat watching him. He picked up his hat.

On the mesa they watched a storm that had made it up to the north. At sundown a troubled light. The dark jade shapes of the lagunillas below them lay in the floor of the desert savanna like piercings through to another sky. The laminar bands of color to the west bleeding out under the hammered clouds. A sudden violetcolored hooding of the earth.

They sat tailorwise on ground that shuddered under the thunder and they fed the fire out of the ruins of an old fence. Birds were coming down out of the half darkness upcountry and shearing away off the edge of the mesa and to the north the lightning stood along the rimlands like burning mandrake.

What else did she say? said Rawlins.

That was about it.

You think she was speakin for Rocha?

I dont think she speaks for anybody but her.

She thinks you got eyes for the daughter.

I do have eyes for the daughter.

You got eyes for the spread?

John Grady studied the fire. I dont know, he said. I aint thought about it.

Sure you aint, said Rawlins.

He looked at Rawlins and he looked into the fire again.

When is she comin back?

About a week.

I guess I dont see what evidence you got that she's all that interested in you.

John Grady nodded. I just do. I can talk to her.

The first drops of rain hissed in the fire. He looked at Rawlins.

You aint sorry you come down here are you?

Not yet.

They sat hooded under their slickers. They spoke out of the hoods as if addressing the night.

I know the old man likes you, said Rawlins. But that dont mean he'll set still for you courtin his daughter.

Yeah, I know.

I dont see you holdin no aces.

Yeah.

What I see is you fixin to get us fired and run off the place.

They watched the fire. The wire that had burned out of the fenceposts lay in garbled shapes all about the ground and coils of it stood in the fire and coils of it pulsed red hot deep in the coals. The horses had come in out of the darkness and stood at the edge of the firelight in the falling rain dark and sleek with their red eyes burning in the night.

You still aint told me what answer you give her, said Rawlins.

I told her I'd do whatever she asked.

What did she ask?

I aint sure.

They sat watching the fire.

Did you give her your word? said Rawlins.

I dont know. I dont know if I did or not.

Well either you did or you didn't.

That's what I'd of thought. But I dont know.

Five nights later asleep in his bunk in the barn there was a tap at the door. He sat up. Someone was standing outside the door. He could see a light through the boardjoinings.

Momento, he said.

He rose and pulled on his trousers in the dark and opened the door. She was standing in the barn bay holding a flashlight in one hand with the light pointed at the ground.

What is it? he whispered.

It's me.

She held the light up as if to verify the truth of this. He couldnt think what to say.

What time is it?

I dont know. Eleven or something.

He looked across the narrow corridor to the groom's door.

We're going to wake Estéban, he said.

Then invite me in.

He stepped back and she came in past him all rustling of clothes and the rich parade of her hair and perfume. He pulled the door to and ran shut the wooden latch with the heel of his hand and turned and looked at her.

I better not turn the light on, he said.

It's all right. The generator's off anyway. What did she say to you?

She must of told you what she said.

Of course she told me. What did she say?

You want to set down?

She turned and sat sideways on the bed and tucked one foot beneath her. She laid the burning flashlight on the bed and then she pushed it under the blanket where it suffused the room with a soft glow.

She didnt want me to be seen with you. Out on the campo.

Armando told her that you rode my horse in.

I know.

I wont be treated in such a manner, she said.

Her face was strange and theatrical in the uplight. She passed one hand across the blanket as if she'd brush something away. She looked up at him and her face was pale and austere in the underlight and her eyes lost in the darkly shadowed hollows save only for the glint of them and he could see her throat move in the light and he saw in her face and in her figure something he'd not seen before and the name of that thing was sorrow.

I thought you were my friend, she said.

Tell me what to do, he said. I'll do anything you say.

The nightdamp laid the dust going up the ciénaga road and they rode the horses side by side at a walk, sitting the animals bareback and riding with hackamores. Leading the horses by hand out through the gate into the road and mounting up and riding the horses side by side up the ciénaga road with the moon in the west and some dogs barking over toward the shearingsheds and the greyhounds answering back from their pens and him closing the gate and turning and holding his cupped hands for her to step into and lifting her onto the black horse's naked back and then untying the stallion from the gate and stepping once onto the gateslat and mounting up all in one motion and turning the horse and them riding side by side up the ciénaga road with the moon in the west like a moon of white linen hung from wires and some dogs barking.

They'd be gone sometimes till near daybreak and he'd put the stallion up and go to the house for his breakfast and an hour later meet Antonio back at the stable and walk up past the gerente's house to the trap where the mares stood waiting.

They'd ride at night up along the western mesa two hours from the ranch and sometimes he'd build a fire and they could see the gaslights at the hacienda gates far below them floating in a pool of black and sometimes the lights seemed to move as if the world down there turned on some other center and they saw stars fall to earth by the hundreds and she told him stories of her father's family and of Mexico. Going back they'd walk the horses into the lake and the horses would stand and drink with the water at their chests and the stars in the lake bobbed and tilted where they drank and if it rained in the mountains the air would be close and the night more warm and one night he left her and rode down along the edge of the lake through the sedge and willow and slid from the horse's back and pulled off his boots and his clothes and walked out into the lake where the moon slid away before him and ducks gabbled out there in the dark. The water was black and warm and he turned in the lake and spread his arms in the water and the water was so dark and so silky and he watched across the still black surface to where she stood on the shore with the horse and watched where she stepped from her pooled clothing so pale, so pale, like a chrysalis emerging, and walked into the water.

She paused midway to look back. Standing there trembling in the water and not from the cold for there was none. Do not speak to her. Do not call. When she reached him he held out his hand and she took it. She was so pale in the lake she seemed to be burning. Like foxfire in a darkened wood. That burned cold. Like the moon that burned cold. Her black hair floating on the water about her, falling and floating on the water. She put her other arm about his shoulder and looked toward the moon in the west do not speak to her do not call and then she turned her face up to him. Sweeter for the larceny of time and flesh, sweeter for the betrayal. Nesting cranes that stood singlefooted among the cane on the south shore had pulled their slender beaks from their wing pits to watch. Me quieres? she said. Yes, he said. He said her name. God yes, he said.

He came up from the barn washed and combed and a clean shirt on and he and Rawlins sat on crates under the ramada of the bunkhouse and smoked while they waited for supper. There was talking and laughing in the bunkhouse and then it ceased. Two of the vaqueros came to the door and stood. Rawlins turned and looked north along the road. Five Mexican rangers were coming down the road riding singlefile. They were dressed in khaki uniforms and they rode good horses and they wore pistols in beltholsters and carried carbines in their saddlescabbards. Rawlins stood. The other vaqueros had come to the door and stood looking out. As the riders passed on the road the leader glanced across at the bunkhouse at the men under the ramada, at the men standing at the door. Then they went on from sight past the gerente's house, five riders riding single file down out of the north through the twilight toward the tileroofed ranch house below them.

When he came back down through the dark to the barn the five horses were standing under the pecan trees at the far side of the house. They hadnt been unsaddled and in the morning they were gone. The following night she came to his bed and she came every night for nine nights running, pushing the door shut and latching it and turning in the slatted light at God knew what hour and stepping out of her clothes and sliding cool and naked against him in the narrow bunk all softness and perfume and the

175

lushness of her black hair falling over him and no caution to her at all. Saying I dont care I dont care. Drawing blood with her teeth where he held the heel of his hand against her mouth that she not cry out. Sleeping against his chest where he could not sleep at all and rising when the east was already gray with dawn and going to the kitchen to get her breakfast as if she were only up early.

Then she was gone back to the city. The following evening when he came in he passed Estéban in the barn bay and spoke to the old man and the old man spoke back but did not look at him. He washed up and went to the house and ate his dinner in the kitchen and after he'd eaten he and the hacendado sat at the diningroom table and logged the stud book and the hacendado questioned him and made notes on the mares and then leaned back and sat smoking his cigar and tapping his pencil against the edge of the table. He looked up.

You dont read french?

No sir.

The bloody French are quite excellent on the subject of horses. Do you play billiards?

Sir?

Do you play billiards?

Yessir. Some. Pool anyways.

The hacendado folded shut the books and pushed back his chair and rose and he followed him out down the hall and through the salon and through the library to the paneled double doors at the far end of the room. The hacendado opened these doors and they entered a darkened room that smelled of must and old wood.

He pulled a tasseled chain and lit an ornate tin chandelier suspended from the ceiling. Beneath it an antique table of some dark wood with lions carved into the legs. The table was covered with a drop of yellow oilcloth and the chandelier had been lowered from the twentyfoot ceiling with a length of common tracechain.

They stood on either side of the table and folded the cloth toward the middle and folded it again and then lifted it away and took it past the end of the table and walked toward each other and the hacendado took the cloth and carried it over and laid it on some chairs.

He racked the balls and handed the cue ball to John Grady. It was ivory and yellow with age and the grain of the ivory was visible in it. He broke the balls and they played straight pool and the hacendado beat him easily, walking about the table and chalking his cue with a deft rotary motion and announcing the shots in spanish. He played slowly and studied the shots and the lay of the table and as he studied and as he played he spoke of the revolution and of the history of Mexico and he spoke of the dueña Alfonsa.

She was educated in Europe. She learned these ideas, these . . .

He moved his hand in a gesture the boy had seen the aunt make also.

She has always had these ideas. Catorce.

He bent and shot and stood and chalked his cue. He shook his head. One country is not another country. Mexico is not Europe. But it is a complicated business.

He bent and shot the sevenball into the side pocket. He walked around the table.

They went to France for their education. All these young people. They all returned full of ideas. But ideas. . . . People of my generation are more cautious. I think we dont believe that people can be improved in their character by reason. That seems a very french idea.

He chalked, he moved. He bent and shot and then stood surveying the new lay of the table.

Beware gentle knight. There is no greater monster than reason.

He looked at John Grady and smiled and looked at the table.

That of course is the spanish idea. You see. The idea of Quixote. But even Cervantes could not envision such a country as Mexico. Alfonsita tells me I am only being selfish in not wanting to send Alejandra. Perhaps she is right. Perhaps she is right. Diez.

Send her where?

The hacendado had bent to shoot. He raised up again and looked at his guest. To France. To send her to France.

He paused and chalked his cue again.

Why do I bother myself? Eh? She will go. Who am I? A father. A father is nothing.

He bent to shoot and missed his shot and stepped back from the table.

There, he said. You see? You see how this is bad for one's billiard game? This thinking? The French have come into my house to mutilate my billiard game. No evil is beyond them.

He sat on his bunk in the dark with his pillow in his two arms and he leaned his face into it and drank in her scent and tried to refashion in his mind her self and voice. He whispered half aloud the words she'd said. Tell me what to do. I'll do anything you say. The selfsame words he'd said to her. She'd wept against his naked chest while he held her but there was nothing to tell her and there was nothing to do and in the morning she was gone.

The following Sunday Antonio invited him to his brother's house for dinner and afterward they sat in the shade of the ramada off the kitchen and rolled a cigarette and smoked and discussed the horses. Then they discussed other things. John Grady told him of playing billiards with the hacendado and Antonio—sitting in an old Mennonite chair the caning of which had been replaced with canvas, his hat on one knee and his hands together—received this news with the gravity proper to it, looking down at the burning cigarette and nodding his head. John Grady looked off through the trees toward the house, the white walls and the red clay rooftiles.

Digame, he said. Cuál es lo peor: Que estoy pobre o que soy Americano?

The vaquero shook his head. Una llave de oro abre cualquier puerta, he said.

He looked at the boy. He tipped the ash from the end of the cigarette and he said that the boy wished to know his thought. Wished perhaps his advice. But that no one could advise him.

Tienes razón, said John Grady. He looked at the vaquero. He said that

when she returned he intended to speak to her with the greatest seriousness. He said that he intended to know her heart.

The vaquero looked at him. He looked toward the house. He seemed
puzzled and he said that she was here. That she was here now.

Cómo?

Sí. Ella está aquí. Desde ayer.

He lay awake all night until the dawn. Listening to the silence in the bay.
The shifting of the bedded horses. Their breathing. In the morning he
walked up to the bunkhouse to take his breakfast. Rawlins stood in the
door of the kitchen and studied him.

You look like you been rode hard and put up wet, he said.

They sat at the table and ate. Rawlins leaned back and fished his
tobacco out of his shirtpocket.

I keep waitin for you to unload your wagon, he said. I got to go to work
here in a few minutes.

I just come up to see you.

What about.

It dont have to be about somethin does it?

No. Dont have to. He popped a match on the underside of the table
and lit his cigarette and shook out the match and put it in his plate.

I hope you know what you're doin, he said.

John Grady drained the last of his coffee and put the cup on his plate
along with the silver. He got his hat from the bench beside him and put it
on and stood up to take his dishes to the sink.

You said you didnt have no hard feelins about me goin down there.

I dont have no hard feelins about you goin down there.

John Grady nodded. All right, he said.

Rawlins watched him go to the sink and watched him go to the door.
He thought he might turn and say something else but he didnt.

He worked with the mares all day and in the evening he heard the airplane start up. He came out of the barn and watched. The plane came out

of the trees and rose into the late sunlight and banked and turned and leveled out headed southwest. He couldnt see who was in the plane but he watched it out of sight anyway.

Two days later he and Rawlins were in the mountains again. They rode hard hazing the wild manadas out of the high valleys and they camped at their old site on the south slope of the Anteojos where they'd camped with Luis and they ate beans and barbecued goat meat wrapped in tortillas and drank black coffee.

We aint got many more trips up here, have we? said Rawlins.

John Grady shook his head. No, he said. Probably not.

Rawlins sipped his coffee and watched the fire. Suddenly three greyhounds trotted into the light one behind the other and circled the fire, pale and skeletal shapes with the hide stretched taut over their ribs and their eyes red in the firelight. Rawlins half rose, spilling his coffee.

What in the hell, he said.

John Grady stood and looked out into the darkness. The dogs vanished as suddenly as they had come.

They stood waiting. No one came.

What the hell, said Rawlins.

He walked out a little ways from the fire and stood listening. He looked back at John Grady.

You want to holler?

No.

Them dogs aint up here by theirselves, he said.

I know.

You think he's huntin us?

If he wants us he can find us.

Rawlins walked back to the fire. He poured fresh coffee and stood listening.

He's probably up here with a bunch of his buddies.

John Grady didnt answer.

Dont you reckon? said Rawlins.

They rode up to the catchpen in the morning expecting to come upon the hacendado and his friends but they did not come upon him. In the days that followed they saw no sign of him. Three days later they set off down the mountain herding before them eleven young mares and they reached the hacienda at dark and put the mares up and went to the bunkhouse and ate. Some of the vaqueros were still at the table drinking coffee and smoking cigarettes but one by one they drifted away.

The following morning at gray daybreak two men entered his cubicle with drawn pistols and put a flashlight in his eyes and ordered him to get up.

He sat up. He swung his legs over the edge of the bunk. The man holding the light was just a shape behind it but he could see the pistol he held. It was a Colt automatic service pistol. He shaded his eyes. There were men with rifles standing in the bay.

Quién és? he said.

The man swung the light at his feet and ordered him to get his boots and clothes. He stood and got his trousers and pulled them on and sat and pulled on his boots and reached and got his shirt.

Vámonos, said the man.

He stood and buttoned his shirt.

Dónde están sus armas? the man said.

No tengo armas.

He spoke to the man behind him and two men came forward and began to look through his things. They dumped out the wooden coffeebox on the floor and kicked through his clothes and his shaving things and they turned the mattress over on the floor. They were dressed in greasy and blackened khaki uniforms and they smelled of sweat and woodsmoke.

Dónde está su caballo?

En el segundo puesto.

Vámonos, vámonos.

They led him out down the bay to the saddleroom and he got his saddle and his blankets and by then Redbo was standing in the barn bay, stepping nervously. They came back past Estéban's cuarto but there was no sign that the old man was even awake. They held the light while he saddled his horse and then they walked out into the dawn where the other horses were standing. One of the guards was carrying Rawlins's rifle and Rawlins was sitting slumped in the saddle on his horse with his hands cuffed before him and the reins on the ground.

They jabbed him forward with a rifle.

What's this about, pardner? he said.

Rawlins didnt answer. He leaned and spat and looked away.

No hable, said the leader. Vámonos.

He mounted up and they cuffed his wrists and handed him the reins and then all mounted up and they turned their horses and rode two by two out of the lot through the standing gate. When they passed the bunkhouse the lights were on and the vaqueros were standing in the door or squatting along the ramada. They watched the riders pass, the Americans behind the leader and his lieutenant, the others six in number riding in pairs behind in their caps and uniforms with their carbines resting across the pommels of their saddles, all riding out along the ciénaga road and upcountry toward the north.

Downstream

Antonya Nelson

Already in McBride's truck bed were two two-man rafts, two two-man tents, three oars, a foot-operated air pump whose bellows was mended with duct tape, four coffin-size waterproof stuff bags stuffed with clothes and other plastic Ziploc bags full of all a child could dream of for playing house and more: bandages, tweezers, moist towelettes, fresh basil, tea bags, instant coffee, retractable metal cups, gorp, a deck of cards, a crossword book and pencil, Chap Stick, croutons, freeze-dried shrimp creole, freeze-dried vegetarian-style tofu burger mix, unlightable waterproof matches, three lighters, *Anna Karenina* (Dart had been reading it since he was a sophomore), marshmallows (the only ones available in Provo's Albertson's were pastel colored), flattened toilet paper (cardboard removed), aspirin, codeine, snakebite kit, chewing gum (to keep McBride's fingernails out of his mouth), bologna, powdered milk, dry cat food (to feed the fish), tampons, stick cinnamon, toothpaste, Kool-Aid, celluloid sponge, ten packs of Marlboros (Dart's), one pack of Carltons (Carmel had been smoking one bad cigarette a day since age sixteen), a series of rolled topographical maps of the Dolores River and the surrounding area, dried fruit-flavored oatmeal, garbanzos, McBride's thirty-year-old lucky Bulova watch, and Carmel's antidepressants (just in case; hidden in a French candy tin).

Forgotten were: Carmel's trashy novels, McBride's condoms, and Dart's spare prescription glasses.

Camping and drinking. McBride, his friend Will Dart, and their friend Carmel, pronounced like Clint Eastwood's town, all on a trip down the Dolores River, rafting the winter's runoff, Slickrock to Bedrock.

The guidebooks advised running the Dolores from late April through May, possibly early June. It was now June tenth; at the put-in point at Slickrock, there were no other rafts and only a few oblique signs of recent human activity: footprints and sunflower-seed shells, a red bandana half-buried in the silt. By now the river was low enough to have begun clearing from its high-water muddiness, still opaque, but more reminiscent of hazel eyes. It was low enough to bump up against its own rock bottom, riffling the surface. At sunset, already drunk, Dart stood knee-deep a few feet from shore, hand shielding his eyes.

He saw cottonwoods, felt the looming, invisible prospect of canyons downstream. The world seemed a long, floating journey, open before him like a promise. Even if he weren't drunk, he reasoned, he would feel this ecstasy, this conviction that if he simply lifted his feet, he would float away upright, that the water would greet him as easily as it would a piece of driftwood, coddling him along until it found him a home. The face he turned to his friends, Carmel squatting in the sand to find a skipping stone, pragmatic, frowning McBride already unloading the truck, was as contained as Dart could make it. His heart had filled his chest cavity; his body had some keen affinity for this place that he had no control over. These yearly trips were like returning to childhood for Dart; he could almost feel as if he had no history—no failed courses, no demeaning jobs, no ex-girlfriends, no disappointed parents. Here, now, he felt powerful enough to discover something, a comet, for instance, or a new species of insect, as if this optimism were wholly fresh and portentous instead of annual and transient.

McBride threw gear from the truck bed, swinging and releasing in an invigorating rhythm while the stuff bags landed with soft thuds on the sand. Soon, of course, all would be chaos and muck, but for now there was a sense of plentitude and order, as if they'd descended into a well-stocked bomb shelter.

Tonight they would camp here, McBride decided, then put in early tomorrow. Their stretch was forty-five river miles, and he'd told the sheep farmer at Bedrock they'd be taking out in three days, which meant fifteen miles tomorrow. McBride wasn't as comfortable in the water as he was on a trail. Every year there was at least one moment when he panicked. He was always in favor of portaging around the most dangerous rapids; every year they rafted over anyway. McBride managed always to be in the second raft so that he could watch Dart in the first one find the river's tongue and ride it out. Then he would follow. Or, if Dart blew it, well, McBride had the advantage of that nonexample also.

But that was tomorrow's anxiety. Today he was happy unloading, knowing tonight they would be right here. He didn't have to worry yet about boulders and undercurrents and those deep black whirling holes that sucked their tiny rafts like toy boats in a draining bathtub. Guidebooks talked about the easiness of the Dolores, but the lower the water got, the less easy it truly was. McBride paused for a moment to look at the river at twilight. It was beautiful, even with Dart flailing in it, and McBride was peaceful, contemplating dinner, scanning the sand for a flat tent space.

In their established division of labor, Carmel built fires. She had a knack. Looking for kindling, she considered her ingenuity at destruction: burning things up, knocking things down, killing things off. The flawless man she'd left in Salt Lake City told her to come back when her ego felt better, when she could begin loving herself. He saw her little sabotages in their relationship as self-hate; she saw them as extensions of the same destructive impulses that had snipped spiders' legs from their bodies or that had sucker-punched her brothers when she was younger. Simple love of conflict and fury and bang-bang. She brought a gun with her last year and shot a fat whistling pig on a rock ledge. Dart had been appalled; McBride, merely startled. She left the gun at home this time.

Still, it was her intention this year to poach a sheep; without a gun, it would be more difficult, but better. There was a pasture they passed tomorrow. Camp was only a mile or so beyond. They could double back in the night, McBride (it had to be McBride; Dart was too soft) would help. Maybe they would drown the sheep.

Carmel's pleasure in these trips, this the seventh one, had dwindled. Their first had been when she was seventeen, rafting with her best friend, the best friend's older brother, and his friend McBride. Four of them, she and Dart in the slow-leak raft because they were thinnest, hefty McBride and Dart's chunky sister Lana Dart in the fully inflated model, navigating the then-unknown Dolores. The first time it was an adventure; every time since had been anticlimactic for Carmel. She'd destroyed her friendship with Lana, so the next year Lana hadn't wanted to come. The year after that she'd decided she'd fallen in love with Dart, but then realized she really hadn't by the end of the trip, which kept them at odds for most of the following year. Anyway, the point was, every year on the Dolores made Carmel realize she'd been better off the year before.

This time, for instance, she'd told her boyfriend, Lawrence, that she was going rafting, as she always did in June, and then didn't even explain why she wasn't inviting him. Maybe he would have understood; it was hard to say, but she so badly didn't want him along that she didn't chance it.

"Some day," Lawrence told her as she knelt mashing her down bag in its preposterously small sack, "you will spontaneously combust. Poof! Nothing left but shoes and the silver from your teeth."

* * *

That night in the tent they'd designated the boys', Will Dart lay in his bag lazily masturbating and considering becoming a hermit. But I *like* people, he kept remembering. Beside him McBride snored out such strong alcoholic vapors, Dart wanted to light an experimental match over his face. Dart himself was so drunk he didn't think it would be possible to get anywhere with his hands. Still, it felt great to be on the Dolores again, and this was his private celebration.

Seeing Carmel had also excited him. He'd been in love with her since he met her, back when she'd been friends with his sister. He despaired when he thought of Lana, how ordinary she'd become, how narrow her vision and aspirations. He'd been flattered to discover Carmel still laughed at his jokes, still was the good sport he'd left in Salt Lake at the end of last year's trip. They'd had a near-miss sort of messy almost-relationship that now and then seemed to get in the way of friendship, but he'd watched closely and was relieved to see she seemed to have put it behind her.

Listening to the water outside, Dart imagined that he and McBride and Carmel might raft past their takeout point in a few days, continue down the Dolores until it emptied into the Colorado, then keep right on going into an exotic outdoor future, which, though clear in his mind, he knew had no reality. Tree houses, rope swings, log cabins, springwater, cords and cords of chopped wood, a continuous campfire. Unrealistic, but pleasurable nonetheless, so much so that he quieted his hands and lay still, reveling in his utopia.

McBride woke with a strictly camper's hangover, sore not only in the head and stomach, but at all major joints and muscles, particularly the back. He'd thrown himself on his bag last night without clearing the ground beneath him of rocks he'd missed when he'd first set up the tent. But if camper's hangovers were the worst kind, they were also the shortest-lived.

Oddly, Carmel was already awake when McBride crawled from the tent. Dart slept the deep sleep of the afternoon riser, but there was Carmel, also usually a late sleeper, sitting on a rock at the river's edge, smoking a cigarette and drinking coffee. A fire, whose smoke probably had wakened him, burned weakly in last night's ashes. McBride and Carmel corresponded during the year, occasionally making vague plans to meet halfway between Salt Lake and Missoula, where McBride lived, but never quite pulling it off. Still, they were friends, and it struck McBride for the first time that she was not happy. He tried to think if she had ever been happy, if he'd been so obtuse all these years as to have missed what now seemed very obvious. Yes, he decided, she'd been happy before, maybe even as recently as last summer, but was no longer. It was somehow nakedly obvious to him in her hunched back and stringy hair.

"Morning," he said, hands in pockets.

"Hey," Carmel answered. "You know, I was just thinking that we've got to transfer all of that booze to plastic bottles."

"I was thinking that, too," McBride said, grateful she was not going to get weepy on him. Every year, he fell a little bit in love with Carmel and those feelings accumulated, making him fonder of her now than he ever had been.

Carmel spotted a sheep in the late morning. She and Dart shared the less leaky of their rafts while McBride and two thirds of the gear rode behind. The sun was brilliant and Carmel had taken off her work shirt and tied it scarflike around her chest. She then reclined sideways in the boat to sunbathe, allowing Dart to row happily along. She only rowed over rapids. This was the arrangement they had come up with years ago, one that Carmel knew would offend McBride's sense of fair play, but one that Dart seemed completely content with.

"Sheep!" she told Dart, rocking the raft in her struggle to sit upright.

"Hey, bubba," Dart yelled out to a stupefied animal watching them listlessly.

"Your days are numbered," Carmel warned it.

The river was wide here, sprawled luxuriously in the midst of farmland. It would narrow soon, be pushed too quickly through the enclosing sandstone canyon walls, but for now it was lazy, shallow, and broad. Carmel felt the same way.

"I forgot my books," she told Dart. "I was going to bring a frothy romance to read to you today." She reclined again.

"I brought *Anna*," Dart offered.

"No way. Only fluff on the Dolores." Carmel opened her eyes long enough to watch Dart smile, light another cigarette in the chain he had going, and readjust his glasses. They were tied to his head with a piece of rope. Every year she meant to buy him a strap designed for the same purpose and every year she forgot. It occurred to her that she could tell McBride to bring it for her next year and he would not let her down. She looked beyond Dart to the rear raft, where McBride paddled three times on the left, then three on the right, cutting a fairly straight line, which did not even approximate the warbly course Dart had the two of them on. There was McBride with his trimmed beard and broad shoulders and khaki outdoorsman shirt, at work on the river. Perhaps she should fall in love with him, perhaps he would be the steady, firm hand she might now need.

"Look at him," Carmel said to Dart.

Dart raised his cigarette to McBride and grinned. "What ho?" he yelled back, but McBride only nodded, busy rowing. His mind was too one-tracked, Carmel decided. She couldn't fall in love with him.

"He thinks I think I'm Cleopatra," she told Dart.

"Aren't you?" he grinned again.

Carmel had the sudden temptation to make him unhappy. People could be too smugly gleeful. "I should have brought my gun," she said, watching his face.

Dart's smile turned to bewilderment. He was a child, she saw, whose feelings not only could be hurt but were always right there on the surface, susceptible. "What for?" he asked.

Carmel's desire to hurt him vanished. She would have given him a kiss on the cheek if that were possible, but instead only laughed. "Just kidding," she said. Why, Carmel wondered, was Dart not right for her? In anyone else, thin shoulders and thick glasses would not have put her off; she'd dated that physical type before. But the one time she'd been able to love him, he'd been too shy in responding, too slow to seduce, asking her permission every step of the way. Embarrassment for him rekindled in her when she remembered his asking if it was all right to kiss her. Embarrassment and a specific kind of anger she had for people weaker than herself.

It was noon when they came upon their traditional first campsite, an idyllic spot just before the big canyons, where they set their tents beneath trees. Though hundreds of rafters must have camped here, the site remained pristine enough to make McBride believe no one had been there since them, one year earlier. In all the rivers he'd rafted, all the trails he'd hiked, there was never a place quite like the Dolores, whose devotees seemed intent on maintaining its wildness. The stretch starting tomorrow had nothing human in it, past or present: no phone wires, no roads, no rusty cans, no fences, no old mining sites: nothing but their toy boats. Tomorrow's campsite was under the shelf of a rock wall in which there were hundreds of little naturally occurring holes. Every year Carmel would find stones to put in the holes, filling a few rows before they left. Every year her stones were still there, the only real indication some person had been at work in paradise.

McBride glided to a clean stop after watching Dart and Carmel's sloppy one. Carmel was hanging on to brush while Dart clambered up the side, kicking mud in behind him. McBride steadied his raft with an oar set in the shallows and then stepped gingerly up a lesser incline a few yards down from his friends. Only his left foot got wet and only the sole at that.

"Lunchtime," Carmel pronounced. Thin as she was, she was a voracious eater. It was she who always made them bring along provisions such as marshmallows and bologna. After lunch, Dart wanted to hike and McBride decided to go with him. The two of them couldn't get Carmel to budge from her spot beneath a tree. "I'll read," she said. "I'll drink." McBride looked over his shoulder as they left, but she hadn't moved to dig out a book, hadn't gotten a drink. She watched the river.

She was still watching when they returned a few hours later. McBride worried until he saw that she'd set up both tents and found firewood.

There was a big pit set with twigs and kindling, a blanket beside it, an aluminum pot full of water, and the makings for shrimp creole laid out.

They waited for dark, drinking Kool-Aid and rum. McBride had tried to fix freeze-dried food in his kitchen in Missoula, but it never tasted even remotely like it did on the river. He ate heartily tonight, ignoring the tiny black flecks of ash.

"Found a great spring," Dart told Carmel. "Beautiful."

She nodded. McBride noticed she'd almost finished a bottle of rum while they were gone but was not her usual boisterous drunk self. Preoccupied, she smiled at their jokes while seeming to wish she were elsewhere. McBride found himself reaching too hard for the funny lines, checking her expression frequently, waiting for approval.

They sang cowboy songs around the red late-night coals, Dart and Carmel passing joints between them. McBride only risked getting high when his self-confidence was up; otherwise, he became impossibly paranoid, struck dumb by all of his inadequacies. Dart and Carmel did not share this problem. Soon, Dart had to call it a night. His eyes, in the camp light, had retreated. Rowing, hiking, boozing, doping. He didn't even bother getting to the tent, just wrapped himself in his sleeping bag too close to the fire.

McBride could have slept then, too, but Carmel worried him and he decided to wait. After a moment she stood, surprisingly well-balanced, and with her boot toe, rolled Dart away from the fire. When she sat down, it was very near McBride, whose cheeks flushed at her proximity. He could see a hair growing on her chin.

"Listen," she said in her husky voice. "You like mutton?"

McBride listened while she explained an outrageous plan to kill a sheep. Apparently, she'd been thinking about it all day. She wanted to rope the animal's ankles like a rodeo rider, then level a blow to its head. McBride was too stunned to answer.

"What rope?"

"We'll use my belt."

"You don't want to hurt a lamb."

"Yes," she said calmly. "I really do. We just have to get back upriver. It's not like we wouldn't eat it," she told McBride. "You guys fish, right? What's the big difference? You think a fuzzy live thing has more rights than a slimy one?" She looked at him with grim amusement. "If you don't come," she said, "I'll do it by myself."

The boat was cold and strange in the dark and the river seemed four times as deep. The canyon downstream beckoned to them like a void. They rowed furiously against the current, moving slowly but steadily. McBride's exhausted muscles, lubricated with liquor, performed without his thinking about them. He didn't believe they'd find any sheep, but Carmel's blood-thirstiness was disturbing enough on its own. He couldn't imagine how it would seem when he was sober.

"No sheep," McBride said gratefully, when they reached the pasture. Carmel grabbed a handful of brush and pulled them ashore.

"We can find them," she said. True, the moon was sufficiently bright to see landmarks—trees, the biggest of the rocks in the river. But beyond a certain point in the pasture, there was nothing but shadow, a tree line or distant row of hay.

"This is ridiculous," McBride said after they had tied the raft to a clump of willows and begun making their way through the field.

Carmel kept thinking she could hear them, just over there, just beyond. But the sheep seemed wilier than she had imagined. Their elusiveness only made her more certain in her desire to kill one; they were fairer game than she'd previously believed. They zigzagged across a rocky field, making sheep noises, McBride still a little drunk. Carmel, on the other hand, didn't feel a thing, not intoxicated, not high, not tired. Only mad. Furious. Her disappointment had grown into a terrible anger. She began throwing rocks, trying at first to hit things, then just pitching them one after another ahead of her. No fucking sheep.

But it wasn't just sheep. It was everything, big and small. It was the chill in the air and the slightly tight corduroys she wore. It was her. It was her boyfriend, Lawrence, and her men friends McBride and Dart. Not one of them knew her, really knew her. Sometimes she thought Lawrence understood the real her. Then there were times like today on the river, when it seemed only Will Dart could know her. They all knew parts of her. But she couldn't be everything around any one of them. She missed having women friends. She missed Lana Dart. Always she was screwing things up. Friendships, romances—when they went awry, the fault was hers.

Next to her, McBride pulled out a pack of gum and offered her a stick. With effort, she was polite. "No, thank you." Her contempt for him was very high. What kind of man was he, trailing her around on this chase? He seemed to find it all very anecdotal. He would tell the Story of the Sheep Hunt some day, Carmel thought. The Story of Crazy Carmel. She began running.

The night opened ahead of her, tripping her but not spilling her. McBride was calling her name. He would wait. He would wait all night if she made him. Her men were, one and all, loyal. Loyal to a fault. She forced herself to run harder, faster, stumbling as she went but not falling. What kept her from falling? To think about falling was to make it impossible. She ran until she was hurting everywhere, cheeks, lungs, thighs, toes. She wanted to hurt more. She wanted to be unconscious in pain. Her fury then reached its apex and, headfirst, she plunged herself down.

Dart woke practically lying in the warm ashes of last night's fire. When he opened his eyes he felt lousy; eyes closed he was okay. "Coffee," he said aloud.

He'd expected one or both of the others to be up, waiting to laugh at him; he was usually the last. But the tent flaps were tied down and all of yesterday's clutter untouched. He decided to skinny-dip.

Sitting on an upturned raft, he stripped, checking as he went for ticks. The sun, just now cresting the trees, caused a wave of goose bumps on his pale skin. The Dolores was snow runoff, just barely above freezing, and there was no good place to ease in slowly. Dart dipped his long, ugly feet in first, then delicately leapt in up to his waist, biting back a scream as cold jolted through him. It took ages too long to scramble out.

But as big a shock as the water had been, the sight of Carmel standing near the stuff bags was a bigger one. She looked as if she'd been mauled by a bear. Even without his glasses, Dart could see scrapes running the length of her jawline, both of her black eyes, the puffy mass of her mouth.

She hadn't seen him, though he wasn't very far away. She was searching through a bag, gingerly pulling things out and dropping them to the ground. Dart dressed rapidly, his heartbeat rampant.

"What happened?" he asked, hating the breathlessness in his voice.

She gave him an indifferent appraisal, bare feet to wet head, and shook a metal candy tin. "I tripped."

The whole morning went like that. Dart felt as if he must have insulted somebody's mother in his sleep or committed some similar unforgivable blunder. All of a sudden he was in the supply raft by himself while McBride went ahead with Carmel. Carmel was rowing, besides. He tried to be angry, as he believed was justified, but all he felt was ashamed. He'd failed, though for the life of him he couldn't figure out how.

When they entered the beginning of the maze that was the canyons, he found himself not paying close attention to the water; instead, he was watching McBride and Carmel, looking for signs they were lovers. That had happened before, two friends began sleeping together and didn't bother to tell him until he'd made a fool of himself. So he tried to tactfully accept the new situation like a good third wheel. He tried to remember that the Dolores was the important part: the beautiful canyons, whose high, smooth walls arched up on either side of him. Black deposits in the sandstone ran down the terra-cotta like spilled paint, tapering at the base. He saw a bald eagle, gliding on a thermal, and nearly lost himself in the wonder of it. Nearly. Overwhelming scenery or no, Dart was unable to let go. He smoked and paddled and looked about in awe, but all he could see was the tiny boat ahead and his two friends.

Since McBride was such an efficient oarsman, they got far ahead, soon completely out of sight. Dart made miscalculations, took the wrong tongue over a rock, touched bottom. Water accumulated in the boat after every rapids. And, for the first time in seven years, he capsized.

He'd decided to circumvent a large, flat rock that the water flowed smoothly over. Sometimes you could raft such a rock, making a small leap so you didn't get caught in the undertow on the other side. But his confidence was shaken today and he chose the narrow stream of water to the left, needing to quickly bear even farther left to avoid a shallows beyond. Halfway through, he saw that the rock jutted under the path he'd taken as well, and that its shape pulled everything to the right, regardless. The correct path was over, and he'd gone around. His raft seemed to be sucked straight down, its vinyl floor pulling away from his feet and the sides narrowing around him. He lost his glasses. There was nothing but foam. White foam and suction. The thrill of being removed from his raft was exhilarating and Dart actually came up laughing with fright. He didn't notice how cold it was until past the undertow, casting about for his broken oar.

Carmel and McBride were gone. Everything was floating downstream, stuff bags and loose clothing, the raft itself, two oar pieces. Flotsam. His glasses had sunk. Dart stood shivering in the shallows of a sandbar and hoped his friends would think he drowned. With a great sadness, he realized this was the last year on the Dolores. He didn't usually recognize the moments in his life when it fell apart, but he thought that right now was an exception.

He sighed, still shaken by his capsizing. McBride and Carmel would have to retrieve the supplies. He was going to sit down and dry out, have a little rest.

McBride kept thinking, *everything has changed*. He rowed distractedly, not speaking to Carmel, just concentrating on her oar ahead of his, watching the water drip off it as she lifted it from the river, over and over. *Everything has changed*.

They'd spent the night at the pasture, McBride holding her until she finally slept. There was blood on his sleeves, blood in his beard. She'd been incoherent, ranting, then clinging, still trying to hurt herself, scraping her bare hands on rocks. At daybreak they'd returned to camp. He'd understood she didn't want to ride with Dart today.

"You better?" he'd asked that morning.

"Than what?" she'd answered, wryly.

They reached their traditional campsite at Bull Spring much earlier than normal. It hadn't been the usual second day of running the rapids and playing capture the flag with each other. Carmel had seemed in a hurry and McBride was willing to accommodate her.

When he saw Dart's raft and the gear float by camp, his throat constricted. He realized he was looking for Dart among it. There was nowhere to get help. They were hours from any kind of phone or town.

"I have to go back upstream," McBride told Carmel. Her eyes were wide and empty. "Maybe you can try to get the supplies?" She looked blankly downstream as two of the stuff bags rounded a bend. The raft had caught in the rocks, along with a third red bag. Carmel nodded.

McBride found himself paddling against the current for the second day in a row. How stupid to let Dart get so far behind. But he'd been sulking, sulking and falling behind. McBride vowed that he'd tell Dart everything, all of Carmel's ramblings and tears, if only he were okay.

The Dolores had never seemed to McBride to be a deadly river. Intimidating at times, threatening but not deadly. It was an important distinction. Of course, the river itself was not the problem. It was the people. What made everyone so unreliable? McBride couldn't think of one time he'd ever been as transparent to another human as Carmel had been to him last night, as out of control. He didn't like the feeling it gave him, power and embarrassment and empathy and pity, all at once. He shook his head.

He tried to imagine Carmel's life in Salt Lake City but found himself drawing all his knowledge about her from the week he spent with her annually. Which could hardly be called her life. He had visited her once in college in Colorado. Just dropped in unexpectedly. Her reaction was not what he had expected. She'd opened her dorm-room door and stared at him for a moment before she'd let him in. Photographs filled her allotted half of the wall space and in every picture, people were smiling. He'd commented on this and she'd told him that in her photographs, people smiled; otherwise, they didn't get their picture taken. The faces were eerie, and soon McBride saw that smiling was just a way of being nice about baring your teeth.

He thought it ironic that Carmel had become a nurse; he couldn't think of anyone less dedicated to healthy habits. But in his mind, when he put her in a white uniform and sensible white shoes, she was no longer Carmel. Carmel was the woman who last year had lain, hands behind her head, with him and Dart on a huge flat rock and watched the moon rise above the canyon walls. He felt that woman had disappeared.

"I'm a parasite," she'd told him. "I get in people and make them sick." She rammed her head into McBride's chest. "Sometimes I think I'm a public contagion, like these cultures at the hospital. Hazards to the general populace. Just like that."

How did you respond, McBride wondered, though it didn't seem to matter.

"I could kill someone," Carmel whispered, last night and right now, in McBride's ear. "I could do it."

He saw Will Dart standing on a sandbar. He rowed more furiously, his eyes tearing in relief. Dart's glasses were gone, his clothing was soaked. A rivulet of blood ran down one calf until it dried at his ankle. His thick black hair stood on end like a fright wig. But there he was, waving his gangly arms and smiling. "What ho?"

Carmel was so happy to see Dart come back alive she started crying. She'd managed to drag in a stuff bag and the raft, which was completely deflated.

"Hey," she said to him, coughing. "I saved the bag with the tequila and the B and B. I knew you'd be glad."

"Good work," Dart said. His eyes, without his glasses, wandered a little. When he looked at Carmel, they skidded to the right, as if she'd moved, then centered again.

"We're a sight," she told him, suddenly happier than she had been in months. They were messy but safe, warm in the sunlight and out of any danger in the water. There would be a fire. They would drink and laugh and sleep underneath the blanket that had made it. Carmel wished suddenly that McBride had some wounds as well. His stern expression reminded her that he'd been the one to rescue both her and Dart. He was humorless as a martyr when he came away from Dart's bedraggled raft.

"Holey?" Dart asked, smiling weakly.

"Ruined," McBride answered unsmiling. "And a full day from Bedrock. Jesus."

Carmel thought he was being melodramatic. "We can squish together in the other one," she said, then remembered last night, when *he'd* indulged *her* theatrics. She wished she could erase the night, erase her long, complicated confessional session with him. Now when he looked at her, he seemed to think he understood something, that he had witnessed her bared soul. Stupid, she thought. He didn't know her at all. In fact, battered and dense Dart seemed closer to her now.

"Let me clean your cuts," Carmel said.

McBride tried to catch her eye, but she wouldn't let him. Fuck him, she thought, leading Dart to the warm sand beneath a rock ledge. She dabbed her shirttail in a capful of tequila and swabbed his knees.

"Pretty incredible undertow," he said, wincing.

"Yeah?"

"Oh yeah. You wouldn't think the Dolores ever got that deep, but I couldn't feel bottom."

"Huh." She sat back, touched her own scrapes. "I wiped out on a rock," she said shyly. "Literally." How necessary it had seemed last night, but foolish now.

"Maybe we should have some shots of this," Dart said, swirling the bottle.

"No limes," Carmel said.

"Emergency substitution?"

"Toothpaste." They laughed, each took a shot with a dollop of Crest afterward to kill the bite. They sat getting drunk while McBride found firewood and tried to patch the raft with first-aid tape. Carmel began absently filling the little holes in the wall behind her. Her work from the last seven years was still untouched. The holes reminded her of a miniature city of ancient cliff dwellings. In the beginning, she sort of thought of her pebbles as inhabitants, but now she just thought of them as rocks, clogging the spaces.

Dart joined her and before long, Carmel curled up on the warm sand and just watched him, content and sleepy. She fell into a dreamless sleep.

She looked like hell, McBride thought, but they both wanted her anyway. He couldn't explain it, but he wanted desperately to make love to her. His feelings for her had run the gamut today, pity to anger to passion. Maybe it was all the same. But he wanted her. He and Will Dart shuffled aimlessly around camp, waiting for her to wake up. Neither wanted to hike, neither wanted to sit and talk to the other. They waited for her.

He'd discovered that Dart's raft could hold a fair amount of air for about fifteen minutes. Then it had to be repumped. Tomorrow they would stop every mile or so to get the air pump. Thankfully, he'd put it in the raft with him and Carmel that morning. Ever since he'd found Dart alive, he'd grown more and more annoyed with him. What kind of idiot capsized on the Dolores? One of the slowest floating rivers in the nation, the easiest stretch. And Dart was supposed to be the expert raftsman.

He looked up at the sky, waiting for dark, waiting to light a campfire, waiting for Carmel to rise.

Carmel was hungry when she woke, but all their carefully packed, water-proofed food had floated away, spices and all. So much preparation quickly rendered moot.

They drank B and B out of the bailing cup, eyeing each other. It began to scare her. No one was stopping it, Carmel thought. No one made a move to stop what was going to happen.

When it got dark Carmel stood and walked out of the fire's light. She stopped when she was far enough away that they could not see her but she could see them. Who would come after her, she wondered. Dutiful McBride? Pathetic Dart?

She watched as they sat on either side of the fire, good friends whom she had set at odds. For a fleeting moment, she savored her destruction of their friendship. Then she dug her fingernails into her forearms and bit her lower lip. Her own dismal unhappiness made her want to infect everyone around her, and yet it was a vicious circle, as causing pain was what she hated in herself. When does it end, she wondered.

Dart stood up at the fire, stretched his long, bruised arms over his head. He said something to McBride, who didn't look up and didn't answer. "I guess I'll go find her," or something else equally as euphemistic. He came toward her with unflagging efficiency, straight to her.

"Can I sit?" he whispered, asking her permission.

She nodded, irritated. As soon as he sat, she grabbed him and kissed his face, over and over, pressing her sore lips ferociously against his soft features—all this before he could begin his own awkward dumb way of doing the same thing.

"Unzip," she commanded. He was hard, and they were fast.

"McBride!" Carmel yelled, before Dart had a chance to gather his wits. He struggled to rise, pulling his sandy pants up as he went, catching pubic hair when he zipped. "McBride, come here!" What was she doing?

Dart watched as Carmel, completely nude, met McBride halfway between the fire's light and the blackness outside of it. McBride apparently had been walking blind for a few yards because his face, when he finally saw her, went slack. She wanted to have sex right there. She embraced McBride, who stood without moving, and lifted one naked thigh to his belt, nuzzling his throat. McBride said something as he tried to push her away. Carmel laughed, then said, ". . . fuck . . ." *Fuck Dart?* Dart wondered. *I want to fuck you?* She jumped against McBride, forcing him to cup his hands around her buttocks to keep her from falling. He kissed her. Dart saw their heads turning in a long, if not passionate, then painful, kiss. His stomach churned—humiliation, shame, self-pity.

To be inside her had been wonderful. He hadn't ever really allowed himself the full fantasy of sex with Carmel. Dart found himself stirred again by the memory, despite what he saw before him, McBride staggering toward the blanket near the fire with Carmel in his arms. They would make love. He would watch. It all happened as if he were imagining it and not actually witnessing it, McBride's muscular body in the firelight, Carmel's savage face over his shoulder, McBride crying out and Dart feeling it as if it were himself.

Then he heard his name. Carmel raised her hands to her mouth and yelled his name into the night, over the sound of the water. He would join them, he realized, he would walk to the fire, he would undress, he would be a willing part of whatever this was, hypnotized but conscious, and he did, *doing* it at the precise moment he could *imagine* it, as if there were no difference between the two.

The farmer, as was previously arranged, had parked McBride's truck near the takeout point. The farmer's sheep, curious and stupid, slow and smelly, milled about it. McBride paid him ten dollars and got behind the wheel. He couldn't believe how great it felt to steer, to start the engine and feel the motor respond to his foot on the pedal.

There'd been no discussion that day as they leapfrogged to Bedrock, stopping three or four times an hour to pump air into the raft. The thing was, there was no one to blame, McBride realized, no one to think worse of than the other two. They would never see one another again, it was clear. There was something freeing about it, something poisonous.

Aimed toward Nucla, clouds on the far horizon bubbling up behind one another like an H-bomb blast, Carmel introduced the peach schnapps from her pack, the last of their $200 cache. She sat between the men in the truck and McBride guessed they'd gotten used to her scabbed face: he couldn't make out the awfulness in it anymore. She waved her bottle by the throat, across Dart and out the window. Once it was empty, she let loose. It smashed onto the pavement behind them. "Happy flat fucking tires, assholes!" she yelled.

They were looking for liquor when they passed a farm. Dart wondered aloud if the children in the yard, three of them playing some odd-looking game, would know how to help. He and Carmel debated this point. Drunk, McBride did not register until they were well past that one of the boys had tied the other to a telephone pole, that the little girl, presumably the boys' sister, was standing by crying, helpless. He presented this evidence to his cohorts, who turned to look out the back window.

"Think he'll get hit by lightning?" Carmel asked scientifically.

"Should we do something?" Dart said. "Us?"

But the rain began and the fuzz of all that peachiness rubbed and chafed McBride's insides and extremities. He shut his eyes and said to himself, What if I weren't here, driving by at this precise moment? Who, besides me, could save that boy? When he opened them, he was crossing the yellow lines and the oval emblem of a Peterbilt was coming at him. "Chicken!!" Carmel screeched happily, and they pushed 85, 90, veering at the last moment, high on not giving one goddamn about it.

Fishtailing, the three of them rode into the storm, lightning striking— Dart told them no, lightning didn't strike, exactly, it met its countercurrent from the ground halfway—and trees bowing, rain in sheets breaking over them like waves on a beach, the rhythm of a pulsing heart, blinding them every other beat.

The B.A.R. Man

Richard Yates

Until he got his name on the police blotter, and in the papers, nobody had ever thought much about John Fallon. He was employed as a clerk in a big insurance company, where he hulked among the file cabinets with a consci-entious frown, his white shirt cuffs turned back to expose a tight gold watch on one wrist and a loose serviceman's identification bracelet, the relic of a braver and more careless time, on the other. He was twenty-nine years old, big and burly with neatly combed brown hair and a heavy white face. His eyes were kindly except when he widened them in bewilderment or narrowed them in menace, and his mouth was childishly slack except when he tightened it to say something tough. For street wear, he preferred slick, gas-blue suits with stiff shoulders and very low-set buttons, and he walked with the hard, ringing cadence of steel-capped heels. He lived in Sunnyside, Queens, and had been married for ten years to a very thin girl named Rose who suffered from sinus headaches, couldn't have children, and earned more money than he did by typing eighty-seven words a minute without missing a beat on her chewing gum.

Five evenings a week, Sunday through Thursday, the Fallons sat at home playing cards or watching television, and sometimes she would send him out to buy sandwiches and potato salad for a light snack before they went to bed. Friday, being the end of the workweek and the night of the fights on television, was his night with the boys at the Island Bar and Grill, just off Queens Boulevard. The crowd there were friends of habit rather than of choice, and for the first half hour they would stand around self-consciously, insulting one another and jeering at each new arrival ("Oh Jesus, looka what just come in!"). But by the time the fights were over they would usually have joked and drunk themselves into a high good humor, and the evening would often end in song and staggering at two or three o'clock. Fallon's Saturday, after a morning of sleep and an afternoon of helping with the housework, was devoted to the entertainment of his wife: they would catch the show at one of the neighborhood movies and go to an ice-cream parlor afterwards, and they were usually in bed by twelve. Then came the drowsy living-room clutter of newspapers on Sunday, and his week began again.

The trouble might never have happened if his wife had not insisted, that particular Friday, on breaking his routine: there was a Gregory Peck picture in its final showing that night, and she said she saw no reason why he couldn't do without his prize fight, for once in his life. She told him this on Friday morning, and it was the first of many things that went wrong with his day.

At lunch—the special payday lunch that he always shared with three fellow clerks from his office, in a German tavern downtown—the others were all talking about the fights, and Fallon took little part in the conversation. Jack Kopeck, who knew nothing about boxing (he had called the previous week's performance "a damn good bout" when in fact it had been fifteen rounds of clinches and cream-puff sparring, with the mockery of a decision at the end), told the party at some length that the best all-around bout he'd ever seen was in the Navy. And that led to a lot of Navy talk around the table, while Fallon squirmed in boredom.

"So here *I* was," Kopeck was saying, jabbing his breastbone with a manicured thumb in the windup of his third long story, "my first day on a new ship, and nothing but these tailor-made dress blues to stand inspection in. Scared? Jesus, I was shakin' like a leaf. Old man comes around, looks at me, says, 'Where dya think *you're* at, sailor? A fancy-dress ball?'"

"Talk about inspections," Mike Boyle said, bugging his round comedian's eyes. "Lemme tell ya, *we* had this commander, he'd take this white glove and wipe his finger down the bulkhead? And brother, if that glove came away with a specka dust on it, you were dead."

Then they started getting sentimental. "Ah, it's a good life, though, the Navy," Kopeck said. "A clean life. The best part about the Navy is, you're somebody, know what I mean? Every man's got his own individual job to do. And I mean what the hell, in the Army all you do is walk around and look stupid like everybody else."

"Brother," said little George Walsh, wiping mustard on his knockwurst, "you can say that again. I had four years in the Army and, believe me, you can say that again."

That was when John Fallon's patience ran out. "Yeah?" he said. "What parta the Army was that?"

"What part?" Walsh said, blinking. "Well, I was in the ordnance for a while, in Virginia, and then I was in Texas, and Georgia—how d'ya mean, what part?"

Fallon's eyes narrowed and his lips curled tight. "You oughta tried an infantry outfit, Mac," he said.

"Oh, well," Walsh deferred with a wavering smile.

But Kopeck and Boyle took up the challenge, grinning at him.

"The *infantry*?" Boyle said. "Whadda they got—specialists in the infantry?"

"You betcher ass they got specialists," Fallon said. "Every son of a bitch *in* a rifle company's a specialist, if you wanna know something. And I'll tellya *one* thing, Mac—they don't worry about no silk gloves and no tailor-made clothes, you can betcher ass on that."

"Wait a second," Kopeck said. "I wanna know one thing, John. What was your specialty?"

"I was a B.A.R. man," Fallon said.

"What's that?"

And this was the first time Fallon realized how much the crowd in the office had changed over the years. In the old days, back around 'forty-nine or 'fifty, with the old crowd, anyone who didn't know what a B.A.R. was would almost certainly have kept his mouth shut.

"The B.A.R.," Fallon said, laying down his fork, "is the Browning Automatic Rifle. It's a thirty-caliber, magazine-fed, fully-automatic piece that provides the major firepower of a twelve-man rifle squad. That answer your question?"

"How d'ya mean?" Boyle inquired. "Like a tommy gun?"

And Fallon had to explain, as if he were talking to children or girls, that it was nothing at all like a tommy gun and that its tactical function was entirely different; finally he had to take out his mechanical pencil and draw, from memory and love, a silhouette of the weapon on the back of his weekly pay envelope.

"So okay," Kopeck said, "tell me one thing, John. Whaddya have to know to shoot this gun? You gotta have special training, or what?"

Fallon's eyes were angry slits as he crammed the pencil and the envelope back into his coat. "Try it sometime," he said. "Try walkin' twenty miles on an empty stomach with that B.A.R. and a full ammo belt on your back, and then lay down in some swamp with the water up over your ass, and you're pinned down by machine-gun and mortar fire and your squad leader starts yellin', 'Get that B.A.R. up!' and you gotta cover the withdrawal of the whole platoon or the whole damn company. *Try* it some time, Mac—*you'll* find out whatcha gotta have." And he took too deep a drink of his beer, which made him cough and sputter into his big freckled fist.

"Easy, easy," Boyle said, smiling. "Don't bust a gut, boy."

But Fallon only wiped his mouth and glared at them, breathing hard.

"Okay, so you're a hero," Kopeck said lightly. "You're a fighting man. Tell me one thing, though, John. Did you personally shoot this gun in combat?"

"Whadda you think?" Fallon said through thin, unmoving lips.

"How many times?"

The fact of the matter was that Fallon, as a husky and competent soldier of nineteen, many times pronounced "a damn good B.A.R. man" by the others in his squad, had carried his weapon on blistered feet over miles of road and field and forest in the last two months of the war, had lain with it under many artillery and mortar barrages and jabbed it at the chests of many freshly taken German prisoners; but he'd had occasion to fire it only twice, at vague areas rather than men, had brought down nothing either time, and had been mildly reprimanded the second time for wasting ammunition.

"Nunnya goddamn business how many!" he said, and the others looked down at their plates with ill-concealed smiles. He glared at them, defying anyone to make a crack, but the worst part of it was that none of them said anything. They ate or drank their beer in silence, and after a while they changed the subject.

Fallon did not smile all afternoon, and he was still sullen when he met his wife at the supermarket, near home, for their weekend shopping. She looked tired, the way she always did when her sinus trouble was about to get worse, and while he ponderously wheeled the wire-mesh cart behind her he kept turning his head to follow the churning hips and full breasts of other young women in the store.

"Ow!" she cried once, and dropped a box of Ritz crackers to rub her heel in pain. "Can't you watch where you're *going* with that thing? You better let me push it."

"You shouldn't of stopped so sudden," he told her. "I didn't know you were gonna stop."

And thereafter, to make sure he didn't run the cart into her again, he had to give his full attention to her own narrow body and stick-thin legs. From the side view, Rose Fallon seemed always to be leaning slightly forward; walking, her buttocks seemed to float as an ungraceful separate entity in her wake. Some years ago, a doctor had explained her sterility with the fact that her womb was tipped, and told her it might be corrected by a course of exercises; she had done the exercises halfheartedly for a while and gradually given them up. Fallon could never remember whether her odd posture was supposed to be the cause or the result of the inner condition, but he did know for certain that, like her sinus trouble, it had grown worse in the years since their marriage: he could have sworn she stood straight when he met her.

"You want Rice Krispies or Post Toasties, John?" she asked him.

"Rice Krispies."

"Well, but we just had that last week. Aren't you tired of it?"

"Okay, the other, then."

"What are you mumbling for? I can't hear you."

"Post Toasties, I said!"

Walking home, he was puffing more than usual under the double armload of groceries. "What's the *matter*?" she asked, when he stopped to change his grip on the bags.

"Guess I'm outa shape," he said. "I oughta get out and play some handball."

"Oh, honestly," she said. "You're always saying that, and all you ever do is lie around and read the papers."

She took a bath before fixing the dinner, and then ate with a bulky housecoat roped around her in her usual state of post-bath dishevelment: hair damp, skin dry and porous, no lipstick and a smiling spoor of milk around the upper borders of her unsmiling mouth. "Where do you think you're going?" she said, when he had pushed his plate away and stood up. "Look at that—a full glass of milk on the table. Honestly, John, you're the one that makes me *buy* milk and then when I buy it you go and leave a full glass on the table. Now come back here and drink that up."

He went back and gulped the milk, which made him feel ill.

When her meal was over she began her careful preparations for the evening out; long after he had washed and dried the dishes she was still at the ironing board, pressing the skirt and blouse she planned to wear to the movies. He sat down to wait for her. "Be late to the show if you don't get a move on," he said.

"Oh, don't be silly. We've got practically a whole hour. What's the *matter* with you tonight, anyway?"

Her spike-heeled street shoes looked absurd under the ankle-length wrapper, particularly when she stooped over, splay-toed, to pull out the wall plug of the ironing cord.

"How come you quit those exercises?" he asked her.

"What exercises? What are you talking about?"

"You know," he said. "You know. Those exercises for your tipped utiyus."

"*Uterus*," she said. "You always say 'utiyus.' It's *uterus*."

"So what the hell's the difference? Whyd'ya quit 'em?"

"Oh, honestly, John," she said, folding up the ironing board. "Why bring that up *now*, for heaven's sake?"

"So whaddya wanna do? Walk around with a tipped utiyus the resta ya life, or what?"

"Well," she said, "I certainly don't wanna get pregnant, if that's what you mean. May I ask where we'd be if I had to quit my job?"

He got up and began to stalk around the living room, glaring fiercely at the lamp shades, the watercolor flower paintings, and the small china figure of a seated, sleeping Mexican at whose back bloomed a dry cactus plant. He went to the bedroom, where her fresh underwear was laid out for the evening, and picked up a white brassiere containing the foam-rubber cups without which her chest was as meager as a boy's. When she came in he turned on her, waving it in her startled face, and said, "Why d'ya *wear* these goddamn things?"

She snatched the brassiere from him and backed against the doorjamb, her eyes raking him up and down. "Now, *look*," she said. "I've had *enough* of this. Are you gonna start acting decent, or not? Are we going to the movies, or not?"

And suddenly she looked so pathetic that he couldn't stand it. He grabbed his coat and pushed past her. "Do whatcha like," he said. "I'm goin' out." And he slammed out of the apartment.

It wasn't until he swung onto Queens Boulevard that his muscles began to relax and his breathing to slow down. He didn't stop at the Island Bar and Grill—it was too early for the fights anyway, and he was too upset to enjoy them. Instead, he clattered down the stairs to the subway and whipped through the turnstile, headed for Manhattan.

He had set a vague course for Times Square, but thirst overcame him at Third Avenue; he went up to the street and had two shots with a beer chaser in the first bar he came to, a bleak place with stamped-tin walls and a urine smell. On his right, at the bar, an old woman was waving her cigarette like a baton and singing "Peg o' My Heart," and on his left one middle-aged man was saying to another: "Well, my point of view is this: maybe you could argue with McCarthy's methods, but son of a bitch, you couldn't argue with him on principle. Am I right?"

Fallon left the place and went to another near Lexington, a chrome-and-leather place where everyone looked bluish green in the subtle light. There he stood at the bar beside two young soldiers with divisional patches on their sleeves and infantry braid on the PX caps that lay folded under their shoulder tabs. They wore no ribbons—they were only kids—but Fallon could tell they were no recruits: they knew how to wear their Eisenhower jackets, for one thing, short and skintight, and their combat boots were soft and almost black with polish. Both their heads suddenly turned to look past him, and Fallon, turning too, joined them in watching a girl in a tight tan skirt detach herself from a party at one of the tables in a shadowy corner. She brushed past them, murmuring, "Excuse me," and all three of their heads were drawn to watch her buttocks shift and settle, shift and settle until she disappeared into the ladies' room.

"Man, that's rough," the shorter of the two soldiers said, and his grin included Fallon, who grinned back.

"Oughta be a law against wavin' it around that way," the tall soldier said. "Bad for the troops."

Their accents were Western, and they both had the kind of blond, squint-eyed, country-boy faces that Fallon remembered from his old platoon. "What outfit you boys in?" he inquired. "I oughta reckanize that patch."

They told him, and he said, "Oh, yeah, sure—I remember. They were in the Seventh Army, right? Back in forty-four and -five?"

"Couldn't say for sure, sir," the short soldier said. "That was a good bit before our time."

"Where the hellya get that 'sir' stuff?" Fallon demanded heartily. "I wasn't no officer. I never made better'n pfc, except for a couple weeks when they made me an acting buck sergeant, there in Germany. I was a B.A.R. man."

The short soldier looked him over. "That figures," he said. "You got the build for a B.A.R. man. That old B.A.R.'s a heavy son of a bitch."

"You're right," Fallon said. "It's heavy, but, I wanna tellya, it's a damn sweet weapon in combat. Listen, what are you boys drinking? My name's Johnny Fallon, by the way."

They shook hands with him, mumbling their names, and when the girl in the tan skirt came out of the ladies' room they all turned to watch her again. This time, watching until she had settled herself at her table, they concentrated on the wobbling fullness of her blouse.

"Man," the short soldier said, "I mean, that's a pair."

"Probably ain't real," the tall one said.

"They're real, son," Fallon assured him, turning back to his beer with a man-of-the-world wink. "They're real. I can spot a paira falsies a mile away."

They had a few more rounds, talking Army, and after a while the tall soldier asked Fallon how to get to the Central Plaza, where he'd heard about the Friday night jazz; then they were all three rolling down Second Avenue in a cab, for which Fallon paid. While they stood waiting for the elevator at the Central Plaza, he worked the wedding ring off his finger and stuck in it in his watch pocket.

The wide, high ballroom was jammed with young men and girls; hundreds of them sat listening or laughing around pitchers of beer; another hundred danced wildly in a cleared space between banks of tables. On the bandstand, far away, a sweating group of colored and white musicians bore down, their horns gleaming in the smoky light.

Fallon, to whom all jazz sounded the same, took on the look of a connoisseur as he slouched in the doorway, his face tense and glazed under the squeal of clarinets, his gas-blue trousers quivering with the slight, rhythmic dip of his knees and his fingers snapping loosely to the beat of the drums. But it wasn't music that possessed him as he steered the soldiers to a table next to three girls, nor was it music that made him get up, as soon as the band played something slow enough, and ask the best-looking of the three to dance. She was tall and well-built, a black-haired Italian girl with a faint shine of sweat on her brow, and as she walked ahead of him toward the dance floor, threading her way between the tables, he reveled in the slow grace of her twisting hips and floating skirt. In his exultant, beer-blurred mind he already knew how it would be when he took her home—how she would feel to his exploring hands in the dark privacy of the taxi, and how she would be later, undulant and naked, in some ultimate vague bedroom at the end of the night. And as soon they reached the dance floor, when she turned around and lifted her arms, he crushed her tight and warm against him.

"Now, *look*," she said, arching back angrily so that the cords stood out in her damp neck, "Is that what you call *dancing?*"

He relaxed his grip, trembling, and grinned at her, "Take it easy, honey," he said. "I won't bite,"

"Never mind the 'honey,' either," she said, and that was all she said until the dance was over.

But she had to stay with him, for the two soldiers had moved in on her lively, giggling girlfriends. They were all at the same table now, and for half an hour the six of them sat there in an uneasy party mood: one of the other girls (they were both small and blonde) kept shrieking with laughter at the things the short soldier was mumbling to her, and the other had the tall soldier's long arm around her neck. But Fallon's big brunette, who had reluctantly given her name as Marie, sat silent and primly straight beside him, snapping and unsnapping the clasp of the handbag in her lap. Fallon's fingers gripped the back of her chair with white-knuckled intensity, but whenever he let them slip tentatively to her shoulder she would shrug free.

"You live around here, Marie?" he asked her.

"The Bronx," she said.

"You come down here often?"

"Sometimes."

"Care for a cigarette?"

"I don't smoke."

Fallon's face was burning, the small curving vein in his right temple throbbed visibly, and sweat was sliding down his ribs. He was like a boy on his first date, paralyzed and stricken dumb by the nearness of her warm dress, by the smell of her perfume, by the way her delicate fingers worked on the handbag and the way the moisture glistened on her plump lower lip.

At the next table a young sailor stood up and bellowed something through cupped hands at the bandstand, and the cry was taken up elsewhere around the room. It sounded like "We want the saints!" but Fallon couldn't make sense of it. At least it gave him an opening. "What's that they're yellin'?" he asked her.

"The Saints," she told him, meeting his eyes just long enough to impart the information. "They wanna hear 'The Saints.'"

"Oh."

After that they stopped talking altogether for a long time until Marie made a face of impatience at the nearest of her girlfriends. "Let's go, hey," she said. "C'mon. I wanna go home."

"Aw, *Marie*," the other girl said, flushed with beer and flirtation (she was wearing the short soldier's overseas cap now). "Don't be such a stupid." Then, seeing Fallon's tortured face, she tried so help him out. "Are you in the Army too?" she asked brightly, leaning toward him across the table.

"Me?" Fallon said, startled. "No, I—I used to be, though. I been outa the Army for quite a while now."

"Oh, yeah?"

"He used to be a B.A.R. man," the short soldier told her.

"Oh, yeah?"

"We want 'The Saints'!" "We want 'The Saints'!" They were yelling it from all corners of the enormous room now, with greater and greater urgency.

"C'mon, hey," Marie said again to her girlfriend. "Let's go. I'm tired."

"So *go* then," the girl in the soldier's hat said crossly. "*Go* if you want to, Marie. Can'tcha go home by yourself?"

"No, wait, listen—" Fallon sprang to his feet. "Don't go yet, Marie—I'll tell ya what. I'll go get some more beer, okay?" And he bolted from the table before she could refuse.

"No more for me," she called after him, but he was already three tables away, walking fast toward the little ell of the room where the bar was. "Bitch," he was whispering. "Bitch. Bitch." And the images that tortured him now, while he stood in line at the makeshift bar, were intensified by rage: there would be struggling limbs and torn clothes in the taxi; there would be blind force in the bedroom, and stifled cries of pain that would turn to whimpering and finally to spastic moans of animal lust. Oh, he'd loosen her up! He'd loosen her up!

"C'mon, c'mon," he said to the men who were fumbling with pitchers and beer spigots and wet dollar bills behind the bar.

"We—want—'The Saints'!" "We—want—'The Saints'!" The chant in the ballroom reached its climax. Then, after the drums built up a relentless, brutal rhythm that grew all but intolerable until it ended in a cymbal smash and gave way to the blare of the brass section, the crowd went wild. It took some seconds for Fallon to realize, getting his pitcher of beer at last and turning away from the bar, that the band was playing "When the Saints Go Marching In."

The place was a madhouse. Girls screamed and boys stood yelling on chairs, waving their arms; glasses were smashed and chairs sent spinning, and four policemen stood alert along the walls, ready for a riot as the band rode it out.

When the saints
Go marching in
Oh, when the saints go marching in . . .

Fallon moved in jostled bewilderment through the noise, trying to find his party. He found their table, but couldn't be sure it was theirs—it was empty except for a crumpled cigarette package and a wet stain of beer, and one of its chairs lay overturned on the floor. He thought he saw Marie among the frantic dancers, but it turned out to be another big brunette in the same kind of dress. Then he thought he saw the short soldier gesturing wildly across the room, and made his way over to him, but it was another soldier with a country-boy face. Fallon turned around and around, sweating, looking everywhere in the dizzy crowd. Then a boy in a damp pink shirt reeled heavily against his elbow and the beer spilled in a cold rush on his hand and sleeve, and that was when he realized they were gone. They had ditched him.

He was out on the street and walking, fast and hard on his steel-capped heels, and the night traffic noises were appallingly quiet after the bedlam of shouting and jazz. He walked with no idea of direction and no sense of time, aware of nothing beyond the pound of his heels, the thrust and pull of his muscles, the quavering intake and sharp outward rush of his breath and the pump of his blood.

He didn't know if ten minutes or an hour passed, twenty blocks or five, before he had to slow down and stop on the fringe of a small crowd that clustered around a lighted doorway where policemen were waving the people on.

"Keep moving," one of the policemen was saying. "Move along, please. Keep moving."

But Fallon, like most of the others, stood still. It was the doorway to some kind of lecture hall—he could tell that by the bulletin board that was just visible under the yellow lights inside, and by the flight of the marble stairs that led up to what must have been an auditorium. But what caught most of his attention was the picket line: three men about his own age, their eyes agleam with righteousness, wearing the blue-and-gold overseas caps of some veterans' organization and carrying placards that said:

SMOKE OUT THIS FIFTH AMENDMENT COMMIE

PROF. MITCHELL GO BACK TO RUSSIA

AMERICA'S FIGHTING SONS PROTEST MITCHELL

"Move along," the police were saying. "Keep moving."

"Civil rights, my ass," said a flat muttering voice at Fallon's elbow. "They oughta lock this Mitchell up. You read what he said in the Senate hearing?" And Fallon, nodding, recalled a fragile, snobbish face in a number of newspaper pictures.

"Look at there—" the muttering voice said. "Here they come. They're comin' out now."

And they were. Down the marble steps they came, past the bulletin board and out onto the sidewalk: men in raincoats and greasy tweeds, petulant, Greenwich Village-looking girls in tight pants, a few Negroes, a few very clean, self-conscious college boys.

The pickets were backed off and standing still now, holding their placards high with one hand and curving the other around their mouths to call, "Boo-oo!" "Boo-oo!"

The crowd picked it up: "Boo-oo!" "Boo-oo!" And somebody called, "Go back to Russia!"

"Keep moving," the cops were saying. "Move along, now. Keep moving."

"There he is," said the muttering voice. "There he comes now—that's Mitchell."

And Fallon saw him: a tall, slight man in a cheap double-breasted suit that was too big for him, carrying a briefcase and flanked by two plain women in glasses. There was the snobbish face of the newspaper pictures, turning slowly from side to side now, with a serene, superior smile that seemed to be saying, to everyone it met: *Oh, you poor fool. You poor fool.*

"KILL that bastard!"

Not until several people whirled to look at him did Fallon realize he was yelling; then all he knew was that he had to yell again and again until his voice broke, like a child in tears: *"KILL that bastard! KILL 'im! KILL 'im!"*

In four bucking, lunging strides he was through to the front of the crowd; then one of the pickets dropped his placard and rushed him, saying, "Easy, Mac! Take it *easy*—" But Fallon threw him off, grappled with another man and wrenched free again, got both hands on Mitchell's coat front and tore him down like a crumpled puppet. He saw Mitchell's face recoil in wet-mouthed terror on the sidewalk, and the last thing he knew, as the cop's blue arm swung high over his head, was a sense of absolute fulfillment and relief.

The Things They Carried

Tim O'Brien

First Lieutenant Jimmy Cross carried letters from a girl named Martha, a junior at Mount Sebastian College in New Jersey. They were not love letters, but Lieutenant Cross was hoping, so he kept them folded in plastic at the bottom of his rucksack. In the late afternoon, after a day's march, he would dig his foxhole, wash his hands under a canteen, unwrap the letters, hold them with the tips of his fingers, and spend the last hour of light pretending. He would imagine romantic camping trips into the White Mountains in New Hampshire. He would sometimes taste the envelope flaps, knowing her tongue had been there. More than anything, he wanted Martha to love him as he loved her, but the letters were mostly chatty, elusive on the matter of love. She was a virgin, he was almost sure. She was an

English major at Mount Sebastian, and she wrote beautifully about her professors and roommates and midterm exams, about her respect for Chaucer and her great affection for Virginia Woolf. She often quoted lines of poetry; she never mentioned the war, except to say, Jimmy, take care of yourself. The letters weighed ten ounces. They were signed Love, Martha, but Lieutenant Cross understood that Love was only a way of signing and did not mean what he sometimes pretended it meant. At dusk, he would carefully return the letters to his rucksack. Slowly, a bit distracted, he would get up and move among his men, checking the perimeter, then at full dark he would return to his hole and watch the night and wonder if Martha was a virgin.

The things they carried were largely determined by necessity. Among the necessities or near-necessities were P-38 can openers, pocket knives, heat tabs, wristwatches, dog tags, mosquito repellent, chewing gum, candy, cigarettes, salt tablets, packets of Kool-Aid, lighters, matches, sewing kits, Military Payment Certificates, C rations, and two or three canteens of water. Together, these items weighed between fifteen and twenty pounds, depending upon a man's habits or rate of metabolism. Henry Dobbins, who was a big man, carried extra rations; he was especially fond of canned peaches in heavy syrup over pound cake. Dave Jensen, who practiced field hygiene, carried a toothbrush, dental floss, and several hotel-size bars of soap he'd stolen on R&R in Sydney, Australia. Ted Lavender, who was scared, carried tranquilizers until he was shot in the head outside the village of Than Khe in mid-April. By necessity, and because it was SOP, they all carried steel helmets that weighed five pounds including the liner and camouflage cover. They carried the standard fatigue jackets and trousers. Very few carried underwear. On their feet they carried jungle boots—2.1 pounds—and Dave Jensen carried three pairs of socks and a can of Dr. Scholl's foot powder as a precaution against trench foot. Until he was shot, Ted Lavender carried six or seven ounces of premium dope, which for him was a necessity. Mitchell Sanders, the RTO, carried condoms. Norman Bowker carried a diary. Rat Kiley carried comic books. Kiowa, a devout Baptist, carried an illustrated New Testament that had been presented to him by his father, who taught Sunday school in Oklahoma City, Oklahoma. As a hedge against bad times, however, Kiowa also carried his grandmother's distrust of the white man, his grandfather's old hunting hatchet. Necessity dictated. Because the land was mined and booby-trapped, it was SOP for each man to carry a steel-centered, nylon-covered flak jacket, which weighed 6.7 pounds, but which on hot days seemed much heavier. Because you could die so quickly, each man carried at least one large compress bandage, usually in the helmet band for easy access. Because the nights were cold, and because the monsoons were wet, each carried a green plastic poncho that could be used as a raincoat or groundsheet or makeshift tent. With its quilted liner, the poncho weighed almost two pounds, but it was worth every ounce. In April, for instance, when Ted Lavender was shot, they used his poncho to wrap him up, then to carry him across the paddy, then to lift him into the chopper that took him away.

They were called legs or grunts.

To carry something was to hump it, as when Lieutenant Jimmy Cross humped his love for Martha up the hills and through the swamps. In its intransitive form to hump meant to walk, or to march, but it implied burdens far beyond the intransitive.

Almost everyone humped photographs. In his wallet, Lieutenant Cross carried two photographs of Martha. The first was a Kodachrome snapshot signed Love, though he knew better. She stood against a brick wall. Her eyes were gray and neutral, her lips slightly open as she stared straight-on at the camera. At night, sometimes, Lieutenant Cross wondered who had taken the picture, because he knew she had boyfriends, because he loved her so much, and because he could see the shadow of the picture taker spreading out against the brick wall. The second photograph had been clipped from the 1968 Mount Sebastian yearbook. It was an action shot—women's volleyball—and Martha was bent horizontal to the floor, reaching, the palms of her hands in sharp focus, the tongue taut, the expression frank and competitive. There was no visible sweat. She wore white gym shorts. Her legs, he thought, were almost certainly the legs of a virgin, dry and without hair, the left knee cocked and carrying her entire weight, which was just over one hundred pounds. Lieutenant Cross remembered touching that left knee. A dark theater, he remembered, and the movie was *Bonnie and Clyde,* and Martha wore a tweed skirt, and during the final scene, when he touched her knee, she turned and looked at him in a sad, sober way that made him pull his hand back, but he would always remember the feel of the tweed skirt and the knee beneath it and the sound of the gunfire that killed Bonnie and Clyde, how embarrassing it was, how slow and oppressive. He remembered kissing her good night at the dorm door. Right then, he thought, he should've done something brave. He should've carried her up the stairs to her room and tied her to the bed and touched that left knee all night long. He should've risked it. Whenever he looked at the photographs, he thought of new things he should've done.

What they carried was partly a function of rank, partly of field specialty.

As a first lieutenant and platoon leader, Jimmy Cross carried a compass, maps, code books, binoculars, and a .45-caliber pistol that weighed 2.9 pounds fully loaded. He carried a strobe light and the responsibility for the lives of his men.

As an RTO, Mitchell Sanders carried the PRC-25 radio, a killer, twenty-six pounds with its battery.

As a medic, Rat Kiley carried a canvas satchel filled with morphine and plasma and malaria tablets and surgical tape and comic books and all the things a medic must carry, including M&Ms for especially bad wounds, for a total weight of nearly twenty pounds.

As a big man, therefore a machine gunner, Henry Dobbins carried the M-60, which weighed twenty-three pounds unloaded, but which was almost always loaded. In addition, Dobbins carried between ten and fifteen pounds of ammunition draped in belts across his chest and shoulders.

As PFCs or Spec 4s, most of them were common grunts and carried the standard M-16 gas-operated assault rifle. The weapon weighed 7.5 pounds unloaded, 8.2 pounds with its full twenty-round magazine. Depending on numerous factors, such as topography and psychology, the riflemen carried anywhere from twelve to twenty magazines, usually in cloth bandoliers, adding on another 8.4 pounds at minimum, fourteen pounds at maximum. When it was available, they also carried M-16 maintenance gear—rods and steel brushes and swabs and tubes of LSA oil—all of which weighed about a pound. Among the grunts, some carried the M-79 grenade launcher, 5.9 pounds unloaded, a reasonably light weapon except for the ammunition, which was heavy. A single round weighed ten ounces. The typical load was twenty-five rounds. But Ted Lavender, who was scared, carried thirty-four rounds when he was shot and killed outside Than Khe, and he went down under an exceptional burden, more than twenty pounds of ammunition, plus the flak jacket and helmet and rations and water and toilet paper and tranquilizers and all the rest, plus the unweighed fear. He was dead weight. There was no twitching or flopping. Kiowa, who saw it happen, said it was like watching a rock fall, or a big sandbag or something—just boom, then down—not like the movies where the dead guy rolls around and does fancy spins and goes ass over teakettle—not like that, Kiowa said, the poor bastard just flat-fuck fell. Boom. Down. Nothing else. It was a bright morning in mid-April. Lieutenant Cross felt the pain. He blamed himself. They stripped off Lavender's canteens and ammo, all the heavy things, and Rat Kiley said the obvious, the guy's dead, and Mitchell Sanders used his radio to report one U.S. KIA and to request a chopper. Then they wrapped Lavender in his poncho. They carried him out to a dry paddy, established security, and sat smoking the dead man's dope until the chopper came. Lieutenant Cross kept to himself. He pictured Martha's smooth young face, thinking he loved her more than anything, more than his men, and now Ted Lavender was dead because he loved her so much and could not stop thinking about her. When the dust off arrived, they carried Lavender aboard. Afterward they burned Than Khe, they marched until dusk, then dug their holes, and that night Kiowa kept explaining how you had to be there, how fast it was, how the poor guy just dropped like so much concrete. Boom-down, he said. Like cement.

* * *

In addition to the three standard weapons—the M-6o, M-16, and M-79—
they carried whatever presented itself, or whatever seemed appropriate as a
means of killing or staying alive. They carried catch-as-catch-can. At various times, in various situations, they carried M-14s and CAR-15s and
Swedish Ks and grease guns and captured AK-47s and Chi-Coms and
RPGs and Simonov carbines and black-market Uzis and .38-caliber Smith
& Wesson handguns and 66-mm LAWs and shotguns and silencers and
blackjacks and bayonets and C-4 plastic explosives. Lee Strunk carried a
slingshot; a weapon of last resort, he called it. Mitchell Sanders carried
brass knuckles. Kiowa carried his grandfather's feathered hatchet. Every
third or fourth man carried a Claymore antipersonnel mine—3.5 pounds
with its firing device. They all carried fragmentation grenades—fourteen
ounces each. They all carried at least one M-18 colored smoke grenade—
twenty-four ounces. Some carried CS or teargas grenades. Some carried
white phosphorus grenades. They carried all they could bear, and then some,
including a silent awe for the terrible power of the things they carried.

In the first week of April, before Lavender died, Lieutenant Jimmy Cross
received a good-luck charm from Martha. It was a simple pebble, an ounce
at most. Smooth to the touch, it was a milky-white color with flecks of
orange and violet, oval-shaped, like a miniature egg. In the accompanying
letter, Martha wrote that she had found the pebble on the Jersey shoreline,
precisely where the land touched water at high tide, where things came
together but also separated. It was this separate-but-together quality, she
wrote, that had inspired her to pick up the pebble and to carry it in her
breast pocket for several days, where it seemed weightless, and then to send
it through the mail, by air, as a token of her truest feelings for him. Lieutenant Cross found this romantic. But he wondered what her truest feelings
were, exactly, and what she meant by separate-but-together. He wondered
how the tides and waves had come into play on that afternoon along the
Jersey shoreline when Martha saw the pebble and bent down to rescue it
from geology. He imagined bare feet. Martha was a poet, with the poet's
sensibilities, and her feet would be brown and bare, the toenails unpainted,

the eyes chilly and somber like the ocean in March, and though it was painful, he wondered who had been with her that afternoon. He imagined a pair of shadows mowing along the strip of sand where things came together but also separated. It was phantom jealousy, he knew, but he couldn't help himself. He loved her so much. On the march, through the hot days of early April, he carried the pebble in his mouth, turning it with his tongue, tasting sea salts and moisture. His mind wandered. He had difficulty keeping his attention on the war. On occasion he would yell at his men to spread out the column, to keep their eyes open, but then he would slip away into daydreams, just pretending, walking barefoot along the Jersey shore, with Martha, carrying nothing. He would feel himself rising. Sun and waves and gentle winds, all love and lightness.

What they carried varied by mission.

When a mission took them to the mountains, they carried mosquito netting, machetes, canvas tarps, and extra bug juice.

If a mission seemed especially hazardous, or if it involved a place they knew to be bad, they carried everything they could. In certain heavily mined AOs where the land was dense with Toe Poppers and Bouncing Betties, they took turns humping a twenty-eight-pound mine detector. With its headphones and big sensing plate, the equipment was a stress on the lower back and shoulders, awkward to handle, often useless because of the shrapnel in the earth, but they carried it anyway, partly for safety, partly for the illusion of safety.

On ambush, or other night missions, they carried peculiar little odds and ends. Kiowa always took along his New Testament and a pair of moccasins for silence. Dave Jensen carried night-sight vitamins high in carotene. Lee Strunk carried his slingshot; ammo, he claimed, would never be a problem. Rat Kiley carried brandy and M&M candy. Until he was shot, Ted Lavender carried the starlight scope, which weighed 6.3 pounds with its aluminum carrying case. Henry Dobbins carried his girlfriend's panty hose wrapped around his neck as a comforter. They all carried ghosts. When dark came, they would move out single file across the meadows and paddies to their ambush coordinates, where they would quietly set up the Claymores and lie down and spend the night waiting.

Other missions were more complicated and required special equipment. In mid-April, it was their mission to search out and destroy the elaborate tunnel complexes in the Than Khe area south of Chu Lai. To blow the tunnels, they carried one-pound blocks of pentrite high explosives, four blocks to a man, sixty-eight pounds in all. They carried wiring, detonators, and battery-powered clackers. Dave Jensen carried earplugs. Most often, before blowing the tunnels, they were ordered by higher command to search them, which was considered bad news, but by and large they just shrugged and carried out orders. Because he was a big man, Henry Dobbins was excused from tunnel duty. The others would draw numbers. Before Lavender died there were seventeen men in the platoon, and whoever drew the number seventeen would strip off his gear and crawl in headfirst with a flashlight and Lieutenant Cross's .45-caliber pistol. The rest of them would fan out as security. They would sit down or kneel, not facing the hole, listening to the ground beneath them, imagining cobwebs and ghosts, whatever was down there—the tunnel walls squeezing in—how the flashlight seemed impossibly heavy in the hand and how it was tunnel vision in the very strictest sense, compression in all ways, even time, and how you had to wiggle in—ass and elbows—a swallowed-up feeling—and how you found yourself worrying about odd things—Will your flashlight go dead? Do rats carry rabies? If you screamed, how far would the sound carry? Would your buddies hear it? Would they have the courage to drag you out? In some respects, though not many, the waiting was worse than the tunnel itself. Imagination was a killer.

On April 6, when Lee Strunk drew the number seventeen, he laughed and muttered something and went down quickly. The morning was hot and very still. Not good, Kiowa said. He looked at the tunnel opening, then out across a dry paddy toward the village of Than Khe. Nothing moved. No clouds or birds or people. As they waited, the men smoked and drank Kool-

225

Aid, not talking much, feeling sympathy for Lee Strunk but also feeling the luck of the draw. You win some, you lose some, said Mitchell Sanders, and sometimes you settle for a rain check. It was a tired line and no one laughed.

Henry Dobbins ate a tropical chocolate bar. Ted Lavender popped a tranquilizer and went off to pee.

After five minutes, Lieutenant Jimmy Cross moved to the tunnel, leaned down, and examined the darkness. Trouble, he thought—a cave-in maybe. And then suddenly, without willing it, he was thinking about Martha. The stresses and fractures, the quick collapse, the two of them buried alive under all that weight. Dense, crushing love. Kneeling, watching the hole, he tried to concentrate on Lee Strunk and the war, all the dangers, but his love was too much for him, he felt paralyzed, he wanted to sleep inside her lungs and breathe her blood and be smothered. He wanted her to be a virgin and not a virgin, all at once. He wanted to know her. Intimate secrets—why poetry: Why so sad? Why that grayness in her eyes? Why so alone? Not lonely, just alone—riding her bike across campus or sitting off by herself in the cafeteria—even dancing, she danced alone—and it was the aloneness that filled him with love. He remembered telling her that one evening. How she nodded and looked away. And how, later, when he kissed her, she received the kiss without returning it, her eyes wide open, not afraid, not a virgin's eyes, just flat and uninvolved.

Lieutenant Cross gazed at the tunnel. But he was not there. He was buried with Martha under the white sand at the Jersey shore. They were pressed together, and the pebble in his mouth was her tongue. He was smiling. Vaguely, he was aware of how quiet the day was, the sullen paddies, yet he could not bring himself to worry about matters of security. He was beyond that. He was just a kid at war, in love. He was twenty-four years old. He couldn't help it.

A few moments later Lee Strunk crawled out of the tunnel. He came up grinning, filthy but alive. Lieutenant Cross nodded and closed his eyes while the others clapped Strunk on the back and made jokes about rising from the dead.

Worms, Rat Kiley said. Right out of the grave. Fuckin' zombie.

The men laughed. They all felt great relief.

Spook City, said Mitchell Sanders.

Lee Strunk made a funny ghost sound, a kind of moaning, yet very happy, and right then, when Strunk made that high happy moaning sound, when he went *Ahhooooo*, right then Ted Lavender was shot in the head on his way back from peeing. He lay with his mouth open. The teeth were broken. There was a swollen black bruise under his left eye. The cheekbone was gone. Oh shit, Rat Kiley said, the guy's dead. The guy's dead, he kept saying, which seemed profound—the guy's dead. I mean really.

The things they carried were determined to some extent by superstition. Lieutenant Cross carried his good-luck pebble. Dave Jensen carried a rabbit's foot. Norman Bowker, otherwise a very gentle person, carried a thumb that had been presented to him as a gift by Mitchell Sanders. The thumb was dark brown, rubbery to the touch, and weighed four ounces at most. It had been cut from a VC corpse, a boy of fifteen or sixteen. They'd found him at the bottom of an irrigation ditch, badly burned, flies in his mouth and eyes. The boy wore black shorts and sandals. At the time of his death he had been carrying a pouch of rice, a rifle, and three magazines of ammunition.

You want my opinion, Mitchell Sanders said, there's a definite moral here.

He put his hand on the dead boy's wrist. He was quiet for a time, as if counting a pulse, then he patted the stomach, almost affectionately, and used Kiowa's hunting hatchet to remove the thumb.

Henry Dobbins asked what the moral was.

Moral?

You know. *Moral.*

Sanders wrapped the thumb in toilet paper and handed it across to Norman Bowker. There was no blood. Smiling, he kicked the boy's head, watched the flies scatter, and said, It's like with that old TV show—Paladin. Have gun, will travel.

Henry Dobbins thought about it.

Yeah, well, he finally said. I don't see no moral.

There it *is*, man.

Fuck off.

They carried USO stationery and pencils and pens. They carried Sterno, safety pins, trip flares, signal flares, spools of wire, razor blades, chewing tobacco, liberated joss sticks and statuettes of the smiling Buddha, candles, grease pencils, *The Stars and Stripes*, fingernail clippers, Psy Ops leaflets, bush hats, bolos, and much more. Twice a week, when the resupply choppers came in, they carried hot chow in green Mermite cans and large canvas bags filled with iced beer and soda pop. They carried plastic water containers, each with a two-gallon capacity. Mitchell Sanders carried a set of starched tiger fatigues for special occasions. Henry Dobbins carried Black Flag insecticide. Dave Jensen carried empty sandbags that could be filled at night for added protection. Lee Strunk carried tanning lotion. Some things they carried in common. Taking turns, they carried the big PRC-77 scrambler radio, which weighed thirty pounds with its battery. They shared the weight of memory. They took up what others could no longer bear. Often, they carried each other, the wounded or weak. They carried infections. They carried chess sets, basketballs, Vietnamese-English dictionaries, insignia of rank, Bronze Stars and Purple Hearts, plastic cards imprinted with the Code of Conduct. They carried diseases, among them malaria and dysentery. They carried lice and ringworm and leeches and paddy algae and various rots and molds. They carried the land itself—Vietnam, the place, the soil—a powdery orange-red dust that covered their boots and fatigues and faces. They carried the sky. The whole atmosphere, they carried it, the humidity, the monsoons, the stink of fungus and decay, all of it, they carried gravity. They moved like mules. By daylight they took sniper fire, at night they were mortared, but it was not battle, it was just the endless march, village to village, without purpose, nothing won or lost. They marched for the sake of the march. They plodded along slowly, dumbly, leaning forward against the heat, unthinking, all blood and bone, simple grunts, soldiering with their legs, toiling up the hills and down into the paddies and across the rivers and up again and down, just humping, one step and then the next and then another, but no volition, no will, because it was automatic, it was anatomy, and the war was entirely a matter of posture and carriage, the hump was everything, a kind of inertia, a kind of emptiness, a dullness of desire and intellect and conscience and hope and human sensibility. Their principles were in their feet. Their calculations were biological. They had no sense of strategy or mission. They searched the villages without knowing what to look for, not caring, kicking over jars of rice, frisking children and old men, blowing tunnels, sometimes setting fires and sometimes not, then forming up and moving on to the next village, then other villages, where it would always be the same. They carried their own lives. The pressures were enormous. In the heat of early afternoon, they would remove their helmets and flak jackets, walking bare, which was dangerous but which helped ease the strain. They would often discard things along the route of march. Purely for comfort, they would throw away rations, blow their Claymores and grenades, no matter, because by nightfall the resupply choppers would arrive with more of the same, then a day or two later still more, fresh watermelons and crates of ammunition and sunglasses and woolen sweaters—the resources were stunning—sparklers for the Fourth of July, colored eggs for Easter—it was the great American war chest—the fruits of science, the smokestacks, the canneries, the arsenals at Hartford, the Minnesota forests, the machine shops, the vast fields of corn and wheat—they carried like freight trains; they carried it on their backs and shoulders—and for all the ambiguities of Vietnam, all the mysteries and unknowns, there was at least the single abiding certainty that they would never be at a loss for things to carry.

After the chopper took Lavender away, Lieutenant Jimmy Cross led his men into the village of Than Khe. They burned everything. They shot chickens and dogs, they trashed the village well, they called in artillery and watched the wreckage, then they marched for several hours through the hot afternoon, and then at dusk, while Kiowa explained how Lavender died, Lieutenant Cross found himself trembling.

He tried not to cry. With his entrenching tool, which weighed five pounds, he began digging a hole in the earth.

He felt shame. He hated himself. He had loved Martha more than his men, and as a consequence Lavender was now dead, and this was something he would have to carry like a stone in his stomach for the rest of the war.

All he could do was dig. He used his entrenching tool like an ax, slashing, feeling both love and hate, and then later, when it was full dark, he sat at the bottom of his foxhole and wept. It went on for a long while. In part, he was grieving for Ted Lavender, but mostly it was for Martha, and for himself, because she belonged to another world, which was not quite real, and because she was a junior at Mount Sebastian College in New Jersey, a poet and a virgin and uninvolved, and because he realized she did not love him and never would.

Like cement, Kiowa whispered in the dark. I swear to God—boom-down. Not a word.

I've heard this, said Norman Bowker.

A pisser, you know? Still zipping himself up. Zapped while zipping.

All right, fine. That's enough.

Yeah, but you had to see it, the guy just—

I *heard*, man. Cement. So why not shut the fuck *up*?

Kiowa shook his head sadly and glanced over at the hole where Lieutenant Jimmy Cross sat watching the night. The air was thick and wet. A warm, dense fog had settled over the paddies and there was the stillness that precedes rain.

After a time Kiowa sighed.

One thing for sure, he said. The lieutenant's in some deep hurt. I mean that crying jag—the way he was carrying on—it wasn't fake or anything, it was real heavy-duty hurt. The man cares.

Sure, Norman Bowker said.

Say what you want, the man does care.

We all got problems.

Not Lavender.

No, I guess not, Bowker said. Do me a favor, though.

Shut up?

That's a smart Indian. Shut up.

Shrugging, Kiowa pulled off his boots. He wanted to say more, just to lighten up his sleep, but instead he opened his New Testament and arranged it beneath his head as a pillow. The fog made things seem hollow and unattached. He tried not to think about Ted Lavender, but then he was thinking how fast it was, no drama, down and dead, and how it was hard to feel anything except surprise. It seemed unchristian. He wished he could find some great sadness, or even anger, but the emotion wasn't there and he couldn't make it happen. Mostly he felt pleased to be alive. He liked the smell of the New Testament under his cheek, the leather and ink and paper and glue, whatever the chemicals were. He liked hearing the sounds of night. Even his fatigue, it felt fine, the stiff muscles and the prickly awareness of his own body, a floating feeling. He enjoyed not being dead. Lying there, Kiowa admired Lieutenant Jimmy Cross's capacity for grief. He wanted to share the man's pain, he wanted to care as Jimmy Cross cared. And yet when he closed his eyes, all he could think was Boom-down, and all he could feel was the pleasure of having his boots off and the fog curling in around him and the damp soil and the Bible smells and the plush comfort of night.

After a moment Norman Bowker sat up in the dark.

What the hell, he said. You want to talk, *talk*. Tell it to me.

Forget it.

No, man, go on. One thing I hate, it's a silent Indian.

For the most part they carried themselves with poise, a kind of dignity. Now and then, however, there were times of panic, when they squealed or wanted to squeal but couldn't, when they twitched and made moaning sounds and covered their heads and said Dear Jesus and flopped around on the earth and fired their weapons blindly and cringed and sobbed and begged for the noise to stop and went wild and made stupid promises to themselves and to God and to their mothers and fathers, hoping not to die. In different ways, it happened to all of them. Afterward, when the firing ended, they would blink and peek up. They would touch their bodies, feeling shame, then quickly hiding it. They would force themselves to stand. As if in slow motion, frame by frame, the world would take on the old logic—absolute silence, then the wind, then sunlight, then voices. It was the burden of being alive. Awkwardly, the men would reassemble themselves, first in private, then in groups, becoming soldiers again. They would repair the leaks in their eyes. They would repair the leaks in their eyes. They would check for casualties, call in dust offs, light cigarettes, try to smile, clear their throats and spit and begin cleaning their weapons. After a time someone would shake his head and say, No lie, I almost shit my pants, and someone else would laugh, which meant it was bad, yes, but the guy had obviously not shit his pants, it wasn't that bad, and in any case nobody would ever do such a thing and then go ahead and talk about it. They would squint into the dense, oppressive sunlight. For a few moments, perhaps, they would fall silent, lighting a joint and tracking its passage from man to man, inhaling, holding in the humiliation. Scary stuff, one of them might say. But then someone else would grin or flick his eyebrows and say, Roger-dodger, almost cut me a new asshole, *almost*.

There were numerous such poses. Some carried themselves with a sort of wistful resignation, others with pride or stiff soldierly discipline or good humor or macho zeal. They were afraid of dying but they were even more afraid to show it.

They found jokes to tell.

They used a hard vocabulary to contain the terrible softness. *Greased*, they'd say. *Offed, lit up, zapped while zipping*. It wasn't cruelty, just stage presence. They were actors. When someone died, it wasn't quite dying, because in a curious way it seemed scripted, and because they had their lines mostly memorized, irony mixed with tragedy, and because they called it by other names, as if to encyst and destroy the reality of death itself. They kicked corpses. They cut off thumbs. They talked grunt lingo. They told stories about Ted Lavender's supply of tranquilizers, how the poor guy didn't feel a thing, how incredibly tranquil he was.

There's a moral here, said Mitchell Sanders.

They were waiting for Lavender's chopper, smoking the dead man's dope.

The moral's pretty obvious, Sanders said, and winked. Stay away from drugs. No joke, they'll ruin your day every time.

Cute, said Henry Dobbins.

Mind-blower, get it? Talk about wiggy. Nothing left, just blood and brains.

They made themselves laugh.

There it is, they'd say. Over and over—there it is, my friend, there it is—as if the repetition itself were an act of poise, a balance between crazy and almost crazy, knowing without going, there it is, which meant be cool, let it ride, because Oh yeah, man, you can't change what can't be changed, there it is, there it absolutely and positively and fucking well *is*.

They were tough.

They carried all the emotional baggage of men who might die. Grief, terror, love, longing—these were intangibles, but the intangibles had their own mass and specific gravity, they had tangible weight. They carried shameful memories. They carried the common secret of cowardice barely restrained, the instinct to run or freeze or hide, and in many respects this was the heaviest burden of all, for it could never be put down, it required perfect balance and perfect posture. They carried their reputations. They carried the soldier's greatest fear, which was the fear of blushing. Men killed, and died, because they were embarrassed not to. It was what had brought them to the war in the first place, nothing positive, no dreams of glory or honor, just to avoid the blush of dishonor. They died so as not to die of embarrassment. They crawled into tunnels and walked point and advanced under fire. Each morning, despite the unknowns, they made their legs move. They endured. They kept humping. They did not submit to the obvious alternative, which was simply to close the eyes and fall. So easy, really. Go limp and tumble to the ground and let the muscles unwind and not speak and not budge until your buddies picked you up and lifted you into the chopper that would roar and dip its nose and carry you off to the world. A mere matter of falling, yet no one ever fell. It was not courage, exactly; the object was not valor. Rather, they were too frightened to be cowards.

By and large they carried these things inside, maintaining the masks of composure. They sneered at sick call. They spoke bitterly about guys who had found release by shooting off their own toes or fingers. Pussies, they'd say. Candyasses. It was fierce, mocking talk, with only a trace of envy or awe, but even so, the image played itself out behind their eyes.

They imagined the muzzle against flesh. Nothing to it: squeeze the trigger and blow away a toe. They imagined it. They imagined the quick, sweet pain, then the evacuation to Japan, then a hospital with warm beds and cute geisha nurses.

And they dreamed of freedom birds.

At night, on guard, staring into the dark, they were carried away by jumbo jets. They felt the rush of takeoff. *Gone!* they yelled. And then velocity—wings and engines—a smiling stewardess—but it was more than a plane, it was a real bird, a big sleek silver bird with feathers and talons and high screeching. They were flying. The weights fell off; there was nothing to fear. They laughed and held on tight, feeling the cold slap of wind and altitude, soaring, thinking *It's over, I'm gone!*—they were naked, they were light and free—it was all lightness, bright and fast and buoyant, light as light, a helium buzz in the brain, a giddy bubbling in the lungs as they were taken up over the clouds and the war, beyond duty, beyond gravity and mortification and global entanglements—*Sin loi!* they yelled, *I'm sorry, motherfuckers, but I'm out of it, I'm goofed, I'm on a space cruise, I'm gone!* and it was a restful, unencumbered sensation, just riding the light waves, sailing that big silver freedom bird over the mountains and oceans, over America, over the farms and great sleeping cities and cemeteries and highways and the Golden Arches of McDonald's, it was flight, a kind of fleeing, a kind of falling, falling higher and higher, spinning off the edge of the earth and beyond the sun and through the vast, silent vacuum where there were no burdens and where everything weighed exactly nothing—*Gone!*—they screamed, *I'm sorry but I'm gone!*—and so at night, not quite dreaming, they gave themselves over to lightness, they were carried, they were purely borne.

On the morning after Ted Lavender died, First Lieutenant Jimmy Cross crouched at the bottom of his foxhole and burned Martha's letters. Then he burned the two photographs. There was a steady rain falling, which made it difficult, but he used heat tabs and Sterno to build a small fire, screening it with his body, holding the photographs over the tight blue flame with the tips of his fingers.

He realized it was only a gesture. Stupid, he thought. Sentimental, too, but mostly just stupid.

Lavender was dead. You couldn't burn the blame.

Besides, the letters were in his head. And even now, without photographs, Lieutenant Cross could see Martha playing volleyball in her white gym shorts and yellow T-shirt. He could see her moving in the rain.

When the fire died out, Lieutenant Cross pulled his poncho over his shoulders and ate breakfast from a can.

There was no great mystery, he decided.

In those burned letters Martha had never mentioned the war, except to say, Jimmy, take care of yourself. She wasn't involved. She signed the letters Love, but it wasn't love, and all the fine lines and technicalities did not matter. Virginity was no longer an issue. He hated her. Yes, he did. He hated her. Love, too, but it was a hard, hating kind of love.

The morning came up wet and blurry. Everything seemed part of everything else, the fog and Martha and the deepening rain.

He was a soldier, after all.

Half smiling, Lieutenant Jimmy Cross took out his maps. He shook his head hard, as if to clear it, then bent forward and began planning the day's march. In ten minutes, or maybe twenty, he would rouse the men and they would pack up and head west, where the maps showed the country to be green and inviting. They would do what they had always done. The rain might add some weight, but otherwise it would be one more day layered upon all the other days.

He was realistic about it. There was that new hardness in his stomach. He loved her but he hated her.

No more fantasies, he told himself.

Henceforth, when he thought about Martha, it would be only to think that she belonged elsewhere. He would shut down the daydreams. This was not Mount Sebastian, it was another world, where there were no pretty poems or midterm exams, a place where men died because of carelessness and gross stupidity. Kiowa was right. Boom-down, and you were dead, never partly dead.

Briefly, in the rain, Lieutenant Cross saw Martha's gray eyes gazing back at him.

He understood.

It was very sad, he thought. The things men carried inside. The things men did or thought they had to do.

The things men did or felt they had to do.

He almost nodded at her, but didn't.

Instead he went back to his maps. He was now determined to perform his duties firmly and without negligence. It wouldn't help Lavender, he knew that, but from this point on he would comport himself as an officer. He would dispose of his good-luck pebble. Swallow it, maybe, or use Lee Strunk's slingshot, or just drop it along the trail. On the march he would impose strict field discipline. He would be careful to send out flank security, to prevent straggling or bunching up, to keep his troops moving at the proper pace and at the proper interval. He would insist on clean weapons. He would confiscate the remainder of Lavender's dope. Later in the day, perhaps, he would call the men together and speak to them plainly. He would accept the blame for what had happened to Ted Lavender. He would be a man about it. He would look them in the eyes, keeping his chin level, and he would issue the new SOPs in a calm, impersonal tone of voice, a lieutenant's voice, leaving no room for argument or discussion. Commencing immediately, he'd tell them, they would no longer abandon equipment along the route of march. They would police up their acts. They would get their shit together, and keep it together, and maintain it neatly and in good working order.

He would not tolerate laxity. He would show strength, distancing himself.

Among the men there would be grumbling, of course, and maybe worse, because their days would seem longer and their loads heavier, but Lieutenant Cross reminded himself that his obligation was not to be loved but to lead. He would dispense with love; it was not now a factor. And if anyone quarreled or complained, he would simply tighten his lips and arrange his shoulders in the correct command posture. He might give a curt little nod. Or he might not. He might just shrug and say, Carry on, then they would saddle up and form into a column and move out toward the villages west of Than Khe.

Marry the One Who Gets There First: Outtakes from the Sheidegger-Krupnik Wedding Album

Heidi Julavits

Photo 1 *June Sheidegger, maid of honor, leans on the porch railing of the Rocky Mountain Lodge.*

Violet's younger sister, June, refuses to wear a slip beneath her sheer silk bridesmaid dress. The startling views of the Sawtooth Range serve as only a momentary distraction from the unfettered swell of June's behind inside the peach fabric, indicating that June also decided to forgo underwear.

Photo 2 *Violet, half dressed, sits before a map of Idaho (circa 1921) while her Grandma Rose pins hot rollers in her hair.*

Earlier in the week, Violet had pored over maps in the Lower Stanley Municipal Building. Violet is a psychology student and an advocate of an experimental method called "language therapy." (Her first paper, "Alleviate Chronic Depression Through Positive Word Usage," has just been accepted at an on-line 'zine called "Psyched!") Thus, she is reluctant to be wed in a place called Lower Stanley. She hoped that a close examination of the zoning maps would reveal that the Rocky Mountain Lodge is actually part of the adjacent township, Diamond Heights.

While Violet fretted over fragile, unwieldy acres of paper, Louis, her husband-to-be, entertained himself with a dirty manila file he found marked SURVEYORS. Now that both his parents are dead, Louis runs the family business—Krupnik Bros. Photographic Supplies and Development—located on the Lower East Side of Manhattan. Unlike his fiancée, he thinks *lower* connotes the humble foundation upon which an island of steel and striving depends.

SURVEYORS contained snapshots of WPA workers from the thirties. All the images were identical save one—strangely enough, a photo of a newly wed couple on the porch of what appeared to be the Rocky Mountain Lodge. Indeed, written on the back was the inscription I KNEW FROM THE MOMENT I SAW HER. STAN AND RHODA, ROCKY MOUNTAIN LODGE, 9/5/33.

Louis wondered how Stan could have been so sure and pegged him as a cocky unimaginative bastard. Still, he believed that this photograph, so out of place amongst the saddle-faced ditchdiggers, was meant as a sign to him, Louis Krupnik: Orphan, Pessimist, Voyeur, Liar.

He shoved the photograph into the pocket of his windbreaker.

Photo 3 *June sorts through a shoe box of letters in front of the lodge's big stone fireplace.*

As the fire crackles and the morning light grows stronger and higher through the lodge windows, June cuts the blue stationery into careful strips and returns them, gently, to the shoe box.

Photo 4 *Violet, flipping through a fashion magazine while receiving a pedicure, holds up a headline*—15 WAYS TO LOOK GOOD NAKED AND WIN THE MAN OF YOUR DREAMS.

Louis was the sort of man who had a drawerful of T-shirts emblazoned with the names of women's fashion magazines. At first, Violet mistook this for the seething undercurrent of Louis's anima. Later, she realized there was a predatory subtext to his T-shirts that she'd chosen, optimistically, not to see. Instead of the one-word innocence of *Vogue* and *Seventeen*, it was "(I slept with a girl who works at) *Seventeen*" and "(I slept with a girl who works at) *Vogue*." And he had. Normally this did not bother her, except when he moved inside of her and it seemed nothing less than a vise grip could coax him into coming.

It's all those girls, she'd think. His prick was a jaded, callused bit of flesh—senseless as a carpenter's thumb. She dreamed of taking a pumice stone to that hardened knob the way the pedicurist sands away at her thick heels, flesh falling like sawdust into the metal sink. She would make it raw and new and hers.

Photo 5 *As Louis and Bart toss a football on the lodge's front lawn, Bart throws long, driving Louis backward into a bramble bush.*

Louis's first date with Violet ended well—the two of them kissing frantically between bushes in a small park near the Hudson River—though the beginning was far from promising. Talking to Violet was like talking to a wine expert, insofar as she found soaring, unlikely virtues in the most basic things. The restaurant he chose was "clerical yet stately," the minestrone soup "balmy and supine," his blue shirt "refreshingly insouciant." At first, he found her relentless chirping nauseating. The restaurant's most distinguishing feature, truth be told, was that it owed him a free dinner, the soup was obviously from a can, and the shirt was stolen.

After a few decanters of rotgut ("spirited," "tumescent") Chianti, however, Violet in her fluffy sweater became increasingly irresistible. By 2:00 A.M., they found themselves rolling around the stale city grass of a tiny park. Violet would later insist that it was her "positive speech" that made Louis change his mind about her, but he maintained, stubbornly, that it was nothing but the wine talking.

Photo 6 *A football, poorly thrown, spooks a horse.*

Norton Black, stable hand at the Rocky Mountain Lodge, is accustomed to bearing the brunt of the guests' stupidity. He picks himself out of the arroyo where his horse has just tossed him. Goddamned weddings every weekend, he thinks. Marrying soft-footed city kids who fancy themselves pioneers.

He brushes off his Wranglers and bullets back the football. It punches Mr. Shitty Quarterback square in the diaphragm.

"Hey, man, really sorry about that," Mr. Shitty Quarterback gasps, winded, obviously scared to offer Norton a hand for fear he'll tear it off.

Norton doesn't give the guy the satisfaction of an answer. He cracks his knuckles as he goes to fetch his horse. In truth, he's not mad at this skinny rich guy or his horse, or anything. Life has never been particularly good to Norton Black, and he sees no reason why it should change its tune today.

Photo 7 *Grandma Rose Sheidegger, arranging flowers on the fireplace mantel, knocks a glass vase to the floor.*

Grandma Rose, like most women of her era, believed in omens and structured her life decisions respectfully around her debatable interpretations of them. She knew, for example, the morning she awoke to a squirrel noisily turning a bone around and around in the copper rain gutter outside her bedroom window that it was time to cut her long, red hair. Likewise, she knew when she met Joe Sheidegger that he was to be her husband. Never mind that he smelled foreign and always would. They were drinking champagne at the Essex Hotel, and Rose, in her nervousness, knocked her flute to the floor. Joe soothed her immediately by saying, "It is better to be a crystal and be broken than to remain perfect like a tile on a housetop." She knew it as a Chinese proverb oft repeated by her own grandfather. In a world full of empty coincidences and accidents, she read this as an omen of their fated union.

Photo 8 *Louis, fresh from the shower, snaps a self-portrait in his towel.* No man could ever accuse him of being unromantic. A thief, perhaps, a pervert, even, but not unromantic. Had he learned nothing from his father? Had he not witnessed Saul Krupnik waste his youth and health on a store, eventually succumbing to an aneurysm directly attributable to the late shipment of the new Fuji X2oo telephoto lens? Had he not watched his mother, Ida, endure unloved by Saul until her heart turned small and mean and weak?

Louis was not the man his father was—the straight man, the coldly determined man, the man without lust. He began what he called the Krupnik Variation during his high school vacations, when he was responsible for slipping the sheeny new photos into yellow envelopes. At first, Louis felt guilty about flipping through the images before putting them behind the appropriate alphabetized tab. Then, he became entranced by the odd pieces of the world people found worth preserving—a door with a brass street number, a tin of muffins, the mole on a woman's forearm.

It was only when he stumbled across the raven-haired girl wearing a red dress in front of a Ferris wheel that he realized his transgression had been in the service of a divine search all along. Here, the Girl of his Dreams.

Photo 9 *Margie Adams, covered in pastry flour, blushes as June catches her licking the buttercream frosting off the feet of a plastic bride and groom.*

In addition to being an accomplished pastry chef, Margie Adams is also Grandma Rose and Grandpa Joe's live-in caretaker, a sprightly yet solidly muscular woman who June is convinced is a lesbian. It is for her sake that June has neglected to wear underwear, in hopes that it will distract

Margie from the oddity of her request to bake a boxful of shredded blue paper into the wedding cake.

"Fortunes," June explains, smiling in that sweet, lying way she imagines Margie will find irresistible.

Photo 10 *Violet does the Dance of the Tacky Wedding Presents in her satin panties, holding a salad bowl over her bare breasts.*

The bowl is hand-painted with a ring of purple coyotes howling at nothing. Violet hates it.

Later, as she is composing an insincere thank-you note, Violet will think of her own family's salad bowl. She remembers also serving platters, salt and pepper shakers, pots and pans, silver trivets, all the utilitarian things that were selected, she assumed, with exquisite care by her parents. Now she realizes that her parents probably received their family salad bowl as a wedding gift, an object that neither had cared for much but that they needed and therefore kept. These were the precious relics of her childhood—these accidental, unwanted things.

Photo 11 *Louis, walking to his rented minivan to get his cuff links, sees June on the porch, examining her reflection in the window.*

She is outside; he is inside. It is precisely as it was the first time he laid eyes on her. He almost makes the same mistake, too, thinking she is gazing with such intensity at him instead of her own reflection. He was in a bookstore in San Francisco. June was (she defensively claimed) merely checking to make sure her earrings weren't half slipped from her ears. She had just pulled her sweater over her head, and she had lost more than a few single earrings that way. Honestly, she'd prefer to lose the pair. She was an advocate of the clean break, she informed him. Nothing to be gained by retaining the partial remainder of a previous whole, there to niggle you every time you open your jewelry box with the things you've lost in life.

He had followed her from the bookstore to a café, recognizing her as the Girl of his Dreams. He also found familiar her calculated attempts to make something different of herself.

Afterward, he wondered if she would have slept with him if he hadn't just been visiting friends for the weekend, if she'd never learned that he actually lived in New York. Suddenly, he loomed as an opportunity to be missed, a potential regret, rather than a local stranger full of possibilities.

Photo 12 *Violet and June's brother Bart, armed with a fleur-de-lis linen napkin, flogs their mother, Tenny Sheidegger, who realized too late that the florist forgot to de-pistil the lilies.*

Bart will never beat his future wife, but he will spend thousands of dollars on a dominatrix service whose billed charges (poorly masquerading as a culinary-supply store called the Whip and Spoon) will be found on Bart's Visa statement by his wife, causing her to reflect lovingly on the inherent Weakness of Men.

Photo 13 *Grandma Rose Sheidegger, crying at the prenuptial luncheon.*

Joe, her husband, has refused to let her have a second helping of turkey tetrazzini and a refill of coffee. He barks and Rose starts to cry. Without a word, he lays his napkin over his uneaten lunch and leaves the dining room.

"He always makes me leave before I'm ready," Rose whimpers to Margie. "Last wedding we went to, I wanted to keep dancing."

Rose looks despondently down the lodge drive at the two wheel ruts that grow closer and closer together as they roll down the hill. Somehow they strike her as dishonest, these two lines pressed into the earth. She feels they should move farther apart as they reach for the far-off horizon. She stands to get a better look, hoping that the two ruts diverge farther on, and knocks her juice glass onto the wide-plank floor.

Rose regards the shattered bits hatefully, as if they had exposed her.

"I married the wrong man," Rose says to Margie loudly and slowly, as if she were hard-of-hearing like Joe. Rose holds Margie's wrist for balance as she steps on the shards of glass with her heel, grinding them into a sharp, iridescent snow.

Photo 14 *Louis nicks himself shaving as he notices June in the mirror, visible on the lawn through his bathroom window.*

When did he first know? Certainly not in San Francisco. He and Violet had only just begun to date, and he didn't think he even knew she had sister. It wasn't until he went to the Sheideggers' summer house on Lake Sunapee for the Fourth of July weekend that the two Junes merged into one spirited dark-haired girl, a bikini strap drifting down her tan shoulder and her hips bound low with a towel batiked by boat grease and wood varnish. He was looking out the picture window, and she was looking in, fiddling with her bare earlobes and appearing to be searching for no one but him.

Photo 15 *June, looking at a photograph.*

It's a self-timed picture of her and Louis in the Eagle's Nest, the small guest shack at Lake Sunapee hidden from the main house behind a tightly ivied trellis. They are both naked beneath a Hudson Bay blanket. The light in the cabin was so poor that their faces moon out from the shadows of the bunk bed, rounder and whiter than they must have been on a holiday weekend in July.

She can remember full well where Violet was—at her friend Susie Minturn's Peace Corps send-off party (two years in Botswana, an unlikely career choice for someone as committed to leg waxing as Susie). Violet asked her to "keep Louis entertained" because Violet was as blond and stupid as June was dark and wise. So there they were, in a shack that smelled of kerosene and pine needles and mold, listening to the water lap viciously at the small stone beach every time a water-skier whished by. Louis loved her then with a power that pried his ribs apart, she could tell.

It was her idea to take the picture. He was reluctant for the obvious reasons, but then his love of perversity overrode reason. Or maybe it was because June insisted so tenaciously, knowing that he would require this sort of evidence loose in the world in order to love her. Then he would be able to encounter it accidentally and spy on a framed snippet of passion. He could make it his, but only if it seemed he was stealing it from a stranger.

Photo 16 *Grandpa Joe starts the car, leaving his weepy wife behind.*

He starts these fights intentionally. He wouldn't want to hurt Rose, so he feels it's better she doesn't know the truth. He looks at the map again to measure the distance to the nearest Indian reservation. Fifteen miles. He feels the folded bills in his pocket thick as a heart and readies himself for the quick banter around the craps table. It makes him think of the mah-jongg parlor he visited just before he took Rose on their first date. The boss, Jimmy Wong, made him memorize some Chinese saying about roof tiles. "Works ladies like charm," Jimmy assured him. It was the first and only time Jimmy hadn't cheated the daylights out of him.

Photo 17 *Violet wearing her bathrobe, hair wet and uncombed, makes a call from an outside pay phone near the open kitchen windows.*

She can smell her own wedding feast in its nascent stages, the ghosts of wilting onions and browning garlic escaping through the greasy screens. She can hear the mindless banter of the summer lodge staff—underage, ill-at-ease college students from Massachusetts, Virginia, Vermont—as they gossip about what a slut Hope is, sleeping with the stable guy so he'll buy her beer. Norton is his name, a hayseed endowed with a penis not entirely dissimilar to that of his equestrian charges. She can't help but pick up the undertones of envy and admiration they feel for Hope the Slut, and possibly longing that she share some of her wanton-woman's bounty with them—Schlitz, Weidemann's, Old Milwaukee.

Violet imagines herself sneaking a few six-packs into the kitchen for these mean, thirsty kids in ski-resort T-shirts and Tevas, but then she stops herself. She is no fairy godmother. Violet has made a life out of knowing others' secrets and desires. She likes to be able to look through people and interpret their promises and loyalties as the ragged, halfhearted things that they are. If she can't control the way people desire her, at least she can comfort herself with the knowledge that she has spied on what lives in their hearts.

Photo 18 *Louis, buttoning his tux trousers, reaches into the back pocket and pulls out an envelope.*

Of course Louis found them. To his credit, his father was half smart about hiding the photos. But Louis discovered them anyway after Saul died, tucked in his leather account ledger. The Ferris wheel rose behind them. The woman wore a red dress and a mink stole that had once belonged to Ida but otherwise bore scant resemblance to his mother. Looking at the photos, Louis couldn't decide which disturbed him more—the fact that his father was actually a cheating, lying bastard or that he was too damned cheap to buy the poor girl her own fur. Then he realized what bothered him most was how eerily similar the photo of his father's mistress was to that of the Girl of his Dreams and how distastefully his current situation with June and Violet Sheidegger mirrored that of his father.

He closed the ledger, feeling ill. As he left the office, he was unable to shake the echoes of his father's business mantra from his head.

"Give a man incentive to buy," his father had always told him. "Two for the price of one, boy. Two for the price of one."

Photo 19 *June in the lodge kitchen, contemplating a cockroach on the wall.*

If only June had been a fly on the wall, or even a cockroach, for that matter, just to know what had transpired to make Louis send her that Dear June letter on his signature blue stationery.

"Get rid of my letters," his final missive demanded. "Shred them. Bury them. I don't care. Just get rid of them."

June looks at the wedding cake, basking on a silver tray in all its frilly splendor, and smiles.

Such a good girl for a change. She has done exactly as he requested.

Photo 20 *Louis fingers a man's antique watch as he stares at his reflection in the dressing-room mirror.*

The watch was given to his father by his mother on their wedding day. It is gold with a bracelet band. Saul stopped wearing it because it gave him a rash, so his mother wore it instead. She wore it until the day before she died, when Louis visited her at the hospital.

"Get out!" she screamed, hurling the watch at him. It hit the wall next to his head, the crystal cracking like a delicate bone.

"Mother, it's Louis," Louis said. She thought he was his dead father. It made him wince.

"The one, the one, you were *the one*. Bah!" Ida spat at him, but the saliva landed on her chin, making a dark stain on her blue-paper hospital robe.

Louis put the broken watch in his coat and closed the door behind him.

He sat on a park bench across from the hospital and watched the pigeons feed on old peanut hulls. As he rummaged for the watch in his pocket, a shard of glass cut him. He sucked his finger as he flipped the watch over with his free hand. TO THE ONE OF MY DREAMS, the inscription read. IDA 12/3/62.

What a fucking trap, he thought. He reached into his pocket for the Girl of his Dreams, bent on tearing her to shreds, but found he had left the photo in another coat.

Suddenly he felt the glass wiggle free of his wound along with a sweet string of blood. Without thinking twice, he swallowed the shard, feeling it scrape past his throat, his larynx, lodging, finally, somewhere near his heart.

Photo 21 *June and Susie Minturn, wearing their matching brides-maid dresses, speak briefly as they apply their lipstick in the washroom.*

June, making small talk, asks Susie how long ago she returned from Botswana. Susie, bewildered, clarifies that she's been living in Atlanta for the past three years as a buyer for a southern department-store chain called Bink's. Susie (Susan, now) has embraced the South completely, finding it to be a far more refined existence. Even the drunks are elegant in Atlanta, she will later tell Bart as he undresses her at the EZ Sleep Motel. Bart will not be able to get it up, and Susan will lie awake as he snores, naked, beside her. She will feel strangely proud of herself as if she'd beaten him at a game women aren't supposed to win, like one-on-one basketball. From the onset of their lives together, Susan's love for her future husband, Bart Sheidegger, is inextricably linked with pity, as well as a heady feeling of superiority.

Photo 22 *Violet at the pay phone, wearing her wedding dress, her hair still in curlers.*

Maybe it was revenge.

Maybe if she hadn't trapped them together in the Eagle's Nest, she wouldn't have exuded the sort of proud, spurned rawness that is so attractive to certain kinds of men, men composed of impulses both carnivorous and maternal.

His name was Shane, a perfectly hushed, ethereal name for a man whose life was committed to adoring things he could never have. She began spending one night a week, then two, then three, sitting in one of Shane's cracked French-leather armchairs, listening to Frank Sinatra recordings and drinking the fine, pale West Indian rum Shane poured into her tumbler. She was intrigued by a certain saintly quality in him, an excessive goodness always verging on perversity.

She lied to Louis, telling him she'd picked up a private tutorial in Queens. Shane insisted on paying her to offset suspicions. Maybe that's why she let him touch her the way she did. He had a signet ring that he liked to press over her eyelids, branding her with his initials so that his ownership would be clear every time she blinked.

Returning to Louis on the train, she would finger the twenties Shane gave her and not feel the slightest twinge of guilt. Rather, she reasoned she was developing her own secrets, her own desires, her own darknesses, that she was no longer the obvious blonde optimist, the girl with her heart on her sleeve, the girl who cheerily urged people to use words like *upper* instead of *lower*, the girl too stupid to know the thrill one can get from deception.

Photo 23 *Louis and June, arguing behind the horse stables before the ceremony.*

June, panicked, has just told Louis that Susie Minturn never went to Botswana.

"Violet framed us," June says.

Louis feels not so much guilty as foolish. She's beaten him at his own game. The thought of being watched is something he's never in his life considered happening to him. He finds it gives him a shiver of something he can't name—loathing, excitement, he isn't sure.

June looks at him all cow-eyed, petting her evening bag. Louis grabs the bag and pushes a rough hand into its silky interior. He pulls out the photo of the two of them at the Eagle's Nest.

"*How dare you,*" he hisses, shaking the photograph in her face.

She tries to snatch it back from him but he holds it high over his head, ripping it into tiny pieces.

The sun shines through her gauzy dress and he can see everything about her. He throws her away from him, disgusted. Just like every other fucking woman, he mutters to himself as he heads back to the lodge. It's not that Louis doesn't like women. He's just disgusted with June for advertising herself as something different.

Not like Violet, he finds himself thinking proudly as he stalks back to the chapel to be married. All along, Violet had him believing she was just another girl when actually she was a soul cut from the same devious cloth.

Photo 24 *Violet stands at the pay phone with the wind blowing her veil over her face.*

Again, the answering machine picks up, the man's voice woven through faint strains of Sinatra. *"I'm not in right now, but if you leave your name and number . . ."*

Violet starts to speak but then goes silent. Instead, she holds the receiver out toward the Sawtooth Range so that she can record for Shane the eagles circling around the snow-capped peaks, the lemony late-afternoon sunshine, the way she feels mere moments before she exchanges her wedding vows. And how *does* she feel? She isn't sure precisely, but a part of her believes she must find meaning in the fact that Shane was not home to comfort her, that she has been pushed to do the right thing despite the secret lives she and Louis lead. As she hangs up the phone, she feels claustrophobic, as if the mountains and the air are crushing in on her like a great expanse of possibilities aligning into the sudden, clear trajectory of her life.

Photo 25 *June, crying behind the stables, stabs a hole in the earth with the heel of her silver sandal.*

When the hole is deep enough, she fills it with the torn pieces of the photograph, then pushes the dirt back with her toe. She tamps the earth down. Tamp, tamp, tamp. As a child, she took clogging lessons and the steps come back to her now. One-two-three, one-two-three, tamp-tamp-tamp, tamp-tamp-tamp.

Hands on her hips, she clogs around to the front of the stables but stops when she sees Louis leaning against the side wall. He motions to her to come toward him, quietly. He puts his hands on her shoulders and turns her, pressing himself against her back. They are looking through a large hole in the wall, staring at a man in a cowboy hat with his jeans around his boots, stroking his monstrous hardness with a dusty hand. He stands over a young girl lying naked on a horse blanket, Tevas on her tanned feet. He regards her with eyes that are as wide and blank as a horse's.

June feels Louis start to swell against her gauzy behind. He hugs her tight as if she were anything—a blanket, a pillow, just something to hold on to—as he starts, with great, silent sobs, to cry.

Photo 26 *Louis, frantic, spots June's handbag by the fireplace.*

He is just about to walk to the chapel, located in the middle of a field behind the lodge. He can hear the strains of Mendelssohn's "Wedding March" warbling through the dry grasses. Suddenly he reaches into his tux jacket. No one sees him stuff the envelope of photos inside June's forgotten handbag. No one sees the relief he seems to feel afterward, as if he had just buried a long-sick relative.

Photo 27 *Violet adjusts her garter beneath the chapel door's rough-hewn lintel.*

She can see Louis at the altar, watching her with astonishment, as if she were a statue that had just stepped off its pedestal. He looks at her and she knows, in a glance, that he knows she knows. A shiver goes through her. She enters the chapel.

Photo 28 *Hope, walking up from the stables, buckling her new, big belt.*

She smells the inside of her elbow, because that's where a person stinks of sex if they're going to. All she smells, however, is horse shit and hay. She alternates between feeling lost and victorious, between the sense that she's located something in herself that she never knew existed or lost something forever. It does not occur to her at any point during her walk up the mile-long drive to the lodge that she has experienced both things, that they are one and the same.

Photo 29 *Violet's veil, lying in the road.*

A chuck wagon drives the newlyweds around the property as the guests walk from the chapel to the lodge. Violet's veil snags on a piece of fencing, pulling with it a fake blond braid that lands, coiled and still as a sleeping rattlesnake, in a wheel rut.

Photo 30 *June crouched in the back of the chuck wagon, recently freed of its nuptial cargo.*

In her hand is what appears to be a length of Rapunzel's escape rope. June is in the process of debraiding it with her hot fingers. (It can rescue no one, certainly not her.) Suddenly, without the aid of any reflective surface, she catches a perfect and absurd image of herself—weeping in the back of a chuck wagon, clinging to a piece of fake hair with nails painted a deep, sad red chosen because of its appropriate name (Other Woman)—and for the first time in a long time, she laughs at herself.

Photo 31 *Grandma Rose, fast asleep at the reception.*

In the background, people lunge and twirl on a parquet dance floor. Grandpa Joe has taken off his suit coat to drape around her shoulders while he goes to fetch their Lincoln from the parking lot. He imagines he will read tonight, or maybe play cribbage alone, being first himself, then Rose, trying to forget what he knows of each hand as he switches chairs in the kitchenette. Maybe, however, he will simply turn off the lights and come as close as he ever does to sleep, flipping between the talk shows and the Weather Channel, alone in the world and yet comfortably so, keeping one protective hand on the upturned hip of his sleeping wife.

Photo 32 *Louis and Violet join hands to cut the cake.*

They both notice the strange texture as the knife sinks through the frosting, like rowing a boat through seaweed.

Photo 33 *June hikes her bridesmaid dress up around her thighs.*

She is striking out, lighter, it seems, into the ocean of burnt-yellow hills behind the lodge. The heels of her shoes dip and teeter into snake holes. She whips them off, hurling them into the low-lying scrub and flushing a pair of pheasants. She searches her purse for a hair clip and finds instead three unfamiliar photos.

The first photo is of an old man who vaguely resembles Louis, his arm around a woman in furs who's young enough to be his daughter. The second is an old black-and-white photo of a just-married couple (*"I knew from the moment I saw her*"). The third photo is of a young girl in a red dress at a carnival. They are meaningless pieces of somebody's life, not hers. June throws the photos into the air and watches them as they catch the air currents like birds and swoop away toward the ravine.

Her ethereal figure grows smaller and smaller as she disappears into the setting sun, the sound of the swing band now barely audible as she hears the drum roll, signaling the cutting of the cake.

Photo 34 *Louis and Violet chew, quizzically.*

Louis reaches into his mouth as if he's removing one of the long, blond hairs Violet occasionally cooks into his dinner. He recognizes his handwriting on the strip of blue paper immediately.

"*. . . no one in the world meant for me but you, June . . .*"

Photo 35 *Louis plunges a hand into the center of the cake and emerges with a fistful of its warm, floury innards entwined with little bits of blue paper like worms around a dog's heart.*

He has a mind to suffocate June with the fucking cake, stuff every last confetti-filled piece of it down her vindictive little throat.

As his eyes pass over the crowd, Louis is alarmed to discover he doesn't recognize a single one of the guests, as if he has arrived to be married at the wrong wedding. Strangely, nor does he recognize the woman beside him with whom he grasps a knife handle.

They avoid each other's eyes like two strangers sharing a table in a café. The guests sense their awkwardness and begin to shift and shuffle and buzz.

Suddenly this woman (his wife, he guesses) reaches over and pulls his hand to her lips, the hand that is smeared with buttercream and bits of cake and slips of blue paper. She pushes his fist into her mouth, his knuckles cutting against her sharp teeth. She eats madly—cake, frosting, paper.

At first, he is horrified. Then he finds he has the strongest urge to kiss her. He does exactly that, tasting the mess of cake and buttercream and lipstick and blood from his cut knuckles as the crowd of strangers cheers them on bawdily. He realizes he barely knows this woman with whom he now shares a name, a bed, a life. At the same time, he feels she knows and loves him for all the ways that he has always been unknowable. Though he can't be sure, he senses himself closing in on a mystery that has governed his parents, his grandparents, his great-grandparents, their loves as fated as they are accidental. After a life spying on other people's intimacy, he is suddenly the man on the inside, slightly less bewildered, looking out.

He, too, takes a bite of the cake, eats his words.

Photo 36 *It is nearly dark now.*

The last dusky bits of day cling to the horizon. June trips along the arroyo that hugs the highway, feeling her way with her bare feet. Suddenly, headlights appear over the ridge. They drift across her cautiously, thinking her a ghost. She hears the gears shift and the engine idle.

"Need a lift?"

June looks up. A man in a pickup leans out his window.

"Where are you headed?" she asks.

He nods his head forward. "Up the road a piece. Going to buy some beer."

June considers this for a moment. She's rather thirsty after all her walking.

"A beer sounds good right about now," she replies, and lets herself into the passenger-side door. The man notices her bare feet, but not in a way that indicates he finds it strange.

"Norton Black," he says, holding out a hand. "Nice dress."

"June Sheidegger," she replies, extending hers. "Thanks." She can tell by his tone that he means it.

Norton puts the truck in gear, and the two of them pull away until they are nothing but two taillights against a purpling sky. Maybe they will drive to the store and decide to grab a bite to eat at the steak house, talk about their notions of themselves. Maybe Norton will see in June a strange resemblance to his dead sister and June will admire the way he wears a pocket watch in his jeans like her Grandpa Joe. Maybe they will decide, by the time they've worked their way through their rhubarb pie, that they were made for each other and keep driving into the sunset that faded ages ago. Maybe they will marry and, more often than not, wake up next to each other lonelier than if one of them had slept on the rec-room couch.

But probably they will thrill in telling their kids about that fated evening, and their grandkids. They will talk and talk about the way that love is an obvious thing and how they just *knew*. And maybe on certain evenings— when they're looking at their carefully posed wedding photographs, and the sun is setting, and the air is like it was the night Norton found June barefoot by the road—they'll believe their own tales about how love is a fixed, unquestionable thing, written in stars and in stones.

The Celebrity

John Dos Passos

The young man from the sticks got into the Grand Central Station too late in the day to start attending to the business he'd come for. He stood swinging his suitcase in the middle of the glowing pavement near the information booth. It was a rainy day. The station looked huge and lonely in spite of the late afternoon crowd. Then he suddenly remembered the phone number of the couple he'd met on the French Line boat. He went over to a phone booth and called. She answered. He recognized her voice at once. She said why didn't he come down and have a sandwich with them, she had some interesting people coming for cocktails. He said he'd be tickled to death, hung up, went and checked his bag, and took the subway downtown.

When he got out at Astor Place he had to ask the newsvendor which way was west. He found the house and the right name over a bell. Then he suddenly felt very shy.

After all he didn't know them very well, he didn't know how well he'd be able to keep up with interesting people. He got up his nerve and gave the bell a jab. The latch on the door buzzed. He went up a flight of creaky stairs and there she was holding open a tall white door.

"I hope you're not dreadfully hungry," she said. "Charles Edward Holden is coming and he's always late."

"Not at all . . . Why that's fine," said the young man from the sticks.

He followed her into a long tall room full of people amid cigarette smoke. The husband came up and pressed a pink cocktail into his hand. "He said maybe he'd come," said the husband. "Well here's how."

"Here's how," said the young man from the sticks, blinking a little around the room.

"Mr. Zbsssk . . . Meet Miss Mmmmtbx . . . I'm sure you know Ttm Krmmt."

The couple he'd met on the French Line boat had vanished. The young man from the sticks held tight to his cocktail glass and moistened his lips with his tongue. He looked around at the men's faces and the women's faces and the cocktail glasses and women's hats round about him. Everybody was talking at once.

He approached a long-nosed lanky man who stood by himself with his back to the wall.

"Nasty day," he said.

"In what way?" said the lanky man without looking at him.

"I mean the rain."

"So it's raining is it?" The lanky man took a cigarette out of a fresh package, looked for a moment as if he was going to offer one but thought better of it and put them back in his pocket. The young man from the sticks brought out a cigarette of his own. The lanky man had just blown out his match and stood staring at the ceiling, letting the blue smoke pour out of his large nostrils. The young man began to stammer. He stuck the cigarette unlighted in the corner of his mouth and managed to get the words out, "MMM mister holder . . . what line . . . er . . . is he in?"

"Holdy," said the lanky man turning his back and walking away. "He's shot his bolt."

At that minute a man grabbed the young man from the sticks by the buttons of his vest. "Where was it we met? . . . you tell me . . . I bet you don't remember."

The young man from the sticks shook his head. Then he smiled and held out his hand. "Maybe it was over on the other side," he said.

"No it was somewhere uptown . . . I never forget a face." The man who never forgot a face had a very pink face with circular lines on it. He was pretty well tanked. It looked as if some of the pink from the cocktails had gotten into his face.

"Very interesting people here . . ." the young man began timidly.

"Why kid ourselves?" the man who never forgot a face broke in. He rolled his boiled codfish eyes. "You know and I know that it's not like the old days . . . Don't you old timer?"

The young man nodded and blushed. "But this feller who's coming . . . Mr. Holdy?"

"Nothing but a clique . . . a collection of logrollers . . ." The man who never forgot a face winked. "After all us old newspaper men understand these things."

"Oh I see," said the young man.

The man who never forgot a face took him by the sleeve and led him through the crowd into the back room. "Scotch in here," he whispered mysteriously over his shoulder.

"Oh I see," said the young man.

It was quieter in the back room. It was possible to hear what people said. The couple he'd met on the boat were sitting quietly eating chicken salad with a few friends with whiskies and sodas beside them. "Oh here you are," they cried out with forced brightness.

"I was telling this young man . . . it turns out we're old friends . . . that it's not like the old days at 63 . . . you remember?"

"Or 321," said a sallow woman with a veil on her nose.

"Or at Marian's," sighed the couple he'd met on the French Line boat.

He was settled on the couch beside them with a plate of chicken salad on his knees. He wasn't following the conversation so well. So he spent his time with the supper and the whiskey and soda. The man who never forgot a face was arguing with a haggard-faced man with black eyebrows as to whether Charles Edward Holden was a communist. One man said he was a communist, the other said he was a paid agent of Wall Street. Every now and then the woman the young man had met on the French Line boat leaned forward and said smiling, "But you're both too silly." The haggard-faced man with the black eyebrows finally got to his feet and said Charles Edward Holden ought to be shot against a white wall.

That broke up the group. The young man from the sticks found that he was getting sleepy what with the heat of the room and the scotch on top of the pink cocktail. He got to his feet. The woman he'd met on the French Line boat looked up at him with her handsome tired long-lidded eyes. "You don't think so do you?"

"No indeed," said the young man. He roamed around looking for the bathroom and instead got into the kitchenette where the husband was washing glasses.

"Lemme help you wipe," he said.

"No. I've got a system," said the husband.

"Say won't those birds get into trouble if they talk like that?" The young man jerked his thumb over his shoulder.

"This is a free country."

"I don't mean they're wrong . . . But I've got my living to make," said the young man from the sticks.

"A man's got a right to his opinions," said the husband pouring out the soapy water into the sink.

"Where I come from," said the young man from the sticks, "the Declaration of Independence stirs up a hornet's nest."

When the glasses were washed they went out through the hall to the front room. People had thinned out a little. The man who was talking about shooting them against a white wall strode up to them as they came in waving a crooked forefinger. "Now you're both office workers . . . you tell us what the white-collar classes think about it. Are they coming round to the side of the working class?"

"It takes plenty work to stay in the working class, these days," said the young man from the sticks.

"Do you mean to tell me . . ." the haggard-faced man began.

There were three long rings on the doorbell. Everybody quieted down. "There he is," said somebody.

"Sounds like his ring," said the husband.

The couple the young man had met on the French Line boat went to the door. A small nattily dressed young man came in. "Oh we thought you were Charles Edward Holden," said a girl.

"Well maybe I am," said the new young man. "I've felt funny all day." The remark didn't go so well. You could feel the silence freezing around people's mouths.

"Well I think I'd better be getting along," said the young man from the sticks. He said good-bye to the husband and added, "And thank our charming hostess for me."

In the hall he found his charming hostess and the new young man talking profoundly together. They didn't notice him. Downstairs on the stoop he found the man who never forgot a face. "So it got a bit too dense for you too? . . . When the dear lady has more than three of her beaux present at one time it becomes positively stifling . . . I suppose you know that Holden is the real number one."

"You don't say," said the young man from the sticks, yanking up the collar of his overcoat because it was still drizzling.

"Better come and have a bite to eat. I know a wonderful place . . . almost like the old days. Those stand-up suppers get you in the long run."

"They sure do," said the young man from the sticks.

They went in by a black door through a corridor that smelt of toilets into a stuffy barroom that had a few tables with dirty tablecloths in a row at the end. They sat down at a table and ordered two ryes.

"I know where it was we met . . . It was years ago at Little Hungary."

"But I've never been to Hungary," said the young man from the sticks.

"Sure . . . Here's how . . . I never forget a face . . . Now I sometimes get confused on names."

On the strength of that they had several more ryes with beer chasers. The man who never forgot a face kept seeing people he knew at the bar. They got up and went over to the bar to join the crowd. A stubby girl in a Bulgarian blouse who had come in with two ash-colored young men was warmly greeted as Darling. He put his arm around her neck and started to introduce her all around. When he came to the young man from the sticks he hesitated. "Oh you're getting old," she singsonged. "Can't remember names anymore."

"Sure I can Darling, meet . . . My very dear friend . . . Meet Colonel . . ." The young man from the sticks had put out his hand and was just going to say his name when the man who never forgot a face came out with "Charles Edward Holden."

The girl had a turned-up nose and blue eyes with dark rings under them. The eyes looked up at the young man from the sticks when she shook his hand. "Not really . . . Oh I've so wanted to meet you Mr. Holden . . . I've read every word you ever wrote."

"But I'm not really . . ." he stammered.

"Not really a colonel," said the girl with her voice full of honest understanding.

"Just a colonel for a night," said the man who never forgot a face, with a wave of a hand, and ordered up a round of whiskies.

They went on drinking.

"Oh Mr. Holden," said the girl, who put her whiskies away without water like a trouper, "isn't it wonderful that we should meet like this. I thought you were much older and not nearly so good-looking. Now Mr. Holden I want you to tell me all about everything."

"Better call me Charley."

"My name's Bobbie . . . you'll call me Bobbie won't you?"

She drew him away down towards the empty end of the bar a little. "I was having a rotten time . . . They are dear boys but they won't talk about anything except how Phyllis drank iodine because Edward doesn't love her anymore . . . I hate personalities, don't you? I like to talk about problems and things that count, don't you? I like the kind of people who do things. I mean world conditions, Marxism, books and things like that, don't you? Did you ever read the first chapter of *Capital* out loud?"

"Well maybe," began the young man from the sticks.

The girl was plucking at his sleeve.

"Suppose we go somewhere quiet and talk. I can't hear myself think in here."

"Do you know some place we can dance?" he asked. The girl nodded.

On the street she took his arm. The wind had gone into the north, cold and gusty. They walked east and down a street full of tenements and crowded little Italian stores. The girl rang at the basement door. While they were waiting she put her hand on his arm. "I got some money . . . Let this be my party."

"But I wouldn't like that."

"All right. We'll make it fifty-fifty . . . I believe in sex equality, don't you?"

While they were waiting for the door to open he leaned over and kissed her. Her lips were there all ready. "Oh this is a wonderful evening for me," she said snuggling up to him. "You are the nicest celebrity I ever met . . . Most of them are pretty stuffy, don't you think so? No joy de vivre . . . When we have time I want you to explain to me your theory of the effect of the commodity dollar on working-class consumption." "But," he stammered, "I'm not . . ."

The door opened. "Hello Jimmy," said the girl to a slick-looking young man in a brown suit as they brushed past him into the narrow passage. "Meet the boyfriend . . . Mr. Grady, Mr. Holden." The young man's eyes flashed. "Not Charles Edward . . ." The girl nodded her head excitedly so that a big lock of her hair flopped over one eye. "Well sir, I'm surely happy to meet you . . . I'm a constant reader, sir."

The girl mussed up Jimmy's hair. "He's one of the toughest mugs in Manhattan, but he's very nice to his friends."

Bowing and blushing Jimmy found them a table next to the dance floor in the stuffy little pale pink cabaret hot from the spotlights and the cigarette smoke and the sweat of people dancing. Then she grabbed his hand and pulled him to his feet. They danced. The girl rubbed close to him till he could feel her little round breasts through the Bulgarian blouse. "My the boy can dance," she whispered. "Let's forget everything . . . Who we are . . . the day of the week."

"Me . . . I forgot two hours ago," he said giving her a squeeze.

"You're just a plain farmer lad and I'm a bashful barefoot girl."

"More truth than poetry to that," he said through his teeth.

"Poetry . . . I love poetry, don't you? I like to go up to the roof and read it in the rain . . . I'm a pagan child at heart, aren't you? . . . And then you'll tell me all about your work."

They danced until the place closed up. They were staggering when they got out on the black empty streets. They stumbled past garbage pails. Cats ran out from under their feet. They stopped at a corner to talk about unemployment with a cop. In every dark doorway they stopped and kissed. The milkman with his frame of empties was just coming out of the door of the house where she lived. Overhead the sky was getting haggard. As she was looking for her latchkey in her purse, she whispered thoughtfully: "People who really do things make the most beautiful lovers, don't you think so?"

It was the young man from the sticks who woke up first. Sunlight was pressing in through the uncurtained window. The girl was asleep, her face crushed into the pillow. Her mouth was open and with the deep rings under her eyes she looked considerably older than she had the night before. Her skin was pasty and green and she had stringy hair. He grabbed his clothes and dressed as quietly as he could. His watch had stopped.

Must be late as hell. On a big table deep in dust and littered with drawings of funny-looking nudes, he found a sheet of yellow paper that had half a poem on the back of it. He scribbled on it: Good-bye good luck Chas. Ed. Holden, and tiptoed out the door with his shoes in his hand. He was so afraid she'd wake up that he didn't put on his shoes until he'd gone down three flights to the street door.

The Remobilization of Jacob Horner

John Barth

In September it was time to see the Doctor again: I drove out to the Remobilization Farm the morning during the first week of the month. Because the weather was fine, a number of the Doctor's other patients, quite old men and women, were taking the air, seated in their wheelchairs or in the ancient cane chairs along the porch. As usual, they greeted me a little suspiciously with their eyes; visitors of any sort, but particularly of my age, were rare at the farm, and were not welcomed. Ignoring their stony glances, I went inside to pay my respects to Mrs. Dockey, the receptionist-nurse. I found her in consultation with the Doctor himself.

"Good day, Horner," the Doctor beamed.

"Good morning, sir. Good morning, Mrs. Dockey."

That large, masculine woman nodded shortly without speaking—her custom—and the Doctor told me to wait for him in the Progress and Advice Room, which along with the dining room, the kitchen, the reception room, the bathroom, and the Treatment Room, constituted the first floor of the old frame house. Upstairs the partitions between the original bedrooms had been removed to form two dormitories, one for the men and one for the women. The Doctor had his own small bedroom upstairs, too, and there were two bathrooms. I did not know at that time where Mrs. Dockey slept, or whether she slept at the farm at all. She was a most uncommunicative woman.

I had first met the Doctor quite by chance on the morning of March 17, 1951, in what passes for the grand concourse of the Pennsylvania Railroad Station in Baltimore. It happened to be the day after my twenty-eighth birthday, and I was sitting on one of the benches in the station with my suitcase beside me. I was in an unusual condition: I couldn't move. On the previous day I had checked out of my room in an establishment on St. Paul and 33rd streets owned by the university. I had roomed there since September of the year before when, halfheartedly, I matriculated as a graduate student and began work on the degree that I was scheduled to complete the following June.

But on March 16, my birthday, with my oral examination passed but my master's thesis not even begun, I packed my suitcase and left the room to take a trip somewhere. Because I have learned not to be much interested in causes and biographies, I shall ascribe this romantic move to simple birthday despondency, a phenomenon sufficiently familiar to enough people so that I need not explain it further. Birthday despondency, let us say, had reminded me that I had no self-convincing reason for continuing for a moment longer to do any of the things that I happened to be doing with myself as of seven o'clock on the evening of March 16, 1951. I had thirty dollars and some change in my pocket: when my suitcase was filled I hailed a taxi, went to Pennsylvania Station, and stood in the ticket line.

"Yes?" said the ticket agent when my turn came.

"Ah—this will sound theatrical to you," I said, with some embarrassment, "but I have thirty dollars or so to take a trip on. Would you mind telling me some of the places I could ride to from here for, say, twenty dollars?"

The man showed no surprise at my request. He gave me an understanding if unsympathetic look and consulted some sort of rate scales.

"You can go to Cincinnati, Ohio," he declared. "You can go to Crestline, Ohio. And let's see, now—you can go to Dayton, Ohio. Or Lima, Ohio. That's a nice town. I have some of my wife's people up around Lima, Ohio. Want to go there?"

"Cincinnati, Ohio," I repeated, unconvinced. "Crestline, Ohio; Dayton, Ohio; and Lima, Ohio. Thank you very much. I'll make up my mind and come back."

So I left the ticket window and took a seat on one of the benches in the middle of the concourse to make up my mind. And it was there that I simply ran out of motives, as a car runs out of gas. There was no reason to go to Cincinnati, Ohio. There was no reason to go to Crestline, Ohio. Or Dayton, Ohio; or Lima, Ohio. There was no reason, either, to go back to the apartment hotel, or for that matter to go anywhere. There was no reason to do anything. My eyes, as the German classicist Winckelmann said inaccurately of the eyes of Greek statues, were sightless, gazing on eternity, fixed on ultimacy, and when that is the case there is no reason to do anything—even to change the focus of one's eyes. Which is perhaps why the statues stand still. It is the malady *cosmopsis*, the cosmic view, that afflicted me. When one has it, one is frozen like the bullfrog when the hunter's light strikes him full in the eyes, only with *cosmopsis* there is no hunter, and no quick hand to terminate the moment—there's only the light.

Shortsighted animals all around me hurried in and out of doors leading down to the tracks; trains arrived and departed. Women, children, salesmen, soldiers, and redcaps hurried across the concourse toward immediate destinations, but I sat immobile on the bench. After a while Cincinnati, Crestline, Dayton, and Lima dropped from my mind, and their place was taken by that test-pattern of my consciousness, *Pepsi-Cola hits the spot,* intoned with silent oracularity. But it, too, petered away into the void, and nothing appeared in its stead.

If you look like a vagrant it is difficult to occupy a train-station bench all night, even in a busy terminal, but if you are reasonably well dressed, have a suitcase at your side, and sit erect, policemen and railroad employees will not disturb you. I was sitting in the same place, in the same position, when the sun struck the grimy station windows next morning, and in the nature of the case I suppose I would have remained thus indefinitely, but about nine o'clock a small, dapper fellow in his fifties stepped in front of me and stared directly into my eyes. He was bald, dark-eyed, and dignified, a Negro, and wore a graying mustache and a trim tweed suit to match. The fact that I did not stir even the pupils of my eyes under his gaze is an index to my condition, for ordinarily I find it next to impossible to return the stare of a stranger.

"Weren't you sitting here like this last night?" he asked me sharply. I did not reply. He came close, bent his face down toward mine, and moved an upthrust finger back and forth about two inches from my eyes. But my eyes did not follow his finger. He stepped back and regarded me critically, then snapped his fingers almost on the point of my nose. I blinked involuntarily, although my head did not jerk back.

"Ah," he said, satisfied, and regarded me again. "Does this happen to you often, young man?"

Perhaps because of the brisk assuredness of his voice, the *no* welled up in me like a belch. And I realized as soon as I deliberately held my tongue (there being in the last analysis no reason to answer his question at all) that as of that moment I was artificially prolonging what had been a genuine physical immobility. Not to choose at all is unthinkable: what I had done before was simply choose not to act, since I had been at rest when the situation arose. Now, however, it was harder—"more of a choice," so to speak— to hold my tongue than to croak out something that filled my mouth, and so after a moment I said, "No."

Then, of course, the trance was broken. I was embarrassed, and rose stiffly from the bench to leave.

"Where will you go?" my examiner asked with a smile.

"What?" I frowned at him. "Oh—get a bus home, I guess. See you around."

"Wait." His voice was mild, but entirely commanding. "Won't you have coffee with me? I'm a physician, and I'd be interested in discussing your case."

"I don't have any case," I said awkwardly. "I was just—sitting there for a minute or so."

"No. I saw you there last night at ten o'clock when I came in from New York," the Doctor said. "You were sitting in the same position. You *were* paralyzed, weren't you?"

I laughed. "Well, if you want to call it that; but there's nothing wrong with me. I don't know what came over me."

"Of course you don't, but I do. My specialty is various sorts of physical immobility. You're lucky I came by this morning."

"Oh, you don't understand—"

"I brought you out of it, didn't I?" he said cheerfully. "Here." He took a fifty-cent piece from his pocket and handed it to me and I accepted it before I realized what he'd done. "I can't go into that lounge over there. Go get two cups of coffee for us and we'll sit here a minute and decide what to do."

"No, listen, I—"

"Why not?" He laughed. "Go on, now. I'll wait here."

Why not, indeed?

"I have my own money," I protested lamely, offering him his fifty-cent piece back, but he waved me away and lit a cigar.

"Now, hurry up," he ordered around the cigar. "Move fast, or you might get stuck again. Don't think of anything but the coffee I've asked you to get."

"All right." I turned and walked with dignity toward the lounge, just off the concourse.

"Fast!" The Doctor laughed behind me. I flushed, and quickened my step.

While I waited for the coffee I tried to feel the curiosity about my invalidity and my rescuer that it seemed appropriate I should feel, but I was too weary in mind and body to wonder at anything. I do not mean to suggest that my condition had been unpleasant—it was entirely anesthetic in its advanced stage, and even a little bit pleasant in its inception—but it was fatiguing, as an overlong sleep is fatiguing, and one had the same reluctance to throw it off that one has to get out of bed when one has slept around the clock. Indeed, as the Doctor had warned (it was at this time, not knowing my benefactor's name, that I began to think of him with a capital *D*), to slip back into immobility at the coffee counter would have been extremely easy: I felt my mind begin to settle into rigidity, and only the clerk's peremptory, "Thirty cents, please," brought me back to action—luckily, because the Doctor could not have entered the white lounge to help me. I paid the clerk and took the paper cups of coffee back to the bench.

"Good," the Doctor said. "Sit down."

I hesitated. I was standing directly in front of him.

"Here!" he laughed. "On this side!"

I sat where ordered and we sipped our coffee. I rather expected to be asked questions about myself, but the Doctor ignored me.

"Thanks for the coffee," I said. He glanced at me impassively for a moment, as though I were a hitherto silent parrot who had suddenly blurted a brief piece of nonsense, and then he returned his attention to the crowd in the station.

"I have one or two calls to make before we catch the bus," he announced without looking at me. "Won't take long. I wanted to see if you were still here before I left town."

"What do you mean, catch the bus?"

"You'll have to come over to the farm—my Remobilization Farm near Wicomico—for a day or so, for observation," he explained coldly. "You don't have anything else to do, do you?"

"Well, I should get back to the university, I guess. I'm a student."

"Oh!" He chuckled. "Might as well forget about that for a while. You can come back in a few days if you want to."

"Say, you know, really, I think you must have a misconception about what was wrong with me a while ago. I'm not a paralytic. It's all just silly. I'll explain it to you if you want to hear it."

"No, you needn't bother. No offense intended, but the things you think are important probably aren't even relevant. I'm never very curious about my patients' histories. Rather not hear them, in fact—just clutters things up. It doesn't much matter what caused it anyhow, does it?" He grinned. "My farm's like a nunnery in that respect—I never bother about why my patients come there. Forget about causes; I'm no psychoanalyst."

"But that's what I mean, sir," I explained, laughing uncomfortably. "There's nothing physically wrong with me."

"Except that you couldn't move," the Doctor said. "What's your name?"

"Jacob Horner. I'm a graduate student up at Johns Hopkins—"

"Ah, ah," he warned. "No biography, Jacob Horner." He finished his coffee and stood up. "Come on, now, we'll get a cab. Bring your suitcase along."

"Oh, wait, now!"

"Yes?"

I fumbled for protests: the thing was absurd. "Well—this is absurd."

"Yes. So?"

I hesitated, blinking, wetting my lips.

"Think, think!" the Doctor said brusquely.

My mind raced like a car engine when the clutch is disengaged. There was no answer.

"Well, I—are you sure it's all right?" I asked, not knowing what my question signified.

The Doctor made a short, derisive sound (a sort of "Huf!") and turned away. I shook my head—at the same moment aware that I was watching myself act bewildered—and then fetched up my suitcase and followed after him, out to the line of taxicabs at the curb.

* * *

Thus began my *alliance* with the Doctor. He stopped first at an establishment on North Howard Street, to order two wheelchairs, three pairs of crutches, and certain other apparatus for the farm, and then at a pharmaceutical supply house on South Paca Street, where he also gave some sort of order. Then we went to the bus terminal and took the bus to the Eastern Shore. The Doctor's Mercury station wagon was parked at the Wicomico bus depot; he drove to the little settlement of Vineland, about three miles south of Wicomico, turned off onto a secondary road, and finally drove up a long, winding dirt lane to the Remobilization Farm, an aged but white-painted clapboard house in a clump of oaks on a knoll overlooking a creek. The patients on the porch, senile men and women, welcomed the Doctor with querulous enthusiasm, and he returned their greeting. Me they regarded with open suspicion, if not hostility, but the Doctor made no explanation of my presence; for that matter, I should have been hard put to explain it myself.

Inside, I was introduced to the muscular Mrs. Dockey and taken to the Progress and Advice Room for my first interview. I waited alone in that clean room—which, though bare, was not really clinical-looking—for some ten minutes, and then the Doctor entered and took his seat very much in front of me. He had donned a white medical-looking jacket and appeared entirely official and competent.

"I'll make a few things clear very quickly, Jacob," he said leaning forward with his hands on his knees and rolling his cigar around in his mouth between sentences. "The Farm, as you can see, is designed for the treatment of paralytics. Most of my patients are old people, but you mustn't infer from that that this is a nursing home for the aged. Perhaps you noticed when we drove up that my patients like me. They do. It has happened several times in the past that for one reason or another I have seen fit to change the location of the farm. Once it was outside of Troy, New York; another time near Fond du Lac, Wisconsin; another time near Biloxi, Mississippi. And we've been other places, too. Nearly all the patients I have on the farm now have been with me at least since Fond du Lac, and if I should have to

273

move tomorrow to Helena, Montana, or The Rockaways, most of them would go with me, and not because they haven't anywhere else to go. But don't think I have an equal love for them. They're just more or less interesting problems in immobility, for which I find it satisfying to work out therapies. I tell this to you, but not to them, because your problem is such that this information is harmless. And for that matter, you've no way of knowing whether anything I've said or will say is the truth, or just a part of my general therapy for you. You can't even tell whether your doubt in this matter is an honestly founded doubt or just a part of your treatment: access to the truth, Jacob, even belief that there is such a thing, is itself therapeutic or antitherapeutic, depending on the problem. The reality of your problem is all that you can be sure of."

"Yes, sir."

"Why do you say that?" the Doctor asked.

"Say what?"

" 'Yes, sir.' Why do you say 'Yes, sir'?"

"Oh—I was just acknowledging what you said before."

"Acknowledging the truth of what I said or merely the fact that I said it?"

"Well," I hesitated, flustered. "I don't know, sir."

"You don't know whether to say you were acknowledging the truth of my statements, when actually you weren't, or to say you were simply acknowledging that I said something, at the risk of offending me by the implication that you don't agree with any of it. Eh?"

"Oh, I agree with *some* of it," I assured him.

"What parts of it do you agree with? Which statements?" the Doctor asked.

"I don't know: I guess—" I searched my mind hastily to remember even one thing that he'd said. He regarded my floundering for a minute and then went on as if the interruption hadn't occurred.

"Agapotherapy—devotion-therapy—is often useful with older patients," he said. "One of the things that work toward restoring their mobility is devotion to some figure, a doctor or other kind of administrator. It keeps their allegiances from becoming divided. For that reason I'd move the farm occasionally even if other circumstances didn't make it desirable. It does them good to decide to follow me. Agapotherapy is one small therapy in a great number, some consecutive, some simultaneous, which are exercised on the patients. No two patients have the same schedule of therapies, because no two people are ever paralyzed in the same way. The authors of medical textbooks," he added with some contempt, "like everyone else, can reach generality only by ignoring enough particularity. They speak of paralysis, and the treatment of paralytics, as though one read the textbook and then followed the rules for getting paralyzed properly. There is no such thing as *paralysis*, Jacob. There is only paralyzed Jacob Horner. And I don't treat paralysis: I schedule therapies to mobilize John Doe or Jacob Horner, as the case may be. That's why I ignore you when you say you aren't paralyzed like the people out on the porch are paralyzed. I don't treat your paralysis; I treat paralyzed you. Please don't say 'Yes, sir.' "

The urge to acknowledge is an almost irresistible habit, but I managed to sit silent and not even nod.

"There are several things wrong with you, I think. I daresay you don't know the seating capacity of the Cleveland Municipal Stadium, do you?"

"What?"

The Doctor did not smile. "You suggest that my question is absurd, when you have no grounds for knowing whether it is or not—you obviously heard me and understood me. Probably you want to delay my learning that you *don't* know the seating capacity of Cleveland Municipal Stadium, since your vanity would be ruffled if the question *weren't* absurd, and even if it were. It makes no difference whether it is or nor, Jacob Horner: it's a question asked you by your Doctor. Now, is there any ultimate reason why the Cleveland Stadium shouldn't seat fifty-seven thousand, four hundred, eighty-eight people?"

"None that I can think of." I grinned.

"Don't pretend to be amused. Of course there's not. Is there any reason why it shouldn't seat eighty-eight thousand, four hundred, seventy-five people?"

"No, sir."

"Indeed not. Then as far as Reason is concerned, its seating capacity could be almost anything. Logic will never give you the answer to my question. Only Knowledge of the World will answer it. There's no ultimate reason at all why the Cleveland Stadium should seat exactly seventy-three thousand, eight hundred and eleven people, but it happens that it does. There's no reason in the long run why Italy shouldn't be shaped like a sausage instead of a boot, but that doesn't happen to be the case. *The world is everything that is the case,* and what the case is is not a matter of logic. If you don't simply *know* how many people can sit in the Cleveland Municipal Stadium, you have no real reason for choosing one number over another, assuming you can make a choice at all—do you understand? But if you have some Knowledge of the World you may be able to say, 'Seventy-three thousand, eight hundred and eleven,' just like that. No choice is involved."

"Well," I said, "you'd still have to choose whether to answer the question or not, or whether to answer it correctly, even if you knew the right answer, wouldn't you?"

The Doctor's tranquil stare told me my question was somehow silly, though it seemed reasonable enough to me.

"One of the things you'll have to do," he said dryly, "is buy a copy of the *World Almanac* for 1951 and begin to study it scrupulously. This is intended as a discipline, and you'll have to pursue it diligently, perhaps for a number of years. Informational Therapy is one of a number of therapies we'll have to initiate at once."

I shook my head and chuckled genially. "Do all your patients memorize the *World Almanac,* Doctor?"

I might as well not have spoken.

"Mrs. Dockey will show you to your bed," the Doctor said, rising to go. "I'll speak to you again presently." At the door he stopped and added, "One, perhaps two of the older men may attempt familiarities with you at night up in the dormitory. They're on Sexual Therapy. But unless you're accustomed to that sort of thing I don't think you should accept their advances. You should keep your life as uncomplicated as possible, at least for a while. Reject them gently, and they'll go back to each other."

There was little I could say. After a while Mrs. Dockey showed me my bed in the men's dormitory. I was not introduced to my roommates, nor did I introduce myself. In fact, during the three days that I remained at the farm not a dozen words were exchanged between us. When I left they were uniformly glad to see me go.

The Doctor spent two or three one-hour sessions with me each day. He asked me virtually nothing about myself; the conversations consisted mostly of harangues against the medical profession for its stupidity in matters of paralysis, and imputations that my condition was the result of defective character and intelligence.

"You claim to be unable to choose in many situations," he said once. "Well I claim that that inability is only theoretically inherent in situations, when there's no chooser. Given a particular chooser, it's unthinkable. So, since the inability *was* displayed in your case, the fault lies not in the situation but in the fact that there was no chooser. Choosing is existence: to the extent that you don't choose, you don't exist. Now, everything we do must be oriented toward choice and action. It doesn't matter whether this action is more or less reasonable than inaction; the point is that it is its opposite."

"But why should anyone prefer it?" I asked.

"There's no reason why you should prefer it, and no reason why you shouldn't. One is a patient simply because one chooses a condition that only therapy can bring one to, not because one condition is inherently better than another. My therapies for a while will be directed toward making you conscious of your existence. It doesn't matter whether you act constructively or even consistently, so long as you act. It doesn't matter to the case whether your character is admirable or not, so long as you think you have one."

"I don't understand why you should choose to treat anyone, Doctor," I said.

"That's my business, not yours."

And so it went. I was charged, directly or indirectly, with everything from intellectual dishonesty and vanity to nonexistence. If I protested, the Doctor observed that my protests indicated my belief in the truth of his statements. If I only listened glumly, he observed that my glumness indicated my belief in the truth of his statements.

"All right, then," I said at last, giving up. "Everything you say is true. All of it is the truth."

The Doctor listened calmly. "You don't know what you're talking about," he said. "There's no such thing as truth as you conceive it."

These apparently pointless interviews did not constitute my only activity at the farm. Before every meal all the patients were made to perform various calisthenics under the direction of Mrs. Dockey. For the older patients these were usually very simple—perhaps a mere nodding of the head or flexing of the arms—although some of the old folks could execute really surprising feats: one gentleman in his seventies was an excellent rope-climber, and two old ladies turned agile somersaults. For each patient Mrs. Dockey prescribed different activities; my own special prescription was to keep some sort of visible motion going all the time. If nothing else, I was constrained to keep a finger wiggling or a foot tapping, say, during meal-times, when more involved movements would have made eating difficult. And I was told to rock from side to side in my bed all night long: not an unreasonable request, as it happened, for I did this habitually anyhow, even in my sleep—a habit carried over from childhood.

"Motion! Motion!" the Doctor would say, almost exalted. "You must be always *conscious* of motion!"

There were special diets and, for many patients, special drugs. I learned of Nutritional Therapy, Medicinal Therapy, Surgical Therapy, Dynamic Therapy, Informational Therapy, Conversational Therapy, Sexual Therapy, Devotional Therapy, Occupational and Preoccupational Therapy, Virtue and Vice Therapy, Theotherapy and Atheotherapy—and, later, Mythotherapy, Philosophical Therapy, Scriptotherapy, and many, many other therapies practiced in various combinations and sequences by the patients. Everything, to the Doctor, was either therapeutic, antithera-peutic, or irrelevant. He was a kind of superpragmatist.

At the end of my last session—it had been decided that I was to return to Baltimore experimentally, to see whether and how soon my immobility might recur—the Doctor gave me some parting instructions.

"It would not be well in your particular case to believe in God," he said. "Religion will only make you despondent. But until we work out something for you it will be useful to subscribe to some philosophy. Why don't you read Sartre and become an existentialist? It will keep you moving until we find something more suitable for you. Study the *World Almanac*: it is to be your breviary for a while. Take a day job, preferably factory work, but not so simple that you are able to think coherently while working. Something involving sequential operations would be nice. Go out in the evenings; play cards with people. I don't recommend buying a television set just yet. Exercise frequently. Take long walks, but always to a previously determined destination; and when you get there, walk right home again, briskly. And move out of your present quarters; the association is unhealthy for you. Don't get married or have love affairs yet, even if you aren't coura-geous enough to hire prostitutes. Above all, act impulsively: don't let your-self get stuck between alternatives, or you're lost. You're not that strong. If the alternatives are side by side, choose the one on the left; if they're con-secutive in time, choose the earlier. If neither of these applies, choose the alternative whose name begins with the earlier letter of the alphabet. These are the principles of Sinistrality, Antecedence, and Alphabetical Priority—there are others, and they're arbitrary, but useful. Good-bye."

"Good-bye, Doctor," I said, and prepared to leave.

"If you have another attack and manage to recover from it, contact me as soon as you can. If nothing happens, come back in three months. My services will cost you ten dollars a visit—no charge for this one. I have a limited interest in your case, Jacob, and in the vacuum you have for a self. That *is* your case. Remember, keep moving all the time. Be *engagé*. Join things."

I left, somewhat dazed, and took the bus back to Baltimore. There, out of it all, I had a chance to attempt to decide what I thought of the Doctor, the Remobilization Farm, the endless list of therapies, and my own position. One thing seemed fairly clear: the Doctor was operating either outside the law or on its fringes. Sexual Therapy, to name only one thing, could scarcely be sanctioned by the American Medical Association. This doubtless was the reason for the farm's frequent relocation. It was also apparent that he was a crank—though perhaps not an ineffective one—and one wondered whether he had any sort of license to practice medicine at all. Because—his rationalizations aside—I was so clearly different from his other patients, I could only assume that he had some sort of special interest in my case: perhaps he was a frustrated psychoanalyst. At worst he was some combination of quack and prophet running a semi-legitimate rest home for senile eccentrics; and yet one couldn't easily laugh off his forcefulness, and his insights frequently struck home. As a matter of fact, I was unable to make any judgment one way or the other about him or the farm or the therapies.

A most extraordinary doctor. Although I kept telling myself that I was just going along with the joke, I actually did move to East Chase Street; I took a job as an assembler on the line of the Chevrolet factory out on Broening Highway, where I operated an air wrench that belted leaf springs on the left side of Chevrolet chassis, and I joined the UAW. I read Sartre, but had difficulty deciding how to apply him to specific situations. (How did existentialism help one decide whether to carry one's lunch to work or buy it in the factory cafeteria? I had no head for philosophy.) I played poker with my fellow assemblers, took walks from Chase Street down to the waterfront and back, and attended B movies. Temperamentally I was already pretty much of an atheist most of the time, and the proscription of women was a small burden, for I was not, as a rule, heavily sexed. I applied Sinistrality, Antecedence, and Alphabetical Priority religiously (though in some instances I found it hard to decide which of those devices best fitted the situation). And every quarter for the next two years I drove over to the Remobilization Farm for advice. It would be idle for me to speculate further on why I assented to this curious alliance, which more often than not was insulting to me—I presume that anyone interested in causes will have found plenty to pick from by now in this account.

I left myself sitting in the Progress and Advice Room, I believe, in September of 1953, waiting for the Doctor. My mood on this morning was an unusual one; as a rule I was almost "weatherless" the moment I entered the farmhouse, and I suppose that weatherlessness is the ideal condition for receiving advice, but on this morning, although I felt unemotional, I was not without weather. I felt dry, clear, and competent, for some reason or other—quite sharp and not a bit humble. In meteorological terms, my weather was *sec supérieur*.

"How are you these days, Horner?" the Doctor asked as he entered the room.

"Just fine, Doctor," I replied breezily. "How's yourself?"

The Doctor took his seat, spread his knees, and regarded me critically, not answering my question.

"Have you begun teaching yet?"

"Nope. Start next week. Two sections of grammar and two of composition."

"Ah." He rolled his cigar around in his mouth. He was studying me, not what I said. "You shouldn't be teaching composition."

"Can't have everything," I said cheerfully, stretching my legs out under his chair and clasping my hands behind my head. "It was that or nothing, so I took it."

The Doctor observed the position of my legs and arms.

"Who is this confident fellow you've befriended?" he asked. "One of the other teachers? He's terribly sure of himself!"

I blushed: it occurred to me that I was imitating one of my office-mates, an exuberant teacher of history. "Why do you say I'm imitating somebody?"

"I didn't," the Doctor smiled. "I only asked who was the forceful fellow you've obviously met."

"None of your business, sir."

"Oh, my. Very good. It's a pity you can't take over that manner consistently—you'd never need my services again! But you're not stable enough for that yet, Jacob. Besides, you couldn't act like him when you're in his company, could you? Anyway, I'm pleased to see you assuming a role. You do it, evidently, in order to face up to me: a character like your friend's would never allow itself to be insulted by some crank with his string of implausible therapies, eh?"

"That's right, Doctor," I said, but much of the fire had gone out of me under his analysis.

"This indicates to me that you're ready for Mythotherapy, since you seem to be already practicing it without knowing it, and therapeutically, too. But it's best you be aware of what you're doing, so that you won't break down through ignorance. Some time ago I told you to become an existentialist. Did you read Sartre?"

"Some things. Frankly I really didn't get to be an existentialist."

"No? Well, no matter now. Mythotherapy is based on two assumptions: that human existence precedes human essence, if either of the two terms really signifies anything; and that a man is free not only to choose his own essence but to change it at will. Those are both good existentialist premises, and whether they're true or false is no concern of us—they're *useful* in your case."

He went on to explain Mythotherapy.

"In life," he said, "there are no essentially major or minor characters. To that extent, all fiction and biography, and most historiography, is a lie. Everyone is necessarily the hero of his own life story. Suppose you're an usher in a wedding. From the groom's viewpoint he's the major character; the others play supporting parts, even the bride. From your viewpoint, though, the wedding is a minor episode in the very interesting history of *your* life, and the bride and groom both are minor figures. What you've done is choose to *play the part* of a minor character: it can be pleasant for you to *pretend to be* less important than you know you are, as Odysseus does when he disguises himself as a swineherd. And every member of the congregation at the wedding sees himself as the major character, condescending to witness the spectacle. So in this sense fiction isn't a lie at all, but a true representation of the distortion that everyone makes of life.

"Now, not only are we the heroes of our own life stories—we're the ones who conceive the story, and give other people the essences of minor characters. But since no man's life story as a rule is ever one story with a coherent plot, we're always reconceiving just the sort of hero we are, and consequently just the sort of minor roles the other people are supposed to play. This is generally true. If any man displays almost the same character day in and day out, all day long, it's either because he has no imagination, like an actor who can play only one role, or because he has an imagination so comprehensive that he sees each particular situation of his life as an episode in some grand overall plot, and can so distort the situations that the same type of hero can deal with them all. But this is most unusual.

"This kind of role-assigning is mythmaking, and when it's done consciously or unconsciously for the purpose of aggrandizing or protecting your ego—and it's probably done for this purpose all the time—it becomes Mythotherapy. Here's the point: an immobility such as you experienced that time in Penn Station is possible only to a person who for some reason or other has ceased to participate in Mythotherapy. At that time on the bench you were neither a major nor a minor character: you were no character at all. It's because this has happened once that it's necessary for me to explain to you something that comes quite naturally to everyone else. It's like teaching a paralytic how to walk again.

"I've said you're too unstable to play any one part all the time—you're also too unimaginative—so for you these crises had better be met by changing scripts as often as necessary. This should come naturally to you; the important thing for you is to realize what you're doing so you won't get caught without a script, or with the wrong script in a given situation. You did quite well, for example, for a beginner, to walk in here so confidently and almost arrogantly a while ago, and assign me the role of a quack. But you must be able to change masks at once if by some means or other I'm able to make the one you walked in with untenable. Perhaps—I'm just suggesting an offhand possibility—you could change to thinking of me as The Sagacious Old Mentor, a kind of Machiavellian Nestor, say, and yourself as The Ingenuous But Promising Young Protégé, a young Alexander, who someday will put all these teachings into practice and far outshine the master. Do you get the idea? Or—this is repugnant, but it could be used as a last resort—The Silently Indignant Young Man, who tolerates the ravings of a Senile Crank but who will leave this house unsullied by them. I call this repugnant because if you ever used it you'd cut yourself off from much that you haven't learned yet.

"It's extremely important that you learn to assume these masks wholeheartedly. Don't think there's anything behind them: *ego* means *I*, and *I* means *ego*, and the ego by definition is a mask. Where there's no ego—this is you on the bench—there's no *I*. If you sometimes have the feeling that your mask is *insincere*—impossible word!—it's only because one of your masks is incompatible with another. You mustn't put on two at a time. There's a source of conflict; and conflict between masks, like absence of masks, is a source of immobility. The more sharply you can dramatize your situation and define your own role and everybody else's role, the safer you'll be. It doesn't matter in Mythotherapy for paralytics whether your role is major or minor, as long as it's clearly conceived, but in the nature of things it'll normally always be major. Now say something."

I could not.

"Say something!" the Doctor ordered. "Move! Take a role!"

I tried hard to think of one, but I could not.

"Damn you!" the Doctor cried. He kicked back his chair and leaped upon me, throwing me to the floor and pounding me roughly.

"Hey!" I hollered, entirely startled by his attack. "Cut it out! What the hell!" I struggled with him, and being both larger and stronger than he, soon had him off me. We stood facing each other warily, panting from the exertion.

"You watch that stuff!" I said belligerently. "I could make plenty of trouble for you if I wanted to, I'll bet!"

"Anything wrong?" asked Mrs. Dockey, sticking her head into the room. I would not want to tangle with her.

"No, not now." The Doctor smiled, brushing the knees of his white trousers. "A little Pugilistic Therapy for Jacob Horner. No trouble." She closed the door.

"Now, shall we continue our talk?" he asked me, his eyes twinkling. "You were speaking in a manly way about making trouble."

But I was no longer in a mood to go along with the whole ridiculous business. I'd had enough of the old lunatic for this quarter.

"Or perhaps you've had enough of The Old Crank for today, eh?"

"What would the sheriff in Wicomico think of this farm?" I grumbled. "Suppose the police were sent out to investigate Sexual Therapy?"

The Doctor was unruffled by my threats.

"Do you intend to send them?" he asked pleasantly.

"Do you think I wouldn't?"

"I've no idea," he said, still undisturbed.

"Do you dare me to?"

This question, for some reason or other, visibly upset him: he looked at me sharply.

"Indeed I do not," he said at once. "I'm sure you're quite able to do it. I'm sorry if my tactic for mobilizing you just then made you angry. I did it with all good intent. You *were* paralyzed again, you know."

"You and your paralysis!" I sneered.

"You *have* had enough for today, Horner!" the Doctor said. He too was angry now. "Get out! I hope you get paralyzed driving sixty miles an hour on your way home!" He raised his voice. "Get out of here, you damned moron!"

His obviously genuine anger immediately removed mine, which after the first instant had of course been only a novel mask.

"I'm sorry, Doctor," I said. "I won't lose my temper again."

We exchanged smiles.

"Why not?" He laughed. "It's both therapeutic and pleasant to lose your temper in certain situations." He relit his cigar, which had been dropped during our scuffle. "Two interesting things were demonstrated in the past few minutes, Jacob Horner. I can't tell you about them until your next visit. Good-bye, now. Don't forget to pay Mrs. Dockey."

Out he strode, cool as he could be, and a few moments later out strode I: A Trifle Shaken, But Sure of My Strength.

Soldier's Joy

Tobias Wolff

On Friday Hooper was named driver of the guard for the third night that week. He had recently been broken in rank again, this time from corporal to Pfc, and the first sergeant had decided to keep Hooper's evenings busy so that he would not have leisure to brood. That was what the first sergeant told Hooper when Hooper came to the orderly room to complain.

"It's for your own good," the first sergeant said. "Not that I expect you to thank me." He moved the book he'd been reading to one side of his desk and leaned back. "Hooper, I have a theory about you," he said. "Want to hear it?"

"I'm all ears, Top," Hooper said. The first sergeant put his boots up on the desk and stared out the window to his left. It was getting on toward 5:00. Work details had begun to return from the rifle range and the post laundry and the brigade commander's house, where Hooper and several other men were excavating a swimming pool without aid of machinery. As the trucks let them out they gathered on the barracks steps and under the live oak beside the mess hall, their voices a steady murmur in the orderly room where Hooper stood waiting for the first sergeant to speak.

"You resent me," the first sergeant said. "You think you should be sitting here. You don't know that's what you think because you've totally sublimated your resentment, but that's what it is all right, and that's why you and me are developing a definite conflict profile. It's like you have to keep fucking up to prove to yourself that you don't really care. That's my theory. You follow me?"

"Top, I'm way ahead of you," Hooper said. "That's night school talking."

The first sergeant continued to look out the window. "I don't know," he said. "I don't know what you're doing in my army. You've put your twenty years in. You could retire to Mexico and buy a peso factory. Live like a dictator. So what are you doing in my army, Hooper?"

Hooper looked down at the desk. He cleared his throat but said nothing.

"Give it some thought," the first sergeant said. He stood and walked Hooper to the door. "I'm not hostile," he said. "I'm prepared to be supportive. Just think nice thoughts about Mexico, okay? Okay, Hooper?"

Hooper called Mickey and told her he wouldn't be coming by that night after all. She reminded him that this was the third time in one week, and said that she wasn't getting any younger.

"What am I supposed to do?" Hooper asked. "Go AWOL?"

"I cried three times today," Mickey said. "I just broke down and cried, and you know what? I don't even know why. I just feel bad all the time anymore."

"What did you do last night?" Hooper asked. When Mickey didn't answer, he said, "Did Briggs come over?"

"I've been inside all day," Mickey said. "Just sitting here. I'm going out of my tree." Then, in the same weary voice, she said, "Touch it, Hoop."

"I have to get going," Hooper said.

"Not yet. Wait. I'm going into the bedroom. I'm going to pick up the phone in there. Hang on, Hoop. Think of the bedroom. Think of me lying on the bed. Wait, baby."

There were men passing by the phone booth. Hooper watched and tried not to think of Mickey's bedroom, but now he could think of nothing else. Mickey's husband was a supply sergeant with a taste for quality. The walls of the bedroom were knotty pine he'd derailed en route to some colonel's office. The brass lamps beside the bed were made from howitzer casings. The sheets were parachute silk. Sometimes, lying on those sheets, Hooper thought of the men who had drifted to earth below them. He was no great lover, as the women he went with usually got around to telling him, but in Mickey's bedroom Hooper had turned in his saddest performances, and always when he was most aware that everything around him was stolen. He wasn't exactly sure why he kept going back. It was just something he did, again and again.

"Okay," Mickey said. "I'm here."

"There's a guy waiting to use the phone," Hooper told her.

"Hoop, I'm on the bed. I'm taking off my shoes."

Hooper could see her perfectly. He lit a cigarette and opened the door of the booth to let the smoke out.

"Hoop?" she said.

"I told you, there's a guy waiting."

"Turn around, then."

"You don't need me," Hooper said. "All you need is the telephone. Why don't you call Briggs? That's what you're going to do after I hang up."

"I probably will," she said. "Listen, Hoop, I'm not really on the bed. I was just pulling your chain."

"I knew it," Hooper said. "You're watching the tube, right?"

"Somebody just won a saw," Mickey said.

"A saw?"

"Yeah, they drove up to this man's house and dumped a truckload of logs in his yard and gave him a chain saw. This was his fantasy. You should see how happy he is, Hoop. I'd give anything to be that happy."

"Maybe I can swing by later tonight," Hooper said. "Just for a minute."

"I don't know," Mickey said. "Better give me a ring first." After Mickey hung up Hooper tried to call his wife, but there was no answer. He stood there and listened to the phone ringing. Finally he put the receiver down and stepped outside the booth, just as they began to sound retreat over the company loudspeaker. With the men around him Hooper came to attention and saluted. The record was scratchy, but, as always, the music caused Hooper's mind to go abruptly and perfectly still. He held his salute until the last note died away, then broke off smartly and walked down the street toward the mess hall.

The officer of the day was Captain King from Headquarters Company. Captain King had also been officer of the day on Monday and Tuesday nights, and Hooper was glad to see him again because Captain King was too lazy to do his own job or to make sure the guards were doing theirs. He stayed in the guardhouse and left everything up to Hooper.

Captain King had gray hair and a long grayish face. He was a West Point graduate with twenty-eight years of service behind him, just trying to make it through another two years so he could retire at three-quarters pay. All his classmates were generals or at least bird colonels, but he himself had been held back for good reasons, many of which he admitted to Hooper their first night together. It puzzled Hooper at first, this officer telling him about his failures to perform, his nervous breakdowns and Valium habit, but finally Hooper understood: Captain King regarded him, a Pfc with twenty-one years' service, as a comrade in dereliction, a disaster like himself with no room left for judgment against anyone.

The evening was hot and muggy. Little black bats swooped overhead as Captain King made his way along the rank of men drawn up before the guardhouse steps. He objected to the alignment of someone's belt buckle. He asked questions about the chain of command but gave no sign whether the answers he received were right or wrong. He inspected a couple of rifles and pretended to find something amiss with each of them, though it was clear that he hardly knew one end from the other, and when he reached the end of the line he began to deliver a speech. He said that he had never seen such sorry troops in his life. He asked how they expected to stand up to a determined enemy. On and on he went. Captain King had delivered the same speech on Monday and Tuesday, and when Hooper recognized it he lit another cigarette and sat down on the running board of the truck he'd been leaning against.

The sky was gray. It had a damp, heavy look and it felt heavy too, hanging close overhead, nervous with rumblings and small flashes in the distance. Just sitting there made Hooper sweat. Beyond the guardhouse a stream of cars rushed along the road to town. From the officers' club farther up the road came the muffled beat of rock music, which was almost lost, like every other sound of the evening, in the purr of crickets that rose up everywhere and thickened the air like heat.

When Captain King had finished talking he turned the men over to Hooper for transportation to their posts. Two of them, both privates, were from Hooper's company, and these he allowed to ride with him in the cab of the truck while everybody else slid around in back. One was a cook named Porchoff, known as Porkchop. The other was a radio operator named Trac, who had managed to airlift himself out of Saigon during the fall of the city by hanging from the skids of a helicopter. That was the story Hooper had heard, anyway, and he had no reason to doubt it; he'd seen the slopes pull that trick, though few of them were as young as Trac must have been then—nine or ten at the most. When Hooper tried to picture his son Wesley at the same age, hanging over a burning city by his fingertips, he had to smile.

But Trac didn't talk about it. There was nothing about him to suggest his past except perhaps the deep, sickle-shaped scar above his right eye. To Hooper there was something familiar about this scar. One night, watching

Trac play the video game in the company rec room, he was overcome with the certainty that he had seen Trac before somewhere—astride a water buffalo in some reeking paddy or running alongside Hooper's APC with a bunch of other kids all begging money, holding up melons or a bag full of weed or a starving monkey on a stick.

Though Hooper had the windows open, the cab of the truck smelled strongly of after-shave. Hooper noticed that Trac was wearing orange Walkman earphones under his helmet liner. They were against regulation, but Hooper said nothing. As long as Trac had his ears plugged he wouldn't be listening for trespassers and end up blowing his rifle off at some squirrel cracking open an acorn. Of all the guards only Porchoff and Trac would be carrying ammunition, because they had been assigned to the battalion communications center, where there was a tie-in terminal to the division mainframe computer. The theory was that an intruder who knew his stuff could get his hands on highly classified material. That was how it had been explained to Hooper. Hooper thought it was a load of crap. The Russians knew everything anyway.

Hooper let out the first two men at the PX and the next two at the parking lot outside the main officers' club, where lately several cars had been vandalized. As they pulled away, Porchoff leaned over Trac and grabbed Hooper's sleeve. "You used to be a corporal," he said.

Hooper shook Porchoff's hand loose. He said, "I'm driving a truck, in case you didn't notice."

"How come you got busted?"

"None of your business."

"I'm just asking," Porchoff said. "So what happened, anyway?"

"Cool it, Porkchop," said Trac. "The man doesn't want to talk about it, okay?"

"Cool it yourself, fuckface," Porchoff said. He looked at Trac. "Was I addressing you?"

Trac said, "Man, you must've been eating some of your own food."

"I don't believe I was addressing you," Porchoff said. "In fact, I don't believe that you and me have been properly introduced. That's another thing I don't like about the Army, the way people you haven't been introduced to feel perfectly free to get right into your face and unload whatever shit they've got in their brains. It happens all the time. But I never heard anyone say 'Cool it' before. You're a real phrasemaker, fuckface."

"That's enough," Hooper said.

Porchoff leaned back and said, "That's enough," in a falsetto voice. A few moments later he started humming to himself.

Hooper dropped off the rest of the guards and turned up the hill toward the communications center. There were oleander bushes along the gravel drive, with white blossoms going gray in the dusky light. Gravel sprayed up under the tires and rattled against the floorboards of the truck. Porchoff stopped humming. "I've got a cramp," he said.

Hooper pulled up next to the gate and turned off the engine. He looked over at Porchoff. "Now what's your problem?" he said.

"I've got a cramp," Porchoff repeated.

"For Christ's sake," Hooper said. "Why didn't you say something before?"

"I did. I went on sick call, but the doctor couldn't find it. It keeps moving around. It's here now." Porchoff touched his neck. "I swear to God."

"Keep track of it," Hooper told him. "You can go on sick call again in the morning."

"You don't believe me," Porchoff said.

The three of them got out of the truck. Hooper counted out the ammunition to Porchoff and Trac and watched as they loaded their clips. "That ammo's strictly for show," he said. "Forget I even gave it to you. If you run into a problem, which you won't, use the phone in the guard shack. You can work out your own shifts." Hooper opened the gate and locked the two men inside. They stood watching him, faces in shadow, black rifle barrels poking over their shoulders. "Listen," Hooper said, "nobody's going to break in here, understand?"

Trac nodded. Porchop just looked at him.

"Okay," Hooper said. "I'll drop by later. Me and the captain." Hooper knew that Captain King wasn't about to go anywhere, but Trac and Porchoff didn't know that. Hooper behaved better when he thought he was being watched and he supposed that the same was true of other people.

Hooper climbed back inside the truck and started the engine. He gave the V sign to the men at the gate. Trac gave the sign back and turned away. Porchoff didn't move. He stayed where he was, fingers laced through the wire. He looked about ready to cry. "Damn," Hooper said, and he hit the gas. Gravel clattered in the wheel wells. When Hooper reached the main road a light rain began to fall, but it stopped before he'd even turned the wipers on.

Hooper and Captain King sat on adjacent bunks in the guardhouse, which was empty except for them and a bat that was flitting back and forth among the dim rafters. As on Monday and Tuesday nights, Captain King had brought along an ice chest filled with little bottles of Perrier water. From time to time he tried pressing one on Hooper, but Hooper declined. His refusals made Captain King apologetic. "It's not a class thing," Captain King said, looking at the bottle in his hand. "I don't drink this stuff because I went to the Point or anything like that." He leaned down and put the bottle between his bare feet. "I'm allergic to alcohol," he said. "Otherwise I'd probably be an alcoholic. Why not? I'm everything else." He smiled at Hooper.

Hooper lay back and clasped his hands behind his head and stared up at the mattress above him. "I'm not much of a drinker myself," he said. He knew that Captain King wanted him to explain why he refused the Perrier water, but there was really no reason in particular.

"I drank eggnog one Christmas when I was a kid, and it almost killed me," Captain King said. "My arms and legs swelled up to twice their normal size. The doctors couldn't get my glasses off because my skin was all puffed up around them. You know the way a tree will grow around a rock.

It was like that. A few months later I tried beer at some kid's graduation party and the same thing happened. Pretty strange, eh?"

"Yes, sir," Hooper said.

"I used to think it was all for the best. I have an addictive personality, and you can bet your bottom dollar I would have been a problem drinker. No question about it. But now I wonder. If I'd had one big weakness like that, maybe I wouldn't have had all these little pissant weaknesses I ended up with. I know that sounds like bull-pucky, but look at Alexander the Great. Alexander the Great was a boozer. Did you know that?"

"No, sir," Hooper said.

"Well he was. Read your history. So was Churchill. Churchill drank a bottle of Cognac a day. And of course Grant. You know what Lincoln said when someone complained about Grant's drinking?"

"Yes, sir. I've heard the story."

"He said, 'Find out what brand he uses so I can ship a case to the rest of my generals.' Is that the way you heard it?"

"Yes, sir."

Captain King nodded. "I'm all in," he said. He stretched out and assumed exactly the position Hooper was in. It made Hooper uncomfortable. He sat up and put his feet on the floor.

"Married?" Captain King asked.

"Yes, sir."

"Kids?"

"Yes, sir. One. Wesley."

"Oh my God, a boy," Captain King said. "They're nothing but trouble, take my word for it. They're programmed to hate you. It has to be like that, otherwise they'd spend their whole lives moping around the house, but just the same it's no fun when it starts. I have two, and neither of them can stand me. Haven't been home in years. Breaks my heart. Of course, I was a worse father than most. How old is your boy?"

"Sixteen or seventeen," Hooper said. He put his hands on his knees and looked at the floor. "Seventeen. He lives with my wife's sister in San Diego."

Captain King turned his head and looked at Hooper. "Sounds like you're not much of a dad yourself."

Hooper began to lace his boots up.

"I'm not criticizing," Captain King said. "At least you were smart enough to get someone else to do the job." He yawned. "I'm whipped," he said. "You need me for anything? You want me to make the rounds with you?"

"I'll take care of things, sir," Hooper said.

"Fair enough." Captain King closed his eyes. "If you need me, just shout."

Hooper went outside and lit a cigarette. It was almost midnight, well past the time appointed for inspecting the guards. As he walked toward the truck mosquitoes droned around his head. A breeze was rustling the tree-tops, but on the ground the air was hot and still.

Hooper took his time making the rounds. He visited all the guards except Porchoff and Trac and found everything in order. There were no problems. Finally he started down the road toward the communications center, but when he reached the turnoff he kept his eyes dead ahead and drove past. Warm, fragrant air rushed into his face from the open window. The road ahead was empty. Hooper leaned back and mashed the accelerator. The engine roared. He was moving now, really moving, past darkened barracks and bare flagpoles and bushes whose flowers blazed up in the glare of the headlights. Hooper grinned. He felt no pleasure, but he grinned and pushed the truck as hard as it would go.

Hooper slowed down when he left the post. He was AWOL now. Even if he couldn't find it in him to care much about that, he saw no point in calling attention to himself.

Drunk drivers were jerking their cars back and forth between lanes. Every half mile or so a police car with flashing lights had someone stopped by the roadside. Other police cars sat idling behind billboards. Hooper stayed in the right lane and drove slowly until he reached his turn, then he gunned the engine again and raced down the pitted street that led to

Mickey's house. He passed a bunch of kids sitting on the hood of a car with cans of beer in their hands. The car door was open, and Hooper had to swerve to miss it. As he went by he heard a blast of music.

When he reached Mickey's block Hooper turned off the engine. The truck coasted silently down the street, and again Hooper became aware of the sound of crickets. He stopped on the shoulder across from Mickey's house and sat listening. The thick pulsing sound seemed to grow louder every moment. Hooper drifted into memory, his cigarette dangling unsmoked, burning its way toward his fingers. At the same instant that he felt the heat of the ember against his skin Hooper was startled by another pain, the pain of finding himself where he was. It left him breathless for a moment. Then he roused himself and got out of the truck.

The windows were dark. Mickey's Buick was parked in the driveway beside another car that Hooper didn't recognize. It didn't belong to her husband and it didn't belong to Briggs. Hooper glanced around at the other houses, then walked across the street and ducked under the hanging leaves of the willow tree in Mickey's front yard. He knelt there, holding his breath to hear better, but there was no sound but the sound of the crickets and the rushing of the big air conditioner Mickey's husband had taken from a helicopter hangar. Hooper saw no purpose in staying under the tree, so he got up and walked over to the house. He looked around again, then went into a crouch and began to work his way along the wall. He rounded the corner of the house and was starting up the side toward Mickey's bedroom when a circle of light burst around his head and a woman's voice said, "Thou shalt not commit adultery."

Hooper closed his eyes. There was a long silence. Then the woman said, "Come here."

She was standing in the driveway of the house next door. When Hooper came up to her she stuck a pistol in his face and told him to raise his hands. "A soldier," she said, moving the beam of light up and down his uniform. "All right, put your hands down." She snapped the light off and stood watching Hooper in the flickering blue glow that came from the open door behind her. Hooper heard a dog bark twice and a man say, "Remember—nothing is too good for your dog. It's 'Ruff ruff' at the sign of the double R." The dog barked twice again.

"I want to know what you think you're doing," the woman said.

Hooper said, "I'm not exactly sure." He saw her more clearly now. She was thin and tall. She wore glasses with harlequin frames, and she had on a white dress of the kind girls called formals when Hooper was in high school—tight around the waist and flaring stiffly at the hip, breasts held in hard-looking cups. Shadows darkened the hollows of her cheeks. Under the flounces of the dress her feet were big and bare.

"I know what you're doing," she said. She pointed the pistol, an Army .45, at Mickey's house. "You're sniffing around that whore over there."

Someone came to the door behind the woman. A deep voice called out, "Is it him?"

"Stay inside, Dads," the woman answered. "It's nobody."

"It's him!" the man shouted. "Don't let him talk you out of it again! Do it while you've got the chance, sweetie pie."

"What do you want with that whore?" the woman asked Hooper. Before he could answer, she said, "I could shoot you and nobody would say boo. I'm within my rights."

Hooper nodded.

"I don't see the attraction," she said. "But then, I'm not a man." She made a laughing sound. "You know something? I almost did it. I almost shot you. I was that close, but then I saw the uniform." She shook her head. "Shame on you. Where is your pride?"

"Don't let him talk," said the man in the doorway. He came down the steps, a tall white-haired man in striped pajamas. "There you are, you sonofabitch," he said. "I'll dance on your grave."

"It isn't him, Dads," the woman said sadly. "It's someone else."

"So he says," the man snapped. He started down the driveway, hopping from foot to foot over the gravel. The woman handed him the flashlight and he turned it on in Hooper's face, then moved the beam slowly down to his boots. "Sweetie pie, it's a soldier," he said.

"I told you it wasn't him," the woman said.

"But this is a terrible mistake," the man said. "Sir, I'm at a loss for words."

"Forget it," Hooper told him. "No hard feelings."

"You are too kind," the man said. He reached out and shook Hooper's hand. He nodded toward the house. "Come have a drink."

"He has to go," the woman said. "He was looking for something and he found it."

"That's right," Hooper told him. "I was just on my way back to base."

The man gave a slight bow with his head. "To base with you, then. Good night, sir."

Hooper and the woman watched him make his way back to the house. When he was inside, the woman turned to Hooper. "Why are you still here?" she asked angrily. "Go back to your post."

Captain King was still asleep when Hooper returned to the guardhouse. His thumb was in his mouth and he made little noises as he sucked it. Hooper lay in the next bunk with his eyes open. He was still awake at 4:00 in the morning when the telephone began to ring.

It was Trac calling from the communications center. He said that Porchoff was threatening to shoot himself, and threatening to shoot Trac if Trac tried to stop him. "This dude is mental," Trac said. "You get me out of here, and I mean now."

"We'll be right there," Hooper said. "Just give him lots of room. Don't try to grab his rifle or anything."

"Fat fucking chance," Trac said. "Man, you know what he called me? He called me a gook. I hope he wastes himself. I don't need no assholes with loaded guns declaring war on me, man."

"Just hold tight," Hooper told him. He hung up and went to wake Captain King, because this was a mess and he wanted it to be Captain King's mess and Captain King's balls that got busted if anything went wrong. He walked over to Captain King and stood looking down at him. Captain King's thumb had slipped out of his mouth, but he was still making sucking noises and pursing his lips. Hooper decided not to wake him after all. Captain King would probably refuse to come anyway, but if he did come he would screw things up for sure. Just the sight of him was enough to make somebody start shooting.

A light rain had begun to fall. The road was empty except for one jeep going the other way. Hooper waved at the two men in front as they went past, and they both waved back. Hooper felt a surge of friendliness toward them. He followed their lights in his mirror until they vanished behind him.

Hooper parked the truck halfway up the drive and walked the rest of the distance. The rain was falling harder now, tapping steadily on the shoulders of his poncho. Sweet, almost unbreathable smells rose from the earth. He walked slowly, gravel crunching under his boots. When he reached the gate a voice to his left said, "Shit, man, you took your time." Trac stepped out of the shadows and waited as Hooper tried to get the key into the lock. "Come on, man," Trac said. He knelt with his back to the fence and swung the barrel of his rifle from side to side.

"Got it," Hooper said. He took the lock off and Trac pushed open the gate. "The truck's down there," Hooper told him. "Just around the turn."

Trac stood close to Hooper, breathing quick, shallow breaths and shifting from foot to foot. His face was dark under the hood of his glistening poncho. "You want this?" he asked. He held out his rifle.

Hooper looked at it. He shook his head. "Where's Porchoff?"

"Around back," Trac said. "There's some picnic benches out there."

"All right," Hooper said. "I'll take care of it. Wait in the truck."

"Shit, man, I feel like shit," Trac said. "I'll back you up, man."

"It's okay," Hooper told him. "I can handle it."

"I never cut out on anybody before," Trac said. He shifted back and forth.

"You aren't cutting out," Hooper said. "Nothing's going to happen."

Trac started down the drive. When he disappeared around the turn, Hooper kept watching to make sure he didn't double back. A stiff breeze began to blow, shaking the trees, sending raindrops rattling down through the leaves. Thunder rumbled far away.

Hooper turned and walked through the gate into the compound. The forms of shrubs and pines were dark and indefinite in the slanting rain. Hooper followed the fence to the right, squinting into the shadows. When he saw Porchoff, hunched over the picnic table, he stopped and called out to him, "Hey, Porchoff! It's me—Hooper."

Porchoff raised his head.

"It's just me," Hooper said, following his own voice toward Porchoff, showing his empty hands. He saw the rifle lying on the table in front of Porchoff. "It's just me," he repeated, monotonously as he could. He stopped beside another picnic table ten feet or so from the one where Porchoff sat, and lowered himself onto the bench. He looked over at Porchoff. Neither of them spoke for a while. Then Hooper said, "Okay, Porchoff, let's talk about it. Trac tells me you've got some kind of problem."

Porchoff didn't answer. Raindrops streamed down his helmet onto his shoulders and dripped steadily past his face. His uniform was soggy and dark, plastered to his skin. He stared at Hooper and said nothing. Now and then his shoulders jerked.

"Are you gay?" Hooper asked.

Porchoff shook his head.

"Well then, what? You on acid or something? You can tell me, Porchoff. It doesn't matter."

"I don't do drugs," Porchoff said. It was the first time he'd spoken. His voice was calm.

"Good," Hooper said. "I mean, at least I know I'm talking to you, and not to some fucking chemical. Now listen up, Porchoff—I don't want you turning that rifle on me. Understand?"

Porchoff looked down at the rifle, then back at Hooper. He said, "You leave me alone and I'll leave you alone."

"I've already had someone throw down on me once tonight," Hooper said. "I'd just as soon leave it at that." He reached under his poncho and took out his cigarette case. He held it up for Porchoff to see.

"I don't use tobacco," Porchoff said.

"Well, I do," Hooper said. He shook out a cigarette and bent to light it. "Hey," he said. "All right. One match." He put the case back in his pocket and cupped the cigarette under the picnic table to keep it dry. The rain was falling lightly now in fine fitful gusts like spray. The clouds had gone the color of ash. Misty gray light was spreading through the sky. Hooper saw that Porchoff's shoulders twitched constantly now, and that his lips were blue and trembling. "Put your poncho on," Hooper told him.

Porchoff shook his head.

"You trying to catch pneumonia?" Hooper asked. He smiled at Porchoff. "Go ahead, boy. Put your poncho on."

Porchoff bent over and covered his face with his hands. Hooper realized that he was crying. He smoked his cigarette and waited for Porchoff to stop, but Porchoff kept crying and finally Hooper grew impatient. He said, "What's all this crap about you shooting yourself?"

Porchoff rubbed at his eyes with the heels of his hands. "Why shouldn't I?" he asked.

"Why shouldn't you? What do you mean, why shouldn't you?"

"Why shouldn't I shoot myself? Give me a reason."

"This is baloney," Hooper said. "You don't run around asking why shouldn't I shoot myself. That's decadent, Porchoff. Now, do me a favor and put your poncho on."

Porchoff sat shivering for a moment. Then he took his poncho off his belt, unrolled it, and began to pull it over his head. Hooper considered making a grab for the rifle but held back. There was no need, he was home free now. People who were going to blow themselves away didn't come in out of the rain.

"You know what they call me?" Porchoff said.

"Who's 'they,' Porchoff?"

"Everyone."

"No. What does everyone call you?"

"Porkchop. *Porkchop.*"

"Come on," Hooper said. "What's the harm in that? Everyone gets called something."

"But that's my *name*," Porchoff said. "That's *me*. It's got so even when people use my real name I hear 'Porkchop.' All I can think of is this big piece of meat. And that's what they're seeing too. You can say they aren't, but I know they are."

Hooper recognized some truth in this, a lot of truth in fact, because when he himself said, "Porkchop," that was what he saw: a pork chop.

"I hurt all the time," Porchoff said, "but no one believes me. Not even the doctors. You don't believe me, either."

"I believe you," Hooper said.

Porchoff blinked. "Sure," he said.

"I believe you," Hooper repeated. He kept his eyes on the rifle. Porchoff wasn't going to shoot himself, but the rifle still made Hooper uncomfortable. He was about to ask Porchoff to give it to him, but decided to wait a little while. The moment was wrong somehow. Hooper pushed back the hood of his poncho and took off his fatigue cap. He glanced up at the pale clouds.

"I don't have any buddies," Porchoff said.

"No wonder," Hooper said. "Calling people gooks, making threats. Let's face it, Porchoff, your personality needs some upgrading."

"But they won't give me a chance," Porchoff said. "All I ever do is cook food. I put it on their plates and they make some crack and walk on by. It's like I'm not even there. So what am I supposed to act like?"

Hooper was still gazing up at the clouds, feeling the soft rain on his face. Birds were starting to sing in the woods beyond the fence. He said, "I don't know, Porchoff. It's just part of this rut we're all in." Hooper lowered his head and looked over at Porchoff, who sat hunched inside his poncho, shaking as little tremors passed through him.

"My dad was in the National Guard back in Ohio," Porchoff said. "He's always talking about the great experiences he and his buddies used to have, camping out and so on. Nothing like that ever happens to me."

Porchoff looked down at the table, then looked up and said, "How about you? What was your best time?"

"My best time," Hooper said. He thought of telling Porchoff some sort of lie, but the effort of making things up was beyond him and the memory Porchoff wanted was close at hand. For Hooper, it was closer than the memory of home. In truth it was a kind of home. It was where he went to be back with his friends again, and his old self. It was where Hooper drifted when he was too low to care how much lower he'd be when he drifted back, and lost it all again. He felt for his cigarettes. "Vietnam," he said.

Porchoff just looked at him.

"We didn't know it then," Hooper said. "We used to talk about how when we got back in the world we were going to do this and we were going to do that. Back in the world we were going to have it made. But ever since then it's been nothing but confusion." Hooper took the cigarette case from his pocket but didn't open it. He leaned forward on the table.

"Everything was clear," he said. "You learned what you had to know and you forgot the rest. All this chickenshit. You didn't spend every living minute of the day thinking about your own sorry-ass little self. Am I getting laid enough. What's wrong with my kid. Should I insulate the fucking house. That's what does it to you, Porchoff. Thinking about yourself. That's what kills you in the end."

Porchoff had not moved. In the gray light Hooper could see Porchoff's fingers spread before him on the tabletop, white and still as if they had been drawn there in chalk. His face was the same color.

"You think you've got problems, Porchoff, but they wouldn't last five minutes in the field. There's nothing wrong with you that a little search-and-destroy wouldn't cure." Hooper paused, smiling to himself, already deep in the memory. He tried to bring it back for Porchoff, tried to put it into words so that Porchoff could see it, too, the beauty of that life, the faith so deep that in time you were not different men anymore but one man.

But the words came hard. Hooper saw that Porchoff did not understand, and that he could not make him understand. He said, "You'll see, Porchoff. You'll get your chance."

Porchoff stared at Hooper. "You're crazy," he said.

"We're all going to get another chance," Hooper said. "I can feel it coming. Otherwise I'd take my walking papers and hat up. You'll see. All you need is a little contact. The rest of us, too. Get us out of this rut."

Porchoff shook his head and murmured, "You're really crazy."

"Let's call it a day," Hooper said. He stood and held out his hand. "Give me the rifle."

"No," Porchoff said. He pulled the rifle closer. "Not to you."

"There's no one here but me," Hooper said.

"Go get Captain King."

"Captain King is asleep."

"Then wake him up."

"No," Hooper said. "I'm not going to tell you again, Porchoff, give me the rifle." Hooper walked toward him but stopped when Porchoff picked up the weapon and pointed it at his chest. "Leave me alone," Porchoff said.

"Relax," Hooper told him. "I'm not going to hurt you." He held out his hand again.

Porchoff licked his lips. "No," he said. "Not you."

Behind Hooper a voice called out, "Hey! Porkchop! Drop it!"

Porchoff sat bolt upright. "Jesus," he said.

"It's Trac," Hooper said. "Put the rifle down, Porchoff—now!"

"Drop it!" Trac shouted.

"Oh Jesus," Porchoff said and stumbled to his feet with the rifle still in his hands. Then his head flapped and his helmet flew off and he toppled backward over the bench. Hooper's heart leaped as the shock of the blast hit him. Then the sound went through him and beyond him into the trees and the sky, echoing on in the distance like thunder. Afterward there was silence. Hooper took a step forward, then sank to his knees and lowered his forehead to the wet grass. He spread his fingers through the grass beside his head. The rain fell around him with a soft whispering sound. A blue jay squawked.

Hooper heard the swish of boots through the grass behind him. He pushed himself up and sat back on his heels and drew a deep breath.

"You okay?" Trac said.

Hooper nodded.

Trac walked on to where Porchoff lay. He said something in Vietnamese, then looked back at Hooper and shook his head.

Hooper tried to stand but went to his knees again.

"You need a hand?" Trac asked.

"I guess so," Hooper said.

Trac came over to Hooper. He slung his rifle and bent down and the two men gripped each other's wrists. Trac's skin was dry and smooth, his bones as small as a child's. This close, he looked more familiar than ever. "Go for it," Trac said. He tensed as Hooper pulled himself to his feet and for a moment afterward they stood facing each other, swaying slightly, hands still locked on one another's wrists. "All right," Hooper said. Each of them slowly loosened his grip.

In a soft voice, almost a whisper, Trac said, "They gonna put me away?"

"No," Hooper said. He walked over to Porchoff and looked down at him. He immediately turned away and saw that Trac was still swaying, and that his eyes were glassy. "Better get off those legs," Hooper said. Trac looked at him dreamily, then unslung his rifle and leaned it against the picnic table farthest from Porchoff. He sat down and took his helmet off and rested his head on his crossed forearms.

The wind had picked up again, carrying with it the whine of distant engines. Hooper fumbled a cigarette out of his case and smoked it down, staring toward the woods, feeling the rain stream down his face and neck. When the cigarette went out Hooper dropped it, then picked it up again and field-stripped it, crumbling the tobacco around his feet so that no trace of it remained. He put his cap back on and raised the hood of his poncho. "How's it going?" he said to Trac.

Trac looked up. He began to rub his forehead, pushing his fingers in little circles above his eyes.

Hooper sat down across from him. "We don't have a whole lot of time," he said.

Trac nodded. He put his helmet on and looked over at Hooper.

"All right, son," Hooper said. "Let's get our story together."

The Bullet's Flight

Denis Johnson

I went out to the farmhouse where Dundun lived to get some pharmaceutical opium from him, but I was out of luck.

He greeted me as he was coming out into the front yard to go to the pump, wearing new cowboy boots and a leather vest, with his flannel shirt hanging out over his jeans. He was chewing on a piece of gum.

"MacInnes isn't feeling too good today. I just shot him."

"You mean killed him?"

"I didn't mean to."

"Is he really dead?"

"No. He's sitting down."

"But he's alive."

"Oh, sure, he's alive. He's sitting down now in the back room."

Dundun went on over to the pump and started working the handle.

I went around the house and in through the back. The room just through the back door smelled of dogs and babies. Beatle stood in the opposite doorway. She watched me come in. Leaning against the wall was Blue, smoking a cigarette and scratching her chin thoughtfully. Jack Hotel was over at an old desk, setting fire to a pipe, the bowl of which was wrapped in tinfoil.

When they saw it was only me, the three of them resumed looking at MacInnes, who sat on the couch all alone with his left hand resting gently on his belly.

"Dundun shot him?" I asked.

"Somebody shot somebody," Hotel said.

Dundun came in behind me carrying some water in a china cup and a bottle of beer and said to MacInnes: "Here."

"*I* don't want that," MacInnes said.

"Okay. Well, here, then." Dundun offered him the rest of his beer.

"No thanks."

I was worried. "Aren't you taking him to the hospital or anything?"

"Good idea," Beatle said sarcastically.

"We started to," Hotel explained, "but we ran into the corner of the shed out there."

I looked out the side window. This was Tim Bishop's farm. Tim Bishop's Plymouth, I saw, which was a very nice old gray-and-red sedan, had sideswiped the shed and replaced one of the corner posts, so that the post lay on the ground and the car now held up the shed's roof.

"The front windshield is in millions of bits," Hotel said.

"How'd you end up way over there?"

"Everything was completely out of hand," Hotel said.

"Where's Tim, anyway?"

"He's not here," Beatle said.

Hotel passed me the pipe. It was hashish, but it was pretty well burned up already.

"How you doing?" Dundun asked MacInnes.

"I can feel it right here. It's just stuck in the muscle."

Dundun said, "It's not bad. The cap didn't explode right, I think."

"It misfired."

"It misfired a little bit, yeah."

Hotel asked me, "Would you take him to the hospital in your car?"

"Okay," I said.

"I'm coming, too," Dundun said.

"Have you got any of that opium left?" I asked him.

"No," he said. "That was a birthday present. I used it all up."

"When's your birthday?" I asked him.

"Today."

"You shouldn't have used it all up before your birthday then," I told him angrily.

But I was happy about this chance to be of use. I wanted to be the one who saw it through and got MacInnes to the doctor without a wreck. People would talk about it, and I hoped I would be liked.

In the car were Dundun, MacInnes, and myself.

This was Dundun's twenty-first birthday. I'd met him in the Johnson County facility during the only few days I'd ever spent in jail, around the time of my eighteenth Thanksgiving. I was the older of us by a month or two. As for MacInnes, he'd been around forever, and in fact I, myself, was married to one of his old girlfriends.

We took off as fast as I could go without bouncing the shooting victim around too heavily.

Dundun said, "What about the brakes? You get them working?"

"The emergency brake does. That's enough."

"What about the radio?" Dundun punched the button, and the radio came on, making an emission like a meat grinder.

He turned it off and then on, and now it burbled like a machine that polishes stones all night.

"How about you?" I asked MacInnes. "Are you comfortable?"

"What do you think?" MacInnes said.

It was a long straight road through dry fields as far as a person could see. You'd think the sky didn't have any air in it and the earth was made of paper. Rather than moving, we were just getting smaller and smaller.

What can be said about those fields? There were blackbirds circling above their own shadows, and beneath them the cows stood around smelling one another's butts. Dundun spat his gum out the window while digging in his shirt pocket for his Winstons. He lit a Winston with a match. That was all there was to say.

"We'll never get off this road," I said.

"What a lousy birthday," Dundun said.

MacInnes was white and sick, holding himself tenderly. I'd seen him like that once or twice even when he hadn't been shot. He had a bad case of hepatitis that often gave him a lot of pain.

"Do you promise not to tell them anything?" Dundun was talking to MacInnes.

"I don't think he hears you," I said.

"Tell them it was an accident, okay?"

MacInnes said nothing for a long moment. Finally he said, "Okay."

"Promise?" Dundun said.

But MacInnes said nothing. Because he was dead.

Dundun looked at me with tears in his eyes. "What do you say?"

"What do you mean, what do I say? Do you think I'm here because I know all about this stuff?"

"He's dead."

"All *right*. I *know* he's dead."

"Throw him out of the car."

"Damn right throw him out of the car," I said. "I'm not taking him any-where now."

For a moment I fell asleep, right while I was driving. I had a dream in which I was trying to tell someone something and they kept interrupting, a dream about frustration.

"I'm glad he's dead," I told Dundun. "He's the one who started every-body calling me Fuckhead."

Dundun said, "Don't let it get you down."

We whizzed along down through the skeleton remnants of Iowa.

"I wouldn't mind working as a hit man," Dundun said.

Glaciers had crushed this region in the time before history. There'd been a drought for years, and a bronze fog of dust stood over the plains. The soybean crop was dead again, and the failed, wilted cornstalks were laid out on the ground like rows of underthings. Most of the farmers didn't even plant anymore. All the false visions had been erased. It felt like the moment before the savior comes. And the savior did come, but we had to wait a long time.

Dundun tortured Jack Hotel at the lake outside of Denver. He did this to get information about a stolen item, a stereo belonging to Dundun's girlfriend, or perhaps to his sister. Later, Dundun beat a man almost to death with a tire iron right on the street in Austin, Texas, for which he'll also someday have to answer, but now he is, I think, in the state prison in Colorado.

Will you believe me when I tell you there was kindness in his heart? His left hand didn't know what his right hand was doing. It was only that certain important connections had been burned through. If I opened up your head and ran a hot soldering iron around in your brain, I might turn you into someone like that.

Memento Mori

Jonathan Nolan

"What like a bullet can undeceive!"
—Herman Melville

Your wife always used to say you'd be late for your own funeral. Remember that? Her little joke because you were such a slob—always late, always forgetting stuff, even before the incident.

Right about now you're probably wondering if you were late for hers.

You were there, you can be sure of that. That's what the picture's for—the one tacked to the wall by the door. It's not customary to take pictures at a funeral, but somebody, your doctors, I guess, knew you wouldn't remember.

They had it blown up nice and big and stuck it right there, next to the door, so you couldn't help but see it every time you got up to find out where she was.

The guy in the picture, the one with the flowers? That's you. And what are you doing? You're reading the headstone, trying to figure out whose funeral you're at, same as you're reading it now, trying to figure why someone stuck that picture next to your door. But why bother reading something that you won't remember?

She's gone, gone for good, and you must be hurting right now, hearing the news. Believe me, I know how you feel. You're probably a wreck. But give it five minutes, maybe ten. Maybe you can even go a whole half hour before you forget.

But you will forget—I guarantee it. A few more minutes and you'll be heading for the door, looking for her all over again, breaking down when you find the picture. How many times do you have to hear the news before some other part of your body, other than that busted brain of yours, starts to remember?

Never-ending grief, never-ending anger. Useless without direction. Maybe you can't understand what's happened. Can't say I really understand, either. Backwards amnesia. That's what the sign says. CRS disease. Your guess is as good as mine.

Maybe you can't understand what happened to you. But you do remember what happened to HER, don't you? The doctors don't want to talk about it. They won't answer my questions. They don't think it's right for a man in your condition to hear about those things. But you remember enough, don't you? You remember his face.

This is why I'm writing to you. Futile, maybe. I don't know how many times you'll have to read this before you listen to me. I don't even know how long you've been locked up in this room already. Neither do you. But your advantage in forgetting is that you'll forget to write yourself off as a lost cause.

Sooner or later you'll want to do something about it. And when you do, you'll just have to trust me, because I'm the only one who can help you.

* * *

Earl opens one eye after another to a stretch of white ceiling tiles inter-rupted by a hand-printed sign taped right above his head, large enough for him to read from the bed. An alarm clock is ringing somewhere. He reads the sign, blinks, reads it again, then takes a look at the room.

It's a white room, overwhelmingly white, from the walls and the cur-tains to the institutional furniture and the bedspread.

The alarm clock is ringing from the white desk under the window with the white curtains. At this point Earl probably notices that he is lying on top of his white comforter. He is already wearing a dressing gown and slippers.

He lies back and reads the sign taped to the ceiling again. It says, in crude block capitals, THIS IS YOUR ROOM. THIS IS A ROOM IN A HOSPITAL. THIS IS WHERE YOU LIVE NOW.

Earl rises and takes a look around. The room is large for a hospital—empty linoleum stretches out from the bed in three directions. Two doors and a window. The view isn't very helpful, either—a close of trees in the center of a carefully manicured piece of turf that terminates in a sliver of two-lane blacktop. The trees, except for the evergreens, are bare—early spring or late fall, one or the other.

Every inch of the desk is covered with Post-it notes, legal pads, neatly printed lists, psychological textbooks, framed pictures. On top of the mess is a half-completed crossword puzzle. The alarm clock is riding a pile of folded newspapers. Earl slaps the snooze button and takes a cigarette from the pack taped to the sleeve of his dressing gown. He pats the empty pock-ets of his pajamas for a light. He rifles the papers on the desk, looks quickly through the drawers. Eventually he finds a box of kitchen matches taped to the wall next to the window. Another sign is taped just above the box. It says in loud yellow letters, CIGARETTE? CHECK FOR LIT ONES FIRST, STUPID.

Earl laughs at the sign, lights his cigarette, and takes a long draw. Taped to the window in front of him is another piece of looseleaf paper headed YOUR SCHEDULE.

It charts off the hours, every hour, in blocks: 10:00 p.m. to 8:00 a.m. is labeled GO BACK TO SLEEP. Earl consults the alarm clock: 8:15. Given the light outside, it must be morning. He checks his watch: 10:30. He presses the watch to his ear and listens. He gives the watch a wind or two and sets it to match the alarm clock.

According to the schedule, the entire block from 8:00 to 8:30 has been labeled BRUSH YOUR TEETH. Earl laughs again and walks over to the bathroom.

The bathroom window is open. As he flaps his arms to keep warm, he notices the ashtray on the windowsill. A cigarette is perched on the ashtray, burning steadily through a long finger of ash. He frowns, extinguishes the old butt, and replaces it with the new one.

The toothbrush has already been treated to a smudge of white paste. The tap is of the push-button variety—a dose of water with each nudge. Earl pushes the brush into his cheek and fiddles it back and forth while he opens the medicine cabinet. The shelves are stocked with single-serving packages of vitamins, aspirin, antidiuretics. The mouthwash is also single-serving, about a shot-glass-worth of blue liquid in a sealed plastic bottle. Only the toothpaste is regular-sized. Earl spits the paste out of his mouth and replaces it with the mouthwash. As he lays the toothbrush next to the toothpaste, he notices a tiny wedge of paper pinched between the glass shelf and the steel backing of the medicine cabinet. He spits the frothy blue fluid into the sink and nudges for some more water to rinse it down. He closes the medicine cabinet and smiles at his reflection in the mirror.

"Who needs half an hour to brush their teeth?"

The paper has been folded down to a minuscule size with all the precision of a sixth-grader's love note. Earl unfolds it and smooths it against the mirror. It reads—

IF YOU CAN STILL READ THIS, THEN YOU'RE A FUCKING COWARD.

Earl stares blankly at the paper, then reads it again. He turns it over. On the back it reads—

P.S.: AFTER YOU'VE READ THIS, HIDE IT AGAIN.

Earl reads both sides again, then folds the note back down to its original size and tucks it underneath the toothpaste.

Maybe then he notices the scar. It begins just beneath the ear, jagged and thick, and disappears abruptly into his hairline. Earl turns his head and stares out of the corner of his eye to follow the scar's progress. He traces it with a fingertip, then looks back down at the cigarette burning in the ashtray. A thought seizes him and he spins out of the bathroom.

He is caught at the door to his room, one hand on the knob. Two pictures are taped to the wall by the door. Earl's attention is caught first by the MRI, a shiny black frame for four windows into someone's skull. In marker, the picture is labeled YOUR BRAIN. Earl stares at it. Concentric circles in different colors. He can make out the big orbs of his eyes and, behind these, the twin lobes of his brain. Smooth wrinkles, circles, semicircles. But right there in the middle of his head, circled in marker, tunneled in from the back of his neck like a maggot into an apricot, is something different. Deformed, broken, but unmistakable. A dark smudge, the shape of a flower, right there in the middle of his brain.

He bends to look at the other picture. It is a photograph of a man holding flowers, standing over a fresh grave. The man is bent over, reading the headstone. For a moment this looks like a hall of mirrors or the beginnings of a sketch of infinity: the one man bent over, looking at the smaller man, bent over, reading the headstone. Earl looks at the picture for a long time. Maybe he begins to cry. Maybe he just stares silently at the picture. Eventually, he makes his way back to the bed, flops down, seals his eyes shut, tries to sleep.

The cigarette burns steadily away in the bathroom. A circuit in the alarm clock counts down from ten, and it starts ringing again.

Earl opens one eye after another to a stretch of white ceiling tiles, interrupted by a hand-printed sign taped right above his head, large enough for him to read from the bed.

You can't have a normal life anymore. You must know that. How can you have a girlfriend if you can't remember her name? Can't have kids, not unless you want them to grow up with a dad who doesn't recognize them. Sure as hell can't hold down a job. Not too many professions out there that value forgetfulness. Prostitution, maybe. Politics, of course.

No. Your life is over. You're a dead man. The only thing the doctors are hoping to do is teach you to be less of a burden to the orderlies. And they'll probably never let you go home, wherever that would be.

So the question is not "to be or not to be," because you aren't. The question is whether you want to do something about it. Whether revenge matters to you.

It does to most people. For a few weeks, they plot, they scheme, they take measures to get even. But the passage of time is all it takes to erode that initial impulse. Time is theft, isn't that what they say? And time eventually convinces most of us that forgiveness is a virtue. Conveniently, cowardice and forgiveness look identical at a certain distance. Time steals your nerve.

If time and fear aren't enough to dissuade people from their revenge, then there's always authority, softly shaking its head and saying, We understand, but you're the better man for letting it go. For rising above it. For not sinking to their level. And besides, says authority, if you try anything stupid, we'll lock you up in a little room.

But they already put you in a little room, didn't they? Only they don't really lock it or even guard it too carefully because you're a cripple. A corpse. A vegetable who probably wouldn't remember to eat or take a shit if someone wasn't there to remind you.

And as for the passage of time, well, that doesn't really apply to you anymore, does it? Just the same ten minutes, over and over again. So how can you forgive if you can't remember to forget?

You probably were the type to let it go, weren't you? Before.

But you're not the man you used to be. Not even half. You're a fraction; you're the ten-minute man.

Of course, weakness is strong. It's the primary impulse. You'd probably prefer to sit in your little room and cry. Live in your finite collection of memories, carefully polishing each one. Half a life set behind glass and pinned to cardboard like a collection of exotic insects. You'd like to live behind that glass, wouldn't you? Preserved in aspic.

You'd like to but you can't, can you? You can't because of the last addition to your collection. The last thing you remember. His face. His face and your wife, looking to you for help.

And maybe this is where you can retire to when it's over. Your little collection. They can lock you back up in another little room and you can live the rest of your life in the past. But only if you've got a little piece of paper in your hand that says you got him.

You know I'm right. You know there's a lot of work to do. It may seem impossible, but I'm sure if we all do our part, we'll figure something out. But you don't have much time. You've only got about ten minutes, in fact. Then it starts all over again. So do something with the time you've got.

Earl opens his eyes and blinks into the darkness. The alarm clock is ringing. It says 3:20, and the moonlight streaming through the window means it must be the early morning. Earl fumbles for the lamp, almost knocking it over in the process. Incandescent light fills the room, painting the metal furniture yellow, the walls yellow, the bedspread, too. He lies back and looks up at the stretch of yellow ceiling tiles above him, interrupted by a handwritten sign taped to the ceiling. He reads the sign two, maybe three times, then blinks at the room around him.

It is a bare room. Institutional, maybe. There is a desk over by the window. The desk is bare except for the blaring alarm clock. Earl probably notices, at this point, that he is fully clothed. He even has his shoes on under the sheets. He extracts himself from the bed and crosses to the desk. Nothing in the room would suggest that anyone lived there, or ever had, except for the odd scrap of tape stuck here and there to the wall. No pictures, no books, nothing. Through the window, he can see a full moon shining on carefully manicured grass.

Earl slaps the snooze button on the alarm clock and stares a moment at the two keys taped to the back of his hand. He picks at the tape while he searches through the empty drawers. In the left pocket of his jacket, he finds a roll of hundred-dollar bills and a letter sealed in an envelope. He checks the rest of the main room and the bathroom. Bits of tape, cigarette butts. Nothing else.

Earl absentmindedly plays with the lump of scar tissue on his neck and moves back toward the bed. He lies back down and stares up at the ceiling and the sign taped to it. The sign reads, GET UP, GET OUT RIGHT NOW. THESE PEOPLE ARE TRYING TO KILL YOU.

Earl closes his eyes.

They tried to teach you to make lists in grade school, remember? Back when your day planner was the back of your hand. And if your assignments came off in the shower, well, then they didn't get done. No direction, they said. No discipline. So they tried to get you to write it all down somewhere more permanent.

Of course, your grade-school teachers would be laughing their pants wet if they could see you now. Because you've become the exact product of their organizational lessons. Because you can't even take a piss without consulting one of your lists.

They were right. Lists are the only way out of this mess.

Here's the truth: People, even regular people, are never just any one person with one set of attributes. It's not that simple. We're all at the mercy of the limbic system, clouds of electricity drifting through the brain. Every man is broken into twenty-four-hour fractions, and then again within those twenty-four hours. It's a daily pantomime, one man yielding control to the next: a backstage crowded with old hacks clamoring for their turn in the spotlight. Every week, every day. The angry man hands the baton over to the sulking man, and in turn to the sex addict, the introvert, the conversationalist. Every man is a mob, a chain gang of idiots.

This is the tragedy of life. Because for a few minutes of every day, every man becomes a genius. Moments of clarity, insight, whatever you want to call them. The clouds part, the planets get in a neat little line, and everything becomes obvious. I should quit smoking, maybe, or here's how I could make a fast million, or such and such is the key to eternal happiness. That's the miserable truth. For a few moments, the secrets of the universe are opened to us. Life is a cheap parlor trick.

But then the genius, the savant, has to hand over the controls to the next guy down the pike, most likely the guy who just wants to eat potato chips, and insight and brilliance and salvation are all entrusted to a moron or a hedo-nist or a narcoleptic.

The only way out of this mess, of course, is to take steps to ensure that you control the idiots that you become. To take your chain gang, hand in hand, and lead them. The best way to do this is with a list.

It's like a letter you write to yourself. A master plan, drafted by the guy who can see the light, made with steps simple enough for the rest of the idiots to understand. Follow steps one through one hundred. Repeat as necessary.

Your problem is a little more acute, maybe, but fundamentally the same thing.

It's like that computer thing, the Chinese room. You remember that? One guy sits in a little room, laying down cards with letters written on them in a language he doesn't understand, laying them down one letter at a time in a sequence according to someone else's instructions. The cards are supposed to spell out a joke in Chinese. The guy doesn't speak Chinese, of course. He just follows his instructions.

There are some obvious differences in your situation, of course: You broke out of the room they had you in, so the whole enterprise has to be portable. And the guy giving the instructions—that's you, too, just an earlier version of you. And the joke you're telling, well, it's got a punch line. I just don't think anyone's going to find it very funny.

So that's the idea. All you have to do is follow your instructions. Like climbing a ladder or descending a staircase. One step at a time. Right down the list. Simple.

And the secret, of course, to any list is to keep it in a place where you're bound to see it.

He can hear the buzzing through his eyelids. Insistent. He reaches out for the alarm clock, but he can't move his arm.

Earl opens his eyes to see a large man bent double over him. The man looks up at him, annoyed, then resumes his work. Earl looks around him. Too dark for a doctor's office.

Then the pain floods his brain, blocking out the other questions. He squirms again, trying to yank his forearm away, the one that feels like it's burning. The arm doesn't move, but the man shoots him another scowl. Earl adjusts himself in the chair to see over the top of the man's head.

The noise and the pain are both coming from a gun in the man's hand—a gun with a needle where the barrel should be. The needle is digging into the fleshy underside of Earl's forearm, leaving a trail of puffy letters behind it.

Earl tries to rearrange himself to get a better view, to read the letters on his arm, but he can't. He lies back and stares at the ceiling.

Eventually the tattoo artist turns off the noise, wipes Earl's forearm with a piece of gauze, and wanders over to the back to dig up a pamphlet describing how to deal with a possible infection. Maybe later he'll tell his wife about this guy and his little note. Maybe his wife will convince him to call the police.

Earl looks down at the arm. The letters are rising up from the skin, weeping a little. They run from just behind the strap of Earl's watch all the way to the inside of his elbow. Earl blinks at the message and reads it again. It says, in careful little capitals, I RAPED AND KILLED YOUR WIFE.

It's your birthday today, so I got you a little present. I would have just bought you a beer, but who knows where that would have ended?

So instead, I got you a bell. I think I may have had to pawn your watch to buy it, but what the hell did you need a watch for, anyway?

You're probably asking yourself, Why a bell? In fact, I'm guessing you're going to be asking yourself that question every time you find it in your pocket. Too many of these letters now. Too many for you to dig back into every time you want to know the answer to some little question.

It's a joke, actually. A practical joke. But think of it this way: I'm not really laughing at you so much as with you.

I'd like to think that every time you take it out of your pocket and wonder, Why do I have this bell? a little part of you, a little piece of your broken brain, will remember and laugh, like I'm laughing now.

Besides, you do know the answer. It was something you learned before. So if you think about it, you'll know.

Back in the old days, people were obsessed with the fear of being buried alive. You remember now? Medical science not being quite what it is today, it wasn't uncommon for people to suddenly wake up in a casket. So rich folks had their coffins outfitted with breathing tubes. Little tubes running up to the mud above so that if someone woke up when they weren't supposed to, they wouldn't run out of oxygen. Now, they must have tested this out and realized that you could shout yourself hoarse through the tube, but it was too narrow to carry much noise. Not enough to attract attention, at least. So a string was run up the tube to a little bell attached to the headstone. If a dead person came back to life, all he had to do was ring his little bell till someone came and dug him up again.

I'm laughing now, picturing you on a bus or maybe in a fast-food restaurant, reaching into your pocket and finding your little bell and wondering to yourself where it came from, why you have it. Maybe you'll even ring it.

Happy birthday, buddy.

I don't know who figured out the solution to our mutual problem, so I don't know whether to congratulate you or me. A bit of a lifestyle change, admittedly, but an elegant solution, nonetheless.

Look to yourself for the answer.

That sounds like something out of a Hallmark card. I don't know when you thought it up, but my hat's off to you. Not that you know what the hell I'm talking about. But, honestly, a real brainstorm. After all, everybody else needs mirrors to remind themselves who they are. You're no different.

The little mechanical voice pauses, then repeats itself. It says, "The time is 8:00 a.m. This is a courtesy call." Earl opens his eyes and replaces the receiver. The phone is perched on a cheap veneer headboard that stretches behind the bed, curves to meet the corner, and ends at the minibar. The TV is still on, blobs of flesh color nattering away at each other. Earl lies back down and is surprised to see himself, older now, tanned, the hair pulling away from his head like solar flares. The mirror on the ceiling is cracked, the silver fading in creases. Earl continues to stare at himself, astonished by what he sees. He is fully dressed, but the clothes are old, threadbare in places.

Earl feels the familiar spot on his left wrist for his watch, but it's gone. He looks down from the mirror to his arm. It is bare and the skin has changed to an even tan, as if he never owned a watch in the first place. The skin is even in color except for the solid black arrow on the inside of Earl's wrist, pointing up his shirtsleeve. He stares at the arrow for a moment. Perhaps he doesn't try to rub it off anymore. He rolls up his sleeve.

The arrow points to a sentence tattooed along Earl's inner arm. Earl reads the sentence once, maybe twice. Another arrow picks up at the beginning of the sentence, points farther up Earl's arm, disappearing under the rolled-up shirtsleeve. He unbuttons his shirt.

Looking down on his chest, he can make out the shapes but cannot bring them into focus, so he looks up at the mirror above him.

The arrow leads up Earl's arm, crosses at the shoulder, and descends onto his upper torso, terminating at a picture of a man's face that occupies most of his chest. The face is that of a large man, balding, with a mustache and a goatee. It is a particular face, but like a police sketch it has a certain unreal quality.

The rest of his upper torso is covered in words, phrases, bits of information, and instructions, all of them written backward on Earl, forward in the mirror.

Eventually Earl sits up, buttons his shirt, and crosses to the desk. He takes out a pen and a piece of notepaper from the desk drawer, sits, and begins to write.

I don't know where you'll be when you read this. I'm not even sure if you'll bother to read this. I guess you don't need to.

It's a shame, really, that you and I will never meet. But, like the song says, "By the time you read this note, I'll be gone."

We're so close now. That's the way it feels. So many pieces put together, spelled out. I guess it's just a matter of time until you find him.

Who knows what we've done to get here? Must be a hell of a story, if only you could remember any of it. I guess it's better that you can't.

I had a thought just now. Maybe you'll find it useful.

Everybody is waiting for the end to come, but what if it already passed us by? What if the final joke of Judgment Day was that it had already come and gone and we were none the wiser? Apocalypse arrives quietly; the chosen are herded off to heaven, and the rest of us, the ones who failed the test, just keep on going, oblivious. Dead already, wandering around long after the gods have stopped keeping score, still optimistic about the future.

I guess if that's true, then it doesn't matter what you do. No expectations. If you can't find him, then it doesn't matter, because nothing matters. And if you do find him, then you can kill him without worrying about the consequences. Because there are no consequences.

That's what I'm thinking about right now, in this scrappy little room. Framed pictures of ships on the wall. I don't know, obviously, but if I had to guess, I'd say we're somewhere up the coast. If you're wondering why your left arm is five shades browner than your right, I don't know what to tell you. I guess we must have been driving for a while. And, no, I don't know what happened to your watch.

And all these keys: I have no idea. Not a one that I recognize. Car keys and house keys and the little fiddly keys for padlocks. What have we been up to?

I wonder if he'll feel stupid when you find him. Tracked down by the ten-minute man. Assassinated by a vegetable.

I'll be gone in a moment. I'll put down the pen, close my eyes, and then you can read this through if you want.

I just wanted you to know that I'm proud of you. No one who matters is left to say it. No one left is going to want to.

Earl's eyes are wide open, staring through the window of the car. Smiling eyes. Smiling through the window at the crowd gathering across the street.

The crowd gathering around the body in the doorway. The body emptying slowly across the sidewalk and into the storm drain.

A stocky guy, facedown, eyes open. Balding head, goatee. In death, as in police sketches, faces tend to look the same. This is definitely somebody in particular. But really, it could be anybody.

Earl is still smiling at the body as the car pulls away from the curb. The car? Who's to say? Maybe it's a police cruiser. Maybe it's just a taxi.

As the car is swallowed into traffic, Earl's eyes continue to shine out into the night, watching the body until it disappears into a circle of concerned pedestrians. He chuckles to himself as the car continues to make distance between him and the growing crowd.

Earl's smile fades a little. Something has occurred to him. He begins to pat down his pockets; leisurely at first, like a man looking for his keys, then a little more desperately. Maybe his progress is impeded by a set of handcuffs. He begins to empty the contents of his pockets out onto the seat next to him. Some money. A bunch of keys. Scraps of paper.

A round metal lump rolls out of his pocket and slides across the vinyl seat. Earl is frantic now. He hammers at the plastic divider between him and the driver, begging the man for a pen. Perhaps the cabbie doesn't speak much English. Perhaps the cop isn't in the habit of talking to suspects. Either way, the divider between the man in front and the man behind remains closed. A pen is not forthcoming.

The car hits a pothole, and Earl blinks at his reflection in the rearview mirror. He is calm now. The driver makes another corner, and the metal lump slides back over to rest against Earl's leg with a little jingle. He picks it up and looks at it, curious now. It is a little bell. A little metal bell. Inscribed on it are his name and a set of dates. He recognizes the first one: the year in which he was born. But the second date means nothing to him. Nothing at all.

As he turns the bell over in his hands, he notices the empty space on his wrist where his watch used to sit. There is a little arrow there, pointing up his arm. Earl looks at the arrow, then begins to roll up his sleeve.

* * *

"You'd be late for your own funeral," she'd say. Remember? The more I think about it, the more trite that seems. What kind of idiot, after all, is in any kind of rush to get to the end of his own story?

And how would I know if I were late, anyway? I don't have a watch anymore. I don't know what we did with it.

What the hell do you need a watch for, anyway? It was an antique. Deadweight tugging at your wrist. Symbol of the old you. The you that believed in time.

No. Scratch that. It's not so much that you've lost your faith in time as that time has lost its faith in you. And who needs it, anyway? Who wants to be one of those saps living in the safety of the future, in the safety of the moment after the moment in which they felt something powerful? Living in the next moment, in which they feel nothing. Crawling down the hands of the clock, away from the people who did unspeakable things to them. Believing the lie that time will heal all wounds—which is just a nice way of saying that time deadens us.

But you're different. You're more perfect. Time is three things for most people, but for you, for us, just one. A singularity. One moment. This moment. Like you're the center of the clock, the axis on which the hands turn. Time moves about you but never moves you. It has lost its ability to affect you. What is it they say? That time is theft? But not for you. Close your eyes and you can start all over again. Conjure up that necessary emotion, fresh as roses.

Time is an absurdity. An abstraction. The only thing that matters is this moment. This moment a million times over. You have to trust me. If this moment is repeated enough, if you keep trying—and you have to keep trying—eventually you will come across the next item on your list.

The Lonesome Vigilante

John Steinbeck

The great surge of emotion, the milling and shouting of the people fell gradually to silence in the town park. A crowd of people still stood under the elm trees, vaguely lighted by a blue street light two blocks away. A tired quiet settled on the people; some members of the mob began to sneak away into the darkness. The park lawn was cut to pieces by the feet of the crowd.

Mike knew it was all over. He could feel the let-down in himself. He was as heavily weary as though he had gone without sleep for several nights, but it was a dream-like weariness, a grey comfortable weariness. He pulled his cap down over his eyes and moved away, but before leaving the park he turned for one last look.

In the center of the mob someone had lighted a twisted newspaper and was holding it up. Mike could see how the flame curled about the feet of the grey naked body hanging from the elm tree. It seemed curious to him that Negroes turn a bluish grey when they are dead. The burning newspaper lighted the heads of the up-looking men, silent men and fixed; they didn't move their eyes from the hanged man.

Mike felt a little irritation at whoever it was who was trying to burn the body. He turned to a man who stood beside him in the near-darkness. "That don't do no good," he said.

The man moved away without replying.

The newspaper torch went out, leaving the park almost black by contrast. But immediately another twisted paper was lighted and held up against the feet. Mike moved to another watching man. "That don't do no good," he repeated. "He's dead now. They can't hurt him none."

The second man grunted but did not look away from the flaming paper. "It's a good job," he said. "This'll save the county a lot of money and no sneaky lawyers getting in."

"That's what I say," Mike agreed. "No sneaky lawyers. But it don't do no good to try to burn him."

The man continued staring toward the flame. "Well, it can't do much harm, either."

Mike filled his eyes with the scene. He felt that he was dull. He wasn't seeing enough of it. Here was a thing he would want to remember later so he could tell about it, but the dull tiredness seemed to cut the sharpness off the picture. His brain told him this was a terrible and important affair, but his eyes and his feelings didn't agree. It was just ordinary. Half an hour before, when he had been howling with the mob and fighting for a chance to help pull on the rope, then his chest had been so full that he had found he was crying. But now everything was dead, everything unreal; the dark mob was made up of stiff lay-figures. In the flame-light the faces were as expressionless as wood. Mike felt the stiffness, the unreality in himself, too. He turned away at last and walked out of the park.

The moment he left the outskirts of the mob a cold loneliness fell upon him. He walked quickly along the street wishing that some other man might be walking beside him. The wide street was deserted, empty, as unreal as the park had been.

The two steel lines of the car tracks stretched glimmering away down the street under the electroliers, and the dark store windows reflected the midnight globes.

A gentle pain began to make itself felt in Mike's chest. He felt with his fingers; the muscles were sore. Then he remembered. He was in the front line of the mob when it rushed the closed jail door. A driving line forty men deep had crashed Mike against the door like the head of a ram. He had hardly felt it then, and even now the pain seemed to have the dull quality of loneliness.

Two blocks ahead the burning neon word BEER hung over the sidewalk. Mike hurried toward it. He hoped there would be people there, and talk to remove this silence; and he hoped the men wouldn't have been to the lynching.

The bartender was alone in his little bar, a small, middle-aged man with a melancholy moustache and an expression like an aged mouse, wise and unkempt and fearful.

He nodded quickly as Mike came in. "You look like you been walking in your sleep," he said.

Mike regarded him with wonder. "That's just how I feel, too, like I been walking in my sleep."

"Well, I can give you a shot if you want."

Mike hesitated. "No—I'm kind of thirsty. I'll take a beer. Was you there?"

The little man nodded his mouse-like head again. "Right at the last, after he was all up and it was all over. I figured a lot of the fellas would be thirsty, so I came back and opened up. Nobody but you so far. Maybe I was wrong."

"They might be along later," said Mike. "There's a lot of them still in the park. They cooled off, though. Some of them trying to burn him with newspapers. That don't do no good."

"Not a bit of good," said the little bartender. He twitched his thin moustache.

Mike knocked a few grains of celery salt into his beer and took a long drink. "That's good," he said. "I'm kind of dragged out."

The bartender leaned close to him over the bar, his eyes were bright. "Was you there all the time—to the jail and everything?"

Mike drank again and then looked through his beer and watched the beads of bubbles rising from the grains of salt in the bottom of the glass. "Everything," he said. "I was one of the first in the jail, and I helped pull on the rope. There's times when citizens got to take the law in their own hands. Sneaky lawyer comes along and gets some fiend out of it."

The mousy head jerked up and down. "You God-dam right," he said. "Lawyers can get them out of anything. I guess the nigger was guilty all right."

"Oh, sure! Somebody said he even confessed."

The head came close over the bar again. "How did it start, mister? I was only there after it was all over, and then I only stayed a minute and then came back to open up in case any of the fellas might want a glass of beer."

Mike drained his glass and pushed it out to be filled. "Well, of course everybody knew it was going to happen. I was in a bar across from the jail. Been there all afternoon. A guy came in and says, 'What are we waiting for?' So we went across the street, and a lot more guys was there and a lot more come. We all stood there and yelled. Then the sheriff come out and made a speech, but we yelled him down. A guy with a twenty-two rifle went along the street and shot out the street lights. Well, then we rushed the jail doors and bust them. The sheriff wasn't going to do nothing. It wouldn't do him no good to shoot a lot of honest men to save a nigger fiend."

"And election coming on, too," the bartender put in.

"Well the sheriff started yelling, 'Get the right man, boys, for Christ's sake get the right man. He's in the fourth cell down.'

331

"It was kind of pitiful," Mike said slowly. "The other prisoners was so scared. We could see them through the bars. I never seen such faces."

The bartender excitedly poured himself a small glass of whiskey and poured it down. "Can't blame 'em much. Suppose you was in for thirty days and a lynch mob came through. You'd be scared they'd get the wrong man."

"That's what I say. It was kind of pitiful. Well, we got to the nigger's cell. He just stood stiff with his eyes closed like he was dead drunk. One of the guys slugged him down and he got up, and then somebody else socked him and he went over and hit his head on the cement floor." Mike leaned over the bar and tapped the polished wood with his forefinger. " 'Course this is only my idea, but I think that killed him. Because I helped get his clothes off, and he never made a wiggle, and when we strung him up he didn't jerk around none. No, sir. I think he was dead all the time, after that second guy smacked him."

"Well, it's all the same in the end."

"No it ain't. You like to do the thing right. He had it coming to him, and he should have got it." Mike reached into his trousers pocket and brought out a piece of torn blue denim. "That's a piece of the pants he had on."

The bartender bent close and inspected the cloth. He jerked his head up at Mike. "I'll give you a buck for it."

"Oh no you won't!"

"All right. I'll give you two bucks for half of it."

Mike looked suspiciously at him. "What do you want it for?"

"Here! Give me your glass! Have a beer on me. I'll pin it up on the wall with a little card under it. The fellas that come in will like to look at it."

Mike haggled the piece of cloth in two with his pocket knife and accepted two silver dollars from the bartender.

"I know a show card writer," the little man said. "Comes in every day. He'll print me up a nice little card to go under it." He looked wary. "Think the sheriff will arrest anybody?"

" 'Course not. What's he want to start any trouble for? There was a lot of votes in that crowd tonight. Soon as they all go away, the sheriff will come and cut the nigger down and clean up some."

The bartender looked toward the door. "I guess I was wrong about the fellas wanting a drink. It's getting late."

"I guess I'll get along home. I feel tired."

"If you go south, I'll close up and walk a ways with you. I live on south Eighth."

"Why, that's only two blocks from my house. I live on south Sixth. You must go right past my house. Funny I never saw you around."

The bartender washed Mike's glass and took off the long apron. He put on his hat and coat, walked to the door and switched off the red neon sign and the house lights. For a moment the two men stood on the sidewalk looking back toward the park. The city was silent. There was no sound from the park. A policeman walked along a block away, turning his flash into the store windows.

"You see?" said Mike. "Just like nothing happened."

"Well, if the fellas wanted a glass of beer they must have gone someplace else."

"That's what I told you," said Mike.

They swung along the empty street and turned south, out of the business district. "My name's Welch," the bartender said. "I only been in this town about two years."

The loneliness had fallen on Mike again. "It's funny—" he said, and then, "I was born right in this town, right in the house I live in now. I got a wife but no kids. Both of us born right in this town. Everybody knows us."

They walked on for a few blocks. The stores dropped behind and the nice houses with bushy gardens and cut lawns lined the street. The tall shade trees were shadowed on the sidewalk by the street lights. Two night dogs went slowly by, smelling at each other.

Welch said softly—"I wonder what kind of a fella he was—the nigger, I mean."

Mike answered out of his loneliness. "The papers all said he was a fiend. I read all the papers. That's what they all said."

"Yes, I read them, too. But it makes you wonder about him. I've known some pretty nice niggers."

333

Mike turned his head and spoke protestingly. "Well, I've knew some damn fine niggers myself. I've worked right long side some niggers and they was as nice as any white man you could want to meet.—But not no fiends."

His vehemence silenced little Welch for a moment. Then he said, "You couldn't tell, I guess, what kind of a fella he was?"

"No—he just stood there stiff, with his mouth shut and his eyes tight closed and his hands right down at his sides. And then one of the guys smacked him. It's my idea he was dead when we took him out."

Welch sidled close on the walk. "Nice gardens along here. Must take a lot of money to keep them up." He walked even closer, so that his shoulder touched Mike's arm. "I never been to a lynching. How's it make you feel—afterwards?"

Mike shied away from the contact. "It don't make you feel nothing." He put down his head and increased his pace. The little bartender had nearly to trot to keep up. The street lights were fewer. It was darker and safer. Mike burst out, "Makes you feel kind of cut off and tired, but kind of satisfied, too. Like you done a good job—but tired and kind of sleepy." He slowed his steps. "Look, there's a light in the kitchen. That's where I live. My old lady's waiting up for me." He stopped in front of his little house.

Welch stood nervously beside him. "Come into my place when you want a glass of beer—or a shot. Open 'til midnight. I treat my friends right." He scampered away like an aged mouse.

Mike called "Good night."

He walked around the side of his house and went in the back door. His thin petulant wife was sitting by the open gas oven warming herself. She turned complaining eyes on Mike where he stood in the door.

Then her eyes widened and hung on his face. "You been with a woman," she said hoarsely. "What woman you been with?"

Mike laughed. "You think you're pretty slick, don't you? You're a slick one, ain't you? What makes you think I been with a woman?"

She said fiercely, "You think I can't tell by the look on your face that you been with a woman?"

"All right," said Mike. "If you're so slick and know-it-all, I won't tell you nothing. You can just wait for the morning paper."

He saw doubt come into the dissatisfied eyes. "Was it the nigger?" she asked. "Did they get the nigger? Everybody said they was going to."

"Find out for yourself if you're so slick. I ain't going to tell you nothing."

He walked through the kitchen and went into the bathroom. A little mirror hung on the wall. Mike took off his cap and looked at his face. "By God she was right," he thought. "That's just exactly how I do feel."

Monhegan Light

Richard Russo

Well, he'd been wrong, Martin had to admit, as Monhegan began to take shape on the horizon. Wrong about the island, about the ferry. Maybe even wrong to make this journey in the first place. Joyce, Clara's sister, had implied as much, not that he'd paid much attention to her, colossal bitch that she was. Imagine, even now, so long after the fact (after the fact of Clara's death), still trying to make him feel guilty. As if *he* were the one who'd been living a lie for twenty-five years. He could still see her smirking at him.

But he *had* been wrong about the island. About what it was. He'd imagined Monhegan as harboring some sort of retreat or commune inhabited by starving, self-deluded, talentless fringe painters like Joyce.

Wannabes. (Not that Robert Trevor, alas, was one of those.) But a quick scan of the brochure had shown him that this was no commune. The artists who summered here were not hoping to "arrive" one day; they already had. The island's other claim to fame was its hiking trails, for which he was grateful. Otherwise, how would he have explained to Beth his sudden urge to see Monhegan instead of heading up the coast to Bar Harbor as planned? He glanced over at her now to make sure she hadn't caught on to their real purpose.

The woman in question had closed her eyes and reclined her head over the back of the seat so that her smooth throat was exposed to the weakening September sun. Her long hair hung straight down, spilling onto the top of a backpack that a young man sitting behind them had wedged between the seats. Martin gave the boy an apologetic smile and received in return a shrug of camaraderie that suggested the boy understood about pretty women who were careless with their hair.

No, Beth was not the sort of girl, Martin reassured himself, who "caught on" to things. In fact, the way she took in new data without apparent surprise was one of her great life skills. An arched eyebrow seemed to represent the extreme end of her emotional range when it came to revelation, and to Martin's way of thinking, there was much to be said for such economy, especially in a woman. Beth never said I-told-you-so, even in an I-told-you-so situation, of which the ferry was the latest. The whole trip, hastily arranged after the shoot had wrapped, was not going smoothly.

"I think I've discovered why they don't take cars," Martin told her, returning to the island's information brochure. He'd assured her yesterday that all these islands off the coast of Maine had ferries that took automobiles, and that now, after Labor Day, they probably wouldn't even need a reservation. "There are no roads on the island."

There was a downside to Beth's emotional reticence, of course. That arched eyebrow of hers did manage to convey perhaps by intention, perhaps not, that the reason that she was not greatly surprised by the fact that you were wrong about something was that she understood you, knew you better than you knew yourself, and therefore inferred that of course you *would* be wrong about a lot of things. When Martin glanced over at Beth now, he was rewarded with the precise arched eyebrow he'd anticipated, its meaning unmistakable. Fortunately there was a trace of a smile, too, and in that smile a hint of generosity that distinguished her from professional bitches like his sister-in-law, Joyce.

"No paved roads, anyway," he continued, after Beth again allowed her eyes to close sleepily. "Except for the summer, there are only seventy-five full-time residents on the island. Five children attend the local school."

Beth did not open her eyes when she spoke. "I wonder if they have a special program for gifted kids."

Martin chuckled. "Or a remedial one, come to that."

Beth did not smile, causing Martin to wonder if he'd misread her remark about the gifted children. He'd assumed she'd meant it to be funny, since it was, but one never knew. "She looks perfect for you, Martin," Joyce had remarked yesterday, though Beth had remained in the car while Martin climbed the front-porch steps and rang the bell. "How clever of you two to find each other."

"It's suggested here that visitors bring a flashlight, since power out-rages on the island are common," Martin read on in the pamphlet. "I don't suppose you've got a flashlight on you?"

At this, Beth pulled the material of her tube top away from her chest to check. From where Martin sat, her entire right breast was exposed for a full beat before she allowed the elastic to snap back into place. The young man seated behind them had chosen that precise moment to stand up, which meant that he must have gotten, Martin guessed, an even better view.

"Hey," he said, when the boy was safely out of hearing along the boat's opposite rail. "This ain't L.A."

"It's not?" she said, feigning astonishment. "Really?"

"Okay, fine," he said, going back to his brochure. "But people have different ideas about nudity in New England." California born and bred, he'd been to the Northeast only a couple of times on shoots, once to southern Connecticut, which didn't feel much like New England, and once to Boston, which felt like the city it was. But Puritanism had flowered in this rocky soil, hadn't it? And after driving up the coast of Maine from Portland, Martin thought he understood why people who lived in such a harsh, unforgiving physical landscape might come to sterner conclusions about sex than people who lived in Malibu.

"Yeah, well, I've spent a lot of money on these boobs, old man."

Which was true. And not just her boobs, either, Martin was certain. Beth was a firm believer in fixing whatever ailed you. Actually, she was not merely a firm believer, but a believer in firmness. At thirty-five, her body was taut and lean, her long legs tanned and ropelike, her tummy flat from thousands of murderous crunches. Her breasts, truth be told, were a little too firm, at least for Martin's taste, better to look at than to caress. Whatever she'd had done to them caused her nipples to be in a constant state of erection. If the boy over at the rail had gotten a good look, he'd already had the best of them.

"Ugliness," Martin's friend, the director Peter Axelrod, was fond of saying wistfully, "is gradually being bred out of the species in California." And beauty along with it, Martin sometimes thought. Living in L.A. and working in "the industry," Martin saw many beautiful women, and the most beautiful of them were flawed in some way that made them anxious. Audrey Hepburn's eyebrows. Meryl Streep's nose. He'd sat on the sideline of many a tearful, whispered conversation on the set in which some actress had become irrationally convinced that the next shot would reveal or emphasize some terrible imperfection she was determined to conceal. Axelrod, whose face had been badly burned when he was a child, handled them as well as anybody. "Look at me," he'd say quietly. "Look at this face and tell me *you're* ugly." They loved him for that, sometimes, Martin suspected, even sleeping with him out of gratitude. Back in his director's chair, he'd give the actress a few minutes to compose herself, explaining to the waiting crew, in his most confidential tones, "Everybody wants to be perfect. I certainly hope this isn't a perfect movie we're making." Whereupon he would be assured it wasn't.

Strange, though. When Axelrod himself married, late in life, the woman he wed might have been Beth's sister, a flawless beauty about twenty years his junior with a face and body that seemed in their perfect symmetry to be computer generated. Which probably meant that ultimately men *were* to blame. That's what Joyce would say. It was men, after all, who were responsible for setting the standards of feminine beauty. Someday, Martin felt certain, it would be discovered what women were responsible for, though probably not in his lifetime.

When he looked up from his brochure, Martin saw that the island's lighthouse had come into view above the dark line of trees, so he got up and went over to the rail for a better look. A few minutes later the ferry rounded the southernmost tip of the island and chugged into the tiny harbor, with its scattering of small buildings set, seemingly, right into the hillside. Only the lighthouse, high on the hill above the village, was bright white, straight out of an Edward Hopper painting. Everything was starkly brilliant in its detail. Martin could feel his eyes welling up in the stiff breeze, and when he felt Beth at his elbow, he tried to wipe the tear out of the corner of his left eye with the heel of his hand, a gesture he hoped looked natural. She must have noticed, though, because she said, "Don't be jealous, babe. God lit this one."

It wasn't until they'd disembarked from the ferry, until they'd located their bags on the dock and started up the hill toward the second-best accommodations on the island, that Martin turned back and saw the name painted on the ferry's transom: THE CLARA B.

He'd told Beth nothing of his wife, except that she'd died several years ago and that he and Clara had stayed married, he supposed, out of inertia. Beth seemed content with this slender account, but then she never appeared to hunger for more information than what Martin offered. He would have concluded that she was genuinely incurious, except that sometimes, if he'd been particularly evasive, she'd pose a follow-up question, days or even weeks after the fact, as if it had taken her all that time to realize he'd not been terribly forthcoming. Worse, she always remembered his precise words, which meant he couldn't plead misunderstanding when an unwanted subject got revisited. Often her questions took the form of statements, as was the case now.

"That woman didn't appear to like you very much," she observed over her chicken Caesar salad.

They were the only two people in the dining room. They'd come in just after two, having checked in and unpacked their things, to find that the dining room was closed, though the young woman working in the kitchen said she supposed, inasmuch as they were guests of the hotel, they might be fed something if what they wanted wasn't too complicated. Martin had ordered a bowl of chowder, figuring something of that sort was probably what the woman had in mind. Beth had ordered the chicken Caesar, which was what she would have ordered if the woman had been mute on the subject of what they might and might not have. When their food was served a few minutes later, the woman reminded them that the last seating for dinner that evening would be at seven-thirty, which may or may not have registered with Beth, who did not look up from the map of the island's trails that she was studying. She'd changed into hiking clothes in their room.

Martin was about to remark that it was Beth herself whom the kitchen woman was not fond of when it occurred to him that Beth had not been referring to their waitress, but rather to Joyce.

"She was Clara's sister," Martin explained, as if this *were* an explanation, as if it were common knowledge that all sisters despised their brothers-in-law by natural decree.

"Did you fuck her?" Beth asked around a bite of blackened chicken breast.

"Joyce?" Martin snorted.

"Well, I assume you were fucking your wife," Beth pointed out, not unreasonably. Martin might have corrected her but did not. "Men have been known—"

"I'll try to forgive you for that unkind and entirely unwarranted suspicion," he said, blowing on his chowder, the first bite of which had burned his tongue.

"This is an excellent Caesar salad," Beth said.

"Good," Martin told her. "I'm glad."

"Now you're mad at me."

"No."

"Tell me," she said, leaving Martin to wonder for a full beat whether she intended to change the subject or forge ahead. Change it was Martin's guess, and he was right. "What will you be doing while I'm climbing the island's dangerous cliffs, which this publication warns me not to do alone?"

Martin decided not to take this particular bait. "I thought I'd take some pictures, maybe visit a gallery or two. See if I can locate a bottle of wine for dinner." The hotel, they'd been informed when they checked in, had no liquor license.

"One dinner without wine wouldn't kill us, actually," Beth pointed out.

"How do you know?"

"Well, it's true I'm only guessing."

Martin studied her until she pushed her plate away. As usual, about half the food remained on it. In all of the time they'd been together, nearly a year now, Martin had never known her to finish a serving of anything. In restaurants known for their small portions, Beth would order twice as much food so she could leave the same amount. Clara, he recalled, had eaten like a man, with appetite and appreciation. "When have I ever been unable to answer the bell?" he asked Beth. "Any bell."

She gave him a small smile, which meant that their argument, if that's what this was, was over. "I'm not overly fond of boxing metaphors applied to sex," she told him, taking one of his thumbs and pulling on it. "It's not war."

Like hell, Martin thought.

"But yes," she conceded, "you *do* answer every bell, old man."

"Thank you," Martin said, meaning it. The question he'd asked had been risky, he realized, and he was glad the danger had passed.

"I'm going back to the room for some sunscreen," she said, pushing her chair back. "I'll be taking the A trail—"

Martin whistled a few bars of "Take the 'A' Train."

"—in case I need rescuing."

Martin watched her across the room. He had a pretty good idea what the sunscreen was for. She'd sunbathe on a rock, topless, in some secluded, but not too secluded, spot. Martin imagined the young fellow from the ferry watching her through binoculars from an adjacent bluff. "You *could* go with her," he said to himself. "There's nothing preventing you."

But there was.

He'd half expected to discover that Joyce had lied to him, but Robert Trevor's studio was right where she said it would be. By Martin's count roughly a third of the houses on the island were listed as artists' studios, though to the casual eye they looked no different from the other houses, inhabited, presumably, by lobstermen and the owners of the island's few seasonal businesses. All of the buildings were sided with the same weathered gray shingles, as if they'd been subjected, decades ago, to a dress code. Trevor's studio was at the edge of the village, where the dirt road ended and one of the island's dozen or so hiking trails began. Martin had watched Beth disappear up another of these half an hour ago and purposely waited until he was sure she'd forgotten nothing and wouldn't be returning until early evening.

Trevor's studio was unmarked except for a tiny engraved sign to the left of the screen door. The inner door was wide open, and Martin was about to knock at the screen when he heard a loud crash from around back of the house. There, on the elevated deck, Martin found a large man with a flowing mane of silver hair, dressed in paint-splattered jeans and an unbuttoned blue denim work shirt. He was teetering awkwardly on one knee, his other leg stretched out stiffly in front of him like a prosthesis, and trying to prop up a rickety three-legged table with its splintered fourth leg. There were jelly jars and paintbrushes strewn everywhere. One small jar, which looked to Martin like it might have originally contained artichoke hearts, had described a long, wet arc on the floor of the sloping deck and come to a teetering pause at the top of the steps, then thumped down all five, coming to rest at Martin's feet.

Martin picked it up and waited for Robert Trevor—there could be no doubt it was the artist himself—to notice him. The wooden leg that had detached itself from the table fell off again as soon as the man, with considerable difficulty, got back to his feet and tested it. "All right, be that way," Robert Trevor said, tossing the leg on the tabletop and sitting down heavily on a chair that didn't look much sturdier than the table. It groaned mightily under the big man's weight, but ultimately held. Martin saw that Trevor was sweating, that his forehead was smudged with several different colors of paint from his palette.

There was an easel set up next to the table, and Trevor studied the half-finished canvas resting on it, a landscape, as if rickety furniture were the least of his problems. It took him a minute to sense Martin's presence at the foot of his deck, and even then he didn't react with as much surprise as Martin himself would have displayed had their situations been reversed. The painter nodded at Martin as if he'd been expecting him. He did not get up. "You," he said, running his fingers through his hair, "would be Clara's husband."

"Martin."

"Right, Martin."

"Joyce called you?"

Robert Trevor snorted. "I don't have a phone. That's one of the many beauties of this place." He paused to let this vaguely political observation sink in. "No, the sun went behind a cloud and I looked over and there you were. I made the connection."

Okay, Martin thought. So that's the way it's going to be. The sun *had* in that instant disappeared behind a cloud, though, and Martin thought of Beth walking along the cliffs on the back side of the island. She'd be disappointed now, lacking an excuse to sunbathe topless.

"I'm going to need that, Martin," Robert Trevor told him, indicating the artichoke jar.

"Can I come up?" Martin asked.

"Have you come to murder me?" Robert Trevor asked. "Did you bring a gun?"

Martin shook his head. "No, no gun. I just came to have a look at you," he said, pleased that this statement so nicely counterbalanced in its unpleasantness the painter's own remark about the sun.

Robert Trevor apparently appreciated the measured response as well. "Well, I guess I'll have to trust you," he replied, finally struggling to his feet.

Martin climbed the steps to the deck, where there was an awkward moment, since neither man seemed to relish the notion of shaking hands.

"There's another of those jars under the table, if you feel like getting it," the painter pointed out. "I could do it myself, but it would take me an hour."

Martin fetched that jar and two others while Robert Trevor picked up his brushes and arranged them in groupings that made some sort of sense to him, though none to Martin, then added solvent from a tin can to each of the jars. Martin, crouching, had better luck getting the leg wedged back in place than the other man had had.

"I didn't mean for you to stop work," Martin said when he realized that this was what was happening.

The painter regarded him as if he'd said something particularly foolish. He was a very big man, Martin realized. He had a huge belly, but he was tall enough to carry the weight without appearing obese. He'd probably been slimmer before, when he and Clara were lovers. Martin had no doubt that this was what they were from the moment he'd unpacked the painting.

"The light's about finished for today, Martin," the other man shrugged. "The best light's usually early. The rest is memory. Not like that bastard business you're in."

So, Martin thought. Clara had talked about them. First she'd fucked this painter Robert Trevor and then she'd talked to him about their lives, their marriage.

"What's that term movie people use? The last good light of the day?"

"Magic hour?"

"Right. Magic hour," Trevor nodded. "Tell me. Is that real, or just something you movie people made up?"

"It's real enough."

"Real enough," Robert Trevor repeated noncommittally, as if to suggest that maybe he believed Martin and maybe he didn't. "Well, if you aren't here to murder me, why don't you have a seat while I get us a beer. When I come back, you can tell me if my Clara was 'real enough' to suit you."

She had arrived professionally wrapped and crated, and when Martin saw the return address on the label, he set the parcel aside in the corner of his study. Joyce had always been an unpleasant woman, so it stood to reason that whatever she was sending him would be unpleasant. She'd called a week earlier, telling him to expect something, refusing to say what. "I wouldn't be sending it," she explained, "except I hear you have a new girl-friend. Is it serious, Martin?"

"I don't see where it's any of your business, Joyce," he'd told her, glad to have this to say, since he didn't have any idea whether he and Beth were serious or not. How Joyce, who lived clear across the country, would have heard about Beth to begin with was something of a mystery. Why she should care was another. What she had sent him, crated so expertly against the possibility of damage, was a third, but all three mysteries together aroused in Martin little curiosity. That the package contained a painting he suspected from its shape, but from this deduction he'd leapt to an erroneous conclusion, that Joyce herself was the painter.

So he'd put it aside, leaving the parcel unopened for more than a week. Beth had been curious about it, or maybe just curious about his own lack of curiosity. She loved presents and received a great number of them, it seemed to Martin, although the majority were from her doting father, a man not so much older than Martin himself. Daddy, as she referred to him, lived in Minnesota with a wife his own age, and Martin, thankfully, had never met either of them. Beth seemed to have little urgent affection for her parents, but her eyes always lit up when one of her father's packages arrived. "You never buy me presents, Martin," she mock-complained every time she opened one of these. "Why is that?"

Whatever instinct prevented Martin from unwrapping the painting in front of Beth, he was immediately grateful for it. As soon as he tore the outer covering off the skeleton of protective latticework, he knew he'd acted wisely. Seeing Clara there, just behind the grate, he had to suppress a powerful urge to lock the front door against intrusion, to pull the room's curtains against the brilliant California sunlight. After she was uncrated and leaning against the wall, he'd remained transfixed for a long time—he couldn't afterward be sure how long—and for almost as long by Robert Trevor's signature in the lower right of the canvas. He didn't need the signature, of course, to know that Joyce was not the painter. Joyce hadn't anything like this measure of talent, for one thing. For another, she'd never have seen Clara like this. It wasn't just his wife's nakedness, or even her pose, just inside the open doorway, light streaming in on her, all other objects disappearing into shadow. It was something else. The painting's detail was minutely photographic where the light allowed, yet it was very much "painted," interpreted, Martin supposed, an effect no camera could achieve. Joyce would have gotten a charge out of it, he had to admit later, when the spell finally broke, or broke enough to return Martin to himself. The sight of him on his knees before Clara would have been worth both her trouble and the extravagant cost of the packing and shipping.

"So what was it?" Beth asked when she returned from work that evening. He'd opened a bottle of white wine and drunk half of it before he heard the garage door grind open and Beth's Audi pull inside.

"What was what?" he said, affecting nonchalance.

She poured herself a glass of the wine, regarded him curiously, then held up a splintered stick from the latticework he'd broken into small pieces over his knee and stuffed into one of the large rubber trash cans they kept in the garage. Had he forgotten to put the lid on? Or was it Beth's habit to remove all the lids from the trash cans on her way in each evening, to see if he'd thrown away anything interesting that day?

"Something hateful," he finally answered her, believing this to be true, then adding, "Nothing important," as pure a lie as he'd ever told.

She nodded, as if this explanation were full and sufficient, holding the wine in her glass up to the light. "Not our usual white," she remarked, taking a sip.

"No."

"A hint of sweet. You usually hate that."

"Let's go to Palm Springs for the weekend," he suggested.

She continued to study him, clearly puzzled. "You just finished shooting in Palm Springs. You said you hated it."

"It'll be different now," he explained, "with us gone."

"So, Martin," Robert Trevor said when he returned with two bottles of sweating domestic beer, a brand Martin didn't realize was even brewed anymore. Trevor had partially buttoned his blue denim work shirt, Martin noticed, though a tuft of gray, paint-splattered chest hair was still visible at the open neck. The man sat in stages, as if negotiating with the lower half of his body. "Have I seen any of your films?"

"*My* films?" Martin smiled, taking a sip of cold, bitter beer. "I'm not a director, Robert."

The other man was still trying to get settled, lifting his bad leg out straight in front of him by hand, clearly annoyed by the need to do so. "I was trying to remember the word for what you are when I was inside. Clara told me, but I forgot."

"Cuckold?" Martin suggested.

Robert Trevor didn't respond right away. Clearly he was a man whose equilibrium did not tilt easily, and Martin found himself admiring that. His eyes were piercing pale blue. Clara, naked, had allowed him to turn them on her. "Now *there's* a Renaissance word for you," Trevor said finally. "A Renaissance notion, actually."

"You think so?" Martin said, pressing what he felt should have been his advantage. "Have you ever been married, Robert?"

"Never," the painter admitted. "Flawed concept, I always thought."

"Some might say it's people who are flawed, not the concept."

Robert Trevor looked off into the distance, as if he might actually be considering whether Martin's observation had merit, but then he quickly said, "Gaffer! That's what you are. You're a gaffer."

Martin had to smile inwardly. Clearly, if he'd come all this way and looked up this Robert Trevor in the hopes of an apology, he was to be disappointed. The good news was that this was not—he was pretty sure—what he had come for.

"Clara explained it all to me one afternoon," Robert Trevor explained.

"Actually, I'm a D.P. now," Martin told him, and was immediately ashamed of himself, of his need to inform his rival that he'd come up in the world.

Robert Trevor frowned. "Dip?" he said. "You're a dip, Martin?"

"Director of photography."

"Ah," the other man said. "I guess that makes you an artist."

"No," Martin assured him. "Merely a technician."

Though he'd been called an artist. Peter Axelrod considered him one. He'd gotten an urgent call from Peter one night a few years ago, asking him to come to the set where he was shooting a picture that starred a famously difficult actor. It was a small film, serious in content and intent, and the director and star had been embroiled in a quiet struggle over the star's performance for the first three weeks of the shoot. The actor was determined to give a performance that would be hailed as masterfully understated. To the director's way of thinking, his performance, to this point, was barely implied. Worse, the next day they'd be shooting one of the film's pivotal scenes.

Martin found his old friend sitting alone in a makeshift theater near the set, morosely studying the dailies. Martin took a seat in the folding chair next to Axelrod's and together they watched take after take. After half an hour, Axelrod called for the lights. "There's nothing to choose from," the director complained, rubbing his forehead. "He does the same thing every take, no matter what I suggest."

To Martin, perhaps because he was not invested in the picture, and because he could focus on one thing whereas the director had to consider fifty, the problem was obvious. "Don't argue with him. He's just going to dig his heels in deeper, the way they all do. You want a star performance, light him like a star, not like a character actor."

Peter Axelrod considered this advice for about five seconds. "Son of a bitch," he said. "David's in cahoots with him, isn't he?" David, a man Martin knew well, was the D.P. on the film. "I should shitcan the prick and hire you right this second."

Martin, of course, had demurred. The following week he was starting work on another picture, and Axelrod's offer wasn't so much real as symbolic testimony to his gratitude. "You just saved this picture," he told Martin out on the lot. "You just saved me."

The two men had shaken hands then, when Axelrod remembered. "I was sorry to hear about Clara. It must have been awful."

"Pretty bad," Martin had admitted. "She weighed about eighty pounds at the end."

The two men looked around the lot. "Movies," Axelrod said, shaking his head. "I wonder what we'd have done if we'd decided to live real lives and have real careers."

"You love movies," Martin pointed out.

"I know," Axelrod had admitted. "God help me, I do."

"Merely a technician," Robert Trevor repeated now, improbably seated across from Martin on the opposite coast. He'd already drained half his beer, while Martin, never a beer drinker, had barely touched his. "Well, I wouldn't worry about it. In the end, maybe that's all it is, art. Solid technique. A dash of style."

"I don't think I care to talk about art, Robert."

"No, I don't suppose you do," the painter said, running his fingers through his hair. "Joyce told me she sent you that painting. I'd have tried to talk her out of that had I known."

"Why?"

"Because Clara wouldn't have wanted her to. Funny to think of them as sisters, actually. Joyce always after vengeance. Clara so anxious to forgive."

Which was true. Martin had seen photos of them as little girls where it was hard to tell them apart. But by adolescence Clara was already flowering into the healthy, full-figured, ruddily complected woman she would become, whereas Joyce, pale and thin, had begun to look out at the world through dark, aggrieved eyes. It was clear to Martin when he saw Joyce yesterday that not one of her myriad grievances had ever been addressed to her satisfaction.

"So, Robert. How long were you and my wife lovers?"

The painter paused, as if undecided how best, or perhaps whether, to answer. "Why would you want to know that, Martin? How will knowing make things better for you?"

"How long?"

After a beat, he said, "We had roughly twenty years' worth of summers, Martin."

Right, Martin thought. The worst, then. Odd that he couldn't remember whether Clara had ever directly deceived him or whether she'd simply allowed him to deceive himself. He'd assumed that she needed time with her sister each summer. That she'd never asked him to accompany her to visit the sister he'd never been able to tolerate he'd considered a kindness.

"A month one year. Six weeks the next. I painted her every minute I could, then kept at it when she was gone."

Yes. The worst. This was one of the things he'd needed to know, of course. "How many are there?"

"Paintings?" Robert asked. "A dozen finished oils. More watercolors. Hundreds of studies. The one Joyce sent you might be the best of the lot. You should hang on to it."

"Where are they?" he asked, nodding at the studio. "Here?"

"At my farm in Indiana."

"You never sold any of them?"

"I've never *shown* any of them."

"Why not?"

"She wouldn't allow it when she was alive. Joyce kept the one you have in the guest room Clara used when she visited. Clara made her promise never to show anyone."

"She's been dead for several years now."

"Also there were your feelings to consider."

Martin snorted. "Please. You want me to believe you were concerned with my feelings?"

"Not even remotely," Trevor admitted freely. "Clara was, though. And . . . after her death . . . I started thinking of the paintings as private. When I die will be time enough."

"So nobody knows about them?"

"You do. Joyce. My New York agent suspects, and I've given instructions concerning them to my attorney." He finished his beer, then peered into the bottle as if, there at the bottom, the names of others who knew about the paintings might be printed. "That's what you've got to prepare yourself for, Martin. I've never pursued fame, but it appears I've become famous anyway, at least in certain circles. When I die, Clara's going to become a very famous lady. Everybody loves a secret. In fact," he smiled, "you might want to option the movie rights."

"Did you know she was dying?"

"She told me when she was first diagnosed, yes. I painted her that summer, like always."

Martin massaged his temples, the tips of his fingers cool from the beer bottle.

"She insisted. And of course I wanted to. I couldn't not paint her. I would have, right to the end, had that been possible."

"Why?"

"Why paint her disease, you mean?"

No, that wasn't what he'd meant. It shamed him to articulate further. "Why paint her at all, Robert? That's what I've been wondering. She wasn't what you'd call a beautiful woman."

The other man didn't hesitate at all. "No, Martin. She wasn't what *you'd* call a beautiful woman. She was one of the most beautiful women *I* ever laid eyes on."

Yes, Martin thought. That much had been clear from the painting, right from the start. And his next question was the reason he'd come so far. "Why?" he heard himself ask. "What was it about her?"

"I thought you didn't want to talk about art, Martin," the other man replied.

That night, Martin and Beth ate by candlelight in the dining room of the small hotel where they were staying. The candles were a matter of necessity. The electrical storm had come upon them in a hurry, or so it seemed to Martin. The sun had disappeared behind that first cloud when he'd arrived at Robert Trevor's studio. When he'd left, an hour later, the whole sky was rumbling with dark, low thunderheads. The painter, correctly predicting that the island would lose power, had insisted that Martin take a flashlight with him. "Just leave it in the room," he'd instructed. "I run into Dennis and Pat all the time. They'll return it." When Martin had smiled at this and shook his head, Robert Trevor read his thought and nodded agreement. "Island life, Martin. Island life."

Trevor had walked with him as far as the gate, an effort that clearly cost him. "What's wrong with your leg, Robert?" Martin had asked him as he lifted the gate's latch to let himself out.

"It's my hip, actually," the painter told him. "It needs replacing, they tell me. I'm thinking about it."

Martin remembered the battered table Robert Trevor used for his paints, the broken leg he continued to prop under it. Unless he was very much mistaken, Trevor wasn't the sort of man who believed in replacement.

"You didn't come to visit her," Martin remarked—one last-ditch attempt at censure—after the gate swung shut between them.

"No."

"You could have," he said. "You could have shown up with Joyce, claimed to be an old friend. I wouldn't have known."

"I thought about it," Trevor admitted. "But I had it on excellent authority that I wasn't needed. You rose to the occasion, is what I heard."

In the distance, a low rumble of thunder.

"That's what our friend Joyce can't quite forgive you for, by the way," Trevor continued. "Your devotion to Clara during those last months enraged her. Up to that point she'd always felt comfortable and justified in despising you."

"I rose to the occasion of her death, but not her life?"

"Something like that," Robert Trevor nodded. "Look at it this way. You got a damn good painting out of that woman's need to punish you."

"I don't know what to do with it, though," Martin admitted. "I had to rent one of those self-storage units out in the Valley."

"Air-conditioned, I hope."

Martin nodded. "It's the only thing in there."

"I'd love to have it back if you don't want it."

"It'll be even harder to look at now," he admitted, though he knew he'd never return the painting to Robert Trevor. "That look of longing on her face. The way she was standing there. I'm always going to know it was you she was waiting for to come through that door."

"Wrong again, Martin," Robert Trevor had assured him. He was leaning heavily with both hands on the gate, letting Martin know that a handshake wasn't any more necessary now than it had been earlier. It suddenly dawned on Martin that the man had to be in his seventies. "I was the one who did come through that door. You were the one she was waiting for."

"So," Beth said, digging into her steak with genuine appetite. At least, Martin thought, she wasn't one of those L. A. girls who always order the fish and drink nothing but mineral water. "Were you worried about me?"

"Yes," Martin said. She'd come striding down the dirt path minutes ahead of the storm. He'd waited for her in a rocking chair on the inn's front porch as the sky grew blacker and blacker. She'd no more than sat down next to him than the air sizzled with electricity and the first bolt of lightning cleaved the sky.

"You forget I'm from Minnesota," she said, pointing her fork at him. "I spent the first twenty years of my life watching storms develop. How was your lazy afternoon, old man?"

"Fine."

"Just fine?"

"I visited a studio. Took some photos. Like I said."

"You should have come with me. The path through the forest is strewn with fairy houses."

"With what?"

"Little houses built of bark and leaves and pebbles. By children, I suppose, if you don't believe in fairies. People leave pennies near the ones they like best. Isn't that sweet? I can see why Clara loved it here."

Martin just stared at her.

"Well . . . that's why we came all this way, right? This island was your wife's favorite place in the whole world, and this is your way of saying goodbye to her."

"I didn't know you—"

"I'm not *stupid*, Martin. I know how much you loved her."

"But I didn't." The words were right there to be spoken, and for a heartbeat Martin thought he would speak them. But if he did, how would he ever stop? How would he keep from adding, "Any more than I love you."

They used Robert Trevor's flashlight to illuminate the pitch-black staircase and locate their room on the third floor. Undressing in the dark, they lay in the canopied bed and watched the sky through the open window. The storm had moved out to sea, but it was still visible, flickering on the distant horizon. Every twenty seconds or so, the beam from the lighthouse swept past.

"What do you think?" Beth said. "Should we stay an extra day?"

"If you like," he said. "Whatever you want."

"It's up to you."

After a moment he said, "I called Peter while you were out." He would be starting a new picture with Axelrod early next month. "He'd like me to come back early, by the second week of rehearsal instead of the third, if possible. He didn't come right out and say so, but that's what he wants."

"What do *you* want?"

"I wouldn't mind heading back."

"Fine with me."

"Let's, then."

A few minutes later she was snoring gently in the crook of his arm. For a long time Martin lay in the dark thinking about Robert Trevor's farm in Indiana, where there were, if the other man was telling the truth, a dozen more oils of Clara, plus hundreds of smaller studies. And he thought too about Beth, poor girl. She had it, of course, exactly backwards. This trip was not about saying goodbye to his wife as much as hello. He'd fallen in love with her, truly in love, the moment he'd uncrated the package back in L.A. and seen his wife through another man's eyes. Just as Joyce had known, somehow, that he would.

What folly, Martin couldn't help thinking, bitterly, as he lay in the dark, a second lovely woman—no doubt it was his destiny to sell her short as well—sleeping peacefully in the crook of his arm. What absolute folly love was. Talk about a flawed concept. He remembered how he and his friends, all of them junior-high-school shy, without girlfriends, the way they used to congregate in the shadow of the bleachers to evaluate the girls at Friday-night school dances. The best ones were taken, of course, which left the others. "She's kind of pretty, don't you think?" one of his friends, or maybe Martin himself, would venture, and then it would be decided, by popular consensus, if she was or she wasn't.

Now that it had been decided that they would leave the island in the morning, Martin was relieved. He preferred the West Coast, and he was looking forward to the new picture with Axelrod, which was to star an actress he'd worked with shortly after Clara's death. The script had called for partial nudity, and the actress, who was in her mid-forties and had recently had a baby, was worried what she would look like. "Trust me," Axelrod had told her. "Nobody's going to see anything. They're just going to think they do. And this man," he continued, referring to Martin, "is an artist."

The next evening, Martin and Axelrod and the terrified actress—she *was* one of the most beautiful women Martin had ever laid eyes on, and never more beautiful than right then—sat in three folding chairs watching the dailies of the scene that had so frightened her. They'd done only three takes, and midway through viewing the first she began to relax, intuiting that it was going to be all right. Still, Martin couldn't have been more surprised when she took his hand there in the darkness and leaned toward him, without ever taking her eyes off the screen, and whispered, "Oh, I love you, I love you, I love you."

Fleur

Louise Erdrich

The first time she drowned in the cold and glassy waters of Lake Turcot, Fleur Pillager was only a girl. Two men saw the boat tip, saw her struggle in the waves. They rowed over to the place she went down, and jumped in. When they dragged her over the gunwales, she was cold to the touch and stiff, so they slapped her face, shook her by the heels, worked her arms back and forth, and pounded her back until she coughed up lake water. She shivered all over like a dog, then took a breath. But it wasn't long afterward that those two men disappeared. The first wandered off, and the other, Jean Hat, got himself run over by a cart.

It went to show, my grandma said. It figured to her, all right. By saving Fleur Pillager, those two men had lost themselves.

The next time she fell in the lake, Fleur Pillager was twenty years old and no one touched her. She washed onshore, her skin a dull dead gray, but when George Many Women bent to look closer, he saw her chest move. Then her eyes spun open, sharp black riprock, and she looked at him. "You'll take my place," she hissed. Everybody scattered and left her there, so no one knows how she dragged herself home. Soon after that we noticed Many Women changed, grew afraid, wouldn't leave his house, and would not be forced to go near water. For his caution, he lived until the day that his sons brought him a new tin bathtub. Then the first time he used the tub he slipped, got knocked out, and breathed water while his wife stood in the other room frying breakfast.

Men stayed clear of Fleur Pillager after the second drowning. Even though she was good-looking, nobody dared to court her because it was clear that Misshepeshu, the waterman, the monster, wanted her for himself. He's a devil, that one, love-hungry with desire and maddened for the touch of young girls, the strong and daring especially, the ones like Fleur.

Our mothers warn us that we'll think he's handsome, for he appears with green eyes, copper skin, a mouth tender as a child's. But if you fall into his arms, he sprouts horns, fangs, claws, fins. His feet are joined as one and his skin, brass scales, rings to the touch. You're fascinated, cannot move. He casts a shell necklace at your feet, weeps gleaming chips that harden into mica on your breasts. He holds you under. Then he takes the body of a lion or a fat brown worm. He's made of gold. He's made of beach moss. He's a thing of dry foam, a thing of death by drowning, the death a Chippewa cannot survive.

Unless you are Fleur Pillager. We all knew she couldn't swim. After the first time, we thought she'd never go back to Lake Turcot. We thought she'd keep to herself, live quiet, stop killing men off by drowning in the lake. After the first time, we thought she'd keep the good ways. But then, after the second drowning, we knew that we were dealing with something much more serious. She was haywire, out of control. She messed with evil, laughed at the old women's advice, and dressed like a man. She got herself into some half-forgotten medicine, studied ways we shouldn't talk about.

Some say she kept the finger of a child in her pocket and a powder of unborn rabbits in a leather thong around her neck. She laid the heart of an owl on her tongue so she could see at night, and went out, hunting, not even in her own body. We know for sure because the next morning, in the snow or dust, we followed the tracks of her bare feet and saw where they changed, where the claws sprang out, the pad broadened and pressed into the dirt. By night we heard her chuffing cough, the bear cough. By day her silence and the wide grin she threw to bring down our guard made us frightened. Some thought that Fleur Pillager should be driven off the reservation, but not a single person who spoke like this had the nerve. And finally, when people were just about to get together and throw her out, she left on her own and didn't come back all summer. That's what this story is about.

During that summer, when she lived a few miles south in Argus, things happened. She almost destroyed that town.

When she got down to Argus in the year of 1920, it was just a small grid of six streets on either side of the railroad depot. There were two elevators, one central, the other a few miles west. Two stores competed for the trade of the three hundred citizens, and three churches quarreled with one another for their souls. There was a frame building for Lutherans, a heavy brick one for Episcopalians, and a long narrow shingled Catholic church. This last had a tall slender steeple, twice as high as any building or tree.

No doubt, across the low, flat wheat, watching from the road as she came near Argus on foot, Fleur saw that steeple rise, a shadow thin as a needle. Maybe in that raw space it drew her the way a lone tree draws lightning. Maybe, in the end, the Catholics are to blame. For if she hadn't seen that sign of pride, that slim prayer, that marker, maybe she would have kept walking.

But Fleur Pillager turned, and the first place she went once she came into town was to the back door of the priest's residence attached to the landmark church. She didn't go there for a handout, although she got that, but to ask for work. She got that too, or the town got her. It's hard to tell which came out worse, her or the men or the town, although the upshot of it all was that Fleur lived.

The four men who worked at the butcher's had carved up about a thousand carcasses between them, maybe half of that steers and the other half pigs, sheep, and game animals like deer, elk, and bear. That's not even mentioning the chickens, which were beyond counting. Pete Kozka owned the place, and employed Lily Veddar, Tor Grunewald, and my stepfather, Dutch James, who had brought my mother down from the reservation the year before she disappointed him by dying. Dutch took me out of school to take her place. I kept house half the time and worked the other in the butcher shop, sweeping floors, putting sawdust down, running a hambone across the street to a customer's bean pot or a package of sausage to the corner. I was a good one to have around because until they needed me, I was invisible. I blended into the stained brown walls, a skinny, big-nosed girl with staring eyes. Because I could fade into a corner or squeeze beneath a shelf, I knew everything, what the men said when no one was around, and what they did to Fleur.

Kozka's Meats served farmers for a fifty-mile area, both to slaughter, for it had a stock pen and chute, and to cure the meat by smoking it or spicing it in sausage. The storage locker was a marvel, made of many thicknesses of brick, earth insulation, and Minnesota timber, lined inside with sawdust and vast blocks of ice cut from Lake Turcot, hauled down from home each winter by horse and sledge.

A ramshackle board building, part slaughterhouse, part store, was fixed to the low, thick square of the lockers. That's where Fleur worked. Kozka hired her for her strength. She could lift a haunch or carry a pole of sausages without stumbling, and she soon learned cutting from Pete's wife, a string-thin blonde who chain-smoked and handled the razor-sharp knives with nerveless precision, slicing close to her stained fingers. Fleur and Fritzie Kozka worked afternoons, wrapping their cuts in paper, and Fleur hauled the packages to the lockers. The meat was left outside the heavy oak doors that were only opened at 5:00 each afternoon, before the men ate supper.

Sometimes Dutch, Tor, and Lily ate at the lockers, and when they did I stayed too, cleaned floors, restoked the fires in the front smokehouses, while the men sat around the squat cast-iron stove spearing slats of herring onto hardtack bread. They played long games of poker or cribbage on a board made from the planed end of a salt crate. They talked and I listened, although there wasn't much to hear since almost nothing ever happened in Argus. Tor was married, Dutch had lost my mother, and Lily read circulars. They mainly discussed about the auctions to come, equipment, or women.

Every so often, Pete Kozka came out front to make a whist, leaving Fritzie to smoke cigarettes and fry raised doughnuts in the back room. He sat and played a few rounds but kept his thoughts to himself. Fritzie did not tolerate him talking behind her back, and the one book he read was the New Testament. If he said something, it concerned weather or a surplus of sheep stomachs, a ham that smoked green or the markets for corn and wheat. He had a good-luck talisman, the opal-white lens of a cow's eye. Playing cards, he rubbed it between his fingers. That soft sound and the slap of cards was about the only conversation.

Fleur finally gave them a subject.

Her cheeks were wide and flat, her hands large, chapped, muscular. Fleur's shoulders were broad as beams, her hips fishlike, slippery, narrow. An old green dress clung to her waist, worn thin where she sat. Her braids were thick like the tails of animals, and swung against her when she moved, deliberately, slowly in her work, held in and half-tamed, but only half. I could tell, but the others never saw. They never looked into her sly brown eyes or noticed her teeth, strong and curved and very white. Her legs were bare, and since she padded around in beadwork moccasins they never saw that her fifth toes were missing. They never knew she'd drowned. They were blinded, they were stupid, they only saw her in the flesh.

And yet it wasn't just that she was a Chippewa, or even that she was a woman, it wasn't that she was good-looking or even that she was alone that made their brains hum. It was how she played cards.

Women didn't usually play with men, so the evening that Fleur drew a chair up to the men's table without being so much as asked, there was a shock of surprise.

"What's this," said Lily. He was fat, with a snake's cold pale eyes and precious skin, smooth and lily-white, which is how he got his name. Lily had a dog, a stumpy mean little bull of a thing with a belly drum-tight from eating pork rinds. The dog liked to play cards just like Lily, and straddled his barrel thighs through games of stud, rum poker, *vingt-un*. The dog snapped at Fleur's arm that first night, but cringed back, its snarl frozen, when she took her place.

"I thought," she said, her voice soft and stroking, "you might deal me in."

There was a space between the heavy bin of spiced flour and the wall where I just fit. I hunkered down there, kept my eyes open, saw her black hair swing over the chair, her feet solid on the wood floor. I couldn't see up on the table where the cards slapped down, so after they were deep in their game I raised myself up in the shadows, and crouched on a sill of wood.

I watched Fleur's hands stack and ruffle, divide the cards, spill them to each player in a blur, rake them up and shuffle again. Tor, short and scrappy, shut one eye and squinted the other at Fleur. Dutch screwed his lips around a wet cigar.

"Gotta see a man," he mumbled, getting up to go out back to the privy. The others broke, put their cards down, and Fleur sat alone in the lamp-light that glowed in a sheen across the push of her breasts. I watched her closely, then she paid me a beam of notice for the first time. She turned, looked straight at me, and grinned the white wolf grin a Pillager turns on its victims, except that she wasn't after me.

"Pauline there," she said, "how much money you got?"

We'd all been paid for the week that day. Eight cents was in my pocket.

"Stake me," she said, holding out her long fingers. I put the coins in her palm and then I melted back to nothing, part of the walls and tables. It was a long time before I understood that the men would not have seen me no matter what I did, how I moved. I wasn't anything like Fleur. My dress hung loose and my back was already curved, an old woman's. Work had roughened me, reading made my eyes sore, caring for my mother before she died had hardened my face. I was not much to look at, so they never saw me.

When the men came back and sat around the table, they had drawn together. They shot each other small glances, stuck their tongues in their cheeks, burst out laughing at odd moments, to rattle Fleur. But she never minded. They played their *vingt-un*, staying even as Fleur slowly gained. Those pennies I had given her drew nickels and attracted dimes until there was a small pile in front of her.

Then she hooked them with five-card draw, nothing wild. She dealt, discarded, drew, and then she sighed and her cards gave a little shiver. Tor's eye gleamed, and Dutch straightened in his seat.

"I'll pay to see that hand," said Lily Veddar.

Fleur showed, and she had nothing there, nothing at all.

Tor's thin smile cracked open, and he threw his hand in too.

"Well, we know one thing," he said, leaning back in his chair, "the squaw can't bluff."

With that I lowered myself into a mound of swept sawdust and slept. I woke up during the night, but none of them had moved yet, so I couldn't either. Still later, the men must have gone out again, or Fritzie come out to break the game, because I was lifted, soothed, cradled in a woman's arms and rocked so quiet that I kept my eyes shut while Fleur rolled me into a closet of grimy ledgers, oiled paper, balls of string, and thick files that fit beneath me like a mattress.

The game went on after work the next evening. I got my eight cents back five times over, and Fleur kept the rest of the dollar she'd won for a stake. This time they didn't play so late, but they played regular, and then kept going at it night after night. They played poker now, or variations, for one week straight, and each time Fleur won exactly one dollar, no more and no less, too consistent for luck.

By this time, Lily and the other men were so lit with suspense that they got Pete to join the game with them. They concentrated, the fat dog sitting tense in Lily Veddar's lap, Tor suspicious, Dutch stroking his huge square brow, Pete steady. It wasn't that Fleur won that hooked them in so, because she lost hands too. It was rather that she never had a freak hand or even anything above a straight. She only took on her low cards, which didn't sit right. By chance, Fleur should have gotten a full or flush by now. The irritating thing was she beat with pairs and never bluffed, because she couldn't, and still she ended up each night with exactly one dollar. Lily couldn't believe, first of all, that a woman could be smart enough to play cards, but even if she was, that she would then be stupid enough to cheat for a dollar a night. By day I watched him turn the problem over, his hard white face dull, small fingers probing at his knuckles, until he finally thought he had Fleur figured out as a bit-time player, caution her game. Raising the stakes would throw her.

More than anything now, he wanted Fleur to come away with something but a dollar. Two bits less or ten more, the sum didn't matter, just so he broke her streak.

Night after night she played, won her dollar, and left to stay in a place that just Fritzie and I knew about. Fleur bathed in the slaughtering tub, then slept in the unused brick smokehouse behind the lockers, a windowless place tarred on the inside with scorched fats. When I brushed against her skin I noticed that she smelled of the walls, rich and woody, slightly burnt. Since that night she put me in the closet I was no longer afraid of her, but followed her close, stayed with her, became her moving shadow that the men never noticed, the shadow that could have saved her.

August, the month that bears fruit, closed around the shop, and Pete and Fritzie left for Minnesota to escape the heat. Night by night, running, Fleur had won thirty dollars, and only Pete's presence had kept Lily at bay. But Pete was gone now, and one payday, with the heat so bad no one could move but Fleur, the men sat and played and waited while she finished work. The cards sweat, limp in their fingers, the table was slick with grease, and even the walls were warm to the touch. The air was motionless. Fleur was in the next room boiling heads.

Her green dress, drenched, wrapped her like a transparent sheet. A skin of lakeweed. Black snarls of veining clung to her arms. Her braids were loose, half-unraveled, tied behind her neck in a thick loop. She stood in steam, turning skulls through a vat with a wooden paddle. When scraps boiled to the surface, she bent with a round tin sieve and scooped them out. She'd filled two dishpans.

"Ain't that enough now?" called Lily. "We're waiting." The stump of a dog trembled in his lap, alive with rage. It never smelled me or noticed me above Fleur's smoky skin. The air was heavy in my corner, and pressed me down. Fleur sat with them.

"Now what do you say?" Lily asked the dog. It barked. That was the signal for the real game to start.

"Let's up the ante," said Lily, who had been stalking this night all month. He had a roll of money in his pocket. Fleur had five bills in her dress. The men had each saved their full pay.

"Ante a dollar then," said Fleur, and pitched hers in. She lost, but they let her scrape along, cent by cent. And then she won some. She played unevenly, as if chance was all she had. She reeled them in. The game went on. The dog was stiff now, poised on Lily's knees, a ball of vicious muscle with its yellow eyes slit in concentration. It gave advice, seemed to sniff the lay of Fleur's cards, twitched and nudged. Fleur was up, then down, saved by a scratch. Tor dealt seven cards, three down. The pot grew, round by round, until it held all the money. Nobody folded. Then it all rode on one last card and they went silent. Fleur picked hers up and blew a long breath. The heat lowered like a bell. Her card shook, but she stayed in.

Lily smiled and took the dog's head tenderly between his palms.

"Say, Fatso," he said, crooning the words, "you reckon that girl's bluffing?"

The dog whined and Lily laughed. "Me too," he said, "let's show." He swept his bills and coins into the pot and then they turned their cards over.

Lily looked once, looked again, then he squeezed the dog up like a fist of dough and slammed it on the table.

Fleur threw her arms out and drew the money over, grinning that same wolf grin that she'd used on me, the grin that had them. She jammed the bills in her dress, scooped the coins up in waxed white paper that she tied with string.

"Let's go another round," said Lily, his voice choked with burrs. But Fleur opened her mouth and yawned, then walked out back to gather slops for the one big hog that was waiting in the stock pen to be killed.

The men sat still as rocks, their hands spread on the oiled wood table. Dutch had chewed his cigar to damp shreds, Tor's eye was dull. Lily's gaze was the only one to follow Fleur. I didn't move. I felt them gathering, saw my stepfather's veins, the ones in his forehead that stood out in anger. The dog had rolled off the table and curled in a knot below the counter, where none of the men could touch it.

Lily rose and stepped out back to the closet of ledgers where Pete kept his private stock. He brought back a bottle, uncorked and tipped it between his fingers. The lump in his throat moved, then he passed it on. They drank, quickly felt the whiskey's fire, and planned with their eyes things they couldn't say out loud.

When they left, I followed. I hid out back in the clutter of broken boards and chicken crates beside the stock pen, where they waited. Fleur could not be seen at first, and then the moon broke and showed her, slipping cautiously along the rough board chute with a bucket in her hand. Her hair fell, wild and coarse, to her waist, and her dress was a floating patch in the dark. She made a pig-calling sound, rang the tin pail lightly against the wood, froze suspiciously. But too late. In the sound of the ring Lily moved, fat and nimble, stepped right behind Fleur and put out his creamy hands. At his first touch, she whirled and doused him with the bucket of sour slops. He pushed her against the big fence and the package of coins split, went clinking and jumping, winked against the wood. Fleur rolled over once and vanished in the yard.

The moon fell behind a curtain of ragged clouds, and Lily followed into the dark muck. But he tripped, pitched over the huge flank of the pig, who lay mired to the snout, heavily snoring. I sprang out of the weeds and climbed the side of the pen, stuck like glue. I saw the sow rise to her neat, knobby knees, gain her balance, and sway, curious, as Lily stumbled forward. Fleur had backed into the angle of rough wood just beyond, and when Lily tried to jostle past, the sow tipped up on her hind legs and struck, quick and hard as a snake. She plunged her head into Lily's thick side and snatched a mouthful of his shirt. She lunged again, caught him lower, so that he grunted in pained surprise. He seemed to ponder, breathing deep. Then he launched his huge body in a swimmer's dive.

The sow screamed as his body smacked over hers. She rolled, striking out with her knife-sharp hooves, and Lily gathered himself upon her, took her foot-long face by the ears and scraped her snout and cheeks against the trestles of the pen. He hurled the sow's tight skull against an iron post, but instead of knocking her dead, he merely woke her from her dream.

She reared, shrieked, drew him with her so that they posed standing upright. They bowed jerkily to each other, as if to begin. Then his arms swung and flailed. She sank her black fangs into his shoulder, clasping him, dancing him forward and backward through the pen. Their steps picked up pace, went wild. The two dipped as one, box-stepped, tripped each other. She ran her split foot though his hair. He grabbed her kinked tail. They went down and came up, the same shape and then the same color, until the men couldn't tell one from the other in that light and Fleur was able to launch herself over the gates, swing down, hit gravel.

The men saw, yelled, and chased her at a dead run to the smokehouse. And Lily too, once the sow gave up in disgust and freed him. That is where I should have gone to Fleur, saved her, thrown myself on Dutch. But I went stiff with fear and couldn't unlatch myself from the trestles or move at all. I closed my eyes and put my head in my arms, tried to hide, so there is nothing to describe but what I couldn't block out, Fleur's hoarse breath, so loud it filled me, her cry in the old language, and my name repeated over and over among the words.

The heat was still dense the next morning when I came back to work. Fleur was gone but the men were there, slack-faced, hung over. Lily was paler and softer than ever, as if his flesh had steamed on his bones. They smoked, took pulls off a bottle. It wasn't noon yet. I worked awhile, waiting shop and sharpening steel. But I was sick, I was smothered, I was sweating so hard that my hands slipped on the knives, and I wiped my fingers clean of the greasy touch of the customers' coins. Lily opened his mouth and roared once, not in anger. There was no meaning to the sound. His boxer dog, sprawled limp beside his foot, never lifted its head. Nor did the other men.

They didn't notice when I stepped outside, hoping for a clear breath. And then I forgot them because I knew that we were all balanced, ready to tip, to fly, to be crushed as soon as the weather broke. The sky was so low that I felt the weight of it like a yoke. Clouds hung down, witch teats, a tornado's green-brown cones, and as I watched one flicked out and became a delicate probing thumb. Even as I picked up my heels and ran back inside, the wind blew suddenly, cold, and then came rain.

Inside, the men had disappeared already and the whole place was trembling as if a huge hand was pinched at the rafters, shaking it. I ran straight through, screaming for Dutch or for any of them, and then I stopped at the heavy doors of the lockers, where they had surely taken shelter. I stood there a moment. Everything went still. Then I heard a cry building in the wind, faint at first, a whistle and then a shrill scream that tore through the walls and gathered around me, spoke plain so I understood that I should move, put my arms out, and slam down the great iron bar that fit across the hasp and lock.

Outside, the wind was stronger, like a hand held against me. I struggled forward. The bushes tossed, the awnings flapped off storefronts, the rails of porches rattled. The odd cloud became a fat snout that nosed along the earth and sniffled, jabbed, picked at things, sucked them up, blew them apart, rooted around as if it was following a certain scent, then stopped behind me at the butcher shop and bored down like a drill.

I went flying, landed somewhere in a ball. When I opened my eyes and looked, stranger things were happening.

A herd of cattle flew through the air like giant birds, dropping dung, their mouths opened in stunned bellows. A candle, still lighted, blew past, and tables, napkins, garden tools, a whole school of drifting eyeglasses, jackets on hangers, hams, a checkerboard, a lampshade, and at last the sow from behind the lockers, on the run, her hooves a blur, set free, swooping, diving, screaming as everything in Argus fell apart and got turned upside down, smashed, and thoroughly wrecked.

Days passed before the town went looking for the men. They were bachelors, after all, except for Tor, whose wife had suffered a blow to the head that made her forgetful. Everyone was occupied with digging out, in high relief because even though the Catholic steeple had been torn off like a peaked cap and sent across five fields, those huddled in the cellar were unhurt. Walls had fallen, windows were demolished, but the stores were intact and so were the bankers and shop owners who had taken refuge in their safes or beneath their cash registers. It was a fair-minded disaster, no one could be said to have suffered much more than the next, at least not until Fritzie and Pete came home.

Of all the businesses in Argus, Kozka's Meats had suffered worst. The boards of the front building had been split to kindling, piled in a huge pyramid, and the shop equipment was blasted far and wide. Pete paced off the distance the iron bathtub had been flung—a hundred feet. The glass candy case went fifty, and landed without so much as a cracked pane. There were other surprises as well, for the back rooms where Fritzie and Pete lived were undisturbed. Fritzie said the dust still coated her china figures, and upon her kitchen table, in the ashtray, perched the last cigarette she'd put out in haste. She lit it up and finished it, looking through the window. From there, she could see that the old smokehouse Fleur had slept in was crushed to a reddish sand and the stockpens were completely torn apart, the rails stacked helter-skelter. Fritzie asked for Fleur. People shrugged. Then she asked about the others and, suddenly, the town understood that three men were missing.

There was a rally of help, a gathering of shovels and volunteers. We passed boards from hand to hand, stacked them, uncovered what lay beneath the pile of jagged splinters. The lockers, full of the meat that was Pete and Fritzie's investment, slowly came into sight, still intact. When enough room was made for a man to stand on the roof, there were calls, a general urge to hack through and see what lay below. But Fritzie shouted that she wouldn't allow it because the meat would spoil. And so the work continued, board by board, until at last the heavy oak doors of the freezer were revealed and people pressed to the entry. Everyone wanted to be the first, but since it was my stepfather lost, I was let go in when Pete and Fritzie wedged through into the sudden icy air.

Pete scraped a match on his boot, lit the lamp Fritzie held, and then the three of us stood still in its circle. Light glared off the skinned and hanging carcasses, the crates of wrapped sausages, the bright and cloudy blocks of lake ice, pure as winter. The cold bit into us, pleasant at first, then numbing. We must have stood there a couple of minutes before we saw the men, or more rightly, the humps of fur, the iced and shaggy hides they wore, the bearskins they had taken down and wrapped around themselves. We stepped closer and tilted the lantern beneath the flaps of fur into their faces. The dog was there, perched among them, heavy as a doorstop. The three had hunched around a barrel where the game was still laid out, and a dead lantern and an empty bottle, too. But they had thrown down their last hands and hunkered tight, clutching one another, knuckles raw from beating at the door they had also attacked with hooks. Frost stars gleamed off their eyelashes and the stubble of their beards. Their faces were set in concentration, mouths open as if to speak some careful thought, some agreement they'd come to in each other's arms.

Power travels in the bloodlines, handed out before birth. It comes down through the hands, which in the Pillagers were strong and knotted, big, spidery, and rough, with sensitive fingertips good at dealing cards. It comes through the eyes, too, belligerent, darkest brown, the eyes of those in the bear clan, impolite as they gaze directly at a person.

In my dreams, I look straight back at Fleur, at the men. I am no longer the watcher on the dark sill, the skinny girl.

The blood draws us back, as if it runs through a vein of earth. I've come home and, except for talking to my cousins, live a quiet life. Fleur lives quiet too, down on Lake Turcot with her boat. Some say she's married to the waterman, Misshepeshu, or that she's living in shame with white men or windigos, or that she's killed them all. I'm about the only one here who ever goes to visit her. Last winter, I went to help out in her cabin when she bore the child, whose green eyes and skin the color of an old penny made more talk, as no one could decide if the child was mixed blood or what, fathered in a smokehouse, or by a man with brass scales, or by the lake. The girl is bold, smiling in her sleep, as if she knows what people wonder, as if she hears the old men talk, turning the story over. It comes up different every time and has no ending, no beginning. They get the middle wrong too. They only know that they don't know anything.

The Widow Ching—Pirate

Jorge Luis Borges

(Translated from the Spanish by Norman Thomas di Giovanni)

Any mention of pirates of the fair sex runs the immediate risk of awakening painful memories of the neighborhood production of some faded musical comedy, with its chorus line of obvious housewives posing as pirates and hoofing it on a briny deep of unmistakable cardboard. Nonetheless, lady pirates there have been—women skilled in the handling of ships, in the captaincy of brutish crews, and in the pursuit and plunder of seagoing vessels. One such was Mary Read, who once declared that the profession of pirate was not for everyone, and that to engage in it with dignity one had, like her, to be a man of courage. At the flamboyant outset of her career, when as yet she captained no crew, one of her lovers was wronged by the ship's bully. Challenging the fellow to a duel, Mary took him on with both hands, according to the time-honored custom of the West Indies—unwieldy and none-too-sure flintlock in the left, trusty cutlass in the right. The pistol misfired, but the sword behaved as it should. . . . Along about 1720, Mary Read's daring career was cut short by a Spanish gallows at St. Jago de la Vega, in Jamaica.

Another lady buccaneer of those same seas was Anne Bonney, a good-looking, boisterous Irishwoman, with high breasts and fiery red hair, who was always among the first to risk her neck boarding a prize. She was a shipmate and, in the end, gallows mate of Mary Read; Anne's lover, Captain John Rackam, sported a noose on that occasion, too. Contemptuous of him, Anne came up with this harsh variant of Aisha's reproach of Boabdil: "If you had fought like a Man, you need not have been hang'd like a Dog."

A third member of this sisterhood, more venturesome and longer-lived than the others, was a lady pirate who operated in Asian waters, all the way from the Yellow Sea to the rivers of the Annam coast. I speak of the veteran widow Ching.

THE APPRENTICE YEARS

Around 1797, the shareholders of the many pirate squadrons of the China seas formed a combine, to which they named as admiral a man altogether tried and true—a certain Ching. So severe was this Ching, so exemplary in his sacking of the coasts, that the terror-stricken inhabitants of eighty seaboard towns, with gifts and tears, implored imperial assistance. Their pitiful appeal did not go unheard: they were ordered to put their villages to the torch, forget their fishing chores, migrate inland, and there take up the unfamiliar science of agriculture. All this they did, so that the thwarted invaders found nothing but deserted coasts. As a result, the pirates were forced to switch to preying on ships, a form of depredation which, since it seriously hampered trade, proved even more obnoxious to the authorities than the previous one. The imperial government was quick to act ordering the former fishermen to abandon plow and yoke and mend their nets and oars. True to their old fears, however, these fishermen rose up in revolt, and the authorities set upon another course—that of pardoning Ching by appointing him Master of the Royal Stables. Ching was about to accept the bribe. Finding this out in time, the shareholders made their righteous indignation evident in a plate of poisoned greens, cooked with rice. The morsel proving deadly, the onetime admiral and would-be Master of the Royal Stables gave up his ghost to the gods of the sea. His widow, transfigured by this twofold double-dealing, called the pirate crews together, explained to them the whole involved affair, and urged them to reject both the emperor's deceitful pardon and the unpleasant service rendered by the poison-dabbling shareholders. She proposed, instead, the plundering of ships on their own account and the election of a new admiral.

The person chosen was the widow Ching. She was a clinging woman, with sleepy eyes and a smile full of decayed teeth. Her blackish, oiled hair shone brighter than her eyes. Under her sober orders, the ships embarked upon danger and the high seas.

THE COMMAND

Thirteen years of systematic adventure ensued. Six squadrons made up the fleet, each flying a banner of a different color—red, yellow, green, black, purple, and one (the flagship's) emblazoned with a serpent. The captains were known by such names as "Bird and Stone," "Scourge of the Eastern Sea," "Jewel of the Whole Crew," "Wave with Many Fishes," and "Sun on High." The code of rules, drawn up by the widow Ching herself, is of an unappealable severity, and its straightforward, laconic style is utterly lacking in the faded flowers of rhetoric that lend a rather absurd loftiness to the style of Chinese officialdom, of which we shall presently offer an alarming specimen or two. For now, I copy out a few articles of the widow's code:

All goods transshipped from enemy vessels will be entered in a register and kept in a storehouse. Of this stock, the pirate will receive for himself out of ten parts, only two; the rest shall belong to the storehouse, called the general fund. Violation of this ordinance will be punishable by death.

The punishment of the pirate who abandons his post without permission will be perforation of the ears in the presence of the whole fleet; repeating the same, he will suffer death.

375

Commerce with captive women taken in the villages is prohibited on deck; permission to use violence against any woman must first be requested of the ship's purser, and then carried out only in the ship's hold. Violation of this ordinance will be punishable by death.

Information extracted from prisoners affirms that the fare of these pirates consisted chiefly of ship biscuits, rats fattened on human flesh, and boiled rice, and that, on days of battle, crew members used to mix gunpowder with their liquor. With card games and loaded dice, with the metal square and bowl of fantan, with the little lamp and the pipe dreams of opium, they whiled away the time. Their favorite weapons were a pair of short swords, used one in each hand. Before seizing another ship, they sprinkled their cheekbones and bodies with an infusion of garlic water, which they considered a certain charm against shot.

Each crewman traveled with his wife, but the captain sailed with a harem, which was five or six in number and which, in victory, was always replenished.

KIA-KING, THE YOUNG EMPEROR, SPEAKS

Somewhere around the middle of 1809, there was made public an imperial decree, of which I transcribe the first and last parts. Its style was widely criticized. It ran:

Men who are cursed and evil, men capable of profaning bread, men who pay no heed to the clamor of the tax collector or the orphan, men in whose undergarments are stitched the phoenix and the dragon, men who deny the great truths of printed books, men who allow their tears to run toward the North—all these are disrupting the commerce of our rivers and the age-old intimacy of our seas. In unsound, unseaworthy craft, they are tossed by storms both night and day. Nor is their object one of benevolence: they are not and never were the true friends of the seafarer. Far from lending him their aid, they swoop down on him most viciously, inviting him to wrack and ruin, inviting him to death. In such wise do they violate the natural laws of the Universe that rivers overflow their banks, vast acreages are drowned, sons are pitted against fathers, and even the roots of rain and drought are altered. . . .

. . . In consequence, Admiral Kwo-lang, I leave to your hand the administration of punishment. Never forget that clemency is a prerogative of the throne and that it would be presumptuous of a subject to endeavor to assume such a privilege. Therefore, be merciless, be impartial, be obeyed, be victorious.

The incidental reference to unseaworthy vessels was, of course, false. Its aim was to encourage Kwo-lang's expedition. Some ninety days later, the forces of the widow Ching came face-to-face with those of the Middle Kingdom. Nearly a thousand ships joined battle, fighting from early morning until late evening. A mixed chorus of bells, drums, curses, gongs, and prophecies, along with the report of the great ordnance, accompanied the action. The emperor's forces were sundered. Neither the proscribed clemency nor the recommended cruelty had occasion to be exercised. Kwo-lang observed a rite that our present-day military, in defeat, choose to ignore—suicide.

THE TERRORIZED RIVERBANKS

The proud widow's six hundred war junks and forty thousand victorious pirates then sailed up the mouths of the Si'kiang, and to port and starboard they multiplied fires and loathsome revels and orphans. Entire villages were burned to the ground. In one of them alone, the number of prisoners passed a thousand. A hundred and twenty women who sought the confused refuge of neighboring reed fields and paddies were given away by a crying baby and later sold into slavery in Macao. Although at some remove, the tears and bereavement wreaked by this depredation came to the attention of Kia-king, the Son of Heaven. Certain historians contend that this outcry pained him less than the disaster that befell his punitive expedition. The truth is that he organized a second expedition, awesome in banners, in sailors, in soldiers, in the engines of war, in provisions, in augurs, and in astrologers. The command this time fell upon one Ting-kwei. The fearful multitude of ships sailed into the delta of the Si'kiang, closing off passage to the pirate squadron. The widow fitted out for battle. She knew it would be difficult, even desperate; night after night and month after month of plundering and idleness had weakened her men. The opening of battle was delayed. Lazily, the sun rose and set upon the rippling reeds. Men and their weapons were waiting. Noons were heavy, afternoons endless.

THE DRAGON AND THE FOX

And yet, each evening, high, shiftless flocks of airy dragons rose from the ships of the imperial squadron and came gently to rest on the enemy decks and surrounding waters. They were lightweight constructions of rice paper and strips of reed, akin to comets, and their silvery or reddish sides repeated identical characters. The widow anxiously studied this regular stream of meteors and read in them the long and perplexing fable of a dragon which had always given protection to a fox, despite the fox's long ingratitude and repeated transgressions. The moon grew slender in the sky, and each evening the paper and reed figures brought the same story, with almost imperceptible variants. The widow was distressed, and she sank deep into thought. When the moon was full in the sky and in the reddish water, the story seemed to reach its end. Nobody was able to predict whether limitless pardon or limitless punishment would descend upon the fox, but the inexorable end drew near. The widow came to an understanding. She threw her two short swords into the river, kneeled in the bottom of a small boat, and ordered herself rowed to the imperial flagship.

It was dark; the sky was filled with dragons—this time, yellow ones. On climbing aboard, the widow murmured a brief sentence. "The fox seeks the dragon's wing," she said.

THE APOTHEOSIS

It is a matter of history that the fox received her pardon and devoted her lingering years to the opium trade. She also left off being the widow, assuming a name which in English means "Luster of Instruction."

From this period [wrote one Chinese chronicler lyrically], *ships began to pass and repass in tranquillity. All became quiet on the rivers and tranquil on the four seas. Men sold their weapons and bought oxen to plow their fields. They buried sacrifices, said prayers on the tops of hills, and rejoiced themselves by singing behind screens during the daytime.*

Neighbors

Raymond Carver

Bill and Arlene Miller were a happy couple. But now and then they felt they alone among their circle had been passed by somehow, leaving Bill to attend to his bookkeeping duties and Arlene occupied with secretarial chores. They talked about it sometimes, mostly in comparison with the lives of their neighbors, Harriet and Jim Stone. It seemed to the Millers that the Stones lived a fuller and brighter life, one very different from their own. The Stones were always going out for dinner, or entertaining at home, or traveling about the country somewhere in connection with Jim's work.

The Stones lived across the hall from the Millers. Jim was a salesman for a machine-parts firm and often managed to combine business with a pleasure trip, and on this occasion the Stones would be away for ten days, first to Cheyenne, then on to St. Louis to visit relatives. In their absence, the Millers would look after the Stones' apartment, feed Kitty and water the plants.

Bill and Jim shook hands beside the car. Harriet and Arlene held each other by the elbows and kissed lightly on the lips.

"Have fun," Bill said to Harriet.

"We will," said Harriet. "You kids have fun too." Arlene nodded.

Jim winked at her. " 'Bye, Arlene. Take good care of the old man."

"I will," Arlene said.

"Have fun," Bill said.

"You bet," Jim said, clipping Bill lightly on the arm. "And thanks again, you guys."

The Stones waved as they drove away, and the Millers waved too.

"Well, I wish it was us," Bill said.

"God knows, we could use a vacation," Arlene said. She took his arm and put it around her waist as they climbed the stairs to their apartment.

After dinner Arlene said, "Don't forget. Kitty gets liver flavoring the first night." She stood in the kitchen doorway folding the handmade tablecloth that Harriet had bought for her last year in Santa Fe.

Bill took a deep breath as he entered the Stones' apartment. The air was already heavy and it was always vaguely sweet. The sunburst clock over the television said half-past eight. He remembered when Harriet had come home with the clock, how she crossed the hall to show it to Arlene, cradling the brass case in her arms and talking to it through the tissue paper as if it were an infant.

Kitty rubbed her face against his slippers and then turned onto her side, but jumped up quickly as Bill moved to the kitchen and selected one of the stacked cans from the gleaming drainboard. Leaving the cat to pick at her food, he headed for the bathroom. He looked at himself in the mirror and then closed his eyes and then opened them. He opened the medicine chest. He found a container of pills and read the label: *Harriet Stone. One each day as directed*, and slipped it into his pocket. He went back to the kitchen, drew a pitcher of water and returned to the living room. He finished watering, set the pitcher on the rug and opened the liquor cabinet. He reached in back for the bottle of Chivas Regal. He took two drinks from the bottle, wiped his lips on his sleeve and replaced the bottle in the cabinet.

Kitty was on the couch sleeping. He flipped the lights, slowly closing and checking the door. He had the feeling he had left something.

"What kept you?" Arlene said. She sat with her legs turned under her, watching television.

"Nothing. Playing with Kitty," he said, and went over to her and touched her breasts.

"Let's go to bed, honey," he said.

The next day Bill took only ten of the twenty minutes' break allotted for the afternoon, and left at fifteen minutes before five.

He parked the car in the lot just as Arlene hopped down from the bus. He waited until she entered the building, then ran up the stairs to catch her as she stepped out of the elevator.

"Bill! God, you scared me. You're early," she said.

He shrugged. "Nothing to do at work," he said.

She let him use her key to open the door. He looked at the door across the hall before following her inside.

"Let's go to bed," he said.

"Now?" She laughed. "What's gotten into you?"

"Nothing. Take your dress off." He grabbed for her awkwardly, and she said, "Good God, Bill."

He unfastened his belt.

Later they sent out for Chinese food, and when it arrived they ate hungrily, without speaking, and listened to records.

"Let's not forget to feed Kitty," she said.

"I was just thinking about that," he said. "I'll go right over."

He selected a can of fish for the cat, then filled the pitcher and went to water. When he returned to the kitchen the cat was scratching in her box. She looked at him steadily for a minute before she turned back to the litter. He opened all the cupboards and examined the canned goods, the cereals, the packaged foods, the cocktail and wine glasses, the china, the pots and pans. He opened the refrigerator. He sniffed some celery, took two bites of cheddar cheese and chewed on an apple as he walked into the bedroom. The bed seemed enormous, with a fluffy white bedspread draped to the floor. He pulled out a nightstand drawer, found a half-empty package of cigarettes and stuffed them into his pocket. Then he stepped to the closet and was opening it when the knock sounded at the front door.

He stopped by the bathroom and flushed the toilet on his way.

"What's been keeping you?" Arlene said. "You've been over here more than an hour."

"Have I really?" he said.

"Yes, you have," she said.

"I had to go to the toilet," he said.

"You have your own toilet," she said.

"I couldn't wait," he said.

That night they made love again.

In the morning he had Arlene call in for him. He showered, dressed and made a light breakfast. He tried to start a book. He went out for a walk and felt better, but after a while, hands still in his pockets, he returned to the apartment. He stopped at the Stones' door on the chance he might hear the cat moving about. Then he let himself in at his own door and went to the kitchen for the key.

Inside it seemed cooler than his apartment, and darker too. He wondered if the plants had something to do with the temperature of the air. He looked out the window, and then he moved slowly through each room considering everything that fell under his gaze, carefully, one object at a time. He saw ashtrays, items of furniture, kitchen utensils, the clock. He saw everything. At last he entered the bedroom, and the cat appeared at his feet. He stroked her once, carried her into the bathroom and shut the door.

He lay down on the bed and stared at the ceiling. He lay for a while with his eyes closed, and then he moved his hand into his pants. He tried to recall what day it was. He tried to remember when the Stones were due back, and then he wondered if they would ever return. He could not remember their faces or the way they talked and dressed. He sighed, and then with effort rolled off the bed to lean over the dresser and look at himself in the mirror.

He opened the closet and selected a Hawaiian shirt. He looked until he found Bermudas, neatly pressed and hanging over a pair of brown twill slacks. He shed his own clothes and slipped into the shorts and the shirt. He looked in the mirror again, he went to the living room and poured himself a drink and sipped it on his way back to the bedroom. He put on a dark suit, a blue shirt, a blue and white tie, black wing-tip shoes. The glass was empty and he went for another drink.

In the bedroom again he sat on a chair, crossed his legs and smiled, observing himself in the mirror. The telephone rang twice and fell silent. He finished the drink and took off the suit. He rummaged the top drawers until he found a pair of panties and a brassiere. He stepped into the panties and fastened the brassiere, then looked through the closet for an outfit. He put on a black-and-white checkered skirt which was too snug and which he was afraid to zipper, and a burgundy blouse that buttoned up the front. He considered her shoes, but understood they would not fit. For a long time he looked out the living-room window from behind the curtain. Then he returned to the bedroom and put everything away.

He was not hungry. She did not eat much either, but they looked at each other shyly and smiled. She got up from the table and checked that the key was on the shelf, then quickly cleared the dishes.

He stood in the kitchen doorway and smoked a cigarette and watched her pick up the key.

"Make yourself comfortable while I go across the hall," she said. "Read the paper or something." She closed her fingers over the key. He was, she said, looking tired.

He tried to concentrate on the news. He read the paper and turned on the television. Finally he went across the hall. The door was locked.

"It's me. Are you still there, honey?" he called.

After a time the lock released and Arlene stepped outside and shut the door. "Was I gone so long?" she said.

"Well you were," he said.

"Was I?" she said. "I guess I must have been playing with Kitty."

He studied her, and she looked away, her hand still resting on the doorknob.

"It's funny," she said. "You know, to go in someone's place like that."

He nodded, took her hand from the knob and guided her toward their own door. He let them into their apartment. "It is funny," he said. He noticed white lint clinging to the back of her sweater, and the color was high in her cheeks. He began kissing her on the neck and hair and she turned and kissed him back.

"Oh, damn," she said. "Damn, damn," girlishly clapping her hands. "I just remembered. I really and truly forgot to do what I went over there for. I didn't feed Kitty or do any watering." She looked at him. "Isn't that stupid?"

"I don't think so," he said. "Just a minute, I'll get my cigarettes and go back with you."

She waited until he had closed and locked their door, and then she took his arm at the muscle and said, "I guess I should tell you. I found some pictures."

He stopped in the middle of the hall. "What kind of pictures?"

"You can see for yourself," she said, and watched him.

"No kidding." He grinned. "Where?"

"In a drawer," she said.

"No kidding," he said.

And then she said, "Maybe they won't come back," and was at once astonished at her words.

"It could happen," he said. "Anything could happen."

"Or maybe they'll come back and," but she did not finish.

They held hands for the short walk across the hall, and when he spoke she could barely hear his voice.

"The key," he said. "Give it to me."

385

"What?" she said. She gazed at the door.

"The key," he said, "you have the key."

"My God," she said, "I left the key inside."

He tried the knob. It remained locked. Then she tried the knob, but it would not turn. Her lips were parted, and her breathing was hard, expectant. He opened his arms and she moved into them.

"Don't worry," he said into her ear. "For God's sake, don't worry." They stayed there. They held each other. They leaned into the door as if against a wind, and braced themselves.

Lightning Man

David Means

The first time, he was fishing with Danny. Fishing was a sacrament, and therefore, after the strike, when his head was clear, there was the blurry aftertaste of ritual: the casting of the spoon in lazy repetitions, the slow cranking, the utterance of the clicking reel, the baiting of the clean hook, and the cosmic intuitive troll for the deep pools of cool water beneath the gloss of a wind-dead afternoon. Each fish seemed to arrive as a miracle out of the silence: a largemouth bass gasping for air, gulping the sky, gyrating, twisting, turning against the leader's force. But then he was struck by lightning and afterward felt like a fish on the end of the line. There was a paradigm shift: He identified purely—at least for a few months—with the fish, dangling, held by an invisible line tossed down from the heavens.

* * *

Lucy had languid arms and pearly white skin—as smooth as the inside of a seashell, he liked to say—and he smelled, upon returning to the house on the Morrison farm one night, her peaty moistness on his fingers. He'd touched her—just swept his fingers into wetness—and now, unable to sleep, he'd gone outside to the porch swing to let the adrenaline and testosterone subside. His hope was to score with her before he left for boot camp. A storm was coming. Sheets of heat lightning unfurled inside clouds to the west. Deep, laryngeal mumbles of thunder smothered the cricket noise. The bolt that hit him ricocheted off a fence twenty yards away. Later he would recall that he'd half-jokingly spoken to the storm, and even to God, in a surge of testosterone-driven delight. Come on, you bastard, give me what you've got—the same phraseology boys his age were using to address incoming mortar rounds on East Asian battlefields. Come on, you bastard, try another one, he yelled just before the twin-forked purple-mauve bolt twisted down from the front edge of the squall line and tore off the fence at what—in flawed memory—seemed a squared right angle. It hit a bull's-eye on his sternum, so far as the doctors could deduce, leaving a moon-crater burn that never really healed. His father came out shortly to lock up the barn before the storm began (too late)—a cheroot lodged in his teeth—and found his son on his back, smoking slightly. During his two-week observational stay in the hospital, his teeth ached and sang, although he couldn't pick up the apocryphal transmissions of those megawatt, over-the-border Mexican radio stations. Upon his return home, Lucy came to his house and—in the silence of a hot summer afternoon—ran her hand down under the band of his BVDs.

Just before the third strike, a few years later, he saw a stubby orphan bolt, a thumb of spark wagging at him from the fence. (Research would later confirm that these microbolts in truth exist.) When *Life* magazine ran a single-page photo montage titled "Lightning Man," the article stated: "Nick Kelley claims he had a strange vision shortly before being struck. He was with two friends in a field a few hours south of Chicago, showing them some property he planned to develop. A small bolt of lightning was seen along a fence just before he was struck. Visions like this, possibly hallucinatory, have been reported by other eyewitnesses." The photo montage showed him in the backyard with a barbecue fork, pointing it at a sky loaded with thick clouds. The report failed to mention the severe contusion along his cheek and certain neurological changes that would reveal themselves over the course of time. His love for Lucy had been obliterated after the second strike. With the third strike his friendship with Danny was vaporized. And in between the first two, he'd temporarily lost all desire to fish.

The fourth had his name on it and was a barn burner, the kind you see locking horns with the Empire State Building. As it came down, he talked to it, holding his arms up for an embrace. This was again in a boat, out in the middle of Lake Michigan, trolling for coho and steelhead. (He liked the stupid simplicity of fishing in this manner, keeping an eye on the sonar, dragging a downrigger through the depths of the lake, leaning back in his seat, and waiting.) The boat's captain, Pete, caught the edge of the bolt and was burned to a crisp. Nick held a conversation with the big one as he took the full brunt. It went something like this: No matter what, I'll match you, you prick, this story, my story, a hayseed from central Illinois, struck once, twice for good luck, third time a charm, and now, oh by Jupiter! by Jove! or whatever, oh storm of narrative and calamity. Oh glorious grand design of nature. Rage through me. Grant my heart the guts to resist, but not too much. Make me, oh Lord, a good conductor. I will suffer *imitatione Christi*, taking on the burdens of the current and endeavoring to live again.

Shortly after his release from Chicago General, he began weekly attendance at the Second Church of God (or was it the Third?), where he met his first wife, Agnes, who bore an uncanny resemblance to Lucy (same peaches-and-cream complexion). When it came to his past and his history with lightning, scars aside, he had the reticence of a cold-war spy: The book was closed on cloud-to-ground, on hexes, on lightning-rod drummers, and the mystical crowd. (He had been offered gigs selling Pro-teck-o-Charge Safe-T rods—LIGHTNING IS THE NO. 1 CASE OF BARN FIRES!!!!—and

1-800-Know Your Future.) The book was closed on media interviews, on direct one-on-one confrontations with big bolts. (He in no way worried about smaller variants of lightning, those stray electrical fields that haunt most houses, those freak power surges that melt phone lines and blow phones blank, or those bolts of energy that float bemused into farmhouse windows.) Later he'd come to think that he had been willfully ignoring those forms and thereby picked a fight with them. Once, a film crew from France tracked him down to dredge up the past, but for the most part he urged himself into a normal life and felt bereft of charge, working at a PR firm, representing some commodities brokers, so that when the next strike came, it was out of the blue—the blue yonder, a rogue bit of static charge, summer heat lightning. This time he and Agnes were safely ensconced in their summer rental in northern Michigan, watching the Cubs. Agnes lay prone on the divan, wearing only panties and a bra, exposing her long legs and her schoolgirl belly and the dimpled muscles of her thigh. The cobwebby bolt radiated in a blue antimacassar across the window screen, collected itself, swept through the window, and seemed to congeal around her so that in that brief moment before she was killed, before the power failure plunged the room into black, he was granted a photo negative of her glorious form.

To get away from Chicago, he bought the old family farm, rebuilt the big barn, installing along its roofline six rods with fat blue bulbs attached to thick braided aluminum wires dangling from its sides. The horizon in those parts let the sky win. Even the corn seemed to be hunching low in anticipation of the next strike. In the evenings he read Kant and began dating a woman named Stacy, a large-boned farm widow who dabbled in poetry and quoted from T. S. Eliot, the whole first section of "Ash Wednesday," for example, and entire scenes from "The Cocktail Party." Nick was fifty now, lean from the field work, with chronic back pain from driving the combine. But he loved the work. He loved the long stretches of being alone in the cab, listening to Mozart sonatas while the corn marched forward into the arch lights, eager to be engulfed by the mawing machine. Behind the cab—in the starlit darkness—emerged the bald swath of landscape.

No more messing around. His days of heady challenge were over, Nick thought, ignoring the pliant, flexible nature of lightning itself, the dramatically disjointed manner in which it put itself into the air, the double-jointed way it could defy itself. The Morrison homestead was about as dead out-there as you could get. He was working night and day to harvest the soy-beans, trying to compete with the big Iowa industrial farms. Too tired to give a shit. Thunderstorm season was mostly done. Those fall storms that heaved through seemed exhausted and bored with the earth, offering up a pathetic rain, if anything.

The bolt that struck him the sixth time came out from under the veil of the sky—as witnessed by his farmhand Earl, who was unhitching some equip-ment and just happened to glance at Nick resting his back in a yellow lawn chair. The whopper bolt struck twenty feet away, balled itself up, rolled to Nick's feet, and exploded. He flew head over heels against the barn. In the hospital he remembered the medicine-ball exercises from grammar-school gym class, heaving the leather-clad ball at one another, relishing the absurdity of the game: trying like hell to knock the other guy over, to over-come him with the inertia of the object. To properly catch a medicine ball, you had to absorb the force and fall back with it so that at some point both you and the ball's momentum were married to each other. It was a delicate dance. He was pretty good at it.

Nick suffered further neurological damage, strange visions, a sparkling bloom of fireworks under his eyelids. He began to remember. It began to become clear. He had separated from himself during the strike. A doppel-gänger of sorts had emerged from his body: a little stoop-shouldered man, thin and frail, making small poking gestures with his cane as he listed for-ward. A soil sniffer of the old type. A man who could gather up a palmful of dirt and bring it to his nose and give you a rundown of its qualities—moistness and pH and lime content. This was the old dirt farmer of yore who knew his dry-farming methods and gave long intricate dances to the sky urging the beastly drought to come to an end. This man longed more than anything for the clouds to burst open at their seams, for a release of tension in the air, for not just thunder and lightning but for the downpour the land deserved. He was a remnant of all those sodbusters of yesterday: failed and broken by the land, trying as best they could to find the fix—an old, traditional rain dance, or a man who came with a cannon to shoot holes in the sky. Beneath the spot where the lightning ball had landed, the soil had fused to glass, and below that—Earl took a shovel and dug it up—the glass extended in an icicle five feet long, branching down to the underground cable that delivered current from the old barn to the storage shed. A power-company representative explained that these underground cables were as prone as above-ground wires to lightning strikes. God knows why, he added.

For three weeks Stacy sat beside his hospital bed and accompanied his anguish by singing odes and folk songs and small ditties she'd picked up as a kid in Alabama, in addition to going through the complete collected poems of Eliot. She had a pure, hard voice that seemed carved out of the American soil. In the bandage casing, amid the welts of itching and the drips of sweat running down his legs—all unreachable locations—he had acute visions of combat in Korea, the U. S. 1st Cavalry Division taking the full brunt of a barrage of Katyusha rockets—until bolt No. 8 (as he envisioned it) intervened, with its thick girth, the revoltingly huge embrace of the horizon as it came eagerly down. It was the big one, the finalization of several conjoining forks into one, unimaginable fury.

After Stacy took off on him, he put the farm up for sale and moved six miles to the north. He would live a bachelor life in a small Illinois town. He would avoid fate by immersing himself in the lackluster fluidum of the landscape, in the view from his room over the Ellison Feed & Seed store, a vista so boring it made you want to spit (and he did). Boarding in the rooms around him were exiled farm boys who sniffed glue from crumpled brown bags, listened to music, and whiled away days writing on the walls with Magic Markers. There was nobody as deviant and lost as an ex-farm boy, he would come to learn. They were depressed from knowing that the whole concept of the farm—the agrarian mythos of land and human love, not to mention the toil and tribulation of their own kin, who had suffered dust bowls, droughts, and seed molds—had been reduced to a historical joke. Industrial farms ruled. Left perplexed in their skin, they listened to hip-hop, attempted more urbane poses (many had missing limbs), smoked crack and jimsonweed, stalked the night half naked in their overalls, carved tattoos into their own arms. Nick felt akin to them. In their own way, they'd been struck by lightning, too.

Of course the next strike (No. 7) did come. It arrived in a preposterously arrogant manner, in a situation so laden with cliché that even Nick had to laugh it off when he could laugh, weeks later, after the trembles, the delusions, and the spark-filled sideshows. He knew that the next one would be his last. The next one would be the killer. The end. No more after that one. He felt No. 8 at the side of his vision as he stared out the window at the dead town, so dry—caught in a midsummer drought—it made his throat itch. In his field of vision there now appeared a blank spot, empty and deep and dark. The room crackled in the midsummer heat. The window opened to a view of a defunct farm town, circa 1920, with false-front facades in the western style, buildings shell-shocked and plucked clean of life. The beaverboard walls grew rank and emitted a dry, mustard smell. In the long afternoon shadows the farm boys hung out with crumpled bags to their faces—breathing the glue the way injured grunts took bottled oxygen. As if it made a difference. When he ventured downstairs, he walked with a hobble, keeping his weight off the balls of his feet, which were swollen and raw. Now I can safely be called enfeebled, he told the boys. They gathered around him, fingering his scars, showing in kind their own tattoos and flesh wounds, stumps that flicked quickly, glossy twists that traced the half-healed paths of boxcutter slashes and paint-scraper battles. They offered him crumpled bags. He declined. They offered him gasoline to sniff, weed, Valium. They asked him to tell his stories, and he did, giving them long tales, embellishing details at will, watching them nod slowly in appreciation. Here was something they could understand. Nature playing mind games. Nature fucking with him. He dug deep into the nature of lightning. He made himself heroic. He raised his fist like Zeus, catching bolts out of air. He tossed balled lightning, dribbled in for a fast break. This was the least he could do for them. He pitied them for their empty eyes, for the dead, slurry way they spoke.

In the dark room as the days turned and the sun raged over the cracked streets below, shrub-sized weeds driving up through the damaged macadam, Nick let the siege mentality develop. He would hunker down. He would avoid the next one. No. 7 had come just after his complete recovery, when he was called back to Chicago to make a court appearance in litigation over an option fund. He had gone out to the Oak Ridge Country Club with Albert Forster. The club would soon install lightning-detection equipment—the first of its kind in the Chicago metro area—to forewarn of exactly the kind of conditions that led to strike No. 7. A mass of cold air arrived from Canada, dug into the hot reaches of the Central Plains, picked up steam, and formed a storm front that had already spawned a classic F-4 tornado, reducing one trailer park to a salad of pink fluffy insulation material, chips of fiberglass, and chunks of Sheetrock. As he teed up on the second hole, bunching his shoulders in a manner that foretold of his forthcoming slice, the front was tonguing into the sticky summer air overhead. In the end it was just another bolt. Simple as that. It appeared as a surprise. Two blunt rumbles swallowed the golf course, a flick behind them, and then, just as Nick threw his club into his backswing, adjusting his shoulders, head cocked, eyes upward on the sky, No. 7 forked down, split into five wayward crabs of raw voltage, and speared him in the brow the way you'd poke a shrimp with a cocktail fork.

* * *

In the room he listened to the walls crackle and sat in front of an oscillating metal fan and didn't move for hours at a time. Down the street old Ralph the barber told his own kind of lightning stories about the Battle of the Bulge. If the rotating fan failed to keep him company, he'd go down to watch Ralph cut hair. Outside Ralph's establishment a wooden pole turned to rot. Inside, the mirrors were clean and the chrome and white enamel basins were kept shiny. The sad parameters of his life became nicely apparent at Ralph's. Here is a man defined by lightning, the shop said. Here is a man who could use a shave. A bit off the sides, layered in back. In the shop, his story was lore, it was myth, it was good talk. It was clear in those humble confines, amid the snip of shears, the concise irreversible nature of cutting hair. (People just don't realize how tough human hair is to cut, Ralph said.) Amid barbering—flattops, Princetons, layer cuts, wet and dry—the best Nick could do was answer the probing questions that Ralph sent his way. He embellished as much as he could. But he didn't lie. In the barbershop, words felt ponderous and heavy. He filled in with silence as much as he could, and when that didn't work, he hemmed and hawed. But with Ralph the silence seemed necessary. What went unspoken was filled in with Ralph's grunts and his nods and his attention to whoever was getting a cut; if he was between cuts, he might be cleaning the sink or arranging his scissors or stropping his razor with thoughtless Zen strokes. Christ, it's a good story you got, Nick, he said after hearing an account of No. 7. Ralph had a long pale face—the face of a man who seldom saw the sun—with eyes that drooped in sockets that drooped. Ralph sat on a fence between doubt and belief. He would never fully believe this strange man who came out of the blue and claimed to have owned the Morrison tract, the famous farm over in the next county, a farm that was at one time perhaps the best-run bit of land in that part of Lincoln County. He would only half-believe this guy who seemed so weatherworn and odd. Men like this arrived often out of the Great Plains, even now, years after the great wanderings of hobos and tramps, and they often spoke in a reverent voice of preposterous and prophetic events, events that were mostly untrue but that somehow had the ring of truth. Ralph knew the importance of such souls.

They walked the line between fact and fiction, and in doing so lightened the load of the truth. They made you aware of the great, desolate span of the Central States, of the empty space that still prevailed. He snipped with care around the ears and then snapped the buzzers on and cleaned up the neck, working to create a neat line. He would listen to Lightning Man's stories again, and by the time the man's whole repertoire of tales was used up, another year or so would have passed and he'd be ready to hear them again, forgetting enough of the details to make it interesting. Lightning Man would become a fixture in the shop. He'd have his own chair and ashtray. Into the long afternoons his words would pass. A place would be found for this man. Odd chores would be offered so that he might find subsistence, a few bucks here or there. In this manner another soul would be able to conclude his days upon the earth—at least until the odd premonitions came and the air grew absurdly still and above the shop the clouds began their boiling congregation, and then a faint foreshadowing taste of ozone would arrive. Then everything would change, and nothing would be the same again.

The Visit to the Museum

Vladimir Nabokov

(Translated from the Russian by Dmitri Nabokov)

Several years ago a friend of mine in Paris—a person with oddities, to put it mildly—learning that I was going to spend two or three days at Montisert, asked me to drop in at the local museum where there hung, he was told, a portrait of his grandfather by Leroy. Smiling and spreading out his hands, he related a rather vague story to which I confess I paid little attention, partly because I do not like other people's obtrusive affairs, but chiefly because I had always had doubts about my friend's capacity to remain this side of fantasy. It went more or less as follows: after the grandfather died in their St. Petersburg house back at the time of the Russo-Japanese War, the contents of his apartment in Paris were sold at an auction. The portrait, after some obscure peregrinations, was acquired by the museum of Leroy's native town. My friend wished to know if the portrait was really there; if there, if it could be ransomed; and if it could, for what price. When I asked why he did not get in touch with the museum, he replied that he had written several times, but had never received an answer.

I made an inward resolution not to carry out the request—I could always tell him I had fallen ill or changed my itinerary. The very notion of seeing sights, whether they be museums or ancient buildings, is loathsome to me; besides, the good freak's commission seemed absolute nonsense. It so happened, however, that, while wandering about Montisert's empty streets in search of a stationery store, and cursing the spire of a long-necked cathedral, always the same one, that kept popping up at the end of every street, I was caught in a violent downpour which immediately went about accelerating the fall of the maple leaves, for the fair weather of a southern October was holding on by a mere thread. I dashed for cover and found myself on the steps of the museum.

It was a building of modest proportions, constructed of many-colored stones, with columns, a gilt inscription over the frescoes of the pediment, and a lion-legged stone bench on either side of the bronze door. One of its leaves stood open, and the interior seemed dark against the shimmer of the shower. I stood for a while on the steps, but, despite the overhanging roof, they were gradually growing speckled. I saw that the rain had set in for good, and so, having nothing better to do, I decided to go inside. No sooner had I trod on the smooth, resonant flagstones of the vestibule than the clatter of a moved stool came from a distant corner, and the custodian—a banal pensioner with an empty sleeve—rose to meet me, laying aside his newspaper and peering at me over his spectacles. I paid my franc and, trying not to look at some statues at the entrance (which were as traditional and as insignificant as the first number in a circus program), I entered the main hall.

Everything was as it should be: grey tints, the sleep of substance, matter dematerialized. There was the usual case of old, worn coins resting in the inclined velvet of their compartments. There was, on top of the case, a pair of owls, Eagle Owl and Long-eared, with their French names reading

"Grand Duke" and "Middle Duke" if translated. Venerable minerals lay in their open graves of dusty papier-mâché; a photograph of an astonished gentleman with a pointed beard dominated an assortment of strange black lumps of various sizes. They bore a great resemblance to frozen frass, and I paused involuntarily over them for I was quite at a loss to guess their nature, composition and function. The custodian had been following me with felted steps, always keeping a respectful distance; now, however, he came up, with one hand behind his back and the ghost of his other in his pocket, and gulping, if one judged by his Adam's apple.

"What are they?" I asked.

"Science has not yet determined," he replied, undoubtedly having learned the phrase by rote. "They were found," he continued in the same phony tone, "in 1895, by Louis Pradier, Municipal Councillor and Knight of the Legion of Honor," and his trembling finger indicated the photograph.

"Well and good," I said, "but who decided, and why, that they merited a place in the museum?"

"And now I call your attention to this skull!" the old man cried energetically, obviously changing the subject.

"Still, I would be interested to know what they are made of," I interrupted.

"Science . . ." he began anew, but stopped short and looked crossly at his fingers, which were soiled with dust from the glass.

I proceeded to examine a Chinese vase, probably brought back by a naval officer; a group of porous fossils; a pale worm in clouded alcohol; a red-and-green map of Montisert in the seventeenth century; and a trio of rusted tools bound by a funereal ribbon—a spade, a mattock and a pick. "To dig in the past," I thought absentmindedly, but this time did not seek clarification from the custodian, who was following me noiselessly and meekly, weaving in and out among the display cases. Beyond the first hall there was another, apparently the last, and in its center a large sarcophagus stood like a dirty bathtub, while the walls were hung with paintings.

At once my eye was caught by the portrait of a man between two abominable landscapes (with cattle and "atmosphere"). I moved closer and, to my considerable amazement, found the very object whose existence had hitherto seemed to me but the figment of an unstable mind. The man, depicted in wretched oils, wore a frock coat, whiskers and a large pince-nez on a cord; he bore a likeness to Offenbach, but, in spite of the work's vile conventionality, I had the feeling one could make out in his features the horizon of a resemblance, as it were, to my friend. In one corner, meticulously traced in carmine against a black background, was the signature *Leroy* in a hand as commonplace as the work itself.

I felt a vinegarish breath near my shoulder, and turned to meet the custodian's kindly gaze. "Tell me," I asked, "supposing someone wished to buy one of these paintings, whom should he see?"

"The treasures of the museum are the pride of the city," replied the old man, "and pride is not for sale."

Fearing his eloquence, I hastily concurred, but nevertheless asked for the name of the museum's director. He tried to distract me with the story of the sarcophagus, but I insisted. Finally he gave me the name of one M. Godard and explained where I could find him.

Frankly, I enjoyed the thought that the portrait existed. It is fun to be present at the coming true of a dream, even if it is not one's own. I decided to settle the matter without delay. When I get in the spirit, no one can hold me back. I left the museum with a brisk, resonant step, and found that the rain had stopped, blueness had spread across the sky, a woman in besplattered stockings was spinning along on a silver-shining bicycle, and only over the surrounding hills did clouds still hang. Once again the cathedral began playing hide-and-seek with me, but I outwitted it. Barely escaping the onrushing tires of a furious red bus packed with singing youths, I crossed the asphalt thoroughfare and a minute later was ringing at the garden gate of M. Godard. He turned out to be a thin, middle-aged gentleman in high collar and dickey, with a pearl in the knot of his tie, and a face very much resembling a Russian wolfhound; as if that were not enough, he was licking his chops in a most doglike manner, while sticking a stamp on an envelope, when I entered his small but lavishly furnished room with its malachite inkstand on the desk and a strangely familiar Chinese vase on the mantel. A pair of fencing foils hung crossed over the mirror, which reflected the narrow grey back of his head. Here and there photographs of a warship pleasantly broke up the blue flora of the wallpaper.

"What can I do for you?" he asked, throwing the letter he had just sealed into the wastebasket. This act seemed unusual to me; however, I did not see fit to interfere. I explained in brief my reason for coming, even naming the substantial sum with which my friend was willing to part, though he had asked me not to mention it, but wait instead for the museum's terms.

"All this is delightful," said M. Godard. "The only thing is, you are mistaken—there is no such picture in our museum."

"What do you mean there is no such picture?" I explained, "I have just seen it! Portrait of a Russian nobleman, by Gustave Leroy."

"We do have one Leroy," said M. Godard when he had leafed through an oilcloth notebook and his black fingernail had stopped at the entry in question. "However, it is not a portrait but a rural landscape: The Return of the Herd."

I repeated that I had seen the picture with my own eyes five minutes before and that no power on this earth could make me doubt its existence.

"Agreed," said M. Godard, "but I am not crazy either. I have been curator of our museum for almost twenty years now and know this catalog as well as I know the Lord's Prayer. It says here Return of the Herd and that means the herd is returning, and unless perhaps your friend's grandfather is depicted as a shepherd, I cannot conceive of his portrait's existence in our museum."

"He is wearing a frock coat," I cried. "I swear he is wearing a frock coat!"

"And how did you like our museum in general?" M. Godard asked suspiciously. "Did you appreciate the sarcophagus?"

"Listen," I said (and I think there was already a tremor in my voice), "do me a favor—let's go there this minute, and let's make an agreement that if the portrait is there, you will sell it."

"And if not?" inquired M. Godard.

"I shall pay you the sum of money anyway."

"All right," he said. "Here, take this red-and-blue pencil and using the red—the red, please—put it in writing for me."

In my excitement, I carried out his demand. Upon glancing at my signature, he deplored the difficult pronunciation of Russian names. Then he appended his own signature and, quickly folding the sheet, thrust it into his waistcoat pocket.

"Let's go," he said freeing a cuff.

On the way he stepped into a shop and bought a bag of sticky looking caramels which he began offering me insistently; when I flatly refused, he tried to shake out a couple of them into my hand. I pulled my hand away. Several caramels fell on the sidewalk; he stopped to pick them up and then overtook me at a trot. When we drew near the museum we saw the red tourist bus (now empty) parked outside.

"Aha," said M. Godard, pleased. "I see we have many visitors today."

He doffed his hat and, holding it in front of him, walked decorously up the steps.

All was not well at the museum. From within issued rowdy cries, lewd laughter, and even what seemed like the sound of a scuffle. We entered the first hall; there the elderly custodian was restraining two sacrilegists who wore some kind of festive emblems in their lapels and were altogether very purple-faced and full of pep as they tried to extract the municipal councillor's merds from beneath the glass. The rest of the youths, members of some rural athletic organization, were making noisy fun, some of the worm in alcohol, others of the skull. One joker was in rapture over the pipes of the steam radiator, which he pretended to take for an exhibit; another was taking aim at an owl with his fist and forefinger. There were about thirty of them in all and their motion and voices created a condition of crush and thick noise.

M. Godard clapped his hands and pointed at a sign reading "Visitors to the Museum must be decently attired." Then he pushed his way, with me following, into the second hall. The whole company immediately swarmed after us. I steered Godard to the portrait; he froze before it, chest inflated, and then stepped back a bit, as if admiring it, and his feminine heel trod on somebody's foot.

"Splendid picture," he exclaimed with genuine sincerity. "Well, let's not be petty about this. You were right, and there must be an error in the catalog."

As he spoke, his fingers, moving as it were on their own, tore up our agreement into little bits which fell like snowflakes into a massive spittoon.

"Who's the old ape?" asked an individual in a striped jersey, and as my friend's grandfather was depicted holding a glowing cigar, another funster took out a cigarette and prepared to borrow a light from the portrait.

"All right, let us settle on the price," I said, "and, in any case, let's get out of here."

"Make way, please!" shouted M. Godard, pushing aside the curious.

There was an exit, which I had not noticed previously, at the end of the hall and we thrust our way through to it.

"I can make no decision," M. Godard was shouting above the din. "Decisiveness is a good thing only when supported by the law. I must first discuss the matter with the mayor, who has just died and has not yet been elected. I doubt that you will be able to purchase the portrait, but nonetheless I would like to show you still other treasures of ours."

We found ourselves in a hall of considerable dimensions. Brown books, with a half-baked look and coarse, foxed pages, lay open under glass on a long table. Along the walls stood dummy soldiers in jackboots with flared tops.

"Come, let's talk it over," I cried out in desperation, trying to direct M. Godard's evolutions to a plush-covered sofa in a corner. But in this I was prevented by the custodian. Flailing his one arm, he came running after us, pursued by a merry crowd of youths, one of whom had put on his head a copper helmet with a Rembrandtesque gleam.

"Take it off, take it off!" shouted M. Godard, and someone's shove made the helmet fly off the hooligan's head with a clatter.

"Let us move on," said M. Godard, tugging at my sleeve, and we passed into the section of Ancient Sculpture.

I lost my way for a moment among some of the enormous marble legs, and twice ran around a giant knee before I again caught sight of

M. Godard, who was looking for me behind the white ankle of a neighboring giantess. Here a person in a bowler, who must have clambered up her, suddenly fell from a great height to the stone floor. One of his companions began helping him up, but they were both drunk, and, dismissing them with a wave of the hand, M. Godard rushed on to the next room, radiant with Oriental fabrics; there hounds raced across azure carpets, and a bow and quiver lay on a tiger skin.

Strangely, though, the expanse and motley only gave me a feeling of oppressiveness and imprecision, and, perhaps because new visitors kept dashing by or perhaps because I was impatient to leave the unnecessarily spreading museum and amid calm and freedom conclude my business negotiations with M. Godard, I began to experience a vague sense of alarm. Meanwhile we had transported ourselves into yet another hall, which must have been really enormous, judging by the fact that it housed the entire skeleton of a whale, resembling a frigate's frame; beyond were visible still other halls, with the oblique sheen of large paintings, full of storm clouds, among which floated the delicate idols of religious art in blue and pink vestments; and all this resolved itself in an abrupt turbulence of misty draperies, and chandeliers came aglitter and fish with translucent frills meandered through illuminated aquariums. Racing up a staircase, we saw, from the gallery above, a crowd of grey-haired people with umbrellas examining a gigantic mock-up of the universe.

At last, in a somber but magnificent room dedicated to the history of steam machines, I managed to halt my carefree guide for an instant.

"Enough!" I shouted. "I'm leaving. We'll talk tomorrow."

He had already vanished. I turned and saw, scarcely an inch from me, the lofty wheels of a sweaty locomotive. For a long time I tried to find the way back among models of railroad stations. How strangely glowed the violet signals in the gloom beyond the fan of wet tracks, and what spasms shook my poor heart! Suddenly everything changed again: in front of me stretched an infinitely long passage, containing numerous office cabinets and elusive, scurrying people. Taking a sharp turn, I found myself amid a thousand musical instruments; the walls, all mirror, reflected an enfilade of grand pianos, while in the center there was a pool with a bronze Orpheus atop a green rock. The aquatic theme did not end here as, racing back, I ended up in the Section of Fountains and Brooks, and it was difficult to walk along the winding, slimy edges of those waters.

Now and then, on one side or the other, stone stairs, with puddles on the steps, which gave me a strange sensation of fear, would descend into misty abysses, whence issued whistles, the rattle of dishes, the clatter of typewriters, the ring of hammers and many other sounds, as if, down there, were exposition halls of some kind or other, already closing or not yet completed. Then I found myself in darkness and kept bumping into unknown furniture until I finally saw a red light and walked out onto a platform that clanged under me—and suddenly, beyond it, there was a bright parlor, tastefully furnished in Empire style, but not a living soul, not a living soul. . . . By now I was indescribably terrified, but every time I turned and tried to retrace my steps along the passages, I found myself in hitherto unseen places—a greenhouse with hydrangeas and broken windowpanes with the darkness of artificial night showing through beyond; or a deserted laboratory with dusty alembics on its tables. Finally I ran into a room of some sort with coatracks monstrously loaded down with black coats and astrakhan furs; from beyond a door came a burst of applause, but when I flung the door open, there was no theatre, but only a soft opacity and splendidly counterfeited fog with the perfectly convincing blotches of indistinct streetlights. More than convincing! I advanced, and immediately a joyous and unmistakable sensation of reality at last replaced all the unreal trash amid which I had just been dashing to and fro. The stone beneath my feet was real sidewalk, powdered with wonderfully fragrant, newly fallen snow in which the infrequent pedestrians had already left fresh black tracks. At first the quiet and the snowy coolness of the night, somehow strikingly familiar, gave me a pleasant feeling after my feverish wanderings. Trustfully, I started to conjecture just where I had come out, and why the snow, and what were those lights exaggeratedly but indistinctly beaming here and there in the brown darkness. I examined and, stooping, even touched a round spur stone on the curb, then glanced at the palm of my hand, full of wet granular cold, as if hoping to read an explanation there. I felt how lightly, how naïvely I was clothed, but the distinct realization that I had escaped from the museum's maze was still so strong that, for the first two or three minutes, I experienced neither surprise nor fear. Continuing my leisurely examination, I looked up at the house beside which I was standing and was immediately struck by the sight of the iron steps and railings that descended into the snow on their way to the cellar. There was a twinge in my heart, and it was with a new, alarmed curiosity that I glanced at the pavement, at its white cover along which stretched black lines, at the brown sky across which there kept sweeping a mysterious light, and at the massive parapet some distance away. I sensed that there was a drop beyond it; something was creaking and gurgling down there. Further on, beyond the murky cavity, stretched a chain of fuzzy lights. Scuffling along the snow in my soaked shoes, I walked a few paces, all the time glancing at the dark house on my right; only in a single window did a lamp glow softly under its green-glass shade. Here, a locked wooden gate. . . . There, what must be the shutters of a sleeping shop. . . . And by the light of a streetlamp whose shape had long been shouting to me its impossible message, I made out the ending of a sign—". . . *inka Sapog*" *(". . . oe Repair")*—but no, it was not the snow that had obliterated the "hard sign" at the end. (After the Revolution, the "hard sign," appearing after consonants at the end of the word, was eliminated from the alphabet.) "No, no, in a minute I shall wake up," I said aloud, and, trembling, my heart pounding, I turned, walked on, stopped again. From somewhere came the receding sound of hooves, cushioned, lazy and even; the snow sat like a skullcap on a slightly leaning spur stone and indistinctly showed white on the woodpile on the other side of the fence, and already I knew, irrevocably, where I was. Alas, it was not the Russia I remembered, but the factual Russia of today, forbidden to me, hopelessly slavish, and hopelessly my own native land. A semiphantom in a light foreign suit, I stood on the impassive snow of an October night, somewhere on the Moyka or the Fontanka Canal, or perhaps on the Obvodny, and I had to do something, go somewhere, run, desperately protect my fragile, illegal life. Oh, how many times in my sleep I had experienced a similar sensation! Now, though, it was reality. Everything was real—the air that seemed to mingle with scattered snowflakes, the still unfrozen canal, the floating fish house, and that peculiar squareness of the darkened and the yellow windows. A man in a fur cap, with a briefcase under his arm, came toward me out of the fog, gave me a startled glance, and turned to look again when he had passed me. I waited for him to disappear and then, with a tremendous haste, began pulling out everything I had in my pockets, ripping up papers, throwing them into the snow and stamping them down. There were some documents, a letter from my sister in Paris, five-hundred francs, a handkerchief, cigarettes; however, in order to shed all the integument of exile, I would have to tear off and destroy my clothes, my linen, my shoes, everything, and remain ideally naked; and even though I was already shivering from my anguish and from the cold, I did what I could.

But enough. I shall not recount how I was arrested, nor tell of my subsequent ordeals. Suffice it to say that it cost me incredible patience and effort to get back abroad, and that, ever since, I have foresworn carrying out commissions entrusted one by the insanity of others.

Hardy in the Evening

Tony Earley

Evelyn and Hardy have been married fifty-two years. Evelyn's feet inside her bedroom shoes are slowly turning black. Evelyn believes the cars passing her house contain secret agents come to watch her, that the boys who play basketball across the road want to see her naked.

Hardy dabs at a spot on Evelyn's thigh with a cotton ball dipped in alcohol. Evelyn says, "You're not trying to poison me, are you, Hardy?"

Hardy thinks, *Too much medication*. Hardy thinks, *You are just about crazy*. Hardy squints at the numbers on the side of the syringe.

Evelyn says, "It would be easy for you to poison me if you wanted to harm me. You wouldn't ever harm me, would you, Hardy?"

"No, baby," says Hardy. "I would never harm you."

Evelyn says, "I know you love that dog more than you love me."
Hardy says, "Hush. Hold still."

Hardy was a hero during the war. The first man he killed leapt out of a fox-hole in North Africa and tried to run away. Hardy led him slightly and dropped him like a rabbit. The last man Hardy killed was taking a leak, in Czechoslovakia, two days before the war ended. Hardy stepped out from behind a tree. The man smiled and said, "No kraut." Hardy shot him through the heart. By then he didn't care anymore.

The dog is a Brittany named Belle. Hardy walks her across the yard toward the cornfield behind his house. Evelyn yells from the porch. "Where are you going, Hardy? Hardy, you come back here." Hardy hears the basketball stop bouncing across the road. He knows if he answers, he will not make it into the field. He keeps walking. Evelyn slams the back door. The ball starts bouncing again. At the edge of the field, Belle looks up at him and whines. She is the best bird dog Hardy has ever had. He carries the shotgun only because Belle doesn't like to work unless he's armed. He says, "Hunt," and the dog bounds into the corn stubble.

One night, after Hardy came home from the war, he woke up out in the yard. He didn't know where he was. Evelyn stood off to the side in her nightgown, calling his name. Hardy moved his eyes to watch her but didn't dare turn his head. She said, "Hardy, I brought you a blanket. I thought you might be cold." Her nightgown glowed in the moonlight. Hardy motioned for her to get down. Evelyn knelt in the grass. She said, "Hardy? It's me. Evelyn. I'm your wife. We're home. I'm not going to let anything happen to you."

As Hardy steps past the dog, two quail explode into the twilight. Hardy intentionally draws a bead behind the nearest bird and squeezes the trigger. The orange muzzle flame licks out against the darkening sky. The shot claps and echoes. The birds arc unharmed across the field toward the woods. Hardy hears their wings whir. For a moment he is intensely happy. The dog breaks point and turns and looks at him. Hardy says, "I missed him, Belle. It's my fault, girl. It's my fault." Hardy says, "Hunt."

In Belle's dog lot, Hardy discovers four pills inside her bowl: two Elavil, a Lasix, and an aspirin. He imagines Evelyn emptying her medicine onto the kitchen counter, picking through the pills the way a child might choose smooth stones from a creek bank or crayons from a box. Hardy allows his shoulders to shake exactly twice. When he came home from the war, he couldn't hold down a job or sleep in a house. Evelyn loved him back into the shape of himself. That she breaks his heart now seems to him only fair. Hardy drops the pills into the pocket of his hunting coat. He walks toward his house slowly, but in a straight line, without stopping.

Morning in America

Tony Earley

She holds on to Jon's hand and tries to pay attention while he prays but instead imagines a distant future: Someone like Jon—she squints hard to make it Jon, but she can't be sure—is the pastor of a brick church on top of a hill. She is his wife. For a moment, her real life falls away, the one in which Jon sees her only as a high school friend, and she feels this better life slip around her shoulders like a coat. She sits in the front pew beneath a stained-glass window and stares up, filled with love for the man in the pulpit. She feels her children sitting all around her but doesn't want to turn her head. She can't tell who the man in the pulpit is, but she thinks that if she can hear Jon in her imagining she can make it him. She tries to travel back toward reality just far enough to make out the sound of his voice and

411

feels Melinda wetly holding her other hand. She hears a locker door slam, hundreds of kids talking too loudly at once, the front door swinging open, and a bus grumbling by. She tries to stay in the pew, bathed in the warm, stained sunlight, but feels herself slipping back into the body of her life. She hears Jon pray beside her, "And we humbly beseech you, heavenly Father, to make us good students today, to help us learn the lessons you think we should know," and she remembers that three of the six calculus problems in her homework are wrong.

With her head still bowed, she opens her eyes and glances up at the clock—she always feels slightly panicked when the bell rings before Jon finishes his prayer—and sees Kyle staring at her. Kyle looks like a seventh grader, except that his little boy's body perches on top of impossibly long insect legs. She stands up straighter. She is used to being stared at while she prays, used to the kids milling around the lobby pretending not to watch, and she views praying without shame as a kind of testimony. She doesn't have the kind of close, personal relationship with Jesus that Jon does but rather believes in Him the way she believes in the roof of her house: She can't see it when she's under it, but she knows that it protects her. Kyle sees her peeking at him and pretends to look for something in his book bag. She smiles and briefly imagines telling him she just wants to be friends.

Jon prays, "We thank you again, Lord Jesus, for this opportunity to praise your holy name," and she reflexively whispers, Yes, yes, although she really isn't paying attention. Kyle is shoving orange earplugs into his ears. She frowns. The bell isn't that loud. Jon prays, "And we ask that you teach us to love our neighbors as ourselves and to think of you in all that we do. In Jesus' name we pray. Amen." She says amen and watches Kyle pull a pistol out of his book bag and point it at her chest. She feels Jon let go of her hand, hears Melinda gasp. When the bullet enters her heart, she leans back against a locker and watches Kyle fire the pistol again and again, his eyes closed now, his head turned away from the noise. He looks afraid. As she slides slowly to the floor, she comes upon a revelation as if it were a vista, the whole world seen from a mountaintop, heaven and earth contained in an atom of thought: We just didn't love Kyle enough, and he has suffered for it. She holds Kyle's misshapen heart inside her chest as if it were the rarest gift. She wants to tell Kyle he is forgiven and ask him to forgive her. She raises her right hand above her head to get his attention and steps off into brightest sunlight.

Rock Springs

Richard Ford

Edna and I had started down from Kalispell heading for Tampa–St. Pete, where I still had some friends from the old glory days who wouldn't turn me in to the police. I had managed to scrape with the law in Kalispell over several bad checks—which is a prison crime in Montana. And I knew Edna was already looking at her cards and thinking about a move, since it wasn't the first time I'd been in law scrapes in my life. She herself had already had her own troubles, losing her kids and keeping her ex-husband, Danny, from breaking in her house and stealing her things while she was at work, which was really why I had moved in in the first place, that and needing to give my little daughter, Cheryl, a better shake in things.

    I don't know what was between Edna and me, just beached by the same tides when you got down to it. Though love has been built on frailer ground than that, as I well know. And when I came in the house that afternoon, I just asked her if she wanted to go to Florida with me, leave things where they sat, and she said, "Why not? My datebook's not that full."

Edna and I had been a pair eight months, more or less man and wife, some of which time I had been out of work, and some when I'd worked at the dog track as a lead-out and could help with the rent and talk sense to Danny when he came around. Danny was afraid of me because Edna had told him I'd been in prison in Florida for killing a man once, though that wasn't true. I had once been in jail in Tallahassee for stealing tires and had gotten into a fight on the county farm where a man had lost his eye. But I hadn't done the hurting, and Edna just wanted the story worse than it was so Danny wouldn't act crazy and make her have to take her kids back, since she had made a good adjustment to not having them, and I already had Cheryl with me. I'm not a violent person and would never put a man's eye out, much less kill someone. My former wife, Helen, would come all the way from Waikiki Beach to testify to that. We never had violence, and I believe in crossing the street to stay out of trouble's way. Though Danny didn't know that.

But we were half down through Wyoming, going toward 1-80 and feeling good about things, when the oil light flashed on in the car I'd stolen, a sign I knew to be a bad one.

I'd gotten us a good car, a cranberry Mercedes I'd stolen out of an ophthalmologist's lot in Whitefish, Montana. I stole it because I thought it would be comfortable over a long haul, because I thought it got good mileage, which it didn't, and because I'd never had a good car in my life, just old Chevy junkers and used trucks back from when I was a kid swamping citrus with Cubans.

The car made us all high that day. I ran the windows up and down, and Edna told us some jokes and made faces. She could be lively. Her features would light up like a beacon and you could see her beauty, which wasn't ordinary. It all made me giddy, and I drove clean down to Bozeman, then straight on through the park to Jackson Hole. I rented us the bridal suite in the Quality Court in Jackson and left Cheryl and her little dog, Duke, sleeping while Edna and I drove to a rib barn and drank beer and laughed till after midnight.

It felt like a whole new beginning for us, bad memories left behind and a new horizon to build on. I got so worked up, I had a tattoo done on my arm that said FAMOUS TIMES, and Edna bought a Bailey hat with an Indian feather band and a little turquoise-and-silver bracelet for Cheryl, and we made love on the seat of the car in the Quality Court parking lot just as the sun was burning up on the Snake River, and everything seemed then like the end of the rainbow.

It was that very enthusiasm, in fact, that made me keep the car one day longer instead of driving it into the river and stealing another one, like I should have done and *had* done before.

Where the car went bad there wasn't a town in sight or even a house, just some low mountains maybe fifty miles away or maybe a hundred, a barbed-wire fence in both directions, hardpan prairie, and some hawks sailing through the evening air seizing insects.

I got out to look at the motor, and Edna got out with Cheryl and the dog to let them have a pee by the car. I checked the water and checked the oil stick, and both of them said perfect.

"What's that light mean, Earl?" Edna said. She had come and stood by the car with her hat on. She was just sizing things up for herself.

"We shouldn't run it," I said. "Something's not right in the oil."

She looked around at Cheryl and Little Duke, who were peeing on the hardtop side by side like two little dolls, then out at the mountains, which were becoming black and lost in the distance. "What're we doing?" she said. She wasn't worried yet, but she wanted to know what I was thinking about.

"Let me try it again," I said.

"That's a good idea," she said, and we all got back in the car.

When I turned the motor over, it started right away and the red light stayed off and there weren't any noises to make you think something was wrong. I let it idle a minute, then pushed the accelerator down and watched the red bulb. But there wasn't any light on, and I started wondering if maybe I hadn't dreamed I saw it, or that it had been the sun catching an angle off the window chrome, or maybe I was scared of something and didn't know it.

"What's the matter with it, Daddy?" Cheryl said from the back seat. I looked back at her, and she had on her turquoise bracelet and Edna's hat set back on the back of her head and that little black-and-white Heinz dog on her lap. She looked like a little cowgirl in the movies.

"Nothing, honey, everything's fine now," I said.

"Little Duke tinkled where I tinkled," Cheryl said, and laughed.

"You're two of a kind," Edna said, not looking back. Edna was usually good with Cheryl, but I knew she was tired now. We hadn't had much sleep, and she had a tendency to get cranky when she didn't sleep. "We oughta ditch this damn car first chance we get," she said.

"What's the first chance we got?" I said, because I knew she'd been at the map.

"Rock Springs, Wyoming," Edna said with conviction. "Thirty miles down this road."

She pointed out ahead. I had wanted all along to drive the car into Florida like a big success story. But I knew Edna was right about it, that we shouldn't take crazy chances. I had kept thinking of it as my car and not the ophthalmologist's, and that was how you got caught in these things.

"Then my belief is we ought to go to Rock Springs and negotiate ourselves a new car," I said. I wanted to stay upbeat, like everything was panning out right.

"That's a great idea," Edna said, and she leaned over and kissed me hard on the mouth.

"That's a great idea," Cheryl said. "Let's pull on out of here right now."

The sunset that day I remember as being the prettiest I'd ever seen. Just as it touched the rim of the horizon, it all at once fired the air into jewels and red sequins the precise likes of which I had never seen before and haven't seen since. The West has it all over everywhere for sunsets, even Florida, where it's supposedly flat but where half the time trees block your view.

"It's cocktail hour," Edna said after we'd driven awhile. "We ought to have a drink and celebrate something." She felt better thinking we were going to get rid of the car. It certainly had dark troubles and was something you'd want to put behind you.

Edna had out a whiskey bottle and some plastic cups and was measuring levels on the glove-box lid. She liked drinking, and she liked drinking in the car, which was something you got used to in Montana, where it wasn't against the law, where, though, strangely enough, a bad check would land you in Deer Lodge Prison for a year.

"Did I ever tell you I once had a monkey?" Edna said, setting my drink on the dashboard where I could reach it when I was ready. Her spirits were already picked up. She was like that, up one minute and down the next.

"I don't think you ever did tell me that," I said. "Where were you then?"

"Missoula," she said. She put her bare feet on the dash and rested the cup on her breasts. "I was waitressing at the Amvets. It was before I met you. Some guy came in one day with a monkey. A spider monkey. And I said, just to be joking, 'I'll roll you for that monkey.' And the guy said, 'Just one roll?' And I said, 'Sure.' He put the monkey down on the bar, picked up the cup, and rolled out boxcars. I picked it up and rolled out three fives. And I just stood there looking at the guy. He was just some guy passing through, I guess a vet. He got a strange look on his face—I'm sure not as strange as the one I had—but he looked kind of sad and surprised and satisfied all at once. I said, 'We can roll again.' But he said, 'No, I never roll twice for anything.' And he sat and drank a beer and talked about one thing and another for a while, about nuclear war and building a stronghold somewhere up in the Bitterroot, whatever it was, while I just watched the monkey, wondering what I was going to do with it when the guy left. And pretty soon he got up and said, 'Well, goodbye, Chipper'; that was this monkey's name, of course. And then he left before I could say anything.

And the monkey just sat on the bar all that night. I don't know what made me think of that, Earl. Just something weird. I'm letting my mind wander."

"That's perfectly fine," I said. I took a drink of my drink. "I'd never own a monkey," I said after a minute. "They're too nasty. I'm sure Cheryl would like a monkey, though, wouldn't you, honey?" Cheryl was down on the seat playing with Little Duke. She used to talk about monkeys all the time then. "What'd you ever do with that monkey?" I said, watching the speedometer. We were having to go slower now because the red light kept fluttering on. And all I could do to keep it off was go slower. We were going maybe thirty-five and it was an hour before dark, and I was hoping Rock Springs wasn't far away.

"You really want to know?" Edna said. She gave me a quick, sharp glance, then looked back at the empty desert as if she was brooding over it.

"Sure," I said. I was still upbeat. I figured *I* could worry about breaking down and let other people be happy for a change.

"I kept it a week," she said. She seemed gloomy all of a sudden, as if she saw some aspect of the story she had never seen before. "I took it home and back and forth to the Amvets on my shifts. And it didn't cause any trouble. I fixed a chair up for it to sit on, back of the bar, and people liked it. It made a nice little clicking noise. We changed its name to Mary because the bartender figured out it was a girl. Though I was never really comfortable with it at home. I felt like it watched me too much. Then one day a guy came in, some guy who'd been in Vietnam, still wore a fatigue coat. And he said to me, 'Don't you know that a monkey'll kill you? It's got more strength in its fingers than you got in your whole body.' He said people had been killed in Vietnam by monkeys, bunches of them marauding while you were asleep, killing you and covering you with leaves. I didn't believe a word of it, except that when I got home and got undressed I started looking over across the room at Mary on her chair in the dark watching me. And I got the creeps. And after a while I got up and went out to the car, got a length of clothesline wire, and came back in and wired her to the doorknob through her little silver collar, and went back and tried to sleep. And I guess

I must've slept the sleep of the dead—though I don't remember it—because when I got up I found Mary had tipped off her chair back and hanged herself on the wire line. I'd made it too short."

Edna seemed badly affected by that story and slid low in the seat so she couldn't see out over the dash. "Isn't that a shameful story, Earl, what happened to that poor little monkey?"

"I see a town! I see a town!" Cheryl started yelling from the back seat, and right up Little Duke started yapping and the whole car fell into a racket. And sure enough she had seen something I hadn't which was Rock Springs, Wyoming, at the bottom of a long hill, a little glowing jewel in the desert with I-80 running on the north side and the black desert spread out behind.

"That's it, honey," I said. "That's where we're going. You saw it first."

"We're hungry," Cheryl said. "Little Duke wants some fish, and I want spaghetti." She put her arms around my neck and hugged me.

"Then you'll just get it," I said. "You can have anything you want. And so can Edna and so can Little Duke." I looked over at Edna, smiling, but she was staring at me with eyes that were fierce with anger. "What's wrong?" I said.

"Don't you care anything about that awful thing that happened to me?" she said. Her mouth was drawn tight, and her eyes kept cutting back at Cheryl and Little Duke, as if they had been tormenting her.

"Of course I do," I said. "I thought that was an awful thing." I didn't want her to be unhappy. We were almost there, and pretty soon we could sit down and have a real meal without thinking somebody might be hunting us.

"You want to know what I did with that monkey?" Edna said.

"Sure I do," I said.

She said, "I put her in a green garbage bag, put it in the trunk of my car, drove to the dump, and threw her in the trash." She was staring at me darkly, as if the story meant something to her that was real important but that only she could see and that the rest of the world was a fool for.

"Well, that's horrible," I said. "But I don't see what else you could do.

420

You didn't mean to kill it. You'd have done it differently if you had. And then you had to get rid of it, and I don't know what else you could have done. Throwing it away might seem unsympathetic to somebody, probably, but not to me. Sometimes that's all you can do, and you can't worry about what somebody else thinks." I tried to smile at her, but the red light was staying on if I pushed the accelerator at all, and I was trying to gauge if we could coast to Rock Springs before the car gave out completely. I looked at Edna again. "What else can I say?" I said.

"Nothing," she said, and stared back at the dark highway. "I should've known that's what you'd think. You've got a character that leaves something out, Earl. I've known that a long time."

"And yet here you are," I said. "And you're not doing so bad. Things could be a lot worse. At least we're all together here."

"Things could always be worse," Edna said. "You could go to the electric chair tomorrow."

"That's right," I said. "And somewhere somebody probably will. Only it won't be you."

"I'm hungry," said Cheryl. "When're we gonna eat? Let's find a motel. I'm tired of this. Little Duke's tired of it too."

Where the car stopped rolling was some distance from the town, though you could see the clear outline of the interstate in the dark with Rock Springs lighting up the sky behind. You could hear the big tractors hitting the spacers in the overpass, revving up for the climb to the mountains.

I shut off the lights.

"What're we going to do now?" Edna said irritably, giving me a bitter look.

"I'm figuring it," I said. "It won't be hard, whatever it is. You won't have to do anything."

"I'd hope not," she said, and looked the other way.

Across the road and across a dry wash a hundred yards was what looked like a huge mobile-home town, with a factory or a refinery of some kind lit up behind it and in full swing. There were lights on in a lot of the mobile homes, and there were cars moving along an access road that ended near the freeway overpass a mile the other way. The lights in the mobile homes seemed friendly to me, and I knew right then what I should do.

"Get out," I said, and opened my door.

"Are we walking?" Edna said.

"We're pushing," I said.

"I'm not pushing," Edna said, and reached up and locked her door.

"All right," I said. "Then you just steer."

"You pushing us to Rock Springs, are you, Earl? It doesn't look like it's more than about three miles," Edna said.

"I'll push," Cheryl said from the back.

"No, hon. Daddy'll push. You just get out with Little Duke and move out of the way."

Edna gave me a threatening look, just as if I'd tried to hit her. But when I got out she slid into my seat and took the wheel, staring angrily ahead straight into the cottonwood scrub.

"Edna can't drive that car," Cheryl said from out in the dark. "She'll run it in the ditch."

"Yes, she can, hon. Edna can drive it as good as I can. Probably better."

"No, she can't," Cheryl said. "No, she can't either." And I thought she was about to cry, but she didn't.

I told Edna to keep the ignition on so it wouldn't lock up and to steer into the cottonwoods with the parking lights on so she could see. And when I started, she steered it straight off into the trees, and I kept pushing until we were twenty yards into the cover and the tires sank in the soft sand and nothing at all could be seen from the road.

"Now where are we?" she said, sitting at the wheel. Her voice was tired and hard, and I knew she could have put a good meal to use. She had a sweet nature, and I recognized that this wasn't her fault but mine. Only I wished she could be more hopeful.

"You stay right here, and I'll go over to that trailer park and call us a cab," I said.

"What cab?" Edna said, her mouth wrinkled as if she'd never heard anything like that in her life.

"There'll be cabs," I said, and tried to smile at her. "There's cabs everywhere."

"What're you going to tell him when he gets here? Our stolen car broke down and we need a ride to where we can steal another one? That'll be a big hit, Earl."

"I'll talk," I said. "You just listen to the radio for ten minutes and then walk on out to the shoulder like nothing was suspicious. And you and Cheryl act nice. She doesn't need to know about this car."

"Like we're not suspicious enough already, right?" Edna looked up at me out of the lighted car. "You don't think right, did you know that, Earl? You think the world's stupid and you're smart. But that's not how it is. I feel sorry for you. You might've *been* something, but things just went crazy someplace."

I had a thought about poor Danny. He was a vet and crazy as a shit-house mouse, and I was glad he wasn't in for all this. "Just get the baby in the car," I said, trying to be patient. "I'm hungry like you are."

"I'm tired of this," Edna said. "I wish I'd stayed in Montana."

"Then you can go back in the morning," I said. "I'll buy the ticket and put you on the bus. But not till then."

"Just get on with it, Earl," she said, slumping down in the seat, turning off the parking lights with one foot and the radio on with the other.

The mobile-home community was as big as any I'd ever seen. It was attached in some way to the plant that was lighted up behind it, because I could see a car once in a while leave one of the trailer streets, turn in the direction of the plant, then go slowly into it. Everything in the plant was white, and you could see that all the trailers were painted white and looked exactly alike. A deep hum came out of the plant, and I thought as I got closer that it wouldn't be a location I'd ever want to work in.

I went right to the first trailer where there was a light and knocked on the metal door. Kids' toys were lying in the gravel around the little wood steps, and I could hear talking on TV that suddenly went off. I heard a woman's voice talking, and then the door opened wide.

A large Negro woman with a wide, friendly face stood in the doorway. She smiled at me and moved forward as if she was going to come out, but she stopped at the top step. There was a little Negro boy behind her peeping out from behind her legs, watching me with his eyes half closed. The trailer had that feeling that no one else was inside, which was a feeling I knew something about.

"I'm sorry to intrude," I said. "But I've run up on a little bad luck tonight. My name's Earl Middleton."

The woman looked at me, then out into the night toward the freeway as if what I had said was something she was going to be able to see. "What kind of bad luck?" she said, looking down at me again.

"My car broke down out on the highway," I said. "I can't fix it myself, and I wondered if I could use your phone to call for help."

The woman smiled down at me knowingly. "We can't live without cars, can we?"

"That's the honest truth," I said.

"They're like our hearts," she said firmly, her face shining in the little bulb light that burned beside the door. "Where's your car situated?"

I turned and looked over into the dark, but I couldn't see anything because of where we'd put it. "It's over there," I said. "You can't see it in the dark."

"Who all's with you now?" the woman said. "Have you got your wife with you?"

"She's with my little girl and our dog in the car," I said. "My daughter's asleep or I would have brought them."

"They shouldn't be left in that dark by themselves," the woman said, and frowned. "There's too much unsavoriness out there."

"The best I can do is hurry back," I said. I tried to look sincere, since everything except Cheryl being asleep and Edna being my wife was the truth. The truth is meant to serve you if you'll let it, and I wanted it to serve me. "I'll pay for the phone call," I said. "If you'll bring the phone to the door I'll call from right here."

The woman looked at me again as if she was searching for a truth of her own, then back out into the night. She was maybe in her sixties but I couldn't say for sure. "You're not going to rob me, are you, Mr. Middleton?" she said, and smiled like it was a joke between us.

"Not tonight," I said, and smiled a genuine smile. "I'm not up to it tonight. Maybe another time."

"Then I guess Terrel and I can let you use our phone with Daddy not here, can't we, Terrel? This is my grandson, Terrel Junior, Mr. Middleton." She put her hand on the boy's head and looked down at him. "Terrel won't talk. Though if he did he'd tell you to use our phone. He's a sweet boy." She opened the screen for me to come in.

The trailer was a big one with a new rug and a new couch and a living room that expanded to give the space of a real house. Something good and sweet was cooking in the kitchen, and the trailer felt like it was somebody's comfortable new home instead of just temporary. I've lived in trailers, but they were just snailbacks with one room and no toilet, and they always felt cramped and unhappy—though I've thought maybe it might've been me that was unhappy in them.

There was a big Sony TV and a lot of kids' toys scattered on the floor. I recognized a Greyhound bus I'd gotten for Cheryl. The phone was beside a new leather recliner, and the Negro woman pointed for me to sit down and call and gave me the phone book. Terrel began fingering his toys, and the woman sat on the couch while I called, watching me and smiling.

There were three listings for cab companies, all with one number different. I called the numbers in order and didn't get an answer until the last one, which answered with the name of the second company. I said I was on the highway beyond the interstate and that my wife and family needed to be taken to town and I would arrange for a tow later. While I was giving the location, I looked up the name of a tow service to tell the driver in case he asked.

When I hung up, the Negro woman was sitting looking at me with the same look she had been staring with into the dark, a look that seemed to want truth. She was smiling, though. Something pleased her and I reminded her of it.

"This is a very nice home," I said, resting in the recliner, which felt like the driver's seat of the Mercedes and where I'd have been happy to stay.

"This isn't *our* house, Mr. Middleton," the Negro woman said. "The company owns these. They give them to us for nothing. We have our own home in Rockford, Illinois."

"That's wonderful," I said.

"It's never wonderful when you have to be away from home, Mr. Middleton, though we're only here three months, and it'll be easier when Terrel Junior begins his special school. You see, our son was killed in the war, and his wife ran off without Terrel Junior. Though you shouldn't worry. He can't understand us. His little feelings can't be hurt." The woman folded her hands in her lap and smiled in a satisfied way. She was an attractive woman and had on a blue-and-pink floral dress that made her seem bigger than she could've been, just the right woman to sit on the couch she was sitting on. She was good nature's picture, and I was glad she could be, with her little brain-damaged boy, living in a place where no one in his right mind would want to live a minute. "Where do *you* live, Mr. Middleton?" she said politely, smiling in the same sympathetic way.

"My family and I are in transit," I said. "I'm an ophthalmologist, and we're moving back to Florida, where I'm from. I'm setting up practice in some little town where it's warm year-round. I haven't decided where."

"Florida's a wonderful place," the woman said. "I think Terrel would like it there."

"Could I ask you something?" I said.

"You certainly may," the woman said. Terrel had begun pushing his Greyhound across the front of the TV screen, making a scratch that no one watching the set could miss. "Stop that, Terrel Junior," the woman said quietly. But Terrel kept pushing his bus on the glass, and she smiled at me again as if we both understood something sad. Except I knew Cheryl would never damage a television set. She had respect for nice things, and I was sorry for the lady that Terrel didn't. "What did you want to ask?" the woman said.

"What goes on in that plant or whatever it is back there beyond these trailers, where all the lights are on?"

"Gold," the woman said, and smiled.

"It's what?" I said.

"Gold," the Negro woman said, smiling as she had for almost all the time I'd been there. "It's a gold mine."

"They're mining gold back there?" I said, pointing.

"Every night and every day," she said, smiling in a pleased way.

"Does your husband work there?" I said.

"He's the assayer," she said. "He controls the quality. He works three months a year, and we live the rest of the time at home in Rockford. We've waited a long time for this. We've been happy to have our grandson, but I won't say I'll be sorry to have him go. We're ready to start our lives over." She smiled broadly at me and then at Terrel, who was giving her a spiteful look from the floor. "You said you had a daughter," the Negro woman said. "And what's her name?"

"Irma Cheryl," I said. "She's named for my mother."

"That's nice," she said. "And she's healthy, too. I can see it in your face." She looked at Terrel Junior with pity.

"I guess I'm lucky," I said.

"So far you are," she said. "But children bring you grief, the same way they bring you joy. We were unhappy for a long time before my husband got his job in the gold mine. Now, when Terrel starts to school, we'll be kids again." She stood up. "You might miss your cab, Mr. Middleton," she said, walking toward the door, though not to be forcing me out. She was too polite. "If *we* can't see your car, the cab surely won't be able to."

"That's true," I said, and got up off the recliner, where I'd been so comfortable. "None of us have eaten yet, and your food makes me know how hungry we probably all are."

"There are fine restaurants in town, and you'll find them," the Negro

427

woman said. "I'm sorry you didn't meet my husband. He's a wonderful man. He's everything to me."

"Tell him I appreciate the phone," I said. "You saved me."

"You weren't hard to save," the woman said. "Saving people is what we were all put on earth to do. I just passed you on to whatever's coming to you."

"Let's hope it's good," I said, stepping back into the dark.

"I'll be hoping, Mr. Middleton. Terrel and I will both be hoping."

I waved to her as I walked out into the darkness toward the car where it was hidden in the night.

The cab had already arrived when I got there. I could see its little red and green roof lights all the way across the dry wash, and it made me worry that Edna was already saying something to get us in trouble, something about the car or where we'd come from, something that would cast suspicion on us. I thought, then, how I never planned things well enough. There was always a gap between my plan and what happened, and I only responded to things as they came along and hoped I wouldn't get in trouble. I was an offender in the law's eyes. But I always *thought* differently, as if I weren't an offender and had no intention of being one, which was the truth. But as I read on a napkin once, between the idea and the act a whole kingdom lies. And I had a hard time with my acts, which were oftentimes offender's acts, and my ideas, which were as good as the gold they mined there where the bright lights were blazing.

"We're waiting for you, Daddy," Cheryl said when I crossed the road. "The taxicab's already here."

"I see, hon," I said, and gave Cheryl a big hug. The cabdriver was sitting in the driver's seat having a smoke with the lights on inside. Edna was leaning against the back of the cab between the taillights, wearing her Bailey hat. "What'd you tell him?" I said when I got close.

"Nothin'," she said. "What's there to tell?"

"Did he see the car?"

She glanced over in the direction of the trees where we had hid the Mercedes. Nothing was visible in the darkness, though I could hear Little Duke combing around in the underbrush tracking something, his little collar tinkling. "Where're we going?" she said. "I'm so hungry I could pass out."

"Edna's in a terrible mood," Cheryl said. "She already snapped at me."

"We're tired, honey," I said. "So try to be nicer."

"She's never nice," Cheryl said.

"Run go get Little Duke," I said. "And hurry back."

"I guess *my* questions come last here, right?" Edna said.

I put my arm around her. "That's not true," I said.

"Did you find somebody over there in the trailers you'd rather stay with? You were gone long enough."

"That's not a thing to say," I said. "I was just trying to make things look right, so we don't get put in jail."

"So *you* don't, you mean," Edna said and laughed a little laugh I didn't like hearing.

"That's right. So I don't," I said. "I'd be the one in Dutch." I stared out at the big, lighted assemblage of white buildings and white lights beyond the trailer community, plumes of white smoke escaping up into the heartless Wyoming sky, the whole company of buildings looking like some unbelievable castle, humming away in a distorted dream. "You know what all those buildings are there?" I said to Edna, who hadn't moved and who didn't really seem to care if she ever moved anymore ever.

"No. But I can't say it matters, 'cause it isn't a motel and it isn't a restaurant," she said.

"It's a gold mine," I said, staring at the gold mine, which, I knew now from walking to the trailer, was a greater distance from us than it seemed, though it seemed huge and near, up against the cold sky. I thought there should've been a wall around it with guards instead of just the lights and no fence. It seemed as if anyone could go in and take what they wanted, just the way I had gone up to that woman's trailer and used the telephone, though that obviously wasn't true.

Edna began to laugh then. Not the mean laugh I didn't like, but a laugh that had something caring behind it, a full laugh that enjoyed a joke, a laugh she was laughing the first time I laid eyes on her, in Missoula in the Eastgate bar in 1979, a laugh we used to laugh together when Cheryl was still with her mother and I was working steady at the track and not stealing cars or passing bogus checks to merchants. A better time all around. And for some reason it made me laugh just hearing her, and we both stood there behind the cab in the dark, laughing at the gold mine in the desert, me with my arm around her and Cheryl out rustling up Little Duke and the cabdriver smoking in the cab and our stolen Mercedes-Benz, which I'd had such hopes for in Florida, stuck up to its axle in sand, where I'd never get to see it again.

"I always wondered what a gold mine would look like when I saw it," Edna said, still laughing, wiping a tear from her eye.

"Me too," I said. "I was always curious about it."

"We're a couple of fools, ain't we, Earl?" she said, unable to quit laughing completely. "We're two of a kind."

"It might be a good sign, though," I said.

"How could it be?" she said. "It's not our gold mine. There aren't any drive-up windows." She was still laughing.

"We've seen it," I said, pointing. "That's it right there. It may mean we're getting closer. Some people never see it at all."

"In a pig's eye, Earl," she said. "You and me see it in a pig's eye."

And she turned and got into the cab to go.

The cabdriver didn't ask anything about our car or where it was, to mean he'd noticed something queer. All of which made me feel like we had made a clean break from the car and couldn't be connected with it until it was too late, if ever. The driver told us a lot about Rock Springs while he drove, that because of the gold mine a lot of people had moved there in just six months, people from all over, including New York, and that most of them lived out in the trailers. Prostitutes from New York City, who he called "B-girls," had come into town, he said, on the prosperity tide, and Cadillacs with New York plates cruised the little streets every night, full of

Negroes with big hats who ran the women. He told us that everybody who got in his cab now wanted to know where the women were, and when he got our call he almost didn't come because some of the trailers were brothels operated by the mine for engineers and computer people away from home. He said he got tired of running back and forth out there just for vile business. He said that *60 Minutes* had even done a program about Rock Springs and that a blowup had resulted in Cheyenne, though nothing could be done unless the prosperity left town. "It's prosperity's fruit," the driver said. "I'd rather be poor, which is lucky for me."

He said all the motels were sky-high, but since we were a family he could show us a nice one that was affordable. But I told him we wanted a first-rate place where they took animals, and the money didn't matter because we had had a hard day and wanted to finish on a high note. I also knew that it was in the little nowhere places that the police look for you and find you. People I'd known were always being arrested in cheap hotels and tourist courts with names you'd never heard of before. Never in Holiday Inns or Travelodges.

I asked him to drive us to the middle of town and back out again so Cheryl could see the train station, and while we were there I saw a pink Cadillac with New York plates and a TV aerial being driven slowly by a Negro in a big hat down a narrow street where there were just bars and a Chinese restaurant. It was an odd sight, nothing you could ever expect.

"There's your pure criminal element," the cabdriver said, and seemed sad. "I'm sorry for people like you to see a thing like that. We've got a nice town here, but there're some that want to ruin it for everybody. There used to be a way to deal with trash and criminals, but those days are gone forever."

"You said it," Edna said.

"You shouldn't let it get *you* down," I said to the cabdriver. "There's more of you than them. And there always will be. You're the best advertisement this town has. I know Cheryl will remember you and not *that* man, won't you, honey?" But Cheryl was asleep by then, holding Little Duke in her arms on the taxi seat.

The driver took us to the Ramada Inn on the interstate, not far from where we'd broken down. I had a small pain of regret as we drove under the Ramada awning that we hadn't driven up in a cranberry-colored Mercedes but instead in a beat-up old Chrysler taxi driven by an old man full of complaints. Though I knew it was for the best. We were better off without that car, better, really, in any other car but that one, where the signs had turned bad.

I registered under another name and paid for the room in cash so there wouldn't be any questions. On the line where it said "Representing" I wrote "ophthalmologist" and put "M.D." after the name. It had a nice look to it, even though it wasn't my name.

When we got to the room, which was in the back where I'd asked for it, I put Cheryl on one of the beds and Little Duke beside her so they'd sleep. She'd missed dinner, but it only meant she'd be hungry in the morning, when she could have anything she wanted. A few missed meals don't make a kid bad. I'd missed a lot of them myself and haven't turned out completely bad.

"Let's have some fried chicken," I said to Edna when she came out of the bathroom. "They have good fried chicken at the Ramadas, and I noticed the buffet was still up. Cheryl can stay right here, where it's safe, till we're back."

"I guess I'm not hungry anymore," Edna said. She stood at the window staring out into the dark. I could see out the window past her some yellowish foggy glow in the sky. For a moment I thought it was the gold mine out in the distance lighting the night, though it was only the interstate.

"We could order up," I said. "Whatever you want. There's a menu on the phone book. You could just have a salad."

"You go ahead," she said. "I've lost my hungry spirit." She sat on the bed beside Cheryl and Little Duke and looked at them in a sweet way and put her hand on Cheryl's cheek just as if she'd had a fever. "Sweet little girl," she said. "Everybody loves you."

"What do you want to do?" I said. "I'd like to eat. Maybe *I'll* order up some chicken."

"Why don't you do that?" she said. "It's your favorite." And she smiled at me from the bed.

I sat on the other bed and dialed room service. I asked for chicken, garden salad, potato, and a roll, plus a piece of hot apple pie and ice tea. I realized I hadn't eaten all day. When I put down the phone I saw that Edna was watching me, not in a hateful way or a loving way, just in a way that seemed to say she didn't understand something and was going to ask me about it.

"When did watching me get so entertaining?" I said, and smiled at her. I was trying to be friendly. I knew how tired she must be. It was after nine o'clock.

"I was just thinking how much I hated being in a motel without a car that was mine to drive. Isn't that funny? I started feeling like that last night when that purple car wasn't mine. That purple car just gave me the willies, I guess, Earl."

"One of those cars *outside* is yours," I said. "Just stand right there and pick it out."

"I know," she said. "But that's different, isn't it?" She reached and got her blue Bailey hat, put it on her head, and set it way back like Dale Evans. She looked sweet. "I used to like to go to motels, you know," she said. "There's something secret about them and free—I was never paying, of course. But you felt safe from everything and free to do what you wanted because you'd made the decision to be there and paid that price, and all the rest was the good part. Fucking and everything, you know." She smiled at me in a good-natured way.

"Isn't that the way this is?" I said. I was sitting on the bed, watching her, not knowing what to expect her to say next.

"I don't guess it is, Earl," she said, and stared out the window. "I'm thirty-two and I'm going to have to give up on motels. I can't keep that fantasy going anymore."

"Don't you like this place?" I said, and looked around at the room. I appreciated the modern paintings and the lowboy bureau and the big TV. It seemed like a plenty nice enough place to me, considering where we'd been already.

"No, I don't," Edna said with real conviction. "There's no use in my getting mad at you about it. It isn't your fault. You do the best you can for everybody. But every trip teaches you something. And I've learned I need to give up on motels before some bad thing happens to me. I'm sorry."

"What does that mean?" I said, because I really didn't know what she had in mind to do, though I should've guessed.

"I guess I'll take that ticket you mentioned," she said, and got up and faced the window. "Tomorrow's soon enough. We haven't got a car to take me anyhow."

"Well, that's a fine thing," I said, sitting on the bed, feeling like I was in a shock. I wanted to say something to her, to argue with her, but I couldn't think what to say that seemed right. I didn't want to be mad at her, but it made me mad.

"You've got a right to be mad at me, Earl," she said, "but I don't think you can really blame me." She turned around and faced me and sat on the windowsill, her hands on her knees. Someone knocked on the door. I just yelled for them to set the tray down and put it on the bill.

"I guess I *do* blame you," I said. I was angry. I thought about how I could have disappeared into that trailer community and hadn't, had come back to keep things going, had tried to take control of things for everybody when they looked bad.

"Don't. I wish you wouldn't," Edna said, and smiled at me like she wanted me to hug her. "Anybody ought to have their choice in things if they can. Don't you believe that, Earl? Here I am out here in the desert where I don't know anything, in a stolen car, in a motel room under an assumed name, with no money of my own, a kid that's not mine, and the law after me. And I have a choice to get out of all of it by getting on a bus. What would you do? I know exactly what you'd do."

"You think you do," I said. But I didn't want to get into an argument about it and tell her all I could've done and didn't do. Because it wouldn't have done any good. When you get to the point of arguing, you're past the point of changing anybody's mind, even though it's supposed to be the other way, and maybe for some classes of people it is, just never mine. Edna smiled at me and came across the room and put her arms around me where I was sitting on the bed. Cheryl rolled over and looked at us and smiled, then closed her eyes, and the room was quiet. I was beginning to think of Rock Springs in a way I knew I would always think of it, a lowdown city full of crimes and whores and disappointments, a place where a woman left me, instead of a place where I got things on the straight track once and for all, a place I saw a gold mine.

"Eat your chicken, Earl," Edna said. "Then we can go to bed. I'm tired, but I'd like to make love to you anyway. None of this is a matter of not loving you, you know that."

Sometime late in the night, after Edna was asleep, I got up and walked outside into the parking lot. It could've been anytime because there was still the light from the interstate frosting the low sky and the big red Ramada sign humming motionlessly in the night and no light at all in the east to indicate it might be morning. The lot was full of cars all nosed in, most of them with suitcases strapped to their roofs and their trunks weighed down with belongings the people were taking someplace, to a new home or a vacation resort in the mountains. I had laid in bed a long time after Edna was asleep, watching the Atlanta Braves on cable television, trying to get my mind off how I'd feel when I saw that bus pull away the next day, and how I'd feel when I turned around and there stood Cheryl and Little Duke and no one to see about them but me alone, and that the first thing I had to do was get hold of some automobile and get the plates switched, then get them some breakfast and get us all on the road to Florida, all in the space of probably two hours, since that Mercedes would certainly look less hid in the daytime than the night, and word travels fast. I've always taken care of Cheryl myself as long as I've had her with me. None of the women ever did; most of them didn't even seem to like her, though they took care of me in a way so that I could take care of her. And I knew that once Edna left, all that was going to get harder. Though what I wanted most to do was not think about it just for a little while, try to let my mind go limp so it could be strong for the rest of what there was. I thought that the difference between a successful life and an unsuccessful one, between me at that moment and all the people who owned the cars that were nosed in to their proper places in the lot, maybe between me and that woman out in the trailers by the gold mine, was how well you were able to put things like this out of your mind and not be bothered by them, and maybe, too, by how many troubles like this one you had to face in a lifetime. Through luck or design they had all faced fewer troubles, and by their own characters, they forgot them faster. And that's what I wanted for me. Fewer troubles, fewer memories of trouble.

I walked over to a car, a Pontiac with Ohio tags, one of the ones with bundles and suitcases strapped to the top and a lot more in the trunk, by the way it was riding. I looked inside the driver's window. There were maps and paperback books and sunglasses and the little plastic holders for cans that hang on the window wells. And in the back there were kids' toys and some pillows and a cat box with a cat sitting in it staring up at me like I was the face of the moon. It all looked familiar to me, the very same things I would have in my car if I had a car. Nothing seemed surprising, nothing different. Though I had a funny sensation at that moment and turned and looked up at the windows along the back of the Ramada Inn. All were dark except two. Mine and another one. And I wondered, because it seemed funny, what would you think a man was doing if you saw him in the middle of the night looking in the windows of cars in the parking lot of the Ramada Inn? Would you think he was trying to get his head cleared? Would you think he was trying to get ready for a day when trouble would come down on him? Would you think his girlfriend was leaving him? Would you think he had a daughter? Would you think he was anybody like you?

Behold the Husband in His Perfect Agony

Barry Hannah

1. HOMELESS

When I am run-down and flocked around by the world, I go down to Farte Cove off the Yazoo River and take my beer to the end of the pier where the old liars are still snapping and wheezing at one another. The lineup is always different, because they're always dying out or succumbing to constipation, etc., whereupon they go back to the cabins and wait for a good day when they can come out and lie again, leaning on the rail with coats full of bran cookies. The son of the man the cove was named for is often out there. He pronounces his name Far*tay*, with a great French stress on the last syllable. Otherwise you might laugh at his history or ignore it in favor of the name as it's spelled on the sign.

I'm glad it's not my name.

This poor dignified man has had to explain his nobility to the semiliterate of half of America before he could even begin a decent conversation with them. On the other hand, Farte Jr. is a great liar himself. He tells about seeing ghost people around the lake and tells big loose ones about the size of the fish those ghosts took out of Farte Cove in years past.

Last year I turned thirty-three years old and, raised a Baptist, I had a sense of being Jesus and coming to something decided in my life—because we all know Jesus was crucified at thirty-three. It had all seemed especially important, what you do in this year, and holy with meaning.

On the morning after my birthday party, during which I and my wife almost drowned in vodka cocktails, we both woke up to the making of a truth session about the lovers we'd had before we met each other. I had a mildly exciting and usual history, and she had about the same, which surprised me. For ten years she'd sworn I was the first. I could not believe her history was exactly equal with mine. It hurt me to think that in the era when there were supposed to be virgins she had allowed anyone but *me*, and so on.

I was dazed and exhilarated by this information for several weeks. Finally, it drove me crazy, and I came out to Farte Cove to rest, under the pretense of a fishing week with my chum Wyatt.

I'm still figuring out why I couldn't handle it.

My sense of the past is vivid and slow. I hear every sign and see every shadow. The movement of every limb in every passionate event occupies my mind. I have a prurience on the grand scale. It makes no sense that I should be angry about happenings before she and I ever saw each other. Yet I feel an impotent homicidal urge in the matter of her lovers. She has excused my episodes as the course of things, though she has a vivid memory too. But there is a blurred nostalgia women have that men don't.

You could not believe how handsome and delicate my wife is naked.

I was driven wild by the bodies that had trespassed her twelve and thirteen years ago.

My vacation at Farte Cove wasn't like that easy little bit you get as a rich New Yorker. My finances weren't in great shape; to be true, they were about in ruin, and I left the house knowing my wife would have to answer the phone to hold off, for instance, the phone company itself. Everybody wanted money and I didn't have any.

I was going to take the next week in the house while she went away, watch our three kids and all the rest. When you both teach part-time in the high schools, the income can be slow in summer.

No poor-mouthing here. I don't want anybody's pity. I just want to explain. I've got good hopes of a job over at Alabama next year. Then I'll get myself among higher paid liars, that's all.

Sidney Farte was out there prevaricating away at the end of the pier when Wyatt and I got there Friday evening. The old faces I recognized, a few new hearkening idlers I didn't.

"Now, Doctor Mooney, he not only saw the ghost of Lily, he says he had intercourse with her. Said it was involuntary. Before he knew what he was doing, he was on her making cadence and all their clothes blown away off in the trees around the shore. She turned into a wax candle right under him."

"Intercourse," said an old-timer, breathing heavy. He sat up on the rail. It was a word of high danger to his old mind. He said it with a long disgust, glad, I guess, he was not involved.

"MacIntire, a Presbyterian preacher, I seen him come out here with his son-and-law, anchor near the bridge, and pull up fifty or more white perch big as small pumpkins. You know what they was using for bait?"

"What?" asked another geezer.

"*Nuthin.* Caught on the bare hook. It was Gawd made them fish bite," said Sidney Farte, going at it good.

"Naw. There be a season they bite a bare hook. Gawd didn't have to've done that," said another old guy with a fringe of red hair and a racy Florida shirt.

"Nother night," said Sidney Farte, "I saw the ghost of Yazoo hisself with my paw, who's dead. A Indian king with four deer around him."

The old boys seemed to be used to this one. Nobody said anything. They ignored Sidney.

"Tell you what," said a well-built small old boy. "That was somethin when we come down here and had to chase that whole high-school party off the end of this pier, them drunken children. They was smokin dope and two-thirds a them nekid swimmin in the water. Good hunnerd of em. From your so-called *good* high school. What you think's happnin at the bad ones?"

I dropped my beer and grew suddenly sick. Wyatt asked me what was wrong. I could see my wife in 1960 in the group of high schoolers she must have had. My jealousy went out into the stars of the night above me. I could not bear the roving carelessness of teen-agers, their judgeless tangling of wanting and bodies. But I was the worst back then. In the mad days back then, I dragged the panties off girls I hated and talked badly about them once the sun came up.

"Worst time in my life," said a new, younger man, maybe sixty but with the face of a man who had surrendered, "me and Woody was fishing. Had a lantern. It was about eleven. We was catching a few fish but rowed on into that little cove over there near town. We heard all these sounds, like they was ghosts. We was scared. We thought it might be the Yazoo hisself. We known of some fellows the Yazoo had killed to death just from fright. It was the, over the sounds of what was normal human, sighin and amoanin. It was big unhuman sounds. We just stood still in the boat. Ain't nuthin else us to do. For thirty minutes."

"An what was it?" said the old geezer, letting himself off the rail.

"We had a big flashlight. There came up this rustlin in the brush and I beamed it over there. The two of em makin the sounds get up with half they clothes on. It was my own daughter Charlotte and an older guy I didn't even know with a moustache. My *own* daughter, and them sounds over the water scarin us like ghosts."

"My Gawd, that's awful," said the old geezer on the rail. "Is that the truth? I wouldn't've told that. That's terrible."

Sidney Farte was really upset.

"This ain't the place!" he said. "Tell your kind of story somewhere else."

The old man who'd told his story was calm and fixed to his place. He'd told the truth. The crowd on the pier was outraged and discomfited. He wasn't one of them. But he stood his place. He had a distressed pride. You could see he had never recovered from the thing he'd told about.

I told Wyatt to bring the old man back to the cabin. He was out here away from his wife the same as me and Wyatt. Just an older guy with a big hurting bosom. He wore a suit and the only way you'd know he was on vacation was he'd removed his tie. He didn't know where the bait house was. He didn't know what to do on vacation at all. But he got drunk with us and I can tell you he and I went out the next morning with our poles, Wyatt driving the motorboat, fishing for white perch in the cove near the town. And we were kindred.

We were both crucified by the truth.

2. HOME

I threw a party, wore a very sharp suit. My wife had out all sorts of hors d'oeuvres, some ordered from long off—little briny peppery seafoods you wouldn't have thought of as something to eat. We waited for the guests. Some of the food went bad. Hardly anybody came. It was the night of the lunar eclipse, I think. Underwood, the pianist, showed up and maybe twelve other people. Three I never invited were there. We'd planned on sixty-five.

I guess this was the signal we weren't liked anymore in town.

Well, this has happened before.

Several we invited were lushes who normally wouldn't pass up cocktails at the home of Hitler. Also, there were two nymphomaniacs you could trust to come over in their high-fashion halters so as to disappear around one in the morning with some new innocent lecher. We furthermore invited a few good dull souls who got on an occasional list because they were *good* and furnished a balance to the doubtful others. There was a passionate drudge in landscaping horticulture, for example.

But none of them came.

It was a hot evening and my air-conditioner broke down an hour before the party started.

An overall wretched event was in the stars.

Underwood came only for the piano. I own a huge in-tune Yamaha he cannot separate himself from. Late in the evening I like to join him on my electric bass.

Underwood never held much for electric instruments. He's forty-two, a traveler from the old beatnik and Charlie Parker tribe. I believe he thinks electric instruments are cowardly and unmanly. He does not like the basic idea of men joining talents with a wall socket. In the old days it was just hands, head, and lungs, he says. The boys in the Fifties were better all-around men, and the women were proud of being after-set quim.

Underwood liked to play with this particular drummer about his age. But that night the drummer didn't show up, either. This, to my mind, was the most significant absentee at our party. That drummer had always come before. I thought he was addicted to playing with Underwood. So when Underwood had loosened up on a few numbers and the twelve of us had clapped and he came over for a drink, I asked him, "Why isn't Fred Poor here?"

"I don't know. Fred's got a big family now," said Underwood.

"He always came before. Last month. What's wrong with tonight? Something is wrong with tonight," I said.

"The food's good. I can remember twenty friends in the old days around Detroit who'd be grooving up on this table. You'd thank em for taking your food. That's how solid they were," said Underwood, drinking vodka straight off the ice and smelling at one of the fish hors d'oeuvres.

I saw my wife go into the bathroom. I eased back with a greeting to the sweated-up young priest who had the reputation of a terrific sex counselor. He was out there with the great lyrical lie that made everybody feel good. Is that why he showed up and the others not? His message was that modern man had invented psychology, mental illness, the whole arrogant malaise, to replace the soul. Sex he called God's rule to keep us simple and merry, as we were meant to be, lest we forget we are creatures and figure ourselves totally mental. One night I asked him what of Christ and Mary and the cult of celibacy. "Reason is, Mr. Lee, believe or disbelieve and let be," he answered. "I'm only a goddamned priest. I don't have to be smart or be a star in forensics."

He headed out for more bourbon, and I trucked on after my wife. I whispered in the bathroom keyhole and she let me in. She was rebuckling her sandal with a foot on the commode.

"Why didn't anybody come tonight? What do you think's wrong?" I asked her.

"I only know about why five aren't here. Talked to Jill." She paused. One of Carolyn's habits is making you pose a question.

"Why?" I asked.

"The people Jill knew about said there was something about our life they didn't like. It made them feel edgy and depressed."

"*What?*"

"Jill wouldn't ever say. She left right after she told me."

When I went out, there weren't as many as before. Underwood was playing the piano and the priest was leaning on the table talking to one of the uninvited, a fat off-duty cop from about four houses up the row I'd waved to in the mornings when he was going out in his patrol car. Sitting down fanning herself was a slight old friend of my wife's who had never showed up at our other parties. She was some sort of monument to alert age in the neighborhood—about eighty, open mind, colorful anecdotes, crepey skin, a dress overformal and thick stockings.

"Hi, Mrs. Craft," I said.

"Isn't this a dreadful party? Poor Carolyn, all this food and drink. Which one's her husband?" the old lady said.

I realized maybe she'd never got a good look at me, or had poor eyes.

"I really don't know which one's her husband. What would you say was wrong with them, the Lees? Why have people stayed away from their party?" I said.

"I saw it happen to another couple once," she said. "Everyone suddenly quit them."

"Whose fault was it?"

"Oh, definitely theirs. Or rather *his*. She was congenial, similar to Carolyn. And everybody wanted a party. Oh, those gay sultry evenings!" She gave a delicate cough. "We invented gin and tonic, you know."

"What was wrong with the husband?" I asked.

"He suddenly changed. He went bad. A handsome devil too. But we couldn't stand him after the change."

"What sort of change?" I offered her the hearts of palm and the herring, which, I smelled, was getting gamy in the heat. She ate for a while. Then she looked ill.

"A change . . . I've got to leave. This heat is destroying me."

She rose and went out the kitchen, opening the door herself and leaving for good.

Then I went back to the bathroom mirror. The same hopeful man with the sardonic grin was there, the same religious eyes and sensual mouth, sweetened up by the sharp suit and soft violet collar. I could see no diminution of my previous good graces. This was Washington and my vocation was interesting and perhaps even important. I generally tolerated everybody—no worms sought vent from my heart that I knew of. My wife and other women had said I had an unsettling charm.

* * *

I got out the electric bass and played along with Underwood. But I noticed a baleful look from him, something he'd never revealed before. So I quit and turned off the amplifier. I took a hard drink of Scotch in a cup and opened a closet in my study, got in, shut the door, and sat down on all my old school papers and newspaper notices in the cardboard boxes in the corner.

Here was me and the pitch dark, the odor of old paper and some of my outdoor clothes.

How have I offended? I asked. How do I cause depression and edginess? How have I perhaps changed for the bad, as old Mrs. Craft hinted?

By my cigarette lighter I read a few of the newspaper notices on me and my work. I looked at my tough moral face, the spectacles that put me at a sort of intellectual remove, the sensual mouth to balance it, abetted by the curls of my auburn hair. In fact, no man I knew looked nearly anything like me. My wife told me that when we first met at Vanderbilt my looks pure and simple were what attracted her to me. Yet I was not vain. She was a brown-haired comely girl, in looks like many other brown-haired comely girls, and I loved her for her strong cheerful averageness. Salt of the earth. A few minor talents. Sturdy womb for our two children.

It was not her. It was me!

What have I done? I asked myself.

Then I heard heels on the stairs of my study. A pair was coming down, man and woman. They walked into the study and were silent for a while. Then I heard the sucking and the groans. For three or four minutes they must have kissed. Then:

"It's not any good *here*."

"I know. I feel it. Even sex wouldn't be any good *here*."

"You notice how all this good liquor tastes like iodine?"

They moaned and smacked a few more minutes. Then the man said, "Let's get out of here."

When they went away, I let myself out of the closet. Underwood was standing at my desk. He looked at me crawling out of the closet. I had nothing to say. Neither did he for a while.

Then he said, "I guess I better not come over anymore."

"What's wrong?" I said.

"The crazy . . . or *off* chick that lives upstairs that always comes down and leans on the piano about midnight every night. She's good-looking, but she sets me off. I get the creeps."

"Did she come down again? I guess it's the piano. You ought to be flattered. Most of the time she sits up there in her chair reading."

"Somebody said it was your sister. I don't know. She *looks* like you. Got the same curly auburn hair. It's like you with tits, if you think about it."

"Well, of course it *is* my sister. For a while we had a reason for not telling that around. Trust me."

"I trust you. But she makes my hair cold."

"You loved all types back in the time of the beatniks. I always thought of you as a largehearted person."

"Something goes cold when she talks. I can't get with the thing she's after. For a while I thought she was far-out, some kind of philosopheress. But nothing hangs *in* in what she says."

"She can have her moments. Don't you think she has a certain charm?"

"No doubt on that, with her lungs dripping over her gown. But when she talks, well. . . ." He closed his eyes in an unsatisfactory dreaming sort of trance.

"Can't you see it? Can't you see the charm?" I demanded.

"Whatever, it don't sweeten me," he said, setting down his glass.

He went out the study door.

There, leaning on the piano, in her perfect cobalt gown, was Patricia. She was waiting for Underwood. Near her, as I have intimated, I sometimes have no sense of my own petty mobility from one place to another. I appear, I hover, I turn. Her lush curls burned slowly round and round in the fire of the candle on the mantel. A blaze of silver came from her throatpiece, a lash of gemmy light bounced from her earrings.

Not a soul was in the room with her.

"Underwood's left," I said.

"Music gone?" she said, holding out her hand and clutching her fingers.

"It would be cooler upstairs with your little window unit. You could read. What were you reading tonight?"

"*Heidi*. Such a sugar," she said.

"Oh, yes. Much sugar. The old uncle."

"Mountain," she said.

By this time only the priest was left. He was having an almost rabidly sympathetic conversation with my wife. The man was flushed-out and well drunk, a ship's captain crying his *full speed ahead* in the stern house of a boat rotting to pieces.

I looked over the long table of uneaten fish tasties. The heat had worked on them a couple more hours now and had brought them up to a really unacceptable sort of presence.

"Well. Ho ho. Look at all the stuff. All the cost," I said.

"Just garbage God knows who, namely me, has to haul off and bury," said my wife.

"Ah, no, madam. I'll see to all. Trust me. I'm made for it," swore the priest.

With that he began circling the table, grabbing up the fish tasties and cramming them in his pockets, coat and pants, wadding them into his hat. He spun by me with a high tilt of adieu. But then he bumped into Patricia, who had come in, and spilled some of the muck in his hat on the front of her gown. She didn't move. Then she looked downward into her bosom to the grease and fish flesh that smeared her gown.

"Fishies," she said.

"What a *blight* I am! On this one, on this innocent belle! Strike me down!"

The priest wanted to touch her and clean her off, but could not. His hands trembled before the oil and flakes of fish on her stomach. He uttered a groan and ran from the house.

After he'd gone, the three of us stood there, offering no movement or special expression.

*   *   *

"You ought to go up and clean yourself," Carolyn said to Patricia.

Patricia put her foot on the first stair and looked at me with an appeal. But then she went rapidly up and we could hear her air-conditioner going when she opened her door and then nothing when she closed it.

We straightened up awhile, but not very thoroughly. Then we got in bed.

"You've ruined my life," said my wife. "This party showed it."

"What's *wrong?* What do you mean?"

"Stop it. What's to pretend? Your twin goddamned sister. Your wonderful spiritual feebleminded sister."

"Not! Not! It's just not our language she speaks! Don't say that!"

"*You* taught her all the goddamned English she knows. Oh, when you explained, when she first came, that she was just silent, different! We went through all that. Then we've had her out of pity. . . ."

"She doesn't need anybody's pity! Shut your mouth!"

There was a long hot silence. Above us we heard rocking sounds.

My wife hissed: "She's never even cleaned herself up."

"I'll see."

"Oh, yes, you'll *see*! Don't bother to wake me when you come back." Carolyn had drunk a lot. I went to brush my teeth and when I came back out she was snoring.

I rose on the stairs.

The cool in Patricia's room had surpassed what is comfortable. It was almost frigid, and the unit was still heaving more cold into the room. She sat in the rocking chair reading her book. The soiled gown was still on her. She raised her hand as I passed her to turn down the air conditioning, and I held her hand, coming back to stare over her shoulder.

There was a picture of Heidi and her goat upside down.

"Let's get you in your little tub," I said.

I stripped the gown from her. Then I picked her up and put her in the tub, turning on the water very slow as I lathered her all over.

I gave her a shampoo. Pulling an arm up, I saw what was needed, ran the razor gently over her pits, then saw to the slight stubble on her legs. This is when she always sang. A high but almost inaudible melody of the weirdest and most dreamlike temptation, it would never come from another person in this world.

I began sobbing and she detected it.

"I love you with everything that lives me," she said. "You love me the identical?"

"Everything. Yes."

"Mickey," she said. She clutched one breast and with the other hand she raised the red curls and lips of her virgin sex. "Are you like me?"

I had looked away and was getting a towel.

"Yes. I'm exactly like you. We're twins. We're just alike," I said.

"That's why we can love each other everything," she said.

"Exactly. Just the same."

"Show me you."

"We can't. I can't because of the rules."

"Oh, yeah, darling, the rules!"

She'd always shown a peculiar happiness about the rules.

When I got her in bed, I wound up downstairs, no memory of having traveled anywhere.

I was breathless. My heart was big. Sometimes like this I thought it would just burst and spray its nerves into the dark that does not care, into the friends who would not care.

In bed again I found that Carolyn was not asleep at all. She was sitting up.

"Did you finish with her?"

"Yes."

"Don't tell me what went on. I don't want to know. I love you too much to do anything about it. But look what you've dragged me into."

"I know."

"You can't sleep with me tonight. Get out of here."

"I know," I said.

I got the flashlight and got in the closet again, pulling the door to. I went through all the newspaper notices and the college term papers and picked up the love letters. They were on lined paper, grammar-school paper. It was the summer after I'd taught her to write.

Mickey I love you. There isn't anything but love of you for me. I see the way you walk and your shoes are nice. I desire to thank you with my tongue and my legs too. The tongue and legs are good places. But the most is under my chest where it beats.

Sincerely yours,
PATRICIA

I held all the others, her letters, as the handwriting improved, and saw the last ones with their graceful script, even prettier than I could write on a good day. My essence yearned and rose from the closet and my roots tore from me, standing up like a tangled tree in dark heaven. My mother gave Patricia to me before she threw herself into what she called her patriotic suicide— that is, she used Kentucky whiskey and tobacco and overate fried foods in a long faithful ritual before she joined my old man in the soil near Lexington.

I thought heavily and decided I'd go back down South.

I was tired of Washington, D.C.

I was tired of my vocation.

I was tired of me.

Somewhere near the sea we'd go. Carolyn and Patricia both loved the sea. I'd find a town that would appreciate me for my little gifts and we'd move *there*. Have new friends, more privacy. I might turn back into a Democrat.

Changes like that never bothered my heart.

3. HOME FREE

We were very fond of Mrs. Neap's place—even though it was near the railroad. It was a rambling inn of the old days, with its five bathrooms and balcony over the dining room. We had been harboring there for a couple of weeks and thought we were getting on well enough. But then she comes downstairs one morning holding a swab, and she tells me, looking at the rest of them asleep on the couches and rug: "This is enough. Get out by this afternoon."

"Last night you said we were your adorable vagabonds."

"In the light of day you look more like trash. I had too much of that potato liquor you brought," says Mrs. Neap.

I say, "Give us another chance. It might be your hangover talking. Let's have another conference, say two o'clock. Invite down all the tenants. We'll talk it out."

She says, "It's my decision. I own the place. Property is nine-tenths the law," forearm muscles standing out as she kneads the cleaning rag, one of the lenses of her spectacles cracked.

I say, "But we're the tenth that gives existence quality, the quantum of hope and dream, of laughter, of music. Further, please, Miz Neap, we'll clean, keep this place in shape, paint it up."

"Where paint? What paint? It's ten dollars a quart if you can even find it. You can't find more than four quarts in all South and North Carolina."

"We make our own liquor. We can find a way to make paint too. Gardiner there is close to being a bona fide chemist."

She says, "None of you is any good. You never brought any food into the house. Oh, that sack of onions that fell off a truck and a few blackbirds."

I say, "How can you forget the turkey we brought when we came?"

"Sure," says she, "that's what got you in with, the turkey. But what since, besides potato liquor? Then you ate all the magnolias," says she.

"*One* foolish evening. Your other tenants ate some, too," say I.

"You broke the handle on the faucet."

"Nobody ever proved it was one of us."

"There was no fleas before you came, no cockroaches."

451

"Unproven. Besides, seeing as how there's no more turkey. . . ."

The house begins the shiver it does when a train is entering the curve. The train is always, beyond other concerns, an amazement. Mrs. Neap and I walk out to the warped porch to watch. The train is coming in, all right, rolling its fifteen miles an hour, and you can see the people, hundreds and hundreds, standing and sitting on the wooden platforms the company built over the cars, those pipes and chicken wire boxing in about ninety "air-riders" per car top.

Even an air-riding ticket is exorbitant, but that fifteen-mile-an-hour breeze must be nice.

The train passes three times a week. This one must've been carrying about five thousand in all if you were to count the between-car riders and the maintenance-ladder riders.

Resettlers.

When the bad times really came, they brought families back together, and mainly everybody started coming south. Everybody would travel back to the most prosperous member of his family, taking his own light fortune along to pool it. It healed a lot of divorces and feuds. The best thing you could have was a relative with land. You showed up at his place offering your prodigal soul and those of your family as guards of the land, pulling out your soft hands to garden-up the land and watch over it.

There are no idle murders to speak of anymore. Almost all of them are deliberate and have to do with food, water, seeds, or such as a ticket on the train. For example, if I tried to jump that train Mrs. Neap and I are looking at, a man in street clothes (you'd never know which one but usually a fellow mixing with the air-riders) would shoot me in the head. The worst to come of that would be some mother would see her child see the cloud of blood flying out of my face, and she'd have to cover its mouth before it could yell because you don't want a child making noise in a public area. Be seen and not heard applies to them, and better not even to be seen very much.

The little ones are considered emblems of felony.

When bad times first settled into reality, the radio announcers told us what conversationalists and musicians Americans were proving to be and that our natural fine wit was going to be retreasured. People began working on their communication. Tales were told. Every other guy had a harmonica, a tonette, or at least was honking on two blades of grass. But that was before they started *eating* grass in New York and then buying up the rest of the nation's.

On the National Radio two years ago, we heard the Surgeon General report on the studies done on survivors of lost expeditions, polar and mountaintop sorties. The thing of it was that you could stay alive a phenomenal length of time on almost nothing if you *did* almost nothing, counting talking and singing. Which sent communication and melody back into the crapper.

The Surgeon General said you had to be sure whatever food you were after surpassed in calories the effort getting it would burn up. Don't run after a clump of celery, for example. *Chewing* celery takes more calories than eating it gives you. But cockroaches, moths, and butterflies will come *to* you and can be caught and ingested with a *bonus* of calories and protein. Wash the cockroaches if possible, the Surgeon General said.

We were chewing on our rutabagas and radishes when this came out and we considered it all laughable, radical overscience for the ghettos above the Mason-Dixon.

That was in the days of cheese.

Then, all the blacks started returning to the South, walking. Five thousand of them came through Maryland, *eating* three or four swamps around Chesapeake Bay, stripping every leaf, boiling and salting all the greenery in huge iron caldrons they pulled along on carts.

Those blacks hit Virginia and ate a Senator's cotton plantation. People started shooting at them, and some of the nigs had guns themselves.

It was a bloodbath.

There were rumors that the blacks cooked their own dead, and you could see that's where their strength was coming from.

When the walking poor of Chicago went through the fields of South-ern Illinois, over to Kansas, down through Missouri, this sort of thing was avoided. All of America knew about the Virginia horror, and steps were apparently taken among leaders to prevent its recurrence. The radio announcers urged all the walkers to spread out, don't go in large groups. The vegetation of America would feed everybody if all the Resettlers would spread out.

This was good advice, unless you spread out on somebody's acres.

The South was filling up with railroad people from the big defunct hives in the North. Theoretically, everybody could have his own hundred-foot-square place. But too many came back to the South. There were five million Resettlers in Atlanta, they say. Atlanta is very sorry that it prospered as a railroad. The mayor, a Puerto Rican with his Chinese wife, abdicated, leaving everything to the wardens and the stateside C.I.A.

Everybody is quiet. No more music or talking or needless exertion.

Crowds everywhere are immense and docile.

We hear it on the radio.

"They all look at this place covetously. Those air-riders," says Mrs. Neap. "Poor souls."

You also had the right to kill anybody who jumped *off* the train *into* your yard. An old coroner might come by on his bicycle and stare at the body for a while, letting off a few platitudes about the old days. Like as not, a town officer, usually a nig or Vietnamese, appears and digs a hole three feet deep and prods the body over into it. This is slow going because the man will eat every worm, every grub, every spider and juicy root he upturns with his spade.

Even Mrs. Neap's run-down house probably looks as if it has gunners at it. But it had no protection at all before we got here. I carry a knife.

The direly thin guy six and a half feet tall who melted into the dawn fog with his bow and arrow before anybody got up and returned at evening with almost all of his arrows lost and not a goddamn ounce of meat to show—to be fair, four blackbirds and a rabbit smaller than the hunting arrow—wanted you to think he was Slinking Invisible itself on the borders of our landlord, when the truth was he was miles away missing ten-foot shots on trifling birds and sticking his homemade arrows into high limbs where he couldn't retrieve them.

He calls himself JIM, I mean loudly and significantly, like that.

Says he knows the game world. When we walked up on that big wild turkey just before we found Mrs. Neap's house, I watched that sucker fire off three different arrows at it. The turkey stood there just like the rest of us, unbelieving. At this point I sicced soft-spoken Vince on the turkey. Vince is so patient and soft-spoken, he could talk a snake into leaving his poison behind and pulling up a chair for stud or go-fish, whatever you wanted to play.

Vince talked the turkey right into his arms.

Then came the last arrow from JIM.

It went through Vince's hand and into the heart of the turkey.

We didn't need this. You can't get medical help. There's nothing left but home remedies.

We started despising JIM right then and there.

But Vince's hand healed and is merely unusable instead of gangrenous.

"My God, one of them jumped off," says Mrs. Neap.

I saw. It was an Oriental.

He is wobbling on the gravel in front of the yard. I pull my knife. This close in to a town you have to perform the law.

But one of the wardens in the air-rider cages shoots at him—then the next one, who has a shotgun, blasts the gook.

The guy lies down.

I couldn't tell whether he went to the dirt before or after the gun blast.

Mrs. Neap kneels down with delicate attention to the dead man. With her cracked lens, she seems a benevolent patient scholar.

Mrs. Neap says, "He's a handsome little man. We don't need to call the coroner about him. Look at the muscles. He was well fed. I wonder why he come running toward the house. I guess he wanted to end up here. He chose," says Mrs. Neap.

"I'll get the bike and tell the coroner," I say.

"I said *not* get the coroner. This is my property. Look. His head is across my legal property line," says Mrs. Neap.

Say I, "Let's push him back a few feet. Then he's the city's. There's no reason for you to take the responsibility or cost of burying him."

The old lady is intent. She'd been through the minor Depression in the Thirties. She'd seen some things, I guess.

"Have you never?" says Mrs. Neap.

Her spectacles are flaming with the rising sun.

Say I, "Have I never what?" slipping my knife back into my hip scabbard.

"Eaten it?"

"*It?*"

"Human being."

"Human *being?*"

"Neither have I," says Mrs. Neap. "But I'm so starving, and Orientals are so *clean*. I used to know Chinese in the Mississippi delta. They were squeaky clean and good-smelling. They didn't eat much but vegetables. Help me drag him back," she says.

She didn't need help.

She has the man under the arms and drags him at top speed over the scrub weeds and onto her lawn. Every now and then she gives me a ferocious look. There is a huge broken-down barbecue pit behind the house. I can see that is her destination.

I go up the front steps and wake up our "family." Vince is already awake, his hand hanging red and limp. He has watched the whole process since the gook jumped off the train.

JIM is not there. He is out invisible in the woods, taking dramatic inept shots at mountains.

(To complete his history, when we move on, after the end of this, JIM kills a dog and is dressing him out when a landowner comes up on him and shoots him several times with a .22 automatic. JIM strangles the landowner and the two of them die in an epic of trespass.)

My wife wakes up. Then Gardiner, the chemist who keeps us in booze, wakes up.

Vince has grown even softer since the loss of his right hand. Larry (you don't need to know any more about him) and his girl never wake up.

"Mrs. Neap wants to cook the man," I say.

"What strength. She did a miracle," says soft Vince.

When we get to the rotisserie, Mrs. Neap has the man all cleaned. Her Doberman is eating and chasing the intestines around the backyard.

My family goes into a huddle, pow-wowing over whether to eat the Doberman.

We don't know what she did with the man's head.

By this time she is cutting off steaks and has the fire going good.

Two more tenants come out on the patio, rubbing their eyes, waked up by the smell of that meat broiling on the grill.

Mrs. Neap is slathering on the tomato sauce and pepper.

The rest of the tenants come down.

Meat!

They pick it off the grill and bite away.

Vince has taken the main part of the skeleton back to the garage, faithful to his deep emotion for good taste.

When it is all over, Mrs. Neap appears in the living room, where we are all lying around. Her face is smeary with grease and tomato sauce. She is sponging off her hideous cheeks with a rag even as she speaks.

She says, "I accepted you for a while, you romantic nomads. Oh, you came and sang and improved the conversation. Thanks to JIM for protecting my place and my dried-out garden, wherever he is. But you have to get out by this afternoon. Leave by three o'clock," says she.

"*Why?*" say I.

"Because, for all your music and merriment, you make too many of us. I don't think you'll bring in anything," she says.

"But we *will*," says soft Vince. "We'll pick big luscious weeds. We'll drag honeysuckles back to the hearth."

She looks around at all of us severely.

She says, "I hate to get this down to tacks, but I hear noises in the house since you're here." This old amazing woman was whispering. "You know what goes in America. You know all the announcements about food value. You, one of you, had *old dangerous relations* with Clarisse, the tenant next to my room. I heard. You may be romantic, but you are trash."

She places herself with her glasses so as to fix herself in the image of an unanswerable beacon.

She says, "We all know the *Survival News*. Once I was a prude and resisted. But if we're going to win through for America, I go along. *Only* oral relations are allowed. We must not waste the food from each other, the rich minerals, the raw protein. We are our own gardens," Mrs. Neap says, trembling over her poetry.

It costs her a lot to be so frank, I can see.

"But you cooked a human being and ate him," say I.

"I couldn't help it," says she. "I remember the cattle steaks of the old days, the juicy pork, the dripping joints of lamb, the venison."

"The *what?*" say we.

"Get out of here. I give you to four o'clock," says she.

So the four of us hit the road that afternoon.

We head to the shady green by the compass in my head.

I am the leader and my wife is on my arm.

There are plenty of leaves.

I think we are getting over into Georgia.

My wife whispers in my ear: "Did you go up there with Clarisse?"

I grab off a plump leaf from a yearling ash. In my time I've eaten poison ivy and oak too. The rash erupts around your scrotum, but it raises your head and gives you hope when the poison's in your brain.

I confess. "Yes."

She whispers on. "I wanted JIM. He tried. But he couldn't find my place. He never could find my place."

"JIM?" say I. "He just can't hit any target, now can he?"

"I saw Clarisse eating her own eyelashes," she whispers, from the weakness, I suppose.

"It's okay," say I, wanting to comfort her with an arm over to her shoulder. But with that arm I am too busy taking up good leaves off a stout little palmetto. And ahead of us is a real find, rims of fungus standing off a grandfather oak.

I've never let the family down. Something in my head tells me where the green places are. What a pleasure to me it is to see soft Vince, with his useless floppy red hand, looking happy as he sucks the delicious fungus off the big oak.

My wife throws herself into the feast. Near the oak are two terrapins. She munches the fungus and holds them up. They are huge turtles, probably mates. They'd been eating the fungus themselves.

"Meat!" says the wife.

"We won't!" say I. "I won't eat a hungry animal. I just want to hold and pet one!"

The hunting arrow from JIM gets me right in the navel when I take the cuter of the turtles into my arms.

The wife can't cook.

JIM's feeling too awful to pitch in.

So it'll be up to soft Vince to do me up the best he can with only one good hand.

After the Storm

John Updike

Vera Hummel's guest bedroom shone in the aftermath of the snowstorm. My dreams had been a bent extension, like that of a stick thrust into water, of the last waking events—the final mile staggering through the unwinding storm; my father's beating at the door of the dark house, knocking and whinnying and rubbing his hands together in desperation, yet his importunity no longer seeming absurd or berserk to me but necessary, absolutely in my blind numbness necessary; then Vera Hummel yawning and blinking in the bleaching glare of her kitchen, her unbound hair fanning over the shoulders of her blue bathrobe and her hands tucked in the sleeves and her arms hugging herself as she yawned; and the limping clump of her husband descending the stairs to receive my father's outpour of explanation and gratitude. They put us in their guest bedroom, in a postered, sway-backed bed inherited from Mr. Hummel's mother, my grandfather's sister Hannah. It smelled of feathers and starch and was so like a hammock that my father and I, in underclothes, had to cling to the edges to keep from sliding together in the middle. For some minutes I kept tense. I seemed stuffed with the jiggling atoms of the storm. Then I heard the first rasp of my father's snuffly little snore. Then the wind outside the room sighed mightily, and this thrust of sound and motion beyond me seemed to explain everything, and I relaxed.

The room was radiant. Beyond the white mullions and the curtains of dotted swiss, pinned back with metal flowers painted white, the sky was undiluted blue. I thought, *This morning has never occurred before*, and I jubilantly felt myself to be on the prow of a ship cleaving the skyey ocean of time. I looked around the room for my father; he was gone. I had sunk into the center of the bed. I looked for a clock; there was none. I looked to my left to see how the sun lay on the road and field and mailbox, and my gaze met instead a window giving on a brick wall. Next to the window, its chip ping veneer somehow grimacing, was an old-fashioned bureau with fluted glass knobs, a wavy-faced top drawer, and ponderous scroll feet like the toeless feet of a cartoon bear. The radiance beyond the house picked out the silver glints in the stems and leaves of the wallpaper. I closed my eyes to listen for voices, heard a vacuum cleaner humming at some distance, and must have slipped back into sleep.

When I awoke again the strangeness of it all—the house, the day so fair and sane in the wake of madness, the silence, inside and out (Why had I not been wakened? What had happened to the school? Wasn't it Wednes-day?)—held me from falling back, and I arose and dressed as much as I could. My shoes and socks, set to dry on a radiator in the room, were still damp. The strange walls and hallways, demanding thought and courage at every turn, seemed to suck strength from my limbs. I located the bathroom and splashed cold water on my face and ran my wet finger back and forth across my teeth. In bare feet I went down the Hummels' stairs. They were carpeted with a fresh-napped beige strip held in place by a brass rod at the base of each riser. This was the kind of Olinger home, solid and square and orthodox, that I wished my family lived in.

Mrs. Hummel came in from the front room wearing a pinned-up bandana and an apron patterned with starlike anemones. She held a dainty straw wastebasket in her hand and, grinning so her gums flashed, hailed me with "Good morning, Peter Caldwell!" Her pronouncing my name in full somehow made me completely welcome. She led me into the kitchen and in walking behind her I felt myself, to my surprise, her height, or even an inch taller. She was tall as local women went and I still thought of her as the goddess-size she had appeared to me when I first arrived at the high school, a runty seventh-grader, my waist no higher than the blackboard chalk troughs. Now I seemed to fill her eyes. I sat at the little porcelain-topped kitchen table and she served me like a wife. She set before me a thick tumbler of orange juice whose translucence cast on the porcelain in sunlight an orange shadow like a thin slice of the anticipated taste. It was delicious for me to sit and sip and watch her move. She glided in blue slippers from cupboard to refrigerator to sink as if these intervals had been laid out after measuring her strides; her whole spacious and amply equipped kitchen contrasted with the cramped and improvised corner where my mother made our meals. I wondered why some people could solve at least the mechanical problems of living while others, my people, seemed destined for lifetimes of malfunctioning cars and underheated homes. In Olinger, we had never had a refrigerator, but instead a humiliating old walnut icebox, and my grandmother never sat down with us at the table but ate standing up, off the stove with her fingers, her face wincing in the steam. Haste and improvidence had always marked our domestic details. The reason, it came to me, was that our family's central member, my father, had never rid himself of the idea that he might soon be moving on. This fear, or hope, dominated our home.

"Where's my father?" I asked.

"I don't know exactly, Peter," she said. "Which would you prefer—Wheaties or Rice Krispies or an egg some way?"

"Rice Krispies." An oval ivory-colored clock below the lacquered cabinets said 11:10. I asked, "What happened to school?"

"Have you looked outdoors?"

"Sort of. It's stopped."

"Sixteen inches, the radio said. All the schools in the county have canceled. Even the parochial schools in Alton."

"I wonder if they're going to have swimming practice tonight."

"I'm sure not. You must be dying to get to your home."

"I suppose so. It seems forever since I *was* home."

"Your father was very funny this morning, telling us your adventures. Do you want a banana with the cereal?"

"Oh, gee. Sure, if you have it." That surely was the difference between these Olinger homes and my own: they were able to keep bananas on hand. In Firetown, on the rare times my father thought to buy them, they went from green to rotten without a skip. The banana she set beside my bowl was perfect. Its golden skin was flecked evenly all over just as in the four-color magazine ads. As I sliced it with my spoon, each segment in dropping into the cereal displayed that ideal little star of seeds at the center.

"Do you drink coffee?"

"I try to every morning, but there's never any time. I'm being an awful lot of trouble."

"Hush. You sound like your father." Her "hush," emerging from an intimacy that someone else had created for me, evoked a curious sense of past time, of the few mysterious hours ago when, while I was sound asleep in my great-aunt Hannah's bed, my father had told of his adventures and they had listened to the radio. I wondered if Mr. Hummel had been here also; I wondered what event had spread through the house this aftermath of peaceful, reconciled radiance.

I made bold to ask, "Where is Mr. Hummel?"

"He's out with the plow. Poor Al, he's been up since five. He has a contract with the town to help clear the streets after a storm."

"Oh. I wonder how our poor car is. We abandoned it last night at the bottom of Coughdrop Hill."

"Your father said. When Al comes home, he'll drive you out in the truck to it."

"These Rice Krispies are awfully good."

She looked around from the sink in surprise and smiled. "They're just the ones that come out of the box." Her kitchen seemed to bring out a Dutchness in her intonation. I had always vaguely associated Mrs. Hummel with sophistication, New York, and the rest of it; she shone to such advantage among the other teachers, and sometimes wore mascara. But in her house she was, plainly, of this county.

"How did you like the game last night?" I asked her. I felt awkwardly constrained to keep a conversation up. My father's absence challenged me to put into practice my notions of civilized behavior, which he customarily frustrated. She brought me two slices of glinting toast and dollop of amber crab-apple jelly on a black plate.

"I didn't pay that much attention." She laughed in memory. "Really, that Reverend March amuses me so. He's half a boy and half an old man and you never know which you're talking to."

"He has some medals, doesn't he?"

"I suppose. He went all up through Italy."

"It's interesting, I think, that after all that he could return to the ministry."

Her eyebrows arched. Did she pluck them? Seeing them close, I doubted it. They were naturally fine. "I think it's good; don't you?"

"Oh, it's good, sure. I mean, after all the horrors he must have seen."

"Well—they say there's some fighting even in the Bible."

Not knowing what she wanted, I laughed nevertheless. It seemed to please her. She asked me playfully, "How much attention did *you* pay to the game? Didn't I see you sitting with the little Fogleman girl?"

I shrugged. "I had to sit next to somebody."

"Now, Peter, you watch out. She has the look in her eye."

"Ha. I doubt if I'm much of a catch."

She held up a finger, gay-making in the county fashion. "Ahhh. You have the possibilities."

The interposed "the" was so like my grandfather's manner of speech that I blushed as if blessed. I spread the bright jelly on my toast and she continued about the business of the house.

The next two hours were unlike any previous in my life. I shared a house with a woman, a woman tall in time, so tall I could not estimate her height in years, which at the least was twice mine. A woman of overarching fame; legends concerning her love life circulated like dirty coins in the student underworld. A woman fully grown and extended in terms of property and authority; her presence branched into every corner of the house. Her touch on the thermostat stirred the furnace under me. Her footsteps above me tripped the vacuum cleaner into a throaty, swarming hum. Here and there in the house she laughed to herself, or made a piece of furniture cry as she moved it; sounds of her flitted across the upstairs floor as a bird flits unseen and sporadic through the high reaches of a forest. Intimations of Vera Hummel moved toward me from every corner of her house, every shadow, every curve of polished wood; she was a glimmer in the mirrors, a breath moving the curtains, a pollen on the nap of the arms of the chair I was rooted in.

I heavily sat in the dark front parlor reading from a little varnished rack *Reader's Digests* one after another. I read until I felt sick from reading. I eagerly discovered and consumed two articles side by side in the table of contents: *Miracle Cure for Cancer?* and *Ten Proofs That There Is a God.* I read them and was disappointed, more than disappointed, overwhelmed— for the pang of hope roused fears that had been lulled. For the past two days I had lived with the possibility that my father had cancer, and had grown a little numb to it. Now the demons of dread freshly injected their iron into my blood. It was clear, clear for all the smart rattle of the prose and the encyclopedic pretense of the trim double columns, that there were no proofs, there was no miracle cure. In my terror of words I experienced a panicked hunger for things and I took up, from the center of the lace doily on the small table by my elbow, and squeezed in my hand a painted china figurine of a smiling elf with chunky polka-dot wings. The quick blue slippers sounded on the carpeted stairs and Mrs. Hummel made lunch for the two of us. In the brightness of the kitchen I was embarrassed for my complexion. I wondered if it would be manners to offer to leave, but I had no strength to leave this house, felt unable even to look out the window; and if I did leave, where would I look, and for what? My father's mysterious absence from me seemed permanent. I was lost. The woman talked to me; her words were trivial but they served to make horror habitable. Into the shining plane of the tabletop between our faces I surfaced; I made her laugh. She had taken off her bandana and clipped her hair into a horsetail. As I helped her clear the table and took the dishes to the sink, our bodies once or twice brushed. And so, half sunk in fear and half alive and alight with love, I passed the two hours of time.

My father returned a little after one. Mrs. Hummel and I were still in the kitchen. We had been talking about a wing, an L with a screened porch, which she wanted to have built onto the back of her house; here in the summers she could sit overlooking the yard, away from the traffic and noise of the pike. It would be a bower and I believed I would share it with her.

My father looked, in his bullethead cap and snow-drenched overcoat, like a man just shot from a cannon. "Boy," he told us, "Old Man Winter made up for lost time."

"Where have you *been*?" I asked. My voice ignobly stumbled on a threat of tears.

He looked at me as if he had forgotten I existed. "Out and around," he said. "Over at the school. I would have gotten you up, Peter, but I figured you needed the sleep. You were beginning to look drawn as hell. Did my snoring keep you awake?"

"*No.*" The snow on his coat and pants and shoes, testimony of adventure, made me jealous. Mrs. Hummel's attention had shifted all to him; she was laughing without his even saying anything. His bumpy face was ruddy. He whipped his cap off like a boy and stamped his feet on the cocoa mat inside the door. I yearned to torment him; I became shrill. "What did you *do* at the school? How could you be so *long*?"

"Jesus, I love that building when there aren't any kids in it." He was speaking not to me but to Mrs. Hummel. "What they ought to do with that brick barn, Vera, is turn the kids out on the street and let us teachers live there alone; it's the only place I've ever been in my life where I didn't feel like somebody was sitting on the back of my neck all the time."

She laughed and said, "They'd have to put in beds."

"An old Army cot is all I'd need," he told her. "Two feet wide and six feet long; whenever I get in bed with somebody they take all the covers. I don't mean you, Peter. Tired as I was last night I probably took 'em from you. In answer to your question, what was I doing over there, I brought all my books up to date. For the first time since last marking period everything is apple-pie; I feel like they lifted a concrete block out of my belly. If I don't show up tomorrow, the new teacher can step right in and take over, poor devil. Biff, bang; move over, buddy, next stop, the dump."

I had to laugh.

Mrs. Hummel moved to her refrigerator asking, "George, have you had lunch? Can I give you a roast-beef sandwich?"

"Vera, that's kind as hell of you. To tell you the truth, I couldn't chew a roast-beef sandwich. I had a back tooth pulled last night. I feel a hundred percent better but it's like the lost Atlantis in there. To be perfectly honest with you though, if you and the kid were having coffee, I'd take a cup. I forget if the kid drinks coffee."

"How can you forget it?" I asked. "I try to drink it every morning at home but there's never any *time*."

"Jesus, that reminds me. I tried to get through to your mother but the lines are out. She doesn't have a scrap of food in the house and if I know Pop Kramer he'll be trying to eat the dog. Provided he hasn't fallen down the stairs. That would be just my luck; no doctor can get in there."

"Well when are *we* going to get there?"

"Any minute, kid, any minute. Time and tide for no man wait." He called to Mrs. Hummel, "Never take a boy away from his mother." Then he pinched his lips in; I knew he was wondering if this had been tactless because she, for reasons that were dark to me, had no children herself.

With the pointed quiet of a servant she set the smoking coffee on the counter near him. A coil of hair came loose and trailed across her cheek like a comment. He tried to subdue the excitement in his voice and told her, "I saw Al over by Spruce Street and he's on his way home. He and that truck have been performing miracles out there; this borough does a bang-up job when the chips are down. Traffic's moving on everything but the alleys and the section around Shale Hill. Boy, if I was running this town we'd all be on snowshoes for a month." He clenched and unclenched his hands happily as he gazed into this vision of confusion. "They say a trolley was derailed over in West Alton late last night."

Mrs. Hummel tucked back her hair and asked, "Was anybody hurt?"

"Nobody. It jumped the rails but stayed on its feet. Our own trolleys didn't get through to Ely until around noon. Half the stores in Alton are shut." I marveled at all this information and imagined him gathering it, wading through snowbanks, halting snowplows to question the drivers, running up and down raggedly heaped mounds in his too-small overcoat like an overgrown urchin. He must have circled the town while I was asleep.

I finished my coffee and the odd torpor that my nerves had been holding at bay now was permitted to invade. I ceased to listen as my father told Mrs. Hummel of his further adventures. Mr. Hummel came in the door, grey with fatigue, and shook snow from his hair. His wife fed him lunch; when it was over he looked at me and winked. "Do you want to go home, Peter?"

I went and put on my coat and socks and wrinkled clammy shoes and came back to the kitchen. My father took his empty cup to the sink and restored his cap to his head. "This is awfully white of you, Al; the kid and I really appreciate it." To Mrs. Hummel he said, "Thanks a lot, Vera, you've treated us like princes," and then, the strangest of all the strange things I have told, my father bent forward and kissed the woman on the cheek. I averted my eyes and saw on the spatter-pattern linoleum floor her narrow feet in their blue slippers go up on their toes as she willingly received the kiss.

Then her heels returned to the floor and she was holding my father's wart-freckled hands in her own. "I'm glad you came to us," she told him, as if they were alone. "It filled up the house for a little while."

When my turn to thank her came I didn't dare a kiss and pulled my face back to indicate I was not going to give one. She smiled as she took my offered hand and then put her other hand over it. "Are your hands always so warm, Peter?"

Outside their door, the twigs of a lilac bush had become antlers. Hummel's truck was waiting between the pumps and the air hose; it was a middle-sized rust-splotched Chevrolet pickup with a flaring orange plow coupled to the front bumper. When it went into gear ten different colors of rattle seemed to spring into being around us. I sat between my father and Al Hummel; there was no heater in the front and I was glad to be between the men. We drove out Buchanan Road. Along the street, children in passing had shaken the snow loose from the hedges and now and then above us a loosened batch poured down in a shuffling quick cascade through the branches of a horse-chestnut tree. As the houses thinned, the snow reigned undisturbed over the curved fields beyond the steady ridge, as high as a man, of stained snow heaped by the plow.

The weariness I felt overtakes me in the telling. I sat in the cab of the truck while, framed in the windshield like the blurred comics of an old silent movie, my father and Hummel shoveled out our Buick, which the plows in clearing Route 122 had buried up to the windows. I was bothered by an itching that had spread from my nose through my throat and that I felt to have some connection with the clammy chill of my shoes. The shoulder of the hill threw its shadow over us and a little wind ignited. The sunlight grew long, golden, and vanished from all but the tips of the trees. Expertly Hummel started the motor, backed the rear tires onto the chains, and made them fast with a plier-like tool. Little better than blurs now in the bluish twilight, the men enacted a pantomime with a wallet whose conclusion I did not comprehend. They both gestured widely and then hugged each other farewell. Hummel opened the door of the cab, cold air swept over me, and I transferred my brittle body to our hearse.

469

As we drove home, the days since I had last seen this road sealed shut like a neat scar. Here was the crest of Coughdrop Hill, here was the Clover Leaf Dairy where conveyor belts removed the cow dung, and all the silver chimneys on the barn roof were smoking against the salmon flush of the sky; here was the straightaway where we had once killed a confused oriole, here was Galilee and, beside the site of the old Seven Mile Inn, Potteiger's Store, where we stopped for food. Item by item, as if he were a druggist filling a prescription, my father went around the shelves gathering bread and sliced peaches and Ritz Crackers and Shredded Wheat, piling them up on the counter in front of Charlie Potteiger, who had been a farmer and had come back from the Pacific to sell his farm to developers and set up this store. He kept our debt in a little brown five-cent notebook and, though it ran as high as sixty dollars between paydays, never forgave us so much as an odd penny. "And a loop of that pork sausage my father-in-law loves so much and a half-pound of Lebanon baloney for the kid to nibble," my father told him. An extravagance had entered his shopping, which was customarily niggardly, a day's food at a time, as if the next day there might be fewer mouths to feed. He even bought a bunch of fresh bananas. As Potteiger with his pencil stub effortfully toted up the bill, my father looked at me and asked, "Did you get a soft drink?"

I usually did, as a last sip of civilization before we descended into that rural darkness that by some mistake had become our home. "No," I told him. "I have no appetite. Let's go."

"This poor son of mine," my father announced loudly to the little pack of loafers in red hunting caps who even on this day of storm had showed up to stand around and chew in here, "he hasn't been home for two nights and he wants to see his mamma."

Furious, I pushed through the door into the air. The lake across the road, rimmed in snow, looked black as the back of a mirror. It was that twilight in which some cars have turned on their headlights, some their parking lights, and some no lights at all. My father drove as fast as if the road were bare. In some parts the road had been scraped clean and on these patches our chains changed tune. Halfway up Fire Hill (above us the church and its tiny cross were inked onto an indigo sky) a link snapped. It racketed against the rear right fender for the remaining mile. The few houses of Firetown patched the dusk with downstairs windows glowing dimly as embers. The Ten Mile Inn was dark and boarded shut.

Our road had not been plowed. My father rammed the Buick through the heaped snow and it sagged to a stop perhaps ten feet off the highway. The motor stalled. He turned off the ignition and snapped off the lights. "How will we get out tomorrow?" I asked.

"One thing at a time," he said. "I want to get you home. Can you walk it?"

"What *else* can I do?"

The unplowed road showed as a long stretch of shimmering grey set in perspective by two scribbled lines of young trees. Not a house light showed from here. Above us, in a sky still too bright a blue to support stars, sparse pale clouds like giant flakes of marble drifted westward so stilly their motion seemed lent by the earth's revolution. The snow overwhelmed my ankles and inundated my shoes. I tried to walk in my father's footsteps, but his strides were too great. As the sound of traffic on the highway faded behind us, a powerful silence strengthened. There was a star before us, one, low in the sky and so brilliant its white light seemed warm.

I asked my father, "What's that star?"

"Venus."

"Is it always the first to come out?"

"No. Sometimes it's the last to go. Sometimes when I get up the sun is coming up through the woods and Venus is still hanging over the Amishman's hill."

"Can you steer by it?"

"I don't know. I've never tried. It's an interesting question."

I told him, "I can never find the North Star. I always expect it to be bigger than it is."

"That's right. I don't know why the hell they made it so small."

His shape before me was made less human by the bag of groceries he was carrying and it seemed, my legs having ceased to convey the sensations of walking, that his was the shape of the neck and head of a horse I was riding. I looked straight up and the cobalt dome was swept clean of marble flakes and a few faint stars were wearing through. The branches of the young trees we walked between fell away to disclose the long low hump, sullenly lustrous, of our upper field. The land was silver like a corpse.

"Peter?"

My father's voice startled me, I felt so alone. "What?"

"Nothing. I just wanted to make sure you were still behind me."

"Well, where else would I be?"

"You got me there."

"Shall I carry the bag for a while?"

"No. It's clumsy but it's not heavy."

"Why'd you buy all those bananas if you knew we were going to have to lug everything half a mile?"

"Insanity," he answered. "Hereditary insanity." It was a favorite concept of his.

Lady, hearing our voices, began to bark behind the field. The quick dim doublets of sound like butterflies winged toward us close to the earth, skimming the feathery crust rather than risking a plunge upward into the steep smooth dome that capped a space of Pennsylvania a hundred miles wide. From the spot where the lower road led off from the upper we could see on a clear day to the first blue beginnings of the Alleghenies. We walked downward into the shelter of our hillside. The trees of our orchard came first into view, then our barn and, through the crotches and tangled barren branches of the orchard, our house. Our downstairs light was on, yet as we moved across the silent yard I became convinced that the light was an illusion, that the people inside had died and left the light burning. My father beside me moaned, "Jesus, I know Pop's stumbled down those damn stairs."

But footsteps had beaten a path around the corner of the house ahead of us, and on the porch there were plentiful signs that the pump had been used. Lady, free, raced out of the darkness with the whir of a growl in her throat and then, recognizing us, leaped like a fish from the splashing snow, jabbing her muzzle at our faces, her throat stuck fast on a weak, agonized note of whimpering love. She battered and bustled through the double kitchen door with us and in the warm indoors released an unmistakable tang of skunk.

Here was the kitchen, honey-colored, lit; here were the two clocks, the red electric thrown all out of right time by the power failure but running gamely nevertheless; here was my mother, coming forward with large arms and happy girlish face to take the bundle from my father and welcome us home. "My heroes," she said.

My father explained, "I tried to call you this morning, Cassie, but the lines were down. Have you had a rough time? There's an Italian sandwich in the bag."

"We've had a *won*derful time," my mother said. "Dad's been sawing wood and this evening I made some of that dried-beef soup with apples Granny used to make when we ran out of food." An ambrosial smell of warm apples did breathe from the stove, and a fire was dancing in the fireplace.

"Huh?" It seemed to daze my father that the world had gone on without him. "Pop's okay? Where in hell is he?"

Even as he spoke he walked into the other room and there, sitting in his accustomed place on the sofa, was my grandfather, his shapely hands folded across his chest, his little worn Bible, shut, balanced on one knee.

"Did you cut some wood, Pop?" my father asked loudly. "You're a walking miracle. At some point in your life you must have done something right."

"George, now I don't wish to be ac-quis-i-tive, but by any chance did you remember to bring the *Sun*?" The mailman of course hadn't gotten through, a sore deprivation for my grandfather, who wouldn't believe it had snowed until he read it in the newspaper.

"Hell, no, Pop," my father bellowed. "I forgot. I don't know why, it was insanity."

My mother and the dog came into the living room with us. Lady, unable to keep the good news of our return to herself any longer, jumped up on the sofa and with a snap of her body thrust her nose into my grandfather's ear.

"Hyar, *yaar*," he said, and stood up, rescuing the Bible from his knee in the same motion.

"Doc Appleton called," my mother said to my father.

"Huh? I thought the lines were out."

"They came on this afternoon, after the electricity. I called Hummel's and Vera said you had gone. She sounded more pleasant to me than I've ever heard her over the phone."

"What did Appleton say?" my father asked, crossing the room and looking down at my globe of the Earth.

"He said the X rays showed nothing."

"Huh? Is that what he said? Do you think he's lying, Cassie?"

"You know he never lies. Your X rays are clear. He said it's all in your nerves; he thinks you have a mild case of, now I forget—I wrote it down." My mother passed to the telephone and read from a slip of paper she had left on top of the directory, "*Mucinous colitis*. We had a nice talk; but Doc sounds older."

Abruptly I felt exhausted, empty; still in my coat, I sat down on the sofa and leaned back into its cushions. It seemed imperative to do this. The dog rested her head on my lap and wriggled her ice-cold nose into place beneath my hand. Her fur felt stuffed fluffy with chill outdoor air. My parents looked enormous and dramatic above me.

My father turned, his great face tense, as if refusing to undo the last clamp on hope. "Is that what he said?"

"He did think, though, you need a rest. He thinks teaching is a strain for you and wondered if there was something else you could do."

"Huh? Hell, it's all I'm good for, Cassie. It's my one talent. I can't quit."

"Well, that's what he and I thought you'd say."

"Do you think he can read X rays? Cassie? Do you think the old bluffer knows what he's talking about?"

I had closed my eyes by way of giving thanks. Now a large cool dry hand came and cupped itself over my forehead. My mother's voice said, "George. What have you done with this child? He has a roaring fever."

Muffled somewhat by the wooden wall of the staircase, my grandfather called down to us, "Pleasant dreams."

My father strode across the vibrating kitchen floor and called up the stairs after him, "Don't be sore about the *Sun*, Pop. I'll get you one tomorrow. Nothing'll happen until then, I promise you. The Russians are still in Moscow and Truman's still king."

My mother asked me, "How long has this been?"

"I don't know," I told her. "I've felt sort of weak and unreal all afternoon."

"Do you want some soup?"

"Maybe a little, not much. Isn't it a relief about Daddy? His not having cancer."

"Yes," she said. "Now he'll have to think up some new way of getting sympathy." A little bitter frown came and went in the soothing oval of her face.

I tried to get back into the little intricate world my mother and I had made, where my father was a fond, strange joke, by agreeing, "He *is* good at that. Maybe that's his talent."

He came back into the room and announced to us, "Boy, that man has a temper! He is really and truly sore about my not bringing home a newspaper. He's a powerhouse, Cassie; at his age I'll be dead for twenty years."

Though I was too dizzy and sleepy for calculations, this sounded like an upward revision in his expectations.

My parents fed me and put me to bed and took a blanket off their own bed so I would be warm. My teeth had begun to chatter and I made no attempt to repress this odd skeletal vibration, which both released swarms of chill spirits within me and brought down from my mother warm, helpless, fluttery gusts of concern. My father stood by, kneading his knuckles.

"Poor kid, he's too ambitious," he moaned aloud.

"My little sunbeam," my mother seemed to say.

To the tune of their retreating voices I fell asleep. My dreams seemed to take place in a sluggish whirling world where only my grandmother's face, flashing by on the periphery with the startled, fearful expression with which she used to call me down from a tree I was climbing, kept me company in the shifting, rootless flux of unidentifiable things. My own voice seemed throughout to be raised in protest and when I awoke, with an urgent need to urinate, my parents' voices below me seemed a grappling extension of my own. Morning light the tone of lemon filled the frame of my window. I remembered that in the middle of the night I had almost surfaced from my exitless nightmare at the touch of hands on my face and the sound of my father's voice in a corner of my room saying, "Poor kid, I wish I could give him my mulish body."

Now he was saying downstairs in the high, strained pitch he used like a whip on my mother, "I tell you, Cassie, I have it licked. Kill or be killed, that's my motto. Those bastards don't give me any quarter and I don't give them any."

"Well, that's certainly a very poor attitude for a teacher to have. No wonder your insides are all mixed up."

"It's the *only* attitude, Cassie. Any other attitude is suicide. If I can just hang in there for ten more years, I'll get my twenty-five-years' pension and have it licked."

A pause.

"I think the doctor's right," my mother said. "You should quit."

"Don't be a *femme*, Cassie. That's just Doc Appleton baloney, he has to say something. What else could I do? I'm an unemployable."

"Couldn't you quit and, if you can't find other work, farm this place with me?" Her voice had become shy and girlishly small; my throat contracted with grief for her. "It's a good farm," she said. "We could do like my parents; they were happy before they left this place, weren't you, Pop?"

My grandfather did not answer. My mother hurried nervous little jokes into the gap. "Work with your hands, George. Get close to Nature. It would make a whole man of you."

My father's voice in turn had become grave. "Cassie, I want to be frank with you, because you're my wife. I hate Nature. It reminds me of death. All Nature means to me is garbage and confusion and the stink of skunk—*brroo!*"

"Nature," my grandfather pronounced in his stately way, after clearing his throat vehemently, "is like a mother; she com-forts and chas-tises with the same hand."

An invisible membranous tension spread through the house and I knew that my mother had begun to cry. Her tears were half my own, yet I was glad she had been defeated, for the thought of my father as farmer frightened me. It would sink me too into the soil.

They had left a potty by the bed and, kneeling humbly, I used it. Only the medallions of my wallpaper watched. Like a flayed hide stiff with blood my red shirt lay crumpled on the floor against the baseboard. The action of getting out of bed threw into relief my condition. I was weak-legged and headachy and my throat felt glazed with dry glass. But my nose had begun to run and I could scrape together a small cough.

As I resettled myself in bed I relaxed into the comfortable foreknowledge of the familiar cycle of a cold: the loosening cough, the clogging nose, the subsiding fever, the sure three days in bed. It was during these convalescences that my future seemed closest to me, that the thought of painting excited me most and sprang the most hopeful conceptions. Lying in bed sick, I marshaled vast phantoms of pigment, and the world seemed to exist as the occasion of my dreams.

My father had heard me get out of bed and he came upstairs. He was dressed in his too-short coat and his imbecile knit cap. He was ready to go, and today my sleepiness wouldn't hold him back. His face wore a gaiety. "How is it, kid? Boy, I gave you a rough three days."

"It wasn't your fault. I'm glad it worked out."

"Huh? You mean about the X rays? Yeah, I've always been lucky. God takes care of you if you let Him."

"Are you sure there's school today?"

"Yep, the radio says they're all ready to go. The monsters are ready to learn."

"Hey, Daddy."

"Huh?"

"If you want to quit or take a sabbatical or something, don't not do it on my account."

"Don't you worry about that. Don't you worry about your old man, you got enough on your mind. I never made a decision in my life that wasn't one hundred percent selfish."

I turned my face away and looked through the window. In time my father appeared in this window, an erect figure dark against the snow. His posture made no concession to the pull underfoot; upright he waded out through our yard and past the mailbox and up the hill until he was lost to my sight behind the trees of our orchard. The trees took white on their sun side. The two telephone wires diagonally cut the blank blue of the sky. The bare stone wall was a scumble of umber; my father's footsteps thumbs of white in white. I knew what this scene was—a patch of Pennsylvania in 1947—and yet I did not know, was in my softly fevered state mindlessly soaked in a rectangle of colored light. I burned to paint it, just like that, in its puzzle of glory; it came upon me that I must go to Nature disarmed of perspective and stretch myself like a large transparent canvas upon her in the hope that, my submission being perfect, the imprint of a beautiful and useful truth would be taken.

Then—as if by permitting this inchoate excitement to pass through me I had done an honest piece of work—I went weary and closed my eyes and nearly dozed, so that when my mother brought up my orange juice and cereal I ate with an unready mouth.

Heart of a Champion

T. Coraghessan Boyle

Here are the corn fields and the wheat fields winking gold and goldbrown and yellowbrown in midday sun. Up the grassy slope we go, to the barn redder than red against sky bluer than blue, across the smooth stretch of the barnyard with its pecking chickens, and then right on up to the screen door at the back of the house. The door swings open, a black hole in the sun, and Timmy emerges with his cornsilk hair. He is dressed in crisp overalls, striped T-shirt, stubby blue Keds. There must be a breeze—and we are not disappointed—his clean fine cup-cut hair waves and settles as he scuffs across the barnyard to the edge of the field. The boy stops there to gaze out over the wheat-manes, eyes unsquinted despite the sun, eyes blue as tinted lenses. Then he brings three fingers to his lips in a neat triangle and whistles long and low, sloping up sharp to cut off at the peak. A moment passes: he whistles again. And then we see it—out there at the far corner of the field—the ripple, the dashing furrow, the blur of the streaking dog, white chest, flashing feet.

They are in the woods now. The boy whistling, hands in pockets, kicking along with his short darling strides, the dog beside him wagging the white tip of her tail, an all-clear flag. They pass beneath an arching black-barked oak. It creaks, and suddenly begins to fling itself down on them: immense, brutal: a panzer strike. The boy's eyes startle and then there's the leap, the smart snout clutching his trousers, the thunder-blast of the trunk, the dust and spinning leaves. "Golly, Lassie, I didn't even see it," says the boy, sitting safe in a mound of moss. The collie looks up at him—the svelte snout, the deep gold logician's eyes—and laps at his face.

Now they are down by the river. The water is brown with angry suppurations, spiked with branches, fence posts, tires, and logs. It rushes like the sides of boxcars, chews deep and insidious at the bank under Timmy's feet. The roar is like a jetport—little wonder the boy cannot hear the dog's warning bark. We watch the crack appear, widen to a ditch, then the halves splitting—snatch of red earth, writhe of worm—the poise and pitch, and Timmy crushing down with it. Just a flash—but already he is way downstream, his head like a plastic jug, dashed and bobbed, spinning toward the nasty mouth of the falls. But there is the dog—fast as a flashcube—bursting along the bank, all white and gold, blended in motion, hair sleeked with the wind of it . . . yet what can she hope to do? The current surges on, lengths ahead, sure bet to win the race to the falls. Timmy sweeps closer, sweeps closer, the falls loud as a hundred timpani now, the war drums of the Sioux, Africa gone bloodlust mad! The dog forges ahead, lashing over the wet earth like a whipcrack, straining every ganglion, until at last she draws abreast of the boy. Then she is in the air, then the foaming yellow water. Her paws churning like pistons, whiskers chuffing with exertion—oh, the roar!—and there, she's got him, her sure jaws clamping down on the shirt collar, her eyes fixed on the slip of rock at falls' edge. The black brink of the falls, the white paws digging at the rock—and they are safe. The dog sniffs at the inert little form, nudges the boy's side until she manages to roll him over. She clears his tongue and begins mouth-to-mouth.

Night: the barnyard still, a bulb burning over the screen door. Inside, the family sits at dinner, the table heaped with pork chops, mashed potatoes, applesauce and peas, home-baked bread, a pitcher of immaculate milk. Mom and Dad, good-humored and sympathetic, poised at attention, forks in mid-swoop, while Timmy tells his story.

"So then Lassie grabbed me by the collar and, golly, I guess I blanked out because I don't remember anything more till I woke up on the rock—"

"Well, I'll be," says Mom.

"You're lucky you've got such a good dog, son," says Dad, gazing down at the collie where she lies serenely, snout over paw, tail wapping the floor. She is combed and washed and fluffed, her lashes mascaraed and curled, chest and paws white as soap. She looks up humbly. But then her ears leap, her neck jerks around—and she's up at the door, head cocked, alert. A high yipping yowl, like a stuttering fire whistle, shudders through the room. And then another. The dog whines.

"Darn," says Dad. "I thought we were rid of those coyotes. Next thing you know they'll be after the chickens again."

The moon blanches the yard, leans black shadows on trees, the barn. Upstairs in the house, Timmy lies sleeping in the pale light, his hair gorgeously mussed, his breathing gentle. The collie lies on the throw rug beside the bed, her eyes open. Suddenly she rises and slips to the window, silent as shadow, and looks down the long elegant snout to the barnyard below, where the coyote slinks from shade to shade, a limp pullet dangling from his jaws. He is stunted, scabious, syphilitic, his forepaw trap-twisted, eyes running. The collie whimpers softly from the window. The coyote stops in mid-trot, frozen in a cold shard of light, ears high on his head—

then drops the chicken at his feet, leers up at the window and begins a crooning, sad-faced song.

The screen door slaps behind Timmy as he bolts from the house, Lassie at his heels. Mom's head pops forth on the rebound. "Timmy!" The boy stops as if jerked by a rope, turns to face her. "You be home before lunch, hear?"

"Sure, Mom," the boy says, already spinning off, the dog at his side.

In the woods, Timmy steps on a rattler and the dog bites its head off. "Gosh," he says. "Good girl, Lassie." Then he stumbles and flips over an embankment, rolls down the brushy incline and over a sudden precipice, whirling out into the breathtaking blue space, a sky diver. He thumps down on a narrow ledge twenty feet below—and immediately scrambles to his feet, peering timorously down the sheer wall to the heap of bleached bones at its base. Small stones break loose, shoot out like asteroids. Dirt-slides begin. But Lassie yarps reassuringly from above, sprints back to the barn for winch and cable, hoists the boy to safety.

On their way back for lunch Timmy leads them through a still and leaf-darkened copse. But notice that birds and crickets have left off their cheeping. How puzzling! Suddenly, around a bend in the path before them, the coyote appears. Nose to the ground, intent. All at once he jerks to a halt, flinches as if struck, hackles rising, tail dipping between his legs. The collie, too, stops short, yards away, her chest proud and shaggy and white. The coyote cowers, bunches like a cat, glares. Timmy's face sags with alarm. The coyote lifts his lip. But the collie prances up and stretches her nose out to him, her eyes liquid. She is balsamed and perfumed; her full chest tapers to sleek haunches and sculpted legs. The coyote is puny, runted, half her size, his coat a discarded doormat. She circles him now, sniffing. She whimpers, he growls, throaty and tough—and stands stiff while she licks at his whiskers, noses his rear, the bald black scrotum. Timmy is horror-struck as the coyote slips behind her, his black lips tight with anticipation.

*   *   *

"What was she doing, Dad?" Timmy asks over his milk, good hot soup, and sandwich.

"The sky was blue today, son," Dad says. "The barn was red."

Late afternoon: the sun mellow, orange. Purpling clots of shadow hang from the branches, ravel out from tree trunks. Bees and wasps and flies saw away at the wet full-bellied air. Timmy and the dog are far out beyond the north pasture, out by the old Indian burial ground, where the boy stoops to search for arrowheads. The collie is pacing the crest above, whimpering voluptuously, pausing from time to time to stare out across the forest, eyes distant and moonstruck. Behind her, storm clouds, dark exploding brains, spread over the horizon.

We observe the wind kicking up: leaves flapping like wash, saplings quivering. It darkens quickly now, clouds scudding low and smoky over treetops, blotting the sun from view. Lassie's white is whiter than ever, highlighted against the heavy horizon, wind-whipped hair foaming around her. Still, she does not look down at the boy as he digs.

The first fat random drops, a flash, the volcanic blast of thunder. Timmy glances over his shoulder at the noise just in time to see the scorched pine plummeting toward the constellated freckles in the center of his forehead. Now the collie turns—too late!—the *swoosh-whack* of the tree, the trembling needles. She is there in an instant, tearing at the green welter, struggling through to his side. The boy lies unconscious in the muddying earth, hair cunningly arranged, a thin scratch painted on his cheek. The trunk lies across his back, the tail of a brontosaurus. The rain falls.

Lassie tugs doggedly at a knob in the trunk, her pretty paws slipping in the wet—but it's no use—it would take a block and tackle, a crane, a corps of engineers to shift that stubborn bulk. She falters, licks at the boy's ear, whimpers. See the troubled look in Lassie's eye as she hesitates, uncertain, priorities warring: stand guard—or dash for help? Her decision is sure and swift—eyes firm with purpose, she's off like shrapnel, already up the hill, shooting past dripping trees, over river, cleaving high wet banks of wheat.

A moment later she dashes through the puddled and rain-screened barnyard, barking right on up to the back door, where she pauses to scratch daintily, her voice high-pitched, insistent. Mom swings open the door and Lassie pads in, toenails clacking on the shiny linoleum.

"What is it, girl? What's the matter? Where's Timmy?"

"Yarf! Yarfata-yarf-yarf!"

"Oh, my! Dad! Dad, come quickly!"

Dad rushes in, face stolid and reassuring "What is it, dear? . . . Why, Lassie!"

"Oh, Dad, Timmy's trapped under a pine tree out by the old Indian burial ground—"

"Arpit-arp."

"—a mile and a half past the north pasture."

Dad is quick, firm, decisive. "Lassie, you get back up there and stand watch over Timmy. Mom and I will go for Doc Walker. Hurry now!"

The dog hesitates at the door: "Rarfarrar-ra!"

"Right!" says Dad. "Mom, fetch the chain saw."

See the woods again. See the mud-running burial ground, the fallen pine, and there: Timmy! He lies in a puddle, eyes closed, breathing slow. The hiss of the rain is nasty as static. See it work: scattering leaves, digging trenches, inciting streams to swallow their banks. It lies deep now in the low areas, and in the mid areas, and in the high areas. Now see the dam some indeterminate distance off, the yellow water, like urine, churning over its lip, the ugly earthen belly distended, bloated with the pressure. Raindrops pock the surface like a plague.

Now see the pine once more . . . and . . . what is it? There! The coyote! Sniffing, furtive, the malicious eyes, the crouch, the slink. He stiffens when he spots the boy—but then he slouches closer, a rubbery dangle drooling from between his mismeshed teeth. Closer. Right over the prone figure now, stooping, head dipping between shoulders, irises caught in the corners of his eyes: wary, sly, predatory: a vulture slavering over fallen life.

But wait! Here comes Lassie! Sprinting out of the wheat field, bounding rock to rock across the crazed river, her limbs contourless with speed and purpose.

The jolting front seat of the Ford. Dad, Mom, the Doctor, all dressed in slickers and flap-brimmed hats, sitting shoulder to shoulder behind the clapping wipers, their jaws set with determination, eyes aflicker with downright gumption.

The coyote's jaws, serrated grinders, work at the bones of Timmy's hand. The boy's eyelids flutter with the pain, and he lifts his head feebly—but slaps it down again, flat, lifeless, in the mud. Now see Lassie blaze over the hill, show-dog indignation aflame in her eyes. The scrag of a coyote looks up at her, drooling blood, choking down choice bits of flesh. He looks up from eyes that go back thirty million years. Looks up unmoved, uncringing, the ghastly snout and murderous eyes less a physical than a philosophical challenge. See the collie's expression alter in mid-bound—the countenance of offended A.K.C. morality giving way, dissolving. She skids to a halt, drops her tail and approaches him, a buttery gaze in her golden eyes. She licks the blood from his vile lips.

The dam. Impossibly swollen, the rain festering the yellow surface, a hundred new streams rampaging in, the pressure of those millions of gallons hard-punching millions more. There! The first gap, the water flashing out, a boil splattering. The dam shudders, splinters, blasts to pieces like crockery. The roar is devastating.

The two animals start at the terrible rumbling. Still working their gummy jaws, they dash up the far side of the hill. See the white-tipped tail retreating side by side with the hacked and tick-crawling one—both tails like banners as the animals disappear into the trees at the top of the rise. Now look back to the rain, the fallen pine in the crotch of the valley, the spot of the boy's head. Oh, the sound of it, the wall of water at the far end of the valley, smashing through the little declivity, a God-sized fist prickling with shattered trunks and boulders, grinding along, a planet dislodged. And see Timmy: eyes closed, hair plastered, arm like meatmarket leftovers.

But now see Mom and Dad and the Doctor struggling over the rise, the torrent seething closer, booming and howling. Dad launches himself in full charge down the hillside—but the water is already sweeping over the fallen pine, lifting it like paper. There is a confusion, a quick clip of a typhoon at sea—is that a flash of golden hair?— and it is over. The valley fills to the top of the rise, the water ribbed and rushing.

But we have stopped looking. For we go sweeping up and out of the dismal rain, back to magnificent wheat fields in midday sun. There is a boy cupping his hands to his mouth and he is calling: "Laahh-sie! Laahh-sie!"

Then we see what we must see—way out there at the end of the field— the ripple, the dashing furrow, the blur of the streaking dog, white chest, flashing feet.

Verona: A Young Woman Speaks

Harold Brodkey

I know a lot! I know about happiness! I don't mean the love of God either: I mean I know the human happiness with the crimes in it.

Even the happiness of childhood.

I think of it now as a cruel, middle-class happiness.

Let me describe one time—one day, one night.

I was quite young, and my parents and I—there were just the three of us—were travelling from Rome to Salzburg, journeying across a quarter of Europe to be in Salzburg for Christmas, for the music and the snow. We went by train because planes were erratic, and my father wanted us to stop in half a dozen Italian towns and see paintings and buy things. It was absurd, but we were all three drunk with this; it was very strange: we woke every morning in a strange hotel, in a strange city. I would be the first one to wake; and I would go to the window and see some tower or palace; and then I would wake my mother and be justified in my sense of wildness and belief and adventure by the way she acted, her sense of romance at being in a city as strange as I had thought it was when I had looked out the window and seen the palace or the tower.

We had to change trains in Verona, a darkish, smallish city at the edge of the Alps. By the time we got there, we'd bought and bought our way up the Italian peninsula: I was dizzy with shopping and new possessions: I hardly knew who I was, I owned so many new things: my reflection in any mirror or shopwindow was resplendently fresh and new, disguised even, glittering, I thought. I was seven or eight years old. It seemed to me we were almost in a movie or in the pages of a book: only the simplest and most light-filled words and images can suggest what I thought we were then. We went around shiningly: we shone everywhere. *Those clothes*. It's easy to buy a child. I had a new dress, knitted, blue and red, expensive as hell, I think; leggings, also red; a red loden-cloth coat with a hood and a knitted cap for under the hood; marvelous lined gloves; fur-lined boots and a fur purse or carry-all, and a tartan skirt—and shirts and a scarf, and there was even more: a watch, a bracelet: more and more.

On the trains we had private rooms, and Momma carried games in her purse and things to eat, and Daddy sang carols off-key to me; and sometimes I became so intent on my happiness I would suddenly be in real danger of wetting myself; and Momma, who understood such emergencies, would catch the urgency in my voice and see my twisted face; and she—a large, good-looking woman—would whisk me to a toilet with amazing competence and unstoppability, murmuring to me. "Just hold on for a while," and she would hold my hand while I did it.

So we came to Verona, where it was snowing, and the people had stern, sad faces, beautiful, unlaughing faces. But if they looked at me, those serious faces would lighten, they would smile at me in my splendor. Strangers offered me candy, sometimes with the most excruciating sadness, kneeling or stooping to look directly into my face, into my eyes; and

Momma or Papa would judge them, the people, and say in Italian we were late, we had to hurry, or pause, and let the stranger touch me, talk to me, look into my face for a while. I would see myself in the eyes of some strange man or woman; sometimes they stared so gently I would want to touch their eyelashes, stroke those strange, large, glistening eyes. I knew I decorated life. I took my duties with great seriousness. An Italian count in Siena said I had the manners of an English princess—at times—and then he laughed because it was true I would be quite lurid; I ran shouting in *galleria*, a long room, hung with pictures, and with a frescoed ceiling: and I sat on his lap and wriggled: I was a wicked child, and I liked myself very much; and almost everywhere, almost every day, there was someone new to love me, briefly, while we traveled.

I understood I was special. I understood it *then*.

I knew that what we were doing, everything we did, involved money. I did not know if it involved mind or not, or style. But I knew about money somehow, checks and traveler's checks and the clink of coins. Daddy was a fountain of money: he said it was a spree; he meant for us to be amazed; he had saved money—we weren't really rich but we were to be for this trip. I remember a conservatory in a large house outside Florence and orange trees in tubs; and I ran there too. A servant, a man dressed in black, a very old man, mean-faced—he did not like being a servant anymore after the days of servants were over—and he scowled but he smiled at me, and at my mother, and even once at my father: we were clearly so separate from the griefs and weariness and cruelties of the world. We were at play, we were at our joys, and Momma was glad, with a terrible and naïve inner gladness, and she relied on Daddy to make it work: oh, she worked too, but she didn't know the secret of such—unreality: is that what I want to say? Of such a game, of such an extraordinary game.

There was a picture in Verona Daddy wanted to see; a painting; I remember the painter because the name Pisanello reminded me I had to go to the bathroom when we were in the museum, which was an old castle, Guelf or Ghibelline, I don't remember which; and I also remember the painting because it showed the hind end of the horse, and I thought that was not nice and rather funny, but Daddy was admiring; and so I said nothing.

He held my hand and told me a story so I wouldn't be bored as we walked from room to room in the museum/castle, and then we went outside into the snow, into the soft light when it snows, light coming though snow; and I was dressed in red and had on boots and my parents were young and pretty and had on boots too; and we could stay out in the snow if we wanted; and we did. We went to a square, a piazza—the Scaligera, I think; I don't remember—and just as we got there, the snowing began to bellow and then subside, to fall heavily and then sparsely, and then it stopped: and it was very cold, and there were pigeons everywhere in the piazza, on every cornice and roof, and all over the snow on the ground, leaving little tracks as they walked, while the air trembled in its just-after-snow and just-before-snow weight and thickness and grey seriousness of purpose. I had never seen so many pigeons or such a private and haunted place as that piazza, me in my new coat at the far rim of the world, the far rim of who knew what story, the rim of foreign beauty and Daddy's games, the edge, the white border of a season.

I was half mad with pleasure, anyway, and now Daddy brought five or six cones made of newspaper, wrapped, twisted; and they held grains of something like corn, yellow and white kernels of something; and he poured some on my hand and told me to hold my hand out; and then he backed away.

At first there was nothing, but I trusted him and I waited; and then the pigeons came. On heavy wings. Clumsy pigeony bodies. And red, unreal bird's feet. They flew at me, slowing at the last minute they lit on my arm and fed from my hand. I wanted to flinch, but I didn't. I closed my eyes and held my arm stiffly; and felt them peck and eat—from my hand, these free creatures, these flying things. I liked that moment. I liked my happiness. If I were mistaken about life and pigeons and my own nature, it didn't matter *then*.

The piazza was very silent, with snow; and Daddy poured grains on both my hands and then on the sleeves of my coat and on the shoulders of the coat, and I was entranced with yet more stillness, with this idea of his. The pigeons fluttered heavily in the heavy air, more and more of them, and sat on my arms and on my shoulders; and I looked at Momma and then at my father and then at the birds on me.

Oh, I'm sick of everything as I talk. There is happiness. It always makes me slightly ill. I lose my balance because of it.

The heavy birds, and the strange buildings, and Momma near, and Daddy too: Momma is pleased that I am happy and she is a little jealous; she is jealous of everything Daddy does; she is a woman of enormous spirit; life is hardly big enough for her; she is drenched in wastefulness and prettiness. She knows things. She gets inflexible, though, and foolish at times, and temperamental; but she is a somebody, and she gets away with a lot, and if she is near, you can feel her, you can't escape her, she's that important, that echoing, her spirit is that powerful in the space around her.

If she weren't restrained by Daddy, if she weren't in love with him, there is no knowing what she might do: she does not know. But she manages almost to be gentle because of him; he is incredibly watchful and changeable and he gets tired; he talks and charms people; sometimes, then, Momma and I stand nearby, like moons; we brighten and wane; and after a while, he comes to us, to the moons, the big one, and the little one, and we welcome him, and he is always, to my surprise, he is always surprised, as if he didn't deserve to be loved, as if it were time he was found out.

Daddy is very tall, and Momma is watching us, and Daddy anoints me again and again with the grain. I cannot bear it much longer. I feel joy or amusement or I don't know what; it is all through me, like a nausea—I am ready to scream and laugh, that laughter that comes out like magical, drunken, awful and yet pure spit or vomit or God knows what, that makes me a child mad with laughter. I become brilliant, gleaming, soft: an angel, a great bird-child of laughter.

I am ready to be like that, but I hold myself back.

There are more and more birds near me. They march around my feet and peck at falling and fallen grains. One is on my head. Of those on my arms, some move their wings, fluff those frail, feather-loaded wings, stretch them. I cannot bear it, they are so frail, and I am, at the moment, the kindness of the world that feeds them in the snow.

All at once, I let out a splurt of laughter: I can't stop myself and the birds fly away but not far; they circle around me, above me; and some wheel high in the air and drop as they return; they all returned, some in clouds and clusters driftingly, some alone and angry, pecking at others; some with a blind, animal-strutting abruptness. They gripped my coat and fed themselves. It started to snow again.

I was there in my kindness, in that piazza, within reach of my mother and father.

Oh, how will the world continue? Daddy suddenly understood I'd had enough, I was at the end of my strength—Christ, he was alert—and he picked me up, and I went limp, my arm around his neck, and the snow fell. Momma came near and pulled the hood lower and said there were snowflakes in my eyelashes. She knew he had understood, and she wasn't sure she had; she wasn't sure he ever watched her so carefully. She became slightly unhappy, and so she walked like a clumsy boy beside us, but she was so pretty: she had powers, anyway.

We went to a restaurant, and I behaved very well, but I couldn't eat, and then we went to the train and people looked at us, but I couldn't smile; I was too dignified, too sated; some leftover—pleasure, let's call it—made my dignity very deep. I could not stop remembering the pigeons, or that Daddy loved me in a way he did not love Momma; and Daddy was alert, watching the luggage, watching strangers for assassination attempts or whatever; he was on duty; and Momma was pretty and alone and *happy*, defiant in that way.

And then, you see, what she did was wake me in the middle of the night when the train was chugging up a very steep mountainside; and outside the window, visible because our compartment was dark and the sky was clear and there was a full moon, were mountains, a landscape of mountains everywhere, big mountains, huge ones, impossible, all slanted and pointed and white with snow, and absurd, sticking up into an ink-blue sky and down into blue, blue shadows, miraculously deep. I don't know how to say what it was like: they were not like anything I knew: they were high things; and we were up high in the train and we were climbing higher, and it was not at all true, but it was, you see. I put my hands on the window and stared at the wild, slanting, unlikely marvels, whiteness and dizziness and moonlight and shadows cast by moonlight, not real, not familiar, not pigeons, but a clean world.

We sat a long time, Momma and I, and stared, and then Daddy woke up and came and looked too. "It's pretty," he said, but he didn't really understand. Only Momma and I did. She said to him, "When I was a child, I was bored all the time, my love—I thought nothing would ever happen to me—and now these things are happening—and you have happened." I think he was flabbergasted by her love in the middle of the night; he smiled at her, oh, so swiftly that I was jealous, but I stayed quiet; and after a while, in his silence and amazement at her, at us, he began to seem different from us, from Momma and me; and then he fell asleep again; Momma and I didn't; we sat at the window and watched all night, watched the mountains and the moon, the clean world. We watched together.

Momma was the winner.

We were silent, and in silence we spoke of how we loved men and how dangerous men were and how they stole everything from you no matter how much you gave—but we didn't say it aloud.

We looked at mountains until dawn, and then when dawn came, it was too pretty for me—there was pink and blue and gold, in the sky, and on icy places, brilliant pink and gold flashes, and the snow was colored too, and I said, "Oh," and sighed; and each moment was more beautiful than the one before and I said, "I love you, Momma." Then I fell asleep in her arms.

That was happiness then.

His Son, in His Arms, in Light, Aloft

Harold Brodkey

My father is chasing me.

My God, I feel it up and down my spine, the thumping on the turf, the approach of his hands, his giant hands, the huge ramming increment of his breath as he draws near: a widening effort. I feel it up and down my spine and in my mouth and belly—Daddy is so swift: who ever heard of such swiftness? Just as in stories. . . .

I can't escape him, can't fend him off, his arms, his rapidity, his will. His interest in me.

I am being lifted into the air—and even as I pant and stare blurredly, limply, mindlessly, a map appears, of the dark ground where I ran: as I hang limply and rise anyway on the fattened bar of my father's arm, I see that there's the grass, there's the path, there's a bed of flowers.

I straighten up. There are the lighted windows of our house, some distance away. My father's face, full of noises, is near: it looms: his hidden face: is that you, old money-maker? My butt is folded on the trapeze of his arm. My father is as big as an automobile.

In the oddly shrewd-hearted torpor of being carried home in the dark, a tourist, in my father's arms, I feel myself attached by my heated-by-running dampness to him: we are attached, there are binding oval stains of warmth.

In most social talk, most politeness, most literature, most religion, it is as if violence didn't exist—except as sin, something far away. This is flattering to women. It is also conducive to grace—because the heaviness of fear, the shadowy henchmen selves that fear attaches to us, that fear sees in others, is banished.

Where am I in the web of jealousy that trembles at every human movement?

What detectives we have to be.

What if I am wrong? What if I remember incorrectly? It does not matter. This is fiction—a game—of pleasures, of truth and error, as at the sensual beginning of a sensual life.

My father, Charley, as I knew him, is invisible in any photograph I have of him. The man I hugged or ran toward or ran from is not in any photograph: a photograph shows someone of whom I think: *Oh, was he like that?*

But in certain memories, *he* appears, a figure, a presence, and I think, *I know him.*

It is embarrassing to me that I am part of what is unsayable in any account of his life.

* * *

When Momma's or my sister's excesses, of mood, or of shopping, angered or sickened Daddy, you can smell him then from two feet away: he has a dry, achy little stink of a rapidly fading interest in his life with us. At these times, the women in a spasm of wit turn to me; they comb my hair, clean my face, pat my bottom or my shoulder, and send me off; they bid me to go cheer up Daddy.

Sometimes it takes no more than a tug at his newspaper: the sight of me is enough; or I climb on his lap, mimic his depression; or I stand on his lap, press his head against my chest. . . . His face is immense, porous, complex with stubble, bits of talcum on it, unlikely colors, unlikely features, a bald brow with a curved square of lamplight in it. About his head there is a nimbus of sturdy wickedness, of unlikelihood. If his mood does not change, something tumbles and goes dead in me.

Perhaps it is more a nervous breakdown than heartbreak: I have failed him: his love for me is very limited: I must die now. I go somewhere and shudder and collapse—a corner of the dining room, the back stoop or deck: I lie there, empty, grief-stricken, literally unable to move—I have forgotten my limbs. If a memory of them comes to me, the memory is meaningless. . . .

Momma will then stalk in to wherever Daddy is and say to him, "Charley, you can be mad at me, I'm used to it, but just go take a look and see what you've done to the child. . . ."

My uselessness toward him sickens me. Anyone who fails toward him might as well be struck down, abandoned, eaten.

Perhaps it is an animal state: I-have-nothing-left, I-have-no-place-in-this-world.

Well, this is his house. Momma tells me in various ways to love him. Also, he is entrancing—he is so big, so thunderish, so smelly, and has the most extraordinary habits, reading newspapers, for instance, and wiggling his shoe: his shoe is gross: kick someone with that and they'd fall into next week.

Some memories huddle in a grainy light. What it is is a number of similar events bunching themselves, superimposing themselves, to make a false memory, a collage, a mental artifact. Within the boundaries of one such memory one plunges from year to year, is small and helpless, is a little older: one remembers it all but it is nothing that happened, that clutch of happenings, of associations, those gifts and ghosts of a meaning.

I can, if I concentrate, whiten the light—or yellow-whiten it, actually— and when the graininess goes, it is suddenly one afternoon.

I could not live without the pride and belonging-to-himness of being that man's consolation. He had the disposal of the rights to the out-of-doors— he was the other, the other-not-a-woman: he was my strength, literally, my strength if I should cry out.

Flies and swarms of the danger of being unfathered beset me when I bored my father: it was as if I were covered with flies on the animal plain where some ravening wild dog would leap up, bite and grip my muzzle, and begin to bring about my death.

I had no protection: I was subject now to the appetite of whatever inhabited the dark.

A child collapses in a sudden burst of there-is-nothing-here, and that is added onto nothingness, the nothing of being only a child concentrating on there being nothing there, no hope, no ambition: there is a despair but one without magnificence except in the face of its completeness: *I am a child and am without strength of my own.*

I have—in my grief—somehow managed to get to the back deck: I am sitting in the early evening light; I am oblivious to the light. I did and didn't hear his footsteps, the rumble, the house thunder dimly (behind and beneath me), the thunder of his-coming-to-rescue-me. . . . I did and didn't hear him call my name.

I spoke only the gaping emptiness of grief—that tongue—I understood I had no right to the speech of fathers and sons.

My father came out on the porch. I remember how stirred he was, how beside himself that I was so unhappy, that a child, a child he liked, should suffer so. He laid aside his own mood—his disgust with life, with money, with the excesses of the women—and he took on a broad-winged, malely flustering, broad-winged optimism—he was at the center of a great beating (of the heart, a man's heart, of a man's gestures, will, concern), dust clouds rising, a beating determination to persuade me that the nature of life, of *my* life, was other than I'd thought, other than whatever had defeated me—he was about to tell me there was no need to feel defeated, he was about to tell me that I was a good, or even a wonderful, child.

He kneeled—a mountain of shirt-front and trousers; a mountain that poured, clambered down, folded itself, re-formed itself: a disorderly massiveness, near to me, fabric-hung-and-draped: Sinai. He said, "Here, here, what is this—what is a child like you doing being so sad?" And: "Look at me. . . . It's all right. . . . Everything is all right. . . ." The misstatements of consolation are lies about the absolute that require faith—and no memory: the truth of consolation can be investigated if one is a proper child—that is to say, affectionate—only in a nonskeptical way.

"It's not all right!"

"It is—it is." It was and wasn't a lie: it had to do with power—and limitations: my limitations and his power: he could make it all right for me, everything, provided my everything was small enough and within his comprehension.

Sometimes he would say, "Son—" He would say it heavily—"Don't be sad—I don't want you to be sad—I don't like it when you're sad—"

I can't look into his near and, to me, factually incredible face—incredible because so large (as at the beginning of a love affair): I mean as a *face:* it is the focus of so many emotions and wonderments: he could have been a fool or was—it was possibly the face of a fool, someone self-centered, smug, an operator, semi-criminal, an intelligent psychoanalyst; it was certainly a mortal face—but what did the idea or word mean to me then—*mortal?*

There was a face; it was as large as my chest; there were eyes, inhumanly big, humid—what could they mean? How could I read them? How do you read eyes? I did not know about comparisons: how much more affectionate he was than other men, or less, how much better than common experience or how much worse in this area of being fathered my experience was with him: I cannot say even now: it is a statistical matter, after all, a matter of averages: but who at the present date can phrase the proper questions for the poll? And who will understand the hesitations, the blank looks, the odd expressions on the faces of the answerers?

The odds are he was a—median—father. He himself had usually a conviction he did pretty well: sometimes he despaired—of himself: but blamed me: my love: or something: or himself as a father: he wasn't good at managing stages between strong, clear states of feeling. Perhaps no one is.

Anyway, I knew no such terms as *median* then: I did not understand much about those parts of his emotions which extended past the rather clear area where my emotions were so often amazed. I chose, in some ways, to regard him seriously: in other ways, I had no choice—he was what was given to me.

I cannot look at him, as I said: I cannot see anything: if I look at him without seeing him, my blindness insults him: I don't want to hurt him at all: I want nothing: I am lost and have surrendered and am really dead and am waiting without hope.

He knows how to rescue people. Whatever he doesn't know, one of the things he knows in the haste and jumble of his heart, among the blither of tastes in his mouth and opinions and sympathies in his mind and so on, is the making yourself into someone who will help someone who is wounded. The dispersed and unlikely parts of him come together for a while in a clucking and focused arch of abiding concern. Oh how he plows ahead; oh how he believes in rescue! He puts—he *shoves*—he works an arm behind my shoulders, another under my legs: his arms, his powers shove at me, twist, lift and jerk me until I am cradled in the air, in his arms: "You don't have to be unhappy—you haven't hurt anyone—don't be sad—you're a *nice* boy. . . ."

I can't quite hear him, I can't quite believe him. I can't be *good*—the confidence game is to believe him, is to be a good child who trusts him—we will both smile then, he and I. But if I hear him, I have to believe him still. I am set up that way. He is so big; he is the possessor of so many grandeurs. If I believe him, hope and pleasure will start up again—suddenly—the blankness in me will be relieved, broken by these—meanings—that it seems he and I share in some big, attaching way.

In his pride he does not allow me to suffer: I belong to him.

He is rising, jerkily, to his feet and holding me at the same time. I do not have to stir to save myself—I only have to believe him. He rocks me into a sad-edged relief and an achingly melancholy delight with the peculiar lurch as he stands erect of establishing his balance and rectifying the way he holds me, so he can go on holding me, holding me aloft, against his chest: I am airborne: I liked to have that man hold me—in the air: I knew it was worth a great deal, the embrace, the gift of altitude. I am not exposed on the animal plain. I am not helpless.

The heat his body gives off! It is the heat of a man sweating with regret. His heartbeat, his burning, his physical force: ah, there is a large rent in the nothingness: the mournful apparition of his regret, the proof of his loyalty wake me: I have a twin, a massive twin, mighty company: Daddy's grief is at my grief: my nothingness is echoed in him (if he is going to have to live without me): the rescue was not quite a secular thing. The evening forms itself, a classroom, a brigade of shadows, of phenomena—the tinted air slides: there are shadowy skaters everywhere; shadowy cloaked people step out from behind things which are then hidden behind their cloaks. An alteration in the air proceeds from openings in the ground, from leaks in the sunlight which is being disengaged, like a stubborn hand, or is being stroked shut like my eyelids when I refuse to sleep: the dark rubs and bubbles noiselessly—and seeps—into the landscape. In the rubbed distortion of my inner air, twilight soothes: there are two of us breathing in close proximity here (he is telling me that grownups sometimes have things on their minds, he is saying mysterious things which I don't comprehend; I don't want to look at him: it takes two of my eyes to see one of his—and then I mostly see myself in his eye: he is even more unseeable from here, this holder: my head falls against his neck: "I know what you like—you'd like to go stand on the wall—would you like to see the sunset?" Did I nod? I think I did: I nodded gravely: but perhaps he did not need an answer since he thought he knew me well.

We are moving, this elephant and I, we are lumbering, down some steps, across grassy, uneven ground—the spoiled child in his father's arms—behind our house was a little park—we moved across the grass of the little park. There are sun's rays on the dome of the moorish bandstand. The evening is moist, fugitive, momentarily sneaking, half welcomed in this hour of crime. My father's neck. The stubble. The skin where the stubble stops. Exhaustion has me: I am a creature of failure, a locus of childishness, an empty skull: I am this being-young. We overrun the world, he and I, with his legs, with our eyes, with our alliance. We move on in a ghostly torrent of our being like this.

My father has the smell and feel of wanting to be my father. Guilt and innocence stream and re-stream in him. His face, I see now in memory, held an untiring surprise: as if some grammar of deed and purpose—of comparatively easy tenderness—startled him again and again, startled him continuously for a while. He said, "I guess we'll just have to cheer you up—we'll have to show you life isn't so bad—I guess we weren't any too careful of a little boy's feelings, were we?" I wonder if all comfort is alike.

A man's love is, after all, a fairly spectacular thing.

He said—his voice came from above me—he spoke out into the air, the twilight—"We'll make it all right—just you wait and see. . . ."

He said, "This is what you like," and he placed me on the wall that ran along the edge of the park, the edge of a bluff, a wall too high for me to see over, and which I was forbidden to climb: he placed me on the stubbed stone mountains and grouting of the wall-top. He put his arm around my middle: I leaned against him: and faced outward into the salt of the danger of the height, of the view (we were at least one hundred and fifty feet, we were, therefore, hundreds of feet in the air); I was flicked at by narrow, abrasive bands of wind, evening wind, veined with sunset's sun-crispness, strongly touched with coolness.

The wind would push at my eyelids, my nose, my lips. I heard a buzzing in my ears which signaled how high, how alone we were: this view of a river valley at night and of parts of four counties was audible. I looked into the hollow in front of me, a grand hole, an immense, bellying deep sheet or vast sock. There were numinous fragments in it—birds in what sunlight was left, bits of smoke faintly lit by distant light or mist, hovering inexplicably here and there: rays of yellow light, high up, touching a few high clouds.

It had a floor on which were creeks (and the big river), a little dim, a little glary at this hour, rail lines, roads, highways, houses, silos, bridges, trees, fields, everything more than half hidden in the enlarging dark: there was the shrinking glitter of far-off noises, bearded and stippled with huge and spreading shadows of my ignorance: it was panorama as a personal privilege. The sun at the end of the large, sunset-swollen sky was a glowing and urgent orange; around it were the spreading petals of pink and stratospheric gold: on the ground were occasional magenta flarings; oh it makes you stare and gasp; a fine, astral (not a crayon) red rode in a broad, magnificent band across the middlewestern sky: below us, for miles, shadowiness tightened as we watched (it seemed); above us, tinted clouds spread across the vast shadowing sky: there were funereal lights and sinkings everywhere. I stand on the wall and lean against Daddy, only somewhat awed and abstracted: the view does not own me as it usually does: I am partly in the hands of the jolting amusement—the conceit—of having been resurrected—by my father.

I understood that he was proffering me oblivion plus pleasure, the end of a sorrow to be henceforth remembered as Happiness. This was to be my privilege. This amazing man is going to rescue me from any anomaly or barb or sting in my existence: he is going to confer happiness on me: as a matter of fact, he has already begun.

"Just you trust me—you keep right on being cheered up—look at that sunset—that's some sunset, wouldn't you say?—everything is going to be just fine and dandy—you trust me—you'll see—just you wait and see. . . ."

* * *

Did he mean to be a swindler? He wasn't clear-minded—he often said, "I mean well." He did not think other people meant well.

I don't feel it would be right to adopt an Oedipal theory to explain what happened between him and me: only a sense of what he was like as a man, what certain moments were like, and what was said.

It is hard in language to get the full, irregular, heavy sound of a man.

He liked to have us "all dressed and nice when I come home from work," have us wait for him in attitudes of serene all-is-well contentment. As elegant as a Spanish prince I sat on the couch toying with an oversized model truck—what a confusion of social pretensions, technologies, class disorder there was in that. My sister would sit in a chair, knees together, hair brushed: she'd doze off if Daddy was late. Aren't we happy! Actually, we often are.

One day he came in plungingly, excited to be home and to have us as an audience rather than outsiders who didn't know their lines and who often laughed at him as part of their struggle to improve their parts in his scenes. We were waiting to have him approve of our tableau—he usually said something about what a nice family we looked like or how well we looked or what a pretty group or some such thing—and we didn't realize he was the tableau tonight. We held our positions, but we stared at him in a kind of mindless what-should-we-do-besides-sit-here-and-be-happy-and-nice? Impatiently he said, "I have a surprise for you, Charlotte—Abe Last has a heart after all." My father said something on that order: or "—a conscience after all"; and then he walked across the carpet, a man somewhat jerky with success—a man redolent of vaudeville, of grotesque and sentimental movies (he liked grotesquerie, prettiness, sentiment). As he walked, he pulled banded packs of currency out of his pockets, two or three in each hand. "There," he said, dropping one, then three in Momma's dressed-up lap. "There," he said, dropping another two: he uttered a "there" for each subsequent pack. "Oh, let me!" my sister cried and ran over to look—and then she grabbed two packs and said, "Oh, Daddy, how much *is* this?"

It was eight or ten thousand dollars, he said. Momma said, "Charley,

503

what if someone sees—we could be robbed—why do you take chances like this?"

Daddy harrumphed and said, "You have no sense of fun—if you ask me, you're afraid to be happy. I'll put it in the bank tomorrow—if I can find an honest banker—here, young lady, put that money down: you don't want to prove your mother right, do you?"

Then he said, "I know one person around here who knows how to enjoy himself—" and he lifted me up, held me in his arms.

He said, "We're going outside, this young man and I."

"What should I do with this money!"

"Put it under your mattress—make a salad out of it: you're always the one who worries about money," he said in a voice solid with authority and masculinity, totally pieced out with various self-satisfactions—as if he had gained a kingdom and the assurance of appearing as glorious in the histories of his time; I put my head back and smiled at the superb animal, at the rosy—and cowardly—panther leaping; and then I glanced over his shoulder and tilted my head and looked sympathetically at Momma.

My sister shouted. "I know how to enjoy myself—I'll come too! . . ."

"Yes, yes," said Daddy, who was *never* averse to enlarging spheres of happiness and areas of sentiment. He held her hand and held me on his arm.

"Let him walk," my sister said. And: "He's getting bigger—you'll make a sissy out of him, Daddy. . . ."

Daddy said, "Shut up and enjoy the light—it's as beautiful as Paris and in our own backyard."

Out of folly, or a wish to steal his attention, or greed, my sister kept on: she asked if she could get something with some of the money; he dodged her question; and she kept on; and he grew peevish, so peevish, he returned to the house and accused Momma of having never taught her daughter not to be greedy—he sprawled, impetuous, displeased, semifrantic in a chair: "I can't enjoy myself—there is no way a man can live in this house with all of you—I swear to God this will kill me soon. . . ."

Momma said to him, "I can't believe in the things you believe in—I'm not a girl anymore: when I play the fool, it isn't convincing—you get angry with me when I try. You shouldn't get angry with her—you've spoiled her more than I have—and how do you expect her to act when you show her all that money—how do you think money affects people?"

I looked at him to see what the answer was, to see what he would answer. He said, "Charlotte, try being a rose and not a thorn."

At all times, and in all places, there is always the possibility that I will start to speak or will be looking at something and I will feel his face covering mine, as in a kiss and as a mask, turned both ways like that: and I am inside him, his presence, his thoughts, his language: *I* am languageless then for a moment, an automaton of repetition, a bagged piece of an imaginary river of descent.

I can't invent everything for myself: some always has to be what I already know: some of me always has to be him.

When he picked me up, my consciousness fitted itself to that position: I remember it—clearly. He could punish me—and did—by refusing to lift me, by denying me that union with him. Of course, the union was not one-sided: I was his innocence—as long as I was not an accusation, that is. I censored him—in that when he felt himself being, consciously, a father, he held back part of his other life, of his whole self: his shadows, his impressions, his adventures would not readily fit into me—what a gross and absurd rape that would have been.

So he was *careful*—he *walked on eggs*—there was an odd courtesy of his withdrawal behind his secrets, his secret sorrows and horrors, behind the curtain of what-is-suitable-for-a-child.

Sometimes he becomes simply a set of limits, of walls, inside which there is the caroming and echoing of my astounding sensibility amplified by being his son and in his arms and aloft; and he lays his sensibility aside or models his on mine, on my joy, takes his emotional coloring from me, like a mirror or a twin: his incomprehensible life, with its strengths, ordeals, triumphs, crimes, horrors, his sadness and disgust, is enveloped and momentarily assuaged by my direct and indirect childish consolation.

My gaze, my enjoying him, my willingness to be him, my joy at it, supported the baroque tower of his necessary but limited and maybe dishonest optimism.

One time he and Momma fought over money and he left: he packed a bag and went. Oh it was sad and heavy at home. I started to be upset, but then I retreated into an impenetrable stupidity: not knowing was better than being despairing. I was put to bed and I did fall asleep: I woke in the middle of the night; he had returned and was sitting on my bed—in the dark— a huge shadow in the shadows. He was stroking my forehead. When he saw my eyes open, he said in a sentimental, heavy voice, "I could never leave *you*—"

He didn't really mean it: I was an excuse: but he did mean it—the meaning and not-meaning were like the rise and fall of a wave in me, in the dark outside of me, between the two of us, between him and me (at other moments he would think of other truths, other than the one of he-couldn't-leave-me sometimes). He bent over sentimentally, painedly, not nicely, and he began to hug me; he put his head down, on my chest; my small heartbeat vanished into the near, sizable, anguished, angular, emotion-swollen one that was his. I kept advancing swiftly into wakefulness, my consciousness came rushing and widening blurredly, embracing the dark, his presence, his embrace. It's Daddy, it's Daddy—it's dark still—wakefulness rushed into the dark grave or grove of his hugely extended presence. His affection. My arms stumbled: there was no adequate embrace in me—I couldn't lift *him*—I had no adequacy yet except that of my charm or what-have-you, except things the grownups gave me—not things: traits, qualities. I mean my hugging his head was nothing until he said, "Ah, you love me. . . . You're all right. . . ."

Momma said: "They are as close as two peas in a pod—they are just alike— that child and Charley. That child is God to Charley. . . ."

*　*　*

He didn't always love me.

In the middle of the night that time, he picked me up after a while, he wrapped me in a blanket, held me close, took me downstairs in the dark; we went outside, into the night; it was dark and chilly but there was a moon—I thought he would take me to the wall but he just stood on our back deck. He grew tired of loving me; he grew abstracted and forgot me: the love that had just a moment before been so intently and tightly clasping and nestling went away, and I found myself released, into the cool night air, the floating damp, the silence, with the darkened houses around us.

I saw the silver moon, heard my father's breath, felt the itchiness of the woolen blanket on my hands, noticed its wool smell. I did this alone and I waited. Then when he didn't come back, I grew sleepy and put my head down against his neck: he was nowhere near me. Alone in his arms, I slept.

Over and over a moment seems to recur, something seems to return in its entirety, a name seems to be accurate: and we say it always happens like this. But we are wrong, of course.

I was a weird choice as someone for him to love.

So different from him in the way I was surprised by things.

I am a child with this mind. I am a child he has often rescued.

Our attachment to each other manifests itself in sudden swoops and grabs and rubs of attention, of being entertained, by each other, at the present moment.

I ask you, how is it possible it's going to last?

Sometimes when we are entertained by each other, we are bold about it, but just as frequently, it seems embarrassing, and we turn our faces aside.

His recollections of horror are more certain than mine. His suspicions are more terrible. There are darknesses in me I'm afraid of, but the ones in him don't frighten me but are like the dark in the yard, a dark a child like me might sneak into (and has)—a dark full of unseen shadowy almost-glowing presences—the fear, the danger—are desirable—difficult—with the call-to-be-brave: the childish bravura of *I must endure this* (knowing I can run away if I choose).

The child touches with his pursed, jutting, ignorant lips the large, handsome, odd, humid face of his father who can run away too. More dangerously.

He gave away a car of his that he was about to trade in on a new one: he gave it to a man in financial trouble; he did it after seeing a movie about crazy people being loving and gentle with each other and everyone else: Momma said to Daddy, "You can't do anything you want—you can't listen to your feelings—you have a family. . . ."

After seeing a movie in which a child cheered up an old man, he took me to visit an old man who probably was a distant relative, and who hated me at sight, my high coloring, the noise I might make, my father's affection for me: "Will he sit still? I can't stand noise. Charley, listen, I'm in bad shape—I think I have cancer and they won't tell me—"

"Nothing can kill a tough old bird like you, Ike. . . ."

The old man wanted all of Charley's attention—and strength—while he talked about how the small threads and thicker ropes that tied him to life were being cruelly tampered with.

Daddy patted me afterward, but oddly he was bored and disappointed in me as if I'd failed at something.

He could not seem to keep it straight about my value to him or to the world in general; he lived at the center of his own intellectual shortcomings and his moral price: he needed it to be true, as an essential fact, that goodness—or innocence—was in him or was protected by him, and that, therefore, he was a good *man* and superior to other men, and did not deserve—certain common masculine fates—horrors—tests of his courage—certain pains. It was necessary to him to have it be true that he knew what real goodness was and had it in his life.

Perhaps that was because he didn't believe in God, and because he felt (with a certain self-love) that people, out in the world, didn't appreciate him and were needlessly difficult—"unloving": he said it often—and because it was true he was shocked and guilty and even enraged when he was "forced" into being unloving himself, or when he caught sight in himself of such a thing as cruelty, or cruel nosiness, or physical cowardice— God, how he hated being a coward—or hatred, physical hatred, even for me, if I was coy or evasive or disinterested or tired of him: it tore him apart literally—bits of madness, in varying degrees, would grip him as in a Greek play: I see his mouth, his salmon-colored mouth, showing various degrees of sarcasm—sarcasm mounting into bitterness and even a ferocity without tears that always suggested to me, as a child, that he was near tears but had forgotten in his ferocity that he was about to cry.

Or he would catch sight of some evidence, momentarily inescapable— in contradictory or foolish statements of his or in unkept promises that it was clear he had never meant to keep, had never made any effort to keep— that he was a fraud; and sometimes he would laugh because he was a fraud—a good-hearted fraud, he believed—or he would be sullen or angry, a fraud caught either by the tricks of language so that in expressing affection absentmindedly he had expressed too much; or caught by greed and self-concern: he hated the evidence that he was mutable as hell: that he loved sporadically and egotistically, and often with rage and vengeance, and that madness I mentioned earlier: he couldn't stand those things: he usually forgot them; but sometimes when he was being tender, or noble, or self-sacrificing, he would sigh and be very sad—maybe because the good stuff was temporary. I don't know. Or sad that he did it only when he had the time and was in the mood. Sometimes he forgot such things and was superbly confident—or was that a bluff?

I don't know. I really can't speak for him.

I look at my hand and then at his; it is not really conceivable to me that both are hands: mine is a sort of a hand. He tells me over and over that I must not upset him—he tells me of my power over him—I don't know how to take such a fact—is it a fact? I stare at him. I gasp with the ache of life stirring in me—again: again: *again*—I ache with tentative and complete and then again tentative belief.

For a long time piety was anything at all sitting still or moving slowly and not rushing at me or away from me but letting me look at it or be near it without there being any issue of safety-about-to-be-lost.

This world is evasive.

But someone who lets you observe him is not evasive, is not hurtful, at that moment: it is like in sleep where *the other* waits—the Master of Dreams—and there are doors, doorways opening into farther rooms where there is an altered light, and which I enter to find—what? That someone is gone? That the room is empty? Or perhaps I find a vista, of rooms, of archways, and a window, and a peach tree in flower—a tree with peach-colored flowers in the solitude of night.

I am dying of grief, Daddy. I am waiting here, limp with abandonment, with exhaustion: perhaps I'd better believe in God. . . .

My father's virtues, those I dreamed about, those I saw when I was awake, those I understood and misunderstood, were, as I felt them, in dreams or wakefulness, when I was a child, like a broad highway opening into a small dusty town that was myself; and down that road came bishops and slogans, Chinese processions, hasidim in a dance, the nation's honor and glory *in its young people*, baseball players, singers who sang "with their whole hearts," automobiles and automobile grilles, and grave or comic bits of instruction. This man is attached to me and makes me light up with festal affluence and oddity; he says, "I think you love me."

He was right.

He would move his head—his giant face—and you could observe in his eyes the small town which was me in its temporary sophistication, a small town giving proof on every side of its arrogance and its prosperity and its puzzled contentment.

He also instructed me in hatred: he didn't mean to, not openly: but I saw and picked up the curious buzzing of his puckered distastes, a nastiness of dismissal that he had: a fetor of let-them-all-kill-each-other. He hated lots of people, whole races: he hated ugly women.

He conferred an odd inverted splendor on awfulness—because *he* knew about it: he went into it every day. He told me not to want that, not to want to know about that: he told me to go on being just the way I was— "a nice boy."

When he said something was unbearable, he meant it; he meant he could not bear it.

In my memories of this time of my life, it seems to be summer all the time, even when the ground is white: I suppose it seems like summer because I was never cold.

Ah: I wanted to see. . . .

My father, when he was low (in spirit) would make rounds, inside his head, checking on his consciousness, to see if it was safe from inroads by *"the unbearable"*: he found an all-is-well in a quiet emptiness. . . .

In an uninvadedness, he found the weary complacency and self-importance of All is Well.

(The woman liked invasions—up to a point).

One day he came home, mysterious, exalted, hatted and suited, roseate, handsome, a little sweaty—it really was summer that day. He was exalted— as I said—but nervous toward me—anxious with promises.

And he was, oh, somewhat angry, justified, toward the world, toward me, not exactly as a threat (in case I didn't respond) but as a jumble.

He woke me from a nap, an uneasy nap, lifted me out of bed, me, a child who had not expected to see him that afternoon—I was not particularly happy that day, not particularly pleased with him, not pleased with him at all, really.

He dressed me himself. At first he kept his hat on. After a while, he took it off. When I was dressed, he said, "You're pretty sour today," and he put his hat back on.

He hustled me down the stairs; he held my wrist in his enormous palm—immediate and gigantic to me and blankly suggestive of a meaning I could do nothing about except stare at blankly from time to time in my childish life.

We went outside into the devastating heat and glare, the blathering, humming afternoon light of a midwestern summer day: a familiar furnace.

We walked along the street, past the large, silent houses, set, each one, in hard, pure light. You could not look directly at anything, the glare, the reflections were too strong.

Then he lifted me in his arms—aloft.

He was carrying me to help me because the heat was bad—and worse near the sidewalk which reflected it upward into my face—and because my legs were short and I was struggling, because he was in a hurry and because he liked carrying me, and because I was sour and blackmailed him with my unhappiness, and he was being kind with a certain—limited—mixture of exasperation-turning-into-a-degree-of-mortal-love.

Or it was another time, really early in the morning, when the air was partly asleep, partly adance, but in veils, trembling with heavy moisture. Here and there, the air broke into a string of beads of pastel colors, pink, pale green, small rainbows, really small, and very narrow. Daddy walked rapidly. I bounced in his arms. My eyesight was unfocused—it bounced too. Things were more than merely present: they pressed against me: they had the aliveness of myth, of the beginning of an adventure when nothing is explained as yet.

All at once we were at the edge of a bankless river of yellow light. To be truthful, it was like a big, wooden beam of fresh, unweathered wood: but we entered it: and then it turned into light, cooler light than in the hot humming afternoon but full of bits of heat that stuck to me and then were blown away, a semi-heat, not really friendly, yet reassuring: and very dimly sweaty; and it grew, it spread: this light turned into a knitted cap of light, fuzzy, warm, woven, itchy: it was pulled over my head, my hair, my forehead, my eyes, my nose, my mouth.

So I turned my face away from the sun—I turned it so it was pressed against my father's neck mostly—and then I knew, in a childish way, knew from the heat (of his neck, of his shirt collar), knew by childish deduction, that his face was unprotected from the luminousness all around us: and I looked; and it was so: his face, for the moment unembarrassedly, was caught in that light. In an accidental glory.

The Misfits

Arthur Miller

Wind blew down from the mountains for two nights, pinning them to their little camp on the desert floor. Around the fire on the grand plateau between the two mountain ranges, they were the only moving things. But awakening now with the first pink of dawn they heard the hush of a windless morning. Quickly the sky flared with true dawn like damp paper catching fire, and the shroud of darkness slipped off the little plane and the truck standing a few yards away.

As soon as they had eaten breakfast they took their accustomed positions. Perce Howland went to the tail, ready to unlash the ropes, Gay Langland stood near the propeller, and both watched the pilot, Guido Racanelli, loading his shotgun pistol and stowing it under the seat in the cockpit. He looked thoughtful, even troubled, zipping up the front of his ripped leather jacket. "Sumbitch valve is rattling," he complained.

"It's better than wages, Guido," Perce called from the tail.

"Hell it is if I get flattened up there," Guido said.

"You know them canyons," Gay Langland said.

"Gay, it don't mean a damn thing what the wind does down here. Up there's where it counts." He thumbed toward the mountains behind them. "I'm ten feet from rocks at the bottom of a dive; the wind smacks you down then and you never pull up again."

They saw he was serious so they said nothing. Guido stood still for a moment, studying the peaks in the distance, his hard, melon cheeks browned by wind, the white goggle marks around his eyes turning him into some fat jungle bird. At last he said, "Oh, hell with it. We'll get the sumbitches." He climbed into the cockpit calling to Gay, "Turn her over!"

Perce Howland quickly freed the tail and then the wing tips and Gay hurried to the propeller, swung the blade down and hopped back. A puff of white smoke floated up from the engine ports.

"Goddam car gas," Guido muttered. They were buying low octane to save money. Then he called, "Go again, Gay-boy; ignition on!" Gay reached up and pulled the propeller down and jumped back. The engine said its "Chaahh!" and the fuselage shuddered and the propeller turned into a wheel in the golden air. The little, stiff-backed plane tumbled toward the open desert, bumping along over the sage clumps and crunching whitened skeletons of winter-killed cattle, growing smaller as it shouldered its way over the broken ground, until its nose turned upward and space opened between the doughnut tires and the desert, and it turned and flew back over the heads of Gay and Perce. Guido waved down, a stranger now, fiercely goggled and wrapped in leather. The plane flew away, losing itself against the orange and purple mount which vaulted from the desert to hide from the cowboys' eyes the wild animals they wanted for themselves.

They had at least two hours before the plane would fly out of the mountains, driving the horses before it, so they washed the plates and the cups and stored them in the aluminum grub box. If Guido did find horses, they would break camp and return to Bowie tonight, so they packed up their bedrolls with sailors' tidiness and laid them neatly side by side on the ground. Six great truck tires, each with a rope coiled within, lay on the open truck bed. Gay Langland looked them over and touched them with his hand, trying to think if there was anything they were leaving behind. Serious as he was he looked a little amused, even slightly surprised. He was forty-six years old but his ears still stuck out like a little boy's and his hair lay in swirls from the pressure of his hat. After two days and nights of lying around he was eager to be going and doing and he savored the pleasurable delay of this final inspection.

Perce Howland watched, his face dreamy and soft with his early morning somnambulist's stare. He stood and moved, bent over the tires and straightened himself as effortlessly as wheat, as though he had been created full-grown and dressed as he now was, hipless and twenty-two in his snug dungarees and tight plaid shirt and broad-brimmed hat pushed back on his blond head. Now Gay got into the cab and started the engine and Perce slid into the seat beside him. A thin border collie leaped in after him. "You nearly forgot Belle," he said to Gay. The dog snuggled down behind Gay's feet and they started off.

Thirty miles ahead stood the lava mountains which were the northern border of this desert, the bed of a bowl seven thousand feet in the air, a place no one ever saw excepting a few cowboys searching for strays. People in Bowie, sixty miles away, did not know of this place.

Now that they were on the move, following the two-track trail through the sage, they felt between them the comfort of purpose and their isolation. It was getting warm now. Perce slumped in his seat, blinking as though he would go to sleep, and the older man smoked a cigarette and let his body flow from side to side with the pitching of the truck. There was a moving cloud of dust in the distance, and Gay said, "Antelope," and Perce tipped his hat back and looked. "Must be doin' sixty," he said, and Gay said, "More."

After a while Perce said, "We better get over to Largo by tomorrow if we're gonna get into that rodeo. They's gonna be a crowd trying to sign up for that one."

"We'll drive down in the morning," Gay said.

"Like to win some money. I just wish I get me a good horse down there."

"They be glad to fix you up. You're known pretty good around here now."

Perce tucked his thumbs into his belt so his fingers could touch his prize, the engraved belt buckle with his name spelled out under the raised figure of the bucking horse. He had been coming down from Nevada since he was sixteen, picking up money at the local rodeos, but this trip had been different. Sometime, somewhere in the past weeks, he had lost the desire to go back home.

They rode in silence. Gay had to hold the gearshift lever in high or it would slip out into neutral when they hit a bump. The transmission fork was worn out, he knew, and the front tires were going, too. He dropped one hand to his pants pocket and felt the four silver dollars he had left from the ten Roslyn had given him.

As though he had read Gay's mind, Perce said, "Roslyn would've liked it up here. She'd liked to have seen that antelope, I bet."

Through the corner of his eye Gay watched the younger man, who was looking ahead with a little grin on his face. "Yeah. She's a damned good sport, old Roslyn." He watched Perce for any sign of guile.

"Only educated women I ever knew before was back home near Teachers College," Perce said. "I was learning them to ride for awhile, and I used to think, hell, education's everything. But when I saw the husbands they got married to, why I don't give them much credit. And they just as soon climb on a man as tell him good morning."

"Just because a woman's educated don't mean much. Woman's a woman," Gay said. The image of his wife came into his mind. For a moment he wondered if she was still living with the same man.

"You divorced?" Perce asked.

"No. I never bothered with it," Gay said. It surprised him how Perce said just what was on his mind sometimes. "How'd you know I was thinking of that?" he asked, grinning with embarrassment.

"Hell, I didn't know," Perce said.

"You're always doin' that. I think of somethin' and you say it,"

"That's funny," Perce said.

They rode on in silence. They were nearing the middle of the desert where they would turn east. Gay was driving faster now, holding onto the gearshift lever to keep it from springing into neutral. The time was coming soon when he would need about fifty dollars or sell the truck, because it would be useless without repairs. Without a truck and without a horse he would be down to what was in his pocket.

Perce spoke out of the silence. "If I don't win Saturday I'm gonna have to do something for money."

"Goddam, you always say what's in my mind."

Perce laughed. His face looked very young and pink. "Why?"

"I was just now thinkin'," Gay said, "what I'm gonna do for money."

"Well, Roslyn give you some," Perce said.

He said it innocently, and Gay knew it was innocent, and yet he felt angry blood moving into his neck. Something had happened in these five weeks since he'd met Perce and let him come home to Roslyn's house to sleep, and Gay did not know for sure what it was. Roslyn had taken to calling Perce cute, and now and again she would bend over and kiss him on the back of the neck when he was sitting in the living-room chair, drinking with them.

Not that that meant anything in itself because he'd known eastern women before, and it was just their way. What he wondered at was Perce's hardly noticing what she did to him. Sometimes it was like he'd already had her and could ignore her the way a man will who knows he's boss. Gay sensed the bottom of his life falling if it turned out Roslyn had really been loving this boy beside him. It had happened to him once before, but this frightened him even more and he did not know exactly why. Not that he couldn't do without her. There wasn't anybody or anything he couldn't do without. He had been all his life like Perce Howland, a man moving on or ready to. Only when he had discovered his wife with a stranger in a parked car did he understand he had never had a stake to which he'd been pleasantly tethered.

He had not seen her or his children for years, and only rarely thought about any of them. Any more than his father had thought of him very much after the day he had gotten on his pony, when he was fourteen, to go to town from the ranch, and had kept going into Montana and stayed there for three years. He lived in his country and his father did and it was the same endless range wherever he went and it connected him sufficiently with his father and his wife and his children. All might turn up sometime in some town or at some rodeo where he might happen to look over his shoulder and see his daughter or one of his sons, or they might never turn up. He had neither left anyone nor not-left as long as they were all alive on these ranges, for everything here was always beyond the furthest shot of vision and far away, and mostly he had worked alone or with one or two men between distant mountains anyway.

He drove steadily across the grand plateau, and he felt he was going to be afraid. He was not afraid now, but something new was opening up inside him. He had somehow passed the kidding point: he had to work again and earn his way as he always had before he met Roslyn. Not that he didn't work for her, but it wasn't the same. Driving her car, repairing her house, running errands wasn't what you'd call work. Still it was too. Yet it wasn't either. He grew tired of thinking about it.

In the distance now he could see the shimmering wall of heat rising from the clay flatland they wanted to get to—a beige waste as bare and hard as pavement, a prehistoric lake bed thirty miles long by seventeen miles wide couched between two mountain ranges, where a man might drive a car at a hundred miles an hour with his hands off the wheel and never hit anything at all.

* * *

When they had rolled a few hundred yards onto the clay lake bed, Gay pulled up and shut off the engine. The air was still, in a dead, sunlit silence. Opening his door, he could hear a squeak in the hinge he had never noticed before. When they walked around out here they could hear their shirts rasping against their backs and the brush of a sleeve against their trousers. They looked back toward the mountains at whose feet they had camped and scanned the ridges for Guido's plane.

Perce Rowland said, "I sure hope they's five up in there."

"Guido spotted five last week, he said."

"He said he wasn't sure if one wasn't only a colt."

Gay let himself keep silence. He felt he was going to argue with Perce. "How long you think you'll be stayin' around here?" he asked.

"Don't know," Perce said, and spat over the side of the truck. "I'm gettin' a little tired of this, though."

"Well, it's better than wages."

"Hell, yes. Anything's better than wages."

Gay's eyes crinkled. "You're a real misfit, boy."

"That suits me fine," Perce said. They often had this conversation and savored it. "Better than workin' for some goddam cow outfit buckarooin' so somebody else can buy gas for his Cadillac."

"Damn right," Gay said.

"Hell, Gay, you are the most misfitted man I ever saw and you done all right."

"I got no complaints," Gay said.

"I don't want nothin' and I don't want to want nothin'."

"That's the way, boy."

Gay felt closer to him again and he was glad for it. He kept his eyes on the ridges far away. The sun felt good on his shoulders. "I think he's havin' trouble with them sumbitches up in there."

Perce stared out at the ridges. "Ain't two hours yet." Then he turned to Gay. "These mountains must be cleaned out by now, ain't they."

"Just about," Gay said. "Just a couple small herds left."

"What you goin' to do when you got these cleaned out?"

"Might go north, I think. Supposed to be some big herds in around Thighbone Mountain and that range up in there."

"How far's that?"

"North about a hundred miles. If I can get Guido interested."

Perce smiled. "He don't like movin' around much, does he?"

"He's just misfitted like us," Gay said. "He don't want nothin." Then he added, "They wanted him for an airline pilot flyin' up into Montana and back. Good pay too."

"Wouldn't do it, huh?"

"Not Guido," Gay said, grinning. "Might not like some of the passengers, he told them."

Both men laughed and Perce shook his head in tickled admiration for Guido. Then he said, "They wanted me take over the riding academy up home. Just stand around and see the customers get satisfied and put them girls off and on."

He fell silent. Gay knew the rest. It was the same story. It brought him closer to Perce and it was what he had liked about him in the first place. He had come on Perce in a bar where the boy was buying drinks for everybody with his rodeo winnings, and his hair still clotted with blood from a bucking horse's kick an hour earlier. Roslyn had offered to get a doctor for him and he had said, "Thank you, kindly. But if you're bad hurt you gonna die and the doctor can't do nothin', and if you ain't bad hurt you get better anyway without no doctor."

Now it suddenly came upon Gay that Perce must have known Roslyn before they had met in the bar. He stared at the boy's straight profile. "Want to come up north with me if I go?" he asked.

Perce thought a moment. "Think I'll stay around here. Not much rodeoin' up north."

"I might find a pilot up there if Guido won't come. And Roslyn drive us up in her car."

Perce turned to him, a little surprised. "Would she go up there?"

"Sure. She's a damn good sport," Gay said. He watched Perce's eyes, which had turned interested and warm.

Perce said, "Well, maybe; except to tell you the truth, Gay, I never feel comfortable takin' these horses."

"Somebody's goin' to take them if we don't."

"I know," Perce said. He turned to watch the far ridges again. "Just seems to me they belong up there."

"They ain't doin' nothin' up there but eatin' out good cattle range. The cow outfits shoot them down if they see them."

"I know," Perce said.

There was silence. Neither bug nor lizard nor rabbit moved on the great basin around them. Gay said, "I'd a soon sell them for riding horses, but they ain't big enough. And the freight's more than they're worth. You saw them—they ain't nothin' but skinny horses."

"I just don't know if I'd want to see like a hundred of them goin' for chicken feed, though. I don't mind like five or six, but a hundred's a lot of horses. I don't know."

Gay thought. "Well, if it ain't this it's wages. Around here anyway." He was speaking of himself and explaining himself.

They heard the shotgun off in the sky somewhere and they stopped moving. Gay slid out of the tire in which he had been lounging and off the truck. He went to the cab and brought out a pair of binoculars, blew dust off the lenses, mounted the truck and, with his elbows propped on his knees, he focused on the far mountains.

"See anything?" Perce asked.

"He's still in the pass, I guess," Gay said.

They sat still, watching the empty sky over the pass. The sun was making them perspire now and Gay wiped his wet eyebrows with the back of one hand. They heard the shotgun again. Gay spoke without lowering the glasses: "He's probably blasting them out of some corner."

"I see him," Perce said quickly. "I see him glintin', I see the plane."

It angered Gay that Perce had seen it first without glasses. In the glasses Gay could see the plane clearly now. The plane was flying out of the pass, circling back and disappearing into the pass again. "He's got them in the pass now. Just goin' back in for them."

Now Gay could see moving specks on the ground where the pass opened onto the desert table. "I see them," he said. "One, two, three, four. Four and a colt."

"We gonna take the colt?" Perce asked.

"Hell, can't take the mare without the colt."

Gay handed him the glasses. "Take a look."

Gay went forward to the cab and opened its door. His dog lay shivering on the floor under the pedals. He snapped his fingers and she leaped down to the ground and stood there, quivering as though the ground had hidden explosives everywhere. He climbed back onto the truck and sat on a tire beside Perce, who was looking through the glasses.

"He's divin' down on them. God, they sure can run."

"Let's have a look," Gay said.

The plane was dropping down from the arc of its climb and as the roaring motor flew over them they lifted their heads and galloped faster. They had been running now for over an hour and would slow down when the plane had to climb after a dive and the motor's noise grew quieter. As Guido climbed again Gay and Perce heard a shot, distant and harmless, and the shot sped the horses on as the plane took time to climb bank and turn. Then as the horses slowed to a trot the plane dived down over their backs again and their heads shot up and they galloped until the engine's roar receded. The sky was clear and lightly blue and only the little plane swung back and forth across the desert like the glinting tip of a magic wand, and the horses came on toward the vast striped clay bed where the truck was parked, and at its edge they halted.

The two men waited for the horses to reach the edge of the lake bed when Guido would land the plane and they would take off with the truck.

"They see the heat waves," Gay said, looking through the glasses. The plane dived down on them and they scattered but would not go forward onto the unknowable territory from the cooler, sage-dotted desert behind them. The men on the truck heard the shotgun again. Now the horses broke their formation and leaped onto the lake bed, all heading in different directions, but only trotting, exploring the ground under their feet and the

523

strange, superheated air in their nostrils. Gradually, as the plane wound around the sky to dive again, the horses closed ranks and slowly galloped shoulder to shoulder out onto the borderless waste, the colt a length behind with its nose nearly touching the mare's long tail.

"That's a big mare," Perce said. His eyes were still dreamy and his face was calm, but his skin had reddened.

"She's a bigger mare than usual up there, ya," Gay said. Both men knew the mustang herds lived in total isolation and that inbreeding had reduced them to the size of large ponies. The herd swerved now and they could see the stallion. He was smaller than the mare, but still larger than any they had brought down before. The other two horses were small, the way mustangs ought to be.

The plane was hurrying down for a landing now. Gay and Perce Howland got to their feet and each reached into a tire behind him and drew out a coil of rope whose ends hung in a hoop. They glanced out and saw Guido taxiing toward them and they strapped themselves to stanchions sticking up from the truck bed and stood waiting for him. He cut the engine twenty yards away and leaped out of the open cockpit before the plane had halted, its right wing tilted down, as always, because of the weak starboard shock absorber. He trotted over to the truck, lifting his goggles off and stuffing them into his torn jacket pocket. His face was puffed with preoccupation. He jumped into the cab of the truck and the collie dog jumped in after him and sat on the floor, quivering. He started the truck and they roared across the flat clay.

The herd was standing still in a small clot of dots more than two miles off. The truck rolled smoothly past sixty. Gay on the right front corner of the truck bed and Perce on the left pulled their hats down to their eyebrows against the rush of air and hefted the looped ropes which the wind was threatening to coil and foul in their palms. Guido knew that Gay was a good roper and that Perce was unsure, so he headed for the herd's left in order to come up to them on Gay's side of the truck if he could. This whole method of mustanging—the truck, the tires attached to ropes and the plane—was his idea, and once again he felt the joy of having thought of it all. It had awakened him to life after a year's hibernation. His wife dying in childbirth had been like a gigantic and insane ocean wave rising out of a calm sea, and it had left him stranded in his cousin's house in Bowie, suddenly a bachelor after eleven married years. Only this had broken the silence of the world for him, this roaring across the lake bed with his left boot ready over the brake pedal should the truck start to overturn on a sudden swerve.

The horses, at a standstill now, were staring at the oncoming truck, and the men saw that this herd was beautiful.

A wet spring had rounded them out, and they shone in the sunlight. The mare was almost black and the stallion and the two others were deeply brown. The colt was curly-coated and had a grey sheen. The stallion dipped his head suddenly and turned his back on the truck and galloped. The others turned and clattered after him, with the colt running alongside the mare. Guido pressed down on the gas and the truck surged forward, whining. They were a few yards behind the animals now and they could see the bottoms of their hoofs, fresh hoofs that made a gentle tacking clatter because they had never been shod. The truck was coming abreast of the mare now and beside her the others galloped, slim-legged and wet after roaming almost two hours.

As the truck drew alongside the mare and Gay began twirling his loop above his head, the whole herd wheeled away to the right and Guido jammed the gas peddle down and swung with them, but the truck tilted violently so he slowed down and fell behind them a few yards until they would straighten out and move ahead again. At the edge of their strength they wheeled like circus horses, almost tamely in their terror, and suddenly Guido saw a breadth between the stallion and the two browns and he sped in between, cutting the mare off at the heft with her colt. Now the horses stretched, the clatter quickened. Their hind legs straight back and their necks stretched low and forward. Gay whirled his loop over his head and the truck came up alongside the stallion whose lungs were screaming with exhaustion and Gay flung the noose. It fell on the stallion's head and, with a whipping of the lead, Gay made it slip down over his neck. The horse swerved away to the right and stretched the rope until the tire was pulled off the truck bed and dragged along the hard clay. The three men watched from the slowing truck as the stallion, with startled eyes, pulled the giant tire for a few yards, then reared up with his forelegs in the air and came down facing the tire and trying to back away from it. Then he stood there, heaving, his hind legs dancing in an arc from right to left and back again as he shook his head in the remorseless noose.

As soon as he was sure the stallion was secure, Guido turned sharply left toward the mare and the colt which were trotting idly together by themselves in the distance. The two browns were already disappearing toward the north, but they would halt soon because they were tired, while the mare might continue back into her familiar hills where the truck could not follow. He straightened the truck and jammed down the gas pedal. In a minute he drew up on her left side because the colt was running on her right. She was very heavy, he saw, and he wondered if she were a mustang at all. Then through his right window he saw the loop flying out and down over her head, and he saw her head fly up and then she fell back. He turned to the right, braking with his left boot, and he saw her dragging a tire and coming to a halt, with the free colt watching her and trotting beside her very close. Then he headed straight ahead across the flat toward two specks which rapidly enlarged until they became the two browns which were at a standstill and watching the oncoming truck. He came in between them and they galloped; Perce on the left roped one and Gay roped the other almost at the same time. And Guido leaned his head out of his window and yelled up at Perce. "Good boy!" he hollered, and Perce let himself return an excited grin, although there seemed to be some trouble in his eyes.

Guido made an easy half circle and headed back to the mare and the colt and slowed to a halt twenty yards away and got out of the cab.

The three men approached the mare. She had never seen a man and her eyes were wide in fear. Her rib cage stretched and collapsed very rapidly and there was a trickle of blood coming out of her nostrils. She had a heavy, dark brown mane and her tail nearly touched the ground. The colt with dumb eyes shifted about on its silly bent legs trying to keep the mare between itself and the men, and the mare kept shifting her rump to shield the colt from them.

They wanted now to move the noose higher up on the mare's neck because it had fallen on her from the rear and was tight around the middle of her neck where it could choke her if she kept pulling against the weight of the tire. Gay was the best roper, so Perce and Guido stood by as he twirled a noose over his head, then let it fall open softly, just behind the forefeet of the mare. They waited for a moment, then approached her and she backed a step. Then Gay pulled sharply on the rope and her forefeet were tied together. With another rope Gay lassoed her hind feet and she swayed and fell to the ground on her side. Her body swelled and contracted, but she seemed resigned. The colt stretched its nose to her tail and stood there as the men came to the mare and spoke quietly to her, and Guido bent down and opened the noose and slipped it up under her jaw. They inspected her for a brand, but she was clean.

"Never see a horse that size up here," Gay said to Guido.

Perce said, "She's no mustang. Might even be standard bred." He looked to Guido for confirmation.

Guido sat on his heels and opened the mare's mouth and the other two looked in with him. "She's fifteen if she's a day," Gay said. "She wouldn't be around much longer anyway."

"Ya, she's old." Perce's eyes were filled with thought.

Guido stood up and the three went back to the truck, and drove across the lake bed to the stallion.

"Ain't a bad-lookin' horse," Perce said.

He was standing still, heaving for breath. His head was down, holding the rope taut, and he was looking at them with deep brown eyes that were like the lenses of enormous binoculars. Gay got his rope ready. "He ain't nothin' but a misfit," he said. "You couldn't run cattle with him; he's too small to breed and too old to cut."

"He is small," Perce conceded. "Got a nice neck though."

"Oh, they're nice-*lookin'* horses, some of them," Guido said. "What the hell you goin' to do with them, though?"

Gay twirled the loop over his head and they spread out around the stallion. "They're just old misfit horses, that's all," he said, and he flung the rope behind the stallion's forelegs and the horse backed a step and he drew the rope and the noose bit into the horse's fetlocks drawing them together, and he swayed but he would not fall. "Take hold here," Gay called to Perce, who ran around the horse and took the rope from him and held it taunt. Then Gay went back to the truck, got another rope, returned to the rear of the horse and looped his hind legs. But the stallion would not fall. Guido stepped closer to push him over, but he swung his head and showed his teeth and Guido stepped back. "Pull him down!" Guido yelled to Gay and Perce, and they jerked their ropes to trip the stallion, but he righted himself and stood there, bound by the head to the tire and by his feet to the two ropes which the men held. Then Guido hurried over to Perce and took the rope from him and walked with it toward the rear of the horse and pulled hard. The stallion's forefeet slipped back and he came down on his knees and his nose struck the clay ground and he snorted as he struck, but he would not topple over and stayed there on his knees as though he were bowing to something, with his nose propping up his head against the ground and his sharp bursts of breath blowing up dust in little clouds under his nostrils. Now Guido gave the rope back to young Perce Howland who held it taut and he came up alongside the stallion's neck and laid his hands on the side of the neck and pushed and the horse fell over onto his flank and lay there and, like the mare, when he felt the ground against his body he seemed to let himself out and for the first time his eyes blinked and his breath came now in sighs and no longer fiercely. Guido shifted the noose up under his jaw, and they opened the ropes around his hoofs and when he felt his legs free he first raised his head curiously and then clattered up and stood there looking at them, from one to the other, blood dripping from his nostrils and a stain of deep red on both dusty knees.

Then the men moved without hurrying to the truck and Gay stored his two extra ropes and got behind the wheel with Guido beside him, and Perce climbed onto the back of the truck and lay down facing the sky and made a pillow with his palms.

Gay headed the truck south toward the plane. Guido was slowly catching his breath, and now he lighted a cigarette, puffed it and rubbed his left hand into his bare scalp. He sat gazing out the windshield and the side window. "I'm sleepy," he said.

"What you reckon?" Gay asked.

"What you?" Guido said.

"That mare might be six hundred pounds."

"I'd say about that, Gay."

"About four hundred apiece for the browns and a little more for the stallion. What's that come to?"

"Nineteen hundred, maybe two thousand," Guido said.

They fell silent figuring the money. Two thousand pounds at six cents a pound came to a hundred and twenty dollars. The colt might make it a few dollars more, but not much. Figuring the gas for the plane and the truck, and twelve dollars for their groceries, they came to the figure of a hundred dollars for the three of them. Guido would get forty-five, since he had used his plane, and Gay would get thirty-five, including the use of his truck, and Perce Howland, if he agreed, as he undoubtedly would, had the remaining twenty.

"We should've watered them the last time," Gay said. "They can pick up a lot of weight if you let them water."

"Yeah, let's be sure to do that," Guido said.

They knew they would as likely as not forget to water the horses before they unloaded them at the dealer's lot in Bowie. They would be in a hurry to unload and be free of the animals, free to pitch and roll with time in the bars or asleep in Roslyn's house or making a try in some rodeo. Once they had figured their shares they stopped thinking of money, and they divided it and even argued about it only because it was the custom of men. They had not come up here for the money.

Gay stopped the truck beside the plane. Guido opened his door and said, "See you in town. Let's get the other truck tomorrow morning."

"Perce wants to go over to Largo and sign up for the rodeo tomorrow," Gay said. "Tell ya—we'll go in and get the truck and come back here this afternoon maybe. Maybe we bring them in tonight."

"All right, if you want to. I'll see you boys tomorrow," Guido said, and he got out and stopped for a moment to talk to Perce.

"Perce?"

Guido smiled. "You sleeping?"

"I was about to."

"We figure about a hundred dollars clear. Twenty all right for you?"

"Ya, twenty's all right," Perce said. He hardly seemed to be listening.

"See you in town," Guido said, and turned on his bandy legs and waddled off to the plane where Gay was already standing with his hands on the propeller blade. Guido got in and Gay swung the blade down and the engine started immediately. Guido gunned the plane and she trundled off and into the sky and the two men on the ground watched her as she flew toward the mountains and away.

Now Gay returned to the truck and said, "Twenty all right?" And he said this because he thought Perce looked hurt.

"Heh? Ya, twenty's all right," Perce answered. Then he let himself down and stood beside the truck and wet the ground while Gay waited for him. Then Perce got into the cab and they drove off.

Perce agreed to come back this afternoon with Gay in the larger truck and load the horses, although as they drove across the lake bed in silence they both knew, gradually, that they would wait until morning, because they were tired now and would be more tired later. The mare and her colt stood between them and the sage desert toward which they were heading. Perce stared out the window at the mare and he saw that she was watching them, apprehensively but not in real alarm, and the colt was lying upright on the clay. Perce looked long at the colt as they approached and he thought about it waiting there beside the mare, unbound and free to go off, and he said to Gay, "Ever hear of a colt leave a mare?"

"Not that one," Gay said. "He ain't goin' nowhere."

Perce laid his head back and closed his eyes. His tobacco swelled out his left cheek and he let it soak there.

Now the truck left the clay lake bed and it pitched and rolled over the sage clumps. They would return to their camp and pick up their bedrolls.

"Think I'll go back to Roslyn's tonight," Gay said.

"Okay," Perce said and did not open his eyes.

"We can pick them up in the morning, then take you to Largo."

"Okay," Perce said.

Gay thought about Roslyn. She would probably razz them about all the work they had done for a few dollars, saying they were too dumb to figure in their labor time and other hidden expenses. To hear her sometimes they hadn't made any profit at all. "Roslyn going to feel sorry for the colt," Gay said, "so might as well not mention it."

Perce opened his eyes and looked out at the mountains. "Hell, she feeds that dog of hers canned dog food, doesn't she?"

Gay felt closer to Perce again and he smiled. "Sure does."

"Well, what's she think is in the can?"

"She knows what's in it."

"There's wild horses in the can," Perce said, as though it was part of an angry argument with himself.

They were silent for a while.

"You comin' back to Roslyn's with me or you gonna stay in town?"

"I'd just as soon go back with you."

"Okay," Gay said. He felt good about going into her cabin now. There would be her books on the shelves he had built for her, and they would have some drinks, and Perce would fall asleep on the couch and they would go into the bedroom together. He liked to come back to her after he had worked, more than when he had only driven her here and there or just stayed around her place. He liked his own money in his pocket when he came to her. And he tried harder to visualize how it would be with her and he thought of himself being forty-seven soon, and then nearing fifty. She would go back east one day, maybe this year, maybe next. He wondered again when he would begin turning grey and he set his jaw against the idea of himself grey and an old man.

Perce spoke, sitting up in his seat. "I want to phone my mother. Damn, I haven't called her all year." He sounded angry. He stared out the window at the mountains. He had the memory of how the colt looked and he felt an almost violent wish for it to be gone when they returned. Then he said, "I got to get to Largo tomorrow and register."

"We'll go," Gay said, sensing the boy's unaccountable irritation.

"I could use a good win," he said. He thought of five hundred dollars now, and of the many times he had won five hundred dollars. "You know something, Gay? I'm never goin' to amount to a damn thing." Then, suddenly, he laughed without restraint for a moment and then laid his head back and closed his eyes.

"I told you that the first time I met you, didn't I?" Gay grinned. He felt a bravery between them now, and he was relieved to see that Perce was grinning. He felt the mood coming on for some drinks at Roslyn's.

"That colt won't bring two dollars anyway," Perce said. "What you say we just left him there?"

"Why, you know he'd just follow the truck right into town."

After they had driven fifteen minutes without speaking, Gay said he wanted to go north very soon for the hundreds of horses that were supposed to be in the mountains there. But Perce had fallen fast asleep beside him. Gay wanted to tell about that expedition because as they rolled onto the highway from the desert he began to visualize Roslyn razzing them again, and it was clear to him that he had somehow failed to settle anything for himself; he had put in three days for thirty-five dollars and there would be no way to explain it so it made sense and it would be embarrassing. And yet he knew that it had all been the way it ought to be even if he could never explain it to her or anyone else. He reached out and nudged Perce, who opened his eyes and lolled his head over to face him. "You comin' up to Thighbone with me, ain't you?"

"Okay," Perce said, and went back to sleep.

Gay felt more peaceful now the younger man would not be leaving him. There was a future again, something to head for.

The sun shone hot on the beige plain all day. Neither fly nor bug nor snake ventured out on the waste to molest the four horses tethered there, or the colt. They had run nearly two hours at a gallop and as the afternoon settled upon them they pawed the hard ground for water, but there was none.

Toward evening the wind came up and they backed into it and faced the mountains from which they had come. From time to time the stallion caught the scent of the pastures up there and he started to walk toward the vaulted fields in which he had grazed, but the tire bent his neck around and after a few steps he would turn to face it and leap into the air with his forelegs striking at the sky and then he would come down and be still again. With the deep blue darkness the wind blew faster, tossing their manes and flinging their long tails in between their legs. The cold of night raised the colt onto its legs and it stood close to the mare for warmth. Facing the southern range five horses blinked under the green glow of the risen moon and they closed their eyes and slept. The colt settled again on the hard ground and lay under the mare. In the high hollows of the mountains the grass they had cropped this morning straightened in the darkness. On the lusher swards which were still damp with the rains of spring their hoof-prints had begun to disappear. When the first pink glow of another morning lit the sky, the colt stood up and, as it had done at every dawn, it walked waywardly for water. The mare shifted warningly and her bone hoofs ticked the clay. The colt turned its head and returned to her and stood at her side with vacant eye, its nostrils sniffing the warming air.

The Last Generation

Joy Williams

He was nine.

"Nine," his father would say, "there's an age for you. When I was nine . . ." and so on.

His father's name was Walter. He had a seventeen-year-old brother named Walter Jr. and he was Tommy. The boys had no mother, she had been killed in a car wreck a while before.

It had not been her fault.

Tommy's father was a mechanic at a Chevrolet garage in Tallahassee. His foot had been mangled in a lift there once so that he now walked with a limp, in a ragged, wide-hipped way. The mother had taken care of houses that people rented on the river. She cleaned them and managed them for the owners. Just before she died, there had been this one house and the toilet got stopped up. I told the plumber, Tommy's mother told them, that I wanted to know just what was in that toilet because I didn't trust those tenants. I knew there was something deliberate there, not normal. I said, you tell me what you find there, and when he called back he said, well, you wanted to know what I found there and it was fat meat and paper towels.

She had been very excited about what the plumber had told her. Tommy worried that his mother had still been thinking about this when she died—that she had been driving along, still marveling about it—fat meat and paper towels!—and that then she had been struck, and died.

She had slowed for an emergency vehicle with its lights flashing that was tearing through an intersection and a truck had crashed into her from behind. The emergency vehicle had a destination but there hadn't been an emergency at the time. It was supposed to be stationed at the stockcar races and it was late. The races—the first of the season—were just about to begin at the time of the wreck. Walter Jr. was sitting in the old bleachers with a girl, waiting for the start, and the announcer had just called for the drivers to fire up their engines. There had been an immense roar in the sunny, dusty field, and a great cloud of insects had flown up from the rotting wood of the bleachers. The girl beside Walter Jr. had screamed and spilled her Coke all over him. There had been thousands of the insects, which were long red flying ants of some sort with transparent wings.

Tommy had not seen the alarming eruption of insects. He had been home, putting together a little car from a kit and painting it with silver paint.

Tommy liked rope. Sometimes he ate dirt. Fog thrilled him. He was small for his age, a weedy child. He wore blue jeans with deeply rolled cuffs for growth, although he grew slowly. Weeks often went by when he did not grow. He wore white, rather formal shirts.

The house they lived in on the river was a two-story house with a big porch, surrounded by trees. There was a panel in the ceiling that gave access to a particularly troublesome water pipe. The pipe would leak whenever it felt like it but not all the time. Apparently it had been placed by the builders on such an angle that it could neither be replaced nor repaired. Walter had placed a bucket in the space between the floors above Tommy's ceiling to catch water, and this he emptied every few weeks. Tommy believed that some living thing existed up there that needed water as all living things do, some quiet, listening, watching thing that shared his room with him. At the same time, he knew there was nothing there. Walter would throw the water from the bucket into the yard. It was important to Tommy that he always be there to see the bucket being brought down, emptied, then replaced.

In the house, with other photographs, was a photograph of Tommy and his mother, taken when he was six. It had been taken on the bank of the river, the same river the rest of them still lived on, but not the same place. This place had been farther upstream. Tommy was holding a fish by the tail. His mother was fat and had black hair and she was smiling at him and he was looking at the fish. He was holding the fish upside down and it was not very large, but it was large enough to keep, apparently. Tommy had been told that he had caught the fish and that his mother had fried it up just for him in a pan with butter and salt and that he had eaten it, but Tommy could remember none of this. What he remembered was that he had found the fish, which was not true.

Tommy loved his mother but he didn't miss her. He didn't like his father, Walter, much, and never had. He liked Walter Jr.

Walter Jr. had a moustache and his own Chevy truck. He liked to ride around at night with his friends and sometimes he would take Tommy on these rides. The big boys would drink beer and holler at people in Ford trucks and, in general, carry on as they tore along the river roads. Once Tommy saw a fox, and once they all saw a naked woman in a lighted window. The headlights swept past all kinds of things. One night, one of the boys pointed at a mailbox.

"See that mailbox. That's a three-hundred-dollar mailbox."

"Mailbox can't be three hundred dollars," one of the other boys screamed.

"I seen it advertised. It's totally indestructible. Door can't be pulled off. Ya hit it with a ball bat or a two-by-four, it just busts up the wood, don't hurt the box. Toss an M-80 in there, won't hurt the box."

"What's an M-80?" Tommy asked.

The big boys looked at him.

"He don't know what an M-80 is," one of them said.

Walter Jr. stopped the truck and backed it up. They all got out and stared at the mailbox. "What kind of mail you think these people get anyway?" Walter Jr. said.

The boys pushed at the box and peered inside. "It's just asking for it, isn't it," one of the boys said. They laughed and shrugged, and one of them pissed on it. Then they got back in the truck and drove away.

Walter Jr. had girlfriends too. For a time, his girl was Audrey, only Audrey. Audrey had thick hair and very white, smooth skin and Tommy thought she was beautiful. Together, he thought, she and his brother were like young gods who made the world after many trials and tests, accomplishing everything only through wonders, only through self-transformations. In reality, the two were quite an ordinary couple. If anything, Audrey was peculiar looking, even ugly.

"If you marry my brother, I'll be your brother-in-law," Tommy told her.

"Ha," she said.

"Why don't you like me?" He adored her, he knew she had some power over him.

"Who wants to know?"

"Me. I want to know. Tommy."

"Who's that?" And she would laugh, twist him over, hang him upside down by the knees so he swung like a monkey, dump him on his feet again, and give him a stale stick of gum.

Then Walter Jr. began going out with other girls.

"He dropped me," Audrey told Tommy, "just like that."

It was the end of the summer that his mother had died at the start of. Her clothes still hung in the closet. Her shoes were there, too, lined up. It was the shoes that looked as though they most expected her return. Audrey came over every day and she and Tommy would sit on the porch of the house on the river in two springy steel chairs painted piggy pink. Audrey told him,

"You can't trust anybody,"

and

"Don't agree to anything."

When Walter Jr. walked by, he never glanced at her. It was as though Audrey wasn't there. He would walk by whistling, his hair dark and crispy, his stomach flat as a board. He wore sunglasses, even though the summer had been far from bright. It had been cool and damp. The water in the river was yellow with the rains.

"Does your dad miss the Mom?" Audrey asked Tommy.

"Uh-huh."

"Who misses her the most?"

"I don't know," Tommy said. "Dad, I think."

"That's right," Audrey said. "That's what true love is. Wanting something that's missing."

She brought him presents. She gave him a big book about icebergs with colored pictures. He knew she had stolen it. They looked at the book together and Audrey read parts of it aloud.

"Icebergs were discovered by monks," Audrey said. "That's not exactly what it says here, but I'm trying to make it easier for you. Icebergs were discovered by monks who thought they were floating crystal castles." She pointed toward the river. "Squeeze your eyes up and look at the river. It looks like a cloud lying on the ground instead, see?"

He squeezed up his eyes. He could not see it.

"I like clouds," he said.

"Clouds aren't as pretty as they used to be," Audrey said. "That's a known fact."

Tommy looked back at the book. It was a big book, with nothing but pictures of icebergs, or so it seemed. How could she have stolen it? She turned the pages back and forth, not turning them in any order that he could see.

"Later explorers came and discovered the sea cow," she read. "The sea

538

cows munched seaweed in the shallows of the Bering Strait. They were colossal and dim-witted, their skin was like the bark of ancient oaks. Discovered in 1741, they were extinct by 1768."

"I don't know what extinct is," Tommy said.

"In 1768, it was the eighteenth century. Then there was the nineteenth century and we are in the twentieth century. This is the century of destruction. The earth's been around for 4.6 billion years and it may take only fifty more years to kill it."

He thought for a while. "I'll be fifty-nine," he said. "You'll be sixty-five."

"We don't want to be around when the earth gets killed," Audrey said.

She went into the kitchen and helped herself to two Popsicles from the freezer. They ate them quickly, their lips and tongues turned red.

"Do you want me to give you a kiss?" Audrey said.

He opened his mouth.

"Look," she said. "You don't drool when you kiss and you don't spit either. How'd you learn such a thing?"

"I didn't," he said.

"Never mind," she said. "We don't ever have to kiss. We're the last generation."

Walter drank more than he had when the boys' mother was alive. Still, he made them supper every night when he came home from work. He set the table, poured the milk.

"Well, men," he would say, "here we are." He would begin to cry. "I'm sorry, men," he'd say.

The sun would be setting in a mottled sky over the wet woods, and the light would linger in a smeared radiance for a while.

Tommy would scarcely be able to sleep at night, waiting for the morning to come and go so it would be the afternoon and he would be with Audrey, rocking in the metal chairs.

"The last generation has got certain responsibilities," Audrey said, "though you might think we wouldn't. We should know nothing and want nothing and be nothing, but at the same time we should want everything and know everything and be everything."

Upstairs in his room, Walter Jr. was lifting weights. They could hear him breathing, gasping.

Audrey's strange, smooth face looked blank. It looked empty.

"Did you love my brother?" Tommy asked. "Do you still love him?"

"Certainly not," Audrey said. "We were just passing friends."

"My father says we are all passing guests of God."

"He says that kind of thing because the Mom left so quick." She snapped her fingers.

Tommy was holding tight to the curved metal arms of the chair. He put his hands up to his face and sniffed them. He had had dreams of putting his hands in Audrey's hair, hiding them there, up to his wrists. Her hair was the color of gingerbread.

"Love isn't what you think anyway," Audrey said.

"I don't," Tommy said.

"Love is ruthless. I'm reading a book for English class, *Wuthering Heights*. Everything's in the book, but mostly it's about the ruthlessness of love."

"Tell me the whole book," Tommy said.

"Emily Brontë wrote *Wuthering Heights*. I'll tell you a story about her."

He picked at a scab on his knee.

"Emily Brontë had a bulldog named Keeper that she loved. His only bad habit was sleeping on the beds. The housekeeper complained about this and Emily said that if she ever found him sleeping on the clean white beds again, she would beat him. So Emily found him one evening sleeping on a clean white bed and she dragged him off and pushed him in a corner and beat him with her fists. She punished him until his eyes were swelled up and he was bloody and half blind, and after she punished him, she nursed him back to health."

Tommy rocked on his chair, watching Audrey. He stopped picking. The scab didn't want to come off.

"She had a harsh life," Audrey said, "but she was fair."

"Did she tell him later that she was sorry?" Tommy asked.

"No. Absolutely not."

"Did Keeper forgive her?"

"Dogs aren't human. They can't forgive."

"I've never had a dog," Tommy said.

"I had a dog when I was little. She was a golden retriever. She looked exactly like all golden retrievers. Her size was the same, the color of her fur, and her large, sad eyes. Her behavior was the same. She was devoted, expectant, and yet resigned. Do you see what I mean? But I liked her a lot. She was special to me. When she died, I wanted them to bury her under my window, but you know what they said to me? They said, 'The best place to bury a dog is in your heart.'"

She looked at him until he finally said, "That's right."

"That's a crock," she said. "A crock of you know what. Don't agree to so much stuff. You've got to watch out."

"All right," he said, and shook his head.

Sometimes Audrey visited him at school. He told her when his recess was and she would walk over to the playground and talk with him through the playground's chain link fence. Once she brought a girlfriend with her. Her name was Flan, and she wore large clothes, a long, wide skirt and a big sweater with little animals running in rows. There were only parts of the little animals where the body of the sweater met the sleeves and collar.

"Isn't he cute," Flan said. "He's like a little doll, isn't he?"

"Now don't go and scare him," Audrey said.

Flan had a cold. She held little wadded tissues to her mouth and eyes. The tissues were blue and pink and green and she would dab at her face with them and push them back in her pockets, but one spilled out and fluttered in the weeds beside the school-yard fence. It would not blow away but stayed fluttering there.

"I ain't scaring him. Where'd you get all them moles around your neck?" she said to Tommy.

"What do you mean, where'd he get them," Audrey said. "He didn't get them from anywhere."

"Don't you worry about them moles?" the girl persisted.

"Naw," Tommy said.

"You're a brave little guy, aren't you," Flan said. "There's other stuff, I know. I'm not saying it's all moles." She tugged at the front of the frightful sweater. "Audrey gave me this sweater. She stole it. You know how she steals things and after a while she puts them back? But I like this, so it's not going to get put back."

Tommy gazed at the sweater and then at Audrey.

"Sometimes putting stuff back is the best part," Audrey said. "Sometimes it isn't."

"Audrey can steal anything," Flan said.

"Can she steal a house?" Tommy asked.

"He's so *cute*," Flan shrieked.

"I gotta go in," Tommy said. Behind him, in the school yard, the children were playing a peculiar game. Running, crouching, calling, there didn't seem to be any rules. He trotted toward them and heard Flan say, "He's a cute little guy, isn't he?"

Tommy never saw Flan again and he was glad of that. He asked Audrey if Flan was in the last generation.

"Yes," Audrey said. "She sure is."

"Is my brother in the last generation, too?"

"Technically he is, of course," Audrey said. "But he's not really. He has too much stuff."

"I have stuff," Tommy said. He had his little cars. "You've given me stuff."

"But you don't have possessions, because what I gave you I stole. Anyway, you'll stop caring about that soon. You'll forget all about it, but Walter Jr. really likes possessions and he likes to think about what he's going to do. He has his truck and his barbells and those shirts with the pearl buttons."

"He wants a pair of lizard boots for his birthday," Tommy said.

"Isn't that pathetic," Audrey said.

Every night, Walter would come home from work, scrub down his hands and arms, set the table, pour the milk. The boys sat on either side of him. The chair where their mother used to sit looked out at the yard, at a woodpile there.

"Men," Walter began, "when I was your age, I didn't know . . ." He shook his head and drank his whiskey, his eyes filling with tears.

He had been forgetting to empty the bucket in the space above Tommy's room. A pale stain had spread upon the ceiling. Tommy showed it to Audrey.

"That's nice," she said, "the shape, all dappled brown and yellow like that, but it doesn't tell you anything really. It's just part of the doomed reality all around us." She climbed up and brought the bucket down.

"A monk would take this water and walk into the desert and pour it over a dry and broken stick there," she said. "That's why people become monks, because they get sick of being around doomed reality all the time."

"Let's be monks," he said.

"Monks love solitude," Audrey said. "They love solitude more than anything. When monks started out, long, long ago, they were waiting for the end of time."

"But the end of time didn't happen."

"It was too soon then. They didn't know what we know today."

She wore silver sandals. Once she had broken a strap on the sandal and Tommy had fixed it with his Hot Stuff Instant Glue.

"Someday we could have a little boy just like you," she said. "And we'd call him Tommy Two."

But he was not fond of this idea. He was afraid that it would come out of him somehow, this Tommy Two, that he would make it and be ashamed. So, together, they dismissed the notion.

One day Walter Jr. said to him, "Look, Audrey shouldn't be hanging around here all the time. She's weird. She's no mommy, believe me."

"I don't need a mommy," Tommy said.

"She's mad at me and she's trying to get back at me through you. She's just practicing on you. You don't want to be practiced on, do you? She's just a very unhappy person."

"I'm unhappy," Tommy said.

"You need to get out and play some games. Soccer, maybe."

"Why?" Tommy said. "I don't like Daddy."

"You're just trying that out," Walter Jr. said. "You like him well enough."

"Audrey and me are the last generation and you're not," Tommy said.

"What are you talking about?"

"You should be but you're not. Nothing can be done about it."

"Let's drive around in the truck," Walter Jr. said.

Tommy still enjoyed riding around in the truck. They passed by the houses their mother had cleaned. They looked all right. Someone else was cleaning them now.

"You don't look good," Walter Jr. said. "You're too pale. You mope around all the time."

Hard little leaves whirled across the road. Inside the truck, the needle of the black compass on the dashboard trembled. The compass box was filled with what seemed like water. Maybe it was water. Tommy was looking at everything carefully but trying not to think about it. Audrey was teaching him how to do this. He remembered at some point to turn toward his brother and smile, and this made his brother feel better, it was clear.

The winter nights were cool. Audrey and Tommy still sat in their chairs at dusk on the porch but now they wrapped themselves in blankets.

"Walter Jr. is dating a lot anymore," Audrey said. "It's nice we have these evenings to ourselves but we should take little trips, you know? I have a lot to show you. Have you ever been to the TV tower north of town?"

The father, Walter, was already in bed. He worked and drank and slept. He had saved the fragments of soap his wife had left behind in the shower. He had wrapped them in tissue paper and placed them in a drawer. But he was sleeping in the middle of the bed these nights, hardly aware of it.

"No," Tommy said. "Is it in the woods?"

"It's a lot taller than the woods and it's not far away from here. It's called Tall Timbers. It's right smack in the middle of birds' migration routes. Thousands of birds run into it every year, all kinds of them. We can go out there and look at the birds."

Tommy was puzzled. "Are the birds dead?"

"Yes," she said. "In an eleven-year period, 30,000 birds of 170 species have been found at the base of the tower."

"Why don't they move it?"

"They don't do things like that," Audrey said. "It would never occur to them."

He did not want to see the birds around the tower. "Let's go," he said.

"We'll go in the spring. That's when the birds change latitudes. That's when they move from one place to another. There's a little tiny warbler bird that used to live around here in the spring, but people haven't seen it for years. They haven't found it at the base of any of the TV towers. They used to find it there, that's how they knew it wasn't extinct."

"Monks used to live on top of tall towers," Tommy said, for she had told him this. "If a monk stayed up there, he could keep the birds away, he could wave his arms around or something so they wouldn't hit."

"Monks live in a cool, crystalline half-darkness of the mind and heart," Audrey said. "They couldn't be bothered with that."

They rocked in their chairs on the porch. The porch had been painted a succession of colors. Where the chairs had scraped the wood there was light green, dark green, blue, red. Bugs crawled around the lights.

"If I got sick, would you stay with me?" Tommy asked.

"I'm not sure. It would depend."

"My mommy would have stayed."

"Well, you never know," Audrey said. "You got to realize mommys get tired. They're willing to let things go sometimes. They get to thinking and they're off."

"Do you have a mommy?" he asked cautiously.

"Technically I do," Audrey said, "but she's gone as your mommy, actually. Before something's gone, it has to be there, right? Even so, I don't feel any rancor about her. It's important not to feel rancor."

"I don't feel rancor," Tommy said.

Then one afternoon, Walter came home from his work at the garage and it was as though he had woken from a strange sleep. It wasn't as though he appeared startled by awakening. His days and nights of grief came to an end with no harder shock than that of a boat's keel grounding upon a river's shore. He stopped drinking and weeping. He put his wife's things in cardboard boxes and stored the boxes. In fact, he stored them in the space above Tommy's room.

"Why's that girl here all the time?" Walter asked. "She's not still Walter Jr.'s girlfriend, is she?"

He said, "She shouldn't be here all the time."

"Audrey's my friend," Tommy said.

"She's not a nice girl. She's too old to be your friend."

"Then I'm too young to be your friend."

"No, honey, you're my son."

"I don't like you," Tommy said.

"You love me, but you don't like me, is that it?" Walter was thinner and cleaner. He spoke cheerfully.

Tommy considered this. He shook his head.

At school, at the edge of the playground, Audrey talked through the chain link fence to Tommy.

"You know that pretty swamp close-by? It's full of fish, all different kinds. You know how they know?"

He didn't.

"They poison little patches of it. They put out nets and then they drop the poison in. It settles in the gills of the fish and suffocates them. The fish pop up to the surface and then they drag them out and classify and weigh and measure each one."

"Who?" Tommy said.

"They do it a couple times a year to see if there's as many different kinds and as many as before. That's how they count things. That's their attitude. They act as though they care about stuff, but they don't. They're just pretending."

Tommy told her that his father didn't want her to come over to the house, that he wasn't supposed to talk to her anymore.

"The Dad's back, is he?" Audrey said. "He thinks he can start over. Pathetic."

"What are we going to do?" Tommy said.

"You shouldn't listen to him," Audrey said. "Why are you listening to him? We're the last generation, there's something else we're listening to."

They were silent for a while, listening. The other children had gone inside.

"What is it?" Tommy asked.

"You'll recognize it when you hear it. Something will happen, something unusual for which we were always prepared. The Dad's life has already taken a turn for the worse, it's obvious. It's like he's a stranger now, walking down the wrong road. Do you see what I mean? I could put it another way."

"Put it another way," he said.

"It's his life that's like the stranger, standing real still. A stranger standing alongside a dark road, waiting for him to pass."

It appeared his father was able to keep Audrey away. Tommy wouldn't have thought it was possible. He knew his father was powerless, but Audrey wasn't coming around. His father moved through the house in his dark, oiled boots, in his ragged, limping way. He was fixing things. He painted the kitchen, restacked the woodpile. He replaced the pipe above the ceiling in Tommy's room. It had long been accepted that this could not be done, but now it was done, it did not leak, there was no need for the bucket. The bucket was used now to take ashes from the wood stove. Walter Jr. had a job in the gym he worked out in. He had long, hard muscles, a distracted air. He worried about girls, about money. He wanted an apartment of his own, in town.

Tommy lived alone with his father. "Talk to me, son," Walter said. "I love you."

Tommy said nothing. His father disgusted him a little. He was like a tree walking, strange but not believable. He was trying to start over. It was pathetic.

Tommy saw Audrey only on school days, at recess. He waited by the fence for her in the vitreous intractable light of the southern afternoon.

"I had a boy tell me once my nipples were like bowls of Wheaties," Audrey said.

"When?" Tommy said. "No."

"That's a simile. Similes are a crock. There's no more time for similes. There used to be that kind of time, but no more. You shouldn't see what you're seeing, thinking it looks like something else. They haven't left us with much, but the things that are left should be seen as they are."

Some days she did not come by. Then he would see her waiting at the fence, or she would appear suddenly, while he was waiting there. But then days passed, more days than there had been before. Days with Walter saying, "We need each other, son. We're not over this yet. We have to help each other. I need your help."

It was suppertime. They were sitting over the last of a meal Walter had fixed.

"I want Audrey back," Tommy said.

"Audrey?" Walter looked surprised. "Walter Jr. heard about what happened to Audrey. She made her bed, as they say, now she's got to lie in it." He looked at Tommy, then startled, looked away.

"Who wants you?" Tommy said. "Nobody."

Walter rubbed his head with his hands. He looked around the room, at some milk on the floor that Tommy had spilled. The house was empty except for them. There were no animals around, nothing. It was all beyond what was possible, he knew.

In the night, Tommy heard his father moving around, bumping into things, moaning. A glass fell. He heard it breaking for what seemed a long time. The air in the house felt close, sour. He pushed open his bedroom window and felt the air fluttering warmly against his skin. Down along the river, the water popped and smacked against the muddy bank. It was close to the season when he and Audrey could go to the tower where all the birds were. He could feel it in the air. Audrey would come for him from wherever she was, from wherever they had made her go, and they would go to the tower and find the little warbler bird. Then they would know that it still existed because they had found it dead there. He and Audrey would be the ones who would find it. They were the last generation, the ones who would see everything for the last time. That's what the last generation does.

The Beggar Said So

Isaac Bashevis Singer

(Translated from the Yiddish by Gertrude Hirschler)

One hot summer day a big wagon, drawn by one horse, lumbered into the marketplace of Yanov. It was piled high with motley rags and bedding, laden with cans and buckets, and from the axis between the rear wheels a lantern hung. On top of everything a flowerpot and a cage with a little yellow bird swayed precariously. The driver of the wagon was dark with a pitch-black beard. He wore a cap with a leather visor and a coat not cut in the usual style. At first glance one could have taken him for an ordinary Russian. But the woman with him wore on her head the familiar Jewish coif. Jews, then, after all. Instantly, from all the little shops round about, the Jews of the town rushed out to meet the new arrivals. The stranger stood there in the marketplace with his whip in his hand.

"Wher-r-re's your magistr-r-rate?" he demanded. He pronounced his "r's" in the dialect of Great Poland, hard and sharp.

"And what would you need the magistrate for?"

"I want to be a chimney sweep," said the newcomer.

"And why should a Jew want to be a chimney sweep?"

"I served in the army for twenty-five years. I have my working papers."

"There's a chimney sweep in town already."

"But the beggar said there wasn't," the newcomer insisted.

"What beggar?"

"Why, the one that came to our town."

It seemed that the man—his name was Moshe—had been a chimney sweep in some small town on the other side of the river Vistula, not far from the Prussian border. One day a beggar who traveled from place to place had come to that town and had said something about a chimney sweep being needed in Yanov. Moshe and his wife had lost no time; they had loaded all their worldly goods onto a wagon and set out for Yanov.

The young men watching them smiled, nudged each other and exchanged meaningful glances. The older householders shrugged their shoulders.

"Why didn't you write a letter first?" they asked Moshe.

"I can't w-r-rite," was the answer.

"So you can get someone else to write for you. Beggars have made up stories before."

"But the beggar said . . ."

All talk and counterarguments proved vain. To every question the man had only one answer: "The beggar said so." One might have thought his wife would have had more sense, but she, too, had the same stock rejoinder: "The beggar said so." The crowd of townspeople grew swiftly and the strange tale passed from mouth to mouth. The onlookers began to whisper to each other about it; they shook their heads and made crude puns. One of the men, a flour dealer, called out: "Just think, believing a poor tramp like that!"

"Maybe the beggar was the Prophet Elijah in disguise," jeered another.

The schoolchildren came out from the *Cheder* and mimicked the new arrivals. "The beggar said so," they hooted after them. The young girls giggled while the older women wrung their hands and lamented the lot of these poor fools from Great Poland. In the meantime, Moshe the Chimney Sweep filled one of his cans with water at the town pump and gave his horse a drink. Then he proceeded to fasten a bag of oats around the animal's jaws. From the horse's collar, which was studded with bits of brass, two pine branches protruded stiffly. The shaft was painted blue. Everyone soon saw that the two travelers had with them, besides the horse and the bird, an odd assortment of geese, ducks, chickens, and one black rooster with a red comb—all in one big cage.

In Yanov at the time there were no vacant dwellings; temporarily, therefore, the two strangers were put up at the poorhouse. A coachman took their horse into his own stable, and someone else bought the fowl. Moshe's spouse, Mindel, immediately joined the other *shnorrers'* wives in the kitchen of the poorhouse where she cooked some porridge. Moshe, himself, went off to the study house to recite a few chapters from the Book of Psalms. And a new byword became fashionable in Yanov: "But the beggar said so . . ."

The schoolboys never tired of questioning Moshe and of laughing up their sleeves.

"Tell us," they would query, "just what did he look like, that beggar?"

"Like all other beggars," Moshe would reply.

"What kind of a beard did he have?"

"Yellow."

"Don't you know that men who grow yellow hair are cheaters?"

"How should I know?" Moshe would retort. "I'm a simple man. The beggar said so, and I believed him."

"If he had told you that the rabbi's wife lays eggs, would you have believed that too?"

Moshe did not answer. He was a man well into his fifties, though still without one grey hair. His face was tanned like that of a gypsy. His back was straight; his shoulders and chest, broad. He produced for the schoolteacher's inspection two medals which he had got in the Tsar's service for proficiency in riding and marksmanship, and he told of his experiences as a soldier. He had been one of the young boys inducted by force. His father had been a blacksmith. He, Moshe, had still been a student at the *Cheder* when child-snatchers from the Tsar's army had taken him away. But he, Moshe, had refused to eat forbidden foods and had fasted until he was faint with hunger. The village priest had tried to convert him, but he had a *mezuzah* which his mother had given him, as well as the fringed ritual garment worn next to the body to remind him of his God at all times. Yes, they had whipped him, flogged him too with wet switches, but he had not given in. He had remained a Jew. When they tortured him, he had cried out, "Hear, O Israel, the Lord our God is One."

Moshe also told about the time, years later, when he had fallen asleep while on sentry duty and his gun had slipped from his hand. If he had been caught napping, he would have been sent to Siberia. But, lo, his dead grandfather had appeared to him in a dream and awakened him. He had had another close call: while crossing a frozen river, he had been stranded on an ice floe. Once too he had been attacked by a wild ox. But he had managed to grab the beast by its horns; he still bore the scar on his wrist. The Tsar's veterans had a reputation for telling tall tales, but everyone believed Moshe; it was clear from the way he told his stories that he had not made them up.

Not long after the arrival of Moshe and his wife, a room was found for them to live in and a stable for the horse. Just at that time one of the Yanov water carriers died; Moshe procured a wooden yoke and became a water carrier. His wife, Mindel, went every Thursday to knead dough in the baking troughs and, besides that job, she stripped feathers for the bedding of new brides. Gradually the two newcomers grew accustomed to Yanov. Yet one question still burrowed deep in the heart of Moshe. Why should the beggar have deceived him so? Had not he, Moshe, given his guest, the beggar, his own bed while he himself tossed about on the ground all night? Not to brag about it, but on that Sunday morning, hadn't he given his guest a loaf of bread and a slab of cheese to take on the way? Why, then, should the beggar have wanted to make a fool of him? Moshe often discussed the riddle with his wife. But she did not know the answer either, and each time he broached the subject, she would say:

"Moshe, take my advice and stop thinking about it."

"But . . . why should the beggar have said so if it wasn't true?" he would persist.

Moshe knew that wandering beggars can turn up anywhere. Every Sabbath he looked over the transients gathered at the synagogue entrance to see if this one beggar was among them. But the years passed and the beggar never came. Was the man afraid that Moshe might take revenge? Or perhaps, Moshe thought, God had punished him and he had died on the road. In time, the odd thing was that Moshe was not even angry any longer. He had made up his mind that he would not even give the beggar a beating if he were to meet him again. He would simply take him by the neck and say:

"Why did you make a fool of me, contemptible creature?"

Several coachmen tried to persuade Moshe to sell his horse. The wells from which water was drawn for the town of Yanov were nearby so that a water carrier had no need of a horse. And why, they argued, should he have to feed an animal for nothing? But Moshe refused to part with his old mare. He and his wife were fond of animals. God had not granted them any children, but a variety of living things—stray dogs, cats, birds that could no longer fly—had joined their household. The wife would buy a live carp for the Sabbath, but instead of cleaning it and chopping it up she would let it swim about in a washtub for weeks until it finally died of natural causes. Even though one beggar had misused their kindness, these two did not take out their chagrin on other little people. Moshe's wife carried groats to the poorhouse, and every Friday night Moshe would take a wayfarer home as his guest for the Sabbath. To every one of them he would tell the story of what had happened to him and at the end would ask, "Now, why should the beggar have said so?"

Late one winter night, Moshe was sitting in his chair soaking his feet in a tub of water. His wife had opened the door of a little cage and a tiny yellow bird was flying about the room. They had taught it a number of tricks. For instance, Moshe would place some millet seeds between his fingers and the bird would take them. Or else he would put one single grain on his lips and the bird would snatch it with its beak, exchanging a kiss with the master.

The oven was warm and the door locked tightly against the cold outside. The woman sat in a corner darning socks. Suddenly, Moshe's head sank down on his chest; he fell asleep and at once began to dream. He dreamed that the soot in the chimney of the poorhouse had caught fire. A bright flame shot out from the chimney and was melting the snow on the shingle roof. He awoke with a start.

"Mindel," he called to his wife, "there's a fire at the poorhouse."

"How do you know?"

"I saw it in a dream."

"A dream can fool."

"No, it's true."

In vain did his wife argue that it was bitter outside and that he might catch cold—Heaven forbid—if he went out so soon after soaking his feet. Hurrying, Moshe put on his boots, his fur coat and his sheepskin cap. In his closet he still had had his chimney-sweep's broom with the rope and iron plummet. He took them with him now as he left the house. He walked through Lublin Street and the street of the Synagogue and then arrived at the poorhouse. There he saw everything exactly as it had been in his dream. The chimney spouted fiery sparks. The snow near it had melted. Moshe began to shout as loud as he could, but the people in the poorhouse did not hear him. Indeed, even if they had waked immediately, they would hardly have been able to save themselves for all of them were old, sick and lame. There was no ladder. Moshe attempted to scale the wall. He caught hold of a giant icicle, but that broke off. Then he clung to a shingle but it, too, fell from the eaves before he could climb up. Already part of the roof was on fire. In desperation, Moshe grabbed his broom with the iron plummet and with a forceful heave aimed it at the chimney. Amazingly, at the first try it landed in the chimney. The rope hung out; Moshe grasped it and like an acrobat he swung himself onto the roof. There was no water; quickly he scooped up snow and patting it into balls threw them into the chimney, all the while bellowing at the top of his voice. But no one heard him. The poorhouse was some distance away from the town; besides the wind was howling. And the people of Yanov were sound sleepers.

When Moshe failed to return home, his wife put on her boots and padded jacket and went to the poorhouse to see what was keeping him. The dream was true: there he was, standing on the roof. The fire was out, but the chimney was still smoking. Pale moonlight shone on the eerie scene. By now some of the old people inside had waked and come out, carrying a scoop and shovel. They crowded around. All declared that had it not been for Moshe, the building would have burned to cinders and they would all have perished inside. What with the wind blowing in the direction of the town, the fire could have spread to the synagogue, the bathhouse, the study house and, yes, even to the houses in the marketplace. And then not only would the houses have been burned-out shells, but there would have been more deaths from cold and exposure.

By the next day the report of the feat of Moshe the Water Carrier had spread through the town. The mayor appointed a commission to inspect all the chimneys, and the investigation revealed that the town chimney sweep had not done his job in months. They found him in his room, dead drunk, with a straw in his mouth, still sipping vodka from a cask. He was sent packing and, in his place, Moshe became the official chimney sweep of the town of Yanov.

And now a marvelous thing came to pass.

A few days later, when Moshe went to the poorhouse and the inmates crowded round him to thank him and to shower him with blessings, he noticed someone whose features seemed familiar. The man's beard was a mixture of yellow and grey. He was lying on a straw sack covered with rags. The face from which the eye bulged out was yellow with jaundice. Moshe stopped short and thought in wonder: *Where have I met him before? I could swear that I know this man.* And then he clasped his hands together in amazement. Why, this was none other than the beggar, the very same one who, years ago, had told him that they needed a chimney sweep in Yanov. A stream of tears gushed forth from Moshe's eyes.

Yes, it was the beggar. He had long forgotten his words, but he did recall that in that year and at that time he had spent the Sabbath in that village in Great Poland. He even recalled that he had stayed with some chimney sweep there.

And what was the fruit of all this questioning, of this investigation? Why, it had become quite clear to Moshe that the whole chain of events had been directed from On High. Years ago, this one beggar had been ordained to find a man who would one day save him and all the other people of Yanov from death. It was plain, then, that this beggar had been an instrument of God. Besides, his words had come true after all. Not at the time he said them, to be sure, but much later, for now Moshe had indeed become the official chimney sweep of Yanov. The longer Moshe thought about it, the more clearly did he see the hand of Divine Providence in it all. It was beyond his grasp. Imagine! Holy angels in Heaven thinking of Moshe the Chimney Sweep and sending him messengers with prophecies, just as in the story of Father Abraham!

Moshe was overcome by awe and humility. Had the poorhouse floor not been so dirty he would have fallen upon his face right there and prostrated himself and given thanks to the Almighty. A sob came from his throat and his beard grew sodden with his tears. After he had recovered his composure, he lifted the beggar's frail body in his arms and bore him home upon his shoulders. He washed him, bathed him, dressed him in a clean shirt and laid him on his bed. Mindel immediately went to the stove and made some soup. And the people of the town, who for so many years had poked fun at Moshe and had dubbed him "But-The-Beggar-Said-So," took the events to heart and told their children to stop using that name.

For over three months the beggar lay in Moshe's bed while Moshe slept on the floor. Gradually the poor man regained some of his strength and wanted to go on the road again, but Moshe and his wife would not hear of it. The beggar had neither wife nor child and he was much too old and weak to wander about. He remained with the pair. Regularly he went to the study house to pray and recite psalms. His eyes failed and he grew almost blind. Other wayfarers told story after story of noblemen, merchants and rabbis, but this beggar was silent. When he finished his reading of the Book of Psalms, he would immediately start all over again. He had also memorized whole passages from the Mishnah. When the Talmud students came to him to inquire why, so many years ago, he had told Moshe that there was no chimney sweep in Yanov, he would raise his eyebrows, shrug his shoulders and answer:

"I really don't know."

"And where do you come from?" they would ask him.

He would give some sort of reply, but his words did not come out clearly. The people thought he was deaf. And yet he had no trouble at all hearing the Reader's prayers from his remote corner of the study house. Mindel catered to him, pampering him with chicken and oatmeal, but he ate less and less as time went by. He would absently raise a spoonful of soup to his lips and then forget to put it in his mouth. The little bird which Moshe had brought with him to Yanov had long since died, but his wife had bought another bird from the gypsies. The cage was never closed, and the bird would fly out and perch on the beggar's shoulder for hours on end.

After some time had passed, the beggar was taken ill again. Moshe and his wife sent for a doctor who spared neither time nor remedies, but apparently the man had no more years left. He died during the Passover month and was buried on a Friday. The burial society set aside a plot for him among the graves of residents of long standing. Half of Yanov followed the funeral procession. When Moshe and Mendel returned home from the cemetery, they found that their bird had gone. It never came back. And in Yanov the word went around that the old beggar who had died had been a *Lamed-Vavnik*, one of the Thirty-Six Righteous Men who, living out their days in obscurity, were keeping the world from destruction by the strength of their virtues.

One night, not long after the beggar's death, Moshe and his wife could not sleep. They began to speak of all sorts of things, talking on till sunrise. That morning Moshe announced in the study house that he and his wife wanted to have a new Scroll of the Law made for the community.

The scribe of Yanov labored over the Scroll for three years, and during all that time Moshe and Mindel talked of their Scroll as if it had been their only daughter. Moshe skimped and saved on household expenses, but for the Scroll she bought remnants of silk and velvet, golden thread, and she hired poor maidens to fashion these into embroidered mantelets. Moshe went all the way to Lublin to order the rollers, a crown with bells, a breastplate and a silver pointer, all to adorn the Scroll. Both the mantelets and the rollers bore the beggar's name—Abraham, the son of Chaim.

On the day the Scroll was dedicated, Moshe gave a festive meal for all the poor of Yanov. Just before dusk the guests assembled in the courtyard of the synagogue. The final sheet of the Scroll had been left incomplete, and after evening services the respected citizens of the community each bought the privilege of having one letter on the last sheet inscribed in his behalf. When all the ink had dried on the parchment and the sheet had been sewn into place, the festive procession began. A wedding canopy was spread out on its poles, and held aloft by four of the most distinguished members of the congregation. Beneath the canopy marched the rabbi, carrying the new Scroll in his arms. The little bells on the shining crown tinkled softly. The men and boys sang; the maidens held up braided candles. Waxen tapers had been lit. Moshe and his wife shone in their holiday best. Simple man that he was, Moshe had pinned his two Russian medals to his lapel. Some of the more learned congregants took this amiss and wanted to tell him in no uncertain terms to take them off, but the rabbi would not allow them to humiliate Moshe in public.

Not even the very old in the congregation could recall ever having witnessed a dedication feast like this one. Two bands played without pause. The night was mild and the moon shone brightly. The sky looked like a star-studded curtain for a Heavenly Ark. The girls and the women danced together, apart from the men. One young man strode about merrily on stilts, and a jester serenaded the host and hostess—Moshe and his wife.

There was plenty of wine and ginger cake, supplied by Moshe and Mindel. The band played a real wedding march, a Shear Dance, an Angry Dance, and a Good Morning Dance; it was all just like a regular wedding feast. And then Moshe hitched up his coattails and Mindel her skirts and they danced a *Kasatske* together, bumping fronts and backsides as they pranced.

Moshe called out: "The Beggar-r-r's right next to God!"

And Mindel sang out in reply:

"We are not worthy even of the dust of his feet."

Moshe and Mindel still lived on for quite a few years after this celebration. Before he died, Moshe reserved a burial place for himself next to the grave of the beggar, and he asked to have the broom, the rope and the plummet, with which he had saved the old people at the poorhouse, placed in his coffin.

And as for Mindel—each day she went to the study house and drew aside the velvet curtain of the Ark to bestow a reverent kiss upon her own beloved Scroll. Early every morning without fail, until the last day of her life, she performed this ritual. And in her last will and testament she stipulated that she be buried next to her husband and the beggar who had, after all, spoken the truth.

Cutting Losses

Thomas McGuane

In 1968, a now-ancient time, full of scathing situations, trying love but preferring lust and, for many, one meretricious *scène à faire*, the flushing of narcotics down the toilet, Frank was banished from the family business by his father. This involved a long autobiographical recitation in which his father told about his early years on the ranch, the formulaic (in Frank's eyes) long walk to a poorly heated country school, the pain of being Catholic in a community of Norwegians, the early success in getting calf weights up, the malt-barley successes, the highest certifications and the prize ribbons, the sod-farm successes, the nursery, the Ford dealership, the implement dealership, and the four apartment buildings including the one regularly demolished by the fraternity boys "and their concubines."

Frank's father was a self-taught, almost bookish individual, and he wore his education on his sleeve. Among the fraternity boys was Frank, the son of the landlord, who had graduated a year earlier but who was now "managing the building" for his family, hoping to make it one of the family's successes. The occasion was a theme party, the theme being farm life, a kind of witticism on Frank's part involving hauling three tons of straw into the building and piling it higher not only than the furniture but the heads of the occupants. Barnyard animals, chiefly pigs, were turned loose in this lightless wilderness and the party began. It lasted two days. Tunnels quickly formed not only to the beer kegs but to small clearings where people could gather. There was a prescribed area for bodily functions, a circular clearing in the hay with dove-gray shag carpet for a floor, and another area for the operations of the stereo and its seemingly endless loop of the beloved Neil Young—"Are you ready for the country, 'cause it's time to go!" The world of straw became damp and odorous with beer, marijuana, sperm, perfume, and pig droppings. Frank would remember ever afterward the terror of crawling stoned, in his underwear, down a small side tunnel to meet headlong in the semidarkness a bristling, frightened, three-hundred-pound pig. Right after that, clutching a beer and a joint and hearing the approach of another pig, he withdrew into the straw alongside the tunnel to let the pig pass, watched it go by, ridden by the most beautiful, naked sorority girl he had ever seen, Janet Otergaard from Wolf Point, now vice-president of First National Bank. Frank crawled after her but fell behind a bit and when he caught up she was already going off into the straw with Barry Danzig, who was home from Northwestern Law School. This disappointment had the effect of making Frank long for fresh air. He made his way toward the entrance; and, crawling out of the straw in his underwear, a bleak and tarry roach hanging from one of his slack lips, he met his father. Mr. Copenhaver continued to wear suspenders long after they had gone out of fashion. He wore wide ones with conspicuous brass hardware to remind people of his agricultural origins. Most people hadn't gotten the news that farmers were as liable to be envy-driven crooks as anybody else, the stream of information having been interrupted by the Civil War; so, wearing wide suspenders was like wearing an I AM SINCERE sign. Today, curving over the powerful chest of his father, they stood for all the nonsense he was not brooking. A bleary girl in a straw-flecked blue sweater emerged, pulling the sweater down at the sides over her bare hips. She peered unwelcomingly at Frank's father and said, "Who's this one?"

"The owner of the building!" boomed Mr. Copenhaver. She dove back into the straw. Frank was now overpowered by fear of his father. He felt his drugged and drunken vagueness in muzzy contrast to his father's forceful clarity next to him, a presence formed by a lifetime of unstinting forward movement, of farming, warfare, and free-market capitalism as found in a small Montana city. Next to his father, Frank felt like a pudding. As against making a world, he was prepared to offer the quest for pussy and altered states; an edgeless generation, dedicated to escaping the self and to inconsequential fornicating, dedicated to the idea of the Relationship and all-terrain shoes that didn't lie to your feet. Frank's fear was that his father would strike him. Worse, he said to get the people out, clean it up, and appear at his office in the morning.

That didn't start out well, either. His companions were unwilling to help until they had had a night's sleep. He found himself shouting, on the verge of tears. "Is this friendship? You know my back is against the wall? I'm about to get my ass handed to me! I need you to help me!" We need sleep, they said. So he cleaned the mess up himself hauling twenty-seven loads in the back of his car out to the landfill and simply, hopelessly, releasing the pigs into the neighborhood. They belonged to the family of one of the fellows who hadn't stayed to help. Frank found the most awful things on the floor: false teeth taped to the end of a stick, hot dogs and half-finished bags of miniature doughnuts dusted with powdered sugar, rotten panties, a Bible, a catcher's chest protector. He showered, changed into a clean shirt, clean jeans, and a corduroy sport jacket. Then, having been up all night, he headed for his father's office. He drove up Assiniboine Avenue and then turned at College Street. His nerves were shattered by the sight of three of the pigs jogging up the center of Third Street, loosely glancing over their shoulders. Here and there, people stopped to watch these out-of-place animals.

He parked his car, an old blue Mercury with sarcastic tail fins and speckled bumpers, in front of his father's office, a handsomely remodeled farmhouse on West Deadrock, and went in. He presented himself shakily to the secretary, the very Eileen who now worked for him, who waved him on with a gesture that suggested she knew all about people like Frank and his friends. And perhaps she did, he thought. It's easy to detect motion when you're frozen in position, an old hunter's trick.

"Come in, Frank," said his father evenly.

"Hi, Dad."

His father stayed at his desk while Frank sank subdued into an upholstered chair placed in front of the desk, a chair so ill-sprung that Frank, at six one, was barely able to see over the front of his father's desk. The view of his father's head and neck rising from the horizontal line in front was reminiscent of a poorly lit documentary shot of a sea serpent, and added to the state begun by Frank's shattered condition.

Mr. Copenhaver made a steeple with his fingertips. The high color in his cheeks, the silver-and-sand hair combed straight across his forehead, and the blue suit gave him an ecclesiastical look, and Frank felt a fleeting hope that this was no accident and Christian forgiveness lay just around the corner.

"Frank, you're interested in so many things." His father glanced down; Frank could see he had the desk drawer slightly opened so that he could see some notes he had made for this conversation.

"Yes, sir."

"You like to hunt and fish."

"Yes, sir."

"You like the ladies. You like a high old time. You like to meet your buddies for a drink in the evening and you read our daily newspaper—indicating, I might have hoped, an interest in current events, but probably only the ball scores. I rarely see you with anything uplifting in your hand book-wise, and the few you've left around the place are the absolute utmost in prurience, illustrated with photographs for those who are unable to follow the very descriptive text. So far, so good: At least it was confined between the covers of a book. There was a day in time when I had my own Tilly the Toiler comics, and I am not here setting myself up to moralize about your condition. I have for a long time now, heaving a great sigh, accepted that I was the father of a drunken sports lecher and let it go at that. But when I gave you the opportunity to find some footing in the day-to-day world that would have implications for your livelihood many years down the road, you gave it the kind of disrespect I have to assume was directed at me. Last night, I felt personally smothered in straw and pig manure. That was your valentine to your father, Frank, thank you. And Frank, see how this flies: I'm not going to put up with it anymore. You're not going to run that building anymore, and my hope that you would one day manage the old home place is dead. I think your brother, Mike, is the man for that job."

Mr. Copenhaver tipped back in his chair and began to talk about growing up on the old home place, the long walk to school, the cold, some parenthetical remarks about rural electrification and rural values. Frank tried to stare out the window but his eyes were too weak to get past the glass. He was cotton-mouthed with exhaustion and prepared to endorse any negative view of his character. At the same time, he'd had enough. He got to his feet on his leaden legs and raised his hand, palm outward, to his father.

"I'll see you," Frank said; but it wasn't so. He went out the door and never saw his father again. Mike saw him frequently, even driving down from the school of dentistry. They had a nice, even relationship that Frank envied. Mike never made an attempt to be a businessman like his father. That, much later, would be Frank's job, seeking approval from someone who had departed this world.

Frank sat in the bleachers at the sale yard reading *The Wall Street Journal* and ignoring a bunch of black baldie heifers being steered under the auctioneer's gavel. In landing the Sony account, the Burnett advertising firm announced it wanted to "communicate not only our products, but the lifestyles and emotions that surround us as a company." *What sincerity there is out there in the business community*, thought Frank, *what personnel and marketing resources.* Burnett claimed its paternalistic and excellence-oriented approach to business helped land the thirty-five-million-dollar deal; that and changing the slogan "It's a Sony" to "Be Sony." Jesus fucking Christ. Frank looked up. They were bidding on a group of steers. He raised his hand at seventy-eight dollars a hundredweight and went back out at eighty-six. Then immediately he thought, *I should have bought them, it was scarcely a highly leveraged transaction for the dumb shit in the overalls who got them at eighty-eight.*

There was plenty to be interested in, but living alone, Frank had found it hard to be interested in anything. He had set so many things in motion in his business that he could tap into that as he wished. He had several income properties scattered around the town, including the very remunerative clinic. He dabbled in yearling cattle and even owned a set of royally bred show pigs, though he never found time to go see them.

After his wife, Gracie, had left, for a while he couldn't quite think of his work in an orderly way. If he couldn't see how to get insanely rich or change the world in one or two days, he hardly wanted to go to work at all. Finally, he began to take it seriously again. His work had a fairly large value to him viewed purely as routine. At forty-four (his friends made him a cake, a corona of birthday candles and a chocolate pistol with the number 44 in red), he couldn't make out whether he was young or old, and for many reasons he didn't want to find out through the women in his life. Without Gracie, Frank detected that most people found him a little eerie. He could make them laugh, yet they always felt scrutinized. Some people could stand that and some couldn't. Examination was his disease. He often saw it in the faces of the people he cared for the most. Some of his adversaries in business saw him as a person of subdued and calculating malice. Frank was kind of proud of that. But it was too bad when people he cared about felt eroded by his attention.

On a Tuesday afternoon, he drove to Harlowton for lunch with Bob Cheney, who managed the JA ranch. The JA was a pioneer cattle ranch that once belonged to the Melwood family; Mrs. Melwood, the widow of the last rancher in the family, left it to the Salvation Army and Bob Cheney managed it for them. Frank met Cheney at the Graves Hotel, waiting for him a short time on its veranda and staring out at the summer clouds over the prairie. Cheney arrived in a truck filled with fencing materials and salt blocks, and parked right in front of the hotel. They went inside and ordered lunch.

"How long has it been since you had yearlings on us, Frank?"

"Long time ago. Eighty-one, anyway. Are you going to have any room for me this year?"

"I don't quite know yet. How many head?"

"I'll have to see where the market is, where the bank is."

"I don't think I'll be able to tend them. I'm short a man this season. I could find you a fellow, if you want to pay him."

"That will work. Do you think you'll have room for three hundred head of steers?"

"I might," said Bob. Their lunch arrived and he smiled up at the waitress. Bob had a thin mouth, sharp nose and chin. He looked like an English pirate. "Did you bring your clubs, Frank?"

"You know, I didn't. I have to go straight from you back to Bozeman."

"What a shame. Can't even make nine holes?"

"I can't. And you know what else? I haven't played since the year I last had cattle on you. I just kind of pulled my business life over my head and that was that."

Some war was on the radio and the café was quieter than usual. Conversations murmured on about the eroding price supports for grain, baseball, the cattle-feeder monopolies.

"Your boy still at the college?" Frank asked.

"Getting ready to graduate."

"Is he going to come back to the ranch?"

"I don't think so."

Bob smiled, shrugged. You didn't work your way up in ranching. You might get the job but the owner was always somebody else. A man appeared in the doorway with his dog. The continuity was going out of ranching, and Frank felt sorry for the people who had seen so much in it and couldn't go on with that, in their families or in any other way. Frank thought he himself must be a transitional figure, unlike his father, who had never wanted anything but a business life; he himself had waffled into it, then grown to like it.

Frank's father used to eat here regularly, when he had an interest in the hardware store and then an insurance agency that later moved to Grass Range, where it was absorbed by an office in Lewistown. Then he had a ranch at Straw, west of Eddie's Corner, and it was easy to use the Lewistown office for the ranch business. The ranch, as far as he was concerned, was just another file at the Lewistown office. Payroll, government programs, expenses, everything was just that one file, ran almost a thousand mother cows. Bob Cheney started at the Straw place when he was a young cowboy, later went to work on the JA for Mrs. Melwood and then the Salvation Army. All the same job except the Salvation Army didn't speculate but ran it as a conservative cow-calf place and in good years leased some grass. And it was good grass—buffalo grass and some bluestem. Bob and Frank had always got along, once even worked together; so Frank got the first call on the grass. It wasn't insider trading—he paid the going rate—but it was an awfully good grass deal. Frank thought be could make some money on it, a little anyway. He only did these yearling deals when he thought he was having a good year. You took out a big loan and bet it on one throw of the dice. He liked being in business with people like Bob Cheney, liked talking to them.

"Frank," said Bob, "I believe a man could put five hundred head out there."

Bingo. That was what Frank was waiting to hear. He kept talking but he was already running the numbers in his mind, already picturing the strategy with the bank, perhaps deferring some interest. He wanted a reason to have to come out here. Something about the other stuff was starting to go.

"Here's where we left off," Frank was saying. He was back in town.

The banker was standing between Frank and the Dolan Building, which housed a shoe store and a row of second-floor apartments. There was a man in the window of the shoe store hunkered down in his stocking feet arranging shoe samples. "You were going to go halves with me on the cattle. We were going to fix the rate at nine and there wasn't going to be any points or other charges."

"That's where we left off?"

"Yeah."

The banker had a young face and white hair. His mouth was small and level and it was right under his nose. It was like a face by someone who couldn't draw too well.

"Where did we have to go from there?" smiled the banker.

"Size," said Frank.

"Size?" asked the banker.

"Size," said Frank. "This is going to be what you guys call a jumbo product. I'd like a quarter of a million dollars. More or less. It's five hundred yearlings, basically. You'll have to get back to me, right?"

"Right."

"And remember this, it's only money."

"I'll let you know, Frank."

"And I hope we won't be talking about other collateral than the yearlings."

"Right, Frank. Frank, we walk it through. Don't always be so adversarial. I think it makes you feel you haven't sold out if you act like you're always in a fight with the banks." He laughed; it was really a sharp remark and he was quite proud of it.

This was beginning to absolve Frank of the further need that he seemed to start each day with. He had come to rely on this fiscal narcosis in the last few years. He suspected it had to do with insufficient spiritual values, but those seemed to have gone out the window with his wife. *Press forward*, he thought. *Buy things, then sell them. Try to make a profit. Imbed yourself in the robust flux, the brush fire of commerce.*

He got the loan, and in the wild fluctuations of the cattle market, it was a dangerous loan. They were happy to walk it through when they thought it might blow up in your face. Despite his bold speech to the banker, it cost Frank a lien on the clinic. The yearlings arrived in nine bunches from Chouteau, Camas Prairie, Sumatra, Sedan, Wise River, White Sulphur Springs, Ekalaka, Cat Creek, and Geraldine. Frank stayed at the Graves and met each load with his summer cowboy, a very competent twenty-eight-year-old nephew of Bob's named John Jones. When Frank sat down in the restaurant of the Graves with John Jones to do his W-2 form, he found that this bright young man could neither read nor write. For some reason, as he helped Jones, whose face blazed with shame, fill out his form, he felt like a transubstantiated version of his father, a patient and unambiguous man who would see Jones's illiteracy as just a small impediment in getting the yearlings onto the grass in an orderly way where they could begin to gain weight and be worth more money. To Frank's father, every animal had a dollar meter on its back and the needle was always in motion. Sometimes it was going down. If you ran a thousand head, you had a thousand meters, and you had to keep those needles going up. Frank wondered what his father would have thought at a time when big calves were going for five hundred dollars a round and that quarter-million-dollar note was dragging its ass at nine and a half percent compound interest all summer long, rain or shine, secured by a note on a medical clinic! He would have made money, Frank concluded, for the simple reason that he never saw any romance in cattle. There's a little money in cattle, he used to say, not much, and no romance. A hundred years ago there was big romance in cattle because there was big money in it. There is no big romance combined with small money. Period. Frank's uncle Rusty once said, "The lady doesn't marry the carpenter unless he's got a second home in Santa Monica or a two-foot dick."

Frank went to a breakfast meeting with doctors Jensen, Popelko, Dumars, and Frame in the dining room of the Dexter. They were his renters. The clinic had minimal equipment, an EKG machine, an X-ray machine, no lab. He got there a few minutes late and the doctors were telling stories over their first cup of coffee. Dr. Popelko, an obstetrician who had taught his specialty, explained how he had tried to get his university to hire prostitutes. He chuckled, his little round face completely wrinkled, his bow tie bobbing, and the shoulders of his loud plaid sport jacket shuddering. "How do you teach students to do a vaginal?" he bayed across the dining room. "It's no different than learning to ride a horse. *You need vaginas!* Where are you going to get them? In the old days, we used poor people's vaginas in exchange for medical treatment. Now everyone has insurance. The chancellor's wife isn't going to let you use her vagina, is she? The chairman of the English department is not liable to suggest that the medical students train on his daughter's vagina. The only answer seemed to be prostitutes. But when I suggested this as a budget item to the university, I damn near lost my job. It made the papers and the Born Agains were marching! I went into private practice. I had to!"

"Morning, Frank," said Dr. Dumars. Frank carried his own coffee and roll and set them among the more complete breakfasts of the doctors. Dr. Dumars was an older doctor, close to retirement, and bore himself with the kind of gravity old doctors sometimes had as a result of all they had seen. Jensen and Frame were young and ambitious, with huge split-level homes out in the canyons. Jensen had blond hair, which he had arranged in pixieish bangs, a modern and alert young man with staring eyes. Frame was somber; the skin under his eyes was dark and his lower lip hung in a permanent pout. He was gazing at Frank.

"Been fishing, Frank?" Jensen asked.

"Yeah, I went yesterday over on the Sixteen. It was pretty darn good," Frank said.

"Huh," said Jensen, "we went to the Big Horn over the weekend. Sixteen-foot leaders. Antron emergers. Size 22."

"A little tough for me, sounds like." Frame was still staring at him.

Jensen shrugged. "I wanted to get a couple of days in. There's a marathon in Billings next weekend, then a prostate seminar in Sun Valley the following weekend, and so on, and there goes your life."

Dr. Frame spoke abruptly. "Do you, um, know what?" He was trying to look right through Frank.

"I shudder to think."

"The rent in the, um, clinic is too high."

"No, it's not," said Frank.

"Too high, too low, it's more than we're, um, willing to pay." Frame was teaching Frank the ABCs about the facts of running his building.

Frank sipped his coffee, peered over the top of it at the other doctors who were not tipping their hands, letting Frame run point. Popelko had a purely inquiring look on his face; he just wanted a factual outcome. Jensen was just being serious about whatever it was. No one was going to mediate on Frank's behalf, that was clear. Frank said, "Why don't you move out?"

"We haven't paid last month's rent."

"I hadn't noticed."

"We just wanted to, um, send a signal."

"I don't understand signals. I understand English."

"I tried English," said Dr. Frame. "You didn't seem to, um, understand."

"I understood. I was short on information. I didn't realize you hadn't paid the rent last month. You're evicted."

At this the other doctors clamored. Dumars immediately pulled Jensen toward him by the coat and spoke into his ear. Frank stood up. The doctors were all trying to look like one unit, a little tribal dance group or something. Frank knew they didn't want to move out; they just wanted to improve their deal. Frank read once that 90 percent of them went to medical school for business reasons. That made it easier to keep their rent where it ought to be rather than imagine they were sheltering sick orphans.

"Get your stuff out. Or hand-deliver last month's rent. I'll be able to give you the new figures for next month, if you decide to stay. I don't see last month's check in my office today, you're going to have to work out of your upstairs bedrooms."

Frank walked out into the street. The sunshine hit him. He could never think about property or its problems if the sun was in his face. A ranch couple walked by in matching denim; she had a dramatically tooled purse and he wore a bandanna. They were gazing around at the buildings and gesturing to each other with show-business savvy about projecting their feelings. What a big town this is! they seemed to say.

He kept trying to make an entire day in the office. Eileen had him stacked up with calls to return and letters to respond to. He had to sort out gas-line easements across the ranch. The city was asking him to abandon an old head gate that was now on the grounds of a small park. There was a request from the doctors to confirm that they could always lease at their current rates, which Frank responded to with a number of built-in slides for inflation, cost of living, exhausted depreciation schedules, and the offer to raise the rent at once. He felt quite absent but he immersed himself in paperwork and returning calls. Eileen checked each sheet of paper before handing it to him and tried to characterize it with a phrase. "Payment to the beef council," or "Holly, Blue Cross." *I've got to get levered*, he thought, *and quit dicking around*. He thought about the land; the land, he currently felt, was nowhere. How had he lost his grip on that one? And the cattle, all the young people wanted the cattle off the land altogether and replaced by ferns or some damn thing.

"Del Dawson," said Eileen, pressing a sheaf his way, "wants to know if he can pass on the prepayment privileges you extended to him to a potential new buyer."

"Depends on the potential new buyer. Laurance Rockefeller, yes; Donald Trump, no."

"This is the old Dairy Freeze."

"I don't care if it's Monticello."

"I'll tell Mr. Dawson."

"Good, you tell Dawson."

Frank's father was free of these doubts, and this clarity often made Frank think of him with simple love. He was a boy coming home and his

573

father hugged him into his wintry overcoat in the train station. Other times, his father was slack-faced with alcohol and anger and his family was nothing but ballast.

He recognized that he was going to have to move his mind more into the foreground and out of the world of regrets and ambiguities. The desk was piled high with reminders of neglect. He couldn't run a business this way. "You can't run a business this way!" he said aloud. He thought he heard Eileen say, "Amen," but he knew very well she didn't have that sort of wit. He must have imagined it. It did seem though that he had heard an "amen."

Frank had been slow to face the implication of the emptying of his clinic. It was, as they say, a highly leveraged transaction in the first place. If the prospects of failure had crept toward him from the day Gracie left, they were now at a full gallop. He quickly reckoned whether he could slow this down. He was conscious of a kind of force bearing against him. He drove home and stopped in front of his house. He looked around as though checking the address. The wind up the street in front of his building seemed like the movie wind that blows away footprints.

The two cattle buyers from Nebraska were in his office, smelling of the lots and the diesel fuel of the outbound loads, snap-button cotton shirts, Copenhagen lumps under their lower lips, and Stetson Open Road hats pulled just over the top of their eyes. The older of the two wore eyeglasses with colorless frames. He had buckteeth and looked like he never smiled in his life, not once. His counterpart had a round chipmunky face and eager brown eyes. Frank started out by denying everything. He used a booming voice he only used around cattle buyers. His mind quietly ran on in several directions, one of which was that the bank, noticing poor crop-growing conditions and consequent low feeder replacements, was desperately trying to keep itself, and Frank, from taking a bad blow. The bank must have alerted these boys. Force him to take the loss now and suck it out of his other collateral.

"What do you mean I stole those cattle?" Frank boomed.

"I don't mean literally stole," said the older man.

"I paid about what their owners wanted for them," shouted Frank in a voice that would have been unfamiliar to his own mother. "But I sure picked my time and I bought them right. If you want yearlings, that's one thing. But I don't allow folks to discuss valuation with me at that level. Now, I know where these are going and I know what feed is. I can background them till hell freezes over, you know that. But I have told you like a white man what I've got to have, and the two of you look at me like a pair of Chinamen. You tell me that not only have I stolen these cattle in the first place but that I am not entitled to fair market value for them. Which is: eighty-four cents a hundredweight with a nickel slide at, what? Six hundred pounds?'"

"Five-seventy-five slide," said the young man. Frank shrugged. He minced over to another spot in the room in a golden fatigue. Even he could feel a sort of doom. At least these fellows weren't rubbing his nose in it. A pleasant, protective code was in the air.

"Five-seventy-five," he said. Part of the formula, which comforted everyone in a cattle deal, was to lose deal points without losing face. This price slide really knocked the wind out of Frank but he didn't let it show. His mind was going fast. He knew he wanted to be out from under these cattle but this thing on the slide was a fucking double hernia. He was in too good a mood when he bought them; and lately he had quit tracking them in the marketplace, a loss of interest that could get costly if it went much beyond this. With the doctors out of his building, the bank was surely wondering about him. It was time for the parachute before the USDA issued one of its devastating inventory reports or some bullshit about lighter cattle going on feed, various ruinous allegations about seasonal erosion of Fed cattle marketings.

"I guess we could write you a deposit," said the man in the glasses.

"No, I don't expect you could," Frank said, trying not to get in a rush, trying not to spill, trying not to let on that this was something he wanted out of now. He wanted to get this thing down to the bone. They had to know he was hurting.

"Mister, we're a good ways from home."

"Yeah," said Frank, "this one I've also heard. You don't dare show your face without ten pots of yearlings. You can't even go up to the house without a thousand head because of what people expect of you in the Sandhills." He thought this would warm things up toward a closure, and he was right.

The older man looked at him. "They expect quite a little, don't deny that."

"If you're shipping as quick as you say, I need to show this stock paid in full. Get out your checkbook and start writing." Frank was saying, Don't tell me you can't write me a great big check for these cattle, I know you're plenty stout.

The older man slid his eyes to his companion, moved his chin very slightly. They were going to leave Frank his shred of dignity. It wasn't costing them anything. The round-faced younger man reached under his coat without looking and elevated his checkbook from his shirt pocket.

"I used to know a man who wrote checks for a million dollars," Frank said, "then lit his cigar with them. Can you tell me who I can call to verify the funds in your account?"

Frank was back out of the cattle business again. If the check didn't bounce, he could go to the bank and tell them that though they just lost fifty thousand dollars, it could have been way worse, blah, blah, blah. No surprise to them. Changing times like an ice-water enema. They sent these guys. They knew there was a loss. It was just a question of how bad a one a man could take. That evening, he walked home from the office, sat down at the table, and looked out through the window into the declining light of that day. "Gracie," he said aloud, perfectly aware that it is not a great thing to begin talking to yourself. "I think I'm going broke."

This feeling stayed with him so long that it was not exactly a surprise when his accountant asked to see him in his offices. John Coleman was one of the most reputable accountants in the city, and Frank enjoyed going to his offices for a sense of pulse, a cool office with muted traffic sounds below, an undisturbed air. He showed Frank a chair, then swung sideways in his own after asking his secretary to hold his calls. He always gave Frank the feeling that he had made more time than they would ever need. "Are you all right?" he asked. John still wore wide, soft ties restrained in the middle by a tie clasp with a little chain.

"I'm fine."

"You haven't been by."

"Not much happening. It takes almost a year to absorb the blow of last year's taxes."

"You're a success, Frank. It's expensive to be a success.

"In more ways than one."

"Quite right. It's either too much or too little, isn't it? I mostly see too little. But Frank, you've always had a nice, light touch, a nice feel for the situation."

"John, I appreciate the valentines. What's up?"

"I don't know."

"What do you think it is?"

"I think I see problems."

"Are you talking about my cattle deal?"

"Partly."

"I'll tell you what that was. That was a bum deal and we all have them."

"The clinic?"

"That was a case of drawing the line. Where'd those assholes go, anyway?"

John said in the tone of an elementary-school teacher, "They went elsewhere. They went to the new clinic."

"There's a new clinic?"

"Out near Nineteenth."

"Oh. I thought that was a school."

"See, Frank? You would have known that before."

"Anyway, we'll fill the building."

"You will."

"I believe so."

John laced his fingers over the top of his head and looked straight at Frank. Frank thought it was a rather artificial gesture. He asked, "What about Gracie?"

"What about her?"

"Hear anything?"

"Nope."

"She divorce you yet?"

"Not yet. I don't really care. I guess she'll get around to it."

"I'm just trying to imagine its impact on your finances."

"I guess she'll take me to the cleaners," Frank yawned. "Little coaching from the boyfriend, they'll see a big future. I'm having trouble with the future. It's my least favorite tense."

"Frank, I'm your accountant. Are you saying you don't care?"

"No, I'm saying my focus is elsewhere." He wanted to get up. "Do what you can, John. I'm not much help just now."

"Do you have a plan?"

"Yeah, yeah, I do."

"What is it?"

"I'm just gonna drive around. Take in the sights."

Frank felt very heavy in his chair. John's healthy interest was unbearable. His comfortable office had become a cell. Frank resolved to make a smooth, unjerky exit so that he didn't seem disturbed or alarming to John, who always had his best interests at heart.

"Well I gotta go," said Frank, not knowing where to put his gaze.

"It was good of you to come," said John with an averted look of his own. This was torture for both of them.

"So long, John," said Frank. He was sweating bullets.

"So long, Frank. Hope everything goes okay."

"It will, John."

"Good, Frank."

"This is me then," Frank bleated, "heading on out."

The bank agreed to treat the loss as a simple debt, to be repaid over the year at simple interest, one above prime. At first they wanted to exploit their position on the clinic, and Frank told them where they could put their position. He felt so blue, walked around his block, then down toward town, where he looked at wolf tapes through the window of Sage Records. When the wolf was extinct, you could go to Sage Records and get a wolf tape. Frank even felt that he would feel less dolorous about his situation if there was a good tape of himself.

It was early evening and Frank walked along the sidewalk in front of his building, formerly a clinic. It was a cool, low, sanitary shape with an even hedge of potentillas along the front and specimens of paper birch and seed-less cottonwoods in bark-filled beds. An old man was running a weed-eater along the base of the building with a fanatical small engine raving, a monofilament hiss as the weeds tumbled neatly. The building was pale-ocher brick, and overhead the sky was deepest cobalt, the clouds white, white, white. The street seemed to climb into a magnificent cloudland.

The weed-eater man watched Frank let himself in with a key. The doors were self-closing and made a soft, cushioning sound as they shut off the outside and exposed the silence of the interior. Frank hiked himself up on the receptionist's desk and looked out into the waiting room. Maga-zines, fireproof curtains, green Naugahyde (unborn Naugahyde, Gracie called it) chairs, shin-high tables; no anxiety, nobody waiting to hear what was wrong with them, no news of a baby they weren't supposed to have, no maintenance reports on wearing out bodies, no heartbroken fat girls wad-dling back to the doctors' offices carrying their own records. It was a true dead zone, with decorations by Cézanne, Matisse, and Charlie Russell. He picked up the phone, also dead. The Rolodex was opened to Bungalow Pharmacy, and some wag had written on the desk blotter, "Eat Shit and Die, Motherfucker."

Frank sensed he was not alone. He listened and heard someone walk-ing in a neighboring office, more than one person. He opened his door an inch or two and watched. In a moment, he made out the forms of men carrying out the scales, the doctors, in jogging spandex. He couldn't quite remember who actually owned the scales and so he hesitated before stepping into the corridor; but finally he did emerge and the doctors stopped just a moment, played it as if they knew he was there all along. Then, when they steadied the scales on their shoulders, the weights ran across the bar and clattered to a stop, and Dr. Wood said, "Frank."

"Get 'er all, boys," said Frank. "She'll never be a clinic again."

Dr. Jensen said from beneath his bangs, "We'll only get what belongs to us."

"My lucky day," said Frank.

Frank looked at these remarkably uniform phantoms and felt suddenly sleepy. He went out ahead of them and drove five hard hours to Whitefish, where he took a room on the lake. He watched the cat's-paws on the blue water move the length of the lake for a day and listened to the train travel through the woods above the dark, stony beach. He lay out on the dock and watched the cutthroats fin around the pilings. There were numerous smoke-blackened fireworks parts from the recent Fourth, and Frank, lying face down with his nose between the boards, smelled gunpowder. He loved that smell. He occasionally thought it would be pleasing to shoot several people in particular, accompanied as that would be by this fine smell. A plane went over, no reason he couldn't be in that plane, and a boat went by and there was no reason he couldn't be on that boat. Just at sundown he paddled a floating cushion out to the middle of the lake, where he met a radiologist, a woman in her forties, also on a cushion, hers with parti-colored sea horses and an inflated pillow. She worked in Kalispell and came here, she said, anytime she found a cancer, to float between earth and sky and to sustain, on her sea-horse floatie, a sense of deep time that could accommodate life and death. Frank looked at her long, melancholy face with its thick, seemingly puffy lips, her stringy hair, and short, square brow, and said, "You have a hard job."

"Yes, I do. My job is to search for something I hope I don't find. That is a hard job, sport." Darkness seemed to be forming overhead, a circle of contracting shadows from the shoreline and faint stars overhead. There wasn't a breath of wind and when Frank reached out to take the tip of the radiologist's finger, he was able to draw her raft to him with an ounce of pressure. Her face was an inch away and they both moved imperceptibly toward each other to kiss. Her mouth was open and he tasted a Halls Mentho-lyptus cough drop. He slipped his hand a small distance inside the top of her bathing suit and felt a hard nipple. He opened his eyes and thought he could make out trembling water around her raft. The bottom of her bathing suit was drawn across the points of her hips and a flat stomach. Very quietly, Frank moved to board the radiologist's raft, a delicate matter that worked, right up to the point that it didn't work; and with a sudden rotary motion the radiologist shot out of sight. "Hey!" shouted Frank from impulse and trod water between the plunging shapes of the floaties. He felt the radiologist's head under the arch of his foot and struggled to get ahold of her. She came up spraying water from her mouth and with a minimum of floundering got onto her raft again, on her stomach, and began to paddle toward shore. Frank followed her. "What's your problem?" she said when he overtook her.

"Same problem as everybody else."

"Oh, this'll be good," she said. "What is it?"

"I'm just trying to get some meaning in my life." Frank felt he was leaping from line to line.

"Ha, ha."

They walked together along the railroad track in the last light. There was enough curve in the lakeside route that the rails were always disappearing on the geometry of creosote sleepers just ahead in the woods. Honeysuckle grew wild down the steep banks, where lake water glimmered through the trunks of the tall, old pines. Elise, that was her name, chatted along amiably and was very good at naming the birds they saw, the chipping sparrows, the yellowthroats, the kinglets. There was something about the way she touched her fingertip to the droplets of resin on the pine bark that made Frank think, *I may be headed for a world of poontang.* He wasn't off by much.

In Frank's room, she peered examiningly at his cock, and said, "The baleful instrument of procreation. Ooh," she said squeezing hard, "I can tell I shouldn't have said that!"

"Don't worry about it."

"Are you having a nice time?" she asked.

"Like my grandpa used to say, 'If this ain't it, you can mail mine.'"

They kissed and she slipped her Halls Mentho-lyptus cough drop from her mouth into his; it was like a cool breeze. He slid down the length of her and spanning the backs of her knees with his hands licked deep into her. She moaned, then jumped out of bed. "That cough drop has set me on fire!" she hollered and ran into the bathroom. He heard her running cold water on a washcloth and tried to decide what to do with the cough drop. Finally, he spit it down the wall behind the bed. She came back in with the washcloth clamped to her crotch, got into bed, and sent the washcloth back toward the bathroom with a kind of hook shot.

"Just quit pussyfooting around," she said, "and stick it in."

She had a long, firm body that she must have worked hard to keep in such shape; and she flung it around with great confidence in its appearance. Frank hadn't made such buoyant love in memory. He got happier and happier until he wondered briefly if her energy was connected by some means to having found a cancer that day. He felt very good and did not consider asking about it. Then he thought about that. They were through, lying there, and he must have been looking off and she caught it, scrutinizing him. The room was silent. She leaned across him and picked up the phone and dialed. After a moment, she spoke. She just said, "Hi." Then the other person spoke. Then she said, "Sorry, I couldn't make it" and hung up. It was out of the question to ask who was on the other end; something in the flat way she spoke made Frank know that she was supposed to have been fucking this other person and not over here at the lake fucking him.

It was late and the only thing they could get was the weather channel. Elise was smart and it was fun to talk to her about the possibilities of weather. There was a stalled-out high where they were and you could see it on the national weather map. Elise knew where it was going when it began to move; it was going to the Dakotas. She stood naked beside the television set and pointed to where it was going. Their drought was over but it looked like others had just begun. She came back to bed. You could see where the heat spread west from Bullhead City, Arizona, then hit a kind of Pacific wall and stalled, rising slowly up the coast of California . . . she had her mouth on him now and the antics of the weatherman with his pointer didn't make any sense.

When they'd finished, Frank turned the weather off and got back into bed. It was late. They talked awhile about property. Frank said housing starts were way up in his part of the state. "The contractors who hung in during the Eighties were really booked. Everybody's working. We're all trying to woo these new businesses but our unemployment rates are so low and our warehouses so full, we know we're askew on their shopping lists. I've got a little building I rent as a kind of clinic slash boutique to five doctors."

"Oh, that's great."

"Yeah."

"I'm just there at the Valley Hospital. It's okay. I don't pack anything home with me. I'm still in my hippie mode, down deep."

"Were you a hippie?" he asked.

"Yup."

"Huh, so was I."

"I mean, I was pretty motivated compared to some of them but I consider myself an old hippie. What do you think I'm doing here?"

"People were doing this before the hippies."

"Not with the same spirit," said Elise. "I was hitchhiking around Europe, and in Italy they called us *I Amici di Liverpool* because they thought all the hippies came from Liverpool, kind of a hangover from the Beatles era."

"I guess Italians get the news a little late."

"They just get it when they want it. . . ." She seemed to drift off and then spoke again. "What's the policy on your toothbrush?"

"You can use it."

"Mm." He could feel her drift off, her back to him. He put his arms around her and thought about considering the weather with someone else . . . thundershowers in Indiana . . . lake effect. . . Then he thought, *To be living.*

* * *

He woke up in the dark. He was alone. That was probably why he woke up. The bathroom light was on. He made out a knee beyond the lighted doorway with the corner of a newspaper over it. He heard a deep, solid fart. He thought of a map-reading scene in a movie about the Civil War, and the cannon fire reduced so you could hear the dialogue of strategy. She sensed something.

"Are you awake?"

"Just."

"Is this your *Journal*?"

"Yup."

"Have you read it?"

"No, I haven't."

"It says, 'Natural gas is the fuel of the future.'"

"I see."

"It's a joke. I know you were awake when I made that little noise."

"I'm afraid I was."

"'The 1990s were supposed to bring a golden era for the gas industry. Repeated threats of oil shortages, ever-toughening pollution laws, and federal tax credits refunding up to 70 percent of exploration costs seemed to guarantee that gas would become the dominant fossil fuel.' What do you think?"

"I don't have a strong feeling about this one way or the other."

"Yet you lay there like a secretive little mouse because I cut one lousy fart in the privacy of a motel bathroom."

"I wasn't being secretive. I was asleep."

Elise came back to bed in a flood of warmth, immediately cuddled. "You married?"

"Separated."

"Since when, since breakfast?"

"Long time. How about you?"

"Yup, nice husband, two nice kids, boys."

"So, what's this all about?"

"I belong to a dick-of-the-month club."

"Seriously."

"How should I know? You paddle out to the middle of a northern Montana lake to be alone and a decent-looking guy paddles out and rolls your raft. There's nobody else out there. It's determinism, it's fate. Fate says: Put out, Elise. So, Elise puts out. You seemed to welcome the fate of Elise and its atmosphere of festivity. You seemed to salute the cheating heart of Elise."

"This is an unusual thing for you?"

"Not particularly."

"Was that your husband on the phone?"

"Nope."

"What about the cancer?"

"That was pretty much true. I confess that it's also sort of an unimpeachable excuse. But don't you think that most personal freedom is built on other people's misfortune?"

"Good grief."

"I never look at a set of X-rays without being reminded how short life is. Lust follows. It's like living in a city under siege. And here's another weird thought: I'd hate to ever have to X-ray someone I've had sex with."

What an adorable woman, Frank thought, a little crush forming, so full of life and now asleep with an untroubled conscience. Her peace was catching and he was soon asleep.

In the morning, they got coffee in Styrofoam cups from a gas-station convenience store. The sky was clear except for a huge white thunderhead to the west that caught a pink-orange effulgence from the morning sun. Elise slid into her yellow Jeep Cherokee. Traffic headed toward Flathead streamed past behind her. She nodded, smiled as if to say yes or yep or uh-huh, and pulled into traffic.

He finished his coffee and went back to the motel to check out. He felt a goofy pride to see the thrashed and discomposed bed. "Good job, Frank," he said aloud and climbed into the shower, letting the needles of hot water drive into his revitalized flesh. Then he shaved. Frank loved to shave. It was interesting to get the little groove in his upper lip and to make the sideburns come out even. He had to stretch the skin of his neck to shave it smoothly as it no longer stayed taut on its own. What difference does it make if my flesh is firm, he thought smugly, if they're going to put out like that anyway? That simple fiesta of venery has restored me. I'm like the happy duck that spots the decoys.

A Man in the Way

F. Scott Fitzgerald

Pat Hobby could always get on the lot. He had worked there fifteen years on and off—chiefly off during the past five—and most of the studio police knew him. If tough customers on watch asked to see his studio card he could get in by phoning Lou, the bookie. For Lou also, the studio had been home for many years.

Pat was forty-nine. He was a writer but he had never written much, nor even read all the "originals" he worked from, because it made his head bang to read much. But the good old silent days you got somebody's plot and a smart secretary and gulped benzedrine "structure" at her six or eight hours every week. The director took care of the gags. After talkies came he always teamed up with some man who wrote dialogue. Some young man who liked to work.

"He got a list of credits second to none," he told Jack Berners. "All I need is an idea and to work with somebody who isn't all wet."

He had buttonholed Jack outside the production office as Jack was going to lunch and they walked together in the direction of the commissary.

"You bring *me* an idea," said Jack Berners. "Things are tight. We can't put a man on salary unless he's got an idea."

"How can you get ideas off salary?" Pat demanded—then he added hastily: "Anyhow I got the germ of an idea that I could be telling you all about at lunch."

Something might come to him at lunch. There was Baer's notion about the boy scout. But Jack said cheerfully, "I've got a date for lunch, Pat. Write it out and send it around, eh?"

He felt cruel because he knew Pat couldn't write anything out but he was having story trouble himself. The war had just broken out and every producer on the lot wanted to end their current stories with the hero going to war. And Jack Berners felt he had thought of that first for his production.

"So write it out, eh?"

When Pat didn't answer Jack looked at him—he saw a sort of whipped misery in Pat's eye that reminded him of his own father. Pat had been in the money before Jack was out of college—with three cars and a chicken over every garage. Now his clothes looked as if he'd been standing at Hollywood and Vine for three years.

"Scout around and talk to some of the writers on the lot," he said. "If you can get one of them interested in your idea, bring him up to see me."

"I hate to give an idea without money on the line," Pat brooded pessimistically. "These young squirts'll lift the shirt off your back."

They had reached the commissary door.

"Good luck, Pat. Anyhow we're not in Poland."

—*Good* you're not, said Pat under his breath. They'd slit your gizzard.

Now what to do? He went up and wandered along the cellblock of writers. Almost everyone had gone to lunch and those who were in he didn't know. Always there were more and more unfamiliar faces. And he had thirty credits; he had been in the business, publicity and script-writing, for twenty years.

The last door in the line belonged to a man he didn't like. But he wanted a place to sit a minute so with a knock he pushed it open. The man wasn't there—only a very pretty, frail-looking girl sat reading a book.

"I think he's left Hollywood," she said in answer to his question. "They gave me his office but they forgot to put up my name."

"You a writer?" Pat asked in surprise.

"I work at it."

"You ought to get 'em to give you a test."

"No—I like writing."

"What's that you're reading."

She showed him.

"Let me give you a tip," he said. "That's not the way to get the guts out of a book."

"Oh."

"I've been here for years—I'm Pat Hobby—and I *know*. Give the book to four of your friends to read it. Get them to tell you what stuck in their minds. Write it down and you've got a picture—see?"

The girl smiled.

"Well, that's very—very original advice, Mr. Hobby."

"Pat Hobby," he said. "Can I wait here a minute? Man I came to see is at lunch."

He sat down across from her and picked up a copy of a photo magazine.

"Oh, just let me mark that," she said quickly.

He looked at the page which she checked. It showed paintings being boxed and carted away to safety from an art gallery in Europe.

"How'll you use it?" he said.

"Well, I thought it would be dramatic if there was an old man around while they were packing the pictures. A poor old man, trying to get a job helping them? But they can't use him—he's in the way—not even good cannon fodder. They want strong young people in the world. And it turns out he's the man who painted the pictures many years ago."

Pat considered.

"It's good but I don't get it," he said.

"Oh, it's nothing, a short short maybe."

"Got any good picture ideas? I'm in with all the markets here."

"I'm under contract."

"Use another name."

Her phone rang.

"Yes, this is Pricilla Smith," the girl said.

After a minute she turned to Pat.

"Will you excuse me? This is a private call."

He got it and walked out, and along the corridor. Finding an office with no name on it he went in and fell asleep on the couch.

II

Late that afternoon he returned to Jack Berners' waiting rooms. He had an idea about a man who meets a girl in an office and he thinks she's a stenographer but she turns out to be a writer. He engages her as a stenographer, though, and they start for the South Seas. It was a beginning, it was something to tell Jack, he thought—and, picturing Pricilla Smith, he refurbished some old business he hadn't seen used for years.

He became quite excited about it—felt quite young for a moment and walked up and down the waiting room mentally rehearsing the first sequence. "So here we have a situation like *It Happened One Night*—only *new*. I see Hedy Lamarr—"

Oh, he knew how to talk to these boys if he could get to them, with something to say.

"Mr. Berners still busy?" he asked for the fifth time.

"Oh, yes, Mr. Hobby. Mr. Bill Costello and Mr. Bach are in there."

He thought quickly. It was half-past five. In the old days he had just busted in sometimes and sold an idea, an idea good for a couple of grand because it was just the moment when they were very tired of what they were doing at present.

He walked innocently out and to another door in the hall. He knew it led through a bathroom right in to Jack Berners' office. Drawing a quick breath he plunged. . . .

". . . So that's the notion," he concluded after five minutes. "It's just a flash—nothing really worked out, but you could give me an office and a girl and I could have something on paper for you in three days."

Berners, Costello and Bach did not even have to look at each other. Berners spoke for them all as he said firmly and gently, "That's no idea, Pat. I can't put you on salary for that."

"Why don't you work it out further by yourself," suggested Bill Costello. "And then let's see it. We're looking for ideas—especially about the war."

"A man can think better on salary," said Pat.

There was silence. Costello and Bach had drunk with him, played poker with him, gone to the races with him. They'd honestly be glad to see him placed.

"The war, eh," he said gloomily, "Everything is war now, no matter how many credits a man has. Do you know what it makes me think of. It makes me think of a well-known painter in the discard. It's war time and he's useless—just a man in the way." He warmed to his conception of himself, "—but all the time they're carting away *his own paintings* as the most valuable thing worth saving. And they won't even let him help. That's what it reminds me of."

There was again silence for a moment.

"That isn't a bad idea," said Bach thoughtfully. He turned to the others, "You know? In itself?"

Bill Costello nodded.

"Not bad at all. And I know where we could spot it. Right at the end of the fourth sequence. We just change old Ames to a painter."

Presently they talked money.

"I'll give you two weeks on it," said Berners to Pat. "At two-fifty."

591

"Two-fifty!" objected Pat. "Say there was one time you paid me ten times that!"

"That was ten years ago," Jack reminded him. "Sorry. Best we can do now."

"You make me feel like that old painter—"

"Don't oversell it," said Jack, rising and smiling. "You're on the payroll."

Pat went out with a quick step and confidence in his eyes. Half a grand—that would take the pressure off for a month and you could often stretch two weeks into three—sometimes four. He left the studio proudly through the front entrance, stopping at the liquor store for a half-pint to take back to his room.

By seven o'clock things were even better. Santa Anita tomorrow, if he could get an advance. And tonight—something festive ought to be done tonight. With a sudden rush of pleasure he went down to the phone in the lower hall, called the studio and asked for Miss Pricilla Smith's number. He hadn't met anyone so pretty for years. . . .

In her apartment Pricilla Smith spoke rather firmly into the phone.

"I'm awfully sorry," she said, "but I couldn't possibly . . . No—and I'm tied up all the rest of the week."

As she hung up, Jack Berners spoke from the couch. "Who was it?"

"Oh, some man who came in the office," she laughed, "and told me never to read the story I was working on."

"Shall I believe you?"

"You certainly shall. I'll even think of his name in a minute. But first I want to tell you about an idea I had this morning. I was looking at a photo in a magazine where they were packing up some works of art in the Tate Gallery in London. And I thought—"

Plains of Abraham

Russell Banks

Had he known everything then that he'd know later, Vann still would have called it a coincidence, nothing more. His was a compact, layered mind with only a few compartments connected. He had been married three times and was unmarried now, and this morning he couldn't shake Irene, his second wife, from his mind. He shaved and dressed for work, tightened the covers and slid the bed back under the sofa, all the while swatting at thoughts of Irene, the force of his swipes banging doors and walls, making him feel clumsy and off-balance. *Thinking about problems only aggravates problems,* but the way these random scraps of memory, emotion, and reflection flew at him—even now, four years after the divorce from Irene, with the lump of a whole third marriage and divorce in between—was strange. Vann

593

and Irene had not seen each other or spoken in person once in those years.

It was a coincidence, that's all, and would have been one even if Vann had known that on this particular morning, a Wednesday in November, Irene, who was forty-eight years old and close to a hundred pounds overweight and suffering from severe coronary disease, who normally would herself be getting ready for work, was instead being prepared at Saranac Lake General Hospital for open-heart surgery. The procedure, to be performed by the highly regarded vascular surgeon Dr. Carl Ransome, was to be a multiple bypass. It was a dangerous although not an uncommon operation, even up here in the north country, and had Irene not collapsed in pain two days earlier while grocery shopping at the Grand Union in Lake Placid with her daughter, Frances, the procedure would have been put off until she had lost a considerable part of her excess weight. Too late for that now.

"Jesus," Dr. Ransome had said to the night nurse after visiting Irene in her room for the first time, "this'll be like flaying a goddamned whale." The nurse winced and looked away, and the young surgeon strode whistling down the corridor.

Vann stirred a cup of instant coffee and wondered if he ever crowded Irene's mornings the way she was crowding his. Probably not. Irene was tougher than he, a big-bellied joker who had seemed nothing but relieved when he left her, although he himself had been almost surprised by his departure, as if she had tricked him into it.

"Good riddance," she liked saying to Frances. "Never marry a construction man, doll baby. They're hound dogs with hard hats."

Vann wasn't quite that bad. He was one of those men who protect themselves by dividing themselves. He regarded love and work as opposites—he loved to work but had to work at love. Yet, with Irene, what Vann thought of as love had come easy, at least at first. When they married, Irene and Vann were in their mid-thirties, lonely, and still shaky from the aftershocks of belligerent first divorces, and for a few years they managed to meet each other's needs almost without trying. Vann was a small man, wiry, with muscles like doorknobs, and back then he had liked Irene's size, her soft amplitude. He had regarded her as a large woman, not fat. And she had liked and admired his crisp, intense precision, his pale crew-cut hair, his tight smile.

To please her, and to suit himself, too, he had come in off the road and for a while kept his tools in the trunk of his car and worked locally. He started his own one-man plumbing-and-heating business, limited mostly to small repairs and renovations, operating out of a shop that he built into the basement of Irene's house in Lake Placid. Frances, who was barely a teenager then, had resented Vann's sudden, hard presence in her mother's life and home and stayed away at boarding school, except for holidays, which was fine by Vann, especially since Irene's first husband was paying the tuition.

Irene quit her job at the real-estate office and kept Vann's books. But after four barely break-even and two losing years in a row, his credit at the bank ran out, and the business collapsed, and Vann went on the road again. Soon he saw his needs differently. He guessed Irene saw her needs differently then, too. He knew he had disappointed her. He allowed himself a couple of short-term dalliances, and she found out about one. He told her about one other. He drank a lot, maybe too much, and there were some dalliances he barely remembered. Those he kept to himself. A year later, they were divorced.

Vann had known from the moment he and Irene first spoke of marriage that if he failed at this, his second shot at domestic bliss, he would have to revise his whole view of life with women. This was going to be his second and probably last chance to get love and marriage right. Vann knew that much. You can't make a fresh start on anything in life three times. By then, if a man gets divorced and still goes on marrying, he's chasing something other than romance and domestic life; he's after something strictly private. Vann had gone on anyhow. And now, in spite of the third divorce, or perhaps because of it, whenever he told himself the story of his life, the significance of his second marriage remained a mystery to him and a persistent irritant. Vann remembered his ten years with Irene the way men remember their war years: the chapter in the story of his life so far that was both lumi-nous and threatening and loomed way too large to ignore.

He picked up his coffee cup and went outside and stood on the rickety, tilted porch of the cottage, where he deliberately studied the smear of pink in the eastern sky and the rippling ribbons of light on the small, man-made lake in front of him. *Lake Flower. Weird name for a lake.* He decided that it was going to be a fine day. Which pleased him. He'd scheduled the duct-work test for today and did not want to run it in a nasty, bone-chilling autumn rain. Vann was field superintendent for Sam Guy, the mechanical contractor out of Lake Placid, on the addition to Saranac Lake General Hospital. Tomorrow, if today's test went smoothly—he had no reason to think it wouldn't—he'd have the heat turned on in the new wing. After that, they'd be working comfortably inside.

It was still dark—dark and cold, a few degrees below freezing—when he got into his truck and drove from the Harbor Hill Cottages on Lake Flower out to the hospital, and despite his studied attempts to block her out, here came Irene again. He remembered how they used to sit around the supper table and laugh together. She had a loose, large face and no restrictions on distorting it to imitate fools and stupid people. Her tongue was as rough as a wood rasp, and she had a particular dislike of Sam Guy, who, the day after Vann's business folded, had hired him and sent him back on the road. "That man needs you because without you he can't pour pee from a boot," she'd declare, and she'd yank one of her own boots off and hold it over her head and peer up into it quizzically.

Vann had never known a woman that funny. Toward the end, however, she had started turning her humor on him, and from then on, there was no more laughing at Irene's comical faces and surprising words. His only recourse had been to slam the door behind him while she shouted, "G'wan, go! Good riddance to bad rubbish!"

He switchbacked along tree-lined streets, crossing the ridge west of the narrow lakeside strip of hotels, motels, stores, and restaurants, and entered a neighborhood of small wood-frame houses and duplexes. The pale light from his headlights bounced off frost that clung like a skin to yellowed lawns, glassed-in porches, and steeply pitched rooftops. Strings of smoke floated from chimneys, and kitchen lights shone from windows. *Jesus, family life.* Which, despite all, Vann still thought of as normal life. *And a proper breakfast.* Vann could almost smell eggs and bacon frying. Moms, dads, and kids cranking up their day together: He could hear their cheerful, sleepy voices.

Vann had lived that sort of morning, but not for nearly fifteen years now, and he missed it. Who wouldn't? Way back in the beginning, up in Plattsburgh, with his own mom and dad, he'd been one of the kids at the table; then later, for a few years, with his first wife, Evelyn, and the boys, he had been the dad. But family life had slipped from his grasp without his having noticed, as if, closing his eyes to drink from a spring, he'd lost a handful of clear water and was unable afterward to imagine a way to regain it. The spring must have dried up. A man can't blame his hands, can he?

Instead, he'd learned to focus his thoughts on how, when he was in his twenties and married to Evelyn and the boys were young, he simply had not appreciated his good luck. That was all. Evelyn had remarried happily and wisely right after the divorce, and the boys, Neil and Charlie, raised more by their stepfather than by Vann, had turned into young men themselves—gone from him forever, or so it seemed. A postcard now and then was all, and the occasional embarrassed holiday phone call. Nothing, of course, from Evelyn—his child bride, as he referred to her—but that, especially as the years passed, was only as it should be.

The way Vann viewed it, his main sin in life had been not to have appreciated his good luck back when he had it. If he'd done that, he probably would have behaved differently. His was a sin of omission, then. To reason that way seemed more practical to him and more dignified than to wallow in regret. It helped him look forward to the future. It had helped him marry Irene. And it had eased his divorce from Inger, his third wife. The Norwegian, was how he thought of her now.

At the variety store where Broadway turned onto Route 86, he picked up a *Daily Enterprise* and coffee to go and a fresh pack of Marlboros. He was driving one of Sam Guy's company pickups, a spruce-green three-quarter-ton Jimmy, brand-new. It had been assigned to him directly from the dealer, and though he liked to pretend, at least to himself, that the vehicle belonged to him and not his boss, Vann would not have said aloud that it was his. That wasn't his style. He was forty-nine, too old to say he owned what he didn't. And too honest.

Besides, he didn't need to lie: He was making payments to the Buick dealer in Plattsburgh on a low-mileage, two-year-old black Riviera that he'd bought last spring to celebrate his divorce from the Norwegian. She'd gotten sole ownership of the house he'd built for them in Keene Valley, but she was also stuck with the mortgage, which gave him some satisfaction. His monthly payments for the car had worked out to six dollars less than his monthly alimony checks, a coincidence Vann found oddly pleasant and slightly humorous, although, when he told people about it, no one else thought it funny or even interesting, which puzzled him.

The Riviera was loaded. A prestige car. It cheered Vann to be seen driving it, and he hoped that over the summer the Norwegian, who was a legal aide for the Adirondack Park Agency in Ray Brook, had accidentally spotted him in it once or twice. He didn't particularly want to see her, but he sure hoped that she had seen him and had noted that Vann Moore, yes indeedy, was doing just fine, thanks.

Out on Route 86 a few miles west of town, he turned right at Lake Colby and pulled into the hospital parking lot, drove to the rear of the three-story brick building, and passed along the edge of the rutted field to the company trailer, where he parked next to a stack of steel pipe. From the outside, the new wing, a large cube designed to merge discreetly with the existing hospital building, appeared finished—walls, roof, and windows cemented solidly into place. Despite appearances, however, the structure was little more than a shell. The masons hadn't started the interior walls yet, the plumbers hadn't set any of the fixtures or run the aboveground water, vacuum, and air lines, and the electricians were still hanging overhead conduit. The painters hadn't even hauled their trailer to the site.

The ductwork for the air-conditioning and heat was finished, though.

Three days ahead of schedule. Vann was a good super. He'd risen in the ranks from journeyman pipe fitter to foreman to super. He'd run his own business and could read drawings and engineering specs, could do estimates for new work in Sam Guy's shop in Lake Placid when the weather turned bad and everyone else got laid off. And he was a good boss, respected and liked by his men. Sam Guy regarded Vann as his right hand and had no compunctions about saying so, and he paid him appropriately. To people who wondered about Vann's way of life, and there were a few, Sam said that if Vann hadn't been tagged over the years with alimony payments and hadn't lost three houses, one to each wife, he'd be living well on what he earned as a super. He wouldn't be renting furnished rooms and shabby, unused vacation cottages, following the work from town to town across the north country. To Vann, however, the opposite was true: If he hadn't followed the work, he'd not have been divorced three times.

Inside the hospital, in the physicians' scrub room, Dr. Ransome and his assistant this morning, Dr. Clark Rabideau, the resident cardiologist who was Irene's regular physician, and Dr. Alan Wheelwright, the anesthesiologist, were discussing the incoming governor's environmental policies while they slowly, methodically washed their hands and arms.

Their patient, Irene Moore, dozy with sedatives, her belly shaved from chin to crotch, was being wheeled on a gurney down the long, windowless second-floor hallway from her room to the main operating room at the end. Her twenty-year-old daughter, Frances, sat alone by the window in Irene's room, flipping through a copy of *Cosmopolitan*. Frances was a tall, big-hipped girl, a second-year student at St. Lawrence University planning to major in psychology. Her straight, slate-colored hair fell limply to her shoulders, and her square face was tight with anxiety.

With her mother unconscious, or nearly so, Frances felt suddenly, helplessly alone. *I'm over my head in this*, she said to herself, *way over*, and quickly turned the pages, one after the other. *What the hell am I supposed to be thinking about? What?*

It was nearly daylight. In the northeast, the flattened sky over Whiteface Mountain was pale gray. In the southeast, over Mount Marcy and

Algonquin Peak, a bank of clouds tinted pink was breaking apart, promising a clear day. The other workers were rumbling onto the job site—electricians, masons, plumbers, steamfitters—driving their own cars and pickups while the foremen and supers arrived in company vehicles. It was light enough for Vann, smoking in his truck, sipping his coffee, to read the front page of the paper and check the NFL scores. It got his mind finally off Irene.

He folded his paper and left the warm truck, but as he crossed to the trailer, key in hand, he glanced out across Lake Colby at the pink morning sky and the dark line of pines below, and the scenery sent him drifting again. He remembered an afternoon four years ago, shortly after the divorce. He was running the public high school job over in Elizabethtown and living in the Arsenal Motel on Route 9 at the edge of town, and one Friday when he drove in from work, a large, flat package was waiting for him at the front desk.

Vann knew at once that it was from Irene—he recognized her hand-writing and the return address, their old Lake Placid address. He lugged the crate back to his room and lay it flat on the bed and studied it for a while. What the hell kind of joke was she playing on him this time?

Finally, he pried open the crate and removed several layers of brown paper and plastic bubble-wrap from the object inside. It was a large, framed picture. He recognized it instantly and felt a rush of fear that made his heart pound as if he had unwrapped a bomb. It was a signed color photograph of Adirondack scenery by a well-known local photographer. Very expensive, he knew. A few years back, when they were still happily married, he and Irene had strolled into a Lake Placid crafts shop, and Vann had glanced up at a picture on the wall and had felt himself leap straight up and into it, as if into someone's dream. It was called *Plains of Abraham* and the scene was of a late-summer day, looking across a field of tall grasses and wildflowers toward Algonquin Peak. The golden field, wide and flat, lay in sunshine in the foreground at eye level. A dark, jagged line of trees cut across the middle, and the craggy, plum-colored mountain towered in the distance, a pure and endless blue sky behind and above it.

This was the first and only picture Vann had ever wanted to own. He asked the saleswoman how much, figuring he could maybe spring for a hundred bucks.

"Twenty-two hundred dollars," she said.

He felt his ears and face flush. "Pretty pricey," he said and moved quickly on to the maple cutting boards and ceramic bowls.

For months afterward, Irene had teased him about it, imitating his high, thin voice and pursed lips. "Pretty pricey," she chirped, checking out a restaurant menu. Or speculating about local real estate: "Pretty pricey." But she had seen the strange, distant, pained look on her husband's face as he gazed at the picture on the wall of the crafts shop. And now here it was before him, as if staring at him from his bed, while he stood over it, confused, frightened, stubbornly resisting awe. He no more wanted to live with that picture than he wanted to live with the woman who had sent it to him. It made him feel invaded, trapped, guilty. Just as she did. If he kept it, what was he supposed to do, write her a thank-you note? What he *should* do, he thought, is return the picture to the crafts shop and pocket the money himself. Serve Irene right.

He took down the large print of an antlered deer that hung above his bed in the motel room and replaced it with *Plains of Abraham* and stepped back to examine it. It was like a window that opened onto a world larger and more inviting than any he had ever seen. No, the picture was too personal between him and Irene and too mysterious to return for cash, he decided. He would wrap it up and recrate the thing and mail it back to her tomorrow. She's so damned smart, let *her* figure out why she sent it to him.

He washed and changed out of his work clothes and went for supper and a few drinks at the Ausable Inn in Keene Valley, where he'd arranged to meet Inger, the Norwegian, whom at that time he'd not quite decided to marry, although he was sleeping with her three and four nights a week. He didn't return to the motel until halfway through the next day, Saturday, and by then, hungover, fuddled with sex and sleeplessness, he had all but forgotten the picture. But when he entered the small room and saw the photograph hanging above his bed, he remembered everything. He sat down on the chair facing it, and his eyes filled with tears. He could not believe that he was actually crying. Crying over what? An overpriced picture of some *scenery*? A damned *divorce*? An *ex-wife*?

He took down the photograph and rehung the deer print. Carefully, he wrapped the picture, returned it to its crate, and stuck the crate into his closet, where it remained more or less forgotten for the entire summer. When the school job was finished and Vann moved fifty miles south to Glens Falls, where a shopping mall was going in, he lugged the picture along and stashed it in the back of his motel-room closet down there. He still owned the thing, although it remained in its crate, and the crate stayed in his closet, hidden, barely acknowledged by Vann, except when one job was over and he packed to move to the next. He'd pull it out and sit on the bed and study Irene's original mailing label as if it could somehow tell him why he couldn't seem to get rid of the damned thing.

To Irene, her mind and body muffled by sedatives, the washed-out blue tile walls of the operating room looked almost soft, as if covered with terry cloth. The operating table, shaped like a cruciform, was in the middle of the room under a bank of white lights. Irene felt her body being eased off the cart by a female nurse and the two male attendants who had brought her here. They arranged themselves alongside her in a line and slid her smoothly onto the table. Her body felt like cold butter. She could see what was happening, but it seemed to be going on elsewhere, in a room beyond glass, and to someone else. Her arms were extended and strapped down, and a long, dark-blue curtain was drawn around her upper and lower parts, leaving only her enormous trunk exposed.

"We're outta here, Dale," one of the attendants said, and Irene heard the squeaky wheels of the cart and the swish of the closing door.

Hidden behind her, Alan Wheelwright, the anesthesiologist, in a blue cotton gown and cap and white surgical mask, stood at the head of the table preparing bags of blood for transfusion, while the nurse, her flecked green eyes expressionless above her mask, swabbed Irene's belly with orange antiseptic, covering her mounded body from hip to throat, back to front, humming as she worked, as if she were home alone painting her toenails. Then, into each of Irene's thick, chalk-white arms, the nurse inserted an intravenous catheter.

Irene saw a man's face, which she recognized, despite the mask, as Dr. Rabideau's, and next to him another man, taller, with bushy white eyebrows, whom she did not recognize but felt she should. There were more nurses now, and the room suddenly seemed crowded and small. A man laughed, genuinely pleased. Someone sang, *I'm forever blowing bubbles.*

She wondered where in the room Vann was standing. Maybe he was one of the people in the masks. She looked at the eyes; she knew Vann's eyes. Her own eyelids seemed to be semitransparent sheets, shutting over and over, in layers. She blinked and left a film; then another. She wondered if her eyes had been shut for a long time already.

What we have here, folks, is hard labor.

Vann's eyes were sapphire-blue and crinkly at the corners, even when he wasn't smiling, like now.

Break out the retractors, Dale. We have liftoff.

Vann was down in the dim basement of the new wing, a huge, cold, open space cluttered with cinder blocks, unused rolls of pink insulation, and stacks of conduit. It took him several tries, but he finally got the gas-powered Briggs & Stratton compressor chugging smoothly. The pump was tied to the overhead ductwork through a three-quarter-inch gate valve with a pressure gauge that Vann had installed strictly for the purposes of the test. He had a kid, Tommy Farr, to help him, but Vann made the connections himself, using Tommy to hand him the tools as he needed them—hose clamps, screwdriver, pipe-joint compound, Stillson wrench. His bare hands were red and stiff from the cold; Vann didn't like working with gloves.

The rest of his crew was scattered over the first and second floors of the wing, installing plumbing fixtures in the lavatories and running the vacuum and oxygen lines. The sheet-metal guys had been released for a new job, a supermarket in a mini-mall over in Tupper Lake. He figured if any blowouts or blocks in the ductwork showed up, he and Tommy could locate and fix them themselves. He wasn't worried. It was a routine test under fairly low pressure, twenty-five pounds per square inch. It wasn't as if the ducts were going to carry water. Just heated air from the large, dark furnace that sat ready to be fired in a shadowed corner of the basement and cooled air from the crated air-conditioning units that had been lifted to the rooftop by crane a week ago.

"All right, Tommy," Vann said, and he stood away from the valve and handed the skinny kid the wrench. "You wanna do the honors?" Vann lit a cigarette, clenched it between his lips, inhaled deeply, and stuck his chilled hands into his jacket pockets.

"Just turn the sucker on?"

"Let her rip. When you hit twenty-five psi's on the gate-valve gauge, close 'er up."

The kid knelt down and with one large hand slowly opened the valve and released a jet of compressed air into the pipeline that led to the threaded gate valve soldered to the side of the sheet-metal duct directly overhead. That duct in turn led from the cold furnace behind them to elaborate crosses and intersections at several places in the basement, where it split into smaller ducts that passed through the reinforced concrete ceiling on to the floors above. At each floor the ducts split again and snaked between and above the yet-to-be-installed walls and ceilings of the new rooms and corridors. These ducts, carefully blocked and baffled at the openings, turns, T's, and Y's, eventually crossed out of the new wing into the old hospital and tied into its system, which carried heated air from the outdated but still adequate furnace in the basement of the main wing of the hospital to the 150 private and semiprivate rooms and wards, the scrub rooms and surgeons' dressing rooms, the physical-therapy center, the operating rooms, the emergency room, the maternity ward and nursery, and all the large and small, public and private lavatories, the janitors' closets, kitchens, dining rooms, nurses' lounges, computer center, labs, billing offices, administrative offices, and the gift shop and florist shop, which was closed this early in the day, and the nearly empty waiting rooms, and even into the large, glass-fronted lobby, where Frances, the daughter of Irene Moore, was at this moment strolling from the hospital, down the steps to the parking lot. Frances was on a run into town for some small present to greet her mom when she woke, something sentimental and silly, like a teddy bear, that her mom would pretend to hate, the way she always did, but Frances knew that her mom would store the gift in a secret drawer so that she could take it out and look at it whenever she wanted to realize anew how much her daughter loved her.

Something was going wrong. The first sign was a cool puff of air that carried a gray plume of ash—probably cigarette ash—from a wall register into the cafeteria on the first floor of the old wing. A janitor leaned against his mop and with some annoyance watched the gray powder float onto his clean floor.

In a laboratory on the second floor, bits of dirt fell from the ceiling vent onto the head and shoulders of a puzzled technician, causing her to jump from her seat and stare at the vent for a moment. When no further debris fell, she sat back down and resumed cataloging urine samples.

Then along one corridor after another and in the maternity ward and in several of the private rooms, on all three floors of the hospital, nurses, doctors, maintenance people, and even some patients began to see tiny scraps of paper, ashes, shreds of pink insulation, metal filings, sawdust, and unidentifiable bits of dirt fly from the registers and ceiling vents, float through the air, and land on sheets and pillows, sterilization cabinets, stainless-steel counters, computers, desks, spotless equipment, and tools of all kinds, dusting hairdos, nurses' caps, starched white uniforms, and even the breakfast trays. Nurses, doctors, administrators, and staff people strode up and down hallways and made phone calls, trying to locate the cause of this invasion of flying debris. Attendants grabbed sheets and blankets and covered the newborn infants in the nursery and patients in the wards, shouting orders and firing angry questions at one another, while patients pressed their buzzers and hollered for help and brushed the floating bits of dirt and trash away from their faces, bandages, casts, and bedding. Those patients who were mobile ran, limped, and rolled in wheelchairs from their rooms and wards to the hallways and nurses' stations, demanding to know what was happening. Had there been an explosion? Was there a fire?

In the operating room, Dr. Rabideau shouted, *Close her up! For Christ's sake, close her up and get her the hell out of here!*

In the cold basement of the new wing, Vann stood in the light of a single bulb and puzzled over the gauge on his compressor. He rubbed his cigarette out on the cement floor.

"She's not holding any pressure at all now. Not a damn bit," he said to Tommy Farr. "Something's open that shouldn't be. Or else we've got one hell of a blowout someplace," he said and reached up and shut off the air to the main duct. He switched off the compressor motor, and the basement was suddenly silent.

"How we gonna find out what's open?" Tommy asked.

"We got to check everything that's supposed to be closed. One of you guys must've left a cap off one of the register openings."

"Hey, not me! I ain't no sheet-metal guy. I was in the trailer counting fittings all day Friday."

"I know, I know. I just need somebody to blame," Vann said, smiling. He clapped the kid on the shoulder. "C'mon, let's get the drawings from the trailer. We'll go room to room and check every vent until we find the missing cap. Then we'll cap 'er and try again."

Vann had done his job the way he was supposed to, and his men had done theirs. He could not have known what had occurred beyond the thick fire wall that separated the new wing from the old, could not have known that over there, when he finally shut his compressor down, the debris had instantly ceased to fall. And he could not have known that seconds after Drs. Ransome, Rabideau, and Wheelwright in a panic had closed their incisions and rushed her from the operating room, his ex-wife Irene had gone into cardiac arrest in the recovery room. They had managed to get her heart pumping again and her blood pressure back, but an embolism had formed in her left carotid artery and had started working its way toward her neck. Shortly after noon, a blood vessel between the left temporal and parietal lobes of her brain burst, and Irene Moore suffered a massive stroke and immediately lapsed into a coma.

The only surgeon in the area capable of removing the clot from her brain was driving over from Plattsburgh. They hoped to have the operating room cleaned up and ready for him by early evening. With her heart condition, however, and the trauma inflicted on her by the interrupted surgery this morning, the likelihood of still more embolisms, the anticoagulants, and now the stroke, "I'm sorry, but it truly does not look good," Dr. Rabideau told Frances.

She did not know where to turn for consolation or advice. She was the only one left in the world who loved her mother, and her mother was the only one left who loved her. Frances's father, Irene's long-gone first husband, had his new life, a new wife and new kids out in California. Irene's second husband, Vann, had his new life, too, Frances supposed. He and Frances had never liked each other much, anyhow.

A little after lunch, the supervisor of maintenance in the hospital found Vann on the second floor of the new wing, still tracing the overhead ducts with Tommy Farr. The supervisor, Fred Noelle, was a man in his mid-sixties who had worked for the hospital since high school. He knew every inch of the old building, every valve, switch, pump, and fitting, and had been an especially useful consultant when they were designing the addition. Cautiously, Fred asked Vann if earlier this morning he might have done something in the way of connecting the heat and ventilation ducts of the new wing to the ducts of the old. Tied them together, say, and then opened them up, maybe.

"No," Vann said. "Why? You got problems over there?"

"Have we got problems? Yes, we've got problems. We'll be cleaning the place up for the rest of the year." He was a balding, heavyset man with a face like a bull terrier, and he looked very worried. He knew there were law-suits coming. A lot of finger-pointing and denials.

"What the hell happened?" Vann asked him.

Fred told him. "They got crap on patients, in the labs, all over. Even in the operating rooms."

Vann was silent. Then he spoke slowly and clearly, directing his words to the kid but speaking mainly for Fred Noelle's benefit. "It couldn't have been us. There are baffles between the two systems, blocks, and they don't come out till after we get everything installed and blown out and balanced and the whole wing is nice and clean and ready for use. Then we open it to the old system. And that won't be till next summer," he said, his voice ris-ing. He knew he was telling the truth. He also knew that he was dead wrong.

Somewhere, somehow, one of the baffles between the two networks had not been installed by his men or else had been left off the drawing by the mechanical engineer who had designed the system for the architect. Either way, Vann knew the fault was his. This morning, before cranking up the compressor, on the off chance that one of his sheet-metal guys had screwed up, he should have checked the baffles, every damned one of them. No one ever did that, but he should've.

He placed the drawing on the floor and got down on his hands and knees to examine it. "See," he said to Fred. "Take a look right here. Baffle. And here. Baffle. And here," he said, pointing to each of the places where the ducts crossed through the thick wall between the two wings of the hospital.

But then he saw it. No baffle. The mechanical engineer had made a ter-rible mistake, and Vann, back when they'd installed the ducts, hadn't caught it.

Fred got down beside him, and he saw it, too. "Uh-oh," he said, and he placed his fingertip where a barrier should have been indicated and where, instead, the drawing showed a main duct flowing through the old exterior wall and connecting directly to the heat and ventilation system of the hos-pital. A straight shot.

Tommy squatted down on the other side of Vann and furrowed his brow and studied the drawing. He didn't see anything wrong. "Bad, huh, Vann?"

Vann followed Fred Noelle out of the structure and across the parking lot and through the main entrance of the hospital. They went straight to the large carpeted office of Dr. Christian Snyder, the hospital director. Fred made the introductions, and Dr. Snyder got up and shook Vann's hand firmly.

"We think we got this thing figured out," Fred said. Dr. Snyder was a crisply efficient fellow in his early forties with blond, blow-dried hair. He wore a dark pinstripe suit and to Vann looked more like a downstate lawyer than a physician. Fred unrolled the drawing on Dr. Snyder's large mahogany desk, and the three men stood side by side and examined the plan together, while Fred described Vann's test and how it was supposed to work and how it had failed.

"You're the subcontractor for the sheet-metal work?" Dr. Snyder said to Vann.

"No. No, I'm just the field super for him. Sam Guy, he's the subcontractor."

"I see. But you're responsible for the installation."

"Well, yes. But I just follow the drawings, the blueprints."

"Right. And this morning you were testing the new ductwork, blowing compressed air through it, right?"

"Yes, but I didn't realize—"

Dr. Snyder cut him off. "I understand." He went around his desk, sat down heavily, and picked up a pencil and tapped his teeth with it. "Fred, will you be able to attend a meeting here this evening? Seven-thirty, say?"

Fred said sure, and Dr. Snyder reached for his phone. Vann picked up the drawing and started to roll it up. "Please, leave that here," Dr. Snyder said, and then he was speaking to his secretary. "Celia, for that meeting with Baumbach, Beech, and Warren? Fred Noelle, who's in charge of maintenance, he'll be joining us."

He glanced up at Vann as if surprised to see him still standing there.

"You can go, if you want. Thanks for your help. We'll be in touch," he said and went back to his telephone.

Outside in the lobby, alone, Vann pulled out a cigarette and stuck it between his lips.

"Sir! No smoking!" the receptionist barked at him, and he shoved the cigarette back into the pack and made for the door.

On the steps he stopped and lit up and looked across the road at Lake Colby and the pine trees and hills beyond. There was a stiff, cold breeze off the lake, and it was starting to get dark. Vann checked his watch. Three-thirty-five. Off to his left he saw a woman with her back to him, also smoking and regarding the scenery. Vann couldn't remember when he had done anything this bad. Not at work, anyhow. In life, sure—he'd messed up his life, messed it up lots of ways, most people do. But, Jesus, never at work.

The woman tossed her cigarette out to the parking lot below and turned to go back inside, and Vann recognized her—Frances, his ex-wife's daughter. For a second, he was afraid of her, but then he realized that he was glad to see her and blurted, "Hey, Frances! What're you doing here?" Startled, she looked up at him, and he saw that she was crying. He took a step toward her. She was taller than he remembered, a few inches taller than he, and heavier. Her face was swollen and red and wet with tears. "Is it your mom?"

She nodded yes, like a child, and he reached out to her. She kept her arms tight to her sides but let him hold her close. He was all she had; he would have to be enough.

"Come on inside and sit down, honey, and tell me what's happened," Vann said, and with one arm around her, he walked her back into the lobby, where they sat down on one of the blond sofas by the window. "Jeez," he said, "I don't have a handkerchief."

"That's okay, I got a tissue." She pulled a wrinkled tissue from her purse and wiped her cheeks.

"So tell me what happened, Frances. What's wrong with your mom?"

She hesitated a second. Then she inhaled deeply and said, "I don't understand it. She's in a coma. She went in for open-heart surgery this morning and something happened, something went wrong, and they had to bring her out in the middle of it."

"Oh," Vann said. "Oh, Jesus." He lowered his head. He put his hands over his face and closed his eyes behind them.

"There were complications. She had a stroke. The doctors don't think she'll come out of it," she said, and started to cry again.

Vann took his hands away from his face and sat there staring at the floor. The beige carpet was decorated with the outlines of orange and dark-green rectangles. Vann let his gaze follow the interlocking colored lines from his feet out to the middle of the room and then back again. Out and back, out and back. There were six or eight other people seated in the sofas and chairs scattered around the lobby, reading magazines or talking quietly with one another, waiting for news of their mothers and fathers, their husbands and wives and children in the rooms above.

"Do you think maybe could I go and see her?" he said in a low voice.

"I don't think so. She's in intensive care, Vann. She won't even know you're there. I saw her a little while ago, but she didn't know it was me in the room."

Slowly Vann got to his feet and moved toward the receptionist by the elevator. He wanted to see Irene. He could say it to himself. It didn't matter if she knew he was there or not; he had to see her. He needed to fill his mind with her actual, physical presence. No fading memories of her, no tangled feelings of guilt for things done and undone, no dimly remembered hurts and resentments. Too late for all that. He needed to look at her literal existence, see her in the here and now, and take full-faced whatever terrible thoughts and feelings came to him there.

"I need to see my wife," he said to the receptionist. "She's in intensive care."

The woman peered at him over her horn-rimmed glasses. "Who's your wife?"

"Irene. Irene Moore."

He signed the book that the woman pushed at him and stepped

quickly toward the elevator. "Third floor," she said. He got into the elevator, turned back, and saw Frances seated across the lobby, looking mournfully at him. Then the door slid closed.

At the nurses' station outside the intensive-care unit, an elderly nurse pointed him down a hallway to a closed door. "Second bed on the right. You can't miss her; she's the only one there."

The room was dark, windowless, lit only by the wall lamp above the bedstead. Irene's body was very large; it filled the bed. Vann didn't remember her as that big. She made him feel suddenly small, shrunken, fragile. There were IV stands and oxygen tanks and tubes that snaked in and out of her body and several thick black wires attached to cabinet-sized machines that blinked and whirred, monitoring her blood pressure, heart, and breathing.

For a long time he stood at the foot of the bed peering through the network of tubes and wires at his ex-wife's body. She was covered to her neck by a sheet. Her arms lay limp and white outside the sheet. A tube dripped clear liquid into a vein at one wrist. On the other wrist she wore a plastic identification band.

No wedding ring, he noticed. He looked down at his own left hand. No wedding ring there, either. *Irene, you're the one I loved.* He said the words silently to himself, straight out. *And I'm only loving you now. And, Jesus, look at what I've done to you, before I could love you.*

What's that love worth now, I wonder, to you or me or anybody?

He felt a strong wind blow over him, and he had to grab hold of the metal bed frame to keep from staggering backward. The wind was warm, like a huge breath, an exhalation, and though it pummeled him, he wasn't afraid of it. He turned sideways and made his way along the bed. The wind abated, and he found himself looking down at Irene's face. There was a tube in her slightly open mouth and another in one of her nostrils. Her eyes were closed. Somewhere behind her face, Irene was curled in on herself like a child, naked, huddled in the darkness, alone, waiting.

Vann slipped his hands into his jacket pockets and stood with his feet apart and looked down on the woman he had been able to love for only a moment. He stood there for a long time, long after he had ceased to love her and had only the memory of it left. Then he turned away from her.

When he emerged from the elevator to the lobby, he quickly looked around for Frances and found her seated in a far corner of the room, slumped in a chair with her head on one arm and her eyes closed as if she was asleep. He sat down next to her, and her eyes fluttered open.

"Did you see her?" Frances asked.

"Yeah. I did. I saw her."

"She didn't know you were there, did she?"

"No. No, she didn't," he said. "But that didn't matter."

"Where're you going now, Vann? From here."

"Well, I don't know. I thought maybe I'd wait here, Frances. Keep you company. If you don't mind, I mean."

The girl didn't answer him. They both knew that Irene was going to die, probably before morning. Like a father, Vann would wait here with her and help the girl endure her mother's death.

People coming into the lobby were brushing snow off their shoulders and hats. Vann looked out the window at the parking lot and the lake. It had been snowing for a while, and the cars in the lot were covered with powdery white sheets. Sam Guy would fire him, no doubt about it, and both Vann and Sam would be lucky if no one sued them. Vann would go back to working locally out of his car, like he'd done when he first married Irene. He was coming in off the road, too late, maybe, to make anyone happy, but here he was anyhow, trying.

Bess

Jayne Anne Phillips

You have to imagine: this was sixty, seventy, eighty years ago, more than the lifetimes allotted most persons. We could see no other farms from our house, not a habitation or the smoke of someone's chimney; we could not see the borders of the road anymore but only the cover of snow, the white fields, and mountains beyond. Winters frightened me, but it was summers I should have feared. Summers, when the house was large and full, the work out-of-doors so it seemed no work at all, everything done in company—summers all the men were home, the farm was crowded, lively; it seemed nothing could go wrong then.

Our parents joked about their two families, first the six sons, one after the other; then a few years later the four daughters, Warwick, and me.

Another daughter after the boy was a bad sign, Pa said; there were enough children. I was the last, youngest of twelve Hampsons, and just thirteen months younger than Warwick. Since we were born on each other's heels, Mam said, we would have to raise each other.

The six elder brothers had all left home at sixteen to homestead some-where on the land, each going first to live with the brother established before him. They worked mines or cut timber for money to start farms and had an eye for women who were not delicate. Once each spring they were all back to plant garden with Pa, and the sisters talked amongst themselves about each one.

By late June the brothers had brought their families, each a wife and several children. All the rooms in the big house were used, the guesthouse as well, swept and cleaned. There was always enough space because each family lived in two big rooms, one given to parents and youngest baby and the other left for older children to sleep together, all fallen uncovered across a wide cob-stuffed mattress. Within those houses were many children, fif-teen, twenty, more. I am speaking now of the summer I was twelve, the sum-mer Warwick got sick and everything changed.

He was nearly thirteen. We slept in the big house in our same room, which was bay-windowed, very large and directly above the parlor, the huge oak tree lifting so close to our window it was possible to climb out at night and sit hidden on the branches. Adults on the porch were different from high up, the porch lit in the dark and chairs creaking as the men leaned and rocked, murmuring, drinking homemade beer kept cool in cel-lar crocks.

Late one night that summer, Warwick woke me, pinched my arms inside my cotton shift and held his hand across my mouth. He walked like a shadow in his white nightclothes, motioning I should follow him to the window. Warwick was quickly through and I was slower, my weight still on the sill as he settled himself, then lifted me over when I grabbed a higher branch, my feet on his chest and shoulders. We climbed into the top branches that grew next to the third floor of the house and sat cradled where three branches sloped; Warwick whispered not to move, stay behind the leaves in case they look. We were outside Claude's window, seeing into the dim room.

Claude was youngest of the older brothers and his wife was hugely with child, standing like a white column in the middle of the floor. Her white chemise hung wide round her like a tent and her sleeves were long and belled; she stood, both hands pressed to the small of her back, leaning as though to help the weight at her front. Then I saw Claude kneeling, darker than she because he wasn't wearing clothes. He touched her feet and I thought at first he was helping her take off her shoes, as I helped the young children in the evenings. But he had nothing in his hands and was lifting the thin chemise above her knees, higher to her thighs, then above her hips as she was twisting away but stopped and moved toward him, only holding the cloth bunched to conceal her belly. She pressed his head away from her, the chemise pulled to her waist in back and his one hand there trying to hold her. Then he backed her three steps to the foot of the bed and she half leaned, knees just bent; he knelt down again, his face almost at her feet and his mouth moving like he was biting her along her legs. She held him just away with her hands and he touched over and over the big globed belly, stroking it long and deeply like you would stroke a scared animal. Suddenly he stood quickly and turned her so her belly was against the heaped sheets. She grasped the bed frame with both hands so when he pulled her hips close she was bent prone forward from the waist; now her hands were occupied and he uncovered all of her, pushing the chemise to her shoulders and past her breasts in front; the filmy cloth hid her head and face, falling even off her shoulders so it hung halfway down her arms. She was all naked globes and curves, headless and wide-hipped with the swollen belly big and pale beneath her like a moon; standing that way she looked all dumb and animal like our white mare before she foaled. All the time she was whimpering, Claude looking at her. We saw him, he started to prod himself inside her very slow, tilting his head and listening. . . . I put my cool hands over my eyes then, hearing their sounds until Warwick pulled my arms down and made me look. Claude was tight behind her, pushing in and flinching like he couldn't get out of her, she bawled once. He let her go, stumbling; they staggered onto the bed, she lying on her back away from him with the bunched chemise in her mouth. He pulled her to him and took the cloth from her lips and wiped her face.

This was perhaps twenty minutes of a night in July 1900. I looked at Warwick as though for the first time. When he talked he was so close I could feel the words on my skin distinct from night breeze. "Are you glad you saw?" he whispered, his face frightened.

He had been watching them from the tree for several weeks.

In old photographs of Coalton that July 4, the town looks scruffy and blurred. The blue of the sky is not shown in those black-and-white studies. Wooden sidewalks on the two main streets were broad and raised; that day people sat along them as on low benches, their feet in the road, waiting for the parade. We were all asked to stay still as a photographer took pictures of the whole scene from a nearby hillside. There was a prayer blessing the new century and the cornet band assembled. The parade was forming out of sight, by the river; Warwick and Pa had already driven out in the wagon to watch. It would be a big parade; we had word that local merchants had hired part of a circus traveling through Bellington. I ran up the hill to see if I could get a glimpse of them; Mam was calling me to come back and my shoes were blond to the ankles with dust. Below me the crowd began to cheer. The ribboned horses danced with fright and kicked, jerking reins looped over low branches of trees and shivering the leaves. From up the hill I saw dust raised in the woods and heard the crackling of what was crushed. There were five elephants; they came out from the trees along the road and the trainer sat on the massive harnessed head of the first. He sat in a sort of purple chair, swaying side to side with the lumbering swivel of the head. The trainer wore a red cap and jacket; he was dark and smooth on his face and held a boy close around his waist. The boy was moving his arms at me and it was Warwick; I was running closer and the trainer beat with his staff on the shoulders of the elephant while the animal's snaky trunk, all alive, ripped small bushes. Warwick waved; I could see him and ran

617

dodging the men until I was alongside. The earth was pounding and the animal was big like a breathing wall, its rough side crusted with dirt and straw. The skin hung loose, draped on the limbs like sacking crossed with many creases. The enormous creature worked, wheezing, and the motion of the lurching walk was like the swing of a colossal gate. Far, far up, I saw Warwick's face; I was yelling, yelling for them to stop, stop and take me up, but they kept on going. Just as the elephants passed, wind lifted the dust and ribbons and hats, the white of the summer skirts swung and billowed. The cheering was a great noise under the trees and birds flew up wild. Coalton was a sea of yellow dust, the flags snapping in that wind and banners strung between the buildings broken, flying.

Warwick got it in his head to walk a wire. Our Pa would not hear of such foolishness, so Warwick took out secretly to the creek every morning and practiced on the sly. He constructed a thickness of barn boards lengthwise on the ground, propped with nailed supports so he could walk along an edge. First three boards, then two, then one. He walked barefoot tensing his long toes and cradled a bamboo fishing pole in his arms for balance. I followed along silently when I saw him light out for the woods. Standing back a hundred feet from the creek bed, I saw through dense summer leaves my brother totter magically just above the groundline; thick ivy concealed the edges of the boards and made him appear a jerky magician. He often walked naked since the heat was fierce and his trousers too-large hand-me-downs that obstructed careful movement. He walked parallel to the creek and slipped often. Periodically he grew frustrated and jumped cursing into the muddy water. Creek bottom at that spot was soft mud and the water perhaps five feet deep; he floated belly-up like a seal and then crawled up the bank mud-streaked to start again. I stood in the leaves. He was tall and still coltish then, dark from the sun on most of his body, long-muscled; his legs looked firm and strong and a bit too long for him, his buttocks were tight and white. It was not his nakedness that moved me to stay hidden, barely breathing lest he hear the snap of a twig and discover me—it was the way he touched the long yellow pole, first holding it close, then opening his arms gently as the pole rolled across his flat still wrists to his hands; another movement, higher, and the pole balanced like a visible thin line on the tips of his fingers. It vibrated as though quivering with a sound. Then he clasped it lightly and the pole turned horizontally with a half rotation; six, seven, eight quick flashes, turning hard and quick, whistle of air, snap of the light wood against his palms. Now the pole lifted, airborne a split second and suddenly standing, earthward end walking Warwick's palm. He moved, watching the sky and a wavering six feet of yellow needle. The earth stopped in just that moment, trees still, Warwick moving, and then as the pole toppled in a smooth arc to water he followed in a sideways dive. While he was under, out of earshot and rapturous in the olive water, I ran quick and silent back to the house, through forest and vines to the clearing, the meadow, the fenced boundaries of the high-grown yard and the house, the barn where it was shady and cool and I could sit in the mow to remember his face and the yellow pole come to life. You had to look straight into the sun to see its airborne end and the sun was a blind white burn the pole could touch. Like Warwick was prodding the sun in secret, his whole body a prayer partly evil.

One day of course he saw me watching him, and knew in an instant I had watched him all along; by then he was actually walking a thick rope strung about six feet off the ground between two trees. For a week he'd walked only to a midpoint, as he could not rig the rope so it didn't sag and walking all the way across required balance on the upward slant. That day he did it; I believe he did it only that once, straight across. I made no sound but as he stood there poised above me his eyes fell upon my face; I had knelt in the forest cover and was watching as he himself had taught me to watch. Perhaps this explains his anger—I see still, again and again, Warwick jumping down from the rope, bending his knees to an impact as dust clouds his feet but losing no balance, no stride, leaping toward me at a run. His arms are still spread, hands palm-down as though for support in the air and then I hear rather than see him because I'm running, terrified—shouting his name in supplication through the woods as he follows, still coming after me wild with rage as I'd never seen anyone. Then I was nearly out of breath and just screaming, stumbling—

It's true I led him to the thicket, but I had no idea where I was going. We never went there, as it was near a rocky outcropping where copperheads bred, and not really a thicket at all but a small apple orchard gone diseased and long dead. The trees were oddly dwarfed and broken, and the ground cover thick with vines. Just as Warwick caught me I looked to see those rows of small dead trees; then we were fighting on the ground, rolling. I fought with him in earnest and scratched his eyes; already he was covered all over with small cuts from running through the briars. This partially explains how quickly he was poisoned but the acute nature of the infection was in his blood itself. Now he would be diagnosed severely allergic and given antibiotics; then we knew nothing of such medicines. The sick were still bled. In the week he was most ill, Warwick was bled twice daily, into a bowl. The doctor theorized, correctly, that the poison had worsened so as to render the patient's blood toxic.

Later Warwick told me, if only I'd stopped yelling—now that chase seems a comical as well as nightmarish picture; he was only a naked enraged boy. But the change I saw in his face, that moment he realized my presence, foretold everything. Whatever we did from then on was attempted escape from the fact of the future.

"Warwick? Warwick?"

In the narrow sun porch, which is all windows but for the house wall, he sleeps like a pupa, larva wrapped in a woven spit of gauze and never turning. His legs weeping in the loose bandages, he smells of clear fluid seeped from wounds. The seepage clear as tears, clear as sweat, but sticky on my hands when my own sweat never sticks but drips from my forehead into his flat stomach where he says it stings like salt.

"Warwick. Mam says to turn you now."

Touching the wide gauze strips in the dark. His ankles propped on rolls of cloth so his legs air and the blisters scab after they break and weep. The loose gauze strips are damp when I unwrap them, just faintly damp; now we don't think he is going to die.

He says, "Are they all asleep inside?"

"Yes. Except Mam woke me."

"Can't you open the windows. Don't flies stop when there's dew?"

"Yes, but the mosquitoes. I can put the netting down but you'll have that dream again."

"Put it down but come inside, then I'll stay awake."

"You shouldn't, you should sleep."

Above him the net is a canopy strung on line, rolled up all the way round now and tied with cord like a bedroll. It floats above him in the dark like a cloud the shape of the bed. We keep it rolled up all the time now since the bandages are off his eyes; he says looking through it makes everyone a ghost and fools him into thinking he's still blind.

Now I stand on a chair to reach the knotted cords, find them by feel, then the netting falls all around him like a skirt.

"All right, Warwick, see me? I just have to unlatch the windows."

Throw the hooks and windows swing outward all along the sun porch walls. The cool comes in, the lilac scent, and now I have to move everywhere in the dark because Mam says I can't use the lamp, have kerosene near the netting—

"I can see you better now," he says from the bed.

I can tell the shadows, shapes of the bed, the medicine table, the chair beside him where I slept the first nights we moved him to the sun porch. Doctor said he'd never seen such a poison, Warwick's eyes swollen shut, his legs too big for pants, soles of his feet oozing in one straight seam like someone cut them with scissors. Mam with him day and night until her hands broke out and swelled; then it was only me, because I don't catch poison, wrapping him in bandages she cut and rolled wearing gloves.

"Let me get the rose water," I whisper.

Inside the tent he sits up to make room. I hold the bowl of rose water and the cloth, crawl in and it's like sitting low in high fields hidden away, except there isn't even sky, no opening at all.

"It's like a coffin, that's what," he'd said when he could talk.

"A coffin is long and thin," I told him, "with a lid."

"Mine has a ceiling," Warwick said.

Inside everything is clean and white and dry; every day we change the white bottom sheet and he isn't allowed any covers. He's sitting up—I still can't see him in the dark, even the netting looks black, so I find him, hand forehead nose throat.

"Can't you see me. There's a moon, I see you fine."

"Then you've turned into a bat. I'll see in a moment, it was light in the kitchen."

"Mam?"

"Mam and three lamps. She's rolling bandages this hour of the night. She doesn't sleep when you don't."

"I can't sleep."

"I know."

He only sleeps in daytime when he can hear people making noise. At night he wakes up in silence, in the narrow black room, in bandages in the tent. For a while when the doctor bled him he was too weak to yell for someone.

He says, "I won't need bandages much longer."

"A little longer," I tell him.

"I should be up walking. I wonder if I can walk, like before I wondered if I could see."

"Of course you can walk, you've only been in bed two weeks, and a few days before upstairs—"

"I don't remember when they moved me here, so don't it seem like always I been here."

Pa and two brothers and Mam moved him, all wearing gloves and their forearms wrapped in gauze I took off them later and burned in the wood stove.

"Isn't always. You had deep sleeps in the fever, you remember wrong." I start at his feet, which are nearly healed, with the sponge and the cool water. Water we took from the rain barrel and scented with torn roses, the petals pounded with a pestle and strained, since the doctor said not to use soap.

The worst week I bathed him at night so he wouldn't get terrified alone. He was delirious and didn't know when he slept or woke. When I touched him with the cloth he made such whispers, such inside sounds; they weren't even words but had a cadence like sentences. If he could feel this heat and the heat of his fever, blind as he was then in bandages, and tied, if he could still think, he'd think he was in hell. I poured the alcohol over him, and the water from the basin, I was bent close to his face just when he stopped raving and I thought he had died. He said a word.

"Bessic," he said.

Bless me, I heard. I knelt with my mouth at his ear, in the sweat, in the horrible smell of the poison. "Warwick," I said. He was there, tentative and weak, a boy waking up after sleeping in the blackness three days. "Stay here, Warwick. Warwick."

I heard him say the word again, and it was my name, clearly.

"Bessie," he said.

So I answered him. "Yes, I'm here. Stay here."

Later he told me he slept a hundred years, swallowed in a vast black belly like Jonah, no time any more, no sense but strange dreams without pictures. He thought he was dead, he said, and the moment he came back he spoke the only word he'd remembered in the dark.

Sixteen years later, when he did die, in the mine—did he say a word again, did he say that word? Trying to come back. The second time, I think he went like a streak. I had the color silver in my mind. A man from Coalton told us about the cave-in. The man rode out on a horse, a bay mare, and he galloped the mare straight across the fields to the porch instead of taking the road. I was sitting on the porch and saw him coming from a ways off. I stood up as he came closer; I knew the news was Warwick, and that whatever had happened was over. I had no words in my mind, just the color silver, everywhere. The fields looked silver too just then, the way the sun slanted. The grass was tall and the mare moved through it up to her chest, like a powerful swimmer. I did not call anyone else until the man arrived and told me, breathless, that Warwick and two others were trapped, probably suffocated, given up for dead. The man, a Mr. Forbes, was surprised at my composure. I simply nodded; the news came to me like an echo. I had not thought of that moment in years—the moment Warwick's fever broke and I heard him speak—but the moment returned in an instant. Having felt it once, that disappearance, even so long before, I was prepared. Memory does not work according to time. I was twelve years old, perceptive, impressionable, in love with Warwick as a brother and sister can be in love. I loved him then as one might love one's twin, without a thought. After that summer I understood too much. I don't mean I was ashamed; I was not. But no love is innocent once it has recognized its own existence.

At eighteen I went away to a finishing school in Lynchburg. The summer I came back, foolishly, I ran away west. I eloped partially because Warwick found fault with anyone who courted me, and made a case against him to Mam. The name of the man I left with is unimportant. I do not really remember his face. He was blond but otherwise he did resemble Warwick—in his movements, his walk, his way of speaking. All told, I was in his company eight weeks. We were traveling, staying in hotels. He'd told me he was in textiles but it seemed actually he gambled at cards and roulette. He had a sickness for the roulette wheel, and other sicknesses. I could not bear to stand beside him in the gambling parlors; I hated the noise and the smoke, the perfumes mingling, the clackings of the wheels like speeded-up clocks and everyone's eyes following numbers. Often I sat in a hotel room with a blur of noise coming through the floor, and imagined the vast space of the barn around me: dark air filling a gold oval, the tall beams, the bird sounds ghostly like echoes. The hay, ragged heaps that spilled from the mow in pieces and fell apart.

The man who was briefly my husband left me in St. Louis. Warwick came for me; he made a long journey in order to take me home. A baby boy was born the following September. It was decided to keep my elopement and divorce, and the pregnancy itself, secret. Our doctor, a country man and friend of the family, helped us forge a birth certificate stating that Warwick was the baby's father. We invented a name for his mother, a name unknown in those parts, and told that she'd abandoned the baby to us. People lived so far from one another, in isolation, that such deceit was possible. My boy grew up believing I was his aunt and Warwick his father, but Warwick could not abide him. To him, the child was a living reminder of my abasement, my betrayal in ever leaving the farm.

The funeral was held at the house. Men from the mine saw to it Warwick was laid out in Coalton, then they brought the box to the farm on a lumber wagon. The lid was kept shut. That was the practice then; if a man died in the mines his coffin was closed for services, nailed shut, even if the man was unmarked.

The day after Warwick's funeral, all the family was leaving back to their homesteads having seen each other in a confused picnic of food and talk and sorrowful conjecture. Half the sorrow was Warwick alive and half was Warwick dead. His dying would make an end of the farm. I would leave now for Bellington, where, in a year, I would meet another man. Mam and Pa would go to live with Claude and his wife. But it was more than losing the farm that puzzled and saddened everyone; no one knew who Warwick was, really. They said it was hard to believe he was inside the coffin, with the lid nailed shut that way. Touch the box, anywhere, with the flat of your hand, I told them. They did, and stopped that talk.

The box was thick pine boards, pale white wood; I felt I could barely look through it like water into his face, like he was lying in a piece of water on top of the parlor table. Touching the nailed lid you felt first the cool slide of new wood on your palm, and a second later the depth—a heaviness inside like the box was so deep it went clear to the center of the earth, his body contained there like a big caged wind. Something inside, palpable as the different air before flash rains, with clouds blown and air clicking before the crack of downpour.

625

I treated the box as though it were living, as though it had to accustom itself to the strange air of the house, of the parlor, a room kept for weddings and death. The box was simply there on the table, long and pure like some deeply asleep, dangerous animal. The stiff damask draperies at the parlor windows looked as though they were about to move, gold tassels at the hems suspended and still.

The morning before the service most of the family had been in Coalton, seeing to what is done at a death. I had been alone in the house with the coffin churning what air there was to breathe. I had dressed in my best clothes as though for a serious, bleak suitor. The room was just lighted with sunrise, window shades pulled halfway, their cracked sepia lit from behind. One locust began to shrill as I took a first step across the floor; somehow one had gotten into the room. The piercing, fast vibration was very loud in the still morning: suddenly I felt myself smaller, cramped as I bent over Warwick inside his white tent of netting, his whole body afloat below me on the narrow bed, his white shape in the loose bandages seeming to glow in dusk light while beyond the row of open windows hundreds of locusts sang a ferocious pattering. I could scarcely see the parlor anymore. My vision went black for a moment, not black but dark green, like the color of the dusk those July weeks years before.

Among the Paths to Eden

Truman Capote

One Saturday in March, an occasion of pleasant winds and sailing clouds, Mr. Ivor Belli bought from a Brooklyn florist a fine mass of jonquils and conveyed them, first by subway, then foot, to an immense cemetery in Queens, a site unvisited by him since he had seen his wife buried there the previous autumn. Sentiment could not be credited with returning him today, for Mrs. Belli, to whom he had been married twenty-seven years, during which time she had produced two now-grown and matrimonially-settled daughters, had been a woman of many natures, most of them trying: he had no desire to renew so unsoothing an acquaintance, even in spirit. No; but a hard winter had just passed, and he felt in need of exercise, air, a heart-lifting stroll through the handsome, spring-prophesying weather; of course, rather as an extra dividend, it was nice that he would be able to tell his daughters of a journey to their mother's grave, especially so since it might a little appease the elder girl, who seemed resentful of Mr. Belli's too comfortable acceptance of life as lived alone.

The cemetery was not a reposeful, pretty place; was, in fact, a damned frightening one: acres of fog-colored stone spilled across a sparsely grassed and shadeless plateau. An unhindered view of Manhattan's skyline provided the location with beauty of a stage-prop sort—it loomed beyond the graves like a steep headstone honoring these quiet folk, its used-up and very former citizens: the juxtaposed spectacle made Mr. Belli, who was by profession a tax accountant and therefore equipped to enjoy irony however sadistic, smile, actually chuckle—yet, oh God in heaven, its inferences chilled him, too, deflated the buoyant stride carrying him along the cemetery's rigid, pebbled paths. He slowed until he stopped, thinking: "I ought to have taken Morty to the zoo"; Morty being his grandson, aged three. But it would be churlish not to continue, vengeful: and why waste a bouquet? The combination of thrift and virtue reactivated him; he was breathing hard from hurry when, at last, he stooped to jam the jonquils into a rock urn perched on a rough grey slab engraved with Gothic calligraphy declaring that

SARAH BELLI

1901–1959

had been the

DEVOTED WIFE OF IVOR

BELOVED MOTHER OF IVY AND REBECCA.

Lord, what a relief to know the woman's tongue was finally stilled. But the thought, pacifying as it was, and though supported by visions of his new and silent bachelor's apartment, did not relight the suddenly snuffed-out sense of immortality, of glad-to-be-aliveness, which the day had earlier kindled. He had set forth expecting such good from the air, the walk, the aroma of another spring about to be. Now he wished he had worn a scarf; the sunshine was false, without real warmth, and the wind, it seemed to him, had grown rather wild. As he gave the jonquils a decorative pruning, he regretted he could not delay their doom by supplying them with water; relinquishing the flowers, he turned to leave.

A woman stood in his way. Though there were few other visitors to the cemetery, he had not noticed her before, or heard her approach. She did not step aside. She glanced at the jonquils; presently her eyes, situated behind steel-rimmed glasses, swerved back to Mr. Belli.

"Uh. Relative?"

"My wife," he said, and sighed as though some such noise was obligatory.

She sighed, too; a curious sigh that implied gratification. "Gee, I'm sorry."

Mr. Belli's face lengthened. "Well."

"It's a shame."

"Yes."

"I hope it wasn't a long illness. Anything painful."

"No-o-o," he said, shifting from one foot to the other. "In her sleep." Sensing an unsatisfied silence, he added, "Heart condition."

"Gee. That's how I lost my father. Just recently. Kind of gives us something in common. Something," she said, in a tone alarmingly plaintive, "something to talk about."

"—know how you must feel."

"At least they didn't suffer. That's a comfort."

The fuse attached to Mr. Belli's patience shortened. Until now he had kept his gaze appropriately lowered, observing, after his initial glimpse of her, merely the woman's shoes, which were of the sturdy, so-called sensible type often worn by aged women and nurses. "A great comfort," he said, as he executed three tasks: raised his eyes, tipped his hat, took a step forward.

Again the woman held her ground; it was as though she had been

629

employed to detain him. "Could you give me the time? My old clock," she announced, self-consciously tapping some dainty machinery strapped to her wrist, "I got it for graduating high school. That's why it doesn't run so good any more. I mean, it's pretty old. But it makes a nice appearance."

Mr. Belli was obliged to unbutton his topcoat and plow around for a gold watch embedded in a vest pocket. Meanwhile, he scrutinized the lady, really took her apart. She must have been blonde as a child, her general coloring suggested so: the clean shine of her Scandinavian skin, her chunky cheeks, flushed with peasant health, and the blueness of her genial eyes— such honest eyes, attractive despite the thin silver spectacles surrounding them; but the hair itself, what could be discerned of it under a drab felt hat, was a poorly permanented frizzle of no particular tint. She was a bit taller than Mr. Belli, who was five-foot-eight with the aid of shoe lifts, and she may have weighed more; at any rate he couldn't imagine that she mounted scales too cheerfully. Her hands: kitchen hands; and the nails: not only nibbled ragged, but painted with a pearly lacquer queerly phosphorescent. She wore a plain brown coat and carried a plain black purse. When the student of these components recomposed them he found they assembled themselves into a very decent-looking person whose looks he liked; the nail polish was discouraging; still he felt that here was someone you could trust. As he trusted Esther Jackson, Miss Jackson, his secretary. Indeed, that was who she reminded him of, Miss Jackson; not that the comparison was fair—to Miss Jackson, who possessed, as he had once in the course of a quarrel informed Mrs. Belli, "intellectual elegance and elegance otherwise." Nevertheless, the woman confronting him seemed imbued with that quality of goodwill he appreciated in his secretary, Miss Jackson, Esther (as he'd lately, absentmindedly, called her). Moreover, he guessed them to be about the same age: rather on the right side of forty.

"Noon. Exactly."

"Think of that! Why, you must be famished," she said, and unclasped her purse, peered into it as though it were a picnic hamper crammed with sufficient treats to furnish a smorgasbord. She scooped out a fistful of peanuts. "I practically live on peanuts since Pop—since I haven't anyone to cook for. I must say, even if I do say so, I miss my own cooking; Pop always said I was better than any restaurant he ever went to. But it's no pleasure cooking just for yourself, even when you *can* make pastries light as a leaf. Go on. Have some. They're fresh-roasted."

Mr. Belli accepted; he'd always been childish about peanuts and, as he sat down on his wife's grave to eat them, only hoped his friend had more. A gesture of his hand suggested that she sit beside him; he was surprised to see that the invitation seemed to embarrass her; sudden additions of pink saturated her cheeks, as though he'd asked her to transform Mrs. Belli's bier into a love bed.

"It's okay for you. A relative. But me. Would she like a stranger sitting on her—resting place?"

"Please. Be a guest. Sarah won't mind," he told her, grateful the dead cannot hear, for it both awed and amused him to consider what Sarah, that vivacious scene-maker, that energetic searcher for lipstick traces and stray blonde strands, would say if she could see him shelling peanuts on her tomb with a woman not entirely unattractive.

And then, as she assumed a prim perch on the rim of the grave, he noticed her leg. Her left leg; it stuck straight out like a stiff piece of mischief with which she planned to trip passersby. Aware of his interest, she smiled, lifted the leg up and down. "An accident. You know. When I was a kid. I fell off a roller coaster at Coney. Honest. It was in the paper. Nobody knows why I'm alive. The only thing is I can't bend my knee. Otherwise it doesn't make any difference. Except to go dancing. Are you much of a dancer?"

Mr. Belli shook his head; his mouth was full of peanuts.

"So that's something else we have in common. Dancing. I *might* like it. But I don't. I like music, though."

Mr. Belli nodded his agreement.

"And flowers," she added, touching the bouquet of jonquils; then her fingers traveled on and, as though she were reading Braille, brushed across the marble lettering of his name. "Ivor," she said, mispronouncing it. "Ivor Belli. My name is Mary O'Meaghan. But I wish I were Italian. My sister is;

well, she married one. And oh, he's full of fun; happy-natured and outgoing, like all Italians. He says my spaghetti's the best he's ever had. Especially the kind I make with seafood sauce. You ought to taste it."

Mr. Belli, having finished the peanuts, swept the hulls off his lap. "You've got a customer. But he's not Italian. Belli sounds like that. Only I'm Jewish."

She frowned, not with disapproval, but as if he had mysteriously daunted her.

"My family came from Russia; I was born there."

This last information restored her enthusiasm, accelerated it. "I don't care what they say in the papers. I'm sure Russians are the same as everybody else. Human. Did you see the Bolshoi Ballet on TV? Now didn't that make you proud to be a Russian?"

He thought: she means well; and was silent.

"Red cabbage soup—hot or cold—with sour cream. Hmnn. See," she said, producing a second helping of peanuts, "you *were* hungry. Poor fellow." She sighed. "How you must miss your wife's cooking."

It was true, he did; and the conversational pressure being applied to his appetite made him realize it. Sarah had set an excellent table: varied, on time, and well flavored. He recalled certain cinnamon-scented feast days. Afternoons of gravy and wine, starchy linen, the "good" silver; followed by a nap. Moreover, Sarah had never asked him to dry a dish (he could hear her calmly humming in the kitchen), had never complained of housework; and she had contrived to make the raising of two girls a smooth series of thought-out, affectionate events; Mr. Belli's contribution to their upbringing had been to be an admiring witness; if his daughters were a credit to him (Ivy living in Bronxville, and married to a dental surgeon; her sister the wife of A. J. Krakower, junior partner in the law firm of Finnegan, Loeb and Krakower), he had Sarah to thank; they were her accomplishment. There was much to be said for Sarah, and he was glad to discover himself thinking so, to find himself remembering not the long hell of hours she had spent honing her tongue on his habits, supposed poker-playing, woman-chasing vices, but gentler episodes: Sarah showing off her self-made hats, Sarah scattering crumbs on snowy window sills for winter pigeons: a tide of visions that towed to sea the junk of harsher recollections. He felt, was all at once happy to feel, mournful, sorry he had not been sorry sooner; but, though he did genuinely value Sarah suddenly, he could not pretend regret that their life together had terminated, for the current arrangement was, on the whole, preferable by far. However, he wished that, instead of jonquils, he had brought her an orchid, the gala sort she'd always salvaged from her daughters' dates and stored in the icebox until they shriveled.

"—aren't they?" he heard, and wondered who had spoken until, blinking, he recognized Mary O'Meaghan, whose voice had been playing along unlistened to: a shy and lulling voice, a sound strangely small and young to come from so robust a figure.

"I said they must be cute, aren't they?"

"Well," was Mr. Belli's safe reply.

"Be modest. But I'm sure they are. If they favor their father; ha ha, don't take me serious, I'm joking. But, seriously, kids just slay me. I'll trade any kid for any grown-up that ever lived. My sister has five, four boys and a girl. Dot, that's my sister, she's always after me to baby-sit now that I've got the time and don't have to look after Pop every minute. She and Frank, he's my brother-in-law, the one I mentioned, they say Mary, nobody can handle kids like *you*. At the same time have fun. But it's so easy; there's nothing like hot cocoa and a mean pillow fight to make kids sleepy. Ivy," she said, reading aloud the tombstone's dour script. "Ivy and Rebecca. Sweet names. And I'm sure you do your best. But two little girls without a mother."

"No, no," said Mr. Belli, at last caught up. "Ivy's a mother herself. And Becky's expecting."

Her face restyled momentary chagrin into an expression of disbelief. "A grandfather? You?"

Mr. Belli had several vanities: for example, he thought he was *saner* than other people; also, he believed himself to be a walking compass; his digestion, and an ability to read upside down, were other ego-enlarging items. But his reflection in a mirror aroused little inner applause; not that he disliked his appearance; he just knew that it was very so-what. The harvesting of his hair had begun decades ago; now his head was an almost barren field. While his nose had character, his chin, though it made a double effort, had none. His shoulders were broad; but so was the rest of him. Of course he was neat: kept his shoes shined, his laundry laundered, twice a day scraped and talcumed his bluish jowls; but such measures failed to camouflage, actually they emphasized, his middle-class, middle-aged ordinariness. Nonetheless, he did not dismiss Mary O'Meaghan's flattery; after all, an undeserved compliment is often the most potent.

"Hell, I'm fifty-one," he said, subtracting four years. "Can't say I feel it." And he didn't; perhaps it was because the wind had subsided, the warmth of the sun grown more authentic. Whatever the reason, his expectations had reignited, he was again immortal, a man planning ahead.

"Fifty-one. That's nothing. The prime. Is if you take care of yourself. A man your age needs tending to. Watching after."

Surely in a cemetery one was safe from husband stalkers? The question, crossing his mind, paused midway while he examined her cozy and gullible face, tested her gaze for guile. Though reassured, he thought it best to remind her of their surroundings. "Your father. Is he"—Mr. Belli gestured awkwardly—"nearby?"

"Pop? Oh, no. He was very firm; absolutely refused to be buried. So he's at home." A disquieting image gathered in Mr. Belli's head, one that her next words, "His ashes are," did not fully dispel. "Well," she shrugged, "that's how he wanted it. Or—I see—you wondered why *I'm* here? I don't live too far away. It's somewhere to walk, and the view. . . ." They both turned to stare at the skyline where the steeples of certain buildings flew pennants of cloud, and sun-dazzled windows glittered like a million bits of mica. Mary O'Meaghan said, "What a perfect day for a parade!"

Mr. Belli thought, *You're a very nice girl*; then he said it, too, and wished he hadn't, for naturally she asked him why. "Because. Well, that was nice what you said. About parades."

"See? So many things in common! I never miss a parade," she told him triumphantly. "The bugles. I play the bugle myself; used to, when I was at Sacred Heart. You said before—" She lowered her voice, as though approaching a subject that required grave tones. "You indicated you were a music lover. Because I have thousands of old records. Hundreds. Pop was in the business and that was his job. Till he retired. Shellacking records in a record factory. Remember Helen Morgan? She slays me, she really knocks me out."

"*Jesus* Christ," he whispered. Ruby Keeler, Jean Harlow: those had been keen but curable infatuations; but Helen Morgan, albino-pale, a sequinned wraith shimmering beyond Ziegfeld footlights—truly, truly he had loved her.

"Do you believe it? That she drank herself to death? On account of a gangster?"

"It doesn't matter. She was lovely."

"Sometimes, like when I'm alone and sort of fed up, I pretend I'm her. Pretend I'm singing in a nightclub. It's fun; you know?"

"Yes, I know," said Mr. Belli, whose own favorite fantasy was to imagine the adventures he might have if he were invisible.

"May I ask: would you do me a favor?"

"If I can. Certainly."

She inhaled, held her breath as if she were swimming under a wave of shyness; surfacing, she said: "Would you listen to my imitation? And tell me your honest opinion?" Then she removed her glasses: the silver rims had bitten so deeply their shape was permanently printed on her face. Her eyes, nude and moist and helpless, seemed stunned by freedom; the skimpily lashed lids fluttered like long-captive birds abruptly let loose. "There: everything's soft and smoky. Now you've got to use your imagination. So pretend I'm sitting on a piano—gosh, for*give* me, Mr. Belli."

"Forget it. Okay. You're sitting on a piano."

"I'm sitting on a piano," she said, dreamily drooping her head backward until it assumed a romantic posture. She sucked in her cheeks, parted her lips; at the same moment Mr. Belli bit into his. For it was a tactless visit that glamour made on Mary O'Meaghan's filled-out and rosy face; a visit that should not have been paid at all; it was the wrong address. She waited, as though listening for music to cue her; then, "*Don't ever leave me, now*

635

that you're here! Here is where you belong. Everything seems so right when you're near, When you're away it's all wrong," and Mr. Belli was shocked, for what he was hearing was exactly Helen Morgan's voice, and the voice, with its vulnerable sweetness, refinement, its tender quaver toppling high notes, seemed not to be borrowed, but Mary O'Meaghan's own, a natural expression of some secluded identity. Gradually she abandoned theatrical poses, sat upright singing with her eyes squeezed shut: *"—I'm so depend-ent, When I need comfort, I always run to you. Don't ever leave me! 'Cause if you do, I'll have no one to run to."* Until too late, neither she nor Mr. Belli noticed the coffin-laden entourage invading their privacy: a black caterpil-lar composed of sedate Negroes who stared at the white couple as though they had stumbled upon a pair of drunken grave robbers—except one mourner, a dry-eyed little girl who started laughing and couldn't stop; her hiccuplike hilarity resounded long after the procession had disappeared around a distant corner.

"If that kid was mine," said Mr. Belli.

"I feel so ashamed."

"Say, listen. What for? That was beautiful. I mean it; you can sing."

"Thanks," she said; and, as though setting up a barricade against impending tears, clamped on her spectacles.

"Believe me, I was touched. What I'd like is, I'd like an encore."

It was as if she were a child to whom he'd handed a balloon, a unique balloon that kept swelling until it swept her upward, danced her along with just her toes now and then touching ground. She descended to say: "Only not here. Maybe," she began, and once more seemed to be lifted, lilted through the air, "maybe sometime you'll let me cook you dinner. I'll plan it really Russian. And we can play records."

The thought, the apparitional suspicion that had previously passed on tiptoe, returned with a heavier tread, a creature fat and foursquare that Mr. Belli could not evict. "Thank you, Miss O'Meaghan. That's something to look forward to," he said. Rising, he reset his hat, adjusted his coat. "Sitting on cold stone too long, you can catch something."

"When?"

"Why, never. You should *never* sit on cold stone."

"When will you come to dinner?"

Mr. Belli's livelihood rather depended upon his being a skilled inventor of excuses. "Anytime," he answered smoothly. "Except anytime soon. I'm a tax man; you know what happens to us fellows in March. Yes sir," he said, again hoisting out his watch, "back to the grind for me." Still he couldn't—could he?—simply saunter off, leave her sitting on Sarah's grave? He owed her courtesy; for the peanuts, if nothing more, though there was more—perhaps it was due to her that he had remembered Sarah's orchids withering in the icebox. And anyway, she *was* nice, as likeable a woman, stranger, as he'd ever met. He thought to take advantage of the weather, but the weather offered none: clouds were fewer, the sun exceedingly visible. "Turned chilly," he observed, rubbing his hands together. "Could be going to rain."

"Mr. Belli. Now I'm going to ask you a very personal question," she said, enunciating each word decisively. "Because I wouldn't want you to think I go about inviting just anybody to dinner. My intentions are—" Her eyes wandered, her voice wavered, as though the forthright manner had been a masquerade she could not sustain. "So I'm going to ask you a very personal question. Have you considered marrying again?"

He hummed, like a radio warming up before it speaks; when he did, it amounted to static: "Oh, at *my* age. Don't even want a dog. Just give me TV. Some beer. Poker once a week. Hell. Who the hell would want me?" he said; and, with a twinge, remembered Rebecca's mother-in-law, Mrs. A. J. Krakower, Sr., Dr. Pauline Krakower, a female dentist (retired) who had been an audacious participant in a certain family plot. Or what about Sarah's best friend, the persistent "Brownie" Pollock? Odd, but as long as Sarah lived he had enjoyed, upon occasion taken advantage of, "Brownie's" admiration; afterwards—finally he had *told* her not to telephone him any more (and she had shouted: "Everything Sarah ever said, she was right. You fat little *hairy* little bastard"). Then; and then there was Miss Jackson. Despite Sarah's suspicions, her in fact devout conviction, nothing untoward, very untoward, had transpired between him and the pleasant Esther, whose hobby was bowling. But he had always surmised, and in recent months known, that if one day he suggested drinks, dinner, a workout in some bowling alley. . . . He said: "I *was* married. For twenty-seven years. That's enough for any lifetime"; but as he said it, he realized that, in just this moment, he had come to a decision, which was: he *would* ask Esther to dinner, he would take her bowling and buy her an orchid, a gala purple one with a lavender-ribbon bow. And where, he wondered, do couples honeymoon in April? At the latest May. Miami? Bermuda? Bermuda! "No, I've never considered it. Marrying again."

One would have assumed from her attentive posture that Mary O'Meaghan was raptly listening to Mr. Belli—except that her eyes played hooky, roamed as though she were hunting at a party for a different, more promising face. The color had drained from her own face; and with it had gone most of her healthy charm. She coughed.

He coughed. Raising his hat, he said: "It's been very pleasant meeting you, Miss O'Meaghan."

"Same here," she said, and stood up. "Mind if I walk with you to the gate?"

He did, yes; for he wanted to mosey along alone, devouring the tart nourishment of this spring-shiny, parade weather, be alone with his many thoughts of Esther, his hopeful, zestful, live-forever mood. "A pleasure," he said, adjusting his stride to her slower pace and the slight lurch her stiff leg caused.

"But it *did* seem like a sensible idea," she said argumentatively. "And there was old Annie Austin: the living proof. Well, nobody had a *better* idea. I mean, everybody was at me: Get married. From the day Pop died, my sister and everybody was saying: Poor Mary, what's to become of her? A girl that can't type. Take shorthand. With her leg and all; can't even wait on tables. What happens to a girl—a *grown* woman—that doesn't know anything, never done anything? Except cook and look after her father. All I heard was: Mary, you've got to get married."

"So. Why fight that? A fine person like you, you ought to be married. You'd make some fellow very happy."

"Sure I would. But *who*?" She flung out her arms, extended a hand toward Manhattan, the country, the continents beyond. "So I've looked; I'm not lazy by nature. But honestly, frankly, how does anybody ever find a husband? If they're not very, very pretty; a terrific dancer. If they're just— oh, ordinary. Like me."

"No, no, not at all," Mr. Belli mumbled. "Not ordinary, no. Couldn't you make something of your talent? Your voice?"

She stopped, stood clasping and unclasping her purse. "Don't poke fun. Please. My life is at stake." And she insisted: "I *am* ordinary. So is old Annie Austin. And she says the place for me to find a husband—a decent, comfortable man—is in the obituary column."

For a man who believed himself a human compass, Mr. Belli had the anxious experience of feeling he had lost his way; with relief he saw the gates of the cemetery a hundred yards ahead. "She does? She says that? Old Annie Austin?"

"Yes. And she's a very practical woman. She feeds six people on fifty-eight dollars and seventy-five cents a week: food, clothes, everything. And the way she explained it, it certainly *sounded* logical. Because the obituaries are full of unmarried men. Widowers. You just go to the funeral and sort of introduce yourself: sympathize. Or the cemetery: come here on a nice day, or go to Woodlawn, there are always widowers walking around. Fellows thinking how much they miss home life and maybe wishing they were married again."

When Mr. Belli understood that she was in earnest, he was appalled; but he was also entertained: and he laughed, jammed his hands in his pockets and threw back his head. She joined him, spilled a laughter that restored her color, that, in skylarking style, made her rock against him. "Even I—" she said, clutching at his arm, "even *I* can see the humor." But it was not a lengthy vision; suddenly solemn, she said: "But that is how Annie met her husbands. Both of them: Mr. Cruikshank, and then Mr. Austin. So it *must* be a practical idea. Don't you think?"

"Oh, I do think."

She shrugged. "But it hasn't worked out too well. Us, for instance. *We* seemed to have such a lot in common."

"One day," he said, quickening his steps. "With a livelier fellow."

"I don't know. I've met some grand people. But it always ends like this. Like us. . . ." she said, and left unsaid something more, for a new pilgrim, just entering through the gates of the cemetery, had attached her interest: an alive little man spouting cheery whistlings and with plenty of snap to his walk. Mr. Belli noticed him, too, observed the black band sewn round the sleeve of the visitor's bright green tweed coat, and commented: "Good luck, Miss O'Meaghan. Thanks for the peanuts."

I Look Out for Ed Wolfe

Stanley Elkin

He was an orphan, and, to himself, he seemed like one, looked like one. His orphan's features were as true of himself as are their pale, pinched faces to the blind. At twenty-seven he was a neat, thin young man in white shirts and light suits with lintless pockets. Something about him suggested the ruthless isolation, the hard self-sufficiency of the orphaned, the peculiar dignity of men seen eating alone in restaurants on national holidays. Yet it was this perhaps which shamed him chiefly, for there was a suggestion, too, that his impregnability was a myth, a smell not of the furnished room which he did not inhabit, but of the three-room apartment on a good street which he did. The very excellence of his taste, conditioned by need and lack, lent to him the odd, maidenly primness of the lonely.

He saved the photographs of strangers and imprisoned them behind clear plastic windows in his wallet. In the sound of his own voice he detected the accent of the night school and the correspondence course, and nothing of the fat, sunny ring of the world's casually afternooned. He strove against himself, a supererogatory enemy, and sought by a kind of helpless abrasion, as one rubs wood, the gleaming self beneath. An orphan's thinness, he thought, was no accident.

Returning from lunch he entered the office building where he worked. It was an old building, squat and gargoyled, brightly patched where sandblasters had once worked and then quit before they had finished. He entered the lobby, which smelled always of disinfectant, and walked past the wide, dirty glass of the cigarette-and-candy counter to the single elevator, as thickly barred as a cell.

The building was an outlaw. Low rents and a downtown address and the landlord's indifference had brought together from the peripheries of business and professionalism a strange band of entrepreneurs and visionaries, men desperately but imaginatively failing: an eye doctor who corrected vision by massage; a radio evangelist; a black-belt judo champion; a self-help organization for crippled veterans; dealers in pornographic books, in paper flowers, in fireworks, in plastic jewelry, in the artificial, in the artfully made, in the imitated, in the copied, in the stolen, the unreal, the perversion, the plastic, the schlock.

On the sixth floor the elevator opened and the young man, Ed Wolfe, stepped out.

He passed the Association for the Indians, passed Plasti-Pens, passed *Coffin & Tombstone*, passed Soldier Toys, passed Prayer-a-Day. He walked by the opened door of C. Morris Brut, Chiropractor, and saw him, alone, standing at a mad attention, framed in the arching golden nimbus of his inverted name on the window, squeezing handballs.

He looked quickly away but Dr. Brut saw him and came toward him putting the handballs in his shirt pocket, where they bulged awkwardly. He held him by the elbow. Ed Wolfe looked at the yellowing tile beneath his feet, infinitely diamonded, chipped, the floor of a public toilet, and saw Dr. Brut's dusty shoes. He stared sadly at the jagged, broken glass of the mail chute.

"Ed Wolfe, take care of yourself," Dr. Brut said.

"Right."

"Regard your posture in life. A tall man like yourself looks terrible when he slumps. Don't be a *schlump*. It's not good for the organs."

"I'll watch it."

"When the organs get out of line the man begins to die."

"I know."

"You say so. How many guys make promises. Brains in the brainpan. Balls in the strap. The bastards downtown." He meant doctors in hospitals, in clinics, on boards, nonorphans with M.D. degrees and special license plates and respectable patients who had Blue Cross, charts, died in clean hospital rooms. They were the bastards downtown, his personal New Deal, his neighborhood Wall Street banker. A disease cartel. "They won't tell you. The white bread kills you. The cigarettes. The whiskey. The sneakers. The high heels. They won't tell you. Me, *I'll* tell you."

"I appreciate it."

"Wise guy. Punk. I'm a friend. I give a father's advice."

"I'm an orphan."

"I'll adopt you."

"I'm late for work."

"We'll open a clinic. 'C. Morris Brut and Adopted Son.'"

"It's something to think about."

"Poetry," Dr. Brut said and walked back to his office, his posture stiff, awkward, a man in a million who knew how to hold himself.

Ed Wolfe went on to his own office. He walked in. The sad-faced telephone girl was saying, "Cornucopia Finance Corporation." She pulled the wire out of the board and slipped her headset around her neck, where it hung like a delicate horse collar. "Mr. La Meck wants to see you. But don't go in yet. He's talking to somebody."

He went toward his desk at one end of the big main office. Standing, fists on the desk, he turned to the girl. "What happened to my call cards?"

"Mr. La Meck took them," the girl said.

"Give me the carbons," Ed Wolfe said. "I've got to make some calls."

She looked embarrassed. The face went through a weird change, the sadness taking on an impossible burden of shame so that she seemed massively tragic, like a hit-and-run driver. "I'll get them," she said, moving out of the chair heavily. Ed Wolfe thought of Dr. Brut.

He took the carbons and fanned them out on the desk. He picked one in an intense, random gesture like someone drawing a number on a public stage. He dialed rapidly.

As the phone buzzed brokenly in his ear he felt the old excitement. Someone at the other end greeted him sleepily.

"Mr. Flay? This is Ed Wolfe at Cornucopia Finance." (*Can you cope, can you cope?* he hummed to himself.)

"Who?"

"Ed Wolfe. I've got an unpleasant duty," he began pleasantly. "You've skipped two payments."

"I didn't skip nothing. I called the girl. She said it was okay."

"That was three months ago. She meant it was all right to miss a few days. Listen, Mr. Flay, we've got that call recorded, too. Nothing gets by."

"I'm a little short."

"Grow."

"I couldn't help it," the man said. Ed Wolfe didn't like the cringing tone. Petulance and anger he could meet with his own petulance, his own anger. But guilt would have to be met with his own guilt and that, here, was irrelevant.

"Don't con me, Flay. You're a troublemaker. What are you, Flay, a Polish person? Flay isn't a Polish name, but your address . . ."

"What's that?"

"What are you? Are you Polish?"

"What's that to you? What difference does it make?" That was more like it, Ed Wolfe thought warmly.

"That's what you are, Flay. You're a Pole. It's guys like you who give your race a bad name. Half our bugouts are Polish persons."

"Listen. You can't . . ."

He began to shout. "*You* listen. You wanted the car. The refrigerator. The chintzy furniture. The sectional you saw in the funny papers. And we paid for it, right?"

"Listen. The money I owe is one thing, the way . . ."

"We paid for it, right?"

"That doesn't . . ."

"Right? Right?"

"Yes, you . . ."

"Okay. You're in trouble, Warsaw. You're in terrible trouble. It means a lien. A judgment. We've got lawyers. You've got nothing. We'll pull the furniture the hell out of there. The car. Everything."

"Wait," he said. "Listen, my brother-in-law . . ."

Ed Wolfe broke in sharply. "He's got some money?"

"I don't know. A little. I don't know."

"Get it. If you're short, grow. This is America."

"I don't know if he'll let me have it."

"Steal it. This is America. Good-bye."

"Wait a minute. Please."

"That's it. There are other Polish persons on my list. This time it was just a friendly warning. Cornucopia wants its money. Cornucopia. Can you cope? Can you cope? Just a friendly warning, Polish-American. Next time we come with the lawyers and the machine guns. Am I making myself clear?"

"I'll try to get it to you."

Ed Wolfe hung up. He pulled a handkerchief from his drawer and wiped his face. His chest was heaving. He took another call card. The girl came by and stood beside his desk. "Mr. La Meck can see you now," she mourned.

"Later. I'm calling." The number was already ringing.

"Please, Mr. Wolfe."

"Later, I said. In a minute." The girl went away. "Hello. Let me speak with your husband, madam. I am Ed Wolfe of Cornucopia Finance. He can't cope. Your husband can't cope."

The woman said something, made an excuse. "Put him on, goddamn it. We know he's out of work. Nothing gets by. Nothing." There was a hand on the receiver beside his own, the wide male fingers pink and vaguely perfumed, the nails manicured. For a moment he struggled with it fitfully, as though the hand itself were all he had to contend with. He recognized La Meck and let go. La Meck pulled the phone quickly toward his mouth and spoke softly into it, words of apology, some ingenious excuse Ed Wolfe couldn't hear. He put the receiver down beside the phone itself and Ed Wolfe picked it up and returned it to its cradle.

"Ed," La Meck said, "come into the office with me."

Ed Wolfe followed La Meck, his eyes on La Meck's behind.

La Meck stopped at his office door. Looking around he shook his head sadly and Ed Wolfe nodded in agreement. La Meck let Ed Wolfe pass in first. While La Meck stood, Ed Wolfe could discern a kind of sadness in his slouch, but once La Meck was seated behind his desk he seemed restored, once again certain of the world's soundness. "All right," La Meck began. "I won't lie to you."

Lie to me. Lie to me, Ed Wolfe prayed silently.

"You're in here for me to fire you. You're not being laid off. I'm not going to tell you that I think you'd be happier someplace else, that the collection business isn't your game, that profits don't justify our keeping you around. Profits are terrific, and if collection isn't your game it's because you haven't got a game. As far as your being happier someplace else, that's bullshit. You're not supposed to be happy. It isn't in the cards for you. You're a fall-guy type, God bless you, and though I like you personally, I've got no use for you in my office."

I'd like to get you on the other end of a telephone someday, Ed Wolfe thought miserably.

"Don't ask me for a reference," La Meck said. "I couldn't give you one."

"No, no," Ed Wolfe said. "I wouldn't ask you for a reference." A helpless civility was all he was capable of. If you're going to suffer, *suffer*, he told himself.

"Look," La Meck said, his tone changing, shifting from brutality to compassion as though there were no difference between the two, "you've got a kind of quality, a real feeling for collection. I'm frank to tell you, when you first came to work for us I figured you wouldn't last. I put you on the phones because I wanted you to see the toughest part first. A lot of people can't do it. You take a guy who's down and bury him deeper. It's heart-wringing work. But you, you were amazing. An artist. You had a real thing for the deadbeat soul, I thought. But we started to get complaints, and I had to warn you. Didn't I warn you? I should have suspected something when the delinquent accounts started to turn over again. It was like rancid butter turning sweet. So I don't say this to knock your technique. Your technique's terrific. With you around we could have laid off the lawyers. But Ed, you're a gangster. A gangster."

That's it, Ed Wolfe thought. *I'm a gangster. Babyface Wolfe at nobody's door.*

"Well," La Meck said, "I guess we owe you some money."

"Two weeks' pay," Ed Wolfe said.

"And two weeks in lieu of notice," La Meck said grandly.

"And a week's pay for my vacation."

"You haven't been here a year," La Meck said.

"It would have been a year in another month. I've earned the vacation."

"What the hell," La Meck said. "A week's pay for vacation."

La Meck figured on a pad and tearing off a sheet handed it to Ed Wolfe. "Does that check with your figures?" he asked.

Ed Wolfe, who had no figures, was amazed to see that his check was so large. Leaving off the deductions he made $92.73 a week. Five $92.73's was evidently $463.65. It was a lot of money. "That seems to be right," he told La Meck.

La Meck gave him a check and Ed Wolfe got up. Already it was as though he had never worked there. When La Meck handed him the check he almost couldn't think what it was for. It was as if there should have been a photographer there to record the ceremony. ORPHAN AWARDED CHECK BY BUSINESSMAN.

"Good-bye, Mr. La Meck," he said. "It has been an interesting association," he added foolishly.

"Good-bye, Ed," La Meck answered, putting his arm around Ed Wolfe's shoulders and leading him to the door. "I'm sorry it had to end this way." He shook Ed Wolfe's hand seriously and looked into his eyes. He had a hard grip.

Quantity and quality, Ed Wolfe thought.

"One thing, Ed. Watch yourself. Your mistake here was that you took the job too seriously. You hated the chiselers."

No, no, I loved them, he thought.

"You've got to watch it. Don't love. Don't hate. That's the secret. Detachment and caution. Look out for Ed Wolfe."

"I'll watch out for him," he said giddily and in a moment he was out of La Meck's office, and the main office, and the elevator, and the building itself, loose in the world, as cautious and as detached as La Meck could want him.

He took the car from the parking lot, handing the attendant the two dollars. The man gave him fifty cents back. "That's right," Ed Wolfe said, "it's only two o'clock." He put the half dollar in his pocket, and, on an impulse, took out his wallet. He had twelve dollars. He counted his change. Eighty-two cents. With his finger, on the dusty dashboard, he added $12.82 to $463.65. He had $476.47. *Does that check with your figures?* he asked himself and drove into the crowded traffic.

Proceeding slowly, past his old building, past garages, past bar and grills, past second-rate hotels, he followed the traffic further downtown. He drove into the deepest part of the city, down and downtown to the bottom, the foundation, the city's navel. He watched the shoppers and tourists and messengers and men with appointments. He was tranquil, serene. It was something he would be content to do forever. He could use his check to buy gas, to take his meals at drive-in restaurants, to pay tolls. It would be a pleasant life, a great life, and he contemplated it thoughtfully. To drive at fifteen or twenty miles an hour through eternity, stopping at stoplights and signs, pulling over to the curb at the sound of sirens and the sight of funerals, obeying all traffic laws, making obedience to them his very code. Ed Wolfe, the Flying Dutchman, the Wandering Jew, the Off and Running Orphan, "Look out for Ed Wolfe," a ghostly wailing down the city's corridors. *What would be bad?* he thought.

In the morning, out of habit, he dressed himself in a white shirt and light suit. Before he went downstairs he saw that his check and his twelve dollars were still in his wallet. Carefully he counted the eighty-two cents that he had placed on the dresser the night before, put the coins in his pocket, and went downstairs to his car.

Something green had been shoved under the wiper blade on the driver's side.

YOUR CAR WILL NEVER BE WORTH MORE THAN IT IS WORTH RIGHT NOW.

WHY WAIT FOR DEPRECIATION TO MAKE YOU AUTOMOTIVELY BANKRUPT?

I WILL BUY THIS CAR AND PAY CASH! I WILL NOT CHEAT YOU!

Ed Wolfe considered his car thoughtfully a moment and got in. He drove that day through the city playing the car radio softly. He heard the news each hour and each half hour. He listened to Arthur Godfrey far away and in another world. He heard Bing Crosby's ancient voice, and thought sadly, *Depreciation.* When his tank was almost empty he thought wearily of having to have it filled and could see himself, bored and discontented behind the bug-stained glass, forced into a patience he did not feel, having to decide whether to take the Green Stamps the attendant tried to extend. *Put money in your purse, Ed Wolfe,* he thought. *Cash!* he thought with passion.

He went to the address on the circular.

He drove up onto the gravel lot but remained in his car. In a moment a man came out of a small wooden shack and walked toward Ed Wolfe's car. If he was appraising it he gave no sign. He stood at the side of the automobile and waited while Ed Wolfe got out.

"Look around," the man said. "No pennants, no strings of electric lights." He saw the advertisement in Ed Wolfe's hand. "I ran the ad off on my brother-in-law's mimeograph. My kid stole the paper from his school."

Ed Wolfe looked at him.

"The place looks like a goddamn parking lot. When the snow starts falling I get rid of the cars and move the Christmas trees right onto it. No overhead. That's the beauty of a volume business."

Ed Wolfe looked pointedly at the nearly empty lot.

"That's right," the man said. "It's slow. I'm giving the policy one more chance. Then I cheat the public just like everybody else. You're just in time. Come on, I'll show you a beautiful car."

"I want to sell my car," Ed Wolfe said.

"Sure, sure," the man said. "You want to trade with me. I give top allowances. I play fair."

"I want you to buy my car."

The man looked at him closely. "What do you want? You want me to go into the office and put on the ten-gallon hat? It's my only overhead so I guess you're entitled to see it. You're paying for it. I put on this big frigging hat, see, and I become Texas Willie Waxelman, the Mad Cowboy. If that's what you want, I can get it in a minute."

It was incredible, Ed Wolfe thought. *There were bastards everywhere who hated other bastards downtown everywhere.* "I don't want to trade my car in," Ed Wolfe said. "I want to sell it. I, too, want to reduce my inventory."

The man smiled sadly. "You want me to buy *your* car. You run in and put on the hat. I'm an automobile *salesman,* kid."

"No, you're not," Ed Wolfe said. "I was with Cornucopia Finance. We handled your paper. You're an automobile *buyer.* Your business is in buying up four- and five-year-old cars like mine from people who need dough fast and then auctioning them off to the trade."

The man turned away and Ed Wolfe followed him. Inside the shack the man said, "I'll give you two hundred."

"I need six hundred," Ed Wolfe said.

"I'll lend you the hat. Hold up a goddamn stagecoach."

"Give me five."

"I'll give you two fifty and we'll part friends."

"Four hundred and fifty."

"Three hundred. Here," the man said, reaching his hand into an opened safe and taking out three sheaves of thick, banded bills. He held the money out to Ed Wolfe. "Go ahead, count it."

Absently Ed Wolfe took the money. The bills were stiff, like money in a teller's drawer, their value as decorous and untapped as a sheet of postage stamps. He held the money, pleased by its weight. "Tens and fives," he said, grinning.

"You bet," the man said, taking the money back. "You want to sell your car?"

"Yes," Ed Wolfe said. "Give me the money," he said hoarsely.

He had been to the bank, had stood in the patient, slow, money-conscious line, had presented his formidable check to the impassive teller, hoping the four hundred and sixty-three dollars and sixty-five cents she counted out would seem his week's salary to the man who waited behind him. *Fool*, he thought, *it will seem two weeks' pay and two weeks in lieu of notice and a week for vacation for the hell of it, the three-week margin of an orphan.*

"Thank you," the teller said, already looking beyond Ed Wolfe to the man behind him.

"Wait," Ed Wolfe said. "Here." He handed her a white withdrawal slip.

She took it impatiently and walked to a file. "You're closing your savings account?" she asked loudly.

"Yes," Ed Wolfe answered, embarrassed.

"I'll have a cashier's check made out for this."

"No, no," Ed Wolfe said desperately. "Give me cash."

"Sir, we make out a cashier's check and cash it for you," the teller explained.

651

"Oh." Ed Wolfe said. "I see."

When the teller had given him the two hundred fourteen dollars and twenty-three cents, he went to the next window, where he made out a check for $38.91. It was what he had in his checking account.

On Ed Wolfe's kitchen table was a thousand dollars. That day he had spent a dollar and ninety cents. He had twenty-seven dollars and seventy-one cents in his pocket. For expenses. "For attrition," he said aloud. "The cost of living. For streetcars and newspapers and half gallons of milk and loaves of white bread. For the movies. For a cup of coffee." He went to his pantry. He counted the cans and packages, the boxes and bottles. "The three weeks again," he said. "The orphan's nutritional margin." He looked in his icebox. In the freezer he poked around among white packages of frozen meat. He looked brightly into the vegetable tray. A whole lettuce. Five tomatoes. Several slices of cucumber. Browning celery. On another shelf four bananas. Three and a half apples. A cut pineapple. Some grapes, loose and collapsing darkly in a white bowl. A quarter pound of butter. A few eggs. Another egg, broken last week, congealing in a blue dish. Things in plastic bowls, in jars, forgotten, faintly mysterious left-overs, faintly rotten, vaguely futured, equivocal garbage. He closed the door, feeling a draft. "Really," he said, "it's quite cozy." He looked at the thousand dollars on the kitchen table. "It's not enough," he said. "It's not enough," he shouted. "It's not enough to be cautious on. La Meck, you bastard, detachment comes higher, what do you think? You think it's cheap?" He raged against himself. It was the way he used to speak to people on the telephone. "Wake up. Orphan! Jerk! Wake up. It costs to be detached."

He moved solidly through the small apartment and lay down on his bed with his shoes still on, putting his hands behind his head luxuriously. *It's marvelous,* he thought. *Tomorrow I'll buy a trench coat. I'll take my meals in piano bars.* He lighted a cigarette. *I'll never smile again,* he sang, smiling. "All right, Eddie, play it again," he said. "Mistuh Wuf, you don' wan' ta heah dat ol' song no maw. You know whut it do to you. She ain' wuth it, Mistuh Wuf." He nodded. "Again, Eddie." Eddie played his black ass off. "The way I see it, Eddie," he said, taking a long, sad drink of warm Scotch, "there are orphans and there are orphans." The overhead fan chuffed slowly, stirring the potted palmetto leaves.

He sat up in bed, grinding his heels across the sheets. "There are orphans and there are orphans," he said. "I'll move. I'll liquidate. I'll sell out."

He went to the phone and called his landlady and made an appointment to see her.

It was a time of ruthless parting from his things, but there was no bitterness in it. He was a born salesman, he told himself. A disposer, a natural dumper. He administered severance. As detached as a funeral director, what he had learned was to say good-bye. It was a talent of a sort. And he had never felt quite so interested. He supposed he was doing what he had been meant for, what, perhaps, everyone was meant for. He sold and he sold, each day spinning off, reeling off little pieces of himself, like controlled explosions of the sun. Now his life was a series of speeches, of nearly earnest pitches. What he remembered of the day was what he had said. What others said to him, or even whether they spoke at all, he was unsure.

Tuesday he told his landlady, "Buy my furniture. It's new. It's good stuff. It's expensive. You can forget about that. Put it out of your mind. I want to sell it. I'll show you bills for over seven hundred dollars. Forget the bills. Consider my character. Consider the man. Only the man. That's how to get your bargains. Examine. Examine. I could tell you about innersprings; I could talk to you of leather. But I won't. I don't. I smoke, but I'm careful. I can show you the ashtrays. You won't find cigarette holes in *my* tables. Examine. I drink. I'm a drinker. I drink. But I hold it. You won't find alcohol stains. May I be frank? I make love. Again, I could show you the bills. But I'm cautious. My sheets are virginal, white.

"Two hundred fifty dollars, landlady. Sit on that sofa. That chair. Buy my furniture. Rent the apartment furnished. Deduct what you pay from your taxes. Collect additional rents. Realize enormous profits. Wallow in gravy. Get it, landlady? Get it? Just two hundred fifty dollars. Don't disclose the figure or my name. I want to remain anonymous."

He took her into his bedroom. "The piece of resistance, landlady. What you're really buying is the bedroom stuff. I'm selling you your own bare floor. What charm. Charm? Elegance. Elegance! I throw in the living-room rug. That I throw in. You have to take that or it's no deal. Give me cash and I move tomorrow."

Wednesday he said, "I heard you buy books. That must be interesting. And sad. It must be very sad. A man who loves books doesn't like to sell them. It would be the last thing. Excuse me. I've got no right to talk to you this way. You buy books and I've got books to sell. There. It's business now. As it should be. My library—" He smiled helplessly. "Excuse me, Such a grand name. Library." He began again slowly. "My books, my books are in there. Look them over. I'm afraid my taste has been rather eclectic. You see, my education has not been formal. There are over eleven hundred. Of course many are paperbacks. Well, you can see that. I feel as if I'm selling my mind."

The book buyer gave Ed Wolfe one hundred twenty dollars for his mind.

On Thursday he wrote a letter:

American Annuity & Life Insurance Company,
Suite 410,
Lipton-Hill Building,
2007 Beverly Street, S.W.,
Boston 19, Massachusetts

Dear Sirs,
I am writing in regard to Policy Number 593-00034-78, a $5,000,
twenty-year annuity held by Edward Wolfe of the address below.

Although only four payments have been made, sixteen years remain before the policy matures, I find I must make application for the immediate return of my payments and cancel the policy.

I have read the "In event of cancellation" clause in my policy, and realize that I am entitled to only a flat three percent interest on the "total paid-in amount of the partial amortizement." Your records will show that I have made four payments of $198.45 each. If your figures check with mine this would come to $793.80. Adding three percent interest to this amount ($23.81), your company owes me $817.61.

Your prompt attention to my request would be gratefully appreciated, although I feel, frankly, as though I were selling my future.

On Monday someone came to buy his record collection. "What do you want to hear? I'll put something comfortable on while we talk. What do you like? Here, try this. Go ahead, put it on the machine. By the edges, man. By the edges! I feel as if I'm selling my throat. Never mind about that. Dig the sounds. Orphans up from Orleans singing the news of chain gangs to café society. You can smell the freight trains, man. Recorded during actual performance. You can hear the ice cubes clinkin' in the glasses, the waiters picking up their tips. I have jazz. Folk. Classical. Broadway. Spoken Word. Spoken Word, man! I feel as though I'm selling my ears. The stuff lives in my heart or I wouldn't sell. I have a one-price throat, one-price ears. Sixty dollars for the noise the world makes, man. But remember. I'll be watching. By the edges. Only by the edges!"

On Friday he went to a pawnshop in a Checker Cab.

"You? You buy gold? You buy clothes? You buy Hawaiian guitars? You buy pistols for resale to suicides? I wouldn't have recognized you. Where's the skullcap, the garters around the sleeves? The cigar I wouldn't ask you about. You look like anybody. You look like everybody. I don't know what to say. I'm stuck. I don't know how to deal with you. I was going to tell you something sordid, you know? You know what I mean? Okay, I'll give you facts.

"The fact is, I'm the average man. That's what the fact is. Eleven shirts, 15 neck, 34 sleeve. Six slacks, 32 waist. Five suits at 38 long. Shoes 10-C. A 7½ hat. You know something? Those marginal restaurants where you can never remember whether they'll let you in without a jacket? Well the jackets they lend you in those places always fit me. That's the kind of guy you're dealing with. You can have confidence. Look at the clothes. Feel the material. And there's one thing about me. I'm fastidious. Fastidious. Immaculate. You think I'd be clumsy. A fall guy falls down, right? There's not a mark on the clothes. Inside? Inside it's another story. I don't speak of inside. Inside it's all Band-Aids, plaster, iodine, sticky stuff for burns. But outside—fastidiousness, immaculation, reality! My clothes will fly off your racks. I promise. I feel as if I'm selling my skin. Does that check with your figures?

"So now you know. It's me, Ed Wolfe. Ed Wolfe, the orphan? I lived in the orphanage for sixteen years. They gave me a name. It was a Jewish orphanage so they gave me a Jewish name. Almost. That is they couldn't know for sure themselves so they kept it deliberately vague. I'm a foundling. A lostling. Who needs it, right? Who the hell needs it? I'm at loose ends, pawnbroker. I'm at loose ends out of looser beginnings. I need the money to stay alive. All you can give me.

"Here's a good watch. Here's a bad one. For good times and bad. That's life, right? You can sell them as a package deal. Here are radios, I'll miss the radios. A phonograph. Automatic. Three speeds. Two speakers. The politic bastard shuts itself off. And a pressure cooker. It's valueless to me, frankly. No pressure. I can live only on cold meals. Spartan. Spartan.

"I feel as if I'm selling—this is the last of it, I have no more things—I feel as if I'm selling my things."

On Saturday he called the phone company: "Operator? Let me speak to your supervisor, please.

"Supervisor? Supervisor, I am Ed Wolfe, your subscriber at TErrace 7-3572. There is nothing wrong with the service. The service has been excellent. No one calls, but you can have nothing to do with that. However, I must cancel. I find that I no longer have any need of a telephone. Please connect me with the business office.

"Business office? Business office, this is Ed Wolfe. My telephone number is TErrace 7-3572. I am closing my account with you. When the service was first installed I had to surrender a twenty-five-dollar deposit to your company. It was understood that the deposit was to be refunded when our connection with each other had been terminated. Disconnect me. Deduct what I owe on my current account from my deposit and refund the rest immediately. Business office, I feel as if I'm selling my mouth."

When he had nothing left to sell, when that was finally that, he stayed until he had finished all the food and then moved from his old apartment into a small, thinly furnished room. He took with him a single carton of clothing—the suit, the few shirts, the socks, the pajamas, the underwear and overcoat he did not sell. It was in preparing this carton that he discovered the hangers. There were hundreds of them. His own. Previous tenants'. Hundreds. In each closet on rods, in dark, dark corners was this anonymous residue of all their lives. He unpacked his carton and put the hangers inside. They made a weight. He took them to the pawnshop and demanded a dollar for them. They were worth, he argued, more. In an A&P he got another carton free and went back to repack his clothes.

At the new place the landlord gave him his key.

"You got anything else?" the landlord asked. "I could give you a hand."

"No," he said. "Nothing."

Following the landlord up the deep stairs he was conscious of the $2,479.03 he had packed into the pockets of the suit and shirts and pajamas and overcoat inside the carton. It was like carrying a community of economically viable dolls.

When the landlord left him he opened the carton and gathered all his money together. In fading light he reviewed the figures he had entered in the pages of an old spiral notebook:

Pay	$463.65
Cash	12.82
Car	300.00
Savings	214.23
Checking	38.91
Furniture (& bedding)	250.00
Books	120.00
Insurance	817.61
Records	60.00
Pawned:	
Clothes	110.00
2 watches	18.00
2 radios	12.00
Phonograph	35.00
Pressure cooker	6.00
Phone deposit (less bill)	19.81
Hangers	1.00
Total	$2,479.03

So, he thought, that was what he was worth. That was the going rate for orphans in a wicked world. Something under $2,500. He took his pencil and lined through all the nouns on his list. He tore the list carefully from top to bottom and crumpled the half which inventoried his ex-possessions. Then he crumpled the other half.

He went to the window and pushed the loose, broken shade. He opened the window and set both lists on the ledge. He made a ring of his forefinger and thumb and flicked the paper balls into the street. "Look out for Ed Wolfe," he said softly.

In six weeks the season changed. The afternoons failed. The steam failed. He was as unafraid of the dark as he had been of the sunlight. He longed for a special grief, to be touched by anguish or terror, but when he saw the others in the street, in the cafeteria, in the theater, in the hallway, on the stairs, at the newsstand, in the basement rushing their fouled linen from basket to machine, he stood, as indifferent to their errand, their appetite, their joy, their greeting, their effort, their curiosity, their grime, as he was to his own. No envy wrenched him, no despair unhoped him, but, gradually, he became restless.

He began to spend, not recklessly so much as indifferently. At first he was able to recall for weeks what he spent on a given day. It was his way of telling time. Now he had difficulty remembering and could tell how much his life was costing only by subtracting what he had left from his original two thousand four hundred seventy-nine dollars and three cents. In eleven weeks he had spent six hundred seventy-seven dollars and thirty-four cents. It was almost three times more than he had planned. He became panicky. He had come to think of his money as his life. Spending it was the abrasion again, the old habit of self-buffing to come to the thing beneath. He could not draw infinitely on his credit. It was limited. Limited. He checked his figures. He had eighteen hundred and one dollars, sixty-nine cents. He warned himself, "Rothschild, child. Rockefeller, feller. Look out, Ed Wolfe. Look out."

He argued with his landlord, won a five-dollar reduction in his rent. He was constantly hungry, wore clothes stingily, realized an odd reassurance in his thin pain, his vague fetidness. He surrendered his dimes, his quarters, his half-dollars in a kind of sober anger. In seven weeks he spent only one hundred thirty dollars, fifty-one cents. He checked his figures. He had sixteen hundred seventy-one dollars, eighteen cents. He had spent almost twice what he had anticipated. "It's all right," he said. "I've reversed the trend. I can catch up." He held the money in his hand. He could smell his soiled underwear. "Nah, nah," he said. "It's not enough."

It was not enough, it was not enough, it was not enough. He had painted himself into a corner. Death by cul-de-sac. He had nothing left to sell, the born salesman. The born champion, long-distance, Ed Wolfe of a salesman, and he lay in his room winded, wounded, wondering where his next pitch was coming from, at one with the ages.

He put on his suit, took his sixteen hundred, seventy-one dollars and eighteen cents, and went down into the street. It was a warm night. He would walk downtown. The ice which just days before had covered the sidewalk was dissolved in slush. In darkness he walked through a thawing, melting world. There was, on the edge of the air, something, the warm, moist odor of the change of the season. He was, despite himself, touched. "I'll take a bus," he threatened. "I'll take a bus and close the windows and ride over the wheel."

He had dinner and some drinks in a hotel. When he finished he was feeling pretty good. He didn't want to go back. He looked at the bills thick in his wallet and went over to the desk clerk. "Where's the action?" he whispered. The clerk looked at him, startled. He went over to the bell captain. "Where's the action?" he asked and gave the man a dollar. He winked. The man stared at him helplessly.

"Sir?" the bell captain said, looking at the dollar.

Ed Wolfe nudged him in his gold buttons. He winked again. "Nice town you got here," he said expansively. "I'm a salesman, you understand, and this is new territory for me. Now if I were in Beantown or Philly or L.A. or Vegas or Big D or Frisco or Cincy, why I'd know what was what. I'd be okay, you know what I mean?" He winked once more. "Keep the buck, kid," he said. "Keep it, keep it," he said, walking off.

In the lobby a man sat in a deep chair, *The Wall Street Journal* opened widely across his face. "Where's the action?" Ed Wolfe said, peering over the top of the paper into the crown of the man's hat.

"What's that?" the man asked.

Ed Wolfe, surprised, saw that the man was a Negro.

"What's that?" the man repeated, vaguely nervous. Embarrassed, Ed Wolfe watched him guiltily, as though he had been caught in an act of bigotry.

"I thought you were someone else," he said lamely. The man smiled and lifted the paper to his face. Ed Wolfe stood before the man's opened paper, conscious of mildly teetering. He felt lousy, awkward, complicatedly irritated and ashamed, the mere act of hurting someone's feelings suddenly the most that could be held against him. It came to him how completely he had failed to make himself felt. "Look out for Ed Wolfe, indeed," he said aloud. The man lowered his paper. "Some of my best friends are Comanches," Ed Wolfe said. "Can I buy you a drink?"

"No," the man said.

"Resistance, eh?" Ed Wolfe said. "That's good. Resistance is good. A deal closed without resistance is no deal. Let me introduce myself. I'm Ed Wolfe. What's your name?"

"Please, I'm not bothering anybody. Leave me alone."

"Why?" Ed Wolfe asked.

The man stared at him and Ed Wolfe sat suddenly down beside him. "I won't press it," he said generously. "Where's the action? Where *is* it? Fold the paper, man. You're playing somebody else's gig." He leaned across the space between them and took the man by the arm. He pulled at him gently, awed by his own boldness. It was the first time since he had shaken hands with La Meck that he had touched anyone physically. What he was risking surprised and puzzled him. In all those months to have touched only two people, to have touched even two people! To feel their life, even, as now, through the unyielding wool of clothing, was disturbing. He was unused to it, frightened and oddly moved. The man, bewildered, looked at Ed Wolfe timidly and allowed himself to be taken toward the cocktail lounge.

They took a table near the bar. There, in the alcoholic dark, within earshot of the easy banter of the regulars, Ed Wolfe seated the Negro and then himself. He looked around the room and listened for a moment. He turned back to the Negro. Smoothly boozy, he pledged the man's health when the girl brought their drinks. He drank stolidly, abstractedly. Coming to life briefly, he indicated the men and women around them, their suntans apparent even in the dark. "Pilots," he said. "All of them. Airline pilots. The girls are all stewardesses and the pilots lay them." He ordered more drinks. He did not like liquor and liberally poured ginger ale into his bourbon. He ordered more drinks and forgot the ginger ale. "*Goyim*," he said. "White *goyim*. American *goyim*." He stared at the Negro. "These are the people, man. The mothered and fathered people." He leaned across the table. "Little Orphan Annie, what the hell kind of an orphan is that with all her millions and her white American *goyim* friends to bail her out?"

He watched them narrowly, drunkenly. He had seen them before—in good motels, in airports, in bars—and he wondered about them, seeing them, he supposed, as Negroes or children of the poor must have seen him when he had had his car and driven sometimes through slums. They were removed, aloof—he meant it—a different breed. He turned and saw the Negro and could not think for a moment what the man could have been doing there. The Negro slouched in his chair, his great white eyes hooded. "You want to hang around here?" Ed Wolfe asked him.

"It's your party," the man said.

"Then let's go someplace else," Ed Wolfe said. "I get nervous here."

"I know a place," the Negro said.

"*You* know a place. You're a stranger here."

"No, man," the Negro said. "This is my hometown. I come down here sometimes just to sit in the lobby and read the newspapers. It looks good, you know what I mean? It looks good for the race."

"*The Wall Street Journal*? You're kidding Ed Wolfe. Watch that."

"No," the Negro said. "Honest."

"I'll be damned," Ed Wolfe said. "I come for the same reasons."

"Yeah," the Negro said. "No shit."

"Sure, the same reasons." He laughed. "Let's get out of here." He tried to stand, but fell back again in his chair. "Hey, help me up," he said loudly. The Negro got up and came around to Ed Wolfe's side of the table. Leaning over, he raised him to his feet. Some of the others in the room looked at them curiously. "It's all right," Ed Wolfe said. "He's my man. I take him with me everywhere. It looks good for the race." With their arms around each other's shoulders they stumbled out of the room and through the lobby.

In the street Ed Wolfe leaned against the building and the Negro hailed a cab, the dark left hand shooting up boldly, the long black body stretching forward, raised on tiptoes, the head turned sharply along the left shoulder.

Ed Wolfe knew he had never done it before. The Negro came up beside Ed Wolfe and guided him toward the curb. Holding the door open he shoved him into the cab with his left hand. Ed Wolfe lurched against the cushioned seat awkwardly. The Negro gave the driver an address and the cab moved off. Ed Wolfe reached for the window handle and rolled it down rapidly. He shoved his head out the window of the taxi and smiled and waved at the people along the curb.

"Hey, man. Close the window," the Negro said after a moment. "Close the window. The cops, the cops."

Ed Wolfe laid his head along the edge of the taxi window and looked up at the Negro who was leaning over him and smiling and seemed trying to tell him something.

"Where we going, man?" he asked.

"We're there," the Negro said, sliding along the seat toward the door.

"One ninety-five," the driver said.

"It's your party," Ed Wolfe told the Negro, waving away responsibility.

The Negro looked disappointed, but reached into his pocket to pull out his wallet.

Did he see what I had on me? Ed Wolfe wondered anxiously. *Jerk, drunk, you'll be rolled. They'll cut your throat and then they'll leave your skin in an alley. Be careful.*

"Come on, Ed," the Negro said. He took him by the arm and got him out of the taxi.

Fake. Fake, Ed Wolfe thought. *Murderer. Nigger. Razor man.*

The Negro pulled Ed Wolfe toward a doorway. "You'll meet my friends," he said.

"Yeah, yeah," Ed Wolfe said. "I've heard so much about them."

"Hold it a second," the Negro said. He went up to the window and pressed his ear against the opaque glass.

Ed Wolfe watched him without making a move.

"Here's the place," the Negro said proudly.

"Sure," Ed Wolfe said. "Sure it is."

"Come on, man," the Negro urged him.

"I'm coming, I'm coming," Ed Wolfe mumbled, "but my head is bending low."

The Negro took out a ring of keys, selected one, and put it in the door. Ed Wolfe followed him through.

"Hey, Oliver," somebody called. "Hey, baby, it's Oliver. Oliver looks good. He looks *good*."

"Hello, Mopiani," the Negro said to a short black man.

"How is stuff, Oliver?" Mopiani said to him.

"How's the market?" a man next to Mopiani asked, with a laugh.

"Ain't no mahket, baby. It's a *sto'*," somebody else said.

A woman stopped, looked at Ed Wolfe for a moment, and asked: "Who's the ofay, Oliver?"

"That's Oliver's broker, baby."

"Oliver's broker looks good," Mopiani said. "He looks *good*."

"This is my friend, Mr. Ed Wolfe," Oliver told them.

"Hey, there," Mopiani said.

"Charmed," Ed Wolfe said.

"How's it going, man," a Negro said indifferently.

"Delighted," Ed Wolfe said.

He let Oliver lead him to a table.

"I'll get the drinks, Ed," Oliver said, leaving him.

Ed Wolfe looked at the room glumly. People were drinking steadily, gaily. They kept their bottles under their chairs in paper bags. Ed Wolfe watched a man take a bag from beneath his chair, raise it, and twist the open end of the bag carefully around the neck of the bottle so that it resembled a bottle of champagne swaddled in its toweling. The man poured into his glass grandly. At the dark far end of the room some musicians were playing and three or four couples danced dreamily in front of them. He watched the musicians closely and was vaguely reminded of the airline pilots.

In a few minutes Oliver returned with a paper bag and some glasses. A girl was with him. "Mary Roberta, Ed Wolfe," he said, very pleased. Ed Wolfe stood up clumsily and the girl nodded.

"No more ice," Oliver explained.

"What the hell," Ed Wolfe said.

Mary Roberta sat down and Oliver pushed her chair up to the table. She sat with her hands in her lap and Oliver pushed her as though she were a cripple.

"Real nice little place here, Ollie," Ed Wolfe said.

"Oh, it's just the club," Oliver said.

"Real nice," Ed Wolfe said.

Oliver opened the bottle and poured liquor in their glasses and put the paper bag under his chair. Oliver raised his glass. Ed Wolfe touched it lamely with his own and leaned back, drinking. When he put it down empty, Oliver filled it again from the paper bag. He drank sluggishly, like one falling asleep, and listened, numbed, to Oliver and the girl. His glass never seemed to be empty anymore. He drank steadily but the liquor seemed to remain at the same level in the glass. He was conscious that someone else had joined them at the table. "Oliver's broker looks good," he heard somebody say. Mopiani. Warm and drowsy and gently detached, he listened, feeling as he had in barbershops, having his hair cut, conscious of the barber, unseen behind him, touching his hair and scalp with his warm fingers. "You see Bert? He looks good," Mopiani was saying.

With great effort Ed Wolfe shifted in his chair, turning to the girl.

"Thought you were giving out on us, Ed," Oliver said. "That's it. That's it."

The girl sat with her hands folded in her lap.

"Mary Roberta," Ed Wolfe said.

"Uh huh," the girl said.

"Mary Roberta."

"Yes," the girl said. "That's right."

"You want to dance?" Ed Wolfe asked.

"All right," she said. "I guess so."

"That's it, that's it," Oliver said. "Stir yourself."

He got up clumsily, cautiously, like one standing in a stalled Ferris wheel, and went around behind her chair, pulling it far back from the table with the girl in it. He took her warm, bare arm and moved toward the dancers. Mopiani passed them with a bottle. "Looks good, looks good," Mopiani said approvingly. He pulled her against him to let Mopiani pass, tightening the grip of his pale hand on her brown arm. A muscle leaped beneath the girl's smooth skin, filling his palm. At the edge of the dance floor Ed Wolfe leaned forward into the girl's arms and they moved slowly, thickly across the floor, he held the girl close, conscious of her weight, the life beneath her body, just under her skin. Sick, he remembered a jumping bean he had held once in his palm, awed and frightened by the invisible life, jerking and hysterical, inside the stony shell. The girl moved with him in the music, Ed Wolfe astonished by the burden of her life. He stumbled away from her deliberately. Grinning, he moved urgently back against her. "Look out for Ed Wolfe," he crooned.

The girl stiffened and held him away from her, dancing self-consciously. Ed Wolfe, brooding, tried to concentrate on the lost rhythm. They danced in silence for a while.

"What do you do?" she asked him finally.

"I'm a salesman," he told her gloomily.

"Door to door?"

"Floor to ceiling. Wall to wall."

"Too much," she said.

"I'm a pusher," he said, suddenly angry. She looked frightened. "But I'm not hooked myself. It's a weakness in my character. I can't get hooked. Ach, what would you *goyim* know about it?"

"Take it easy," she said. "What's the matter with you? Do you want to sit down?"

"I can't push sitting down," he said.

"Hey," she said, "don't talk so loud."

"Boy," he said, "you black Protestants. What's that song you people sing?"

"Come on," she said.

"Sometimes I feel like a motherless child," he sang roughly. The other dancers watched him nervously. "That's our national anthem, man," he said to a couple that had stopped dancing to look at him. "That's our song, sweethearts," he said, looking around him. "All right, mine then. I'm an orphan."

"Oh, come on," the girl said, exasperated, "an orphan. A grown man."

He pulled away from her. The band stopped playing. "Hell," he said loudly, "from the beginning. Orphan. Bachelor. Widower. Only child. All my names scorn me. I'm a survivor. I'm a goddamned survivor, that's what." The other couples crowded around him now. People got up from their tables. He could see them, on tiptoes, stretching their necks over the heads of the dancers. *No*, he thought. *No, no. Detachment and caution. The La Meck Plan. They'll kill you. They'll kill you and kill you.* He edged away from them, moving carefully backward against the bandstand. People pushed forward onto the dance floor to watch him. He could hear their questions, could see heads darting from behind backs and suddenly appearing over shoulders as they strained to get a look at him.

He grabbed Mary Roberta's hand, pulling her to him fiercely. He pulled and pushed her up onto the bandstand and then climbed up beside her. The trumpet player, bewildered, made room for him. "Tell you what I'm going to do," he shouted over their heads. "Tell you what I'm going to do."

Everyone was listening to him now.

"Tell you what I'm going to do," he began again.

Quietly they waited for him to go on.

"I don't *know* what I'm going to do," he shouted. "I don't *know* what I'm going to do. Isn't that a hell of a note?"

"Isn't it?" he demanded.

"Brothers and sisters," he shouted, "and as an only child bachelor orphan I use the term playfully you understand. Brothers and sisters, I tell you what I'm *not* going to do. I'm no consumer. Nobody's death can make me that. I won't consume. I mean it's a question of identity, right? Closer, come up closer, buddies. You don't want to miss any of this."

"Oliver's broker looks good up there. Mary Roberta looks good. She looks good," Mopiani said below him.

"Right, Mopiani. She looks good, she looks *good*," Ed Wolfe called loudly. "So I tell you what I'm going to do. What am I bid? What am I bid for this fine strong wench? Daughter of a chief, masters. Dear dark daughter of a dead dinge chief. Look at those arms. Those arms, those arms. What am I bid?"

They looked at him, astonished.

"What am I bid?" he demanded. "Reluctant, masters? Reluctant masters, masters? Say, what's the matter with you darkies? Come on, what am I bid?" He turned to the girl. "No one wants you, honey," he said. "Folks, folks, I'd buy her myself, but I've already told you. I'm not a consumer. Please forgive me, miss."

He heard them shifting uncomfortably.

"Look," he said patiently, "the management has asked me to remind you that this is a living human being. This is the real thing, the genuine article, the goods. Oh, I told them I wasn't the right man for this job. As an orphan I have no conviction about the product. Now you should have seen me in my old job. I could be rough. Rough. I hurt people. Can you imagine? I actually caused them pain. I mean, what the hell, I was an orphan. I *could* hurt people. An orphan doesn't have to bother with love. An orphan's like a nigger in that respect. Emancipated. But you people are another problem entirely. That's why I came here tonight. There are parents among you. I can feel it. There's even a sense of parents behind those parents. My God, don't any of you folks ever die? So what's holding us up? We're not making any money. Come on, what am I bid?"

"Shut up, mister." The voice was raised hollowly someplace in the back of the crowd.

Ed Wolfe could not see the owner of the voice.

"He's not in," Ed Wolfe said.

"Shut up. What right you got to come down here and speak to us like that?"

"He's not in, I tell you. I'm his brother."

"You're a guest. A guest got no call to talk like that."

"He's out. I'm his father. He didn't tell me and I don't know when he'll be back."

"You can't make fun of us," the voice said.

"He isn't here. I'm his son."

"Bring that girl down off that stage!"

"Speaking," Ed Wolfe said.

"Let go of that girl!" someone called angrily.

The girl moved closer to him.

"She's mine," Ed Wolfe said. "I danced with her."

"Get her down from there!"

"Okay," he said giddily. "Okay. All right." He let go of the girl's hand and pulled out his wallet. The girl did not move, he took out the bills and dropped the wallet to the floor.

"Damned drunk!" someone shouted.

"That white man's crazy," someone else said.

"Here," Ed Wolfe said. "There's over sixteen hundred dollars here," he yelled, waving the money. It was, for him, like holding so much paper. "I'll start the bidding. I hear over sixteen hundred dollars once. I hear over sixteen hundred dollars twice. I hear it three times. Sold! A deal's a deal," he cried, flinging the money high over their heads. He saw them reach helplessly, noiselessly toward the bills, heard distinctly the sound of paper tearing.

He faced the girl. "Good-bye," he said.

She reached forward, taking his hand.

"Good-bye," he said again. "I'm leaving."

She held his hand, squeezing it. He looked down at the luxuriant brown hand, seeing beneath it the fine articulation of bones, the rich sudden rush of muscle. Inside her own he saw, indifferently, his own pale hand, lifeless and serene, still and infinitely free.

The Deep Sleep

Aleksandar Hemon

The slumbering guard, about to slide off his chair, had his fingers on the holstered revolver. Pronek passed him by, pushed the grille door aside, and stepped into the elevator. The elevator was rife with a woman's fragrant absence: peachy, skinny, dense. Pronek imagined the woman who might have exuded that scent, and she was worth a stare. She was tall and rangy and strong looking; her hair was black and wiry and parted in the middle; she had black eyes and a sulky droop to her lips. She took a cigarette out of her purse, which was heavier than it needed to be, turned to him, and said, expecting a friendly lighter: "I've been searching for someone, and now I know who."

Pronek's eyes narrowed as he looked at the space where the woman would have stood, and he saw himself through her eyes: tall, formerly lanky, so his relaxed movements did not match his fat-padded trunk; his head almost shaved, marred by a few pale patches (he cut his own hair); a gray sweatshirt that read ILLINOIS across the chest; worn-out jeans with a few pomegranate-juice splotches; and boots that had an army look, save for the crack in his left sole—September rains had already soaked his left sock. As he stepped out of the elevator, a whiff of the fragrant cloud followed him out. He stood in the empty hall: On the left and on the right, there were rows of doors standing at attention in the walls. Above a door on the right was a lit exit sign. Pronek made an effort to remember the position—in case he was too much in a hurry to wait for an elevator. He was looking for office number 909 and decided to go right. The colorless carpet muffled his careful steps. The elbow-shaped ball reeked of bathroom ammonia and sweet cigars, and the fragrant whiff dissipated in it. Pronek tried to open the bathroom door—green, sturdy, with a silhouette of a man—but it was locked. When he pushed the door with his shoulder, it rattled: He could break it open without too much force. He figured that there would be fire stairs behind a milky bathroom window, and that the alley led to Michigan Avenue, where he could safely disappear in the street mass.

All of a sudden, Pronek became aware of a sound that had been in his ears for a while but had not quite reached his brain: It was a smothered, popping sound—first one, then two—with a click at the end. Much like the sound of a gun with a silencer. Pronek's muscles tensed and his heart started thumping like a jungle drum—he was convinced that the hall was echoing his accelerating pulse. He felt his eyebrows dewing, thick loaves of pain forming in his calves. He tiptoed past the doors: 902 (Sternwood Steel Export); 904 (Van Bure Software); 906 (Bernard Ohls Legal Services); 908 (empty); 910 (Riordan & Florian Dental Office)—the popping, along with the murky light, came from behind the dim glass of 910. Pronek imagined bodies lined up on the floor facedown, some of them already dead, with their blood and hair on the wall, their brains bubbling on the carpet. They were shivering, waiting for a quiet man with a marble-gray face to pop them in their napes, knowing they would end up in unmarked graves. They reacted to the surprising bullet with a spasm, then death relaxation, then their blood placidly soaking the carpet. There was another pop. There had been at least six of them, and Pronek reckoned that the killer must be running out of bullets. It was risky, it was none of his business, so he twisted the door handle and peeked in.

A large man in a yellow helmet was pressing his orange staple gun against the far wall. He sensed Pronek and turned around slowly. He had on dirty overalls and a green shirt underneath, with tiny golf balls instead of buttons. He stood firmly facing Pronek, his jaw tense, as if expecting a punch, with his booted feet apart, his staple gun pointing to the floor. "Can I help you with something?" he said, frowning under his helmet. "Sorry," Pronek said. "I look for the office 909."

Office 909 had a sign that read GREAT LAKES EYE and a black-and-white eye with long, upward-curling eyelashes. Pronek hesitated for a moment before knocking at the door—his fingers levitated, angled, in front of the eye. Pronek knocked using three of his knuckles, the glass shook perilously, then he opened the door and entered an empty waiting room. There was another door, closed, and there were magazines strewn on the few chairs, even on the musty floor, as if someone had searched through them all. The waiting room was lit by a thin-necked lamp in the corner, leaning slightly as if about to snap. A picture of an elaborate ocean sunset—somebody lit a match under the water—hung on the opposite wall. "Acapulco," it said in the lower right corner, "where you want to dream." Pronek stood in front of the picture, imagining Acapulco and all the pretty, tawny people there. It would be a good place to disappear for a while.

The door opened and a man and a woman came out. They were laughing convivially with someone who remained invisible. The man—tall and black—put on a fedora with a little bluish feather, which went perfectly with his dapper navy-blue suit, snug on his wide shoulders, and his alligator boots with little explosions on his toes. The woman was pale and slim, with blond, boyish hair and a pointy chin. She had a tight, muscular body, like a long-distance runner, and a beautiful lean neck. She kept the tip of her finger on her chin as she listened to the man inside, who said: "What you wanna do is get some pictures." Pronek imagined touching gently the back of her neck, below the little tail of hair on her nape, and he imagined the tingle that would make her shudder. "You bet," the woman said, stepping out of the waiting room, barely glancing at Pronek. "You got yourself a client, Owen," the dapper man said, following the woman, and a head sprung out of the door, eyes bulging to detect Pronek. "Gee, a client," the head said, and the couple giggled as they closed the door. "Why don't you come in?"

Pronek followed the man inside, closing the croaking door behind him. The room was bright, its windows looking at Grant Park and the dun lake beyond it, waves gliding toward the shore. There was a sofa with a disintegrating lily pattern and a coffee table with a chessboard on it. Pronek landed in the sofa, and the fissures between the cushions widened and gaped at his thighs.

"My name is Taylor Owen," the man said.

"I am Pronek," Pronek said. "Jozef Pronek."

"Good to meet you, Joe," Owen said.

Owen had sweat shadows under his armpits and a hump on his back, as if there were a pillow under his beige shirt. His tie was watermelon-red, tightly knotted under his Adam's apple, which flexed sprightly like a Ping-Pong ball as he spoke. He was bald, with a little island of useless hair above his forehead and a couple of grayish tufts fluffing over his ears. He sat behind a narrow desk piled with papers, the back of his head touching the wall as he leaned in his chair.

"I called. I talked to somebody," Pronek said, "about the job. I thought you need the detective."

"The detective?" Owen chortled. "Lemme guess: You seen a few detective movies, right? The Bogart kind of stuff?"

"No," Pronek said. "Well, yes. But I know it is not like that."

Owen stared at him for a long instant, as if deciding what to do with him, then asked: "Where you from?"

"Bosnia."

"Never heard of it."

"It was in Yugoslavia."

"Ah!" Owen said, relieved. "It's a good place not to be there right now."

"No," Pronek said.

"You a war veteran?"

"No. I came here just before the war."

"You have a blue card?"

"What?"

"You have any security experience?"

"No."

"See, son, we don't have detectives around here no more. Detectives are long gone. We used to be private investigators, but that's over, too. We're operatives now. See what I mean?"

"Yeah," Pronek said. There was a black-and-gray pigeon on the windowsill, huddled in the corner as if freezing.

"No Bogey around here, son. I been in this business for a good long time. Started in the sixties, worked in the seventies. Still work. Know what I mean?"

"Yeah."

"I worked when Papa Daley was running the Machine. . . ."

The phone rang behind the parapet of papers, startling Pronek. Owen snatched the earpiece out of its bed and said: "Yup." He turned away from Pronek, toward the window, but looked over the shivering pigeon, out to the lake. It was a sunny day, cold and blustery still. The wind gasped abruptly, then pushed the windowpane with a thump, overriding the grumbling hum of Michigan Avenue.

"You can kiss that son of a bitch goodbye," Owen said, throwing his feet up on the corner of his desk and rocking in his chair. "You're kidding me. Shampoo? You gotta be kidding me."

On the desk, there was a pile of letters ripped open, apparently with little patience, and a couple of thick black files. Owen scratched the hair island, the size of a quarter, with his pinkie, beginning to rock faster. The pigeon barely had its eyes open, but then it turned its head back and looked straight at Pronek, smirking. Pronek crossed his legs and tightened his butt muscles, repressing a flatulence.

"I know what you up against. It sure is tough. Join the rest of the fucking world." He listened for a moment. "Skip the wisecracks, darling, all right?"

The pigeon was bloated, as if there were a little balloon under the feathers. What if the pigeon was a surveillance device, Pronek thought, a dummy pigeon with a tiny camera in its head, pretending to be sick, watching them.

"All right, I'll see you after the fight tonight. Love ya too," Owen said and hung up. He swung back on his chair toward Pronek, sighed, and said: "My wife is a boxing judge. Can you believe that? A boxing judge. She sits by the ring, watching two guys pummel each other, counting punches. Hell, people think I'm making that up when I tell them."

"It's normal," Pronek said, not knowing what to say.

Owen opened a drawer in his desk, the drawer resisting with a blood-curdling screech, and produced a bottle of Wild Turkey. He poured a generous gulp into a cup that had CHICAGO BULLS written around it, shaking his head as if already regretting his decision. He slurped from the cup and his face cramped, as if he'd swallowed urine, then it settled down, a little redder now, as he looked at Pronek, trying to see through him.

"So you wanna be an operative?"

"I would like to be," Pronek said.

"We don't solve big cases here. Rich women don't make passes at us. We don't tell off big bosses. And we don't wake up in a ditch with a cracked head. We just earn our daily bread doing divorces, checking backgrounds, chasing down deadbeat dads, know what I mean? It's all work, no adventure, pays the rent. Got it?"

"Yeah," Pronek said.

"Do you know where the Board of Education is?"

"In the downtown," Pronek said.

"Do you know where the Six Corners is?"

"No."

"Irving Park and. . . . Oh, fuck it! Do you have a car?"

"No. But I want to buy the car." Pronek started fidgeting in his chair. A drop of sweat rolled down from his left armpit.

"Do you have a camera?"

"No."

"Do you know how to tail?"

"Tale?" Pronek asked, perplexed. "You mean, tell the tale?"

Owen formed a pyramid from his hands and put its tip under his nose, then pushed his nose up a little so the bridge of his nose wrinkled. He glared at Pronek, as if affronted by his sheer presence, curling his lips inward until his mouth was just a straight line. Pronek wanted to tell him that he could learn, that he was really smart, that he used to be a journalist, talked to people—he could make himself over to be an operative. But it was too late: Owen was blinking in slow motion, gathering strength to finish the interview off. He dismantled the pyramid, unfurled his lips, and said:

"Listen, son, I like you. I admire people like you, that's what this country's all about: the wretched refuse coming and becoming American. My mother's family was like that, all the way from Poland. But I ain't gonna give you a job just 'cause I like you. Tell you what I'll do: Give me your phone and I'll call you if something comes up, okay?"

"Okay," Pronek said.

Owen was watching him, probably expecting him to get up, shake hands, and leave, but Pronek's body was suddenly heavy, and he could not get up from the sofa. Nothing in the room moved or produced a sound. They could hear the ill cooing of the pigeon.

"Okay," Owen repeated, as if to break the spell.

Pronek stood at the corner of Granville and Broadway, watching his breath clouding and dissolving before his eyes, waiting for Owen. The picture-frame shop across the street had nicely framed Halloween paintings in the window—ghosts hovering over disheveled children, ghouls rising out of graves. A man with a rotund goiter growing sideways on his neck was entering the diner on

Granville. Pronek thought that the man was growing another, smaller head and imagined a relief of a little, wicked face under the taut goiter skin. Just in front of Pronek, a throbbing car stopped at the streetlight, inhabited by a teenager who had a shield of gold chains on his chest. He was drumming on the wheel with his index fingers, then looked up, pointed one of his fingers at Pronek, and pretended to shoot him. Pronek smiled, as if getting the joke, but then the teenager turned east and disappeared down Granville. Pronek was cold; Owen was late. A *Chicago Tribune* headline behind the filthy glass of a newspaper box read THOUSANDS MISSING IN SREBRENICA. In the distance, Pronek saw a boxy Broadway bus stopping every once in a while on the empty street, sunlight shimmering in its windshield.

Owen pulled up, materializing out of nowhere, brakes screeching, right in front of Pronek. He drove an old Cadillac that looked like the hideous offspring of a tank and a wheel cart. Before Pronek could move toward the car, Owen honked impatiently, and the sound violated the early-morning hum, irking Pronek. Pronek opened the door and an eddy of cigarette smoke and coffee smell escaped into the street. Owen said nothing, put the car in gear, and drove off—a bus whizzed by, barely missing them. He drove with both his hands on top of the wheel, alternately looking at the street and frowning at the tip of his cigarette as it was being transformed into its own ashen ghost. Finally, the ash broke off and fell into his lap. Owen said, as if on cue: "Damn, it's early. But what can we do? We gotta get this guy while he's home sleeping."

Pronek was silent, mulling over a question that would not require too many words. They were waiting at the light on Hollywood. The car in front of them had a bumper sticker reading: IF YOU DON'T LIKE MY DRIVING CALL 1-800-EATSHIT.

"Who is this man?" Pronek asked.

"He's a character, lemme tell you. He's Serbian, I believe. Been here for fifteen years or so, married an American girl, had a child, and then split after years of marriage. He's a runaway daddy is what he is. Couldn't find the son of a bitch, wouldn't show up in court, the lady couldn't get child support. I gotta get him to accept the court summons, so if he doesn't show up in court, we can get cops on his ass. Are you all like that over there, son of a bitches?"

He put out his cigarette in the ashtray already teeming with butts, a few of them falling on the floor. Pronek imagined himself snorting up all those ashes and butts: It would be a good way to exhort a confession under torture. He coughed nauseously.

"What are you?" Owen asked. "It's Serbs fighting Muslims over there, right? Are you a Serb or a Muslim?"

"I am complicated," Pronek said and retched. The car was like a gas chamber, and Pronek felt an impulse to rise and breathe from the pocket of air just under the roof. "You can say I'm the Bosnian."

"I don't give a damn myself, as long as you speak the same language. You speak the same language, right? Yugoslavian?"

"I guess," Pronek said.

"Good," Owen said. "That's why I called you. You get the job done, you get sixty bucks, you're a happy man."

Owen lit another cigarette, snapped his Zippo shut, and inhaled solemnly, as if inhaling a thought. The hair island developed into a vine growing out of his forehead, nearly reaching his eyebrows. He drove past Bryn Mawr, where a crew of crazies was already operating: a man who kept lighting matches over a bunch of cigarettes strewn on the pavement before him, muttering to himself, as if performing a recondite ritual; an old toothless woman in tights with a wet stain spreading between her thighs. They stopped at Lawrence, then turned right.

As they were moving westward, Pronek felt the warmth of a sunbeam tickling his neck. The windshield had thick eyebrows of dirt and a few splattered insects under them. As if reading his mind, Owen said:

"Lemme ask you something: What's the last thing that goes through a fly's head as it hits the windshield?"

He glanced sideways at Pronek with a mischievous grin, apparently proud of his cleverness. "What is it?" he asked again and slammed the brakes, honking violently at the car in front.

"I don't know," Pronek said. "I should have gone the other way."

"Went," Owen said.

"What?"

"Went. You say I should've went the other way." He slammed the brakes again. "But no, that's not what it is. Think again."

"I don't know."

"It's the ass. The last thing that goes through a fly's head as it hits the windshield is its ass." He started laughing, nudging Pronek, until his guffawing turned into coughing and then nearly choking. They stopped at the Clark light and he thumped his chest like a gorilla, his vine of hair quivering, his throat convulsing.

Pronek realized that there was an entire world of people he knew nothing about—the early-morning people. Their faces had different colors in the morning sunlight. They seemed to be comfortable so early in the morning, even if they were already tired going to work. He could tell they had had their breakfast; their eyes were wide open, their faces developed into alertness—in contrast to Pronek's daze: the itching eyes, the tense, tired muscles, the crumpled face, the growling stomach, the pus taste in his mouth, and a general thought shortage. The 6:00 A.M. people, the people who existed when Owen and his people were sleeping: old twiggy ladies with a plastic cover over their meticulously puffed-up hair, like wrapped-up gray lettuce heads; kids in McDonald's uniforms on their way to the morning shift, already burdened with the midday drowsihead; workers unloading crates of strawberries onto a stuck-up dolly—they all seemed to be involved in something purposeful.

Owen completed his coughing, cleared his throat confidently, and asked:

"You still have family there?"

"Where?" Pronek responded, confused by a sudden change in the communication pace.

"Phnom Penh, that's where! Wherever you're from, you still have folks there?"

"Yeah, my parents are still there. But they're still alive."

"Now, who's trying to kill them? I can never get this right. Are they Muslim?"

"No," Pronek said. "They are in Sarajevo. Some Serbs try to kill the Muslims in Sarajevo and Bosnia, and also the people who don't want to kill the Muslims."

"You probably gonna hate this son of a bitch then."

"I don't know yet," Pronek said. What if, he thought, what if he were dreaming this? What if he were one of those 6:00 A.M. people, just about to wake up, slap the snooze button, and linger a few more minutes in bed? Owen hit the brakes again, and Pronek slapped the dashboard, lest he go through the windshield. They were at Western: A Lincoln statue was making a step forward, worried as ever, its head and shoulders dotted with dried pigeon shit. "That son of a bitch lives around here," Owen announced. He crossed Western, almost running over a chunky businessman who was hugging his briefcase as he scurried across the street.

They parked the car on an empty street with two rows of ochre-brick houses facing each other. Owen adjusted his curl, adhering it to his dome. He was looking in the rearview mirror, his hump breathing on his back, his eyes shrunk because of the fuming cigarette in his mouth. The houses all looked the same, as if they were made in the same lousy factory. Owen pointed at the house that had a FOR SALE sign, like a flag, in front of it.

"What I want you to do," he said, handing Pronek a grim envelope, "is to go to that door, ring the bell, and when he asks who it is, talk to him in your monkey language and give him this. He takes it, you leave, I give you sixty bucks, we're all happy. How's that?"

"That's fine," Pronek said and wiped his sweaty palms against his pants. He considered getting out of the car, passing the house, and running away—it would take him forty minutes to walk back to his place.

"Piece of cake," Owen said. "Just do it."

"What is his name?" Pronek asked.

"It's Branko something. Here, you can read it," he pointed at the envelope.

Pronek read: "Brdjanin. It means the mountain man."

"Whatever," Owen said and excavated a gun from under his armpit—two black, perpendicular, steely rectangles, the nozzle eye glancing at Pronek. He looked at it as if he hadn't seen it for a while and offered it to Pronek: "You want it?"

"No, thanks," Pronek said. He wondered what would be the last thing going through his head.

"Nah, you probably don't need it," Owen said. "I'll be right here, caring about you."

Pronek stepped out of the car and walked toward the house. The number on a brass plate next to the door was 2345, and the orderliness of the digits seemed absurd against the scruffy house: blinds with holes, dusty windows, a mountain of soggy coupon sheets at the bottom of the stairs, blisters of paint on the faded-brown door with a red-letter sign reading: NO TRESPASSING in its window. There was a squirrel sitting in an empty birdbath padded with damp leaves, watching him, with its little paws together, as if ready to applaud. Pronek walked up the stairs to the door, clenching the envelope, his heart steadily thumping. He pressed the hard bell-nipple and heard a muffled, deep ding-dong. To the right, a grinning Halloween pumpkin was sagging to the porch floor. He looked toward Owen in the car, who looked back at him over the folded *Sun-Times* with an eager pen in his hand. "If this is a detective novel," Pronek thought, "I will hear shooting now." He imagined going around the house, jumping over the wire fence, looking in, and seeing a body in the middle of a carmine puddle spreading all over the floor, a mysterious fragrance still in the air. Then running back to Owen, only to find him with a little powder-black hole in his left temple, his hand petrified under his armpit, too slow to save him. There was no doubt that he would have to find the killer and prove his own innocence. He rang the bell again. *"Dobro jutro,"* Pronek muttered, rehearsing the first contact with Brdjanin. *"Dobro jutro. Evo ovo je za Vas."* He would give him the envelope then, Brdjanin would take it, confused by the familiarity of the language. Piece of cake.

But then he heard keys rattling, the lock snapping, and a bare-chested man with a beard spreading down his hirsute front and a constellation of brown birthmarks on his pink dome—a man said: "What?" Pronek stared at him paralyzed, his throat clogged with the sounds of *dobro jutro.*

"What you want?" The man had a piece of lint sticking out of his navel and a cicatrix stretching across his rotund stomach.

"This is for you," Pronek garbled and handed him the envelope. The man snatched it out of Pronek's hand, looked at it, and snorted. Should've went the other way.

"You no understand nothing," the man said, waving the envelope in front of Pronek's face.

"I don't know," Pronek said. "I must give this to you."

"Where you from?"

"I am," Pronek said, reluctantly, "from Ukraine."

"Oh, *pravoslavni* brother!" the man exclaimed. "Come in, we drink coffee, we talk. I explain you."

"No, thank you," Pronek uttered. "I must go."

"Come," the man said, growled, and grabbed Pronek's arm and pulled him in. "We drink coffee. We talk."

Pronek felt the disturbed determination of the man's fingers on his forearm. The last thing he saw before he was sucked into the house by the man's will was Owen getting out of the car with an unhappy, worried scowl on his face.

As Pronek was walking in Brdjanin's onionesque wake, he saw a gun handle—gray with two symmetrical dots, like teeny beady eyes—peering out of his pants descending down his butt. Brdjanin led him through a dark hall, through a couple of uncertainly closed doors, into a room that had a table in its center and five chairs summoned around it. On the lacy tablecloth there was a pear-shaped bottle of reddish liquid with a wooden Orthodox cross in it.

"Sit," Brdjanin said. "Here."

"I must go," Pronek uttered and sat down, facing a window. A fly was buzzing against the windowpane, as if trying to cut through it with a minikin circular saw. There was an icon on the wall: a sad saint with a tall forehead and a triangular beard, his head slightly tilted under the halo weight, his hands touching each other gently.

"Sit," Brdjanin said and pulled the gun out of his ass, only to slam it on the table. The window looked out at the garden: There was a shovel sticking out of the ground like a javelin, next to a muddy hole and a mound of dirt overlooking it. Brdjanin sat across the table from Pronek and pushed the gun aside. "No fear. No problem," he said, then turned toward the kitchen and yelled: *"Rajka, kafu!"* He put the envelope right in front of himself, as if about to dissect it. "We talk with coffee," he said.

A woman with a wrinkled, swollen face and a faint bruise on her cheek, like misapplied makeup, peeked out of the kitchen, pulling the flaps of her striped black-and-white bathrobe together, and then retreated. There was a din of drawers and gas hissing, ending with an airy boom.

"You Ukrainian," Brdjanin said and leaned toward him, as if to detect Ukrainianness in his eyes. "How is your name?"

"Pronek." Pronek said, and leaned back in his chair.

"Pronek," Brdjanin repeated. "Good *pravoslav* name. *Pravoslav* brothers help Serbs in war against crazy people."

Pronek looked at Brdjanin, whose beard had a smile crevice in the middle, afraid that a twitch on his face or a diverted glance would blow his feeble cover. Brdjanin was staring at him enthusiastically, then pushed the envelope aside with contempt, leaned further toward Pronek, and asked fervently:

"You know what is this?"

"No," Pronek said.

"Is nothing," Brdjanin said and thrust his right hand forward (the gun comfortably on his left-hand side), all his fingers tight together and his thumb erect, as if he were making a wolf hand-shadow. His thumb was a grotesque stump, like a truncated hot dog, but Pronek was cautious not to pay too much attention to it.

"You must understand," Brdjanin said. "I was fool, *budala*. Wife to me was whore, was born here, but was Croat. Fifteen years. Fifteen years! I go see her brothers, they want to kill me." He made the motion of cutting his throat with the thumb stump, twice, as if they couldn't kill him in the first try. "They Ustashe, want to cut my head because I Serb. Is war now, no more wife, no more brothers. My woman is Serb now, you brother to me now. I trust only *pravoslav* people now. Other people, other people. . . ." He shook his head, signifying suspicion, and pulled his thumb across his throat again.

Pronek nodded automatically, helpless. He wanted to say that Croats are just like everyone else: good people and bad people, or some reasonable platitude like that, but in this room whatever it was he used to think just an hour ago seemed ludicrous now. He wanted the woman to be in the room with him, as if she could protect him from Brdjanin's madness and his cutthroat thumb stump. The room reeked of coffee and smoke, stale sweat and Vegeta, a coat of torturous, sleepless nights over everything. The woman trudged out of the kitchen and put a tray with a coffeepot and demitasse between the two of them, and then dragged her feet back, as if she were ready to collapse. Pronek looked after her longingly, but Brdjanin didn't notice. "This Serbian coffee. They say Turkish coffee. It's Serbian coffee," Brdjanin said, lit a cigarette, and let two smoke-snakes out of his nostrils. Pronek imagined saving the woman from this lair, taking her home (wherever it may be), and taking care of her until she recovered and regained her beauty, slouching somewhere in her heart now—and he would ask for nothing in return. Brdjanin slurped some coffee from his demitasse, then reached behind his chair and produced a newspaper. The headline said: THOUSANDS MISSING IN SREBRENICA.

"Missing?" Brdjanin cried. "No missing. Is war. They kill, they killed. No missing."

He threw the paper across the table and it landed right in front of Pronek, so he had to look at it: a woman clutching her teary face wrapped in a colorless scarf, as if trying to unscrew her head.

"Hmm," Pronek said, only because he thought silence might be conspicuous.

"You know what is this?" Brdjanin asked and spurted out an excited flock of spit drops. "You know?"

"Nothing," Pronek mumbled.

"No, is not nothing. Is Muslim propaganda."

"Oh," Pronek said. Where was Owen? If Owen broke in now, taking out Brdjanin as he was trying to reach his gun, Pronek would run to the kitchen, grab the woman's hand, and escape with her. "Come with me," he would say. *"Podji sa mnom."*

"You know when bomb fall on market in Sarajevo?" Brdjanin asked, frowning and refrowning, sweat collecting in the furrows. "They say hundred people die. They all dolls, *lutke*. Muslims throw bomb on market. Propaganda! Then they put dolls for television, it look bad, like many people killed."

Pronek's mother had barely missed the shell. She had just crossed the street when it landed. She wandered back, dazed, and trudged through bloody pulp, torn limbs banging off the still-standing counters, shell-shocked people slipping on brains. She almost stepped on someone's heart, she said, but it was a tomato—what a strange thing, she thought, a tomato. She hadn't seen a tomato for a couple of years.

"I have the friend," Pronek said, trying to appear disinterested, his heart throttling in his chest, "from Sarajevo. He says the people really died. His parents are in Sarajevo. They saw it."

"What is he?"

"He's the Bosnian."

"No, what is he? He is Muslim? He is Muslim. He lie."

"No, he's not Muslim. He is from Sarajevo."

"He is from Sarajevo, he is Muslim. They want Islamic Republic, many *mudjahedini*."

Pronek slurped his coffee. The gun lay on the left-hand side, comfortably stretched like a sleeping dog—he wouldn't have been surprised if the gun scratched its snout with its trigger. Pronek could see the woman's shadow moving around the kitchen. Brdjanin sighed and put both of his hands on the table, pounding it slowly as he spoke:

"How long you been here? I been here twenty years. Leave my parents, my sister. I come here. Good country, good people. I work in factory, twenty years. But not my country. I die for my country. American die for his country. You die for Ukraine. We all die. Is war."

Pronek looked out and saw Owen getting around the shovel, the paper and pen still in his hands, almost falling into the hole. Owen looked up to the window, saw Pronek, and nodded upward, asking if everything was all right. Pronek quickly looked at Brdjanin, who was looking at his hand, gently hacking the table surface, muttering: "I Serb, no nothing."

"I must go," Pronek said. "I must go to work."

"You go," Brdjanin shrugged and stroked his beard. "No problem."

Pronek stood up. Brdjanin put his hand on the gun. Pronek walked toward the door. Brdjanin held the gun casually, no finger near the trigger. Pronek opened the door, Brdjanin behind him. It was the bathroom: A radiator was wheezing, a cat-litter box underneath was full of sandy lumps. As Pronek was turning around, slowly, Brdjanin grasped Pronek's jacket, his left hand still holding the gun, and looked at him: He was shorter than Pronek, with an exhausted, yeasty smell; his eyes were moist green. Pronek nodded meaninglessly, paralyzed with fear. Brdjanin bowed his head, saying nothing. Pronek could see the woman framed by the kitchen door, watching them. He looked at her, hoping she would come and save him from Brdjanin's grasp. She would come and embrace him and say it was all okay. But she was not moving, as if she were used to seeing men in a clinch. She had her hands in her robe pockets, but then took out a cigarette and a lighter. She lit the cigarette, and Pronek saw the lighter flame flickering with uncanny clarity. She inhaled with a deep sough and tilted her head slightly backward, keeping the smoke in for the longest time, as if she had died an instant before exhaling. Brdjanin was sobbing: squeally gasps ending with stertorous shy snorts, his shoulders heaving in short leaps, his hand tightening its grip on Pronek's jacket. Pronek imagined Brdjanin's gun rising to his temple, the index finger pulling the trigger in slow motion—a loud pop and the brains all over Pronek, blood and slime, dripping down.

The woman looked down, drained, her bosom heaving, patiently not looking up, as if waiting for the two men to disappear.

"It's okay," Pronek said and put his hand on Brdjanin's shoulder. It was sticky and soft, with a few solitary hairs curling randomly. "It will be okay."

"What the hell were you doing in there?" Owen asked curtly, standing at the bottom of the stairs with his hands on his hips. "I almost went in there shooting to save your ass."

Pronek descended the stairs. The sun was creeping up from behind the building across the street, making the black trees gray. The same squirrel stopped, now upside down, midway down a tree, and looked at Pronek. It was skinny and its tail fluff was deflated—it was going to be a long winter.

"Did he take the thing?"

"Yeah," Pronek said. "But I don't think he cares."

"Oh, he'll have to care, believe you me, he'll care."

"There is the woman in there," Pronek said, wistfully.

"There always is," Owen said.

Owen patted Pronek on the back and softly pushed him toward the car. All the weight of Pronek's body was in his feet now, and his neck hurt, as if it were cracking under the head. They walked slowly. Owen offered him a cigarette and Pronek took it. Owen held the lighter in front of Pronek's face, and Pronek saw the yellow flame with a blue root flickering under his breath—he recognized with wearisome detachment that he was alive. He inhaled and said, exhaling:

"I don't smoke."

"Now," Owen said, "now you do."

The Language of Men

by Norman Mailer

In the beginning, Sanford Carter was ashamed of becoming an Army cook. This was not from snobbery, at least not from snobbery of the most direct sort. During the two and a half years Carter had been in the Army he had come to hate cooks more and more. They existed for him as a symbol of all that was corrupt, overbearing, stupid, and privileged in Army life. The image which came to mind was a fat cook with an enormous sandwich in one hand, and a bottle of beer in the other, sweat pouring down a porcine face, foot on a flour barrel, shouting at the K.P.'s, "Hurry up, you men, I ain't got all day." More than once in those two and a half years, driven to exasperation, Carter had been on the verge of throwing his food into a cook's face as he passed on the serving line. His anger often derived from nothing: the set of a pair of fat lips, the casual heavy thump of the serving spoon into his plate, or the resentful conviction that the cook was not serving him enough. Since life in the Army was in most aspects a marriage, this rage over apparently harmless details was not a sign of unbalance. Every soldier found some particular habit of the Army spouse impossible to support.

Yet Sanford Carter became a cook and, to elaborate the irony, did better as a cook than he had done as anything else. In a few months he rose from a Private to a first cook with the rank of Sergeant, Technician. After the fact, it was easy to understand. He had suffered through all his Army career from an excess of eagerness. He had cared too much, he had wanted to do well, and so he had often been tense at moments when he would better have been relaxed. He was very young, twenty-one, had lived the comparatively gentle life of a middle-class boy, and needed some success in the Army to prove to himself that he was not completely worthless.

In succession, he had failed as a surveyor in Field Artillery, a clerk in an Infantry headquarters, a telephone wireman, and finally a rifleman. When the war ended, and his regiment went to Japan, Carter was still a rifleman; he had been a rifleman for eight months. What was more to the point, he had been in the platoon as long as any of its members; the skilled hard-bitten nucleus of veterans who had run his squad had gone home one by one, and it seemed to him that through seniority he was entitled to at least a corporal's rating. Through seniority he was so entitled, but on no other ground. Whenever responsibility had been handed to him, he had discharged it miserably, tensely, overconscientiously. He had always asked too many questions, he had worried the task too severely, he had conveyed his nervousness to the men he was supposed to lead. Since he was also sensitive enough and proud enough never to curry favor with the noncoms in the platoons, he was in no position to sit in on their occasional discussions about who was to succeed them. In a vacuum of ignorance, he had allowed himself to dream that he would be given a squad to lead, and his hurt was sharp when the squad was given to a replacement who had joined the platoon months after him.

The war was over, Carter had a bride in the States (he had lived with her for only two months), he was lonely, he was obsessed with going home. As one week dragged into the next, and the regiment, the company, and his own platoon continued the same sort of training which they had been doing ever since he had entered the Army, he thought he would snap. There were months to wait until he would be discharged and meanwhile it was intolerable to him to be taught for the fifth time the nomenclature of the machine gun, to stand a retreat parade three evenings a week. He wanted some niche where he could lick his wounds, some Army job with so many hours of work and so many hours of complete freedom, where he could be alone by himself. He hated the Army, the huge Army which had proved to him that he was good at no work, and incapable of succeeding at anything. He wrote long, aching letters to his wife, he talked less and less to the men around him and he was close to violent attacks of anger during the most casual phases of training—during close-order drill or cleaning his rifle for inspection. He knew that if he did not find his niche it was possible that he would crack.

So he took an opening in the kitchen. It promised him nothing except a day of work, and a day of leisure which would be completely at his disposal. He found that he liked it. He was given at first the job of baking the bread for the company, and every other night he worked till early in the morning, kneading and shaping his fifty-pound mix of dough. At two or three he would be done, and for his work there would be the tangible reward of fifty loaves of bread, all fresh from the oven, all clean and smelling of fertile accomplished creativity. He had the rare and therefore intensely satisfying emotion of seeing at the end of an Army chore the product of his labor.

A month after he became a cook the regiment was disbanded, and those men who did not have enough points to go home were sent to other outfits. Carter ended at an ordnance company in another Japanese city. He had by now given up all thought of getting a noncom's rating before he was discharged, and was merely content to work each alternate day. He took his work for granted and so he succeeded at it. He had begun as a baker in the new company kitchen; before long he was the first cook. It all happened quickly. One cook went home on points, another caught a skin disease, a third was transferred from the kitchen after contracting a venereal infection. On the shift which Carter worked there were left only himself and a man who was illiterate. Carter was put nominally in charge, and was soon actively in charge. He looked up each menu in an Army recipe book, collected the items, combined them in the order indicated, and after the proper time had elapsed, took them from the stove. His product tasted neither better nor worse than the product of all other Army cooks. But the mess sergeant was impressed. Carter had filled a gap. The next time ratings were given out Carter jumped at a bound from Private to Sergeant T/4.

On the surface he was happy; beneath the surface he was overjoyed. It took him several weeks to realize how grateful and delighted he felt. The promotion coincided with his assignment to a detachment working in a small seaport up the coast. Carter arrived there to discover that he was in charge of cooking for thirty men, and would act as mess sergeant. There was another cook, and there were four permanent Japanese K.P.'s, all of them good workers. He still cooked every other day, but there was always time between meals to take a break of at least an hour and often two; he shared a room with the other cook and lived in comparative privacy for the first time in several years; the seaport was beautiful; there was only one officer, and he left the men alone; supplies were plentiful due to a clerical error which assigned rations for forty men rather than thirty; and in general everything was fine. The niche had become a sinecure.

This was the happiest period of Carter's life in the Army. He came to like his Japanese K.P.'s. He studied their language, he visited their homes, he gave them gifts of food from time to time. They worshiped him because he was kind to them and generous, because he never shouted, because his good humor bubbled over into games, and made the work of the kitchen seem pleasant. All the while he grew in confidence. He was not a big man, but his body filled out from the heavy work; he was likely to sing a great deal, he cracked jokes with the men on the chow line. The kitchen became his property, it became his domain, and since it was a warm room, filled with sunlight, he came to take pleasure in the very sight of it. Before long his good humor expanded into a series of efforts to improve the food. He began to take little pains and make little extra efforts which would have been impossible if he had been obliged to cook for more than thirty men. In the morning he would serve the men fresh eggs scrambled or fried to their desire in fresh butter. Instead of cooking sixty eggs in one large pot he cooked two eggs at a time in a frying pan, turning them to the taste of each soldier. He baked like a housewife satisfying her young husband; at lunch and dinner there was pie or cake, and often both. He went to great lengths. He taught the K.P.'s how to make the toast come out right. He traded excess food for spices in Japanese stores. He rubbed paprika and garlic on the chickens. He even made pastries to cover such staples as corn beef hash and meat and vegetable stew.

It all seemed to be wasted. In the beginning the men might have noticed these improvements, but after a period they took them for granted. It did not matter how he worked to satisfy them; they trudged through the chow line with their heads down, nodding coolly at him, and they ate without comment. He would hang around the tables after the meal, noticing how much they consumed, and what they discarded; he would wait for compliments, but the soldiers seemed indifferent. They seemed to eat without tasting the food. In their faces he saw mirrored the distaste with which he had once stared at cooks.

The honeymoon was ended. The pleasure he took in the kitchen and himself curdled. He became aware again of his painful desire to please people, to discharge responsibility, to be a man. When he had been a child, tears had come into his eyes at a cross word, and he had lived in an atmosphere where his smallest accomplishment was warmly praised. He was the sort of young man, he often thought bitterly, who was accustomed to the attention and the protection of women. He would have thrown away all he possessed—the love of his wife, the love of his mother, the benefits of his education, the assured financial security of entering his father's business— if he had been able just once to dig a ditch as well as the most ignorant farmer.

Instead, he was back in the painful unprotected days of his first entrance into the Army. Once again the most casual actions became the most painful, the events which were most to be taken for granted grew into the most significant, and the feeding of the men at each meal turned progressively more unbearable.

So Sanford Carter came full circle. If he had once hated the cooks, he now hated the troops. At mealtimes his face soured into the belligerent scowl with which he had once believed cooks to be born. And to himself he muttered the age-old laments of the housewife: how little they appreciated what he did.

Finally there was an explosion. He was approached one day by Corporal Taylor, and he had come to hate Taylor, because Taylor was the natural leader of the detachment and kept the other men endlessly amused with his jokes. Taylor had the ability to present himself as inefficient, shiftless, and incapable, in such a manner as to convey that really the opposite was true. He had the lightest touch, he had the greatest facility, he could charm a geisha in two minutes and obtain anything he wanted from a supply sergeant in five. Carter envied him, envied his grace, his charmed indifference; then grew to hate him.

Taylor teased Carter about the cooking, and he had the knack of knowing where to put the knife. "Hey, Carter," he would shout across the mess hall while breakfast was being served, "you turned my eggs twice, and I asked for them raw." The men would shout with laughter. Somehow Taylor had succeeded in conveying all of the situation, or so it seemed to Carter, insinuating everything, how Carter worked and how it meant nothing, how Carter labored to gain their affection and earned their contempt. Carter would scowl, Carter would answer in a rough voice, "Next time I'll crack them over your head." "You crack 'em, I'll eat 'em," Taylor would pipe back, "but just don't put your fingers in 'em." And there would be another laugh. He hated the sight of Taylor.

It was Taylor who came to him to get the salad oil. About twenty of the soldiers were going to have a fish fry at the geisha house; they had bought the fish at the local marker, but they could not buy oil, so Taylor was sent as the deputy to Carter. He was charming to Carter, he complimented him on the meal, he clapped him on the back, he dissolved Carter to warmth, to private delight in the attention, and the thought that he had misjudged Taylor. Then Taylor asked for the oil.

Carter was sick with anger. Twenty men out of the thirty in the detachment were going on the fish fry. It meant only that Carter was considered one of the ten undesirables. It was something he had known, but the proof of knowledge is always more painful than the acquisition of it. If he had been alone his eyes would have clouded. And he was outraged at Taylor's deception. He could imagine Taylor saying ten minutes later, "You should have seen the grease job I gave to Carter. I'm dumb, but man, he's dumber."

Carter was close enough to giving him the oil. He had a sense of what it would mean to refuse Taylor, he was on the very edge of mild acquiescence. But he also had a sense of how he would despise himself afterward.

"No," he said abruptly, his teeth gritted, "you can't have it."

"What do you mean we can't have it?"

"I won't give it to you." Carter could almost feel the rage which Taylor generated at being refused.

"You won't give away a lousy five gallons of oil to a bunch of G.I.'s having a party?"

"I'm sick and tired," Carter began.

"So am I." Taylor walked away.

Carter knew he would pay for it. He left the K.P.'s and went to change his sweat-soaked work shirt, and as he passed the large dormitory in which most of the detachment slept he could hear Taylor's high-pitched voice. Carter did not bother to take off his shirt. He returned instead to the kitchen, and listened to the sound of men going back and forth through the hall and of a man shouting with rage. That was Hobbs, a Southerner, a big man with a big bellowing voice.

There was a formal knock on the kitchen door. Taylor came in. His face was pale and his eyes showed a cold satisfaction. "Carter," he said, "the men want to see you in the big room."

Carter heard his voice answer huskily. "If they want to see me, they can come into the kitchen."

He knew he would conduct himself with more courage in his own kitchen than anywhere else. "I'll be here for a while."

Taylor closed the door, and Carter picked up a writing board to which was clamped the menu for the following day. Then he made a pretense of examining the food supplies in the pantry closet. It was his habit to check the stocks before deciding what to serve the next day, but on this night his eyes ranged thoughtlessly over the canned goods. In a corner were seven five-gallon tins of salad oil, easily enough cooking oil to last a month. Carter came out of the pantry and shut the door behind him.

He kept his head down and pretended to be writing the menu when the soldiers came in. Somehow there were even more of them than he had expected. Out of the twenty men who were going to the party, all but two or three had crowded through the door.

Carter took his time, looked up slowly. "You men want to see me?" he asked flatly.

They were angry. For the first time in his life he faced the hostile expressions of many men. It was the most painful and anxious moment he had ever known.

"Taylor says you won't give us the oil," someone burst out.

"That's right, I won't," said Carter. He tapped his pencil against the scratchboard, tapping it slowly and, he hoped, with an appearance of calm.

"What a stink deal," said Porfirio, a little Cuban whom Carter had always considered his friend.

Hobbs, the big Southerner, stared down at Carter. "Would you mind telling the men why you've decided not to give us the oil?" he asked quietly.

" 'Cause I'm blowed if I'm going to cater to you men. I've catered enough," Carter said. His voice was close to cracking with the outrage he had suppressed for so long, and he knew that if he continued he might cry. "I'm the acting mess sergeant," he said as coldly as he could, "and I decide what goes out of this kitchen." He stared at each one in turn, trying to stare them down, feeling mired in the rut of his own failure. They would never have dared this approach to another mess sergeant.

"What crud," someone muttered.

"You won't give a lousy five-gallon can of oil for a G.I. party," Hobbs said more loudly.

"I won't. That's definite. You men can get out of here."

"Why, you lousy little snot," Hobbs burst out, "how many five-gallon cans of oil have you sold on the black market?"

"I've never sold any." Carter might have been slapped with the flat of a sword. He told himself bitterly, numbly, that this was the reward he received for being perhaps the single honest cook in the whole United States Army. And he even had time to wonder at the obscure prejudice which had kept him from selling food for his own profit.

"Man, I've seen you take it out," Hobbs exclaimed. "I've seen you take it to the market."

"I took food to trade for spices," Carter said hotly.

There was an ugly snicker from the men.

"I don't mind if a cook sells," Hobbs said. "Every man has his own deal in this Army. But a cook ought to give a little food to a G.I. if he wants it."

"Tell him," someone said.

"It's bull," Taylor screeched. "I've seen Carter take butter, eggs, every damn thing to the market."

Their faces were red, they circled him.

"I never sold a thing," Carter said doggedly.

"And I'm telling you," Hobbs said, "that you're a two-bit crook. You been raiding that kitchen, and that's why you don't give to us now."

Carter knew there was only one way he could possibly answer if he hoped to live among these men again. "That's a goddamn lie," Carter said to Hobbs. He laid down the scratchboard, he flipped his pencil slowly and deliberately to one corner of the room, and with his heart aching he lunged toward Hobbs. He had no hope of beating him. He merely intended to fight until he was pounded unconscious, advancing the pain and bruises he would collect as collateral for his self-respect.

To his indescribable relief Porfirio darted between them, held them apart with the pleased ferocity of a small man breaking up a fight. "Now, stop this! Now, stop this!" he cried out.

Carter allowed himself to be pushed back, and he knew that he had gained a point. He even glimpsed a solution with some honor.

He shrugged violently to free himself from Porfirio. He was in a rage, and yet it was a rage he could have ended at any instant. "All right, you men," he swore, "I'll give you the oil, but now that we're at it, I'm going to tell you a thing or two." His face red, his body perspiring, he was in the pantry and out again with a five-gallon tin. "Here," he said, "you better have a good fish fry, 'cause it's the last good meal you're going to have for quite a while. I'm sick of trying to please you. You think I have to work—" he was about to say, my fingers to the bone—"well, I don't. From now on, you'll see what chow in the Army is supposed to be like." He was almost hysterical. "Take that oil. Have your fish fry." The fact that they wanted to cook for themselves was the greatest insult of all. "Tomorrow I'll give you real Army cooking."

His voice was so intense that they backed away from him. "Get out of this kitchen," he said. "None of you has any business here."

They filed out quietly, and they looked a little sheepish.

Carter felt weary, he felt ashamed of himself, he knew he had not meant what he said. But half an hour later, when he left the kitchen and passed the large dormitory, he heard shouts of raucous laughter, and he heard his name mentioned and then more laughter.

He slept badly that night, he was awake at four, he was in the kitchen by five, and stood there white-faced and nervous, waiting for the K.P.'s to arrive. Breakfast that morning landed on the men like a lead bomb. Carter rummaged in the back of the pantry and found a tin of dehydrated eggs covered with dust, memento of a time when fresh eggs were never on the ration list. The K.P.'s looked at him in amazement as he stirred the lumpy powder into a pan of water. While it was still half-dissolved he put it on the fire. While it was still wet, he took it off. The coffee was cold, the toast was burned, the oatmeal stuck to the pot. The men dipped forks into their food, took cautious sips of their coffee, and spoke in whispers. Sullenness drifted like vapors through the kitchen.

At noontime Carter opened cans of meat and vegetable stew. He

697

dumped them into a pan and heated them slightly. He served the stew with burned string beans and dehydrated potatoes which tasted like straw. For dessert the men had a single lukewarm canned peach and cold coffee.

So the meals continued. For three days Carter cooked slop, and suffered even more than the men. When mealtime came he left the chow line to the K.P.'s and sat in his room, perspiring with shame, determined not to yield and sick with the determination.

Carter won. On the fourth day a delegation of men came to see him. They told him that indeed they had appreciated his cooking in the past, they told him that they were sorry they had hurt his feelings, they listened to his remonstrances, they listened to his grievances, and with delight Carter forgave them. That night, for supper, the detachment celebrated. There was roast chicken with stuffing, lemon meringue pie and chocolate cake. The coffee burned their lips. More than half the men made it a point to compliment Carter on the meal.

In the weeks which followed the compliments diminished, but they never stopped completely. Carter became ashamed at last. He realized the men were trying to humor him, and he wished to tell them it was no longer necessary.

Harmony settled over the kitchen. Carter even became friends with Hobbs, the big Southerner. Hobbs approached him one day, and in the manner of a farmer talked obliquely for an hour. He spoke about his father, he spoke about his girlfriends, he alluded indirectly to the night they had almost fought, and finally with the courtesy of a Southerner he said to Carter, "You know, I'm sorry about shooting off my mouth. You were right to want to fight me, and if you're still mad I'll fight you to give you satisfaction, although I just as soon would not."

"No, I don't want to fight with you now," Carter said warmly. They smiled at each other. They were friends.

Carter knew he had gained Hobbs's respect. Hobbs respected him because he had been willing to fight. That made sense to a man like Hobbs. Carter liked him so much at this moment that he wished the friendship to be more intimate.

698

"You know," he said to Hobbs, "it's a funny thing. You know I really never did sell anything on the black market. Not that I'm proud of it, but I just didn't."

Hobbs frowned. He seemed to be saying that Carter did not have to lie. "I don't hold it against a man," Hobbs said, "if he makes a little money in something that's his own proper work. Hell, I sell gas from the motor pool. It's just I also give gas if one of the G.I.'s wants to take the jeep out for a joy ride, kind of."

"No, but I never did sell anything." Carter had to explain. "If I ever had sold on the black market, I would have given the salad oil without question."

Hobbs frowned again, and Carter realized he still did not believe him. Carter did not want to lose the friendship which was forming. He thought he could save it only by some further admission. "You know," he said again, "remember when Porfirio broke up our fight? I was awful glad when I didn't have to fight you." Carter laughed, expecting Hobbs to laugh with him, but a shadow passed across Hobbs's face.

"Funny way of putting it," Hobbs said.

He was always friendly thereafter, but Carter knew that Hobbs would never consider him a friend. Carter thought about it often, and began to wonder about the things which made him different. He was no longer so worried about becoming a man; he felt that to an extent he had become one. But in his heart he wondered if he would ever learn the language of men.

Under the Pitons

Robert Stone

All the previous day, they had been tacking up from the Grenadines, bound for Martinique to return the boat and take leave of Freycinet. Blessington was trying to forget the anxieties of the deal, the stink of menace, the sick ache behind the eyes. It was dreadful to have to smoke with the St. Vincentian dealers, stone killers who liked to operate from behind a thin film of fear. But the Frenchman was tough.

Off Dark Head there was a near thing with a barge under tow. Blessington, stoned at the wheel, his glass of straight Demerara beside the binnacle, had calmly watched a dimly lighted tug struggle past on a parallel course at a distance of a mile or so. The moon was newly risen, out of sight behind the island's mountains, silvering the line of the lower slopes. A haze of starlight left the sea in darkness, black as the pit, now and then flashing phosphorescence. They were at least ten miles offshore.

With his mainsail beginning to luff, he had steered the big ketch a little farther off the wind, gliding toward the trail of living light in the tug's wake. Only in the last second did the dime drop; he took a quick look over his shoulder. And of course there came the barge against the moon-traced mountains a big black homicidal juggernaut, unmarked and utterly unlighted, bearing down on them. Blessington swore and spun the wheel like Ezekiel, as hard to port as it went, thinking that if his keel was over the cable nothing would save them, that 360 degrees of helm or horizon would be less than enough to escape by.

Then everything not secured came crashing down on everything else, the tables and chairs on the afterdeck went over, plates and bottles smashed, whatever was breakable immediately broke. The boat, the *Sans Regret*, fell off the wind like a comedian and flapped into a flying jibe. A couple of yards to starboard the big barge raced past like a silent freight train, betrayed only by the slap of its hull against the waves. It might have been no more than the wind, for all you could hear of it. When it was safely gone, the day's fear welled up again and gagged him.

The Frenchman ran out on deck cursing and looked to the cockpit, where Blessington had the helm. His hair was cut close to his skull. He showed his teeth in the mast light. He was brushing his shorts; something had spilled in his lap.

"*Qu'est-ce que c'est là?*" he demanded of Blessington. Blessington pointed into the darkness where the barge had disappeared. The French-man knew only enough of the ocean to fear the people on it. "*Quel cul!*" he said savagely. "Who is it?" He was afraid of the Coast Guard and of pirates.

"We just missed being sunk by a barge. No lights. Submerged cable. It's okay now."

"Fuck," said the Frenchman, Freycinet. "Why are you stopping?"

"Stopping?" It took a moment to realize that Freycinet was under the impression that because the boat had lost its forward motion they were stopping, as though he had applied a brake. Freycinet had been around boats long enough to know better. He must be out of his mind, Blessington thought.

"I'm not stopping, Honoré. We're all right."

"I bust my fucking ass below," said Freycinet. "Marie fall out of bed."

Tough shit, thought Blessington. Be thankful you're not treading water in the splinters of your stupidly named boat. "Sorry, man," he said.

Sans Regret, with its fatal echoes of Piaf. The Americans might be culturally deprived, Blessington thought, but surely every cutter in the Yankee Coast Guard would have the sense to board that one. And the cabin stank of the resiny ganja they had stashed, along with the blow, under the cabin sole. No amount of roach spray or air freshener could cut it. The space would probably smell of dope forever.

Freycinet went below without further complaint, missing in his ignorance the opportunity to abuse Blessington at length. It had been Blessington's fault they had not seen the barge sooner, stoned and drunk as he was. He should have looked for it as soon as the tug went by. To stay awake through the night he had taken crystal and his peripheral vision was flashing him little mongoose darts, shooting stars composed of random light. Off the north shore of St. Vincent, the winds were murder.

Just before sunrise, he saw the Pitons rising from the sea off the starboard bow, the southwest coast of St. Lucia. Against the pink sky the two peaks looked like a single mountain. It was hard to take them for anything but a good omen. As the sudden dawn caught fire, they turned green with hope. So many hearts, he thought, must have lifted at the sight of them.

To Blessington, they looked like the beginning of home free. Or at least free. Martinique was the next island up, where they could return the boat and Blessington could take his portion and be off to America on his student visa. He had a letter of acceptance from a hotel-management school in Florida but his dream was to open a restaurant in the Keys.

He took another deep draft of the rum to cut the continuing anxieties. The first sunlight raised a sweat on him, so he took his shirt off and put on his baseball hat. Florida Marlins.

Freycinet came out on deck while he was having a drink.

"You're a drunk Irishman," Freycinet told him.

"That I'm not," said Blessington. It seemed to him no matter how much he drank he would never be drunk again. The three Vincentians had sobered him for life. He had been sitting on the porch of the guesthouse on Canouan when they walked up. They had approached like panthers, no metaphor, no politics intended. Their every move was a dark roll of musculature, balanced and wary. They were very big men with square scarred faces. Blessington had been reclining, tilted backward in a cane chair with his feet on the porch rail, when they came up to him.

"Frenchy?" one had asked very softly.

Blessington had learned the way of hard men back in Ireland and thought he could deal with them. He had been careful to maintain his relaxed position.

"I know the man you mean, sir," he had said. "But I'm not him, see. You'll have to wait."

At Blessington's innocuous words they had tensed in every fiber, although you had to be looking right at them to appreciate the physics of it. They drew themselves up around their hidden weaponry behind a silent, drug-glazed wall of suspicion that looked impermeable to reason. They were zombies, without mercy, and he, Blessington, was wasting their time. He resolved to count to thirty but at the count of ten he took his feet down off the rail.

Freycinet turned and shaded his eyes and looked toward the St. Lucia coast. The Pitons delighted him.

"Ah, là. C'est les Pitons, n'est-ce pas?"

"Oui," said Blessington. *"Les Pitons."* They had gone south in darkness and Freycinet had never seen them before.

The wind shifted to its regular quarter and he had a hard time tacking level with the island. The two women came out on deck. Freycinet's Marie was blonde and very young. She came from Normandy and she had been a waitress in the bistro outside Fort-de-France, where Freycinet and Blessington cooked. Sometimes she seemed so sunny and innocent that it was hard to connect her with a hood like Freycinet. At other times she seemed very knowing indeed. It was hard to tell, she was so often stoned.

Gillian was an American from Texas. She had a hard, thin face with a prominent nose and a big jaw. Her father, Blessington imagined, was one of those Texans, a tough, loud man who cursed the Mexicans. She was extremely tall and rather thin, with very long legs. Her slenderness and height and interesting face had taken her into modeling, to Paris and Milan. In contrast, she had muscular thighs and a big derriere, which, if it distressed the couturiers, made her more desirable. She was Blessington's designated girlfriend on the trip but they rarely made love because, influenced by the others, he had taken an early dislike to her. He supposed she knew it.

"Oh, wow," she said in her Texas voice, "look at those pretty mountains."

It was exactly the kind of American comment that made the others all despise and imitate her—even Marie, who had no English at all. Gillian had come on deck stark naked, and each of them, the Occitan Freycinet, Norman Marie, and Irish Blessington, felt scornful and slightly offended. Anyone else might have been forgiven. They had decided she was a type and she could do no right.

Back on Canouan, Gillian had conceived a lust for one of the dealers. At first, when everyone smoked in the safe house, they had paid no attention to the women. The deal was repeated to everyone's satisfaction. As the dealers gave forth their odor of menace Marie had skillfully disappeared herself in plain view. But Gillian, to Blessington's humiliation and alarm, had put out a ray and one of the men had called her on it.

Madness. In a situation so volatile, so bloody *fraught*. But she was full of lusts, was Texan Gillian, and physically courageous, too. He noticed she whined less than the others, in spite of her irritating accent. It had ended with her following the big St. Vincentian to her guesthouse room, walking ten paces behind with her eyes down, making herself a prisoner, a lamb for the slaughter.

For a while Blessington had thought she would have to do all three of them but it had been only the one, Nigel. Nigel had returned her to Blessington in a grim little ceremony, holding her with the chain of her shark's-tooth necklace twisted tight around her neck.

"Wan' have she back, mon?"

Leaving Blessington with the problem of how to react. The big bastard was fucking welcome to her but of course it would have been tactless to say so. Should he protest and get everyone killed? Or should he be complacent and be thought a pussy and possibly achieve the same result? It was hard to find a middle ground but Blessington found one, a tacit, ironic posture, fashioned of silences and body language. The Irish had been a subject race, too, after all.

"I gon' to make you a present, mon. Give you little pink piggy back. Goodness of my ha'art."

So saying, Nigel had put his huge busted-knuckle hand against her pale hard face and she had looked down submissively, trembling a little, knowing not to smile. Afterward, she was very cool about it. Nigel had given her a little Rasta bracelet, beads in the red, yellow, and green colors of Ras Tafari.

"Think I'm a pink piggy, Liam?"

He had not been remotely amused and he had told her so.

So she had walked on ahead laughing and put her palms together and looked up to the sky and said, "Oh, my Lord!" And then glanced at him and wiped the smile off her face. Plainly she'd enjoyed it, all of it. She wore the bracelet constantly.

Now she leaned on her elbows against the chart table with her bare bum thrust out, turning the bracelet with the long, bony fingers of her right hand. Though often on deck, she seemed never to burn or tan. A pale child of night was Gillian.

"What island you say that was?" she asked.

"It's St. Lucia," Blessington told her. "The mountains are called the Pitons."

"The Pee-tuns? Does that mean something cool in French?" She turned to Blessington, then to Freycinet. "Does it, Honoré?"

Freycinet made an unpleasant, ratty face. He was ugly as cat shit,

Blessington thought, something Gillian doubtless appreciated. He had huge soulful brown eyes and a pointed nose like a puppet's. His military haircut showed the flattened shape of his skull.

"It means stakes," Blessington said.

"Steaks? Like . . ."

"Sticks," said Blessington. "Rods. Palings."

"Oh," she said, "stakes. Like Joan of Arc got burned at, right?"

Freycinet's mouth fell open. Marie laughed loudly. Gillian looked slyly at Blessington.

"Honoré," she said. "*Tu es un dindon*. You're a *dindon*, man. I'm shitting you. I understand French fine."

It had become amusing to watch her tease and confound Freycinet. Dangerous work and she did it cleverly, leaving the Frenchman to marvel at the depths of her stupidity until paranoia infected his own self-confidence. During the trip back, Blessington thought he might be starting to see the point of her.

"I mean, I worked the Paris openings for five years straight. I told you that."

Drunk and stoned as the rest of them, Gillian eventually withdrew from the ascending spring sun. Marie went down after her. Freycinet's pointed nose was out of joint.

"You hear what she say?" he asked Blessington. "That she speak French all the time? What the fuck? Because she said before, '*Non*, I don't speak it.' Now she's speaking it."

"Ah, she's drunk, Honoré. She's just a bimbo."

"I 'ope so, eh?" said Freycinet. He looked at the afterdeck to be sure she was out of earshot. "Because . . . because what if she setting us up? All zese time, eh? If she's *agent*. Or she's informer? A grass?"

Blessington pondered it deeply. Like the rest of them he had thought her no more than a fatuous, if perverse, American. Now the way she laughed at them, he was not at all sure.

"I thought she came with you. Did she put money up?"

Freycinet puffed out his hollow cheeks and shrugged.

"She came to me from Lavigerie," he said. The man who called himself Lavigerie was a French-Israeli of North African origin, a hustler in Fort-de-France. "She put in money, *oui*. The same as everyone."

They had all pooled their money for the boat and to pay the Vincentians. Blessington had invested $20,000, partly his savings from the bistro, partly borrowed from his sister and her husband in Providence. He expected to make it back many times over and pay them off with interest.

"Twenty thousand?"

"Yes. Twenty."

"Well, even the Americans wouldn't spend $20,000 to catch us," he told Honoré. "We're too small. And it isn't how they work."

"Now I think I don't trust her, eh?" said Freycinet. He squinted into the sun. The Pitons, no closer, seemed to displease him now. "She's a bitch, *non*?"

"I think she's all right," Blessington said. "I really do."

And for the most part he did. In any case he had decided to, because an eruption of hardcore, coke-and-speed-headed paranoia could destroy them all. It had done so to many others. Missing boats sometimes turned up on the mangrove shore of some remote island, the hulls blistered with bullet holes, cabins attended by unimaginable swarms of flies. Inside, *tableaux morts* not to be forgotten by the unlucky discoverer. Strong-stomached photographers recorded the *tableaux* for the DEA's files, where they were stamped NOT TO BE DESTROYED, HISTORIC INTEREST. The bureau took a certain satisfaction. Blessington knew all this from his sister and her husband in Providence.

Now they were almost back to Martinique and Blessington wanted intensely not to die at sea. In the worst of times, he grew frightened to the point of utter despair. It had been, he realized at such times, a terrible mistake. He gave up on the money. He would settle for just living, for living even in prison in France or America. Or at least for not dying on that horrible bright blue ocean, aboard the *Sans Regret*.

"Yeah," he told Freycinet. "Hell, I wouldn't worry about her. Just a bimbo."

All morning they tacked for the Pitons. Around noon a great crown of puffy cloud settled around Gros Piton and they were close enough to distinguish the two peaks one from the other. Freycinet refused to go below. His presence was so unpleasant that Blessington felt like weeping, knocking him unconscious, throwing him overboard, or jumping over himself. But the Frenchman remained in the cockpit though he never offered to spell Blessington at the wheel. The man drove Blessington to drink. He poured more Demerara and dipped his finger in the bag of crystal. A pulse fluttered under his collarbone, fear, speed.

Eventually Freycinet went below. After half an hour, Gillian came topside, clothed this time, in cutoffs and a halter. The sea had picked up and she nearly lost her balance on the ladder.

"Steady," said Blessington.

"Want a roofie, Liam?"

He laughed. "A roofie? What's that? Some kind of . . ."

Gillian finished the thought he had been too much of a prude to articulate.

"Some kind of blow job? Some kind of sex technique? No, dear, it's a medication."

"I'm on watch."

She laughed at him. "You're shit-faced is what you are."

"You know," Blessington said, "you ought not to tease Honoré. You'll make him paranoid."

"He's an asshole. As we say back home."

"That may be. But he's a very mercurial fella. I used to work with him."

"Mercurial? If you know he's so mercurial how come you brought him?"

"I didn't bring him," Blessington said. "He brought me. For my vaunted seamanship. And I came for the money. How about you?"

"I came on account of having my brains in my ass," she said, shaking her backside. "My talent, too. Did you know I was a barrel racer? I play polo, too. English or Western, man, you name it."

"English or Western?" Blessington asked.

"Forget it," she said. She frowned at him, smiled, frowned again. "You seem, well, scared."

"Ah," said Blessington, "scared? Yes, I am. Somewhat."

"I don't give a shit," she said.

"You don't?"

"You heard me," she said. "I don't care what happens. Why should I? Me with my talent in my ass. Where do I come in?"

"You shouldn't talk that way," Blessington said.

"Fuck you. You afraid I'll make trouble? I assure you I could make trouble like you wouldn't believe."

"I don't doubt it," Blessington said. He kept his eyes on the Pitons. His terror, he thought, probably encouraged her.

"Just between you and me, Liam, I have no fear of dying. I would just as soon be out here on this boat now as in my little comfy bed with my stuffed animals. I would just as soon be dead."

He took another sip of rum to wet his pipes for speech. "Why did you put the money in, then? Weren't you looking for a score?"

"I don't care about money," she said. "I thought it would be a kick. I thought it would be radical. But it's just another exercise in how everything sucks."

"Well," said Blessington, "you're right there."

She looked off at the twin mountains. "They don't seem a bit closer than they did this morning."

"No. It's an upwind passage. Have to tack forever."

"You know what Nigel told me back on Canouan?"

"No," Blessington said.

"He told me not to worry about understanding things. He said understanding was weak and lame. He said you got to *overstand* things." She hauled herself and did the voice of a big St. Vincentian man saddling up a white bitch for the night, laying down wisdom. "You got to *overstand* it. *Overstand* it, right? Funny, huh."

"Maybe there's something in it," said Blessington.

"Rasta lore," she said. "Could be, man."

"Anyway never despise what the natives tell you, that's what my aunt used to say. Even in America."

"And what was your aunt? A dope dealer?"

"She was a nun," Blessington said. "A missionary."

For a while Gillian sunned herself on the foredeck, halter off. But the sun became too strong and she crawled back to the cockpit.

"You ever think about how it is in this part of the world?" she asked him. "The Caribbean and around it? It's all suckin' stuff they got. Suckin' stuff, all goodies and no nourishment."

"What do you mean?"

"It's all turn-ons and illusion," she said. "Don't you think? Like coffee." She numbered items on the long fingers of her left hand. "Tobacco. Emeralds. Sugar. Cocaine. Ganja. It's all stuff you don't need. Isn't even good for you. Perks and pick-me-ups and pogey bait. Always has been."

"You're right," Blessington said. "Things people kill for."

"Overpriced. Put together by slaves and peons. Piggy stuff. For pink piggies."

"I hadn't thought of it," he said. He looked over at her. She had raised a fist to her pretty mouth. "You're clever, Gillian."

"You don't even like me," she said.

"Yes I do."

"Don't you dare bullshit me. I said you don't."

"Well," Blessington said, "to tell you the truth at first I didn't. But now I do."

"Oh, yeah? Why?"

Blessington considered before speaking. The contrary wind was picking up and there were reefs at the south end of the island. Some kind of monster tide was running against them, too.

"Because you're intelligent. I hadn't realized that. You had me fooled, see? Now I think you're amusing."

"Amusing?" She seemed more surprised than angry.

"You really are so bloody clever," he said, finishing the glass of rum. "When we're together I like it. You're not a cop, are you? Anything like that?"

"You only wish," she said. "How about you?"

"Me? I'm Irish, for Christ's sake."

"Is that like not being real?"

"Well," he said, "a little. In many cases."

"You are scared," she said. "You're scared of everything. Scared of me."

"Holy Christ," said Blessington, "you're as bad as Honoré. Look, Gillian, I'm a chef, not a pirate. I never claimed otherwise. Of course I'm scared."

She made him no answer.

"But not of you," he said. "No. Not anymore. I like you here. You're company."

"Am I?" she asked. "Do you? Would you marry me?"

"Hey," said Blessington. "Tomorrow."

Freycinet came up on deck, looked at the Pitons, then up at Blessington and Gillian in the cockpit.

"Merde," he said. "Far away still. What's going on?"

"We're getting there," Blessington said. "We're closer now than we look."

"Aren't the mountains pretty, Honoré?" Gillian asked. "Don't you wish we could climb one?"

Freycinet ignored her. "How long?" he asked Blessington.

"To Martinique? Tomorrow sometime, I guess."

"How long before we're off les Pitons?"

"Oh," Blessington said, "just a few hours. Well before dark so we'll have a view. Better steer clear, though."

"Marie is sick."

"Poor puppy," Gillian said. "Probably all that bug spray. Broth's the thing. Don't you think, Liam?"

"Ya, it's kicking up," Blessington said. "There's a current running and a pretty stiff offshore breeze."

"Merde," said Freycinet again. He went forward along the rail and lay down beside the anchor windlass, peering into the chains.

"He's a cook, too," Gillian said, speaking softly. "How come you're not more like him?"

"An accident of birth," Blessington said.

"If we were married," she said, "you wouldn't have to skip on your visa."

"Ah," said Blessington, "don't think it hasn't occurred to me. Nice to be a legal resident."

"Legal my ass," she said.

Freycinet suddenly turned and watched them. He showed them the squint, the bared canines.

"What you're talking about, you two? About me, eh?"

"Damn, Honoré!" Gillian said. "He was just proposing." When he had turned around again she spoke between her teeth. "Shithead is into the blow. He keeps prying up the sole. Cures Marie's mal de mer. Keeps him on his toes."

"God save us," said Blessington. Leaning his elbow on the helm he took Gillian's right hand and put it to her forehead, her left shoulder, and then her right one, walking through the sign of the cross. "Pray for us like a good girl."

Gillian made the sign again by herself. "Shit," she said, "now I feel a lot better. No, really," she said when he laughed, "I do. I'm gonna do it all the time now. Instead of chanting, '*Om*' or '*Nam myoho renge kyo*.' "

They sat and watched the peaks grow closer, though the contrary current increased.

"When this is over," Blessington said, "maybe we ought to stay friends."

"If we're still alive," she said, "we might hang out together. We could go to your restaurant in the Keys."

"That's what we'll do," he said. "I'll make you a sous-chef."

"I'll wait tables."

"No, no. Not you."

"But we won't be alive," she said.

"But if we are."

"If we are," she said, "we'll stay together." She looked at him sway beside the wheel. "You better not be shitting me."

"I wouldn't. I think it was meant to be."

"Meant to be? You're putting me on."

"Don't make me weigh my words, Gillian. I want to say what occurs to me."

"Right," she said, touching him. "When we're together you can say any damn thing."

The green mountains, in the full richness of afternoon, rose above them. Blessington had a look at the chart to check the location of the off-shore reefs. He began steering to another quarter, away from the tip of the island.

Gillian sat on a locker with her arms around his neck, leaning against his back. She smelled of sweat and patchouli.

"I've never been with anyone as beautiful as you, Gillian."

He saw she had gone to sleep. He disengaged her arms and helped her lie flat on the locker in the shifting shade of the mainsail. Life is a dream, he thought. Something she knew and I didn't.

I love her, Blessington thought. She encourages me. The shadow of the peaks spread over the water.

Freycinet came out on deck and called up to him.

"Liam! We're to stop here. Off les Pitons."

"We can't," Blessington said, though it was tempting. He was so tired.

"We have to stop. We can anchor, yes? Marie is sick. We need to rest. We want to see them."

"We'd have to clear customs," Blessington said. "We'll have bloody cops and boat boys and God knows what else."

He realized at once what an overnight anchorage would entail. All of them up on speed or the cargo, cradling shotguns, peering into the moonlight while they waited for *macheteros* to come on feathered oars and steal their shit and kill them.

"If we anchor," Freycinet said, "if we anchor somewhere, we won't have to clear."

"Yes, yes," Blessington said. "We will, sure. The fucking boat boys will find us. If we don't hire them or buy something they'll turn us in." He picked up the cruising guide and waved it in the air. "It says right here you have to clear customs in Soufrière."

"We'll wait until they have close," said Freycinet.

"Shit," said Blessington desperately, "we'll be fined. We'll be boarded."

Freycinet was smiling at him, a broad demented smile of infinitely self-assured contempt. Cocaine. He felt Gillian put her arm around his leg from behind.

"*Écoutez*, Liam. *Écoutez bien*. We going to stop, man. We going to stop where I say."

He turned laughing into the wind, gripping a stay.

"What did I tell you," Gillian said softly. "You won't have to marry me after all. 'Cause we're dead, baby."

"I don't accept that," Blessington said. "Take the wheel," he told her.

Referring to the charts and the cruising guide, he could find no anchorage that looked as though it would be out of the wind and that was not close inshore. The only possibility was a shallow reef, near the south tip, sometimes favored by snorkeling trips, nearly three miles off the Pitons. It was in the lee of the huge peaks, its coral heads as shallow as a single fathom. The chart showed mooring floats; presumably it was forbidden to anchor there for the sake of the coral.

"I beg you to reconsider, Honoré," Blessington said to Freycinet. He cleared his throat. "You're making a mistake."

Freycinet turned back to him with the same smile.

"Eh, Liam. You can leave, man. You know, there's an Irish pub in Soufrière. It's money from your friends in the IRA. You can go there, eh?"

Blessington had no connection whatsoever with the IRA although he had allowed Freycinet and his friends to believe that and they had chosen to.

"You can go get drunk there," Freycinet told him and then turned again to look at the island.

He was standing near the bow with his bare toes caressing freeboard, gripping a stay. Blessington and Gillian exchanged looks. In the next instant she threw the wheel, the mainsail boom went crashing across the cabin roofs, the boat lurched to port and heeled hard. For a moment Freycinet was suspended over blank blue water. Blessington clambered up over the cockpit and stood swaying there for a moment, hesitating. Then he reached out for Freycinet. The Frenchman swung around the stay like a monkey and knocked him flat. The two of them went sprawling. Freycinet got to his feet in a karate stance, cursing.

"You shit," he said, when his English returned. "Cunt! What?"

"I thought you were going over, Honoré. I thought I'd have to pull you back aboard."

"That's right, Honoré," Gillian said from the cockpit. "You were like a goner. He saved your ass, man."

Freycinet pursed his lips and nodded. "*Bien*," he said. He climbed down into the cockpit in a brisk, businesslike fashion and slapped Gillian across the face, backhand and forehand, turning her head around each time.

He gave Blessington the wheel, then he took Gillian under the arm and pulled her up out of the cockpit. "Get below! I don't want to fucking see you." He followed her below and Blessington heard him speak briefly to Marie. The young woman began to moan. The Pitons looked close enough to strike with a rock and a rich jungle smell came out on the wind. Freycinet, back on deck, looked as though he was sniffing out menace. A divi-divi bird landed on the boom for a moment and then fluttered away.

"I think I have a place," Blessington said, "if you still insist. A reef."

"A reef, eh?"

"A reef about four thousand meters offshore."

"We could have a swim, *non*?"

"We could, yes."

"But I don't know if I want to swim with you, Liam. I think you try to push me overboard."

"I think I saved your life," Blessington said.

They motored on to the reef with Freycinet standing in the bow to check for bottom as Blessington watched the depth recorder. At ten meters of bottom, they were an arm's length from the single float in view. Blessington cut the engine and came about and then went forward to cleat a line to the float. The float was painted red, yellow, and green, Rasta colors like Gillian's bracelet.

It was late afternoon and suddenly dead calm. The protection the Pitons offered from the wind was ideal and the bad current that ran over the reef to the south seemed to divide around these coral heads. A perfect dive site, Blessington thought, and he could not understand why even in June there were not more floats or more boats anchored there. It seemed a steady-enough place even for an overnight anchorage although the cruising guide advised against it because of the dangerous reefs on every side.

The big ketch lay motionless on unruffled water; the float line drifted slack. There was sandy beach and a palm-lined shore across the water. It was a lonely part of the coast, across a jungle mountain track from the island's most remote resort. Through binoculars Blessington could make out a couple of boats hauled up on the strand but no one seemed ready to come out and hustle them. With luck it was too far from shore.

It might be also, he thought, that for metaphysical reasons they presented a forbidding aspect. But an aspect that deterred small predators might in time attract big ones.

Marie came up, pale and hollow-eyed, in her bikini. She gave Blessington a chastising look and lay down on the cushions on the afterdeck. Gillian came up behind her and took a seat on the gear locker behind Blessington.

"The fucker's got no class," she said softly. "See him hit me?"

"Of course. I was next to you."

"Gonna let him get away with that?"

"Well," Blessington said, "for the moment it behooves us to let him feel in charge."

"Behooves us?" she asked. "You say it *behooves* us?"

"That's right."

"Hey, what were you gonna do back there, Liam?" she asked. "Deep-six him?"

"I honestly don't know. He might have fallen."

"I was wondering," she said. "He was wondering, too."

Blessington shrugged.

"He's got the overstanding," Gillian said. "We got the under." She looked out at the water and said, "Boat boys."

He looked where she was looking and saw the boat approaching, a speck against the shiny sand. It took a long time for it to cover the distance between the beach and the *Sans Regret*.

There were two boat boys and they were not boys but men in their thirties, lean and unsmiling. One wore a wool tam-o'-shanter in bright tie-dyed colors. The second looked like an East Indian. His black headband gave him a lascar look.

"You got to pay for dat anchorage, mon," the man in the tam called to them. "Not open to de public widout charge."

"We coming aboard," said the lascar. "We take your papers and passports in for you. You got to clear."

"How much for the use of the float?" Blessington asked.

Suddenly Freycinet appeared in the companionway. He was carrying a big Remington 12-gauge, pointing it at the men in the boat, showing his pink-edged teeth.

"You get the fuck out of here," he shouted at them. A smell of ganja and vomit seemed to follow him up from the cabin. "Understand?"

The two men did not seem unduly surprised at Freycinet's behavior. Blessington wondered if they could smell the dope as distinctly as he could.

"Fuckin' Frenchman," the man in the tam said. "Think he some shit."

"Why don' you put the piece down, Frenchy?" the East Indian asked. "This ain't no Frenchy island. You got to clear."

"You drift on that reef, Frenchy," the man in the tam said. "You be begging us to take you off."

Freycinet was beside himself with rage. He hated *les nègres* more than any Frenchman Blessington had met in Martinique, which was saying a great deal. He had contained himself during the negotiations on Canouan but now he seemed out of control. Blessington began to wonder if he would shoot the pair of them.

"You fucking monkeys!" he shouted. "You stay away from me, eh? Chimpanzees! I kill you quick . . . *mon,*" he added with a sneer.

The men steered their boat carefully over the reef and sat with their outboard idling. They could not stay too long, Blessington thought, their gas tank was small and it was a long way out against a current.

"Well," he asked Gillian, "who's got the overstanding now?"

"Not Honoré," she said.

A haze of heat and doped lassitude settled over their mooring. Movement was labored, even speech seemed difficult. Blessington and Gillian nodded off on the gear locker. Marie seemed to have lured Freycinet belowdecks. Prior to dozing, Blessington heard her imitate the Frenchman's angry voice and the two of them laughing down in the cabin. The next thing he saw clearly was Marie, in her bikini, standing on the cabin, screaming. A shotgun blasted and echoed over the still water. Suddenly the slack breeze had a brisk cordite smell and it carried smoke.

Freycinet shouted, holding the hot shotgun.

The boat with the two islanders in it seemed to have managed to come up on them. Now it raced off, headed first out to sea to round the tip of the reef and then curving shoreward to take the inshore current at an angle.

"Everyone all right?" asked Blessington.

"Fucking monkeys!" Freycinet swore.

"Well," Blessington said, watching the boat disappear, "they're gone for now. Maybe," he suggested to Freycinet, "we can have our swim and go, too."

Freycinet looked at him blankly as though he had no idea what Blessington was on about. He nodded vaguely.

After half an hour Marie rose and stood on the bulwark and prepared to dive, arms foremost. When she went, her dive was a good one, straight-backed and nearly splash-free. She performed a single stroke underwater and sped like a bright shaft between the coral heads below and the crystal surface. Then she appeared prettily in the light of day blinking like a child, shaking her shining hair.

From his place in the bow, Freycinet watched Marie's dive, her under-water career, her pert surfacing. His expression was not affectionate but taut and tight-lipped. The muscles in his neck stood out, his moves were twitchy like a street junkie's. He looked exhausted and angry. The smell of cordite hovered around him.

"He's a shithead and a loser," Gillian said softly to Blessington. She looked not at Freycinet but toward the green mountains. "I thought he was cool. He was so fucking mean, I, like, respected that. Now we're all gonna die. Well," she said, "goes to show, right?"

"Don't worry," Blessington told her. "I won't leave you."

"Whoa," said Gillian. "All right!" But her enthusiasm was not genuine. She was mocking him.

Blessington forgave her.

Freycinet pointed a finger at Gillian. "Swim!"

"What if I don't wanna?" she asked, already standing up. When he began to swear at her in a hoarse voice she took her clothes off in front of them. Everything but the Rasta bracelet.

"I think I will if no one minds," she said. "Where you want me to swim to, Honoré?"

"Swim to fucking *Amérique*," he said. He laughed as though his mood had improved. "You want her, Liam?"

"People are always asking me that," Blessington said. "What do I have to do?"

"You swim to fucking *Amérique* with her."

Blessington saw Gillian take a couple of pills from her cutoff pocket and swallow them dry.

"I can't swim that far," Blessington said.

"Go as far as you can," said Freycinet.

"How about you?" Gillian said to the Frenchman. "You're the one wanted to stop. So ain't you gonna swim?"

"I don't trust her," Freycinet said to Blessington. "What do you think?"

"She's a beauty," Blessington said. "Don't provoke her."

Gillian measured her beauty against the blue water and dived over the side. A belly full of pills, Blessington thought. But her strokes when she surfaced were strong and defined. She did everything well, he thought. She was good around the boat. She had a pleasant voice for country music. He could imagine her riding, a cowgirl.

"Bimbo, eh?" Freycinet asked. "That's it, eh?"

"Yes," Blessington said. "Texas and all that."

"*Oui*," said Freycinet. "Texas." He yawned. "*Bien*. Have your swim with her. If you want."

Blessington went down into the stinking cabin and put his bathing suit on. Propriety to the last. The mixture of ganja, sick, roach spray and pine scent was asphyxiating. If he survived, he thought, he would never smoke hash again. Never drink rum, never do speed or cocaine, never sail or go where there were palm trees and too many stars overhead. A few fog-shrouded winter constellations would do.

"Tonight I'll cook, eh?" Freycinet said when Blessington came back up. "You can assist me."

"Good plan," said Blessington.

Standing on the bulwark, he looked around the boat. There were no other vessels in sight. Marie was swimming backstroke, describing a safe circle about twenty-five yards out from the boat. Gillian appeared to be headed hard for the open sea. She had reached the edge of the current, where the wind raised small horsetails from the rushing water.

If Freycinet was planning to leave them in the water, Blessington wondered, would he leave Marie with them? It would all be a bad idea because Freycinet was not a skilled sailor. And there was a possibility of their being picked up right here or even of their making it to shore, although that seemed most unlikely. On the other hand he had discovered that Freycinet's ideas were often impulses, mainly bad ones. It was his recklessness that had made him appear so capably in charge and that was as true in the kitchen as it was on the Raging Main. He had been a reckless cook.

Besides, there were a thousand dark possibilities on that awful ocean. That he had arranged to be met at sea off Martinique, that there had been some betrayal in the works throughout. Possibly involving Lavigerie or someone else in Fort-de-France.

"Yes," said Blessington. "There's time to unfreeze the grouper."

He looked at the miles of ocean between the boat and the beach at the foot of the mountains. Far off to the right he could see white water, the current running swiftly over the top of a reef that extended southwesterly at a 45 degree angle to the beach. Beyond the reef was a sandspit where the island tapered to its narrow southern end. On their left, the base of the mountains extended to the edge of the sea, forming a rock wall against which the waves broke. According to the charts, the wall plunged to a depth of ten fathoms, and the ocean concealed a network of submarine caves and grottoes in the volcanic rock of which the Pitons were composed. Across the towering ridge, completely out of sight, was a celebrated resort.

"I'll take it out of the freezer," Blessington said.

A swimmer would have to contrive to make land somewhere between the rock wall to the north and the reef and sandspit on the right. There would be easy swimming at first, through the windless afternoon, and a swimmer would not feel any current for the first mile or so. The last part of the swim would be partly against a brisk current, and possibly against the tide. The final mile would seem much farther. For the moment, wind was not in evidence. The current might be counted on to lessen as one drew closer to shore. If only one could swim across it in time.

"It's all right," said Freycinet. "I'll do it. Have your swim."

Beyond that, there was the possibility of big sharks so far out. They might be attracted by the effort of desperation. Blessington, exhausted and dehydrated, was in no mood for swimming miles. Freycinet would not leave them there, off the Pitons, he told himself. It was practically in sight of land. He would be risking too much, witnesses, their survival. If he meant to deep-six them he would try to strike at sea.

Stoned and frightened as he was, he could not make sense of it, regain his perspective. He took a swig from a plastic bottle of warm Evian water, dropped his towel, and jumped overboard.

The water felt good, slightly cool. He could relax against it and slow the beating of his heart. It seemed to cleanse him of the cabin stink. He was at home in the water, he thought. Marie was frolicking like a mermaid, now close to the boat. Gillian had turned back and was swimming toward him. Her stroke still looked strong and accomplished; he set out to intercept her course.

They met over a field of elkhorn coral. Some of the formations were so close to the surface that their feet, treading water, brushed the velvety skin of algae over the sharp prongs.

"How are you?" Blessington asked her.

She had a lupine smile. She was laughing, looking at the boat. Her eyes appeared unfocused, the black pupils huge under the blue glare of afternoon and its shimmering, crystal reflection. She breathed in hungry swallows. Her face was raw and swollen where Freycinet had hit her.

"Look at asshole," she said, gasping.

Freycinet was standing on deck talking to Marie, who was in the water ten feet away. He held a mask and snorkel in one hand and a pair of swim fins in the other. One by one he threw the toys into the water for Marie to retrieve. He looked coy and playful.

Something about the scene troubled Blessington although he could not, in his state, quite reason what it was. He watched Freycinet take a few steps back and paw the deck like an angry bull. In the next moment, Blessington realized what the problem was.

"Oh, Jesus Christ," he said.

Freycinet leaped into space. He still wore the greasy shorts he had worn on the whole trip. In midair he locked his arms around his bent knees. He was holding a plastic spatula in his right hand. He hit the surface like a cannonball, raising a little waterspout, close enough to Marie to make her yelp.

"You know what?" Gillian asked. She had spotted it. She was amazing.

"Yes, I do. The ladder's still up. We forgot to lower it."

"Shit," she said and giggled.

Blessington turned over to float on his back and tried to calm himself. Overhead the sky was utterly cloudless. Moving his eyes only a little he could see the great green tower of Gros Piton, shining like Jacob's ladder itself, thrusting toward the empty blue. Incredibly far above, a plane drew out its jet trail, a barely visible needle stitching the tiniest flaw in the vast perfect seamless curtain of day. Miles and miles above, beyond imagining.

"How we gonna get aboard?" Gillian asked. He did not care for the way she was acting in the water now, struggling to stay afloat, moving her arms too much, wasting her breath.

"We'll have to go up the float line. Or maybe," he said, "we can stand on each other's shoulders."

"I'm not," she said, gasping, "gonna like that too well."

"Take it easy Gillian. Lie on your back."

What bothered him most was her laughing, giggling a little with each breath.

"Okay, let's do it," she said, spitting salt water. "Let's do it before he does."

"Slow and steady," Blessington said.

They slowly swam together, breaststroke toward the boat. A late-afternoon breeze had come up as the temperature began to fall.

Freycinet and Marie had allowed themselves to drift farther and farther from the boat. Blessington urged Gillian along beside him until the big white hull was between them and the other swimmers.

Climbing was impossible. It was partly the nature of the French-made boat; an unusually high transom and the rounded glassy hull made it particularly difficult to board except from a dock or a dinghy. That was the contemporary security-conscious style. And the rental company had removed a few of the deck fittings that might have provided hand- and footholds. Still, he tried to find a grip so that Gillian could get on his shoulders. Once he even managed to get between her legs and push her a foot or so up the hull, sitting on his neck. But there was no place to grab and she was stoned. She swore and laughed and toppled off his shoulders.

He was swimming forward along the hull, looking for the float, when it occurred to him suddenly that the boat must be moving. Sure enough, holding his place, he could feel the hull sliding to windward under his hand. In a few strokes he was under the bow, feeling the ketch's weight thrusting forward, riding him down. Then he saw the Rastafarian float. The float was unoccupied, unencumbered by any line. Honoré and Marie had not drifted from the boat—the boat itself was slowly blowing away, accompanied now by the screech of fiberglass against coral, utterly unsecured. The boys from the Pitons, having dealt with druggies before, had undone the mooring line while they were sleeping or nodding off or scarfing other sorts of lines.

Blessington hurried around the hull, with one hand to the boat's skin, trying to find the drifting float line. It might, he thought, be possible to struggle up along that. But there was no drifting float line. The boat boys must have uncleated it and balled the cleat in nylon line and silently tossed it aboard. They had been so feckless, the sea so glassy and the wind so low that the big boat had simply settled on the float, with its keel fast among the submerged elkhorn, and they had imagined themselves secured. The *Sans Regret*, to which he clung, was gone. Its teak interiors were in another world now, as far away as the tiny jet miles above them on its way to Brazil.

"It's no good," Blessington said to her.

"It's not?" She giggled.

"Please," he said, "please don't do that."

She gasped. "What?"

"Never mind," he said. "Come with me."

They had just started to swim away when a sudden breeze carried the

Sans Regret from between the two couples, leaving Blessington and Gillian and Honoré and Marie to face one another in the water across a distance of twenty yards or so. Honoré and Marie stared at their shipmates in confusion. It was an embarrassing moment. Gillian laughed.

"What have you done?" Honoré asked Blessington. Blessington tried not to look at him.

"Come on," he said to Gillian. "Follow me."

Cursing in French, Freycinet started kicking furiously for the boat. Marie, looking very serious, struck out behind him. Gillian stopped to look after them.

Blessington glanced at his diver's watch. It was 5:15.

"Never mind them," he said. "Don't look at them. Stay with me."

He turned over on his back and commenced an artless backstroke, arms out straight, rowing with his palms, paddling with his feet. It was the most economic stroke he knew, the one he felt most comfortable with. He tried to make the strokes controlled and rhythmic rather than random and splashy to avoid conveying any impression of panic or desperation. To free his mind, he tried counting the strokes. As soon as they were over deep water, he felt the current. He tried to take it at a 45 degree angle, determining his bearing and progress by the great mountain overhead.

"Are you all right?" he asked Gillian. He raised his head to have a look at her. She was swimming in what looked like a good strong crawl. She coughed from time to time.

"I'm cold," she said. "That's the trouble."

"Try resting on your back," he said, "and paddling with your open hands. Like you were rowing."

She turned over and closed her eyes and smiled.

"I could go to sleep."

"You'll sleep ashore," he said. "Keep paddling."

They heard Freycinet cursing. Marie began to scream over and over again. It sounded fairly far away.

Checking on the mountain, Blessington felt a rush of despair. The lower slopes of the jungle were turning dark green. The line dividing sun-bright vegetation from deep-shaded green was withdrawing toward the peak. And it looked no closer. He felt as though they were losing distance, being carried out faster than they could paddle. Marie's relentless screeches went on and on. Perhaps they were actually growing closer, Blessington thought, perhaps an evening tide was carrying them out.

"Poor kid," Gillian said. "Poor little baby."

"Don't listen," he said.

Gillian kept coughing, sputtering. He stopped asking her if she was all right.

"I'm sorry," she said. "I'm really cold now. I thought the water was warm at first."

"We're almost there," he said.

Gillian stopped swimming and looked up at Gros Piton. Turning over again to swim, she got a mouthful of water.

"Like . . . hell," she said.

"Keep going, Gillian."

It seemed to him as he rowed the sodden vessel of his body and mind that the sky was darkening. The sun's mark withdrew higher on the slopes. Marie kept screaming. They heard splashes far off where the boat was now. Marie and Honoré were clinging to it.

"Liam," Gillian said, "you can't save me."

"You'll save yourself," he said. "You'll just go on."

"I can't."

"Don't be a bloody stupid bitch."

"I don't think so," she said. "I really don't."

He stopped rowing himself then although he was loath to. Every interruption of their forward motion put them more at the mercy of the current. According to the cruise book it was only a five-knot current but it felt much stronger. Probably reinforced by a tide.

Gillian was struggling, coughing in fits. She held her head up, greedy for air, her mouth open like a baby bird's in hope of nourishment. Blessington swam nearer to her. The sense of their time ticking away, of distance lost to the current, enraged him.

"You've got to turn over on your back," he said gently. "Just ease onto your back and rest there. Then arch your back. Let your head lie backward so your forehead's in the water."

Trying to do as he told her, she began to thrash in a tangle of her own arms and legs. She swallowed water, gasped. Then she laughed again.

"Don't," he whispered.

"Liam? Can I rest on you?"

He stopped swimming toward her.

"You mustn't. You mustn't touch me. We mustn't touch each other. We might . . ."

"Please," she said.

"No. Get on your back. Turn over slowly."

Something broke the water near them. He thought it was the fin of a black-tipped shark. A troublesome shark but not among the most dangerous. Of course, it could have been anything. Gillian still had the Rasta bracelet around her wrist.

"This is the thing, Liam. I think I got a cramp. I'm so dizzy."

"On your back, love. You must. It's the only way."

"No," she said. "I'm too cold. I'm too dizzy."

"Come on," he said. He started swimming again. Away from her.

"I'm so dizzy. I could go right out."

In mounting panic, he reversed direction and swam back toward her.

"Oh, shit," she said. "Liam?"

"I'm here."

"I'm fading out, Liam. I'll let it take me."

"Get on your back," he screamed at her. "You can easily swim. If you have to swim all night."

"Oh, shit," she said. Then she began to laugh again. She raised the hand that had the Rasta bracelet and splashed a sign of the cross.

"*Nam*," she said "*nam myoho renge kyo*. Son of a bitch." Laughing. What she tried to say next was washed out of her mouth by a wave.

"I can just go out," she said. "I'm so dizzy."

Then she began to struggle and laugh and cry.

"Praise God, from whom all blessings flow," she sang, laughing. "Praise Him, all creatures here below."

"Gillian," he said. "For God's sake." Maybe I can take her in, he thought. But that was madness and he kept his distance.

She was laughing and shouting at the top of her voice.

"Praise Him above, you heavenly host! Praise Father, Son, and Holy Ghost."

Laughing, thrashing, she went under, her face straining, wide-eyed. Blessington tried to look away but it was too late. He was afraid to go after her.

He lost his own balance then. His physical discipline collapsed and he began to wallow and thrash as she had.

"Help!" he yelled piteously. He was answered by a splash and Marie's screaming. Perhaps now he only imagined them.

Eventually he got himself under control. When the entire mountain had subsided into dark green, he felt the pull of the current release him. The breakers were beginning to carry him closer to the sand, toward the last spit of sandy beach remaining on the island. The entire northern horizon was subsumed in the mountain overhead, Gros Piton.

He had one final mad moment. Fifty yards offshore, a riptide was running, it seized him and carried him behind the tip of the island. He had just enough strength and coherence of mind to swim across it. The sun was setting as he waded out, among sea grape and manchineel. When he turned he could see against the setting sun the bare poles of the *Sans Regret*, settled on the larger reef to the south of the island. It seemed to him also that he could make out a struggling human figure, dark against the light hull. But the dark came down quickly. He thought he detected a flash of green. Sometimes he thought he could still hear Marie screaming.

All night, as he rattled through the thick brush looking for a road to follow from concealment, Gillian's last hymn echoed in his mind's ear. He could see her dying face against the black fields of sugarcane through which he trudged.

Once he heard what he was certain was the trumpeting of an elephant. It made him believe, in his growing delirium, that he was in Africa—Africa, where he had never been. He hummed the hymn. Then he remembered he had read somewhere that the resort maintained an elephant in the bush. But he did not want to meet it so he decided to stay where he was and wait for morning. All night he talked to Gillian, joked and sang hymns with her. He saved her again and again and they were together.

In the morning, when the sun rose fresh and full of promise, he set out for the Irish bar in Soufrière. He thought that they might overstand him there.

The Eighty-Yard Run

Irwin Shaw

The pass was high and wide and he jumped for it, feeling it slap flatly against his hands, as he shook his hips to throw off the halfback who was diving at him. The center floated by, his hands desperately brushing Darling's knee as Darling picked his feet up high and delicately ran over a blocker and an opposing linesman in a jumble on the ground near the scrimmage line. He had ten yards in the clear and picked up speed, breathing easily, feeling his thigh pads rising and falling against his legs, listening to the sound of cleats behind him, pulling away from them, watching the other backs heading him off toward the sideline, the whole picture, the men closing in on him, the blockers fighting for position, the ground he had to cross, all suddenly clear in his head, for the first time in his life not a meaningless confusion of men, sounds, speed. He smiled a little to himself as he ran, holding the ball lightly in front of him with his two hands, his knees pumping high, his hips twisting in the almost-girlish run of a back in a broken field. The first halfback came at him and he fed him his leg, then swung at the last moment, took the shock of the man's shoulder without breaking stride, ran right through him, his cleats biting securely into the turf. There was only the safety man now, coming warily at him, his arms crooked, hands spread. Darling tucked the ball in, spurted at him, driving hard, hurling himself along, his legs pounding, knees high, all two hundred pounds bunched into controlled attack. He was sure he was going to get past the safety man. Without thought, his arms and legs working beautifully together, he headed right for the safety man, stiff-armed him, feeling blood spurt instantaneously from the man's nose onto his hand, seeing his face go awry, head turned, mouth pulled to one side. He pivoted away, keeping the arm locked, dropping the safety man as he ran easily toward the goal line, with the drumming of cleats diminishing behind him.

How long ago? It was autumn then and the ground was getting hard because the nights were cold and leaves from the maples around the stadium blew across the practice fields in gusts of wind and the girls were beginning to put polo coats over their sweaters when they came to watch practice in the afternoons.

Fifteen years. Darling walked slowly over the same ground in the spring twilight, in his neat shoes, a man of thirty-five dressed in a double-breasted suit ten pounds heavier in the fifteen years, but not fat, with the years between 1925 and 1940 showing in his face.

The coach was smiling quietly to himself and the assistant coaches were looking at each other with pleasure the way they always did when one of the second stringers suddenly did something fine, bringing credit to them, making their $2,000 a year a tiny bit more secure.

Darling trotted back, smiling, breathing deeply but easily, feeling wonderful, not tired, though this was the tail end of practice and he'd run eighty yards. The sweat poured off his face and soaked his jersey and he liked the feeling, the warm moistness lubricating his skin like oil. Off in a corner of the field some players were punting and the smack of leather against the ball came pleasantly through the afternoon air. The freshmen were running signals on the next field and the quarterback's sharp voice, the pound of the eleven pairs of cleats, the "Dig, now, *dig*!" of the coaches, the laughter of the players all somehow made him feel happy as he trotted back to midfield, listening to the applause and shouts of the students along the sidelines, knowing that after that run the coach would have to start him Saturday against Illinois.

Fifteen years, Darling thought, remembering the shower after the workout, the hot water steaming off his skin and the deep soapsuds and all the young voices singing with the water streaming down and towels going and managers running in and out and the sharp sweet smell of oil of wintergreen and everybody clapping him on the back as he dressed and Packard, the captain, who took being captain very seriously, coming over to him and shaking his hand and saying. "Darling, you're going to go places in the next two years."

The assistant manager fussed over him, wiping a cut on his leg with alcohol and iodine, the little sting making him realize suddenly how fresh and whole and solid his body felt. The manager slapped a piece of adhesive tape over the cut and Darling noticed the sharp clean white of the tape against the ruddiness of the skin, fresh from the shower.

He dressed slowly, the softness of his shirt and the soft warmth of his wool socks and his flannel trousers a reward against his skin after the harsh pressure of the shoulder harness and thigh and hip pads. He drank three glasses of cold water, the liquid reaching down coldly inside of him, soothing the harsh dry places in his throat and belly left by the sweat and running and shouting of practice.

Fifteen years.

The sun had gone down and the sky was green behind the stadium and he laughed quietly to himself as he looked at the stadium, rearing above the trees, and knew that on Saturday when the seventy thousand voices roared as the team came running out onto the field, part of that enormous salute would be for him. He walked slowly, listening to the gravel crunch satisfactorily under his shoes in the still twilight, feeling his clothes swing lightly against his skin, breathing the thin evening air, feeling the wind move in his damp hair, wonderfully cool behind his ears and at the nape of his neck.

Louise was waiting for him at the road, in her car. The top was down and he noticed all over again, as he always did when he saw her, how pretty she was, the rough blond hair and the large, inquiring eyes and the bright mouth, smiling now.

She threw the door open. "Were you good today?" she asked.

"Pretty good," he said. He climbed in, sank luxuriously into the soft leather, stretched his legs far out. He smiled, thinking of the eighty yards. "Pretty damn good."

She looked at him seriously for a moment, then scrambled around, like a little girl, kneeling on the seat next to him, grabbed him, her hands along his ears, and kissed him as he sprawled, head back, on the seat cushion. She let go of him, but kept her head close to his, over his. Darling reached up slowly and rubbed the back of his hand against her cheek, lit softly by a streetlamp a hundred feet away. They looked at each other, smiling.

Louise drove down to the lake and they sat there silently, watching the moon rise behind the hills on the other side. Finally he reached over, pulled her gently to him, kissed her. Her lips grew soft, her body sank into his, tears formed slowly in her eyes. He knew, for the first time, that he could do whatever he wanted with her.

"Tonight," he said. "I'll call for you at seven-thirty. Can you get out?"

She looked at him. She was smiling, but the tears were still full in her eyes. "All right," she said. "I'll get out. How about you? Won't the coach raise hell?"

Darling grinned. "I got the coach in the palm of my hand," he said. "Can you wait till seven-thirty?"

She grinned back at him. "No," she said.

They kissed and she started the car and they went back to town for dinner. He sang on the way home.

*   *   *

Christian Darling, thirty-five years old, sat on the frail spring grass, greener now than it ever would be again on the practice field, looked thoughtfully up at the stadium, a deserted ruin in the twilight. He had started on the first team that Saturday and every Saturday after that for the next two years, but it had never been as satisfactory as it should have been. He never had broken away, the longest run he'd ever made was thirty-five yards, and that in a game that was already won, and then that kid had come up from the third team, Diederich, a blankfaced German kid from Wisconsin, who ran like a bull, ripping lines to pieces Saturday after Saturday, plowing through, never getting hurt, never changing his expression, scoring more points, gaining more ground than all the rest of the team put together, making everybody's All-American, carrying the ball three times out of four, keeping everybody else out of the headlines. Darling was a good blocker and he spent his Saturday afternoons working on the big Swedes and Polacks who played tackle and end for Michigan, Illinois, Purdue, hurling into huge pileups, bobbing his head wildly to elude the great raw hands swinging like meat cleavers at him as he went charging in to open up holes for Diederich coming through like a locomotive behind him. Still, it wasn't so bad. Everybody liked him and he did his job and he was pointed out on the campus and boys always felt important when they introduced their girls to him at their proms, and Louise loved him and watched him faithfully in the games, even in the mud, when your own mother wouldn't know you, and drove him around in her car keeping the top down because she was proud of him and wanted to show everybody that she was Christian Darling's girl. She bought him crazy presents because her father was rich, watches, pipes, humidors, an icebox for beer for his room, curtains, mallets, a fifty-dollar dictionary.

"You'll spend every cent your old man owns." Darling protested once when she showed up at his rooms with seven different packages in her arms and tossed them onto the couch.

"Kiss me," Louise said, "and shut up."

"Do you want to break your poor old man?"

"I don't mind. I want to buy you presents."

"Why?"

"It makes me feel good. Kiss me. I don't know why. Did you know that you're an important figure?"

"Yes," Darling said gravely.

"When I was waiting for you at the library yesterday two girls saw you coming and one of them said to the other, 'That's Christian Darling. He's an important figure.' "

"You're a liar."

"I'm in love with an important figure."

"Still, why the hell did you have to give me a forty-pound dictionary?"

"I wanted to make sure," Louise said, "that you had a token of my esteem. I want to smother you in tokens of my esteem."

Fifteen years ago.

They'd married when they got out of college. There'd been other women for him, but all casual and secret, more for curiosity's sake, and vanity, women who'd thrown themselves at him and flattered him, a pretty mother at a summer camp for boys, an old girl from his home town who'd suddenly blossomed into a coquette, a friend of Louise's who had dogged him grimly for six months and had taken advantage of the two weeks when Louise went home when her mother died. Perhaps Louise had known, but she'd kept quiet, loving him completely, filling his rooms with presents, religiously watching him battling with the big Swedes and Polacks on the line of scrimmage on Saturday afternoons, making plans for marrying him and living with him in New York and going with him there to the night-clubs, the theaters, the good restaurants, proud of him in advance, tall, white-teethed, smiling, large, yet moving lightly, with an athlete's grace, dressed in evening clothes, approvingly eyed by magnificently dressed and famous women in theater lobbies, with Louise adoringly at his side.

Her father, who manufactured inks, set up a New York office for Darling to manage and presented him with three hundred accounts and they lived on Beekman Place with a view of the river with fifteen thousand dollars a year between them, because everybody was buying everything in those days, including ink. They saw all the shows and went to all the speakeasies and spent their fifteen thousand dollars a year and in the afternoons Louise went to the art galleries and the matinees of the more serious plays that Darling didn't like to sit through and Darling slept with a girl who danced in the chorus of *Rosalie* and with the wife of a man who owned three copper mines. Darling played squash three times a week and remained as solid as a stone barn and Louise never took her eyes off him when they were in the same room together, watching him with a secret, miser's smile, with a trick of coming over to him in the middle of a crowded room and saying gravely, in a low voice, "You're the handsomest man I've ever seen in my whole life. Want a drink?"

Nineteen twenty-nine came to Darling and to his wife and father-in-law, the maker of inks, just as it came to everyone else. The father-in-law waited until 1933 and then blew his brains out and when Darling went to Chicago to see what the books of the firm looked like he found out all that was left were debts and three or four gallons of unbought ink.

"Please, Christian," Louise said, sitting in their neat Beekman Place apartment, with a view of the river and prints of paintings by Dufy and Braque and Picasso on the wall, "please, why do you want to start drinking at two o'clock in the afternoon?"

"I have nothing else to do," Darling said, putting down his glass, emptied of its fourth drink. "Please pass the whiskey."

Louise filled his glass. "Come take a walk with me," she said. "We'll walk along the river."

"I don't want to walk along the river," Darling said, squinting intensely at the prints of paintings by Dufy and Braque and Picasso.

"We'll walk along Fifth Avenue."

"I don't want to walk along Fifth Avenue."

"Maybe," Louise said gently, "you'd like to come with me to some art galleries. There's an exhibition by a man named Klee—"

"I don't want to go to any art galleries. I want to sit here and drink Scotch whiskey," Darling said. "Who the hell hung those goddam pictures up on the wall?"

"I did," Louise said.

"I hate them."

"I'll take them down," Louise said.

"Leave them there. It gives me something to do in the afternoon. I can hate them." Darling took a long swallow. "Is that the way people paint these days?"

"Yes, Christian. Please don't drink any more."

"Do you like painting like that?"

"Yes, dear."

"Really?"

"Really."

Darling looked carefully at the prints once more. "Little Louise Tucker. The middle-western beauty. I like pictures with horses in them. Why should you like pictures like that?"

"I just happen to have gone to a lot of galleries in the last few years . . ."

"Is that what you do in the afternoon?"

"That's what I do in the afternoon," Louise said.

"I drink in the afternoon."

Louise kissed him lightly on the top of his head as he sat there squinting at the pictures on the wall, the glass of whiskey held firmly in his hand. She put on her coat and went out without saying another word. When she came back in the early evening, she had a job on a woman's fashion magazine.

They moved downtown and Louise went out to work every morning and Darling sat home and drank and Louise paid the bills as they came up. She made believe she was going to quit work as soon as Darling found a job, even though she was taking over more responsibility day by day at the magazine, interviewing authors, picking painters for the illustrations and covers, getting actresses to pose for pictures, going out for drinks with the right people, making a thousand new friends whom she loyally introduced to Darling.

"I don't like your hat," Darling said, once, when she came in in the evening and kissed him, her breath rich with Martinis.

"What's the matter with my hat, Baby?" she asked, running her fingers through his hair. "Everybody says it's very smart."

"It's too damned smart," he said. "It's not for you. It's for a rich, sophisticated woman of thirty-five with admirers."

Louise laughed. "I'm practicing to be a rich, sophisticated woman of thirty-five with admirers," she said. He stared soberly at her. "Now, don't look so grim, Baby. It's still the same simple little wife under the hat." She took the hat off, threw it into a corner, sat on his lap. "See? Homebody Number One."

"Your breath could run a train," Darling said, not wanting to be mean, but talking out of boredom, and sudden shock at seeing his wife curiously a stranger in a new hat, with a new expression in her eyes under the little brim, secret, confident, knowing.

Louise tucked her head under his chin so he couldn't smell her breath. "I had to take an author out for cocktails," she said. "He's a boy from the Ozark mountains and he drinks like a fish. He's a Communist."

"What the hell is a Communist from the Ozarks doing writing for a woman's fashion magazine?"

Louise chuckled. "The magazine business is getting all mixed up these days. The publishers want to have a foot in every camp. And anyway, you can't find an author under seventy these days who isn't a Communist."

"I don't think I like you to associate with all those people, Louise," Darling said. "Drinking with them."

"He's a very nice, gentle boy," Louise said. "He reads Ernest Dobson." "Who's Ernest Dobson?"

Louise patted his arm, stood up, fixed her hair. "He's an English poet."

Darling felt that somehow he had disappointed her. "Am I supposed to know who Ernest Dobson is?"

"No, dear. I'd better go in and take a bath."

After she had gone, Darling went over to the corner where the hat was lying and picked it up. It was nothing, a scrap of straw, a red flower, a veil, meaningless in his big hand, but on his wife's head a signal of something . . . big city, smart and knowing women drinking and dining with men other than their husbands, conversation about things a normal man wouldn't know much about, Frenchmen who painted as though they used their elbows instead of brushes, composers who wrote whole symphonies without a single melody in them, writers who knew all about politics and women who knew all about writers, the movement of the proletariat, Marx, somehow mixed up with five-dollar dinners and the best-looking women in America and fairies who made them laugh and half-sentences immediately understood and secretly hilarious and wives who called their husbands "Baby." He put the hat down, a scrap of straw and a red flower, and a little veil. He drank some whiskey straight and went into the bathroom where his wife was lying deep in her bath, singing to herself and smiling from time to time like a little girl, paddling the water gently with her hands, sending up a slight spicy fragrance from the bath salts she used.

He stood over her, looking down at her. She smiled up at him, her eyes half closed, her body pink and shimmering in the warm, scented water. All over again, with all the old suddenness, he was hit deep inside him with the knowledge of how beautiful she was, how much he needed her.

"I came in here," he said, "to tell you I wish you wouldn't call me 'Baby.'"

She looked up at him from the bath, her eyes quickly full of sorrow, half-understanding what he meant. He knelt and put his arms around her, his sleeves plunged heedlessly in the water, his shirt and jacket soaking wet as he clutched her wordlessly holding her crazily tight, crushing her breath from her, kissing her desperately, searchingly, regretfully.

He got jobs after that, selling real estate and automobiles, but somehow, although he had a desk with his name on a wooden wedge on it, and he went to the office religiously at nine each morning, he never managed to sell anything and he never made any money.

Louise was made assistant editor and the house was always full of strange men and women who talked fast and got angry over abstract subjects like mural painting, novelists, labor unions. Negro short-story writers drank Louise's liquor, and a lot of Jews, and big solemn men with scarred faces and knotted hands who talked slowly but clearly about picket lines and battles with guns and lead pipe at mine-shaft-heads and in front of factory gates. And Louise moved among them all, confidently, knowing what they were talking about, with opinions that they listened to and argued about just as though she were a man. She knew everybody, condescended to no one, devoured books that Darling had never heard of, walked along the streets of the city, excited, at home, soaking in all the million tides of New York without fear, with constant wonder.

Her friends liked Darling and sometimes he found a man who wanted to go off in the corner and talk about the new boy who played fullback for Princeton, and the decline of the double wingback, or even the state of the stock market, but for the most part he sat on the edge of things, solid and quiet in the high storm of words. "The dialectics of the situation . . . the theater has been given over to expert jugglers . . . Picasso? What man has a right to paint old bones and collect ten thousand dollars for them? . . . I stand firmly behind Trotsky . . . Poe was the last American critic. When he died they put lilies on the grave of American criticism. I don't say this because they panned my last book, but. . . ."

Once in a while he caught Louise looking soberly and consideringly at him through the cigarette smoke and the noise and he avoided her eyes and found an excuse to get up and go into the kitchen for more ice or to open another bottle.

"Come on," Cathal Flaherty was saying, standing at the door with a girl, "you've got to come down and see this. It's down on Fourteenth Street, in the old Civic Repertory, and you can only see it on Sunday nights and I guarantee you'll come out of the theater singing." Flaherty was a big young Irishman with a broken nose who was the lawyer from a longshoreman's union, and he had been hanging around the house for six months on and off, roaring and shutting everybody else up when he got in an argument. "It's a new play, *Waiting for Lefty*, it's about taxi drivers."

"Odets," the girl with Flaherty said. "It's by a guy named Odets."

"I never heard of him," Darling said.

"He's a new one," the girl said.

"It's like watching a bombardment," Flaherty said. "I saw it last Sunday night. You've got to see it."

"Come on, Baby," Louise said to Darling, excitement in her eyes already. "We've been sitting in the Sunday *Times* all day, this'll be a great change."

"I see enough taxi drivers every day," Darling said, not because he meant that, but because he didn't like to be around Flaherty, who said things that made Louise laugh a lot and whose judgment she accepted in almost every subject. "Let's go to the movies."

"You've never seen anything like this before," Flaherty said. "He wrote this play with a baseball bat."

"Come on," Louise coaxed. "I bet it's wonderful."

"He has long hair," the girl with Flaherty said. "Odets. I met him at a party. He's an actor. He didn't say a goddam thing all night."

"I don't feel like going down to Fourteenth Street," Darling said, wishing Flaherty and his girl would get out. "It's gloomy."

"Oh, hell!" Louise said loudly. She looked coolly at Darling, as though she'd just been introduced to him and was making up her mind about him, and not very favorably. He saw her looking at him, knowing there was something new and dangerous in her face, and he wanted to say something, but Flaherty was there and his damned girl, and anyway, he didn't know what to say.

"I'm going," Louise said, getting her coat. "I don't think Fourteenth Street is gloomy."

"I'm telling you," Flaherty was saying, helping her on with her coat, "it's the Battle of Gettysburg, in Brooklynese."

"Nobody could get a word out of him," Flaherty's girl was saying as they went through the door. "He just sat there all night."

The door closed. Louise hadn't said good night to him. Darling walked around the room four times, then sprawled out on the sofa, on top of the Sunday *Times*. He lay there for five minutes looking at the ceiling, thinking of Flaherty walking down the street talking in that booming voice, between the girls, holding their arms.

Louise had looked wonderful. She's washed her hair in the afternoon and it had been soft and light and clung close to her head as she stood there angrily putting her coat on. Louise was getting prettier every year, partly because she knew by now how pretty she was, and made the most of it.

"Nuts," Darling said, standing up. "Oh, nuts."

He put on his coat and went down to the nearest bar and had five drinks off by himself in a corner before his money ran out.

The years since then had been foggy and downhill. Louise had been nice to him, and in a way, loving and kind, and they'd fought only once, when he said he was going to vote for Landon. ("Oh, Christ," she'd said, "doesn't *anything* happen inside you head? Don't you read the papers? The penniless Republican!") She's been sorry later and apologized as she might to a child. He's tried hard, had gone grimly to the art galleries, the concert halls, the bookshops, trying to gain on the trail of his wife, but it was no use. He was bored, and none of what he saw or heard or dutifully read made much sense to him and finally he gave it up. He had thought, many nights as he ate dinner alone, knowing that Louise would come home late and drop silently into bed without explanation, of getting a divorce, but he knew the loneliness, the hopelessness, of not seeing her again would be too much to take. So he was good, completely devoted, ready at all times to go anyplace with her, do anything she wanted. He even got a small job, in a broker's office, and paid his own way, bought his own liquor.

Then he'd been offered the job of going from college to college as a tailor's representative. "We want a man," Mr. Rosenberg had said, "who as soon as you look at him, you say 'There's a university man.'" Rosenberg had looked approvingly at Darling's broad shoulders and well-kept waist, as his carefully brushed hair and his honest, wrinkleless face. "Frankly, Mr. Darling, I am willing to make you a proposition. I have inquired about you, you are favorably known on your old campus, I understand you were in the backfield with Alfred Diederich."

Darling nodded. "Whatever happened to him?"

"He is walking around in a cast for seven years now. An iron brace. He played professional football and they broke his neck for him."

Darling smiled. That, at least, had turned out well.

"Our suits are an easy product to sell, Mr. Darling," Rosenberg said. "We have a handsome, custom-made garment. What has Brooks Brothers got that we haven't got? A name. No more."

"I can make fifty, sixty dollars a week," Darling said to Louise that night. "And expenses. I can save some money and then come back to New York and really get started here."

"Yes, Baby," Louise said.

"As it is," Darling said carefully, "I can make it back here once a month, and holidays and the summer. We can see each other often."

"Yes, Baby." He looked at her face, lovelier now at thirty-five than it had ever been before, but fogged over now as it had been for five years with a kind of patient, kindly, remote boredom.

"What do you say?" he asked. "Should I take it?" Deep within him he hoped fiercely, longing, for her to say, "No, Baby, you stay right here," but she said, as he knew she'd say, "I think you'd better take it."

He nodded. He had to get up and stand with his back to her, looking out the window, because there were things plain on his face that she had never seen in the fifteen years she's known him. "Fifty dollars is a lot of money," he said, "I never thought I'd ever see fifty dollars again." He laughed. Louise laughed too.

Christian Darling sat on the frail green grass of the practice field. The shadow of the stadium had reached out and covered him. In the distance the lights of the university shone a little mistily in the light haze of evening. Fifteen years. Flaherty even now was calling for his wife buying him a drink, filling whatever bar they were in with that voice of his and that easy laugh. Darling half-closed his eyes, almost saw the boy fifteen years ago reach for the pass, slip the halfback, go skittering lightly down the field, his knees high and fast and graceful, smiling to himself because he knew he was going to get past the safety man. That was the high point, Darling thought, fifteen years ago, on an autumn afternoon, twenty years ago and far from death, with the air coming easily into his lungs, and a deep feeling inside him that he could do anything, knock over anybody, outrun whatever had to be outrun. And the shower after and the three glasses of water and the cool night air on his damp head and Louise sitting hatless in the open car with a smile and the first kiss she ever really meant. The high point, an eighty-yard run in the practice, and a girl's kiss and everything after that a decline. Darling laughed. He had practiced the wrong thing, perhaps. He hadn't practiced for 1929 and New York City and a girl who would turn into a woman. Somewhere, he thought, there must have been a point where she moved up to me, was even with me for a moment, when I could have held her hand, if I'd known, held tight, gone with her. Well, he'd never known. Here he was on a playing field that was fifteen years away and his wife was in another city having dinner with another and better man, speaking with him a different, new language, a language nobody had ever taught him.

Darling stood up, smiled a little, because if he didn't smile he knew the tears would come. He looked around him. This was the spot. O'Connor's pass had come sliding out just to here . . . the high point. Darling put up his hands, felt all over again the flat slap of the ball. He shook his hips to throw off the halfback, cut back inside the center, picked his knees high as he ran gracefully over the men jumbled on the ground at the line of scrimmage, ran easily, gaining speed, for ten yards, holding the ball lightly in his two hands, swung away from the halfback diving at him, ran, swinging his hips in the almost girlish manner of a back in a broken field, tore into the safety man, his shoes drumming heavily on the turf, stiff-armed, elbow locked, pivoted, raced lightly and exultantly for the goal line.

It was only after he had sped over the goal line and slowed to a trot that he saw the boy and girl sitting together on the turf, looking at him wonderingly.

He stopped short, dropping his arms. "I . . ." he said, gasping a little though his condition was fine and the run hadn't winded him. "I . . . Once I played here."

The boy and the girl said nothing. Darling laughed embarrassedly, looked hard at them sitting there, close to each other, shrugged, turned and went toward his hotel, the sweat breaking out on his face and running down into his collar.

In the Men's Room of the Sixteenth Century

Don DeLillo

It was the anniversary of the beheading of St. Thomas More, an incandescent night in Times Square, all manner of humanity engaged in vintage decadence.

Thomas Patrick Guffey walked into the precinct house just before midnight. The squad room was full of people arguing and sobbing, another summer night of arsonists, petty thieves, throat-slashers, film projectionists, pimps, dynamiters, lost Iowans, molesters of every kind, hillbilly visionaries with bloody heads, so on and so forth, all of them being informed of their Constitutional rights. Guffey nodded hello here and there and went upstairs to his locker. He took off his sport coat and the pale green tie (embossed initials) which his youngest daughter had given him for his birthday. He transferred the snub-nosed .38 from his shoulder holster to the beige handbag inside the locker. At the far end of the room the precinct captain, Terrible Teddy Effing, was methodically punching and kicking a small hump-chested man in a black overcoat and skullcap. Guffey continued undressing. When he was finished he pounded his right fist into the palm of his left hand nine times. Then he took a padded bra and a pair of India-silk panties out of the locker and put them on. After a good deal of thought he got into a red-and-yellow Mexican maxi-dress—a fantastic flowing creation patterned with stars, mystic eyes and scorpions. He slipped into brown espadrilles and took his makeup kit into the bathroom. He washed his face with cold water. Then he sponged on some pancake, sketched a bit with an eyebrow pencil, applied eye shadow and used a thin sable-tipped brush to anoint his lids with liquid eyeliner. He stuck on false lashes with surgical glue. He followed this by applying mascara, as well as a few strokes of blusher to accent the cheekbones and give them an ascetic look. Then he chose a pastel peach shade of lipstick and followed it with clear gloss. He went back to his locker. It was exactly midnight. He put on a burnt sienna custom wig, brass and silver bracelets, an onyx ring on every finger. He picked up the handbag and went downstairs.

Near the desk his partner Vincent Capezio was questioning a stout bearded man who kept spitting on his right hand and then blessing himself. Capezio gestured to Guffey, who glanced at the clock over the desk and joined his partner.

"I spotted the perpetrator on Forty-third Street," Capezio said. "I took cognizance of the fact that he was peering into the windows of parked motor vehicles. I followed him to Eighth Avenue. At this locale he took out an implement and wedged open the left front window of a 1932 Bugatti Royale with DPL plates. When I identified myself as a law-enforcement officer, the perpetrator began to act in a loud and boisterous manner. He assaulted me with his hands and disarmed me. Then he fled in a westerly direction. I pursued him on foot and with the aid of patrolmen Passacaglia and Fugue I overpowered the son of a bitch and brought him here for booking."

"Why are you telling me this, Vince?"

"Because he denies he's a car booster."

"I deny," the man said.

"He says he's Bernal of Almeria, a saint and former soldier of the Cross. I can't deal with him, Tommy. Effing tried, and Effing can't deal with him either. When Effing can't deal with something, it automatically falls into your category. The guy just won't answer questions. He says saints have traditionally cloaked themselves in silence. It's definitely in your category, Tommy. He says he rode with Cortez."

"I am the one they call Lady Madonna," Guffey said. "If you tell me what's in your heart, I'll do what I can for you. If you refuse to cooperate, you'll probably be tortured and thrown into prison. Mercy is all but unknown and good intentions rot with the meat of dogs."

"You have insulted my dignity," the man said.

Capezio hit him in the mouth and dragged him across the floor toward the cage. Guffey went out into the equatorial night, through humid air palpable as surf, north toward the lights and mad music. Six glossy prostitutes came toward him, shoulder to shoulder across the sidewalk, wearing polymerized thermoplastic dresses and Styrofoam slave bracelets. Right behind them was an individual called Jack & Jill, a known hermaphrodite and suspected dealer in unsterilized hypodermic needles. Guffey crossed the street and went into one of the all-night movie houses, the Basilica, a former showcase for wholesome family movies, now a vaulted haunt of such apathy that the screen often remained blank for days at a time, a fact which seemed to go unnoticed by the patrons. Great silver candlesticks lined the walls of the darkened lobby. Guffey wandered through the theatre. There were busts of desiccated popes and bleak noblemen. Banners and battle standards hung high on the grey walls, reminding him of his honeymoon in Europe, the sublime sense of civilization expressed even in torture chambers and cells. He stood near one of the balcony exits, watching the movie, a necrophile epic, whereupon he was approached by a long-haired, emaciated young man who tried to sell him four capsules of a drug called pseudothalgenomide, a chemically hybrid stimulant so powerful it was able to cause cancer in organically dead tissue.

"I could easily put you under arrest."

"Then you must be Lady Madonna," the young man said. "They talk about you wherever the counter-culture puts down roots."

"What's your story, son?"

"I've sniffed, ate and shot every drug there is. Cyclogen, sleet, moko, gribbies, deecee, flash, sujo pinda. My head's just about inside out."

"The hardest road of all is the road that leads from reason."

"Ain't that the goddamn truth. All I want to do now is get on back to the border states. I'm all through with junk. I want to grow apples and broccoli. I want to spend ten minutes every morning doing squat-jumps and rapping with Jesus."

Guffey opened his handbag and gave the young man a Xeroxed sheet summarizing the *Metaphysical Disputations* of Suárez. Then he went downstairs to make his customary check of the restroom facilities. The men's toilet reminded him of one of the bathrooms in the railroad station in Venice, not cleaned since the Renaissance, an extremely poignant spot, the fecal confluence of many cultures. He scrutinized his makeup in the mirror and then turned and watched as the derelict known as Agony Of The Rose crawled slowly across the wet tile floor to put his lips to the poised tip of Guffey's right shoe. On the wall above the urinals were stone-cold words boldly stroked in black: TIME-SPACE PSYCHOSIS FOLLOWS THE SHATTERING OF THE LOOP OF HISTORY ACCORDING TO THE COMPUTER DEMONS OF GIAMBATTISTA VICO. In the lobby he saw Burgo Swinney, the eunuchoid pornographer, wearing an ecru velveteen jumpsuit and clear vinyl moccasins.

"Quo vadis?" Swinney said.

Dozens of people lounged outside a record store on Forty-second Street. Preadolescent boys for sale. Militant forestry students. Harbingers and importuners. Jackbooted Chinese bikers. Hard-rock guitarists in Vietcong

749

sweatshirts. A teenage girl sat on a suitcase sniffing a handful of oxidized camphor pellets through a long plastic straw, a practice introduced to the East Coast by the followers of a man called Polyplex Comtron, a morgue attendant in Los Angeles. Guffey touched the girl's head, then walked past the Persian baths, the computerized horoscope parlor, the deviation bookstore, the guns-and-ammo discount center, the homoerotic wax museum, the Jansenist reading room, the leper clinic, the paraplegic sex exhibit, the Afro-Cuban ballroom, the jujitsu academy, the pubic-wig boutique, the electric brain-massage outlet. At the end of the block he spotted Teeny Maeve Feeney, a former Ursuline abbess who now walked the streets trying to lure pleasure-seekers to her room. Maeve worked in platonic concert with Longjaw Ed Jolly, a man who claimed to be the last living member of the Castrated Priests of Cybele, a self-mutilation cult. Once Maeve's customer was in the room, Ed Jolly would appear with a sawed-off shotgun and confront the man with a list of questions concerning predestination, idealistic pantheism, the self-knowledge of angels, the existence of the Cynocephali—a race of men with doglike heads mentioned in the writings of St. Augustine. A single wrong answer prompted the two fanatics to initiate the Ravensburg Pattern, a series of cybernetic tortures. Guffey was always saddened to see these men and women in their hopeless roles, sinners in religious fever, poetic desperadoes, carnal martyrs of the Western dream. He turned a corner, away from the traffic noise and buzzing neon, and went into a small dark club called Galileo's Folly, a raided premises and known headquarters for narcotics traffickers. He went straight back to the circular oak table where Niccolò Tancredi, the owner, customarily held forth. Tancredi, a Sicilian of *capo mafioso* ranking, was an impeccably dressed, clear-thinking and unemotional man, somewhat jesuitically inclined, extremely lean of body, his voice a cheese-grating rasp. He commented favorably on Guffey's di Sant'Angelo handbag with its silken ropes and vaguely Middle English motif. They talked a while of Giacomo (Jimmy the Jap) Chikamatsu, missing since spring from his suburban home with its flamingo-studded Zen garden. Tancredi was in a reflective mood.

"Man's salvation is far from assured," he said. "We're in mortal danger of losing the oldest and greatest battle."

"Man is good, Tancredi. He strives, he suffers, he bares his soul to the one true universe. He gives it his all."

"Old friend, the pale light of reason is on my side. We burn slowly and unknowingly. We're aware of nothing but our own search for self-annihilation. Hell is the living electricity."

"Fire is fire," Guffey said. "Light is light."

"But what is apparent is not what is real. I am a sinner, you a saint. But we burn in the same living fire. The fire of earth. The fire of air. The fire of fire. The fire of water. The Greeks knew but four elements. Is our death more glorious than theirs?"

"Man's salvation is wrung minute by minute out of his solitude. Have you read the *Edict of Costa del Sol*?"

"My subscription ran out."

"Your humor refines itself with the years, Tancredi."

"It is perfectable, my friend, as man is not."

Later they sat in Tancredi's dimly lit office and discussed the syndicate's opium holdings. Soon they were joined by four men, one of them Tancredi's brother. Asmodeus, a federal judge; the others, wearing white poppies in their lapels, were enforcers of one kind or another. Tancredi suggested that Guffey remain for the interrogation of a would-be courier for the Mediterranean heroin combine. The candidate was brought in—a young, pale, delicately proportioned man. In questioning him, Tancredi referred to a book that looked to Guffey very much like the *Baltimore Catechism* he had used in grade school.

"Who made you?"

"God made me."

"Who is God?"

"God is the supreme being of heaven and earth Who made all things."

"Why did God make you?"

"God made me to love and honor Him on this earth and in the world to come."

The examination went on for about an hour. Gradually the questions became more difficult, dealing with infinitely compressible theological points, vast mysteries, proofs of refutations of proofs. Tancredi's scorched voice seemed almost eternal, a final moment burning beyond itself.

"It is affirmed that the Holy Ghost is present in raw opium. True or false?"

"True—if by 'present' it is meant that substantial form is not negated by first effects."

"It is affirmed that the One, Holy, Catholic and Apostolic Church, presided over by a Supreme Pontiff, Vicar of Christ on earth, is sole agent for and tributor of cut and uncut white crystalline narcotics on this earth, thus propagating the Holy Spirit and redeeming mankind. True or false?"

"Wait," Guffey said. "The boy needs help. He's no match for you, Tancredi. He can't be more than nineteen. Think of yourself at that age."

"I wrote fascist poems."

"You must be the good cop," the boy said. "We heard about you in North Africa. The drag-saint. Comforter of the afflicted."

"The earth is a woman," Guffey said. "Those who live on the earth are shaped to a woman's shape and comforted by a woman's form. Fortunately the commissioner's office understands this."

"Very well and good," Tancredi said. "Now that we have finished, it's time to begin again. This time you will not give the right answers but only the answers you believe in."

"I've done that."

"You believe nothing of this. We are the only believers. The syndicate is the true mystical body. We are powerful because we believe. We are untouchable because we believe. We are the Church and the Church is us. We live forever because we believe."

"He answered the questions," Guffey said. "How do you know he doesn't believe?"

"He has not the blood."

"Belief is lodged in the most remote places of the heart. You can't reach it even with threats of death."

"You claim to believe?" Tancredi said to the boy.

"Forever, yes."

"You will die for your beliefs?"

"I believe. Now more than ever."

"Then we will begin again. If you give the same answers, you prove you believe, and your life will end violently in a matter of minutes. Are you ready, courier-of-sand-to-the-gods-of-time?"

"I'm ready."

Tancredi reopened the book to the very beginning.

"Who made you?"

"Two normally functioning adults engaged in the act of copulation, with or without intent to engender further life, made me."

Tancredi smiled, his point won, his chilly brand of reason reaffirmed. He approached Guffey and kissed him lightly on each sparsely powdered cheek. Guffey left the club and headed into the night, horns blowing, bells ringing, the lame and the beggarly muttering their supplications. He walked past a woman pushing a baby carriage full of decomposing meat. On Forty-fourth Street he saw Killy Williams, an ex-prizefighter who spent his time directing traffic in the Times Square area. Williams tipped his porkpie hat to Guffey.

"Maybe you recall me," he said. "I fought prelims for six years at the old Garden. I possessed all the equipage to win big. But I was a man who liked to lose. I craved the emotionship of losing. There was a wonderment to it. I've always been complex and introspective. I liked to analyze my defeats. In victory there's nothing to analyze. It was my introspectability that made me a loser. My trainer was Wiggy Abandando, who handled some of the great ones. You probably recall him. Before every fight he'd slap me three times hard in the face. To get the mean blood running. But you can't exteriorize anger. It has to come from inside. I guess I'll head on over to Broadway now. I hear traffic's backed up to infinity."

Guffey hadn't gone half a block when he saw five patrolmen trying to surround the gypsy woman named Dark As The Cave Where My True Love Did Those Things. She seemed to be in a frenzy, scratching and hissing at the men, keeping them at a distance. Vastas Panowski, one of the cops, spotted Guffey and came over.

"Tommy, we can't control her. She won't let us get close enough to put a hand on her."

"What's she done?"

"She's been walking around all night trying to grab the crotches of passersby. I've never seen her this wild. She's been darting at every crotch in sight, like a mongoose. Capezio came by a little while ago and tried to take her in on a nine-fourteen. But she scared him away. He thought she was going to turn him into a wild goat or a lily pad if she ever got her hands on his crotch. He said that's how the curse works. The crotch is the focal point. If she gets to your crotch, she can turn you into one of four different things, depending on your astrological sign. Capezio's on a cusp."

"I want to talk to her," Guffey said.

He followed the patrolman toward the group. Everybody moved out of the way. Dark As The Cave fell to her knees at the sight of the bright maxi-dress.

"Lady Madonna."

"Anxiety is the broken bow of the man-tribe. Once that fact sinks in, you'll no longer be afraid. Go back to your storefront home and try not to get hypertense. Touch my hand and go quickly."

Guffey went down the block and turned a dark corner, aware that someone was following him—white, male, early fifties, grey-templed, six feet two, one ninety-five, tie-dyed snakeskin trousers, gold silk bow tie, buttonless black dinner jacket piped with black satin. Guffey waited in front of a side-street theatre exit, his handbag open and his fingers tickling blissfully at the smoky blue steel of the .38. The stranger approached him now, a Spode-faced man with platinum eyebrows and slightly puckered lips.

"I know who you are," the man said, "and I want to make a deal with you. Let me identify myself. Grambling Douglaston Clapper. The name may ring a bell. For the past three months my wife and I have been hosting a series of buffet dances in order to raise money for the United States Air Force, particularly the Strategic Air Command, one of my favorite branches of the military. But that's scarcely apropos. The point is as follows. We've recently become interested in possession by demons and we plan to start a nationwide chain of clinics, to be run on a franchise basis, devoted to exorcism and general postoperative therapy. We need somebody to run things from the spiritual standpoint. We're basically business-oriented, you see. The job will pay many times your present salary and there are stock options as well."

Guffey withdrew the .38 from his handbag and told the man to face the great metal door of the theatre. He hit him with the gun butt, just once, beneath the right ear. It was beginning to get light. Guffey walked over to Seventh Avenue, there to see Wilkie Kinbote, the perennially unemployed Jonsonian actor, lying in the gutter with his head resting on an empty bottle of eight-year-old Glenfiddich. A boy was divesting him of his Eton jacket, and two girls were using spoons and bottle openers in an attempt to extract some teeth. The kids scattered when they saw Guffey, who bent over the actor and cradled his purplish scabby face.

"Wilkie, it's me."

"I haven't felt this out-of-sorts in twenty years. Give me something to go, Lady M. Some hope. A reason to bear up."

"An English pasture of the mind."

"Is that it?" the actor said.

"A shady nook of the mind. A sort of grassy mental resting place. A leafy ensconcement. A mytho-lyrical bower deep in a dell."

"In actual point of fact, I'm beginning to see what you mean."

"Lemonade amid the trellis-work.

"Yes, go on."

"A greensward of the mind."

"Great God in boots, I think I see it."

Guffey got up, then extended his hand to be kissed. Across the street Erasmus von Hess y Vega, flanked by two catamites holding muzzled

Dobermans on short leashes, was giving a small group of tourists and drifters his standard sermon on the Fourth Reich, the realm of space and relativity brought into man's reach by the new knowledge trickling out of Germany—that the universe is tuba-shaped, that heavy industry is unknown in other solar systems, that the planet Uranus was once part of Germany, having been torn away in a monumental earth spasm countless eons ago, and is soon to be reclaimed by its rightful owner. Guffey listened awhile, standing next to Monsignor Bob Dockery, the abortionist priest. Then he went into an all-night cafeteria and had coffee at a table in the rear. Two groggy flies circled his cup. A girl in khaki screamed at him: "Fascist peeeg power structure! White peeeg police! People's justice for peeegs." The place was full of pigeon feeders, rejected blood donors, men drinking muscatel, eerie female derelicts with newspapered feet, those who fornicated with incubi, those who fingered unholy talismans. A clean-cut young man, remarkably tall and lanky, took the chair across from Guffey.

"They told me I might find you here," he said. "I used to play basketball at the University of Kentucky. We won S.E.C. honors three years running. I had athletic greatness in me. But I soon realized I carry within me a kind of divine spark, a missionary quality that impels me to seek dark corners in which to work some good. My name is Lee ("The Tree") McGee and I want to be a social worker. Tell me how to prepare."

"Read the accounts of the Black Plague," Guffey said. "Read the accounts of the Great Fire of London, the orgies of papal Avignon, the siege of Malta, the self-flagellation cults of the Rhine provinces, the burning of heretics, the Hundred Years' War. Check cross-references and bibliographies. Read on into the night."

"Who are the fallen, Lady Madonna?"

"The fallen are those who sin against God."

"Who are the just?"

"The just are those who sin against man."

"What is the greatest sorrow?"

"The greatest sorrow is simply to be."

Guffey walked slowly toward the precinct house. The sun was visible over silent construction sites, between the bones of partly demolished buildings, against the black glass of condemned skyscrapers. Inside, Capezio was questioning a strange ageless half-naked man; his head and upper body were totally without hair, no eyebrows or lashes or traces of beard, and his face conveyed the character of an off-white eraser at the end of a pencil. Capezio waved Guffey over.

"He says his name is Count Ugo Malatesta. He and his daughter or sister, we're not sure which she is, have been buying up teenage corpses from one of the medical centers in order to use the lungs, sex members and kidneys in some kind of unspeakable rite. The guy's a real wisenheimer; won't say anything without a lawyer. His sister or daughter is pregnant with his child, due any minute, so we sent her over to Rikers Island for delivery or incarceration, whichever comes first. I heard you took care of the gypsy woman before she could get to your crotch."

"She'll be all right for a while."

"We're dealing with medieval forces," Capezio said.

"That's very true, Vincent."

Suddenly the hairless man dropped to the floor in a fit of mad drooling laughter. Guffey went upstairs to his locker, freshly painted in the unruly blue of a Blakean apocalypse. He undressed, got cleaned up and put on his trousers, shoes, shirt and sport coat. He was straightening his tie when he realized he wasn't alone. Sitting at a chessboard in a distant corner of the room, apparently waiting for a challenger, was the man called Blessed Gondolfo, a polydactyl albino dwarf who bore the stigmata.

Guffey returned the .38 to his shoulder holster. He pounded his right fist into the palm of his left hand nine times. Then he left the precinct house and took the subway home to Queens.

The Death of Justina

John Cheever

So help me God, it gets more and more preposterous, it corresponds less and less to what I remember and what I expect, as if the force of life were centrifugal and threw one further and further away from one's purest memories and ambitions; and I can barely recall the old house where I was raised, where in midwinter Parma violets bloomed in a cold frame near the kitchen door and down the long corridor, past the seven views of Rome— up two steps and down three—one entered the library where all the books were in order, the lamps were bright, where there was a fire and a dozen bottles of good bourbon, locked in a cabinet with a veneer like tortoise shell whose silver key my father wore on his watch chain. Just let me give you one example and if you disbelieve me look honestly into your own past and see if you can't find a comparable experience . . .

758

The Death of Justina

* * *

On Saturday the doctor told me to stop smoking and drinking and I did. I won't go into the commonplace symptoms of withdrawal, but I would like to point out that, standing at my window in the evening, watching the brilliant afterlight and the spread of darkness, I felt, through the lack of these humble stimulants, the force of some primitive memory in which the coming of night with its stars and its moon was apocalyptic. I thought suddenly of the neglected graves of my three brothers on the mountainside and that death is a loneliness much crueler than any loneliness hinted at in life. The soul (I thought) does not leave the body, but lingers with it through every degrading stage of decomposition and neglect, through heat, through cold, through the long winter nights when no one comes with a wreath or a plant and no one says a prayer. This unpleasant premonition was followed by anxiety. We were going out for dinner and I thought that the oil burner would explode in our absence and burn the house. The cook would get drunk and attack my daughter with a carving knife, or my wife and I would be killed in a collision on the main highway, leaving our children bewildered orphans with nothing in life to look forward to but sadness. I was able to observe, along with these foolish and terrifying anxieties, a definite impairment to my discretionary poles. I felt as if I were being lowered by ropes into the atmosphere of my childhood. I told my wife—when she passed through the living room—that I had stopped smoking and drinking but she didn't seem to care and who would reward me for my privations? Who cared about the bitter taste in my mouth and that my head seemed to be leaving my shoulders? It seemed to me that men had honored one another with medals, statuary and cups for much less and that abstinence is a social matter. When I abstain from sin it is more often a fear of scandal than a private resolve to improve on the purity of my heart, but here was a call for abstinence without the worldly enforcement of society, and death is not the threat that scandal is. When it was time for us to go out I was so lightheaded that I had to ask my wife to drive the car. On Sunday I sneaked seven cigarettes in various hiding places and drank two Martinis in the downstairs coat closet. At breakfast on Monday my English muffin stared up at me from the plate. I mean I *saw* a face there in the rough, toasted surface. The moment of recognition was fleeting, but it was deep, and I wondered who it had been. Was it a friend, an aunt, a sailor, a ski instructor, a bartender or a conductor on a train? The smile faded off the muffin, but it had been there for a second—the sense of a person, a life, a pure force of gentleness and censure, and I am convinced that the muffin had contained the presence of some spirit. As you can see, I was nervous.

On Monday my wife's old cousin, Justina, came to visit her. Justina was a lively guest, although she must have been crowding eighty. On Tuesday my wife gave her a lunch party. The last guest left at three and a few minutes later, Cousin Justina, sitting on the living-room sofa with a glass of brandy, breathed her last. My wife called me at the office and I said that I would be right out. I was clearing my desk when my boss, MacPherson, came in.

"Spare me a minute," he asked. "I've been bird-dogging all over the place, trying to track you down. Pierson had to leave early and I want you to write the last Elixircol commercial."

"Oh, I can't, Mac," I said. "My wife just called. Cousin Justina is dead."

"You write that commercial," he said. His smile was satanic. "Pierson had to leave early because his grandmother fell off a stepladder."

Now I don't like fictional accounts of office life. It seems to me that if you are going to write fiction you should write about mountain-climbing and tempests at sea and I will go over my predicament with MacPherson briefly, aggravated as it was by his refusal to respect and honor the death of dear old Justina. It was like MacPherson. It was a good example of the way I've been treated. He is, I might say, a tall, splendidly groomed man of about sixty who changes his shirt three times a day, romances his secretary every afternoon between two and two-thirty and makes the habit of continuously chewing gum seem hygienic and elegant. I write his speeches for him and it has not been a happy arrangement for me. If the speeches are successful, MacPherson takes all the credit. I can see that his presence, his tailor and his fine voice are all a part of the performance, but it makes me angry never to be given credit for what was said. On the other hand, if the speeches are unsuccessful—if his presence and his voice can't carry the hour—his threatening and sarcastic manner is surgical and I am obliged to contain myself in the role of a man who can do no good in spite of the piles of congratulatory mail that my eloquence sometimes brings in. I must pretend, I must, like an actor, study and improve on my pretension, to have nothing to do with his triumphs and I must bow my head gracefully in shame when we have both failed. I am forced to appear grateful for injuries, to lie, to smile falsely and to play out a role as asinine and as unrelated to the facts as a minor prince in an operetta, but if I speak the truth it will be my wife and my children who will pay in hardships for my outspokenness. Now he refused to respect or even to admit the solemn fact of a death in our family and if I couldn't rebel it seemed as if I could at least hint at it.

The commercial he wanted me to write was for a tonic called Elixircol and was to be spoken on television by an actress who was neither young nor beautiful, but who had an appearance of ready abandon and who was anyhow the mistress of one of the sponsor's uncles. *Are you growing old?* I wrote. *Are you falling out of love with your image in the looking glass? Does your face in the morning seem rucked and seamed with alcoholic and sexual excesses and does the rest of you appear to be a grayish-pink lump, covered all over with brindle hair? Walking in the autumn woods, do you feel that subtle distance has come between you and the smell of wood smoke? Have you drafted your obituary? Are you easily winded? Do you wear a girdle? Is your sense of smell fading, is your interest in gardening waning, is your fear of heights increasing and are your sexual drives as ravening and intense as ever and does your wife look more and more to you like a stranger with sunken cheeks who has wandered into your bedroom by mistake? If this or any of of this is true you need Elixircol, the true juice of youth. The small economy size* (business with the bottle) *costs seventy-five dollars and the giant family bottle comes at two hundred and fifty. It's a lot of scratch, God knows, but these are inflationary times and who can put a price on youth? If you don't have the cash, borrow it from your neighborhood loan shark or hold up the local bank. The odds are three to one that with a ten-cent water pistol and a slip of paper you can shake ten thousand out of any fainthearted teller. Everybody's doing it.* (Music up and out.)

I sent this into MacPherson via Ralphie, the messenger boy, and took the 4:16 home, traveling through a landscape of utter desolation.

Now my journey is a digression and has no real connection to Justina's death, but what followed could only have happened in my country and in my time and since I was an American traveling across an American landscape, the trip may be part of the sum. There are some Americans who, although their fathers emigrated from the old world three centuries ago, never seem to have quite completed the voyage, and I am one of these. I stand, figuratively, with one wet foot on Plymouth Rock, looking with some delicacy, not into a formidable and challenging wilderness but onto a half-finished civilization embracing glass towers, oil derricks, suburban continents and abandoned movie houses and wondering why, in this most prosperous, equitable and accomplished world—where even the cleaning women practice the Chopin preludes in their spare time—everyone should seem to be so disappointed?

At Proxmire Manor I was the only passenger to get off the random, meandering and profitless local that carried its shabby lights off into the dusk like some game-legged watchman or beadle, making his appointed rounds. I went around to the front of the station to wait for my wife and to enjoy the traveler's fine sense of crises. Above me on the hill was my home and the homes of my friends, all lighted and smelling of fragrant wood smoke like the temples in a sacred grove, dedicated to monogamy, feckless childhood and domestic bliss, but so like a dream that I felt the lack of viscera with much more than poignance—the absence of that inner dynamism we respond to in some European landscapes. In short, I was disappointed. It was my country, my beloved country and there have been mornings when I could have kissed the earth that covers its many provinces and states. There was a hint of bliss—romantic and domestic bliss. I seemed to hear the jingle bells of the sleigh that would carry me to grandmother's house, although in fact grandmother spent the last years of her life working as a hostess on an ocean liner and was lost in the tragic sinking of the *S.S. Lorelei* and I was responding to a memory that I had not experienced. But the hill of light rose like an answer to some primitive dream of homecoming. On one of the highest lawns I saw the remains of a snowman who still smoked a pipe and wore a scarf and a cap, but whose form was wasting away and whose anthracite eyes stared out at the view with terrifying bitterness. I sensed some disappointing greenness of spirit in the scene, although I knew in my bones, no less, how like yesterday it was that my father left the old world to found a new; and I thought of the forces that had brought stamina to the image: the cruel towns of Calabria with their cruel princes, the badlands northwest of Dublin, ghettos, despots, whorehouses, bread lines, the graves of children. Intolerable hunger, corruption, persecution and despair had generated these faint and mellow lights and wasn't all a part of the great migration that is the life of man?

My wife's cheeks were wet with tears when I kissed her. She was distressed, of course, and really quite sad. She had been attached to Justina. She drove me home where Justina was still sitting on the sofa. I would like to spare you the unpleasant details, but I will say that both her mouth and her eyes were wide open. I went into the pantry to telephone Dr. Hunter. His line was busy. I poured myself a drink—the first since Sunday—and lighted a cigarette. When I called the doctor again he answered and I told him what had happened. "Well, I'm awfully sorry to hear about it, Moses," he said. "I can't get over until after six and there isn't much that I can do. This sort of thing has come up before and I'll tell you all I know. You see you live in a B zone—two-acre lots, no commercial enterprises, and so forth. A couple of years ago some stranger bought the old Plewett mansion and it turned out that he was planning to operate it as a funeral home. We didn't have any zoning provision at the time that would protect us and one was rushed through the village council at midnight and they overdid it. It seems that you not only can't have a funeral home in zone B—you can't bury anything there and you can't die there. Of course it's absurd, but we all make mistakes, don't we?

"Now there are two things you can do. I've had to deal with this

ESQUIRE'S BIG BOOK OF FICTION

before. You can take the old lady and put her into the car and drive her over to Chestnut Street where zone C begins. The boundary is just beyond the traffic light by the high school. As soon as you get her over to zone C, it's all right. You can just say she died in the car. You can do that or if this seems distasteful you can call the mayor and ask him to make an exception to the zoning laws. But I can't write you out a death certificate until you get her out of that neighborhood and of course no undertaker will touch her until you get a death certificate."

"I don't understand," I said, and I didn't, but then the possibility that there was some truth in what he had just told me broke against me or over me like a wave, exciting mostly indignation. "I've never heard such a lot of damned foolishness in my life," I said. "Do you mean to tell me that I can't die in one neighborhood and that I can't fall in love in another and that I can't eat. . . ."

"Listen. Calm down, Moses. I'm not telling you anything but the facts and I have a lot of patients waiting. I don't have the time to listen to you fulminate. If you want to move her, call me as soon as you get her over to the traffic light. Otherwise, I'd advise you to get in touch with the mayor or someone on the village council." He cut the connection. I was outraged, but this did not change the fact that Justina was still sitting on the sofa. I poured a fresh drink and lit another cigarette.

Justina seemed to be waiting for me and to be changing from an inert into a demanding figure. I tried to imagine carrying her out to the station wagon, but I couldn't complete the task in my imagination and I was sure that I couldn't complete it in fact. I then called the mayor, but his position in our village is mostly honorary and as I might have known he was in his New York law office and was not expected home until seven. I could cover her, I thought; that would be a decent thing to do, and I went up the back stairs to the linen closet and got a sheet. It was getting dark when I came back into the living room, but this was no merciful twilight. Dusk seemed to be playing directly into her hands and she had gained power and stature with the dark. I covered her with the sheet and turned on a lamp at the other end of the room, but the rectitude of the place with its old furniture, flowers, paintings, etc. was demolished by her monumental shape. The next thing to worry about was the children, who would be home in a few minutes. Their knowledge of death, excepting their dreams and intuitions of which I know nothing, is zero and the bold figure in the parlor was bound to be traumatic. When I heard them coming up the walk I went out and told them what had happened and sent them up to their rooms. At seven I drove over to the mayor's.

He had not come home, but he was expected at any minute and I talked with his wife. She gave me a drink. By this time I was chain-smoking. When the mayor came in we went into a little office or library where he took up a position behind a desk, putting me in the low chair of a supplicant.

"Of course I sympathize with you, Moses," he said, settling back in his chair. "It's an awful thing to have happened, but the trouble is that we can't give you a zoning exception without a majority vote of the village council and all the members of the council happen to be out of town. Pete's in California and Jack's in Paris and Larry won't be back from Stowe until the end of the week."

I was sarcastic. "Then I suppose Cousin Justina will have to gracefully decompose in my parlor until Jack comes back from Paris."

"Oh, no" he said, "oh, *no*. Jack won't be back from Paris for another month, but I think you might wait until Larry comes from Stowe. Then we'd have a majority, assuming of course that they would agree to your appeal."

"For Christ's sake," I snarled.

"Yes, yes," he said, "it is difficult, but after all you must realize that this is the world you live in and the importance of zoning can't be overestimated. Why, if a single member of the council could give out zoning exceptions, I could give you permission right now to open a saloon in your garage, put up neon lights, hire an orchestra and destroy the neighborhood and all the human and commercial values we've worked so hard to protect."

"I don't want to open a saloon in my garage," I howled. "I don't want to hire an orchestra. I just want to bury Justina."

"I know, Moses, I know," he said. "I understand that. But it's just that it happened in the wrong zone and if I make an exception for you I'll have to make an exception for everyone, and this kind of morbidity, when it gets out of hand, can be very depressing. People don't like to live in a neighborhood where this sort of thing goes on all the time."

"Listen to me," I said. "You give me an exception and you give it to me now or I'm going home and dig a hole in my garden and bury Justina myself."

"But you can't do that, Moses. You can't bury anything in zone B. You can't even bury a cat.

"You're mistaken," I said. "I can and I will. I can't function as a doctor and I can't function as an undertaker, but I can dig a hole in the ground and if you don't give me my exception, that's what I'm going to do."

I got out of the low chair before I finished speaking and started for the door.

"Come back, Moses, come back," he said. "Please come back. Look, I'll give you an exception if you'll promise not to tell anyone. It's breaking the law, it's a forgery, but I'll do it if you promise to keep it a secret."

I promised to keep it a secret, he gave me the documents and I used his telephone to make the arrangements. Justina was removed a few minutes after I got home, but that night I had the strangest dream.

I dreamed that I was in a crowded supermarket. It must have been night because the windows were dark. The ceiling was paved with fluorescent light—brilliant, cheerful, but, considering our prehistoric memories, a harsh link in the chain of light that binds us to the past. Music was playing and there must have been at least a thousand shoppers pushing their wagons among the long corridors of comestibles and victuals. Now is there—or isn't there—something about the posture we assume when we push a wagon that unsexes us? Can it be done with gallantry? I bring this up because the multitude of shoppers seemed that evening, as they pushed their wagons, penitential and unsexed. There were all kinds, this being my beloved country. There were Italians, Finns, Jews, Negroes, Shropshiremen, Cubans—anyone who had heeded the voice of liberty—and they were dressed with that sumptuary abandon that European caricaturists record with such bitter disgust. Yes, there were grandmothers in shorts, big-butted women in knitted pants, and men wearing such an assortment of clothing that it looked as if they had dressed hurriedly in a burning building. But this, as I say, is my own country and in my opinion the caricaturist who vilifies the old lady in shorts vilifies himself. I am a native and I was wearing buckskin jump boots, chino pants cut so tight that my sexual organs were discernible and a rayon acetate pajama top printed with representations of the *Pinta*, the *Nina* and the *Santa Maria* in full sail. The scene was strange—the strangeness of a dream where we see familiar objects in an unfamiliar light, but as I looked more closely I saw that there were some irregularities. Nothing was labeled. Nothing was identified or known. The cans and boxes were all bare. The frozen-food bins were full of brown parcels, but they were such odd shapes that you couldn't tell if they contained a frozen turkey or a Chinese dinner. All the goods at the vegetable and the bakery counters were concealed in brown bags and even the books for sale had no titles. In spite of the fact that the contents of nothing was known, my companions of the dream—my thousands of bizarrely dressed compatriots—were deliberating gravely over these mysterious containers as if the choices they made were critical. Like any dreamer, I was omniscient—I was with them and I was withdrawn—and stepping above the scene for a minute I noticed the men at the check-out counters. They were brutes. Now sometimes in a crowd, in a bar or a street, you will see a face so full-blown in its obdurate resistance to the appeals of love, reason and decency—so lewd, so brutish and unregenerate—that you turn away. Men like these were stationed at the only way out and as the shoppers approached them they tore their packages open—I still couldn't see what they contained but in every case the customer, at the sight of what he had chosen, showed all the symptoms of the deepest guilt; that force that brings us to our knees. Once their choice had been opened, to their shame they were pushed—in some cases kicked—toward the door and beyond the door I saw dark water and heard a terrible noise of moaning and crying in the air. They waited at the door in groups to be taken away in some conveyance that I couldn't see. As I watched, thousands and thousands pushed their wagons through the market, made their careful and mysterious choices and were reviled and taken away. What could be the meaning of this?

We buried Justina in the rain the next afternoon. The dead are not, God knows, a minority, but in Proxmire Manor their unexalted kingdom is on the outskirts, rather like a dump, where they are transported furtively as knaves and scoundrels and where they lie in an atmosphere of perfect neglect. Justina's life had been exemplary, but by ending it she seemed to have disgraced us all. The priest was a friend and a cheerful sight, but the undertaker and his helpers, hiding behind their limousines, were not, and aren't they at the root of most of our troubles with their claim that death is a violet-flavored kiss? How can a people who do not mean to understand death hope to understand love and who will sound the alarm?

I went from the cemetery back to my office.

The commercial was on my desk and MacPherson had written across it in large letters in grease pencil: "Very funny, you broken-down bore. Do again."

I was tired but unrepentant and didn't seem able to force myself into a practical posture of usefulness and obedience. I did another commercial.

Don't lose your loved ones because of excessive radioactivity. Don't be a wallflower at the dance because of strontium 90 in your bones. Don't be a victim of fallout. When the tart on 38th Street gives you the big eye, does your body stride off in one direction and your imagination in another? Does your mind follow her up the stairs and taste her wares in revolting detail while your flesh goes off to Brooks Brothers or the foreign-exchange desk of the Chase Manhattan Bank? Haven't you noticed the size of the ferns, the lushness of the grass, the bitterness of the string beans and the brilliant markings on the new breeds of butterflies? You have been inhaling lethal atomic waste for the last twenty-five years and only Elixircol can save you.

I gave this copy to Ralphie and waited perhaps ten minutes, when it was returned, marked again with grease pencil. "Do," he wrote, "or you'll be dead."

I felt very tired. I returned to the typewriter, put another piece of paper into the machine and wrote: *The Lord is my Shepherd, therefore can I lack nothing. He shall feed me in a green pasture and lead me forth beside the waters of comfort. He shall convert my soul and bring me forth in the paths of righteousness for his Name's sake. Yea, though I walk through the valley of the shadow of death I will fear no evil for thou art with me; thy rod and thy staff comfort me. Thou shalt prepare a table for me in the presence of them that trouble me; thou hast anointed my head with oil and my cup shall be full. Surely thy loving kindness and thy mercy shall follow me all the days of my life and I will dwell in the house of the Lord forever.* I gave this to Ralphie and went home.

The Wish

Joanna Scott

Kamon Gilbert woke up on the morning of the last day of his life at 6:19 and in the minute before his alarm went off thought something to this effect: to exist in space, to have a body that can be aroused, senses that give proof of joy, to be in love, to be in love and alive, to love Jenny Templin and to know Jenny loved him, to know the feeling of love, to know they'd have a child soon—why, it was all a fortunate accident, luck, a gift of chance, one sperm out of millions, one egg with the odds against it, the world already crowded, stasis always easier than growth, nothing always dominating something, so life could never be more than a minute fraction of its own potential—

". . . 'Cause the Sunshine Boy got the weather for you right after . . ."

Kamon slammed his hand down on the clock radio's snooze button. Jenny stirred beside him but remained asleep. She'd thrown off the sheets and blankets during the night, and Kamon had only to lift her T-shirt to reveal the mountain of her belly. He lay beside her, resting on an elbow, and with his free hand felt the taut skin hiding the form that would be their child in two months. And he went right on thinking:

An image like stepping-stones, patches of light on custard skin, drawing his mind not from foreground to background, as it would have if he'd composed the shot (knowing as he did a little, far too little, about monocular perspective), but from foreground to that dimension behind any image—the past. All images had stories to tell, causes to explain. In the case of Jenny's swollen belly, the cause was, as Kamon had put it to his friends, "bumping without a body bag." He was proud of what they'd done, their exquisite faith in each other, and yeah, he'd been dismayed when she refused to have it undone, yet by then he was hopelessly in love with her, loving their dark/pale symmetry, loving what he hoped to make her, bringing her along up through life as he went up instead of kicking her to the curb, which is what his cousin Taft told him to do. Oh, Taft liked to give her the red-eye now that they were living in his apartment, never mind what he said. He enjoyed Jenny Templin's good looks even if he liked to say that Kamon's life was damn well over, an opinion that became to Kamon an energizing challenge. He was just beginning—he knew this for a fact, knew that while other guys would have walked away from the situation, he was going to stick it out with Jenny, make himself a family to take care of, and go on loving what he already loved: the girl made of velvet opening her legs to him, going up with him when he went up.

Don't mind that she's white.

Loving her not because of the color of her skin, though not in spite of it, either. He'd admit there were times he minded. He'd even found himself wishing, once things started to get heavy, that she'd spent longer in the oven and been roasted to a darker shade. But he loved what they became together, their contrasts, the balance of light and shadow. Stepping-stones of light. He knew how to look at them together, his hand many shades darker than her belly, the picture enhanced by contrast. Yet what he really wanted was to move the image through the lens of a camera and save it once and for all on paper.

He just had to keep himself from going too fast. Had to learn all he could about the behavior of light during an interval of time. Had to take advantage of time and get himself properly educated. He could look all he wanted, but he had to get educated if he meant to turn looking into a trade and move up from the bottom. He never doubted his potential. He was busting with talent—everyone thought so. Kamon Gilbert, seventeen years old, acting day in and day out like a celebrity, pretending that he couldn't help being as handsome as his daddy, smart to boot, and quick and good at everything he tried out, his special destiny written all over him, bringing girls in a bar over to his table to ask, "Who are you? You must be someone famous. . . ."

Not yet, baby girl, but soon, as long as he didn't lose his way. Sticking to a white girl who was having his child might have added to his journey an extra loop, but he hadn't stopped heading up. If anything, Jenny made him more bent on doing the best he could. Maybe she wasn't busting with talent like Kamon, but she had a kind of courage he could learn from—the courage to try anything, to pick up and start over. She was no average recruit. Why, look at her. Keep looking. The soft point of her chin. The curve downward at the corners of her almond eyes. All the shades of yellow and brown in her hair. Her lips slightly parted. Her tongue moving inside her mouth as she dreamed of love.

Dreaming, wasn't she, of what they'd done? Kamon lying flat as a carpet runner while Jenny licked the salt off him. Jenny straddling Kamon, Kamon straddling Jenny, Kamon building up wet friction, feeling the thrill, again and again, of making love as though for the first time, brown nipple filling his mouth, bodies lying side by side, front to back, upside down, the furnace inside her, cold toes curling against her calves, lips latched onto the ridge of his collarbone, thoughts all jumbled by pleasure, his pleasure shored up by his faith in eternity and hers by fear, Kamon assuming they'd love each other forever, Jenny assuming that something this good couldn't last.

Kamon watched her sleep, thinking about how they'd climb back into this same bed at the end of the day and make love as best they could, lifting themselves up and over the custard mountain of their baby, and when they were done they'd wonder how that mountain could ever come out of her, their baby growing bigger every day.

No denying their lives would have been easier if Jenny had agreed to give up that clump of cells inside her before it got itself a soul. But she wanted a baby, so Kamon made himself want what she wanted, accepting fatherhood as another challenge and thinking ahead, trying to imagine the face of his child but unable to sort through all the possible images to find the one that would greet him in two months, reminding himself as he lay there, his hand still resting on Jenny's belly, that he sure had plenty to learn about photographic composition before his child was born, especially if he wanted to make a record of the baby's opening act. And this kind of thinking made him consider how proud he was to be fathering a child who'd be as lucky as this child, what with Kamon and Jenny and all of Kamon's family loving him as they would, Kamon and Jenny heading up in the world, up and up and up, nothing stopping them as long as they made the necessary effort.

Yeah! exclaimed the baby, shifting abruptly, pressing an eager foot into the wall of its sac, a motion that felt to Kamon like a mouse bouncing against his palm, transforming his pleasant, lazy contemplation into awe. A body inside a body, one asleep, the other awake—Christ almighty! Fucking weird, man! He'd like to catch that on film somehow, some way: motion inside stillness. Except he'd used up his allotment of contact paper at school and couldn't afford to buy more and had sworn off begging extras from his art teacher, Mr. Manelli, a white hot-sauce boss who made it all too clear that Kamon was his favorite.

Which reminded him, oh shit, that he was supposed to have finished *Hamlet* for his English class. *See you later, peanut!* He pulled the sheet over Jenny's bare belly, kissed her lightly on the cheek, and turned off the pending alarm on the clock radio. He dressed quickly in jeans and a ratty T-shirt under his flannel shirt and walked in bare feet along the cold hallway of his cousin Taft's apartment to the kitchen. He made coffee, and while the coffee was dripping, he ate two big bowls of cereal and paged through the final scenes of *Hamlet*, got as far as the sparrow's providential fall, and chose to spend the last minutes before he left the apartment not finishing the play but instead grooming himself in the bathroom, for wasn't it more than likely that his English teacher would assign him the role of Hamlet during class? He'd already read the parts of Romeo and Julius Caesar. And now this: *If it be now, 'tis not to come; if it be not to come, it will be now.*

At 3:05 P.M., two old women in the East Avenue McDonald's waited at the counter for their order. One said, "I got mice. Mice!"

"Mice?" the other asked.

"In my apartment. They wake me up at night."

Kamon stood behind them but moved forward when a girl appeared at another register to take his order. He bought a large milk shake and fries and walked to a far booth so he could be alone and spend a few minutes calming himself down, untying the knot of anger, loops as tight as the muscles in his neck after a day spent at the snake pit that was his school, every student there bent on bringing Kamon down—hating him, if they were white, because he was a nigger, hating him, if they were black, because he was exceptional when measured against the rest of them by the teachers and their standardized tests. *Kamon Gilbert this and Kamon Gilbert that. Kamon, you're jack shit, busting your balls over white pussy.* So he kept to himself between classes, and he stopped eating lunch altogether so he wouldn't have to face the cafeteria mob. And at the end of the school day, he always ended up here, at the McDonald's across from the garage where he worked, so hungry that he ate two fistfuls of fries as he walked to the table.

A few minutes later, he took the lid off his milk shake and shook the last bit into his mouth. He stood up again, noticing with some pleasure that the white lady with mice in her apartment reached for her purse and placed it securely on her lap as he passed behind her chair. She kept her back to him, but her friend followed Kamon with her eyes, that ancient terror making her hands tremble just enough that a few drops of coffee splashed out of her wobbly cup and she had to set it down.

Kamon couldn't leave without saying hello. He stopped in front of the door, swung around, and as he pulled on gloves, filthy black woolen gloves snipped to leave his fingers bare, he said, "Afternoon, ladies!" They didn't reply. "I was wondering if you knew the time?" They were silent for a period that threatened to stretch into tomorrow, until finally the lady with the mice turned to look straight at Kamon and, without glancing at her wristwatch, said, "Three-eighteen," grinning warmly as though to signal her forgiveness.

"That's all right then," Kamon said, returning the smile. But his smile was ineffectual, or else the lady proved more resilient than he'd expected. She kept grinning, leaving him nothing else to do but nod his farewell.

At the garage he found the owner, Paul, at his computer, tapping numbers into the customer-service program. "Fucking gas thief," Paul muttered, banging his index finger against the enter key in an attempt to pound information out of the computer. He snatched a set of keys from a drawer and threw them at Kamon, who had yet to speak.

"Tan Honda Civic, '87 or '88." Paul scribbled the license number on a piece of scrap paper. "Get the bastard," he growled, pressing the paper into Kamon's hand.

So someone had driven away without paying for their gasoline. Another fucking runner, another gas thief, petty stuff—the police had better things to do than respond to such a complaint. If Paul wanted the money for his gasoline, he had to track down the thieves on his own. He'd copy the plate number from the video and try to find the owner's name in the computer's database—with a name and address, he could send a nasty letter. Without the information, his only chance of reimbursement was to catch the crooks on the road. And since Paul himself had better things to do than go chasing cars like a dog, he usually sent one of his mechanics, whoever happened to be close by.

Kamon took Paul's Corvette and headed in the direction Paul had pointed him, knowing that he didn't have much of a chance of catching up to the Civic but thinking that if he did, he'd force the guy off the road, flashing that friendly smile of his, waving through the window, mouthing happily, *I'm gonna kill you!* Problem was, Kamon couldn't read Paul's handwriting, so when he did spot a tan Honda Civic a few miles down the road, he couldn't be sure whether the driver, a middle-aged Asian woman, was really his fugitive. He decided against a confrontation, just drove on in a leisurely way for a while, thinking that he didn't mind working for Paul, not just because the pay was good or because he got to take Paul's Corvette for a spin once in a while, but because the other mechanics didn't despise him. In the garage, unlike at school, Kamon was considered *good enough*, not worse because he was better than the rest of them in any obvious way.

Good enough to grab a quarter-inch ratchet from the toolbox for Paul's cousin Jeff, who when Kamon returned to the garage was in the process of prying off a brake shoe, but not so good he could upload the idle speed into an engine computer or scan information about a malfunctioning brake system or change the setting on a lock. Good enough to work the alignment machine and balance the wheels on an '89 Ford Escort and, of course, to straighten up the drawer of midsized screwdrivers, but not good enough to explain to the owner of a '92 Saab that he would have to pay one hundred thirty-eight dollars and fifty cents just so Paul could take apart the fuel-injection system to find out what was wrong, because the car's diagnostic system couldn't find the problem.

"Kamon, grease the rod ends of this dinky, will ya?"

So Kamon pulled the grease gun away from the bulk oil dispenser and started filling up an outer rod end, stopping a second too late—thick black grease bubbled out of the ball joint and splattered his shirt. Paul was still on the phone with a customer, and Darryl had stepped behind the alignment rack to help Jeff with the brake shoe, so no one noticed Kamon's mistake. He wiped the grease with a gloved hand and moved beneath the car to get at the inner joint, listening as he worked to a song on the radio: *"My snake-hipped, red-lipped, wild revolutionary man . . ."*

Paul was honest and fair, though permanently angry at the world, with his spongy features bunched up in a scowl and his voice crackling with resentment. By his own account, he'd never recovered from the change in the industry, twenty years ago, to the metric system. He had two large cabinets for tools—just to see them made him mad, since back in the old days a mechanic needed a single drawer of tools, sizing was simple, and an experienced mechanic could measure a socket with his eye. With the metric system, the fucking metric system, nothing was simple. Yet Paul continued to blame himself for the confusion and slammed his hand against something hard whenever he grabbed the wrong ratchet. *What's experience worth when everything's changing so fast?* He'd tried out that question on Kamon more than once, and Kamon had tried out an answer:

You learn from experience how to learn from experience.

Kamon, what the fuck are you talking about?

What was he talking about? Smart-ass Kamon, he should have learned from experience to keep his mouth shut, since what he couldn't do was explain himself accurately. He was quick at calculations, could write an elegant sentence, could take a fine photograph, but he couldn't explain how to do any of it and so couldn't make himself understood.

Kamon finished greasing the front rod ends, then moved to the rear of the car, listening as he worked to a song by Blind Willie Johnson on the radio: *"Jesus, make up my dying bed . . ."* And while he squirted grease, Kamon started thinking something like this: How much easier it would be to give up all his ambitions, drop out of school, and work for Paul full-time. If he kept working in the garage the rest of his life, he'd be a good enough mechanic, nothing special. He'd earn good enough money, enough to support his family, and if Jenny went back to work they'd have more than enough, and maybe they'd have a few more babies and eventually they'd buy a house of their own, his folks would watch the babies so Jenny and Kamon could go out, catch a movie, go dancing even, and they'd have friends who wouldn't hate them, they'd have fun, and the only pictures

Kamon would ever take would be the ones for Jenny to put in their albums to serve as a visible measure of time.

Kamon lifted the edges of his gloves and pulled them inside out and off his hands, then held his dirty hands close to his face to breathe deeply that intoxicating smell of oil and gasoline and grease.

Yeah, this would be a good enough life, he thought again. As good a life as any he could imagine.

* * *

6:25, Kamon and Jenny ate sausage-and-pepper pizza and watched a reporter on the local news make a pitch for an animal shelter, asking viewers to consider adopting one or more of the dozens of cats taken from a filthy house on the south side, the owner a feeble, eighty-seven-year-old woman. Then at

6:37 Jenny went to pee and Kamon began his homework, reading the assigned chapter about ionic bonds, the donation of electrons, the positive ion of sodium, the negative ion of chloride, the miracle of sodium chloride, the process of molecular dissociation. While he was reading, Jenny tiptoed behind him and started to massage his shoulders, and Kamon would have given himself over to her if Taft hadn't walked in right at

7:00, ducking into the kitchen, snatching a piece of cold pizza from the table in front of Kamon's textbook, muttering his end-of-the-day greeting, something like *Heya*, or *Hey there*, before sinking his teeth into the pizza and disappearing into his bedroom, leaving Jenny and Kamon alone again, though now Jenny had turned back to the television and with the remote changed the channel to a game show, which she and Kamon watched until

7:15, when a commercial for Worthco Appliances came on and Jenny said about her stepdad, who worked for Worthco, "I wish that asshole would drop dead," and Kamon said, "Make peace with him—maybe he'll give us a washing machine," and Jenny said, "Yeah, right," both of them watching in silence until

7:30, and then Kamon continued with his homework and Jenny lay on the sofa and read a magazine. The basketball game started at

9:00, so she and Kamon sat on the sofa together and Taft sat on his Taft throne, a plump, ragged, pinstriped armchair he'd found on the street. They shouted at the television, cursed the referees, cheered on the players, and threw pillows across the room when someone missed a free throw, until

11:15, when Taft offered to pay Kamon twenty dollars just to go out and get him some cigarettes, so Kamon put on Taft's jacket and his own orange ski hat, kissed Jenny good-bye, and headed to the deli, thinking as he went that his cousin Taft was dumber than dumb and bullish enough that Kamon didn't feel badly about taking advantage of him, charging twenty dollars for an errand that would cost Kamon no more than twenty minutes. Not a bad deal. But shit, he hadn't expected it to be so cold, and as he walked away from the apartment house he pinched the collar of his coat closed and ducked his head against the wind, continuing at a pace just short of a jog, so at

11:24:07 he had reached the corner of Buffalo Avenue and Raymond Street, and at

11:24:12 the door to the deli on the next block opened, and at

11:24:15 Kamon saw the two figures hurtling down the sidewalk toward him. His first confused thought, having spent the last two hours watching basketball, was that he was witnessing a calculated play in some kind of game, with the boys instructed by a coach to run just as they were and at same point to pivot as they continued to run and look back at the deli, gesturing with their handguns at the door, which was still in the process of easing shut on its springs. What they hadn't planned on was this: By the time they had turned their heads back in the direction they were sprinting, Kamon had already arrived on the scene and by his mere presence interrupted the smooth play, forcing the boy in front to sidestep to avoid him and causing the one behind to cross his right leg in front of his left and stumble, catch himself, then hit a patch of watery ice so his left foot slid out from under him and he fell down hard on his ass in front of Kamon, who still confused, reached out a hand for the boy in order to help him to his feet and at

11:24:23 recognized, or thought he recognized, between the scarf wound around the boy's mouth and nose and the ski hat pulled low on his head, the eyes of someone he knew at school—*What was his name?*—someone who belonged to the mob of students who hated Kamon Gilbert, someone Kamon hadn't bothered to distinguish as an individual, so now he couldn't come up with a name, despite his sense of recognition. *Who are you?* Kamon wondered as he bent slightly at the waist, preparing to offer the boy an elbow, since the boy hadn't accepted his hand. *Who are you?* Feeling at once a sharp sense of pity because the boy was obviously scared of him, though Kamon meant no harm and wanted to reassure him, started to consider what he might say, perhaps introduce himself, though if Kamon recognized the boy, then the boy surely recognized Kamon—everyone at school knew Kamon, *Kamon Gilbert this and Kamon Gilbert that*—and in fact he looked at Kamon now with a glittery squint as if to beg Kamon not to recognize him, a look so amusing that Kamon drew in a shallow inhalation, the kind that usually precedes a chuckle, and he would have started to laugh if at

11:24:45 he hadn't become suddenly aware of a pain in the side of his back, only afterward hearing the sound of the first shot, as though time were moving in reverse and whatever had just happened was already starting to undo itself, the pain returning to the sound of the shot, the sound preceding the catch of breath, the inhalation preceding the pity Kamon felt for the boy who'd slipped on the ice, the boy slipping in front of him but going up instead of down, rising toward the bare branches of the maple tree in front of the Presbyterian church while Kamon fell between two parked cars. He heard a brief clatter that reminded him of being a boy shaking a fistful of polished stones his daddy had given him, felt a spasm of pain at the same time, along with a new confusion, for the sequence had reversed itself again, but instead of moving forward, everything was happening at the same time, and the simultaneity seemed natural, as if life had always been this way—instants of multiple sensations, hearing and feeling and seeing the progression of an event within one moment, and within that same moment remembering with dreamy haziness, as Kamon did, that the two players running from the deli had been holding guns, realizing as he fell that he'd forgotten about the guns when he moved to help the second player to his feet, but the gun must have been there somewhere, on the ground, inside the boy's sleeve, somewhere, anywhere, yet the boy had been paralyzed with fear, so he couldn't have had the nerve to pull a trigger. Which immediately brought to mind the capability of the forward player. Yeah, it was possible that the shots still being fired as he fell were coming from the forward player's gun, a clatter of stones, pain within and without, the branches receding, the street rising up between two cars to smack him in the face at

11:24:52 as the boy he'd been trying to help scrambled to his feet and ran away after his teammate, the two players resuming the game that Kamon had interrupted, maybe just practice for the real thing, the important game scheduled for Saturday—you couldn't blame them, really, Kamon had gotten in their way, though you couldn't blame Kamon, he hadn't done anything wrong, he couldn't think of a single thing he'd ever done wrong in his whole life, so at

11:25:03 he asked himself, *How did I come to be here?* The last thing he remembered was the impulse to laugh, but already he'd forgotten what was so funny and felt a residual smile disappear from his face, like a fly taking off after picking up a crumb, leaving behind the itch, which Kamon would have scratched if he could have figured out how to get his hand to his mouth. He'd had a hand once, yeah, and he'd extended the hand to a boy who'd fallen on the sidewalk. But how could that be? Had he extended the hand to himself, left his body in order to lift his body to his feet? Where was he now? Outside with the pain or inside with the night? It was so dark inside, close to midnight, he figured, and he'd done just as his ma expected: *What do you do when you leave the room, Kamon?*

11:25:08 *Turn off the light,* so the room was the color of grease overflowing from a ball joint, and somewhere in the lightless corner, Darryl was laughing at his own bad joke, maybe the joke that had almost spurred Kamon to laughter himself, whatever it was, something that had to do with Jenny. Kamon couldn't feel her, but he could feel how he wanted her to hold him, to warm him with her electric warmth, for wouldn't you know that when pain leaves the body, it transforms into cold, drawing snow from the sky, brittle flakes moistening his cheeks. He would have brushed them away but he had misplaced his hands somewhere between his home and the deli, yeah, he'd been going to the deli, he remembered that much, to the deli for a carton of cigarettes, he'd made a deal with his cousin Taft and would earn twenty dollars for this errand. Go ahead, push Kamon around all you wanted, you owed him twenty dollars now if someone would please find his hands

11:25:17 he'd get up and finish what he'd started, a life beginning with the clatter of stones, a fistful of polished stones and the bark of a magnolia scraping his arm as he climbed, the dribble of a basketball, the echo of voices in windowless hallways, the endless waiting, a beer and a red-hot smothered with onions, sodium chloride, contact paper, the shock of a mouse bouncing against his palm, the pop of a lightbulb, a darkroom, the pissing, the shitting, busting his balls over white pussy, a squirrel caught under the wheels of a moving car, food stamps in an old woman's purse, lemonade, cigarettes, music, magic tricks, and always the waiting, Jenny waiting for him to come home while Kamon waited in line for the Jack

Rabbit and looked forward to the next ride, though the last time he'd coasted straight into a wall and ended up flat as a fruit roll. He'd have to pinch his skin and pull himself into a solid shape, Jenny would expect as much, but he discovered only then that he had lost his stuffing, there was nothing to hold his body together, he couldn't even stand up, he would never stand up, he would never find his hands again,

11:25:18 he would never be himself. He felt now what might be called *panic* but was a feeling too peculiarly Kamon's to be attached to a word and have sensible meaning. The recognition that he would no longer be who he'd been, even as he was still close enough to himself to understand this, produced a change in the pattern of his thinking, a change that felt palpably real, developing as it did from the experience of a loss, understanding as it happened that exactly when 11:25:18 became

11:25:19, the wafer of glass upon which his mind rested shattered, and thought burst from its reservoir like floodwater, traveling through the hollow package of his body in pursuit of the pain,

11:25:20 draining out of him onto the curb, so if he had been able to open his eyes he would have seen the last shreds of his comprehension lying in a wet pool of blood, insoluble thoughts, thoughts that only Kamon Gilbert could have thought, past thoughts and all the potential thought that would have come to him over a lifetime, leaving behind a brain as hollow as the body, knowing nothing about what had happened to him or how it had happened, unable to postulate what would become of the boys who had done this to him, boys who would live into their old age, each of them spending time in jail for other crimes but not for this, and who, by murdering Kamon Gilbert, had deprived him of the one wish he would have wished for, if he'd had a chance:

11:25:21

About the Authors

Russell Banks (1940–), a frequent contributor to *Esquire,* is the author of many novels, including *Cloudsplitter, Affliction, The Sweet Hereafter, Continental Drift,* and, most recently, the short story collection *The Angel on the Roof.* "Plains of Abraham" was published in *Esquire* in July 1999.

For many years a professor in the writing program at Johns Hopkins University, **John Barth** (1930–) is widely hailed as the father of postmodernism. He is the author of the sly collection of stories *Lost in the Funhouse,* and the novels *The Floating Opera, The End of the Road, The Sot-Weed Factor,* the National Book Award–winning *Chimera,* and, most recently, *Coming Soon!!!. Esquire* ran "The Remobilization of Jacob Horner" (an excerpt from his second novel, *The End of the Road*) in July 1958.

Few writers have had an influence on contemporary fiction as far-ranging as **Jorge Luis Borges**'s (1899–1986). He was the author of *A Universal History of Iniquity, Ficciones,* as well as the recently released *Collected Fictions,* and *Selected Non-Fictions.* His story "The Widow Ching—Pirate" appeared in *Esquire* in August 1972.

T. Coraghessan Boyle (1948–) is the author of, among other works, *World's End, The Tortilla Curtain, A Friend of the Earth, After the Plague,* and *Drop City.* "Heart of a Champion" was published in *Esquire* in 1975.

Harold Brodkey (1930–1996) was the author of *First Love and Other Sorrows, Stories in an Almost Classical Mode, Profane Friendship, Women and Angels, The Runaway Soul,* and the memoir *This Wild Darkness: The Story of My Death.* An early champion of his fiction, *Esquire* ran "His Son, in His Arms, in Light, Aloft" in August 1975 and "Verona: A Young Woman Speaks" in July 1977.

Truman Capote (1924–1984) was the author of *Breakfast at Tiffany's, In Cold Blood, The Grass Harp,* and *A Tree of Night.* In the 1980s, *Esquire*'s excerpts of his novel *Answered Prayers* caused much commotion among Capote's socialite subjects. *Esquire* published "Among the Paths to Eden" in July 1960.

Ron Carlson (1947–) is the author of the story collections *At the Jim Bridger, The News of the World, Plan B for the Middle Class,* and *The Hotel Eden. Esquire* published his graceful story "Towel Season" in May 1998.

Raymond Carver (1938–1988) was the author of such classic short story collections as *Will You Please Be Quiet, Please?, What We Talk About When We Talk About Love,* and *Where I'm Calling From.* "Neighbors" ran in the magazine in June 1971.

John Cheever (1912–1982), one of the twentieth century's great practitioners of short fiction, won the Pulitzer Prize in 1979 for his collected stories. He was the author of the novels *The Wapshot Chronicle, The Wapshot Scandal,* and *Falconer,* among other works. He was awarded the National Medal for Literature from the American Academy of Arts and Letters. "The Death of Justina" appeared in *Esquire* in November 1960.

Don DeLillo (1936–) is the author of many distinguished novels, including *White Noise, Underworld, The Names, Mao II,* and *Libra. Esquire* has excerpted many of his books, including *Libra* and *Underworld.* "In the Men's Room of the Sixteenth Century," which *Esquire* ran in December 1971, is one of his earliest published works.

A former newspaper columnist, novelist **Pete Dexter** (1943–) is the author of *Brotherly Love, The Paperboy,* and *Paris Trout,* which won the National Book Award for Fiction in 1988. "The Jeweler," which was published in *Esquire* in April 2002, is his first short story.

John Dos Passos (1896–1970) was the author of numerous works of fiction, among them *The U.S.A. Trilogy: The 42nd Parallel, 1919,* and *The Big Money*; as well as *Manhattan Transfer* and *Three Soldiers.* "The Celebrity" ran in the magazine in August 1935.

Tony Earley (1961–) is the author of the novel *Jim the Boy* and the short story collection *Here We Are in Paradise.* His story "Hardy in the Evening" appeared in *Esquire* in February 1998 and "Morning in America" in July 1998.

Stanley Elkin (1930–1995) was born in New York City and taught for many years at Washington University in St. Louis. He was the author of several highly esteemed novels, among them *Boswell, The Magic Kingdom, The MacGuffin, The Dick Gibson Show,* and *Mrs. Ted Bliss.* In 1982 and 1995, he won the National Book Critics Circle Award for Fiction. "I Look Out for Ed Wolfe" was published in the September 1962 issue of *Esquire.*

Louise Erdrich (1954–) is the author of *Love Medicine, The Beet Queen, Tracks, The Antelope Wife,* and *The Last Report on the Miracles at Little No Horse,* as well as several works of nonfiction and poetry. "Fleur" ran in *Esquire* in August 1986.

F. Scott Fitzgerald (1896–1940) was the author of, most notably, *The Great Gatsby, This Side of Paradise,* and *Tender Is the Night.* His work appeared in the very first issues of *Esquire,* and thereafter appeared in almost every issue until his death. "A Man in the Way" ran in the magazine in February 1940.

"In Desert Waters," which appeared in *Esquire* in 1976, was **Richard Ford**'s (1944–) first national publication. Ford is the author of

The Sportswriter, sections of which ran in the magazine; the Pulitzer Prize–winning *Independence Day*; and the short story collection *Rock Springs*. The story "Rock Springs" was featured in *Esquire* in February 1982.

John Gardner (1933–1982) was the author of many books, including *Grendel, The Sunlight Dialogues, The Art of Living*, and *Mickelsson's Ghosts*. "The Song of Grendel" ran in *Esquire* in October 1971.

Barry Hannah (1942–) is the author of the groundbreaking short story collection *Airships*, as well as the novels *Geronimo Rex, High Lonesome*, and *Yonder Stands Your Orphan*. Writing in *Esquire*, Sven Birkerts praised "the sizzling poetry of his every phrase and sentence." Hannah's miraculous three-part short story "Behold the Husband in His Perfect Agony" ran in the July 1976 issue of the magazine.

Ernest Hemingway (1899–1961) was one of *Esquire*'s earliest and most important contributors; a piece of Hemingway's nonfiction appeared in the very first issue of the magazine. He was the author of *The Sun Also Rises, A Farewell to Arms*, and the story collections *In Our Time, Men Without Women*, and *Winner Take Nothing*. He won the Nobel Prize for Literature in 1954. "The Snows of Kilimanjaro" appeared in the August 1936 issue of *Esquire*.

Originally from Bosnia, **Aleksandar Hemon** (1964–) is the author about whom, in 1999, *Esquire* wrote, "the man is a maestro, a conjurer, a channeler of universes." The book in question was his first story collection, *The Question of Bruno*. "The Deep Sleep," a section of his forthcoming novel *Nowhere Man*, ran in *Esquire* in November 2000.

A maverick voice in contemporary fiction, **Denis Johnson** (1949–) is the author of *The Name of the World, Already Dead, Angels, Fiskadoro, Resuscitation of a Hanged Man*, and the short story collection *Jesus' Son*, many pieces from which appeared in *Esquire*. He is also the author of several volumes of poetry and the nonfiction collection *Seek*. "The Bullet's Flight" appeared in *Esquire* in March 1989.

Heidi Julavits (1968–) is the author of the novel *The Mineral Palace*. Her extraordinary short story "Marry the One Who Gets There

First: Outtakes from the Sheidegger-Krupnik Wedding Album," was published in *Esquire* in April 1998, and appeared in *The Best American Short Stories 1999*.

Norman Mailer (1923–) is the author of numerous books, including *The Naked and the Dead, The Deer Park, Advertisements for Myself*, and *The Executioner's Song*. The magazine has published dozens of his nonfiction pieces, including the famous "Superman Comes to the Supermart." Many of his novels have been excerpted in *Esquire*. "The Language of Men," one of Mailer's few short stories, ran in the magazine in April 1953.

Cormac McCarthy (1933–) is the author of *The Border Triology: All the Pretty Horses, The Crossing*, and *Cities of the Plain*. His other works include the novels *Blood Meridian* and *Suttree*. He is the winner of both the National Book Award and the National Book Critics Circle Award for Fiction. The excerpt from *All the Pretty Horses* was published in the March 1992 issue of *Esquire*.

Thomas McGuane (1939–) is the author of many books, including *The Bushwhacked Piano, Ninety-Two in the Shade, Panama*, and *Nothing but Blue Skies*. "Cutting Losses" was published in the magazine in October 1992.

David Means's (1961–) most recent collection of stories, *Assorted Fire Events*, won the 2000 Los Angeles Times Book Prize for Fiction and was a finalist for the National Book Critics Circle Award. "Lightning Man" appeared in *Esquire* in April 2001.

Arthur Miller (1915–) is the author of many works, including the plays *All My Sons, Death of a Salesman, The Crucible*, and *A View from the Bridge*. Among his many honors is the National Book Medal for Distinguished Contribution to American Letters. *Esquire* published "The Misfits" in October 1957.

Vladimir Nabokov (1899–1977) was one of the greatest prose geniuses of the twentieth century. Among his works are *Lolita; Pale Fire; Speak, Memory;* and *Strong Opinions*. *Esquire* published many of his short stories. "The Visit to the Museum" appeared in the magazine in March 1967.

Antonya Nelson (1961–) is the author of the short story collections

The Expendables, In the Land of Men, Family Terrorists, Female Trouble, and the novels *Talking in Bed, Living to Tell,* and *Nobody's Girl.* "Downstream," one of her earliest stories, ran in *Esquire* in May 1989.

Jonathan Nolan's (1976–) short story "Memento Mori," upon which the 2001 film "Memento" was based, is his first published work of fiction. He lives in California and is writing his first novel. "Memento Mori," which won an O. Henry Award, appeared in *Esquire*'s March 2001 issue.

A native of Minnesota, **Tim O'Brien** (1946–), is the author of the National Book Award–winning novel *Going After Cacciato*, as well as *The Things They Carried, In the Lake of the Woods, The Nuclear Age*, and the upcoming novel *July, July*. He's a frequent contributor to *Esquire*, and a great friend to the magazine. "The Things They Carried" was published in *Esquire* in August 1986, won the National Magazine Award for Fiction in 1987, and was included in *The Best American Short Stories of the Century*.

Flannery O'Connor (1925–1964) wrote the novels *Wise Blood* and *The Violent Bear It Away* and two short story collections, *Everything That Rises Must Converge* and *A Good Man Is Hard to Find. Esquire* published "Parker's Back" posthumously in April 1965.

Jayne Anne Phillips (1952–) grew up in Buckhannon, West Virginia. She is the author of the acclaimed story collections *Black Tickets* and *Fast Lanes*, and the novels *Machine Dreams, Shelter,* and *Motherkind.* "Bess" ran in *Esquire* in August 1984.

Philip Roth (1933–) published his first *Esquire* story, "Expect the Vandals," in 1960. He won the National Book Award for his novels *Goodbye, Columbus* and *Sabbath's Theater*, and the Pulitzer Prize for Fiction for *American Pastoral*. His other books include *Portnoy's Complaint, The Human Stain,* and, most recently, *The Dying Animal.* "A Jewish Patient Begins His Analysis," an excerpt from *Portnoy's Complaint*, was published in the magazine in April 1967.

Richard Russo (1949–) is the author of the novels *Nobody's Fool, The Risk Pool, Straight Man, Empire Falls*, and the upcoming story collection *The Whore's Child*. His story "Monhegan Light" ran in the August 2001 issue of *Esquire*.

Joanna Scott (1960–) grew up in Connecticut and is now a professor at the University of Rochester. She is the author of the novels *Make Believe; The Manikin; The Closest Possible Union; Arrogance; Fading, My Parmacheene Belle*; the story collection *Various Antidotes*; and the upcoming novel *Tourmaline. Esquire* published "The Wish" in February 2000.

Irwin Shaw (1913–1984) published more than a dozen short stories in *Esquire*. He was the author of *The Young Lions; Two Weeks in Another Town; Voices of a Summer Day; Rich Man, Poor Man*; and *Acceptable Losses*. The classic short story "The Eighty-Yard Run" was published in *Esquire* in January 1941.

Isaac Bashevis Singer (1904–1991) was born in Poland and moved to the United States in 1935. Among his works in English are *Gimpel the Fool; Enemies, A Love Story; Satan in Goray*; and *In My Father's Court*. He received the Nobel Prize for Literature in 1978. "The Beggar Said So" appeared in *Esquire* in May 1961.

The author of some of the most important and widely read novels of American literature, **John Steinbeck** (1902–1968) wrote *East of Eden, The Grapes of Wrath, Of Mice and Men,* and *Cannery Row*, among others. He received the Nobel Prize for Literature in 1962. He was an early contributor to the magazine; "The Lonesome Vigilante" was published in *Esquire* in October 1936.

Robert Stone (1937–) is the author of six novels, among them *Damascus Gate, Outerbridge Reach*, and *Dog Soldiers*, which won a National Book Award for Fiction in 1975. "Under the Pitons" appeared in *Esquire* in July 1996.

John Updike (1932–) was born in Shillington, Pennsylvania. He is the author of more than fifty books, including *Rabbit, Run; The Poorhouse Fair; The Centaur*; and *The Complete Henry Bech*. Among his many honors are the National Book Award, the Pulitzer Prize, and the National Book Critics Circle Award for Fiction. "After the Storm" was published in *Esquire* in January 1963 and later appeared as part of *The Centaur*.

David Foster Wallace (1962–) is the author of the story collections *Brief Interviews with Hideous Men* and *Girl with Curious Hair*, the nonfiction collection *A Supposedly Fun Thing I'll Never Do Again*, and the novels *Broom of the System* and *Infinite Jest*. His stories "Adult World (I)" and "Adult World (II)" were published in the July 1998 issue of *Esquire*; "Incarnations of Burned Children" appeared in November 2000.

Esquire has long been an advocate of the daring short fiction of **Joy Williams** (1944–). She is the author of *The Quick and the Dead* and three other novels, as well as two collections of short stories, *Taking Care* and *Escapes*. "The Last Generation" was published in *Esquire* in April 1989.

Tobias Wolff (1945–) is the author of the memoirs *This Boy's Life*, a section of which ran in *Esquire*, and *In Pharaoh's Army*, as well as the story collections *In the Garden of the North American Martyrs*, *Back in the World*, and *The Night in Question*. *Esquire* featured "Soldier's Joy" in its October 1985 issue.

One of the great prose writers of the postwar era, **Richard Yates** (1926–1992) was the author of many novels, among them *Revolutionary Road* and *Cold Spring Harbor*, as well as the short story collections *Liars in Love* and *Eleven Kinds of Loneliness*. A posthumous volume, *The Collected Stories of Richard Yates*, was published in 2001. *Esquire* published several of his stories; "The B.A.R. Man" appeared in the magazine in December 1957.

Acknowledgments

The editor gratefully acknowledges David Granger, Beau Friedlander, Helene Rubinstein, Emily Clark, Zoë Rosenfeld, Alexandra Alter, Suzan Sherman, Rebecca Leece, Dana Stevens, Joe Veltre, David Chan, Nick Einenkel, Brian Allnutt, and, especially, the former *Esquire* fiction editors who brought many of these stories to the magazine, principally, L. Rust Hills, Will Blythe, and Gordon Lish.